THE
MULBERRY
EMPIRE

THE
MULBERRY
EMPIRE

OR

The Two Virtuous Journeys

of

The Amir Dost Mohammed Khan

PHILIP HENSHER

ALFRED A. KNOPF   NEW YORK   2002

For Laurent Rodriguez

C'est toi d'abord, o bien-aimé,
M'apportant avec ta gaité
Dorénavant douce, l'armée
Des victorieux procédés
Par quoi tu m'as toujours dompté,
Conseil juste, forte bonté . . .

—Verlaine

On peut juger du mépris qu'avait pour l'étude des langues un homme qui passait sa vie a découvrir l'epoque précise de la chute des empires et des révolutions qui changent la face du monde.

—*La Chartreuse de Parme*

BELLA

ONE

The Amir Dost Mohammed Khan had fifty-four sons. And his favourite among these sons was Akbar. One day Dost Mohammed feared that he was ill, and close to dying, and he called his fifty-four sons to him. They came from the far peaceful corners of the kingdom of the Amir Dost Mohammed Khan to the great city he had caused to be built, and as they rode through the country, they were not troubled or threatened. The wisdom and strength of their father made straight roads for them, and the justice he had wrought smoothed their passage.

One after another, his four-and-a-half dozen sons came to the great city of Kabul, and the people of Kabul, seeing that the Amir Dost Mohammed Khan had summoned his sons, turned their dust-filled eyes to the dust in grief. One after another, his sons rode through the wide streets, which were crowded but silent in sorrow. They came to the great palace, and came to the bedchamber of their father, the Amir Dost Mohammed Khan. And to each he said with kindness, as he came in, that his speed had been that of one driven by the Wind of a Hundred and Twenty Days. But the great Amir lied, for each had been driven to him by love.

At the end of three days, the Amir Dost Mohammed Khan lay in his bed, and looked around at the silent crowd of his sons, and bid them count themselves. The living counted themselves, and then the dead sons, and then the sons to come, who were not yet born, whom Dost Mohammed loved best, said their names, but only to Dost Mohammed in the dark shade raised over his head. He counted them, and there were fifty-three. It seemed to Dost Mohammed that one was missing.

"Great King," the second youngest of the sons said. "Akbar is not yet here. But he must be fast approaching." Dost Mohammed nodded, and the rough cloth of his bed cover seemed to whisper a denial. "That is not so," the youngest of the sons said. "Akbar my brother has sent a message that he will not come. He has sent a message to the great King my father that he is occupied, and may not turn away from the borders of the country, to mop my father's face and hold my father's head." And the brothers looked away in shame that their father should hear the truth.

But Dost Mohammed nodded, and was pleased by what the youngest of the brothers had said. "He has done right," he said, just that. He raised his head, and looked at the sons who were there, and the sons who were dead, and the sons who were not yet born, and the single son who had better things to do, and the Amir was pleased. And the sons—Afzal, and Azam, and Shams-i Jahan, and Ghulam Haidar, and Sher Ali, and Amin, and Sharif, and Akram and Wali and Faiz and Hawa and Hajira and Ahmad and Zaman and Umar and Ummat al-Mustafa and Bibi Zumurrud and Salih and Muhsin and Nur Jahan and Hasan and Husein and Wafa and Aslam and Qasim and Sher and Nek and Hashim and Sadiq and Shuaib and Rahim and Azim and Sadiq and Sarw-i Jahan and Yusuf and Azim and Habibullah and Mamlakat and Sharaf Sultan and Durr Jan and Sahib Sultan and Bibi Saira and Aisha and Bilqis and Sadiq and Rahim and Saifullah Khan Wakil and Agha and Fatima and Zainab and Banu and Mulk-i Jahan and Badr-i Jahan, youngest of the brothers (for it is written that the women who are born to a great Emperor may be considered sons, too)—the sons of the great King looked at him and saw him revive, and start to live again as he heard that everything was well with his kingdom. Glory be on the names of the sons of the Amir Dost Mohammed Khan, greatest of the Afghans, wisest of his people!

In time, Akbar found that his strength had secured his father's kingdom from his enemies, and, leaving his people with the instruction to be awake and vigilant, hastened to his father's house. But he found the

Dost well, and recovered, and merry, and full of love for the greatest of his sons, and Akbar embraced his father. "My son," the Amir Dost Mohammed Khan said. "You did right not to come to my call, but to remain at the call of the kingdom that will be yours. You, alone among my sons, are truly my son." And after that embrace, the Amir Dost Mohammed Khan lived in peace and plenty for years to come, in the knowledge of his wisdom and the knowledge of the wisdom of his son.

TWO

I

"Emperor of the Afghans," Burnes chanted, "Lord of the most distant horizon, King of the far hills, Heir of Israel, Lord of the Wind of a Hundred, of a Hundred, of a Hundred—"

He opened his eyes, and made a deflating noise. "Ppphhhhhwah," he said. "I always get stuck there."

Outside, in the courtyard, a fight was breaking out between a gang of boys; the sudden close yelling was like a flock of geese, diving over the roofs of the mud-brick house. Burnes knocked his fist against his forehead, as if pretending to think. Dr. Gerard got up from the corner of the room where he had been squatting, awkward as a camel, and went to the shutters to see what, if anything, the fight outside was about.

"Very good," Mohan Lal said smoothly. "Your Persian is really excellent, if I may say so."

There was an embarrassed sort of silence, since Mohan Lal, naturally, ought not to say so. Certainly, it was not for him to tell Burnes whether his Persian was good or not. Still, he seemed to take it upon himself not just to compliment his betters, but, on occasion, to correct them. Anywhere else, of course—but this was not anywhere else, and, knowing that all of them had to rely on Mohan Lal's goodwill, the party had taken a tacit decision to put up with the guide's elegant superiority, perpetually bordering on the supercilious.

"What is it, anyway?" Burnes said finally. "I can't remember. I'm sorry."

"Lord of the Wind of a Hundred and Twenty Days," Mohan Lal said, smiling faintly, as if giving a child the answer to a terribly obvious Christmas puzzle. "An interesting title. The Wind of a Hundred and Twenty Days is a summer wind, a phenomenon fascinating in the abstract, although not something one would wish to experience. It is regarded as a unique property of the kingdom, and therefore an appropriate title for the Amir."

"Not something I'd want to boast about," Dr. Gerard said, turning back to the room, disappointed in the small drama of the courtyard outside. "And I hope we're not here long enough to have to put up with it."

"If he keeps us waiting here long enough," Burnes said, "we may simply have to grit our teeth and endure."

Outside, Kabul continued its usual life.

Burnes found it hard to be quite sure whether, here, they were prisoners or not. Ten days before, they had arrived at the gates of the city—or what passed for the gates, a waist-high mud wall full of holes. An inadequate rampart, one might have thought, but the Afghans came and went quite happily, as if never fearing an enemy, giving no thought to invaders or infidel. Until now, Burnes had remained swathed in his cloth, blanketed up, his face browned first by colouring and after by the weeks trekking in the mountain sun, his blue eyes becoming more startling by the day. Arriving at Kabul, however, it seemed wise to admit to what they were immediately, and take their chances.

Kabul had surprised Burnes. He had read what there was to read about the country, looked with every appearance of care at the drawings, the prints of the city. They hadn't been wrong, exactly; but still the city was not what he expected. No commentator, no artist, had captured what Burnes saw; it was as if they had seen only the outlines of the city, or rather, as if they, like Burnes, had seen it whole, and only cared to convey the city in part. Burnes tried to think of what it was his guides had left out. He could only think of it in two words: the fragrance; the filth.

In other cities, the fruit-and-flower smell of the street, the stench of the shit, human, canine, equine, and more, would have seemed the inessentials of the city's life. It had seemed like that to the observers of the city whose work they had so relied upon; they had removed the fragrance and the filth from their gaze as lying above or below what substance truly mattered. Buildings, thoroughfares, population numbers could be set down, and that was what, it seemed, really counted; not the mere smells of this city. It seemed always in danger of turning into an orchard, a stable, or a vast latrine. To Burnes, on the other hand, it was the intangible but overpowering fact of smell which seemed central to the place. Sitting in this half-prison, with all the time in the world to practise the address to the Amir and pursue absurd speculations, he found himself wondering about a map of the city which would convey this sense of his. In his head was a map of Kabul which did not describe the streets and the buildings, but set down the intangible and rich sudden odours of the place; described where a whiff of horse-shit mingled with the heavy perfume of rotting mulberries, where dead dog and fruit blossom competed. He closed his eyes, and there, in his head, was a weighty flush of sensation, a wave like the colour purple, arriving in his head, foreign, uninvited, irresistible. You did not need to walk the streets to map them in this olfactory manner; you only needed to sit by the window, and wait for a breeze. He had seen nothing of the city, in truth, nothing but a few streets as they had arrived, nothing but the few buildings around the house where they now lived, when their guards occasionally escorted them out. The city came to them, its perfumes carried on the wind.

2

They had arrived, and stood there at the wall, for a moment or two, as if their mere stance could announce their purpose. In front of them, there was the city. It was hard to think of it as a prize worth taking, now. Now that it was here in front of them, it seemed very unlike the great imperial jewel London and Calcutta so easily dreamed of. The hills and hollows of the land had been scattered, it seemed, with detritus; rambling, temporary houses, plastered smooth, scattered where they would fall. It was a city set high in the mountains, and the chill at night was fierce. Between the houses of the city paths, roads of packed-down mud ran; between them a thousand pedlars of goods set up their stalls to sell what they would. But it seemed to Burnes, as he stood there with his companions and waited for the Afghans to come and discover what he wanted, less like a city than a great wild garden. The groves of this high city joined, rambled with fruit trees, with what must be mulberries, blotting on the street and casting their high scent to the wind. What had London and Calcutta dreamed of? A city which could turn into an imperial jewel, certainly, a great imperial city, and not this random assembly, like the careless evening settlement of some wandering people.

Burnes, Mohan Lal the guide, and Gerard had dismounted. They stood there for a while, and it was not long before the curious little boys were succeeded by some more authoritative figures. Mohan Lal had stepped forward, but Burnes spoke first. They had listened to his explanation intently, had exchanged the ritual compliments calmly and gracefully, and, without consulting, had allowed them to remount, and led them into the city. A mounted group approached, shouting hoarsely, wheeled hungrily, curiously, around them like circling buzzards, and, before Burnes could start his explanation again, had ridden off.

First the customs house. The three of them had been hurried into a low white house, its door barely on its hinges. As the eager crowd of short, beakily featured men, all shouting, poured into the garden of the house, a flock of magpies rose clattering like knives from the fruit trees. The packhorses were tied up outside, and quickly stripped of their bundles. Inside, an immensely fat man emerged with great state from a back room, chewing and wiping some grease from his mouth with the bottom of his coat. All the Afghans fell abruptly silent. He gazed at them as mournfully as a dog as their luggage was brought in and dumped on the floor.

Burnes began his explanation. May the sun ever shine, glorious empire of the Afghans, long heard rumours of the wisdom and greatness of the kingdom. All received with gracious nods; tea was called for and brought by two boys of strongly corrupt appearance. Flat sweet bread followed, politely picked at by the Europeans, wolfed by the Afghans. Burnes pressed on. He and his companions were Europeans, returning home from India overland. Long heard rumours of the beauty of Kabul and promised, etc. (A brief pause here as one of the tea boys, after setting down a glass for Burnes, tried to stroke his neck. Burnes pushed him off gently, and the nearest adult hit the boy very hard with the butt of his rifle, to everyone's colossal amusement.) Hoped to stay in Kabul for a month, and their great dream was to meet and talk with the great and famous Emperor of the Afghans, the Amir Dost Mohammed Khan.

Burnes came to the end of his speech, and the customs officer gave a brief side-to-side nod of approbation. It wasn't quite clear what this meant; Burnes, to be sure of indicating what sort of people they were, got out his letters of introduction to the Amir, each carefully prepared in India with a grandiose seal. The official, however, showed almost no interest in them after a quick glance or two. "Oh God," Gerard said in English. "They're going to search the bags." Burnes ignored him; there was nothing to be done about it, and the best way to stay calm was to try not to remember what on earth there was in there.

"My books," Burnes said, as they extracted a dog-eared copy of *Marmion* and flicked through it. A sketchbook he feared might worry them more, but they looked at it cursorily, and set it down.

"Tell me," the customs officer said. "In your country, it is said that pork is eaten. Can that be true?"

Burnes was prepared. "It is a food eaten only by the very poorest people in our country. I myself have never tried it, but it is said that it has the taste, somewhat, of beef. That's a sextant."

"Good, good," the customs officer said as the underlings turned the object upside down, trying to force a noise from it. "And what is it?"

"It is called a sextant in my language," Burnes said. "A sort of talis-man."

"Good, good," the customs officer said. "In my country we have many sextants."

It was a long afternoon, but eventually the possessions had all been examined and packed up again. Nothing seemed to excite their interest except Gerard's bottles of medicine, which they passed around, sniffing at; the maps did not seem to trouble anyone. In the end, Burnes paid the official an enormous bribe in rupees, and gave him a little looking glass.

"I think he was rather disappointed," Mohan Lal said. "He was proba-bly hoping for more guns or a thrilling sort of dagger, I expect. They are said in my country to be frightfully fond of weaponry, these Afghan fel-lows."

Gerard gave a snort, with which Burnes silently concurred. Mohan Lal had long ago started to seem a tedious companion, with his incessant calm explanations of why things had gone wrong.

They had been led to a house. The owner of the house had welcomed them as if they were guests, effusively, ordered them to be given food and drink, and showed them their beds. Were they prisoners? Were they guests? The interminable attentions of the Newab Jubbur Khan, the owner of the house, and of the series of small boys who sat in the corner of the room with muskets seemed to point to different conclusions. They had arrived ten days ago, and seemed no nearer achieving what they were here to do.

What they were was quite a simple matter: two British officers and a native guide. What they were doing there, not even Burnes would, for this moment, quite bring into his mind. If the knowledge was not at the front of his thoughts, even the calmly interrogative brown gaze of his guards would not bring it out. What Kabul was—what Afghanistan was, here at this moment, far from India, further from England in some sense other than yards and feet than even an explorer like Burnes could quite comprehend—was a matter which could not be thought of as simple. There was, too, the question of what an Englishman was doing in Asia. That had been a question which, in this sort of situation, Burnes had had ample time to contemplate, and never managed any kind of answer. He began to be nervous, sitting here; any Englishman grows atavistically restless if he finds himself more than a hundred miles from the nearest sea, and Burnes was somehow aware all the time that this high brown stinking city was a great deal more than a hundred miles from any imaginable sea.

3

"Now, the Lord," Burnes went on. "No, sorry, vocative, O Lord of the Wind of a Hundred and Twenty Days. I always forget Persian numbers over fifty or so."

"It is not particularly complicated," Mohan Lal said, smiling in his infuriating way. "Numbers in Arabic are far more complex a proposition. And we may find we have plenty of time to perfect the address to the Amir."

"I'm sure," Gerard said. "Years, probably. Hi, you, sir."

The guard in the corner of the room moved, minimally.

"Are we to see the Amir today?" Gerard said, as he had asked ten times a day since they had arrived.

The guard made a head-tipping gesture; whether it meant something, or whether it was just the weight of the boy's enormous, mushroom-coloured turban, was not clear.

"In any case," Gerard said, "he knows we are here. Probably."

The boy guard, his loaded *jezail* like a bayonet between his thin dirty hands, considered this, deeply, and then made the same head-tipping gesture. *"Rus?"* he said in the end, nodding three times at the three Europeans. They appeared to know very well what Mohan Lal was.

"No," Burnes said patiently, not for the first time. "No, we are not Russians. We are from England, from Engelstan."

"Yes," Gerard cut in. "Tell the Newab Jubbur Khan to tell the Amir. Go on, go and tell your commanding officer. He will see us then, when he knows where we come from."

The boy looked, as if deeply wounded, appealing to Burnes. *"Rus,"* he said once more, and then, for no reason on earth, started to laugh uproariously. He did not get up.

"I wish they wouldn't do that," Gerard said irritably. "Laugh like that, I mean. It makes me think they know something we don't know. And why do they keep calling us Russians?"

"Rus," the boy said again, murmuring as if entranced, understanding a word in what Gerard said.

"No, no, not *Rus*," Gerard said. "And when do we hear from the damned Emperor of the damned Afghans? Oh, God—oh, God—that damned mutton at breakfast. Gentlemen, excuse me—"

Burnes shrugged, as Gerard rushed from the room, clutching his stomach chaotically like an unfastened valise. He prided himself on the value of patience in these dealings. That was the great thing in the East; patience, because nothing ever happened when it should, nothing ever happened on schedule. Everything, in dealing with the great rulers of the East, was whim and delay. Ten days was nothing; because, in response to whim and delay, there was no sensible behaviour to adopt but a complete, more-than-Oriental patience. That was what everyone said, and Burnes was pleased with himself for having exercised a great deal of patience with every potentate he had ever come across, and usually attained, if not the desired end, then, at least, some interesting conclusion. What no one had ever warned him about was the necessity to exercise some patience with one's fellow travellers; with a supercilious ass like Mohan Lal, forever making superior suggestions about one's Persian or giving one

ridiculous and probably entirely false information about the curious customs of the country, or a bigger ass like Gerard, complaining about the
slightest inconvenience to his blessed dignity, arguing for two *entire days*
about the necessity of shaving his head and dying his beard black before
crossing the Indus, always wanting to tell some outraged and heavily
armed nabob about the greatness of the Empire, or even, once, telling an
imam in response to the invariable question about the European diet that,
yes, he ate bacon daily and very delicious it was too. Unfairly, Burnes
blamed Gerard even for his disastrous digestion, the steady torrential
cataract from his bowels, blamed in turn on the damned mutton at breakfast, the damned beans at dinner, or the damned melon which the rest of
the company had eaten at Jalalabad with no ill effects. Yes, the exercise of
patience with one's damned fellow travellers was the most taxing thing;
compared to that, waiting ten days to see the Amir Dost Mohammed
Khan presented him with no difficulty whatever.

4

Out on the street, debate about the Europeans who rode so badly was
furious and incessant, like the noise of a cloud of swallows.

"The Amir will not see them."

"The Amir will see them tomorrow, fool. He has seen them yesterday,
and knows everything about them."

"How can the Amir have seen them when they have not seen the
Amir?"

At the edges of the market, the old men jogged up and down on their
heels, agitated by debate, and punched at the air, quick as clockwork.
They bothered no one.

"The Amir sent Akbar the son of the Amir, and the Amir saw them
with the eyes of Akbar."

"Did they not know the son of the Amir when Akbar was announced?"

"Many are the ways of the Amir Dost Mohammed Khan, and wise
they are."

Futteh the singer, plump and pale as a dove, his saucy eyes wandering
to make sure of his audience, finished sucking on his plum, pondered,
spat. He began a story.

"You recall the tale of the Vizier's daughter and the son of the King," he started. "And the King did not know how he should know if the daughter of the Vizier was true and good as she was thought to be. Now, this was many, many years ago, in China. And the Vizier had the most marvellous garden of roses in all of China, and he was in the habit of taking a walk in the garden, each morning. And one morning, he was accompanied in his walk by his daughter, who was as beautiful as the first light of the dawn over the mountains. He was glad to walk in the rose garden with his daughter, and, after they had walked together for an hour, the Vizier said to his daughter: My daughter, is it true that . . ."

The story unravelled. Futteh was a good storyteller, and, even in the cold of the early evening, he could hold half a dozen old men with his seamless voice. Their eyes fixed on his, six pairs of eyes, whether crafty, knowing, cynical, for the moment subdued into the quiet trust of the audience. Their knees hunched, their backs against the wall, they listened to the comforting tale they had heard hundreds of times before. Occasionally they interrupted with marginal, concerned comments—"He does not know that the ring has been swallowed by the fish on the King's table," or, "The girl, does she not understand that the man she is marrying is her own brother?" or, as narrative catastrophe threatened, "Allah is great and merciful." But for the most part, they let Futteh tell the story in his own leisurely manner.

When it was over, an hour or two had passed, and the audience sighed, as if wanting more of their own satisfaction.

"The son of the King in the story disguised himself, and went into the marketplace to hear what the common people were saying," one of the audience said.

"Yes, and that is what Akbar, son of the Amir Dost Mohammed Khan, that is what he has done, with the Russians."

"They are not Russians," another man said, passing. "Engelstan."

"Akbar put on a tribesman's clothes, and took a *jezail*," Futteh said, waving his hand in the air impatiently, dismissing either the objection or the flies. "And he went to the house where the English are, and sat with them for two hours, and talked with them. But all the time, they did not know who they were speaking with."

"Great is the mind of the Amir Dost Mohammed Khan, and wise is he in the ways of the world," someone murmured.

"And they ride so badly," Futteh added, with great finality.

"Like the sack of rice on the back of an old donkey," his listeners chorused sagely.

5

The orchard city fell into shade as the afternoon wore on; pale peaches,
espaliered against the wall, plums, apricots, pears; beneath the window of
the Newab Jubbur Khan where they sat all day, a fine apple tree, just like
the trees of Burnes's childhood. He shut his eyes, and sniffed, and sometimes, through all the smell and noise and clear strange mountain air,
there was all his childhood, in the sheltered Montrose garden. Walnuts,
cherries, vines, and more wonderful things, pomegranates growing in the
streets, and, everywhere, mulberry trees; their fruit piled up in market
stalls, lying in the street, and the whole city sucking ceaselessly on fruit.
At the door of their wing in the courtyard, a small boy, padded up with
scraps of cloth, his legs wrapped up puttee-fashion, his dirty feet bare and
hardened in sandals, was sucking on a handful of cherries and mulberries,
cracking walnuts between his hard teeth, and every so often running his
tongue round his mouth to clean off what juice was staining his face,
leaving a fat white clown-smile in a fruit-smeared face. And everywhere
the birds; bright chattering magpies, the fat burble of doves, edging at
each other in their nervous fighting. Burnes watched them for hours
from the window. And the nightingale; he had never known, quite, what
the Persians meant when they wrote about the nightingale, but here, it
was a sharp lemon tang, cutting through the rich sweetness of the dungy
perfumed city, a line of pure song, returning on itself, multiplying, varying, twisting, but always, always, itself. He sat in the evening light, and listened, and found no way to ask the others to be quiet too.

The day wore on, and at some point towards the end of the afternoon,
a procession of dishes began to be carried into the room. The two
women of the house, veiled in brick-red cloaks, carried them in. Their
veils were raw squares of cloth, dropped over their heads. A coarse lattice
was cut in to allow them to see. Burnes seemed to catch the glint of an
eye through the loose weave of the eye-slit, and, before he lowered his
eyes, wondered for a moment if that meant the woman was looking at
him. From their gait, they were both young, and the contours of their
bodies were revealed by the rippling red cloth.

A third woman stood at the door and watched, holding a baby; she too was veiled; even the baby was veiled. She seemed to be supervising the other women. Perhaps a favoured wife. The dishes were set down on the floor without explanation, and, when the entire room was filled with clay dishes, the three women retreated to the door, looked once at the food, and not at the men, and quickly left. And then the Newab Jubbur Khan came in.

The Newab, whose house this was, seemed to regard them with an almost affectionate air. He made a point of eating with them; he also made a point of coming in after the food, and leaving without excusing himself. The three of them scrambled to their feet.

"You have passed an agreeable day, I hope?" the Newab said kindly. He was a slight man, his nose a huge beak in his little face; when he walked, it was with an evident consciousness of grandeur which his appearance did not entitle him to. He walked like a man who has once been fat. "If you do not object, I would like to eat with you."

"We would be honoured," Burnes said.

"Honoured indeed," Gerard said, looking warily at the food. "Thrice honoured."

The Newab nodded agreeably at Gerard's meaningless formulation. "Sit, sit," he said. He rattled off the habitual prayer, lazily looking round, and without taking a breath, fell back from Arabic into Persian. "The lamb is particularly fine, from my own flock." He gestured at a greasy-looking dish, grey and shining in the sun. Burnes leant forward and scooped up some of the cold stew, knowing perfectly well that the Newab was lying politely, since all the food here had to be ordered up from the bazaar. Gerard just looked green.

"Tell me," the Newab asked, after each of the dishes had been commended and accepted, and they were embarked on the task of struggling unsuccessfully with what could be eaten of the Newab's food. "How large a city is London, or Calcutta?"

"They are different cities, Newab, and both large and beautiful," Mohan Lal said.

"I see," the Newab said. He seemed, still, to be under the impression that Calcutta and London were more or less the same place, or perhaps different names for the same city; an impression they had been trying to correct for some time now. "But how big? Is it, for instance, as large as our city?"

"I think it might be even a little larger," Burnes said tactfully. "How many people, for instance, live in Kabul?"

The Newab sucked on his teeth, and gazed at the wall, as if calculating. "Many, many people, and their numbers grow every day, thanks to the wisdom and kindness of the Amir who rules over them."

"I see," Burnes said, making a routine half-incline of the head at the mention of the Amir.

"London has many hundreds of thousands of inhabitants, and is the richest and most beautiful city in the world," Gerard cut in. Burnes looked at him in irritation; what the point of boasting to the Newab about the size of London was, he had no idea. Just an unthinking, involuntary outcrop of Gerard's personality, as frustrating and impossible to argue with as geology.

"Of course, we have seen very little of Kabul," Burnes said. "But the reputation of the beauty and splendour of the city has spread far, and we have travelled from India in the hope that we may see for ourselves."

"How is it that you have seen very little of Kabul?" the Newab abruptly asked. He seemed genuinely puzzled, proffering a dish of boiled aubergines.

Burnes was thrown. "We have been resting here, at your hospitality," he said finally, seeing no way to point out that they were effectively prisoners. At that, as if to make his point, one of the succession of small boys with muskets wandered in. He greeted the Newab elaborately, the English more casually, and sat down in the corner of the room, promptly falling asleep, both hands on the barrel of his gun. "At the gracious hospitality of the Newab," Burnes said, pointedly. "We have been unable to see the famous city of Kabul."

"Great is the city of Kabul," the Newab Jubbur Khan echoed, absently. He took a piece of bread, tearing it in half, and dipped it in some dish of meat; before eating it, he made a vague gesture of invitation towards Gerard, who, with too evident unwillingness, followed his example. "Yes, the city is great, and its fame has spread far. The bazaar of the city is the greatest in the world, where the world comes to marvel at the riches and splendour of the empire. The merchants of China and Russia and Engelstan come to the great markets, laden with goods, and leave laden down with more than they brought, such are the marvels of the city. The beauty and splendour of the city is great, and the beauty of the people of the Emperor is famous throughout the world. And such, willing, it will always be. Over the city is the Bala Hissar, the palace of my brother, the Amir Dost Mohammed Khan, where my brother rules over his family and his wives and his wealth in wisdom and mercy and goodness, willing. And the palace of my brother is famed throughout the world, and the world comes to express its wonder at its beauty and greatness and the greatness of my brother the Amir."

He paused, perhaps considering whether his description of the city would, in the end, be as useful to the English as simply letting them out to look for themselves; perhaps, however, considering what there could possibly be to start praising next in the high stinking city. Not the food, at any rate, Burnes thought unkindly, refusing the offer of another greasy dish.

"The Amir is your brother?" Mohan Lal said.

"The Amir is the brother, it is said, of every Afghan," Burnes said, helping out.

"He is my brother," Jubbur Khan said simply. "The shade of the same mountain shadowed our birth, and may the same stream refresh his parched tongue."

"May friendship be forever between warriors," Burnes said.

"And he is my brother," Jubbur Khan said again.

"He is the brother of every Afghan," Gerard said, conventionally echoing what Burnes had said.

"He is the brother of every Afghan," Jubbur Khan agreed. But then he seemed troubled, and said, once more, more emphatically, "The Amir is my brother."

"He is the brother of every Afghan," Gerard said again, idiotically.

"He is your brother?" Burnes cut in. "He is the son of your father?"

"He is the son of my father," Jubbur Khan said, relieved. "Yes, he is the son of my father."

This explained a great deal. And now Jubbur Khan got up, as if he had said enough to explain who he was, and who the Amir was, and what the Europeans were. He got up, bowing on all sides, and swept out with massive graciousness, hardly waiting for his guests to raise themselves and bow graciously back, as if his good manners were such that no complementary response could possibly improve or complete them, and was out of the door and at the bottom of the stairs before Gerard succumbed to what had clearly been troubling him for some time, a colossal, harrumphing and malodorous fart, like a bough breaking under the sheer weight of fruit. The boy guard looked up, surprised and humorous. Burnes vastly bowed in his direction, the sleeves of his robe collapsing about his arms and hands. "And to you, O Lord of the Wind of a Hundred and Twenty Days," he said. "That, I expect, is a very good sign."

"Indeed," Mohan Lal said. "Your digestion is improving, to venture a fart. You need not have waited until the departure of the Newab, indeed. I have read that the Afghan custom is to fart at table."

"A risky business," Gerard said. "With nothing to eat but this damned greasy food."

6

Outside, there was a flicker of movement. A scarlet-leaved tree against the dense dusk sky trembled suddenly; a gust, quickly over, as if someone had shaken the tree's trunk and run away. Another movement, something which might have been a bird, shooting up from the tree with a raucous squawk, abruptly muted. Gerard raised himself from where he lay, complete with food and boredom, and went to the window, where Burnes was already standing. Underneath the tree, a flash, sudden, of white, like the wink of a fish belly, turning in a black pool. For a moment the faces of the Afghans had turned up to the window, before returning to their usual occupation; their teeth and eyes winking white in the dusk. They could be guards; yes, they could be; or, conceivably, they could merely be sitting there, as they would sit there indifferently, whoever was inside the house of the Newab. Burnes did not know, and could not think who to ask.

Out in the court, the squatting boys were preparing for their street-sport. There were five of them, and each clutched, underneath his arm, something which peeped and squawked, a weak piping squawk like an unoiled hinge. With his free hand, each dipped steadily into a little bag, tied to the sash at his waist next to the knife, and ate shrivelled-up little apricots, crunching and spitting the stones with all the absorption they had. In a moment, a boy threw down the piping bird under his arm, and, as if recognizing the challenge, the boy facing him in the circle threw down his bird, too. The two quails shivered their plumage back into plumpness, and nervously strutted in the other's direction. The boys made an encouraging noise, a quick strange grunting rattle, like a pig eating a snake, and a handful of grain was flung down. The fight began.

It was dark, below, and Burnes could see nothing of the sport; the faces were turned down in excited absorption, and all that could be heard was the occasional fierce cry from a boy, quickly stifled, the pipe and peck of two small birds fighting over a handful of grain. Burnes had seen the sport before, in the daylight, from this window. The rudimentary contest seemed never to weary or tire the street, and they squatted over the two little fat birds, watched them barge each other, pluck at each other with their fierce little beaks like toy birds, a harmless little bout between paint-bright tin birds, wheeling in their tin circles.

Down there, small cries of excitement, quickly muted, were being made; this was not a game for cheering at, but one where the small shrieks of the birds, rending and tearing each other's little flesh for grain, was to be heard and winced over. This was the sport—the one thing, as it were—which kept Kabul quiet, and everyone watched it; underneath the window, Burnes had seen fine horsemen, street boys—even, a couple of times, an idle Newab Jubbur Khan leaving his house for a morning consti-tutional—pause for a moment before the rapt silent bout. It was too dark to see, from the window, what was happening; you could not see which of the two birds was succeeding, which was succumbing. There was only the faint tremulous cries of small fat birds, assaulting each other furiously over grain which neither of them would eat. Burnes drew back into the room.

The guard came in. But instead of sitting down in the corner, he stood at the door, and looked at them; at Burnes and Gerard and Mohan Lal. "He," the guard said finally, "will see you tomorrow." He made a small gesture with his head, the side-to-side twist, an acknowledgement of something, though none of them had said anything, and then left.

They stared at each other.

He will see you tomorrow, the guard had said, just that; and Burnes ran the sentence through his head, over and over again, to see if it was clear, if he had understood it correctly. Language brings opposite meanings so intimately together, and if the guard had said *He will not see you tomorrow,* there was a terrible danger that Burnes would have missed it. He ran through the sentence, over and over, adding words which he might have missed, substituting *they* for *he, never* for *tomorrow, kill* for *see.* He got to the end of it. He was absolutely sure of what he had heard. The Emperor of the Afghans would see them tomorrow.

But with that certainty came an appalling and unanticipated terror. They had travelled to Kabul, never knowing what they would find there;

had presented themselves at the gates; had submitted to their guesthouse garrison without more than a weak tremor of dread. And now, with the certainty that they would do what they had arrived to do, terror set upon Burnes. No; not quite that; it was not that something had struck at him. It was more that something had left him. As if, with the ordinary words, some great certain presence in him had abruptly fled, clearing the walls and windows, the barriers of his own skin without an effort. He sat, trying, almost, not to shake with the black terror of his own certainty, fleeing him, and waited for it to leave. It was the Wind of a Hundred and Twenty Days, and it began in this room, it began its furious flight from this little room, and fled from him, his fear, his terror, his knowledge. He did not know, quite, what it was, what certainty he was losing with this flight, as if of wind; he could only feel it leaving, with no sense at all of what would be left of him when it was gone, what strength to carry out his task. He waited saying nothing, as if in thought, and in a moment it was over; the fleeing strength and certainty had, just at the door, turned and looked at him in quiet curiosity. At him: at the shell of what had housed all that certainty for so long. Turned and looked and left, leaving nothing but Burnes. He sat for a moment in silence, wanting not to show any fear, to anyone, ever again.

7

In these long nights, Burnes dreamt of Montrose. He could not help it.

You went to the door of your chamber, and turned, and looked. The thin curtains were blowing in the summer breeze, and already, at this moment in the morning, the sun was lighting the thin white cloth, there at the narrow windows. You looked down at yourself, and there too, your white nightgown billowed out with the cool Scottish morning breeze, lit with the cool Scottish morning light. And there were your boy's feet, there, on the floor, blue almost with the cold, and veiny. For a moment, you could go back and hug yourself in bed, while the first of the morning; there, your bed, cut and rumpled and squashy with your sleep; or you could do what you could do, run downstairs in your bare feet and throw open the Montrose door to the Montrose morning. Rub your eyes and moan like a dove with your sleep; push your fists into your eye sockets, and fret your sides with your own quick warming embrace. And there.

The blue sky; the birds at song; the smell of the morning's first earth and, behind you, the first clanking noises of the house, preparing itself for the day, as the maids raked the fire and the girl brought in the milk. Yes, he would run, in this cold he could see, and not only feel, down to look at the dreamt Montrose morning.

But then he turned and looked at Montrose, and it too had become an orchard city, high in the dry brown mountains; Scotland turned to Islam, the granite city turned to a city of mulberries, and the perfume wafting over Burnes's sleep was not heather, the song was not that of the starling, but the heavy blossom of mulberry, the clean song of nightingales. It was as if he woke, and went to the Montrose window, and outside, there were orchards and orchards of mulberries. Mulberries outside, weighing the tree down, the tree glimpsed through the open Scottish door. And there, there, was a boy, a curious near-boy, a near-warrior, barely uniformed, a powdery beard against his soft skin, scurrying away outside, peering in at Burnes, in his high gleaming magnificence. And in his wake a sweet whiff of the many-perfumed city, a waft of dung and smoke and the high Scottish, yes, heathery Scottish mountain air; and the scent, too, of mulberries, growing outside somewhere, clotted on the trees, fallen and thick on the roads as dung. Burnes looked down at himself, and his bare night-gowned flesh was glittering with brass, with spurs, his boots bright with polish, but stained with the fruit flesh, the limbs of one who had walked long and far through the orchards. And as he woke, Burnes thought of something he knew, even after waking, to be true: that the fruit for which the English had the single name of *mulberry* had in Persian six separate names, and in Pushto, the language of the far high hills, the fruit had so many names that no one could ever know them all; a fruit which, before, had seemed single turned in Burnes's dream into one with so many names that no man had ever counted them all, and no man would ever risk reciting the many divine names of the divine fruit.

They must have come early, the next morning. Burnes woke from his dream, and already he could hear the whinnying of the strange horses out there in the garden, their unfamiliar-sounding jingle. He lay there on the padded floor, his eyes open, and could see from their unnatural stillness that Gerard and Mohan Lal, too, had woken, and were lying without moving, their eyes closed, feigning sleep so as not to move, not just yet. He lay and listened to the terrifying noise of the horses. They were down there, the men who would take them to the Emperor, of whom they knew nothing, of whose cruelty and goodness they knew nothing. Down there, waiting with all the patience they were born with.

They dressed quickly, and after a breakfast of milk and flat bread, went down to their escorts. They were there, sitting peaceably on their horses, not dismounting, just waiting as they had waited, surely, for an hour or two. Burnes led the other two out. Mohan Lal awkwardly salaamed, a gesture which they returned perfunctorily; their unfamiliar, unwelcoming look at the guide confirming what Burnes had always felt, that his frankly inquiring gaze, noting down, say, a particular stirrup loop as peculiar to the region, was always one guaranteed to bring suspicion and dislike down, not just on him but on the whole party.

It was the first time out of the house in days, and Burnes could not help feeling stiff. He stretched, awkwardly, as the light almost hurt his eyes, and for the first time, he saw the city. Not arriving for the first time, where novelty coloured the vision, not through a window, making distant what was there to be seen, but seeing a city which, it now seemed, he knew from his memory. A scattered city, lying in the scoop of the earth, the brown cubed houses lying against the vast slow rise of the brown mountains like dice in a cupped pair of hands. All the way they had ridden here, the earth had seemed dully brown, unchanging, empty, like the momentarily empty earth after waterless months, from which all colour had been sucked, leaving only brown. But now, coming out into the air, it seemed as if everything had enriched, multiplied in the unchanging earth; the dazed eye, looking down from the dazzling clean blue of the sky, saw a hundred, a thousand tints in the bare mountain earth; browns whitening with chalk, a streak of vivid yellow, a shadow going into mauve in the early-morning sun. Everything, he saw, pausing here before the bleak dazzling sun, could be found here; horses, orchards, sky, water, earth, and now, waiting for the high remote Emperor, he seemed in terror and jubilation to see everything there was, everything, there in the earth.

"Where are we going to?" Burnes shouted to the mounted guards. He was glad to hear his voice sounded authoritative.

"The Bala Hissar," one said, not looking down at him.

"Is it far?" Burnes called.

"No," another horseman said. "Not far."

"The Emperor is waiting," the first horseman said. "It is time to go. Are you ready?"

"Yes," Burnes said. "Yes, we are ready."

They set off, their guard not dismounting but hemming them in between the horses' high flanks. The horses walked with such stately gravity that at one moment, one of them could not bear the tenseness of the slow walk and wheeled abruptly off, circling like a hawk in the street before the rider brought the beast back. There could have been something brutal, a blunt assertion of power, in their making the party walk between the horses, like tethered slaves. They may have felt this—Gerard certainly felt this, to judge by his clenched-buttock stride, now the result of his august pride as much as his fluid bowels—but Burnes couldn't feel any outrage in himself at this treatment. Rather, he felt, in his glittering exotic clothes, dress uniform draped splendidly with the heavy red court robes, like a pilgrim. An unworthy pilgrim, walking humbly up the hill to the great sawn-off blunt rock, the palace, the Bala Hissar, in the middle of which vast plain mass sat the Amir. Up there was the Emperor, politely patient, waiting; you could feel his calm wait here, walking the street between their mounted companions. And the mounted companions, too, seemed quiet, subdued by the Emperor's patient quiet. What splendour was up there, Burnes could not tell; but he felt that there would be none. This city, plain-dressed, the high clean air given its florid perfume by the fruit trees, wasn't ruled by some fabulous potentate; he could feel it. No cushion-fleshed tyrant in a pile of rubies sat up there, watching them approach; just a mind.

As they walked through the narrow mud streets, they were given a thorough inspection. The children came to the windows, and stood, staring; shadows, in the upstairs shuttered windows, showed them that the women of the city, too, were curious. The shops in the bazaar were opening, and, behind the piles of fruit, of bags of spice, the merchants and customers, sitting in the early sun, followed the procession with humorous open eyes. Over the city, the Bala Hissar, a great shapeless piece of power, and they walked the streets, not responding to the keen attention of the city.

They walked on, not speaking to each other or their guards. Occasionally, over their heads, one of the horsemen would call out to another, or to someone in the street. They called out in Pushto, and each time Gerard, walking by Burnes's side, stiffened, knowing that they didn't want to be understood. Burnes worked on his patience; if Gerard could be kept from speaking at least until his easily ignited fury had died down, that would make things a great deal easier. After they had run the gauntlet of the bazaar, the houses seemed to drop away. The hill of the Bala Hissar itself was bare, clear for a siege.

This last stretch, as the road turned upwards, seemed to divide and stretch before them, and it seemed to Burnes, as the Bala Hissar receded from them, that this was the road in the paradox; that with each step, the road doubled in length, that each step grew smaller and more painful, and the great fortress would never be reached, as they laboured at its gates, endlessly. But it was mere minutes before they were there at the open gates, and their escort turned, at some unseen signal, and rode off, calling to each other, now, in Persian.

8

A small man ran up to them and beckoned quickly with his two hands, scowling. He seemed alone, and they followed him into the big square court of the palace. It was quite empty, and they walked briskly across it into another opening, the doors swinging open. Two boys were lounging there, each with a *jezail* slung across his back, each turbanned massively, and they made some side-to-side swing of the head, acknowledging not them, but their little guide. He gestured and beckoned continuously, and they followed him into another hall, where a group of more soldierly youth stood, waiting, and then into another. As they walked through the rooms of the palace, they acquired some kind of attendance behind them, the boys forming a chattering guard behind them, and all the time the little man, dancing, beckoning, in front of them. They walked through one room after another, the heavy blunt-carved dark wood doors opening weightily, and in every room there was almost no furniture, almost nothing, just plain plaster walls, the narrow windows of a palace in a country which knew all about heat, and about cold. Abruptly, they all fell silent, and at a circling gesture from their guide, stopped. The guide looked them over, critically, as if for the first time, and, with a circling gesture, stirring something in the air, a half-smile, a nod at the guards at the door, conveyed somehow that here they were. The doors were brought open and their guards fell back behind them, as they walked, in an awe they tried to subdue, into the great hall of the Amir. And there he was.

The hall was bare, long and square, with a single step at the end rising to a modest platform. There was nothing in the room except a huge

Turkey carpet, rich and deep as rubies. At the far end of the hall, perched on the edge of the step, sat the Amir. A group of courtiers and mullahs, ten or twelve, stood behind him; the courtiers wore swords dangling from their *kummur-bund*. As they entered, the group seemed to stiffen, and drew back, forming a little fan around the Amir, who did not rise. They bowed deeply from the far end of the hall, rose very slowly, and walked forward. Every five paces, they stopped and bowed again, an obeisance returned with a tiny benevolent craning of the neck by the Amir. It wasn't a court ceremonial; just a ritual concocted to show the greatest possible deference, which, it was hoped, the Amir would take as some court ritual of Europe. Finally, at ten paces from the Amir, they dropped to their knees and bowed their heads very slowly to the floor, counted to five, as agreed, and raised them again.

The Amir was smiling. "Welcome, welcome," he said. He was a sharp-featured man, a scimitar of a nose scything through his beautiful humorous face, and his big dark eyes danced, curious or amused, from one to another. His robes were plain, and, like the earth, a dozen shades of brown, and wrapped around his body as he sat, cross-legged, on the edge of the step. By his side, the nobles looked savage, graceless, bundled like washing. He gave a small bow from the neck, not in humility but, as it were, cueing Burnes to speak.

"Emperor," Burnes began. "Lord of the distant horizon, Emperor of the wind, King of the Afghans, Heir of Israel . . ."

That was not quite right. He continued.

"Heir of Israel, we come to offer you the shade of our friendship. May the shade of our friendship always offer you rest and solace, may the waters of the love between our empires never run dry."

"May the song of the nightingale always bless your counsels," the Amir returned, "and may the wise horses of your empire bear you without tiring to your last home. Sit down, sit down."

Burnes, Gerard, and Mohan Lal awkwardly forced themselves into a cross-legged posture; a painful business in high-topped boots.

"Greetings, Sikunder Burnes," the Amir said. "Your name is auspicious."

An old and now familiar joke, from much repetition. Memories were long here, and every single Afghan, on hearing Burnes's name, had asked him if he were Alexander the Great, come to rob the country again. It had seemed unfortunate; now, he had come to see it was just their sense of humour. "There is nothing, thank God, I share with the Greek Alexander, and come not to plunder your kingdom, but in all respect."

The nobles, teetering with nervously thrilled anxiety, now gave way to a general giggling, stopped with one quick sideways jerk of the Amir's head. Behind him, the two pairs of double doors, one on either side of the throne room, were half opened; it had clearly been a great honour that, on their entry into the Bala Hissar, the double doors were all opened. Out of the doors came now a procession of cooks, bearing great dishes of heavy beaten silver, starting with a whole steaming lamb, lying on its back with its legs pathetically upwards in a sea of steaming spinach. It was, Burnes estimated, ten o'clock in the morning, and Gerard was tensing at the sight.

"How many kings are there in Europe?" Dost Mohammed suddenly asked. "And Napoleon, is he still King in Europe?"

"Ah—" Burnes said, thrown off balance. But the Amir seemed hardly to mind.

"I do not understand," the Amir continued. "It seems that the lands of the kings of Europe march with each other. Are they on good terms, or do they fight over their borders? How can they exist without destroying one another? I am most interested, Sikunder Burnes, to have the benefit of your wisdom and knowledge."

Burnes recollected himself. He had been made sleepy by the East, and had been preparing for a long series of introductory gestures; the mutual flattery for half an hour, the commendation and reluctant acceptance of every single dish, the entertainment from the professional anecdotalist. He hadn't anticipated anything like conversation starting up for at least two hours.

"There are many countries in Europe, great Amir," he began. Dost Mohammed, gathering up his retinue, gestured them to their places on the carpet around the colossal morning feast. He drew Burnes to his right side, and seemed to be listening with great attention, the Amir's big dark sad eyes fixed on him as he spoke. When the list had come to an end, he took a deep hissing breath through his nose, like a horse after exercise.

"I see," he said. "It seems to me that your advancement in civilization, as you describe it, does not save you from war and dispute."

"It is to be feared so."

The minor nobility and clergy, all trembling with curiosity, now responded to some kind of sign from the Amir, and fell on the food with a terrible cheerful eagerness.

"It is said," a very young prince asked, "that in your country, the flesh of pigs is eaten. Is this true, Sikunder Burnes?"

The Amir waved away the question before Burnes could answer it. "Tell me about taxation in Europe," he said. "How do your kings collect money to conduct their wars?"

"Such a thing can barely interest the great Amir," Gerard interposed, "so peaceful are his lands and the lives of the people under his wise rule."

"Nevertheless, I want to know," the Amir said, not taking his eyes off Burnes. "Tell me about taxation."

"And you, great Amir," Burnes said. "What do you know of the people of Europe? Have you, with your own eyes, seen the embassies of Russia?"

Dost Mohammed took a piece of bread, and chewed it, thoughtfully.

"Pray, sir," Dr. Gerard said abruptly. "What are your times of prayers?"

The mullah, on safe ground here, immediately began to rattle off the list. Gerard interrupted him. "You are enjoined, I think, by the Koran, to pray before sunrise and after sunset?"

"Yes, yes," the mullah said. "Yes, and damned be the infidel who neglects such prayers."

Gerard could hardly contain himself, his feet twitching with his suppressed theological glee. "Tell me, sir," he went on, his eyebrows shooting up in theatrical amazement, "how one of the faithful would carry out this injunction in the Arctic Circle?"

The mullah hardly paused. "In every part of the world are the injunctions of the Koran to be obeyed, except in some circumstances while travelling, when it is written that—"

"Quite, quite, quite," Gerard went on. "But in the Arctic Circle, man."

"The—" the mullah paused, uncertain.

"The Arctic Circle is the utmost point of the earth, sir, the Ultima Thule, the furthest point on the geographical globe, far north of any inhabited or habitable spot. It exhibits—and this is my query—a seasonal curiosity, for five or six months of the year. In the winter, the sun does not rise; in the summer, the sun does not set, and the barren northern lands are plunged into a night which lasts for months, and, in the summer, a perpetual day. Sir, I repeat my question. How may these prayers be performed in a land where there is neither sunrise nor sunset? Are we to suppose that the faithful Esquimaux are only enjoined to perform their devotions twice a year?"

Gerard was enjoying himself too much, Burnes reflected, and now the mullah had had a moment to consider the question and make something up. He glanced at the Amir, and, to his slight surprise, there was no sense of insult there, but, over the sharp hooked nose, a glittering and amused look in the eyes. Dost Mohammed, too, was enjoying himself.

"Quite, quite," the mullah said. "The Prophet himself visited the faithful Eska, the faithful Eska. It is said. And in such countries it has always been the custom that prayers are not required, in those countries, yes, it is sufficient to repeat the Quluma."

"Permit me to ask, sir," Burnes cut in with a confident feeling that, now, he was entertaining the Dost, "in which chapter of the Koran this doctrine may be found? We poor infidel, alas, may not claim to know or understand the sacred writings."

"Yes," Dost Mohammed added. "Yes, where is this extraordinary idea to be found? I do not remember such a thing. And when is the Prophet supposed to have found time to convert the Eska? I suppose at the same time he was travelling to Engelstan to pay his homage to Sikunder Burnes's grandfather, fool."

The poor mullah started to blush furiously, and the argument was taken up in the far corner of the room. Burnes dared to look directly at the Amir, who was twinkling graciously.

"You see," the Amir said to Burnes, leaning over confidentially and entirely ignoring the gurgle and chatter of the debate, "both our fools and our wise men love to argue, and hope never to conclude their arguments. And in your country, do the wise debate, so as to outlast the nightingale's song?"

"From dusk to dawn, great Amir," Burnes said. "And in every land, I think."

"But your companion has made an interesting point," the Amir said. "And one which the mullahs, now, will never settle. Perhaps you should return in seven years, and see what conclusion they have reached, because I fear they will not agree today."

The Amir looked distinctly amused by this prospect. Burnes looked at him, and the Amir looked, frankly, back; and, for once, looking into the eyes of one of the great princes of the Orient, Burnes did not feel like a rabbit transfixed by a snake.

"The climate of your city is most healthy, great Amir," Burnes said, slipping back into idle compliments. "And the beauty of your people is the most remarkable I have ever seen in my travels."

"If you stay, Sikunder," the Amir said, shrugging briefly, "you will be struck by the Wind of a Hundred and Twenty Days, and you will not think the climate so fine."

"The Wind, Amir?"

"It strikes at travellers, and may take only one. A pestilential wind, which strikes and kills." The other Afghans had fallen silent now. "It attacks like a cold wind, and leaves the traveller senseless. And the flesh of the man struck by the Wind falls from the bones, and limbs soften and fall away from each other, and the hair falls out at the touch. A disease of the low-lands, a curse of the Wind."

"Pray God—" Gerard said.

"And now, Sikunder Burnes," the Amir went on, quite calmly. "Let us speak of your European alchemists."

9

And so, when the infidel had been fed, and watered, and dismissed for the day, Dost Mohammed looked out over his city. Dost Mohammed, son of Sarfraz, son of Hajji Jamal, son of Usaf, son of Yaru, son of Mohammed, son of Omar, son of Khizar, son of Ismail, son of Nek, son of Daru, son of Saifal, son of Barak, son of Abdal, Abdal the Great, father of the Afghans, Heir of Israel, Lord of the Wind, Emperor of the distant horizons; Dost Mohammed looked over the city in his easy splendour, and, in the empty room, let his marvellous mind fill with guile. No noise of feeling crumpled his face, and he thought as long as he could about the English. They, surely, would be useful; the heavy useful English, having money and guns and land, could usefully help the Amir to stay just as he was, just where he was, and continue in his usual ways, without offering interference, preventing trouble without knowing, exactly, what they were doing. Presently the call of the imam to prayer drifted up from the city. Dost Mohammed began, quite slowly, on his devotions. As he rose and fell, his head lifting and dropping over the divine flawed complexity of the prayer-mat, his lips muttering in the empty room, his mind continued to dwell, quite properly, on punishment. It was the Amir's duty each night to determine the punishments to be visited on wrongdoers the next day, and it was to this which, in prayer, he now turned his mind. From the mosques in the city, a rumbling muttering of prayer filled the city with noise, thousands of the devout rising and falling, a single huge multiple sound, and Dost Mohammed rose and fell in prayer, and thought of violence. The wrongdoers the next day were a various bunch. Low thieves, the adulterous twelve-year-old wife of one of the sons of the Amir, the rebellious chief of a tribe whose lands lay just within the uncertain shifting borders of the kingdom. Hanging and beheading and dragging behind horses for the thieves, as was ordained. The adulterous princess to be thrown down the well of the Bala Hissar itself.

And, for the seditious leader—Dost Mohammed thought hard. He despised rebellion, because it always failed; and failure was what Dost Mohammed despised most, being a blot on the face of God. His head lifted and lowered above the glowing ruby prayer-mat, and for the moment he could not think of any punishment. Then he remembered the decreed fate of Sayad Ata, in his youth; he had been caught in rebellion. His fate had been to be tied down on his breast while an elephant trampled on him. Dost Mohammed, deep in prayer, remembered the devout, righteous, and splendid sight of the death of Sayad Ata; how the unworthy descendant of the Prophet himself had groaned and wailed at the approach of the beast! How his followers had groaned in the crowd, not understanding where the path of right had led, as if a thousand elephants were approaching, to tread on them! How his shrieks had been stopped, like a finger placed over the hole in a leaking whistling goatskin, as his bones, all at once, had cracked and popped! How grand and dreadful the sudden gouts of blood from every orifice, bursting out like a spirit-witness to the Faith, spilling into the dust! How right and good, the decreed end of Sayad Ata! Rising and falling in his devotions, his mind filling with the happy contemplation of the exercise of justice and right, the Amir quite forgot that some other means of execution would have to be found for tomorrow's rebellious tribesman, there being, at the moment, no imperial elephant to be had. What had happened to the imperial elephant Dost Mohammed could not, for the moment, quite recollect; whether the dingy, foul-tempered, foul-smelling, and noisy beast had been borrowed by some fool son, given to another recalcitrant tribe as an expensive joke, or had simply wandered off into the hills, Dost Mohammed could not think, so firmly fixed was his mind on the imperial devotions, the imperial punishments. But soon the great Amir, son of Sarfraz, son of Hajji Jamal, all the way back to Abdal and the Heir of Israel himself, would have to think up some new way of putting the better class of criminal to death. Tomorrow, perhaps, he would ask the infidel if he wanted to come and see the executions. Tomorrow, indeed, he would ask the infidel how criminals were put to death in Engelstan. The infidel, after all, was bound to be full of ingenious new ideas.

At the other side of the city, the infidel was sitting or standing, and not saying anything much. Gerard had taken off his full dress uniform, and was sitting in his long thick smalls, holding but not reading a book; his mouth pursed in concentration, he was staring over the top, examining the clean rough floor. Mohan Lal had absented himself, and was in the latrines. Burnes, standing at the window, was giving way to an unfamiliar sensation, the slow scarlet flashes of terror. He had expected relief after his audience with the Amir. He had met emperors before, had met with the great of the Company and the Government. He had been ushered into the presence of the jewelled savage potentates of the East, had sat with tyrants whose teeth were blacked and pointed, as with the blood of their own children, and each time, before, had experienced the same sequence of events. Before, there had been a sort of dread, suppressed by the will like a child's balloon held to the ground by a spreading fist; then the willed exercise of confidence as the great savage potentate, whether a pantomime cannibal king or a savage director of the Company in his Bloomsbury palace, turned his eyes to the pink-and-white stripling and listened to the cautious opinions, buried in carefully lavish flatteries. And afterwards, that sense of relief, as the fist let the balloon go and the dread flew away, away, leaving only a nervous flurry of chat.

Now Burnes did not want to chat. He felt no relief. He felt no nervousness. He felt only the same terror he had felt before they had set off for the Amir's palace, and the kindness of the Amir only augmented the terror he had felt at his quizzing presence. All at once, he felt the full imperial splendour of the Amir's mind, of which he had been permitted to glimpse only the merest fraction; he had recognized that here was no ostentatious potentate, but the weight and show of the imperial, the Napoleonic mind up there could not be greater if it buried itself in rubies. He was not, to be perfectly honest, quite sure what if anything had happened to them, up there in the Bala Hissar; only that tomorrow it was going to happen again. Tomorrow, they would go back, and tomorrow it would be the same. He would walk through the hard-packed mud streets, corralled between horses, walking between hot flanks in his thick shining uniform, and feel himself drenched in sweat and dread.

There was an itch there in him, there, in his hands, and, for the first time since arriving in Kabul, he went to his pack, and took out his note-book, a knife, and the last scrap of a pencil. Slowly, paying no attention to the others in the room, he cut away at the stump, baring the lead, and then squatted on the floor. He took the pencil in his itching hand, and began to write.

"The Afghans," he wrote, "are a nation of children; in their quarrels they fight, and become friends without any ceremony. They cannot conceal their feelings from one another, and a person with any discrimination may at all times pierce their designs. No people are more incapable of managing an intrigue. I was particularly struck with their idleness; they seem to sit listlessly for the whole day, staring at each other; how they live it would be difficult to discover, yet they dress well, and are healthy and happy."

While he wrote, the itch, the uneasy fear, seemed to pass, as he described what he was so certain of, and seemed to bring the Afghans who surrounded them, every one under the point of his pencil. Now, as he wrote, they were a nation of children, and he, describing them, felt for the moment quite safe. But as he stopped and stared at the wall, the feeling returned. "I imbibed a very favourable impression," he wrote, "of their national character."

10

Under the lighted window, five squatting men sat, their attention focused on the eldest of them, his beard thick and square and white on his brown face, like a silver spade. Sadiq, older than he could tell, was telling them a story. His stories were not princesses in gardens and wizards and magic rings, but stories of this city, stories of the past. He was telling them what their fathers had told them many times, the story of how the brave, the great Futteh Khan, great brother of the Amir Dost Mohammed Khan, met his end at the hands of the stinking enemy. They knew the story, had heard it a hundred times, from their fathers, their mothers, and, dozens of times, many many dozens of times, sitting just here, squatting against the wall, listening to just such a storyteller as the fierce-eyed Sadiq, rousing them to vengeance, muttering into the listening night. "And when the Vizier Futteh Khan returned, the treacherous Prince Kamran, chief of the stinking Suddozyes, he fell on him, and seized him, and his eyes were put out. And when he was blind and powerless he was not left to wander the deserts to beg for pity, powerless as he was, but was sliced, and cut, and yet he suffered all in silence. First the treacherous Prince Kamran demanded that he and his brothers surrender to the Persian Emperor, and the Vizier refused. And so Atta Mahmoud Khan, may his torments in hell be unending, sliced off his ear, and another the other ear, and a third his nose. And all the time they lied and said the Vizier had done them wrong. May we rise up and avenge the Vizier and all his enemies! And then his right hand and then his left, and all these torments and lies the Vizier Futteh Khan bore silently and without a sound, as the blood gushed from his face and the stumps of his arms like the fount of a river in spring, so brave was he; but when his enemies took his beard, and with their knives cut it from his face, he wept from his bleeding eyes and cried out from his tongueless mouth, to think how his pride was treated. Vengeance fall on his enemies! Vengeance in the hearts of the subjects of the Amir!"

Above, by the light of a candle which stank of tallow, and burned the walls black and smoked out the room, Burnes, oblivious, wrote on, setting down the Afghans, making sure of what they were and what he knew. For now, this would do. In the end, however, he came to examine his feelings, his sensations; and came to contemplate the particular hollow beating, between dread and excitement, which settled in the stomach at especial moments. Especial moments; standing there, in the hall of the Bala Hissar, waiting to be shown into the presence of the Amir. It was a feeling like that of standing there before a woman who waited only for him to seize her. A feeling like sitting, even, at his desk, taking up a sheaf of paper and beginning to write, to set down what he had seen. Each time the same feeling, each time, a feeling not to be argued with, or explained away. So strong it was, and it remained, that he concluded, in the end, when his life had become what it would become, that it was not, after all, what it so resembled, the awareness of the physical manifestation of sex, nor of the possibility of sex, but merely that of possibility. For him, the excitement which hollowed out his stomach and made his heart beat would always be produced not by what might happen, but what would not, despite all appearances, occur, and it was for the empty promises of chance that his heart beat, and his eyes grew big, and his stomach hollowed, and he stood, and stared at what was there to be stared at. Just that. And, each day, before he began to write, the proverb of the poet came to mind, the proverb carved deep on the tomb of the Emperor Babur, and he spoke it to himself, in his sincere deep rumbling Persian. *Drink wine in the city of Kabul, and send round the cup without stopping; for Kabul is a mountain, a sea, a town, a desert.*

THREE

London, in May.

At any other place in the world, late May would customarily be termed spring, and call forth the songs of birds, and the gambolling of infant mammals, and their attendant poets to sing their praises in the approved manner. Here, in London, in the fourth decade of the last century but one, there are no birds, or only ones so very brown and grey and drooping it is as if their native colours are all washed out with the incessant rinsing which falls from the London skies, birds which make no noise but an occasional croak to clear their throats of dirt. There are no lambs for the poets to celebrate, but only the usual London dogs, lying, their limbs curled up, at every street corner, too dejected to do anything but raise their heads in mild supplication at every passing boy's kick, too far gone in hopelessness to make any noise but a quiet moan, like the wind in a loose pane. You may be sure that the month makes no difference to them, or only in that the earth they find themselves licking ceaselessly off their pelts is dry like dust, or wet like mud. There are poets, it is true, here in London, in the fourth decade of the last century but one, and they write, it is true, about spring and lambs and birds. But to do so, I suppose, they are obliged to shut their eyes against the city they live in, and make something up.

London knows no seasons; knows nothing of spring or summer or winter. It knows nothing but two seasons: Dust, and Mud. Now, at this moment, in May, we seem to be getting towards the end of Mud. Mud settled in more than six months ago, and has shown no sign of taking its leave just yet. The streets have settled into their pristine ooze, and if there be any bedrock beneath the vast sucking mass which London is proud to call a street, no one pretends any longer to know. Anything dropped in the street is instantly swallowed by London and its mud, and is never seen again; a prayer-book, a ring, a hammer, a cloak; all fall to the ground and are forever lost, deep in the mud and slime and filth of the London street. Once a poor musician let his bassoon fall, not far from Seven Dials; the mud deprived him of his livelihood, and the family, tragically bassoonless, now must beg for their merest sufficiencies, there, outside Mrs. Lirriper's drapery shop. Once, as mothers tell their naughtier sons, a small boy let go of his mother's hand while crossing the great swamp of Piccadilly, and, untethered, sank to the bottom of the mud, never to be seen again. Soon, it is to be hoped, the weather will improve, and Mud be succeeded by Dust, though it seems unlikely that any poet will want to sing the praises of that modern season. When that happens, everything changes; the sounds of the city alter from the obscene sucking and splash and brown drain-gurgle of one half the year, to the dry crackle and quiet thudding of the other half. Those who cannot leave the city will start to complain, not of the wet and chill ceaselessly rising around their ankles, but the dry choking heat which gets into the throat, and strangles the Londoner all day and all night.

But if it is true that London knows no seasons, that, perhaps, is because it knows only one Season. It is here, in May, that we find ourselves; here, standing with the linkboys and the cutpurses and the crossing-sweepers, each unpromising youth with the tools of his unpromising trade, standing and gawping at the slow procession unfurling before them, at this hour of early dusk in late spring. It is the height of the Season, and also, nearly, the end of it—a paradox more often stated than relished. The linkboys and cutpurses and crossing-sweepers stand just where Piccadilly turns into Park Lane, and watch the procession before them, silently or raucously calling out, according to their temperament. Up Piccadilly comes a succession of carriages, each a closed black box on wheels, shiny and locked, drawn, mostly, by two black horses, for all the world as if the cashboxes of Threadneedle Street had, with one voice, cried, "Enough of the City!" and, equipped each with a pair of plate-faced footmen and a set of wheels, set off to see if what they had always heard of the West End and its Court could possibly be the case. Up Piccadilly come the melancholy cashboxes, and, at the corner, you can see, as they turn, the whinnying wheels and hooves pulling free of the mud, that each, too, contains a treasure.

The linkboys cry out, with ridicule or amazement, at what they see. At this corner, the inhabitants of each carriage lean forward, and look out. Because here, you see, at this corner, lives the Duke, the old victor of Waterloo, and everyone is curious about the Duke's habits, and will, on passing from Piccadilly into the Park, lean forward in the hope of a brief glimpse of the great man. It is a hope which is often gratified; the Duke is a man who likes to show himself, and strolls, daily, in the Park to accept the homage of strangers. But tonight, there is nothing to be seen. If the inhabitants of the carriages sink back with a minor disappointment, their evenings indefinably clouded now in some way, we have not been disappointed; because now, with the linkboys and the cutpurses, we have caught a marvellous glimpse of a lady or two. Out of the funereal darkness of the inside of a carriage, for all the world like the glitter of a black cashbox being flung open, a glistening white face appears, bathed and almost certainly scented, a white face which allows you to dream of the white flesh, the dream of white lace and silk almost certainly hidden underneath the dark cloak, and, most marvellous of all—something which forces even the wiser cynics of the observing mob into an awed silence—the unmistakable deep glitter of diamonds, brought from the Far East for no reason but to decorate these cool, lovely, clean faces. Everywhere else in the city—everywhere else in the great world, as far as the linkboys know—is mud and filth, and these white faces with their bright white light of diamonds shine like unaccustomed, unimaginable virtue.

They flash in the gaze of the street observers for one second, these costly faces, and then move on in their stately way. Where are they all going, all in the same direction? Why, they are going out, naturally, because this is the Season, and in the Season it does not do, if you are of a certain level in society, to stay at home. It is required of you to put on your least comfortable clothes, ones fitted neither for a London cold nor a London heat, and go and sit for a few hours with people you know nothing of and care nothing for, drawing what satisfaction you may from the fact that when you leave to go home, outside there may be poor people who may be prepared to gawp, who, you hope, are eaten up with envy of you; because if no one in London envies you in your party-going plight, it is hard to see why you should continue the exercise.

2

The carriage now rounding the corner extracts itself with such unpredictable lurchings from the mud beneath the wheels that the cockaded footman on top almost drops his reins. Inside, a startled face lunges towards the window, to the rich appreciation of the street onlookers; they like a nice-looking girl. The nice-looking girl smooths her dress, braces herself as if with cold, and draws back into her seat. By her is an old man, his skin so taut and leathery, his eyes so yellow and unobserving, and the whole effect so quickly angular as he sits there in the clothes for his immaculate evening that you almost expect a forked tongue to dart out, to catch a fly or two. His blood is cold, his movements quick and stiff. He is not in the first flush of fashion, nor of youth; his clothes, though immaculate, have a distinct first-gentleman-of-Europe air, as if remembering on his behalf what he has now forgotten, his high season, so long ago. The fashion of thirty years before, too, accounts for his air; not inattentive, exactly, but strongly attentive to something not in the carriage, something Bella cannot see and does not wish to share. The ruby witch, she once heard him call it; the opium he has been taking, daily, for decades. In recent years, noticing, perhaps, that the young did not care for it and often disapproved of it, he has stopped mentioning it with his customary glee, even to what remains of his family. Bella would not mention it, but has grown used to the idea that when her father hands her into the carriage on their evening round, his touch will not be firm, his gaze fixed on a spot somewhere beyond her. The jerk of the carriage into or out of the mud jolted him into seeing; now his eyes are glazing over again, into their customary blank bliss. His daughter looks at him; she knows the expression very well, and blushes for him.

"I see the Duke is still in town," she says.

"The Duke would never leave town before—before—" her father says, as his look moves back inside the carriage. "I remember, once, many years ago, before you were born or not long after. In the Park we were, and I greeted the Duke. Old acquaintances we were, and he stopped and pinched y'brother's cheek. 'Fine child, that, Colonel,' he said. And Harry took one look at him, with his great beak and his great ramrod shoulders, and started to howl. Never saw the Duke again, not to speak to."

"Poor Harry," Bella Garraway murmurs. Her father has been galvanized by his own anecdote, which Bella has heard many times before; everyone in London has one story about the Duke of Wellington, and—Bella sometimes thinks—each is told and retold until every story has been heard by every man, woman, and child in London, and then they die, stories melting into silence, and oblivion. Her father's story always moves her, strangely, even though it hardly amounts to a story, so ruefully does it reflect on poor Harry and his hopes. She has no response for his story, but it hardly matters, because now Colonel Garraway is sinking back into his sharp-elbowed opiate haze.

The line of wheeled cashboxes moves on, stately as an oriental caravan through the trackless wastes of Piccadilly and Park Lane, all with one end, it seems, in view. At this time of the year, at this time of the afternoon, it is always thus; the upper few thousand, scrubbed and whited like so many peripatetic sepulchres, squeeze themselves into their least comfortable clothes, and set off for the evening's entertainment. To dinner, to a rout, to a dance, to the opera; the upper few thousand, encased in whatever it has been decreed they should wear, limber stiffly through their doors, and into their carriages, to set off to see whatever people they have been seeing every week, all through the Season. Stiffened by their unyielding but undeniably fashionable raiment, you would recognize a member of the upper few thousand even unclad, fresh from the bath, or at the loose-robed gates of heaven; their gait is jointed and unnatural as a puppet's is, and an old dowager walks as smartly as an upright old soldier. You would recognize them naked, but they are held up by their clothes and, stripped of their acquired carapace, they would surely fall, bonelessly, to the ground. As they manoeuvre their much corseted old bodies in or out of the carriage, it is difficult not to fancy that they creak in the exercise. But fashion dictates the stiff brocades and tight corseting, and fashion, here and now, is obeyed as promptly as an admiral.

Of course, everyone who now is making their slow path up Park Lane knows everything that is to be known of their fellow pilgrims. They are a very few, few thousand, and only rarely do they admit a new postulant at the crepuscular shrines of the fashionable London evening. Rarely, and usually by virtue merely of being born, is a new member of Society admitted. Money may admit you as a curiosity; or genius, particularly if displayed by a foreigner about whose origins it is possible to be rather vague, such as that excitingly coiffeured Signor Paganini who was everywhere with his *recitals* two years ago. Adventure, too, or heroism committed by a suitably handsome young man in the East may serve very well to supply the fashionable two-legged curiosity of the Season. A young man with a good tale to tell, possessed of the fortune which accrues so readily in India and the deserts which lie beyond the Bosphorus, may be admitted to have a splendid Season, listened to by every ear from Park to Park, and carry into the country at the end the memory of adoring listening faces, turned up to his, white fans clasped by plump white hands, fluttering off like Cabbage Whites as the marvellously retold anecdote reaches its terrifying climax and the brave young man saves the little Rani from the jaws of the man-eating tiger. He may, also, carry the certainty of hundreds of new friends, many brave Seasons to come, if the hero of the day is foolish; if he is wise, however, he will pack his bags and go back to the scene of his great triumphs after one Season. Next year, as everyone knows, the great world will supply some new excitement, and the great tiger-beating hero will be cut in the Park by all his old friends, now so fascinated by a seven-foot American funambulist, a Russian poetess, or eight-year-old watercolourist that his old stories start to seem very old hat indeed. He will be well advised to retire where he can, and draw what solace he can from his thousands, the vast and grateful emerald the Maharajah awarded him, the rapidly-acquired fat sensible wife.

3

For the moment, the hero of the hour suspects none of this. Burnes is dressing, in as leisurely a fashion as he can manage. Here, in the dressing room of the house he has taken for the Season, he would not think that his time in the stage lights is drawing to a close. If he thinks anything, he probably considers that he is entering on the first stages of a vertiginous ascent. By now, he is intimate with people he barely dared to notice a few months ago; he finds, with a regret that does him credit, that he no longer has much time for those who introduced him to all those salons, before

Christmas; he finds, with a malicious pleasure which quite surprises him, that the Montrose neighbours who snubbed his father twenty years ago now queue to drop their cards in the silver filigree bowl in the hall; they, those Montrose neighbours, have been turned in his eyes into what everyone laughs at, a set of nabob Scotch with raw-skinned ambitious wives. Burnes is decent to everyone, because that is his way. He has started to be noticed by the great—by Dukes—by Royalty, even, once; and, surely, the time will come when the brief notice, the honour graciously conferred in crowded rooms, turns into intimacy, and he finds himself a welcome visitor at every house in town. Perhaps not this year, because the Season is drawing to its brilliant close; but next year. Yes, perhaps next year.

His fingers have slowed, stopped. He stretches out his hand, and Charles hands him the next item in the ritual, in silent deference. For one moment, as he ties the elaborate knot, it occurs to him that he and his valet must be the same age. He looks, critically, in the glass at the final result. He has dined out twenty-one times already this month, and told his story twenty-one times. He looks, critically, at himself in the glass and prepares to go out, to tell it once more. What he sees in the glass is what you expect to see, of the hero of the minute, or more or less so. Not so brown as he was, not so thin as he was. He has been taken in from the heat and dust and wind, and left to pale and fatten on an unaccustomed diet; a diet of drawing rooms, and lobsters and champagne; of morning walks in the Park with no exercise more strenuous than the three-inch raising of the hat; of the ceaseless attentions of the most accomplished young ladies the metropolis can supply wholesale. That the accomplishments of the young ladies run no further than the performance of half a dozen Irish airs on harp or pianoforte hardly troubles Burnes. If he wants other, bolder accomplishments than the ones fashionable London permits of its women, he knows by now where to find them. Under the softening regime, he is quite altered from the man of six months ago; no longer dark and lined and meatless as a piece of old leather that has lain out in the tropical sun for years on end, but pale and soft. He looks at his own veal-face, there in the glass. Only his hard hands betray the fact that he has led quite a different life from his eager listeners; only the bright light in his dark eyes shows that he has seen things they will never see, or wish to.

Charles pauses in his ministrations, looks inquiringly at Burnes in the glass. Burnes becomes aware that the valet said something.

"Yes, Charles?" he says.

"My lady Woodcourt's, sir?" Charles repeats.

"Yes," Burnes says. "Yes, alas."

"Lady Woodcourt," Charles says, managing to sound both approving of Burnes's destination this evening and, shaking his head, disapproving of his master's irreverent tone. Burnes hardly minds; by now, he can afford, he believes, to appear unconcerned by even the most alarming invitation. And who is Lady Woodcourt, after all? A wicked old woman who has lifted her skirts for two kings and who knows how many prime ministers, whose whoring days ought to be over by now. Lady Woodcourt, indeed; a woman he knew nothing of six months ago. Charles takes the brushes and applies them to Burnes's head, the dressing now almost complete. "May I ask—" he continues.

"No," Burnes says. "No, this will be all. I shan't be needing you again tonight, thank you." He has always been good with his men, and, as Charles takes the clothes brush to wipe away the flakes of scurf on the waistcoat, he grins at him. Charles nods, demurely, and finally helps Burnes on with his immaculately shining black coat.

4

Half a mile away, the wicked old woman is descending, very carefully, a staircase. All that perfumes and silk and preservatives can do for her charms has been done, which is not much. Footmen stand around, upright as chessmen on the black and white marble floor, and she comes down the stairs, their bent little old mistress. As usual, the first arrivals have preceded her, and are now kicking their heels in the anteroom. Lady Woodcourt does not hurry on their account, nor does it occur to her to acknowledge them. She moves, a slow bent little old woman, down the stairs as if she would like an arm or a stick to keep her upright. Here, in her house, she seems a nervous little bird in a brilliant gold cage; everything so baby-blue and gold, every wall so hung with looking glasses to entertain its denizen with contemplation of herself. And, between the mirrors, still more representations of Lady Woodcourt. Three or four portraits of her at her peak. In one, she is a girl in her father's grounds. The painter, long ago, saw something in her mind, and has her holding a whip and snaffle. Another is an embarrassing and improbable portrait of her in mythological guise, as—as—as (even Lady Woodcourt, guiding her guests round, has sometimes to pause and think and dredge her old mind) Minerva, the foolish-looking owl just escaping from her limp pale fingers. The third is her wedding portrait, and unwary callers have been known to inquire of each other who the little gentleman in brown could possibly be. That useful and patient Sir Bramley is still to be seen over the fire in his wife's London house, clinging to her arm in fear and disbelief. What happened to him in life, no one quite knows. A very young man ventured once that he had been washed, and dissolved, being nothing, in the end, but varnish and ornament. Certainly it is difficult to believe in Sir Bramley as anything more substantial than his painted past self, but the remark got back, and the very young man was seen no more at Lady Woodcourt's. In reality, it is thought, Sir Bramley lives in Italy for the sake of his health, and leaves Lady Woodcourt to the exercise of her influence and her many protectors.

No smooth-skinned oil-fresh Minerva now, she comes forward into the room and staggers into a chair. Almost at once, the blue-coated chess-man at the door gives a start and calls out the names of the first skulking guests.

"Colonel and Miss Garraway," he calls, blushing and gulping like the boy he is. In through the door pop the old Colonel and his pretty daughter. He, behind some perfect translucent ruby glaze, is a hopeless and declining old beau of hers, a useful stopgap who does no harm to anyone but himself; next to him, his daughter seems alarmingly alert and clean and young. Lady Woodcourt greets them without rising, her hand resting on a bijou gewgaw, a knobbled warty Chinese bronze pig. The girl, she is pleased to see, is as pretty as everyone says, as she follows her father's abstracted bow with a gracefully embarrassed bob, scrutinizing with intense juvenile interest the finer details of the Aubusson, murmuring something which might have been "My lady." A great improvement, all in all, on the Colonel's late wife, who came into a room and waited for the company to rise and say how-de-do, as if she deserved nothing less. This girl, at least, would not laugh in your face and call you her dear Fanny.

Bella Garraway comes into the room, and her feet in their thin slippers are glad not to be kept waiting on marble any longer. It is her first time at the famous, the fascinating Lady Woodcourt's; her papa has taken care not to alarm her, but all the same, she is wearing what diamonds Mama's case has yielded up. Lady Woodcourt sits, smiling vaguely; a woman shrivelled and brown as an old apple, her filmy old eyes drifting perpetually away from the mark. Bella advances, and submits to Lady Woodcourt's grip, a fierce clutch like the clasp of a purse. She just drinks her in; her thin body, her brown wrinkled flesh drifting loosely within the hard carapace of her boned gown like a boat at its moorings. Bella has no idea, in reality, who Fanny Woodcourt is. But Bella, as her sister and governesses always privately remark, is quick on the uptake, and her eyes run quickly over the room, assessing each gift, each bibelot with the commercial eye of an auctioneer. Each object, indeed, has its magnificent provenance, since Lady Woodcourt buys nothing for herself, and takes only from the grandest of her admirers. Anything Bella's father ever gave her is surely in Lady Woodcourt's dressing room by now, if not passed on to the housekeeper. Bella drops her eyes in modesty, but if she will not meet Lady Woodcourt's gaze, she is at least curious enough to inspect her voluble possessions. Whether each porcelain treasure, each glittering glass is the gift of his Grace, Excellency, Majesty hardly matters. Bella looks around, assessing, and sees what Fanny Woodcourt has been.

"My daughter, Lady Woodcourt," Colonel Garraway says, with all his opium-glazed gravity. Lady Woodcourt nods, so calmly that Bella unkindly wonders whether she, too, has been drinking from the phial of the ruby witch. She has learnt how to be suspicious of anything as innocent as composure or boredom in anyone much over the age of forty-five. They all do it, she suspects; and none of them discusses it in her hearing, ever.

"I'm afraid you will find us all," Lady Woodcourt says, "a very dull old company tonight. Do sit down. I am quite mortified, my dear, to inflict such a, such a bundle of dry old sticks on you. I positively fear you may never come again, and that, that, that—"

"That would never do," Colonel Garraway supplies gallantly, handing his daughter to a settle, and sitting down after her. Lady Woodcourt laughs brilliantly, a sound as if her glassy old bones have tumbled loose, all at once, and chimed together into a heap, somewhere inside her skin.

"I'm sure it will be delightful," Bella says, inadequately.

"Such a lot of dry old sticks," Lady Woodcourt says, with a touch of steel, not liking to be contradicted even in this mock-apology. She seems to believe her own polite disclaimer for a second, believing what she says as she says it, as all liars must, and a cloud passes over her brow. "Still— that wonderful young man—the explorer, who, who, who—"

"The hero of Bokhara," Colonel Garraway adds, smiling. "Yes, that very wonderful young man."

"Bokhara," Lady Woodcourt sighs, relieved. "Now that is a place, I swear, not one person in a thousand had heard a jot or, or, or tittle of one year ago. And now we talk of it as readily as we talk of, of—"

"Dorsetshire," Colonel Garraway says.

"Of Dorsetshire," Lady Woodcourt continues. "My young friends talk of nothing else. I think one or two, they fancy taking a house in the better quarter of Bokhara for the winter. Now what do you think of that?"

"I'm sure I don't know," Bella says, faintly alarmed as Lady Woodcourt spectacularly tinkles away.

"All stuff and nonsense, of course, and I don't believe any one of them could point to the wretched place on the map. Still, we talk of nothing else, I find, and all down to this singular, ah, fascinating, ah, ah, remarkable young man, all—"

"Captain Burnes," Bella interjects.

"Indeed. Thank you, my dear," Lady Woodcourt says, looking genuinely as if no one has ever done her a greater favour. "And now, who is this—"

"M. le Duc de Neaud," the footman calls, or rather attempts, since what he announces is the Duck de Nod. "And," as a little woman in a snuff-coloured dress scurries in after her diminutive husband, "Mme la Duchesse."

Everyone rises with an audible relief.

"Delighted—charmed—delighted—quite on time—feared to be early—my dear Fanny—my dear—" the Duchesse de Neaud spills over. She is English, a chatterbox, resented by no one, welcome everywhere, if she does not come first or leave last. The Duc limits himself to a quick bow and a scowl. He came over after the Revolution and, penniless, married one of those spinsters who attended the old Queen Charlotte, to everyone's surprise, including hers; her future had seemed to be mapped out in the series of faintly dictatorial books for children she wrote in dull afternoons at Windsor. She turns from Lady Woodcourt to Bella. "My dear—my dear—"

Colonel Garraway snaps into awareness. "Duchesse," he says. "My daughter, Bella."

"Miss Garraway," the Duc says. "*Charmé.*" But he is already turning, already charmed, it seems, with the next entrants, and Bella sees no reason not to sink back into her chair as the room starts to fill.

5

"Charmed—delighted—couldn't be more—" the Duchesse says, sitting down by Bella. But she is talking, not to Bella but to a fast-approaching young man, pink in his half-worried, half-confident face. He bows rapidly, crumpling at the middle like a man who has been punched hard.

"May I inquire," the young man says to the Duchesse. Bella stops paying any attention, and concentrates on her fan. The old people are coming in, showing no emotion, walking smoothly around each other, bowing automatically, like puppets on casters. The boy at the door is keeping up, but there is now quite a queue outside, waiting to hand their card and have him call their name. She is called back by her name.

"I quite doted on Bella when she was too little to know who was kissing her goodnight," the Duchesse glitters, aiming her smile somewhere beyond the young man, bowing and smiling nervously. "Quite doted on her. I would hug her and affection her, and—such a pretty little thing, and now, quite such a beauty, now, don't blush, my dear."

Bella bows, remembering very well what it was like to be clutched to the swarthy old Duchesse's bosom, heavy and spiked with trinkets; it felt like falling through the window of a jeweller's shop. The Duchesse bows back, and then the young man bows, and they are all precisely like an entire yard full of tired chickens. She was no Duchesse then, but only an old spinster. The young man presents a familiar face to Bella.

"How do you do, Miss Garraway," the familiar face says.

"How do you do," Bella says firmly back, smiling like the audience at a vaudeville.

"Miss Gilbert," the yelping barker cries into the room, "and Miss Jane Gilbert."

She sees from the smiling guest's proprietorial security, his relaxed saunter back into the chair, that this is the son of the house. She corrects herself, looking at Lady Woodcourt, who has no sons. She is no more fecund than a sideboard. This, surely, is the guest of honour. "How do you do, Mr. Burnes. Do you find the climate here suits you? Or do you long for the East?"

"Have you read Mr. Burnes's book, Miss Garraway?" the Duchesse interposes. "I rave over it—the learning—the wit—the fierce fierce tribes of the exotic East. How brave—how heroic you have been, sir. Have you read his book?"

"I have tried, sir, so many times, and each time the bookseller sends me back empty promises, leaving me abandoned. I am not entirely hopeless, but your bookseller is quite the jilt, Mr. Burnes."

The Duchesse laughs brilliantly, flutingly; a youthful and yet historic noise, a descending scale directly from old Queen Charlotte's nurseries. If the Duchesse laughs, there can be no impropriety whatever in this corner of the blue and gold drawing room. Two sisters approach, their faces long as doors: the Gilbert sisters. In mourning, as they so often are, they scrutinize Burnes efficiently. The elder is twenty-seven, and five years ago was sadly disappointed in love; the younger is no older than Bella, but already has her sister's half-angry air, and will come to nothing in the end.

"Quite the jilt," Bella says, as the sisters move on.

"You must tell us," the Duchesse continues, "of your adventures in Bokhara. I long—I pine—for the story, the entire tale, from the horse's mouth."

"So long and dull a story can hardly interest ladies," Burnes says conventionally.

"No, no, Mr. Burnes," the Duchesse says, but she seems to take him at his word, since she rises and goes, smiling, into the crush. The room is crowded now, and Bella's father, there, fifteen yards away, is fixed in his gaze and uncomprehending. One of the Gilbert sisters is talking at him, and directing a fierce laugh at him, the laugh of someone who knows rejection well; he looks like a frightened old man. This is how it is, an hour after his dose. She does not know, and does not wish to know, where he buys what he needs; she only knows, with a wave of shame, that he no longer even talks about it. She wants to rescue her father, there, standing in the embrace of his invisible ruby witch. Burnes, next to her, is twitching like a bird on the branch. It is her duty to carry on talking to him about his East, but she looks at her father and has nothing to say to such a stranger.

6

Through these evenings, these festive London gatherings, people move without any will, like balls on a billiard table. At one end of the space, new balls spill into the confined space, and at the far end, the balls drifting around the smooth space prod each other and drift off unpredictably. An announcement at the door, a pair of new arrivals, somehow nudges the room along a little, and the mass, unwilled, cannons through the room, and the last ripple brings Burnes to his feet, and face to face with Stokes, a brilliant and brilliantly polished writer for the journals, his head smooth and gleaming like marble, his glittering spectacles always ready to be whisked off to make a point. They greet each other, silently.

"I understand, Mr. Burnes, that you have been signally honoured," Stokes begins.

"Beyond my desserts, no doubt, sir," Burnes says.

"I heard that you were signally honoured," Stokes persists. "By our friend in Brighton."

"I would hardly call the King my friend," Burnes says. Or yours, he seems to insist.

"That must have been a thrilling occasion, sir," Stokes said.

"If I were, indeed, honoured by the King's curiosity in my explorations," Burnes says, "you could hardly expect me to tell you the purport of the conversation."

"Come, come, Burnes," Stokes says. "I meant no affront. I did not think it was so very secret. It was from the—no, better not to say—but it was from a gentleman of the Court that I heard the interesting fact. Would you prefer to find some more quiet place to talk?"

"No, sir," Burnes said. "I can have nothing to say to you that I would keep from any person here present. I was honoured by the King's interest, who had read my book with the greatest curiosity, and I received the King's gracious command to Brighton. That is all. A trivial meeting, made remarkable only by the King's majesty. There is really nothing more to say."

(He resists the recall of the jovial bulging maggot in silk stockings and a scrubby wig, thumping the floor with his stick, his nervous Queen clutching the gilt sides of the chair, underneath the vast grand mouldings and velvet and gilt, what passed in his late brother's mind for an oriental palace, and asking such blunt ordinary wrong questions it was not in him to know how to respond, to offer any kind of satisfaction.)

"Your reticence does you credit, sir," Stokes says. "I have read your book, and greatly admire it. You exhibit the greatest faculties of curiosity, erudition, and exposition. But I reached the end of your book with one burning question, ah, as it were, unextinguished. What in heaven's name are we doing in Afghanistan? What, come to that, are we doing in India?"

"Sir, I hardly know what you can mean."

"My meaning is this," Stokes continues. "What drove us to acquire our oriental possessions? And what is driving us to acquire still more? I presume, sir, that you were not in Kabul in pure curiosity. I presume, in short, that your mission was conducted to the sound of those siren voices enjoining us to occupy the whole of Asia, and bankrupt our children and our children's children and our children's children's children. There can be no doubt that you were there to prepare for us to acquire the Punjab, to repeople Afghanistan with our sons and daughters, and open up yet another bottomless pit, to swallow our limited resources—resources which could be put to better use two miles from this house, to clothe and feed the filthy urchins who will beg a farthing from you, and from me, the second we leave our so agreeable hostess's embrace this evening. What, sir, in heaven's name, are we doing in India?"

"You are quite wrong, Mr. Stokes," Burnes says. This is a familiar argument; he has had it, indeed, with Stokes on previous occasions. "There is no intention to add the Punjab or the western tracts of land to our possessions. My mission was purely geographical, purely driven by curiosity. But what, sir, would be the alternative you propose? Were we to stay at home and do nothing?"

"And why not? What is so wrong with being satisfied with what you have?"

"Nothing, sir, unless you have the spirit of a Briton. Our possessions, sir, are vast new markets. Do you suppose our little island can contain our native spirit? Of course it cannot. And should we stay at home, relinquish India tomorrow, what would happen? Would the natives not slide back into all manner of native barbarities—the murder of travellers, the forced suicide of widows? Thuggee and suttee? Would the precious flame of Christianity survive six months in such a poisoned atmosphere? Would India, indeed, be left to its own devices? Would not the French perceive an empty space? Would not Russia send its vast armies to bring new barbarities to a barbarous land? Sir, I suspect you of the worst sort of cynicism."

"Perhaps," Stokes says, smiling, maddeningly, like a teacher praising a moderately bright pupil. "I admire your spirit, Mr. Burnes—I who have never travelled so far as to see the ocean."

Burnes bows, deeply, coldly; he is oddly irritated by the conversation.

7

One of the chessmen comes smoothly into the room, and stops just short of Lady Woodcourt. She breaks off her animated conversation with the latest of the guests, and turns to the footman. The guest bows to her back, and makes his escape into the room. What information the footman bears must be thrilling, for in an instant Lady Woodcourt clasps her hands to her brown wrinkled bosom, as if to stop a pet white mouse escaping from between her dugs, and skips girlishly into the centre of the room. The chatter in the room stops raggedly, and the guests all turn to her, shining with her announcement. She calls out, not raising her voice, and everyone graciously inclines in her direction, like a grove of willows in the breeze.

". . . in honour of our most favoured guest, the hero, I may say, may I not, of Bokhara, M. Mirabolant has graciously consented . . ."

Burnes, who has sat down again, is nodding and smiling; he has had plenty of time to grow used to this announcement.

". . . M. Mirabolant has created a new, a marvellous dish, in honour of his adventures, his great heroism—dear friends, one moment, only . . ."

And the doors are swung open, and, there is M. Mirabolant, the great *chef de cuisine* on whom all London dotes—what all great London used to call a Cook. The great M. Mirabolant, universally agreed to be the greatest Frenchman in existence since—since—since Napoleon, since Voltaire, since time began. And before him is borne a large white china dish, piled high with some white stuff into the approximate semblance of a snowy mountain. M. Mirabolant is all geniality, his broad red face greeting the room without, precisely, greeting anyone. There is a little murmur and patter of applause, as the ladies' hands, soft as the flapping of doves into the sky, acclaim the dish, and the room turns from Mirabolant to the plump hero of the hour, who smilingly discounts any sense that he is worthy of Mirabolant's marvellous pudding.

"M. Mirabolant," Lady Woodcourt insists, "tell me, do not all dishes have a name?"

M. Mirabolant, all geniality, agrees that they do.

"Pray, M. Mirabolant," the Duchesse de Neaud joins in, "charming, quite charming—do tell us, what are we to call this dish?"

M. Mirabolant draws himself up, pulls on the left outer extremity of his marvellous black moustache, gazes in deep thought at the glossy mountain of cream on the shoulders of two trembling footmen. Perhaps no inspiration will come, and the room trembles before M. Mirabolant's genius. But they need not worry; for a light falls on the great Frenchman's face, and genius prepares to speak.

"It calls itself," he growls, his eyes fixed, as if in a trance, on the dish, and not at all on the attending multitudes, *une coupe Bokhara.*"

And now a rapture of applause breaks out in the room, and Mirabolant turns and sweeps out, leaving his adoring public, his ecstatic mistress, quite as if he had hired them for the evening, and not the other way round. Leaves, too, a confection made up entirely of iced cream and crushed meringue, the whole sprinkled with white rose petals.

"Tell me, Mr. Burnes," Bella finds herself saying. "Is this a customary dish of the natives of Bokhara?"

"To the best of my recollection, Miss Garraway," Burnes responds gravely, "they dine on it nightly. Meringue is their staple diet."

"I was certain of it," Bella says. "You must have had more dishes named in your honour than anyone now living."

Burnes laughs heartily, immediately smothering the noise. "Perhaps I am a little ungrateful," he says. "But it seems to me that, like the Dutchman's daughter, the dish has been christened twenty times, and still remains no better than it was at the first."

"Is it always *coupe Bokhara*, Mr. Burnes?" Bella says. "I do hope not—what a melancholy prospect that would be. Not only to have to eat iced cream and meringue every night, but not even to have the solace of variety offered by an occasional change of name."

A cousin of Lady Woodcourt has gone to the piano, and has started up a strange crooning and crackle, which passes for a selection of Welsh airs; a young man stands by to turn the pages, his eyes wandering about the room, his fervour all directed towards finding some means of escape from his sentry duty.

"No, not always, indeed, Miss Garraway," Burnes says. "I think it is only *coupe Bokhara* when M. Mirabolant takes the helm."

"Twice weekly?" Bella says.

"Quite that," Burnes agrees. "Other than that, it may be anything at all; *blanquette à l'Afghanienne, rôti de porc à la mode de Kabul,* or *coupe Bokhara.* Yes, perhaps you are right; it is mostly *coupe Bokhara.*"

"And is it always iced cream and meringue with white rose petals on top?"

"Always. No—I do Mirabolant an injustice—perhaps once the rose petals were pink."

The macabre daughters in their matching grave-gowns, taking a turn about the room, now come to where Burnes sits with Bella. They bow, sourly; Burnes responds, Bella makes a tiny incline, her shoulders trembling with withheld laughter, and they pass on.

"I think your brother was in India, Miss Garraway," Burnes says when they are gone.

"Yes, Harry," Bella says quickly. "Yes, that is right. How did you come to know such a thing?"

"I think it was the first thing I knew about you," Burnes says. Bella blushes and lowers her head, pretending to smooth her gown. "I heard of him in Calcutta. It was a sad end. He was spoken of well by everyone."

"Thank you, sir," Bella says. "My father would be comforted to hear you say that. We hoped India would be the making of him."

"I am sure it would have been," Burnes says. "I would not wish to intrude on your father in such festive—I mean—I would not be the one to bring melancholy thoughts to mind among happy friends."

Bella smiles, seeing where all this talk is leading. All this chatter about poor useless Harry, sent out to India to save his name and put an end to his card debts, dead in three months in an unmentionable duel over an officer's wife or, in official despatches, of the terrible Calcutta cholera. Poor Harry, indeed; but now, at least, he seemed to be serving some kind of useful purpose.

"I wonder if you would permit me to call," Burnes says. "To offer some small solace to your poor father."

"I am sure he would take great pleasure in your conversation, Mr. Burnes," Bella says, smiling warmly. "You are welcome to call at any time." And rests, for one moment, her little white hand on Burnes's; it is cool and pale, his hand, and as she touches him, he does not start, or move, but merely stares, gazes, at the two-second miracle of her hand in his.

"Thank you," Burnes says, helplessly. "And I shall bring my book, if you would permit me."

"We should be delighted," Bella smiles, and her smile is big and white and open. Her little square teeth, her clean pink mouth, her perfect lips. The smile, it makes him pause, and look, and around him, the room is silent, as if a great glass bell has dropped over them, and they move in a slower, bigger atmosphere. She smiles, and she shows her teeth, and glitters at him; there is no modesty in her, but only delight. He thanked her, and she is, for no reason, delighted.

At the other side of the room, Colonel Garraway snaps back into consciousness, his back upright and clean. It is like a window opening in the room. There before him is a girl, sour in the face and wrapped in black, looking at him inquiringly. He has no idea who she is, or what she has just said. At the other end of the room, there is a girl sitting on a sofa with a man. She is his daughter, his daughter Bella. He stands upright, and sees exactly where he is, at Lady Woodcourt's. He bows, for no reason, at the girl in black, by his side, and then sees that behind him is a window, and outside the window is the street, and in the street ten or twenty boys, urchins, are leaping up and down, trying to see into the house, to look in and see Colonel Garraway looking out, just as he is looking out trying to see them looking in. A brilliant thought occurs to him now; the world is full of windows, and some are inside the head, and some are not. He must go home and write that down. He bows again to the girl by his side, whose name is Miss Gilbert. He will go and fetch his girl, Bella, who is looking damned fine, and then they will go home, and he will write down his brilliant thought, whatever it was.

Burnes stays for half an hour after the departure of Bella and her father. He is the guest of honour, but he is allowed to be tired. And tomorrow, he has something to do. He leaves the fluttering gracious crowd, feeling no gratitude to be treated in this luxuriant way, but only relief to be free and once again in the street, in the open air. And tomorrow, he has something to do. He walks out of the door, and there is his carriage, waiting for him. But he does not step into it. He stands on the steps, and, if his feet are in the mud, his eyes are on the night sky, and what he thinks about is something not there, but only in his thoughts. Her teeth, eyes, hands.

FOUR

Alexander Burnes did not come the day after Lady Woodcourt's party—
or the next day—or the day after that. And on the fourth day, just when
Bella and her sister had gone to the Park—just, in fact, at the hour when
they might have been expected to be in the Park—he left his card and a set
of his Bokharan travels.

Bella made no gesture when she saw the bit of pasteboard, showed no
feeling beyond an agitated fumbling with her bonnet's ribbons. But,
walking upstairs as upright as she could manage, as slowly as she could,
she felt cheated of something, as if she had been promised the most
thrilling-sounding of M. Mirabolant's puddings, and, in the event, she had
been presented not even with the customary confection of meringue and
cream, but, four days after she had expected it, an engraving of the promised delight on a card three inches by two. Walking slowly up the stairs,
she ran her fingers over the card, three inches by two, as if it held for her
the slightest promise, as if it had anything in common with her uselessly
unshared hopes. Bella was twenty-four. She expected nothing.

So it was that, when Burnes was announced, a full week after Lady
Woodcourt's famous party, and shown into the drawing room where

Bella was sitting, alone with her work, she stared at him as if she had never seen a man in her life.

The Garraways lived in Hanover Square, in a house so exactly what one would have expected that, Bella thought, none of her family or her family's friends could ever be said to have set eyes upon it. It had precisely the right amount of old furniture to be respectable; it had precisely the right number of new objects to be fashionable. There was a pianoforte and a harp; there were sofas and curtains and a wilderness of walnut, just as other people had; there were portraits by Lely of dear great-great-grandmama, stout in a blue silk gown with her hand resting on a silver globe and pointing to the heavens. There was an ugly one, too, of poor Harry which he had ordered the week after arriving in India, in which his head was inexplicably round as a football ("A native artist," Colonel Garraway was apt to say in mitigation, showing the curious visitor the label, "Executed in the Year 1826 by the Humble Servant of the Brush T. S. Lal, Student and Pupil of the great English Master, Sir Tilly Kettle"). All quite as everyone else had things; all so perfectly appropriate to the Garraways' station in life that one could have predicted the house's exact appearance, and certainly had no need to look at it. It was true that the Garraways, in their dining room, had what, through the gloom, could be perceived to be a lamentable mythology by Hogarth where others might have had a doubtful Claude, but what of that? The Garraways were so completely respectable that they could pass off a small lapse like that as an interesting curiosity, and nobody doubted, since they said so, that an interesting curiosity is what it was. They were respectable to the point of dullness.

It was four in the afternoon, and Colonel Garraway was in his study, taking his second dose of opium of the day. He had unlocked the miniature walnut tantalus, and carefully measured out the drops into a glass. After twenty years establishing a good understanding with the ruby witch, each of his three daily doses was large enough to kill a neophyte. He mixed it with water from the decanter, raised it to the light, and gazed at it sternly. This moment of calm contemplation, which never varied or altered, was an essential part of the Colonel's thrice-daily renewing of his acquaintance with opium; it was his idea of a necessary self-restraint. Presently the world returned to normal. The room deliciously sagged around him, the armchair softened, rose up in an embrace, and all was well again. He never recalled, or noticed, the moment of swallowing; it passed. The Colonel smiled to himself. No, not to himself; to his books.

There they were, all his little books. There they were; now, which was his favourite? There, the one with nice gold lettering, there on the spine; *Dryden Dramatic Works Vol. III.* That was his favourite, wasn't it, because the I, I, I on the spine was so like three nice gold pillars. Perhaps the green stock, for this evening's *tenue,* for Lady Woodcourt's. The Regent would surely approve. But then he remembered, as a dull double knock sounded through the house and the armchair softened under him like warm toffy, that Lady Woodcourt's had taken place a week before, he had no green stock to wear, and the Regent, now, was King—no—was dead. He settled back. The ruby witch! he thought. The ruby witch!

Elizabeth Garraway was in her room, attempting to ignore the clink and knock from her father's study next door. It was the familiar sound of him unlocking the tantalus, taking out the miniature decanter, and settling into oblivion. She was not sure, but she rather thought what she most disapproved of in her father's opium habit was his having had made these appurtenances, acknowledging that there was no hope or desire in him to abandon the habit. Her hair was as smooth as if it had been lacquered onto her head; her velvet dress was as rich and dark as the heart of a poppy. She continued writing her letter.

". . . I feel, however, that the weaker sex, so justly named at present, only occupies so subservient a position due to the manifest inadequacies of feminine education."

She sighed, and thought for a moment. She was writing to her correspondent in Germany. She had had great hopes of Goethe until he died, but Herr R——, although no more effusive in his replies than one would expect of the greatest and most famous novelist in Europe, had been most encouraging. She continued.

"If the conventional female 'accomplishments' stretched to trigonometry and Greek at the expense of the watercolour sketch and the covering of screens, what changes in the helpless position of the sex in society could we hope to see!"

She looked at her sentence, quite satisfied. She wondered for a moment whether Herr R—— would know what was meant by screen-covering, if that were not a usual practice of German virgins, but decided to leave it. What an honour to educate the great R——, even in so small a matter! She was brought from her thoughts by the sound of the double knock. Bella, however, was in the drawing room, she thought, and could best be left. She, turning back to her elevated correspondence, was decidedly not at home.

2

Bella, indeed, was downstairs in the drawing room, her mind quite empty. When the double knock came at the door of the house, she was staring abstractedly at a house fly working its way across the walnut table. Her work was in her lap. The fly seemed lost, cautious, bewildered. Its huge jewelled eyes blank, it seemed to be finding its way over the polished table by touch. It leant on its feelers like an old man on a pair of sticks, as if exhausted; then, suddenly, it reached back and swiftly groomed its wings, back, head with three sleek gestures, and with a single snap, flew off on its own purposes. Bella blinked. In front of her was a young man, pink and ginger as a cake. His hat was apologetically in his hand. She did not recognize him.

"Miss Garraway?" the young man said. "I startled you. I—"

"Mr. Burnes," she said crisply, smiling; and, indeed, Emily had a standing instruction to admit Burnes without question, when she was not at home to all others. She had expected, however, some announcement. "How pleasant. Do sit down."

"I did call," he said. "I was unable directly to call after the evening at—at—"

"At Lady Woodcourt's," Bella said, smiling. There were, it was true, an appalling gaggle of hostesses in London, all rather like Fanny Woodcourt; Bella had spent the previous week accompanying her father to a selection of them, in the unfulfilled hope of seeing Burnes. "A memorable evening for you, was it, Mr. Burnes?"

"Much resembling a great many other evenings it has been my pleasure to attend in the last few months," Burnes said. "Indeed, I think I could hardly distinguish it at this distance from a dozen others this last month."

"What uninterrupted bliss your life must be," Bella said. "For a poor female like me, there could be no higher pleasure than a succession of evenings identical to Lady Woodcourt's. Or perhaps you are weary of them, Mr. Burnes? Surely not. Do not disappoint my youthful hopes."

"I confess," Burnes said, leaning forward in his chair as if she had a lapel to seize, "if I thought my life likely to consist of such evenings, I should return to Kabul and never leave again."

"No pleasures, then?" Bella said. "None, sir?"

"One," Burnes said, and the drop in his manner into a feeling seriousness was as marked as if he had fixed his gaze with hers. She leant forward, unaccountably disconcerted, and rang for tea.

"Have you seen your friend, Mr. Stokes?" Bella said, smoothing her dress down as she settled back.

"Mr. Stokes?" Burnes said, perplexed. He picked up a gold snuffbox, and examined it. "Was that the gentleman's name?"

"You seemed to be holding an energetic conversation with him at Lady Woodcourt's," she said. "A bald gentleman. A writer, I believe. No—I remember now—he is the editor of a periodical. Great things were expected of him, and he wrote a novel—or did he merely promise to write a novel? It is so difficult to remember. Do you plan to write a novel, now, Mr. Burnes? You are certainly promising enough to threaten one."

Burnes took this well. "I fear I shall be too occupied with weightier matters shortly. My time is not entirely my own, Miss Garraway—I return to India in six weeks. Do you suppose six weeks enough time to write a three-volume novel?"

"I feel certain that you, at any rate, possess the dash to carry through such a project. Can it be that the man who bearded the potentates of Asia in their den would shrink from the demands of sending Arabella and Rudolpho through three misunderstandings and the trial of a false suitor before reuniting them in the last pages of the third volume?"

"Stop, Miss Garraway, I beg you," Burnes said, laughing. "I am almost moved by your tale. Perhaps it is you who should write a novel—you, after all, have a great deal more than six weeks to write your masterpiece."

"I hope you are not suggesting that I do not have a great number of highly important calls on my time," Bella said, pretending to be angry. "But, I assure you, I could not write such nonsense—I could not write any novel, nonsensical or no—under any motive less pressing than to save my life. By the by, Mr. Burnes, you will think me remiss for not thanking you directly for the gift of your book."

"It was the smallest task, Miss Garraway," Burnes said. "If you enjoy it, that will be thanks enough."

"I have already enjoyed it," Bella said as the tea came in. She got up and went to the window. Outside, two girls were rolling a hoop past; a man sat in a dark gig, his horse's nose down in a bag of oats. "Perhaps you are right; perhaps I have too little to do, as all my sex. Or perhaps your book was more than commonly engaging. What occupation would you advise for a poor unmarried female? My sister writes to German philosophers, but I know I should burst out laughing before I had written a page. It is a great problem, is it not—how the virgins of England shall occupy their time?"

"I should advise them all," Burnes said solemnly, "to acquire and read my book. Then they would be transported to unfamiliar worlds of thought, I should quickly grow rich, and virtue would flow from this universal unproductive idleness."

She answered him in the same vein, and the conversation lapsed for a moment. It was a fine spring day, almost summer in the promise of heat, and, standing there, she suddenly longed to be in the country, where her eyes could rest upon an expanse of green from her father's house, where there was some relief greater than the Park and the small dusty square of green called Hanover Square, where dogs panted as if in the remotest desert.

She was lost in thought for a moment, and Burnes startled her by saying, "When do you go to the country, Miss Garraway?"

He might have been following her thoughts, although it was not an unnatural thing to ask in May, in London. "I imagine shortly after your departure, Mr. Burnes. I doubt you could have found anything more queer on your travels than our house in Gloucestershire. It is truly something to make a Sultan stare. A moat, castellations, a swarm of savage peacocks, and everything inside so higgledy-piggledy. It is picturesque, as my sister says, to the point of shame."

"I'm sure that I should love it very much," Burnes said, now entirely serious.

"Yes," she said, having nothing contrary to say. "Yes, I think I love it too. Tell me, which of your oriental potentates did you find the most agreeable? From your book, they all seem equally amiable, or almost all."

Burnes drew his chair a little closer to hers, set down his teacup. A light film of sweat was dewing his forehead; it must now be warm in the street. "On the whole," he said. "I think Dost Mohammed, the Prince of Kabul."

"The Prince of Kabul," Bella breathed, turning to him with her luminous grey eyes. "How I envy you, to number such a tremendous personage among your acquaintance. The Prince of Kabul—it truly sounds like the black villain in a Christmas raree show. I see him, entering, stage left, his face and his intentions for the heroine both as black as pitch. Forgive me, Mr. Burnes—I let my tongue run on to no purpose, and I recall now how kind the gentleman was to you from my reading of your book. And now here is my sister."

3

Bella, with relief, rose as her sister came in, gliding as ever, a ready smile on her face. The gliding was a characteristic of Elizabeth. She moved without any impediment to her path, as if, in the kindest possible way, any impediment which did not rapidly remove itself would be crushed beneath the wheels of this mildly smiling female Juggernauth. She was twenty, and, on the whole, got her own way with anyone from Goethe to the stillroom maid. Bella presented them.

"How dull you must find London, Mr. Burnes, after all your exciting travels."

"On the contrary, Miss Garraway," Burnes said. "I have met far more interesting and engaging people in London and, since the greater part of my travels was spent in great discomfort, thirsty and hungry and subject to a succession of trivial ailments, I am glad to exchange the romance of desert life for the unremarkable comforts of Park Lane."

"But surely, Mr. Burnes," Elizabeth continued, "you must find London talk tiresomely dull after the company of your Indian nabobs and Emirs. After the barbaric court of a Maharajah, what possible entertainment can there be for you in an English lady's drawing room?"

Elizabeth was refusing to sit down, the better to clasp her hands and strike minor attitudes against the chimney breast. It was all very well, but Burnes, hat in hand, was beginning to look somewhat awkward standing there, like a footman awaiting his mistress's pleasure. Bella merely looked amused.

"To be frank," Burnes said, "so few of your Eastern princes have anything of interest to say."

"That cannot be true, Mr. Burnes," Bella said. "Why, your book is full of interesting and extraordinary remarks passed by the princes you met. I do not believe you could write such an interesting book filled with the remarks of the ladies of London society."

"To be sure," Burnes said, subsiding with relief as Elizabeth finally sat down at the pianoforte, "their conversation seems extraordinary and full of fascination to us, who have only an imperfect knowledge of their culture, just as the meanest building put up in the Orient seems wonderful to us, as our eyes are not accustomed to what is commonplace."

"The meanest building of the Orient—the garden huts of Bokhara—a tremendous notion, sir," Bella said as Elizabeth started on one of Field's nocturnes, not at all softly.

"There are exceptions to what I say," Burnes said over the intensely genteel din. "As I was saying before Miss Elizabeth Garraway came in—" gracious nod "—I found Dost Mohammed, the Prince of Kabul, to be a remarkable man."

"I have not quite—reached as far as—him in my—perusal of your—book," Elizabeth said, in little gasps between Field's trickier ornamental flourishes; both she and the music seemed to hiccough.

"How did he immediately strike you, Mr. Burnes?" Bella said.

"He has very bad teeth," Burnes said, smiling warmly and incidentally displaying his own very good ones, the fruits of a Scottish childhood eating nothing but roots and thistles. "His conversation is curiously intelligent and penetrating when he asks about us—I felt often that, after my visit, he must surely know far more about the British than this Briton, at least, had succeeded in discovering about him. But in the main, it is a curious, intangible, indefinable quality he has which makes him so remarkable. Do you know what I mean by charm?"

"Of course," Bella said. "I am surprised to hear a Scotsman refer to it. I had thought it a strange and infrequent visitor to your nation. I know from the immortal Kant that properties and qualities may flourish without being named, but this is the first I have heard of the word being used without anything to attach it to. But I forgot, Mr. Burnes, you have spent long in London, and Kabul, where they know, no doubt, all there is to be known of charm."

Even Bella feared this raillery might have gone too far, but Burnes seemed to take it in good part, merely replying, "I would never have thought from your appearance, Miss Garraway, that you had read the immortal Kant."

"Naturally not," Bella said. "I hear most of it from my sister, who is the great reader among us, and that seems to suffice for the normal demands of a lady's conversation."

Elizabeth came to the end of her nocturne with a gulpingly hammered series of chords, and rose to the sincere thanks of Burnes, before excusing herself to the necessity of her correspondence. Burnes got up to take his leave, but before he could speak, Elizabeth had shot through the door and was halfway up the stairs; it was her ostentatiously tactful manner, which never failed to embarrass Bella and make her unable to say anything. She stood there, with Burnes, smiling. Elizabeth had gone, he was alone with her sister; and yet nothing so very terrible seemed to have happened.

"Mr. Burnes," Bella said. It sounded facetious, mocking, said like that, and though she had nothing she wanted to say to him, it would be foolish now to sit down again. She recollected herself. "I am so pleased you came. There must be so many calls on your time, I know."

"I am so sorry I was unable to call before today," he said softly, and that was not quite what she meant.

"We—" Bella stopped. "I am pleased you came at all. Do come again, any time. Truly, any time you can spare from your valuable six weeks."

He bowed, and since his lovely eyes would not quite meet hers, she felt assured that she had now said too much. She could see their next meeting now, in her head; they would be in a crowded room, he surrounded by duchesses, ministers, talking—he had now acquired an emblematical significance—to Stokes the writer and all that shining entourage. And a chill would have fallen between the two of them like a curtain, as he bowed with all the unfeeling profundity at his disposal.

She was so lost in her thoughts that when Burnes, looking mildly puzzled, took his leave and went, she hardly noticed that she was quite alone in the drawing room.

4

"Truly, I like him," she said later, to Elizabeth, upstairs, after dinner.

Elizabeth left off brushing Bella's hair, and turned to her own. It was an unspoken annoyance to Bella that her sister, who was apt to embarrass when strangers were present, and spouted nonsense by the square yard when in correspondence with German philosophers, was perfectly rational and sympathetic alone, after dinner, with no servants listening.

"He seems admirable," she said. "But you say he leaves in six weeks."

"Yes, he does."

"And when does he return?"

"He hasn't named a date. I doubt he knows. But truly, I like him."

Elizabeth pulled at her hair, dragging it in front of her face like a veil, and through it made a vulgar noise with her tongue and lips. Bella shrieked, falling back onto her bed in giggles. "Truly," Elizabeth said. "I like him."

"I *do.*"

"Well, when he returns, perhaps you will still like him. Fancy—Bella Garraway to wait ten years for her betrothed, and he comes back, unable to remember the name of this suddenly old woman, or in a box, a sad early death, dead of the cholera—remember, Bella, George Hathersage, dead after five weeks in Calcutta, dead at twenty-four. Or—fancy, picture, you at the docks, waiting, expectancy bright in your wrinkled old face, and off steps Mr. Burnes, the hero of the age, his left arm firmly linked to a Maharajah's daughter and his right clinging to a case of her family's diamonds."

"If it comes to that," Bella said. "We have diamonds, too."

"But Bella, it may be years—do think."

"It doesn't signify, Elizabeth. I am quite sure he will not call again. Don't ask me how I can be so sure, but I am sure."

But he did call; the next day, and the day after that, and the day after that. He came and he sat, and he submitted to being teased and quizzed until Bella was blue in the face. Always they laughed together—it was a strange sound, in that house, so very genteel—and always they were at ease with each other. The second time Burnes came, he was admitted at once to the empty drawing room, and asked to wait while Miss Bella was sent for. He thought Miss Bella was at home, the footman did—couldn't answer, he was sure, for the remainder of the family. Burnes nodded, satisfied. He looked around him, at the dark quiet room which could be anyone's, and, bearing no trace of her, was Bella's. He wondered where in this abandoned corner of Hanover Square she had left her mark, and the ticking of his watch was loud against the back of his hand. There was a rude rumpus from upstairs; it made him jump. He could have sworn it was the noise of a girl jumping down the stairs, two at a time, and accompanying herself by singing, the sort of unobserved raucous singing he would never have imagined her capable of. The tune was "Men of Harlech," but Burnes, hat and gloves in hand, grew pale as he heard the words Bella, unobserved, as she clearly thought, was applying to the familiar regimental favourite.

> I'm the man (thud!) who came from Scotland
> Shooting (thud!) peas up a nanny-goat's bottom (thud!)
> I'm the man who (thud!) came from Scotland
> Shooting—

With that, she burst incontinently into the silent drawing room, and from the momentary alarmed look on her face, all was clear to Burnes. The footman had failed to find Bella. She had leapt downstairs to the accompaniment of the childhood favourite, believing herself to be alone in the house. Burnes, however, was equal to the situation.

"On the contrary," he said with his best Montrose brogue, "I'm the man who came from Scotland."

After that, they were, so to speak, on all fours with each other, and the casual observer of Mr. Burnes's near-daily calls in Hanover Square might well have been surprised to see the great explorer demonstrating the distinction between the Afghan turban and that of the faithless Sikhs, with the doubtful aid of the drawing room curtains, while the accomplished, beautiful, and respectable Bella Garraway lay supine with laughter on the sofa.

"Truly, I like him." That was all she said to her family, and it was her useful formula. She resisted all suggestions that he should come to dinner, and was not pressed. Colonel Garraway's state made the hosting of a dinner a problematic proposal, and, for her part, Bella could only contemplate the idea of observing Burnes across a plate of soup with a tremor of amusement, when he had spent the previous afternoon teaching her to imitate the precise noise a Bactrian camel makes before spitting.

Only sometimes he fell silent in her company, seemed sadly lost in thought as his eyes fixed on the wallpaper, and she knew quite well what he was thinking, what in all honesty he felt he should now say. If, however, he did come to the point of looking at her and saying, "Bella, I am poor," she knew, for once, what she would say in return; she would say, quite simply, "Burnes, I am rich," and there would be an end on it. Or a beginning; one of the two. But of course he never did say it, having no tongue with which to say such a thing. The truth, unspoken, hung like a curtain between them, and it was, it seemed, only Bella who understood that if he chose, he could take that curtain and wind it, absurdly, about his head, and reduce her, as always, to the point of laughter.

"Truly, I like him," she said, and truly, she did.

"Must you go?" she said. It was late in the afternoon in Hanover Square, and Burnes was standing to leave.

"I must, Bella," he said, but he was smiling, and she knew it meant nothing, and let him go. She shut her eyes, and hugged herself, and smiled, and stayed where she was. She stayed where he had left her, just for a moment, trembling, taut, unseen, like a harp string when the door has been closed on an empty room. She stayed there with her eyes closed until she heard the door to the house close behind him. She opened her eyes on the empty room, and moved swiftly to the window—to the side of the window, where she would be in shadow, and watched him trot down the steps to the house. She saw how gracefully he moved. He must, she thought, be a fine dancer. And then, with an erotic force which made her blush for the weakness of her first thought, she realized from the grace of his few quick movements down the steps in Hanover Square, what he must be good at. What he must be best at. He, surely, was a horseman of superlative accomplishment.

Burnes stopped on the last of the steps, and seemed to realize something. He stood, and began to cast a glance back at the solidly shut door of the Garraways' house. He hovered there for a moment, while Bella watched, puzzled, and then thrust his hands into his coat-tails, and strode off with a pretence of purpose.

When Bella turned round, Emily was in the room. Instead of removing the tea-things, she was hovering over the sofa.

"The gentleman—" she said, almost nervously.

"Yes, Emily?" Bella said, turning back to the sight, once so ordinary, of Hanover Square without an Alexander Burnes in it. "Yes, what is it?"

"The gentleman forgot his gloves, miss," Emily said. She was holding up a pair of pale blue gloves. That was what it had been; Burnes had left his gloves there, and only realized once he had left the house. Casting a glance back at the door of the Garraways' house, he had found that too difficult a challenge; the man who had confronted the Amirs of Bokhara now, apparently, had found some timidity in him which made him shrink from returning to claim his gloves.

"That won't—no—" Bella said, almost snatching the gloves back from Emily. "—no, they are my father's gloves, not Mr. Burnes's. Give them to me—I was on the point of taking them up to him. I need to talk with my father, in any case."

Emily was clearly doubtful. "I think he's asleep presently, miss," she said. "I can take them up later with the six o'clock tray."

Like an invalid, Colonel Garraway had a tray at set times; his six o'clock tray bore what had proved the efficacious restorative of half a pint of dry sherry and some ship's biscuits. Bella was firm, not permitting herself to wonder what Emily and the massively multiplying dependants below stairs would be saying in half an hour about her theft of Burnes's pale blue gloves. Bella, suddenly, simply didn't care. "I'll take them up now," she said, almost furiously, and, walking across the room and snatching the gloves up, almost ran up the stairs with them.

It was only when she was in her room, the door safely shut behind her, that Bella could think of what she had done, and why she had done it. She stood, holding his gloves, and it seemed to her that somewhere, deep in the house, carpets were being beaten; a great regular dull thud, making the walls vibrate and the windows ring. She listened, and it was no noise, but only her heart, the betrayer, rousing the house to her strange desire. She held the gloves to her, and the sound would not stop. The Garraways were so respectable they would never surprise anyone, never disappoint or astonish anyone with their perfect breeding. Now something had come to astonish, to overthrow, to bowl over a Garraway, and she listened to her beating heart with an emotion not far from bewilderment.

In her room, in her bureau, in the third drawer from the top, Bella kept a box of tokens. Tokens of her past life, which no one had seen, or would see. It was this she now reached for, in which she placed Burnes's purloined gloves. A clockwork toy, twenty years old, no longer working; who, now, could say what that meant to Bella? Or a playbill, smudged with a masculine thumb, eloquent only to its collector, and to us, who observe her at this most private juncture, quite silent? A handkerchief, embroidered by hand—not very well, as if by a child, and marked with a D—we would venture so far as to guess that this belonged, once, to Bella's mother, whose name in this house is so sadly neglected, that it is the handkerchief clutched by her mother as she died. Precious things;

most precious things. It was here she placed Burnes's gloves, not quite knowing why, but hearing some imperative voice, which she obeyed.

5

Burnes's book, that summer, was read everywhere. The King did not read it, true. But yet even he had granted the author an audience, had graciously accepted a copy, and had listened, nodding from time to time, while Lady Porchester took it upon herself to describe Burnes's adventures at length to Queen Adelaide. So—since he had never been known to take down any book but the Navy Regulations—even he could, loosely, be said to have read it. All London read it. The hostesses and their daughters read it to each other in the course of their long afternoons. In the city, the busy traders took time from making money to wonder at Burnes's daring, the odd folk he had met, whose existence had never, until that year, been remotely suspected by people whose cellars were filled with the substantial tributes of the far-flung world. Boys at Westminster read it surreptitiously, their eyes shining, and that year, half the poems written for the Prize turned out to be Afghan pastorals, in which a shepherd of the neighbourhood of Herat, longing for his lost herd of fat-tailed sheep (*Pothon platykerkous oies*), came upon a dusky shepherdess. Most people who read Burnes's famous account of his famous travels saw romance in it, and were satisfied to hear of another man's colourful adventures and miserable minor discomforts. Bella, for instance, like a thousand other very similar young ladies between the Park and the Palace, enjoyed it as she might have enjoyed a fancy-dress ball. All these young ladies wondered only at the soft, rather irresolute man who hovered so in drawing rooms, at his having carried out such a mission. The young ladies, like Bella, looked at his white freckled skin and his thin floppy hair, the lightest possible shade of ginger, and wondered.

If many of Burnes's readers, that summer, were taken with a sense of romance, there were others who read his book and found something worth consideration; or rather, there were those who, in reading Burnes's book, felt their own sense of romance quite distinct from that of the herd. Burnes's book recounting his travels to Kabul and beyond ought to have been a simple fact, on which London could agree. There it was, in three volumes, rather large type—it had been written in such a great hurry, so as to meet the public curiosity, that it had altogether been touch and go whether the bookseller could make it stretch to three volumes at all. It ought to have been a simple fact, on which London could agree, like St. James's Palace, or the Strand, or the milkmaid in the Park. But they would not behave like that, these three quite slender volumes. They seemed much more like living beings, or, better, a contagion which takes different forms in each body it attaches itself to. A contagion may not be altogether a bad thing; it may, for instance, form an inoculation, preventing something far worse. And Burnes's books spread from reader to reader. In some of its hosts, its effect was mild; a new curiosity in an unfamiliar part of the world, a burst of romantic enthusiasm. In others it induced a grand desire to change the globe. That, let it be said, was Burnes's intention.

The Prime Minister read it, and wondered why he had never thought about the state of Kabul before; the political classes read it, and often wondered what consequences would flow from our regarding these strange and backward states as mere curiosities. Fat clergymen read it, having little else to do with their time, and badgered anyone who cared to listen on the plain Christian duty to bring the boundaries of Christendom a little wider, to extend our Indian missions westward. Few people took the opinions of clergymen entirely seriously, but they were saying, imperfectly, what their more intelligent elder brothers were starting to feel. These places were, or ought to be, our business, and if we did not acquiesce in our plain duty, there were others who would make it their business.

"The Russians, sir, the Russians," the Duchesse de Neaud said to anyone who would listen—in this case, at the opera, her fervour was being directed at a young protégé of hers, a genius of political economy, a gentleman called Chapman. The old Duchesse, quite uncommonly fervid, was beating him on the breast with her fan as she made her point—an awkward backhanded manoeuvre, since he was sitting behind her in her box. "The Russians—mark my word, sir—are strong, and in want of an empire. No nonsense about Reform there, no worry about the abolition of slavery—nothing, sir, nothing—and Russia would march into India as soon as our backs are turned. I assure you, sir—"

"I hardly think, ma'am, they are in a position—" Chapman began, weakly; the Duchesse's transformation into an observer of the movements of nations had occurred so suddenly, the terrain had abruptly altered, without warning, and the Duchesse's interlocutors felt their way slowly, not entirely sure when they were treading on solid ground.

"Precisely, sir, precisely my point," the Duchesse went on. "It is as in a game of cards. If you sit on what you have won, you quickly see it diminish by the depredations of others. Am I not right, sir?"

Lord Palmerston, who had been attempting to attend to the opera, now gave up with a small inner gesture of regret at the rising shriek of the Duchesse's theorizing. He turned with a tight ready smile to agree with her. Chapman, hovering nervously at her shoulder, sank back into the depths of the red velvet box, hoping to engage the girl in pink with the vast eyes as soon as the Duchesse could be safely handed over to the guest of honour. Lord Palmerston raised a questioning eyebrow. There were few moments when no one was trying to speak to him, and he cultivated the appearance of a melomane, in part, to allow himself a moment free from the rival demands of the town. The Duchesse was in full spate.

". . . most interesting—most interesting young man—remarkable book . . ." she was saying, before spooling back wildly to the outset of her conversation. "You see, sir, it simply is no good to stay as we are, to be satisfied with our Indian possessions as they are."

"I promise you, Duchesse—" Palmerston began.

"What if other hands than ours were to be tempted—yes, tempted, I said, yes, I agree, very fine form, never purer in her top register—tempted by the idea of these virgin lands?"

"India, madam?" Lord Palmerston had no idea how he was allowing himself to be drawn into such a conversation.

"No, sir, the kingdoms of Kabul and Bokhara and—and—if you look at Mr. Burnes's maps, it becomes perfectly apparent that there are others who have as clear an interest in it as we—"

"That interest being none, I suppose, Duchesse, eh?" the old Duc called from the back of the box.

"No, monsieur, no, no—I mean Russia, Lord Palmerston."

"Russia, madam?" Lord Palmerston said, hoping by a display of incredulity to bring an end to a conversation he was being subjected to at all hours of the day and night by the most improbable people. The Duchesse, however, was not so easily cowed.

"And once Russia has established itself in Bokhara, moving on from its Crimean possessions—"

"Madam, I hardly think—"

"Crimean possessions—very true, very possible, not at all—imagine, sir, a Russian empire stretching to Kabul—do you suppose for one instant that they would be satisfied with that? No, sir, it would be onward to the kingdom of the Sikhs, and then, I assure you, our Indian possessions begin to look very vulnerable indeed. I doubt we could defend them against such an onslaught."

"I assure you, Mme la Duchesse," Lord Palmerston said, now entirely giving up on the opera, "that these are all most remote possibilities which I am confident the Governor General would meet appropriately. But, really, madam—"

"Not remote—not possibilities—not for one moment remote," the Duchesse went on, her words spilling out of her snuff-coloured silk. She clutched at ribbons in her enthusiasm. "Have you read Mr. Burnes's travels, sir? The most efficacious manner, I assure you, of meeting the Russian threat—yes, threat, sir—is to move at this exact moment into Kabul, to Bokhara—these vast and peaceful countries, new markets, sir, and labouring under the yoke of an oppressive superstition—sir, do you not think it our plain duty as Christians and Europeans to bring enlightenment to these benighted people and save them—rescue them—from the—the threat of a fate worse, worse, I say," the Duchesse's voice rising as she lost her own thread, "than their own?"

Behind her, Chapman and the pink silk heiress were taking refuge behind her fan, which trembled alarmingly. Lord Palmerston gave up.

"I think, Duchesse," he said wearily, "you make a point which I know many people will agree with."

There was something so final in his tone that even the Duchesse had to sit back in her chair, assuring herself that she, at least, had succeeded in bringing these very important matters to the attention of somebody who would attend to the situation. She turned her attention to the opera, but the act seemed to be over now. Malibran, in a most unbecoming braided blonde wig, was bowing beneath a vast weight of flowers, behaving, at least, as if she were receiving the acclaim of a grateful multitude. The Duchesse, triumphant, prepared to rise and retell her conversation a hundred times.

6

In the Duchesse de Neaud, the infection represented by Burnes's book had found a fertile carrier; truly a carrier, one might say, since she passed on the main features of the contagion without proving profoundly susceptible to the virus itself. Like those wealthy invalids who complain bitterly of an influenza while all the time suffering far less than those to whom they will pass on the illness, she made a great deal of noise for a season on the subject of the central Asian principalities, and, having stirred up a great deal of pained opposition and concern, was satisfied to forget the subject and never again mention Burnes, Kabul or Bokhara with her former fervent tones.

The weather in London changed, quite abruptly. The streets dried into dust which settled like a veil over everything; fruit from the market seemed to have been stored for centuries in the dungeons of some *belle au bois dormant,* so thick did the dust of the streets disguise the bloom of the fruit. The Season began, all at once, to come to an end. There were a few landmarks by which the Season might be considered concluded, but it felt like a rapid collapse of business, and not a cleanly marked boundary. There was no doubt that after the Court had withdrawn, after the last Drawing-Room, after the old Duke's Summer Ball, there was no Season but a hastily convened retreat, as every house from Park to Park resounded with the beating of carpets, the single occupation of dust-sheeting furniture and the sealing-up of trunks, in so much grim-faced hurry that a stranger might have concluded that a marauding army was hammering at the gates of the city, and not merely the unimagined, unexperienced phenomenon of an August in London. But at a certain moment in the year, it was clear that the Season had lost what purpose it had. Perhaps—Bella thought—it ended as soon as an acquaintance remarked, however casually, that he was leaving town early this year. The next day, in fact. The thought presented itself with an attendant melancholy which was quite unfamiliar to her. Never before had the simple fact of having to leave London struck her as so sad a loss, so devastating a revelation of what she must always have known, that the round of parties and Park and dinner was, in truth, at best wearisome and at worst a stale and unprofitable waste of existence. It made no sense to her, to feel like this, and yet that was how she felt. She could only understand it by think-ing that, after the last steamy night at the opera, after the last agonizing Drawing-Room, some wardrobe-faced courtier prodding you in the back and your ostrich feathers shedding by the minute, there would be no more Burnes. She understood that very well. He was this year's novelty, and next year there would be another.

The idea of a different state presented itself to her; the idea of an August where Bella and Burnes together could walk the empty London streets, their happiness observed only by costermongers.

For Bella, now, in this year of Grace, the idea of her departure from London with so much unsaid—even granted that she did not know what she would say, even if she could say it—brought to mind images of col-lapse. Soft yielding sand, collapsing inwards in an hourglass; a bathful of water sliding unstoppably into the drains; Bella alone, in the drawing room at Hanover Square, hearing only the clink and knock of the opium tantalus in the sounding empty house, waiting for departure, and nothing else.

In these last days, there was so much to be done, and the preparations for the months in Gloucestershire were as detailed and solid as for a siege. Gloucestershire was all very well, but there was much which could not be acquired there at any price. For the long siege of dullness, dictated by the fashion which would separate Bella so irresistibly from Burnes, food was needed. The current books, French novels for upstairs, English for the drawing room, old Italian poetry for the library; these things would rep-resent a brave assault on the grim boredom of a Gloucestershire after-noon. New clothes, naturally; it was astonishing how much time could be stolen from the long day by bathing and dressing, but the trick only worked if there were new bonnets, new dresses to hand. Other than that, there remained the resort of driving about the countryside, calling on families; even a country curate's wife, however crass or absurd, would serve to alleviate the ache of ennui as swiftly as her father's unvarying solution. Other amusements were now closed to Bella. Fishing with worms, digging for treasure in the rose garden, dropping grandpapa's folios from the battlements into the moat with a still memorable, pleas-ing, deep-sounding *plop!*—these were things, not newly forbidden to Bella, since they had always been clandestine activities, but since she had grown up and begun to blush, some inner sense, not of decorum but of absurdity, forbade her these previously delightful entertainments. So it was that, to beguile the long August days, purchases had to be made, and Bella and Elizabeth found their last weeks in Hanover Square taken up with visits to the drapers, to the booksellers, in search of some prospective amusement.

7

The bookseller's shop was full, and Bella and Elizabeth had to pick their way through a forest of acquaintances, all despatched on the same desperate errand, to fetch the season's novelties to while away the long country summer. In a street off Piccadilly, the brown little shop was enduring its busiest week of the year, and the gentleman proprietor was wringing his hands as he tried to satisfy each lady with an interesting novelty; and Bella could see, as she quietly picked over the loose-bound piles, that the task of reconciling an individual recommendation with the sort of book which, fashion dictated, all London would be raving over by November, would indeed drive anyone to wring his hands in despair. Just now, Mr. Sandoe was attempting to pacify a substantial marchioness, whose bulk and wide-mouthed face made her, without reason, appear actually to be hungry for a few volumes. Bella, waiting patiently for his attention, picked up an unbound volume; a limp volume of poems about rivers, lakes, mountains, trees—she turned the pages, but no human being was there, only the poet and his trembling emotions laid out for the admiring reader like the last stages of a dissection. There was enough of that, Bella felt, in the country already, and she wanted no slim volume of tremulous awareness, silently deploring her own infallible sense of desolation when she looked at an unpeopled mountain. Bella, who always thought that the one thing the view of an empty meadow wanted to complete it was a picnic of fifteen or twenty well-dressed gentlefolk artistically arranged, set down the exquisitely self-satisfied volume with an uncharacteristic burst of dislike.

"Miss Garraway," a voice broke in. "And Miss Elizabeth Garraway—charmed, how pleasant to meet old friends when out on an errand—so tiring, so enervating, so refreshing to meet, merely, with two such—"

"How do you do, ma'am," Bella said, bobbing to the Duchesse de Neaud, who was accompanied by one of the sour-faced Gilbert girls. "You are, I perceive, on the same errand as we are—" then, recollecting herself, "—though you, ma'am, will have the benefit of a great library to while away your days."

The Duchesse, indeed, was going to Windsor with the Court, as she acknowledged with a profound and unspeaking nod of the head. She was a great favourite of the King, who had known her in his sisters' nurseries for half a century, and was an intimate, she felt able to imply in conversation, of the Queen.

"I long for the day—quite long, my dear—when I am able to spend a moment in a chair with a book at Windsor—quite impossible. HM, you know . . ." (this in a confidential whisper) ". . . remarkable little body, great energy, of course—entirely unable to set down, to lose oneself— quite exhausting, although—" the Duchesse seemed suddenly terrified, as if another pair of listening ears might retell this comparative lack of enthusiasm and cast the Duchesse from her blissful social position into the outer darkness, "—nothing but pleasure in the duty, you know, nothing but, so simple, so easy, so pleased with every small service. And Windsor, you know, where every prospect pleases . . ."

The Duchesse looked around her a trifle wildly, perhaps recalling, far too late, how the second half of the line went. The Gilbert girl took the opportunity to force a simper and bob at Bella and Elizabeth.

"When do you leave town, ma'am?" Bella asked.

"Yes, indeed—Tuesday next, I believe—thank you Miss Garraway—or so I believe, quite, entirely, happily dependent on the wishes of others—"

"I hope M. le Duc is well?" Elizabeth asked.

"Thank you, yes, quite well, quite mad with uncertainty, constantly requiring his trunks to be unpacked for some favourite jewel, naturally, though happy, as I say, to be—I expect, Miss Garraway, you have read this—most entertaining, most instructive—"

This, naturally, was Burnes's book, which the Duchesse seized with both hands from a pile on the bookseller's table. Bella had the presence of mind not to blush, and, though Miss Gilbert was smirking to a painful extent, she could assure herself that the Duchesse probably meant nothing by it. Elizabeth had wandered off, thankfully, affecting to be engaged by some other book.

"Indeed, ma'am," Bella said collectedly. "Mr. Burnes and I, you know, are quite friends."

That did the trick, and Miss Gilbert went off to squeeze Elizabeth for gossip.

"Most timely, his book, I must say," the Duchesse went on, apparently not much caring whether Bella was friends with Burnes or not. "Lord Palmerston—at the opera, you know—only last Wednesday—no, Thursday—most concerned, most intrigued. You see my dear, as Burnes says very truly, nature abhors a vacuum—abhors—and where we refuse to step in, *others may*. You mark my words—" and a black, glittering, and sombre eye now engaged Bella's own, "—*others may*. Thank heaven for Burnes—excellent, splendid, most timely warning, Palmerston was saying so to me—" again that tactful drop in volume, to impress Bella that it was only the significance of what the Duchesse was saying that led her to invoke Lord Palmerston, and not a desire to display her glittering connections to a crowded bookseller's shop, "—he and I were talking about it—Malibran, in *The Sleepwalkerine,* most enchanting, ringing top notes, last Thursday—no, Wednesday—and we agreed, he and I—" now speaking again at normal levels, "—that we must *go to the rescue* of these poor people. Helpless, quite helpless, in need, if anyone is, of our assistance—and, as I was saying—" *sotto voce,* "—to him: if we do not, *others may*. The Russian Bear, my dear, the ravening hungry Russian Bear. Thank heaven for Burnes."

The Duchesse, now finished, fixed Bella again with her gaze, and then, astonishingly, gave a great ursine growl. Bella jumped back, having no response whatever to make to this; she could hardly growl back, as if she were in the nursery with this small brown wrinkled duchess—a mental picture of the Duchesse in her infant frocks, clutching a rusk, shrunken but entirely the same, and growling, shot across Bella's mind. Nor, in all conscience, could she respond in any way to what the Duchesse had said; she understood nothing of what she was referring to.

Elizabeth returned, and Bella felt able to escape. As they left, the Duchesse, still deep in her own thoughts, cried, "A word to the wise, my dear—" and then, as Bella nodded her goodbyes, she made her astonishing bear's growl once more. The surprising fact was that no one else in the bookseller's shop—not even Elizabeth—seemed remotely troubled or interested by the remarkable performance. Bella stepped into the pillbox carriage waiting for them with a persistent and worrying sense that it was she, and not the extravagant old woman, who had made a spectacle of herself.

8

She felt able to plead fatigue, and John took them back to Hanover Square, their errands almost complete. Elizabeth, inexhaustible, let Bella off at Hanover Square before asking John to take her on, wanting to make her farewells to a friend in Green Street.

It was three in the afternoon, and Burnes had been waiting, "no more than five minutes, I assure you."

"How did you know I—we should return soon?"

Burnes smiled. "I did not. I had set a limit on my patient waiting."

"And how long was that, Burnes?" Bella said, long ago having passed to this intimate, military form of address. She began to unpick her bonnet as they sat down. "I would like to know what value you place on my company, and the length of time you would wait for my return seems as accurate a measure as any. For some truly important person—let us say for the Governor General, the King, or my sister's friend Goethe—"

"I believe Herr Goethe is dead, Bella."

"No matter—for these, let us say they would merit a whole afternoon's waiting, hat in hand, jumping to your feet every time the maid enters to feed the fire. On the other hand, let us say, for our friend Stokes—"

"I was truly asking myself whom you were planning to alight on, but Mr. Stokes is a very fair choice."

"Thank you. For Mr. Stokes, I do not suppose you would wait at all; a mere drop of the card in the bowl, and off you would fly like an afrit riding the West Wind. Am I correct?"

"Quite so."

"And yet you waited for me—how long I do not know—and you would, I believe, have waited a minute or two longer. How long the limit you had privately determined is for me to establish, and that, I presume, will inform me what value you place on the conversation of a silly little girl. I wonder with what ingenuity I can discover the true facts of the case."

"No ingenuity is required," Burnes said, laughing at Bella, scratching her head like a regular urchin. "I will tell you—I had decided to wait for fifteen minutes. In any case, I knew you had gone to your bookseller's two hours before, since Emily was so kind as to tell me, and I knew a bookseller could not detain you much longer than that."

"Very well," Bella said. "Fifteen minutes. Now I call that a very valuable contribution to knowledge, though, like the higher mathematics, I hardly know as yet what use I shall put it to."

"I dread your *uses*, Bella," Burnes said, helping himself to tea and, greedily, to sugar. "But how long would you wait for me?"

Bella was silenced, and Burnes, too, in a moment stopped laughing. There was no answer to that; in them both was the unspoken knowledge that the "six weeks," so lightly spoken, so long ago, had shrunk now to one week, that then, he was gone, that after, there was nothing that either could see. In Burnes's pained anxious face was some knowledge that he had not been fair to Bella, and it would have been better not to have come at all; in Bella's face was nothing but a forgiveness for anything Burnes might do, be doing, have done. Bella's forgiveness had no tense, had no aspect, and Burnes dropped his eyes from hers, from her sad, her shining eyes.

"In the interests of coquetry," Bella said, collecting herself, "no woman would ever wait for a man as long as he would wait for her. If I were a flirt, five minutes; if I were a woman of normal self-regard . . ."

But she saw in Burnes's face that he had no heart any longer for their normal banter, that their conversation, like the afternoon, like their lives, had turned in an unexpected direction, and now there was no retrieving it.

"Perhaps ten minutes?" she said, and faltered, her eyes, now, big and swimming and full of ache. She looked at her lap.

"Bella," Burnes said again. "How long would you wait for me?"

She could not think, and she hardly trusted her voice to speak.

"I don't know," she said simply. He could not look at her, perhaps in shame, and he drew back a little in his chair.

"That," he said after a moment, "must be your brother."

For a second she did not know what he meant, and then she saw he was talking about the portrait above the chimney breast. He was right to move away from these dangerous and unstable territories. There could be nothing much gained by talking each other into ultimately painful declarations. She rallied herself.

"Yes, indeed, Harry, my poor brother," she said briskly. "Not a good likeness, but—forgive me, I was about to say something uncharitable."

"I should forgive you," Burnes said, smiling.

"Very well, then; I was about to say that few people would have wanted a good likeness of Harry in a drawing room. He was so very—so very . . ."

"Do go on, Bella," Burnes said. "I think I understand."

"No," Bella said. "He was so very much not at home in a drawing room. He was not quite—not quite *tamed*, I think one might say. He had a knack, a habit, of arriving anywhere early, and then progressing swiftly to the furthest wall. And then he would stand there—I mean, at a rout, if there was any promise of a crowd, of fresh blood and new flesh."

"You make him sound quite the vampyr," Burnes said, looking at the faintly extraordinary portrait with the perfectly round head, the legs crossed at the knees, and the hand resting, extravagantly, on a tiger.

"Perhaps so," Bella said seriously. "If you had seen him against the wall, watching as people came in, assessing himself, preparing himself to spring on his victim—and yet, of course, he could be excellent company and he was my brother. He had to go to India—there was a between-maid, and then another, and debts, cards, and then—you know, Burnes, I feel it shows very bad judgement to attempt to elope with the mother of your principal creditor."

Burnes, despite himself, laughed. "Forgive me," he said. "But yes, not a highly judicious act. May I ask—"

"Really, Burnes, she is still with us. You could hardly expect me to say Emma Franklin, could you? It was decided, then—Harry decided, and we decided, and London gave a great sigh of relief—that he should go to India and make his fortune. Not an unfamiliar story, you must admit, though Harry's *petits péchés* were somewhat more ambitious than the common run. Packed off—dead within months. You heard of him, I recall, in Calcutta."

"Hardly," Burnes said. He had forgotten, by now, how he came first to speak to Bella; it was so very many weeks ago. "As I remember, I heard of him first in London—I heard that you had a brother who went to India and died. Only that."

"Ah," she said, taken by surprise, and all at once, he recalled his ordinary lie, and crimsoned gorgeously from the neck upwards. She was amused. "A very ordinary death; we heard that it was cholera, and cholera does, you know, carry off very many new arrivals in India. A year or so later, the portrait arrived, brought by some fellow Company officer—

wallah, he called himself. They'd all put up a subscription and paid for the portrait to be finished. I heard the true story from him. Another very ordinary death—another officer's wife behaved like an ass, and they were surprised. Did you know duelling was so much the fashion in Calcutta? Pew'aps it ain't, as Harry would have said—Harry would have driven almost anyone to defend his honour with pistols."

She had finished. He saw in her smile and anecdotal glitter how brave she was, and could be again. For herself, she saw only concern in a good man's face.

"You miss him, don't you," he said finally. The room was dark, and quiet; she heard the heavy ticking of his watch in the empty house.

"Yes," she said. "Yes, I do. Now, don't betray me—"

"I would never betray you, Bella," he said, and it was as if there were no other sentence in the world, there to be spoken. She shook her head, not able to look at him, and he understood very well that she meant *Nor I you.* He took her hand, and she moved, suddenly, her body moving in response to his touch like iron to a magnet. "Come with me," he said, rising and advancing to the door. He paused there, and turned, and smiled at her, and, deprived of all will, she rose herself, and followed him.

Out into the street they went, Bella entranced, without a wrap, without a bonnet, and they walked silently southwards through the London streets. No one saw them go; no one paid them any attention as they walked, and through London unfashionable and fashionable they went in silence. She followed him, and it was as if he were drawn by something; what it was, she could not guess, though she could feel that something was pulling him, and it was forty minutes before the streets opened and emptied and there they were, together, at the edge of the river.

Watching the river: watching a perfect chaos of boatmen unloading their goods and passengers onto the wharves. So much to be seen. They stood in bewitched amusement and watched as one lady, stout as a grub in a tight coat, between little shrieks of alarm, allowed herself to be handed into the safe arms of her brass-buttoned husband, waiting with flushed embarrassment on the wharf. Bella and Burnes were interested and uncaring as if the brass-buttoned gentleman had been awaiting a delivery of bales of cotton into his arms, and not merely a wife. By them stood the eager crowd of boys, some ragged, some Sunday-best, which always materializes from nowhere if there is ever the chance that a lady of respectable middle years may fall, shrieking, into a river. The two of them watched, attentively, and would not for the world have admitted that their motives were no more noble than those of the boys. The spectacle came to a disappointing end, safely, and the puerile onlookers almost sighed, waiting for the next entertainment the river's ordinary traffic might afford them.

"I would give ten pounds," Burnes said after a while, "to know the precise contents of every bale, every chest, every warehouse we can see." She had not expected him to say anything romantic, and he had not; he had said something better, something interesting. "To come down here—I feel rather like a novelist must in a crowded room in an inn. To feel that if all the unspeaking secrets contained in it were opened up—then, I should be master of the world, and know everything."

"What would you discover?"

Burnes picked up a stone and sent it skimming into the river.

"Nothing, perhaps," he said. "You could ask people about their passions. That is the way to discover something. No—they would only lie to you."

"Sometimes," Bella said. "Would we discover a great deal by your exercise? Even if we did go down to the wharf and pay the boatman five shillings to allow us to inspect his load, what do you suppose we should find? A boatload of cotton, or coal, or tea, I expect; nothing more interesting or romantic than that."

"Bella, you disappoint me," Burnes said, rubbing his hands together, although it was not cold in the slightest degree. Bella turned and stared at her companion, as if he had gone mad. "Not interesting? Not romantic? The docks of London?"

"Romantic?" Bella said. "Come now, Burnes, be less paradoxical with me. I am too dull for this."

"No paradox whatever," Burnes said. "Merely think—cotton, and coal, and tea—commonplace dull things. Think where they have come from, Bella; think of the journey they have undertaken, through what wastes and deserts, think what hands they have passed through, what fortunes, what hopes rest on these ordinary things. There are men thousands of miles beyond India, whose inner eyes are bent, this very moment, on that exact load of rice, there—"

"You exaggerate, sir."

"Not a whit. Men considering whether, now, their little fortune has reached England safely or is at this moment lying at the bottom of the sea; men wondering whether some shift in weather will double the value of what they sent us, so many months ago, when it comes to sale, or whether it will realize half the poor farmer's expectations. Riches or poverty, competing furiously in a man's mind; a family made or destroyed, there in that bale. Look on that, Bella. Look in front of you. The whole world is here, this afternoon, now. In those cases, being thrown down, coffee and silks and spices, wool and diamonds, all docketed and ticked, all as if it were the most ordinary thing imaginable that the great world should pass through London, like a great haystack passing through the eye of a single needle. Import and export; sending England out to the world, taking the world into England. Cotton, silk, spice, coffee, gold, silver. The world, Bella, the world. Do you not feel it, Bella? Do you not see that I am showing you what I can, showing you the world? You could never find out what people want by going into a room and asking them. But by God, if you could stop this day now, at this moment, and spend as long as you liked examining every bale, every load, every sack of goods you can see, finding out what everything was worth, who sent it, who is about to buy it, by God, you would begin to understand the world. You would begin to understand what the world dreams of."

9

The river continued its placid brown life, unmoved by Burnes's enthusiasm. As Burnes had talked, they had started to walk again, and they now found themselves in the shadow of the great bridge. A boatman clung on to the rope hanging on the nearest pier, the boat under his lurching feet being pushed away by the current. It swung from one side of the great pier to the other. With his left hand, he nonchalantly ate a bit of bread and an onion. The river was low, its stench so strong and heavy that it could be tasted in the mouth. A flock of coal-lighters was secured for the next few hours in the treacle-rich ooze of the river's mud, a stuff almost valuable in itself. On the far bank, boys, almost naked, were plunging into this thick mass of mud, occasionally surfacing with cries to show that some small treasure, some penny had been found. Here surfaced a boy, black and dripping, his hand upstretched with a treasure, and trying to hail a little green tug with his shrieking gull-cry. The traffic of the river continued its furious pace uninterrupted, in the middle stream, like water-insects, handling each other out of the path with busy prodding prongs, hooks, ropes, businesslike and abrupt, not pausing for pleasantry, or apology; the purposeful dancing of a rude public ball. Long and intricate levels of wooden stairs and causeways, eroded and slippery smooth, clung to the river's edge, and each boat, loading, unloading, mooring for a few short hours, seemed like an efficient drab bird which had alighted on one branch rather than another for no particular reason. In a moment it would set off again in a new direction, impelled by nothing more than its own furious energy. As each boat sat there, it seemed as if it cost it more energy to stay still than to move.

Bella said nothing. To her, it had always seemed the river, brown-black, crowded, noisy, and stinking; it had never seemed to matter greatly where her tea came from, what produced the stuff for her linen. She could not suppose that the originators of the stuff worked explicitly to supply her with tribute, like the worshippers of a pagan god. Money and trade; filth and lucre. And yet she did feel it, she did; she felt that here, with Burnes, she was being shown a world; whether it was the great world Burnes descanted on, or the great opening mind of a man she suddenly, incomprehensibly, loved and would give herself to, she did not know.

"It frightens you, the world?" Burnes said suddenly. His eyes were fixed on Bella's face; they were dark and swarming with appraisal. They wavered in their orbs as if searching for some secret that Bella's face held.

"Perhaps it does," Bella said carefully. "Sometimes I don't understand what—quite what the greater part of it has to do with me. You will despise me for that."

"Never," Burnes said, his eyes fiery, fixed on hers, and in one unspoken agreement, they turned, and began to pick their way through London, to return to the place they came from.

The house, still, was empty as they entered, and in the dark hall, Burnes turned to her. She looked with bewilderment upon his face, but he was not preparing to leave her: on the contrary, he was keeping her, and in his expression was a new certainty, as if he knew all at once where to go and what to do. Still with her hand in his, she, all bewildered, submitted to be led forward a pace or two. He hesitated for a moment: it appeared that now he had forgotten what opportunity he had perceived in the course of the journey from the river to this sad empty house; forgotten why he was standing here, why he had taken Bella's hand. But it was, after all, easier than that. She looked at him. His head was cocked like a foxhound's. He was listening for the sound of any other person in the house.

"Very well, then, Burnes," she said, and she had spoken her decision, her right hand in his. What they had understood with the burden of those so few days bearing down upon them, neither would express: she felt that. He led her, then, saying nothing, and she submitted to be led; and together, in the empty house, they walked upstairs.

FIVE

I

A stranger was there, out there, somewhere, somewhere in the haphazard piled-up overlapping streets of Kabul. No one had planned this city, and its many streets were like hundreds of thousands of individual routes. As if a pond was made of the ways that fish find through it. Down there, somewhere in the carpet-mass of pattern and direction and half-intended result, a European stranger had arrived, in an inadequate and fascinating disguise, and the town, quietly, was talking and talking and talking about the new arrival until the muted babble of discussion mounted the hill to the austere halls of the Bala Hissar, and reached—so quickly, so quickly—the ears of the Amir. And to the Amir, the arrival of the new European in town was like the dropping of a rock into the opaque pool of water which was the city, ruffling the surface immediately in ordinary and predictable ways, but disturbing the substance and mass beneath in a manner which could not be seen, or predicted. The Amir sat on the steps of the throne room, with the nobles and the clergy, and listened, noncommittally nodding his head from time to time, as if he were hearing nothing more than gossip.

"His hair is red," the Newab Mohammed Zemaun Khan said. "Red, red as the devil's is."

"And he wears the clothes of the country people," the Newab Jubbur Khan cut in. "He came from the East, from India, but he has been to many, many places. He speaks to everyone about the places he has been, and asks everyone, down to the smallest child, a thousand thousand questions."

"A wise man, then," the Amir said, pretending to reprimand the court. The Newab Jubbur Khan was a poor fellow, the Amir's brother, and if Mohammed Zemaun would one day amount to something, for the moment he was no more than the Amir's gawping boy-nephew.

"A spy, Pearl of the Age," a mullah said. The Amir Dost Mohammed Khan turned, not recognizing the voice; it was the Mir Wa'iz, the teacher of Kabul, speaking through a mouthful of food.

"A spy, Holiness?" the Amir said; the Mir Wa'iz had not, quite, recovered from his display of asininity, weeks and weeks before. He had, after all, allowed the English to question holy doctrine over the question of the faithful Esquimaux, and could still be savagely teased on any subject. "But what enemies can I see on the most distant horizon? Do we not live in peace and plenty?"

"A fool, then," Mohammed Zemaun said. "Or a mere scholar."

"He came from the East," the Mir Wa'iz insisted, in his best holy inscrutable manner.

"A scholar, I expect," the Amir said. "But we shall spy on him, a little, shall we not?"

In truth, Dost Mohammed felt and knew that the arrival of the new Englishman was, in the end, going to prove to be more than gossip, but for the moment there was no reason for the clergy and nobles and wives to know such a thing, and his nodding head was intended to soothe the city into a mood of mere curiosity about the interloper . . .

. . . and down there, in the city, in a hired house, the Amir could almost see the interloper in his absurd and extravagant disguise, writing like a poor scribe, his head down to the page, his tongue almost out. When the Amir concentrated, he could see the arrival, beginning to write, concentrating, his mind on what he was doing, his sudden and uncontrolled movements betraying the angry impatient European fool as he put one word after another down. Like all Europeans, he would be writing about himself, setting down the ease and mastery with which he had come to this point, and the ease and mastery with which he had persuaded the city of what he was. His name the Amir did not need to imagine. He knew it: Masson. And down there in the city, in the far-off distant serene concentrating gaze of the Amir, Masson, the new arrival in his inadequate disguise, started to write . . .

The nobles and the clergy stirred among themselves, restlessly. They were dressed splendidly, and in their thick brocades they seemed to whisper, although nobody spoke. Against them, the Amir looked like an angel, come down from heaven to reprimand them. Today, as every day, he was resplendent in his white muslin; a six-foot angel with a broad curving nose and bad teeth.

"The Sikhs," he said finally. It was the end of a train of thought which had begun with the interloper, Masson, and ended with a British-funded invasion of the Amir's empire. The angel, bad-toothed, imperial in white, looked into the middle distance of the throne room, and saw the far locked doors being flung open by British soldiers, each a fat little red-faced replica of Burnes, armed to the teeth; beyond it, the Amir's empire, so carefully subdued and brought together, like a basket weaved of Jew's-hair thread, was being trampled through by an endless line of similar red-faced replicas, backed up by the filthy stupid—the Amir pursued his own indomitable line of thought, and came to a single sounding conclusion. "The Sikhs," he said.

"The Sikhs, Pearl of the Age?" the Newab Mohammed Zemaun Khan said. None of the heavy crowd of nobles understood what the Amir meant; a moment ago, he had seemed to be talking, or to be about to talk, about the Englishman, and to have dismissed the idea that he could be a spy. And now he had moved on to the Sikhs, the thorn in the side.

"I am talking about the Sikhs," the Amir said, calmly. "Did they send the English spy? What is he here to find out? Who sent him, if not the English? Why, may I ask, do you come here laden with gossip to weary the ears of women, and have no knowledge, no conclusion, nothing, nothing, nothing, of interest for your Emperor?"

Just at that moment, a hammer struck on metal, somewhere, three rooms away, and the court, with thanks, admitted silently that it had nothing to say about the Sikhs. In a moment, more food came in, borne at shoulder height; it was ceremonial food, and everyone gratefully arranged themselves around it. No one was hungry; everybody ate. It was easiest.

2

"We need to know about the English," Dost Mohammed said.

The English? It was an unspoken question around the court. These abrupt changes of subject were familiar in the inner chambers of the Bala Hissar; the court took them as they took the vapid maxims of the mullahs. They demonstrated the workings of a profound mind. When a mullah emerged from deep thought to pronounce that *Life is a dream, and therefore, a dream is life,* he commanded a general flaccid assent. No one would contradict him, not knowing what thoughts had led to a conclusion so perfectly meaningless. Talking to the Amir was rather like that, except that the workings of his mind usually emerged in the end. His brief peremptory comments could be difficult to link, since they were only fragments of a brilliant, involved, silent analysis of a large subject. But the court fell silent when he made these remarks, and observed the Amir, eyes lowered, in respect.

"We need to know about the English," the Amir said again. "So send a boy down to the spy."

The spy? The Mir Wa'iz went so far as to cast a gaze at the Newab Jubbur Khan, raising an eyebrow; perhaps the Newab would know what his brother the Amir's intentions were. The Newab's inscrutable way with a fistful of lamb, however, was most likely due to bafflement. Naturally the Newab would not want to admit that he, too, had no idea. But in a moment the Amir took pity on them.

"We can hardly talk to the English about their ambitions," the Amir said. "And we will not talk to the Sikhs, to find out who is the tool of whom, like the tale of the monkey on the elephant's back. But we seem to have a spy here. Very badly disguised, and he has made no attempt to come and speak to Us, so—a stinking spy it is. Gentlemen!" The Amir clapped his hands, three times. His voice had shrunk to a whisper, and the noise in the bare throne room was explosive as gunshot. The gentlemen of the court came running at the handclaps, like birds magically called back to a branch. "Take this away. No food is required."

The court froze, mid-chew; it was the grossest breach of etiquette to eat while the Amir had refused food, and they were left, suddenly, with cheek pouches full of meat, to swallow slowly without any evidence of chewing.

"Send a boy down to him. Does he like boys? Not a commonplace boy, a boy of parts. Does he like boys?" The Amir, now, was businesslike.

"Yes, Pearl of the Age."

"Have one sent. Not too young. A remarkable boy. We will wish to talk to him afterwards. How old are your sons, Khushhal? How old is the most beautiful of them?"

The least of the nobles, called forward suddenly from the back of the crowd, twitched, terrified, at this direct appeal. His betters parted, let him through, gazed at him with solemn disbelief. He stuttered, nervously, unprepared.

"In my eyes, Pearl of the Age—"

"Yes, yes," the Amir interrupted. "Yes, very estimable, Prince. You know the son I mean."

"Hasan is seventeen, Pearl." Khushhal seemed unaccountably cast down. He had seven sons, the court remembered, or possibly eight.

"Is he a sensible boy, cousin? Is he worthy?"

"He is the finest steed in my stable, Amir, and I give him to any task of his lord's willingly, knowing that he will succeed where many others, where many others—" Khushhal was losing his way in the stately sentence, "—might to their Amir have brought failure and sorrow."

Dost Mohammed seemed content. "Very well, excellent. Make him understand that he may have to do something beyond talking to the English about the Sikhs. Don't tell him what to do, cousin—it wouldn't do to shock the English out of countenance. Or out of bed, I mean, Khushhal?" Everyone laughed at the Amir's heavy joke, covering their mouths genteelly. "You're certain he likes boys, the English spy?"

"Yes, Pearl of the Age, quite sure."

"Well, let us see. Is it Friday?"

"Friday, Amir," Khushhal said, overstepping himself. The Vizier had been trembling at the Amir's coat-sleeves to make this announcement.

"Have the people come to see Us?"

"Naturally, Imperial One," the Vizier leapt in, urgent with his own grandeur.

"Well, show them in. No, no, no more food."

3

Friday was, by decision of the Amir, set aside for any citizen of Kabul with a grievance to come and set it before the court. It was Dost Mohammed's invention. None of his predecessors had carried out such a practice, as the scandalized nobility had muttered among themselves when it had become apparent that the young Sirdar—as he then was— was perfectly serious in proposing that any man at all might come and wear the court's patience into rags with his trivial complaints. Only the Mir Wa'iz, however, had the nerve, as a licensed idiot whom Dost Mohammed liked to contradict, to say bluntly, "But no Amir before you, Lord of the Wind, has ever suggested such a thing."

Dost Mohammed was ready for that, and reminded the court, and, particularly, the Mir Wa'iz (taking his sleeve firmly between thumb and forefinger and drawing the mullah's face terrifyingly close to his own) that, although none of his predecessors had found it necessary to hold a weekly plebeian durbar, every single one of them had met a violent end. An end (beheading, hanging, dismemberment, crushing, and blowing into bits with gunpowder) which, the court would do well to remember, had invariably been meted out to the intimates of the Amir concerned at the same time. The court had swallowed, as one. All at once, precedent and the habitual practice of the court had seemed a much less important thing.

"Remember," Dost Mohammed had said, exercising his imperial prerogative of a broad open unshielded smile, "it is only five hours, every Friday, a short afternoon of boredom for you, and my chance to speak to anyone who wishes to speak to me. And, in return, you probably won't be murdered in the bazaar. Who knows? You might even come to be loved as much as Us."

The court had swallowed again. Five hours! At most, they had envisaged one carefully selected and clean old man, allowed to sit at the far end of the throne room and abase himself for—surely ten minutes would be enough?

But the Amir had been in deadly earnest, and no one found it much consolation to go on thinking of the grim fates of various long-gone Amirs. Frankly, Khushhal for one sometimes thought, after an hour or two standing stiffly behind the mildly nodding Amir while an old man went on and on about his problems, a quick and merciful death might not be such a bad thing. Nor was it the smallest consolation that the Amir himself hardly seemed to look forward to these occasions with enthusiasm. Certainly, the court had suffered enough, and none of them would venture the slightest expression of sympathy at what had now become an official duty.

"Well, well, show them in," the Amir said. "Quick, Jubbur, the grass—quickly now."

The Newab came from the back of the crowd with his appointed task. The Amir settled himself on the upper step of the throne room, while the others drew back. He took a deep breath, and shut his eyes. Jubbur Khan now, concentrating, placed the three blades of grass he had been holding in the second fold of the Amir's turban, five inches above his left ear. He examined his handiwork, then stepped away, feeling for the step with his heel as he walked backwards to his appointed place.

"How many?" Dost Mohammed asked, opening his eyes, rejuvenated.

"Twenty, sir," the Vizier said, straight-faced. The Amir nodded, and in they came. There was a particular approach of the common people on these occasions: they walked in like sheep, driven in by the attendants' impatient shovelling gestures. They could not look at the Amir, of course, and stared instead furiously at the floor. But their movements were sheeplike; they moved in odd little scurries and shuffling panics, all at once in one direction. Some preferred, it seemed, to cling to the wall like blind men, as if the mere open spaces of the throne room terrified them. They moved forward, haphazardly, loosely, their fear palpable. They made no sound but an occasional small mew of alarm. The court watched the progress, unamused. It was like watching a lot of inflated bladders being pushed along a floor. Finally, they were in place in a rough square. At the attendants' double clap, they all fell on their faces, exactly as if praying.

"First," Dost Mohammed said after the terrific ten-minute preliminaries had been got through.

First was a vile old man, as ever. The court rustled, not entirely certain, in fact, whether this particular vile old man hadn't been here a month or two ago. He began to recite his troubles, in a long-drawn-out cracked singing voice, an old bell being beaten again and again; worse, like a bell being beaten by a deaf man, to whom the noise would mean nothing.

"My son is the light of my old age, Amir, the staff on which I lean. Once I was the tree in whose shade he lisped and played, which protected his helpless infancy. And as the lives of men and women teach us, a reversal must come upon us, so that those we once protected with our superior strength must, as the years pass, grow to be stronger than us, and as we grow frail, we may rely on the strength of their arms and the love in their hearts, as they once relied upon ours. Such is the way of human life, lived as it is in a short spell between birth and death."

The man made a small but rhetorically rather effective gesture at his shirt, as if preparing to rend it in his grief. You could see the man had been an admirable and successful storyteller, in his day, though now his voice quavered and he lost his place too easily. He gathered himself, and went on in his amazingly annoying voice.

"Hear then, O Amir, how wrongly I have been treated, how contrary to all human dignity and proper family life! Can such ill-treatment ever have been borne by one poor, neglected old man? Can such suffering ever have been so wilfully, so cruelly inflicted by a son on his helpless father, since the annals of time were started? Can the ears of the great Amir ever have been soiled by the sorrowful retelling of a tale so shocking, of maltreatment so blatant? You see, Amir," the vile old man went on, dropping disconcertingly into prose after his formal encomium, "my son is an ironmonger, with his own shop, in the bazaar. And I was an ironmonger before him, and the shop was mine originally. So two years ago Ahmed, that's my boy's name, he said to me, one day as we were sitting peacefully over a pipe one evening, I think I want to get married. So I said to him, what do you want to do that for? Because, straight away, I could see trouble coming. So he said . . ."

The interminable story wound on, as the daughter-in-law said, so I said to her, and then he said, well; and the court stood stiff as pillars, and wondered at the fantastic patience of the Amir. When it had finally come to an end, the old man looked up, blinking, bewildered, hardly knowing any longer where he was. He had been entirely absorbed by the immense tale of woe and wrong, his eyes fixed on the carpet. Dost Mohammed gave a great cough and a nod, as if commanding a swordsman to scythe through the incredible knots of wrongs and misunderstandings which constituted this unremarkably dull life.

"You have complained that your son wishes you to leave his house, which once was yours," the Amir said. "You say that the wish comes from your son's wife, though her wishes can mean nothing if they are different from your son's. You say, truly, that you yourself freely and without condition gave the house to your son, before he married, and the law is unable to help you. I have heard your story with great interest, and say this to you, old man. Know that the life of man is brief upon this earth, and the happinesses which man may attain are few, and the travails many. Therefore do not complain beneath your load like a bleating ass, but accept joyfully the will of your family as you would the will of God. Go back to your son and say humbly that you deserve nothing, since you gave your love to him freely, and without hope of recompense. Say this to him humbly, in Our name, and if he should remain obdurate, you must accept what he has said, and throw yourself on the mercies of the bountiful world. That is all."

The old man lurched backwards onto his feet, his knees cracking hugely, and, his eyes still cast clumsily downwards in his inexpressive walnut-face, shuffled back to the last row of the company of hapless suppliants. The Vizier called out the name of the second visitor.

Dost Mohammed relaxed, now, giving the supplicants a fine open smile. Around him, the court hardened, fingering their robes. He guessed most of them would prefer never to have to listen to such lowly men at such length. The Amir didn't much care about that. He meant them, a little, to be bored, but, in the main, he wanted them to be insulted. If the Amir was happy to listen to the common people, dressed in their heavy brown robes, to listen to them talking at whatever length they chose, what was the point of serving in the court? What honour could possibly reside in being the noble designed by ancient custom to hand the Amir his rice, if any Kabul ironmonger could just as easily whisper in the Amir's ear, simply by turning up on a Friday morning? Dost Mohammed understood very well that, unlike all those Amirs who had ended so badly, he had no friends, and could not; between the family of the Amir and the rest of Kabul, there was an absolute gulf. What had happened to the kings who hadn't understood this? Shah Shujah, the fool, had immured himself and his court up, and delighted the court with his enclosed fantasies, his entertainments; flattered them with excess. And he was long gone, that old Amir, with his court, long chased out; and now Dost Mohammed was the Amir, and Shah Shujah was, no doubt, in a palace on some Kashmiri lake, disconsolately torturing some small boy to death for the sake of an afternoon's entertainment. Dost Mohammed would not flatter his court with ideas of aristocratic and regal equality; he would insult them by making them see that, in his eyes, the greatest prince and the merest citizen of Kabul were as one. That was the point of the Amir's Fridays. Not to right wrongs, as if the life of great princes were a tale to keep children quiet, but to remind the court, to their helpless indignation, that he, Dost Mohammed, was Amir, with three blades of grass in his turban, and they, the great princes of the court, they might as well be grovelling down there on the carpet, waiting with aching knees to be summoned at their Emperor's whim.

Four hours later, the court was stiff with outrage as a fistful of knives. Dost Mohammed was serene as ever. The pack of mendicants, unanswered and yet somehow satisfied, made their sheeplike progress, backwards, shepherded by the court attendants, out through the double door. As they receded from the awe-struck anteroom into the more distant of the outer chambers, their chatter could be heard to break out again by degrees, merging into the irreverent cackle of starlings in the trees in the courtyard. In a moment, the room was again quiet. Dost Mohammed was thinking, and when he spoke, it was clear that nothing in the previous four hours had occupied much of his mind.

"Send down the boy, Khushhal," he said briefly. "Today or tomorrow. He should stay there a week, and come and tell Us everything next Saturday. You know the particular boy? Good."

"Does the Amir wish to speak with my son before—"

The Amir shook his hands almost irritably at this absurd suggestion. Khushhal had taken the precaution of passing a note to an attendant summoning the boy, and he was at this moment standing in his best and simplest clothes two rooms away, trembling with nerves, no doubt. Still, it did no harm, that sort of thing. Had the Amir suddenly decided to inspect the boy's teeth—the Amir's own being so bad—it would not have done to ask him to wait on the pleasure of a seventeen-year-old boy.

4

You know the one I mean, the Amir had said, querulously, as if it were absurd that anyone should think of another son. And as the court swept past the deeply bowing youth in the third anteroom, shrinking back into one of a file of attendants lining the little route between the throne room and Dost Mohammed's suite of apartments, it was clear from the suddenly drawn eyes, the suddenly checked pace of half the court that they knew the son he meant, too. Dost Mohammed himself gave no sign of recognition in his purposeful stride, but, behind him, the nobility, normally so regulated, cannonaded each into each, tripped over each other as they caught sight of Hasan. For a moment they forgot how to walk. Khushhal himself had no idea. Well, he knew about the boy's beauty, but he had no idea the fame of it had spread beyond the family into the city, and wasn't entirely sure he liked the idea of his son being gazed at in the street, being the cause of lost sleep, being importuned to surrender what virtue, at seventeen, he still possessed, as if he were some bazaar-boy and not the son and grandson of princes. Still—Khushhal reflected—he himself had been famous, in his day (he relished the memory, twenty years back, of a trader at his shop abandoning a transaction and, open-mouthed, clambering up on a chair for a better view). If Hasan could be of use to the Amir, that, at any rate, was a more virtuous and useful end than, as Khushhal had, only using his God-sent gift of beauty to satisfy the lower urges with every bazaar-boy in Kabul, the heavens forgive him.

Hasan, at seventeen, was famous. Of course Dost Mohammed could only mean one of Khushhal's sons. He meant the one who was an angel. Hasan, alone among the sons, was an angel. He had been so beautiful as a baby, as a boy, that his mother had feared for him, knowing that beautiful children often coarsen as they grow older, become overblown like a July rose, their temperament uncertain as they grow too accustomed to the regular supply of love. And when love as it must proves no certainty, they are not resigned to the fact, but are shocked and angry at the seeming injustice. She had veiled him for a time, like a girl baby, to keep off the demons his beauty would summon. Had those demons come? For beautiful children, love occupies too central a place in their mind, pushing other thoughts, wisdom, understanding to the edge, if not altogether out of their thoughts. We are not made for love alone. Love, in the end, is the prerogative of God, the force of whose love we glimpse in shadow, and dimly, when a man loves another. It is, perhaps, only those who for the first decade of their lives have been loved universally and without conditions, on account of their beauty, who go on believing the central fact of their life remains to love and be loved. Those lucky, unlucky people, so secure only in their insecurity, remain as they once were all their lives only in one respect: they always remain children.

The mother of Hasan said some of these things, and thought all of them, confiding the whole only in her prayers. How could this earthly angel not come to harm? But Hasan grew, and the light still shone beneath the soles of his feet as he lightly trod God's earth. With each year, he remained beautiful; with each year, he became beautiful in a different way, since the beauty of a child is a changing thing, even when it is most constant. She never mentioned his name, never, never, in any context, for any purpose, without casting a net around his beloved skin by afterwards slipping in a "God willing." It was so fragile, the radiant beauty which cushioned his steps, and nothing could touch, nothing, not even Time, could destroy it.

Khushhal had made a quick palms-down gesture and a hiss as he passed the boy, wanting him to stay where he was until Khushhal, with the court, had accompanied the Amir to the door of his apartments. The worst of his wives, the lewd contemptuous one, had been waiting there for the Amir; not respectfully, but waiting as if to insult him.

"Dosto," she sang out the second the doors were opened, though she could have no doubt that the court was waiting just there for their dismissal. "I've been waiting for you for the whole day." She had an infuriating voice, with her drawling Suddozye-princess vowels. She had been a prize at the end of one of those footlingly interminable, brutal scraps with the Suddozye pretenders, and never missed a chance to display her contempt of the whole court and the Amir himself before the entire establishment—before Kabul, before the English ambassadors, if she could. Why the Amir didn't simply toss her down a well . . .

"I've been—" the Amir sheepishly said.

"I don't *care*," came the voice. "Shut up with old women and *bores* and your *sisters* all day long. And you with *your* bores, I expect. Well, I need you here, now. I've lost my slippers, and you're the only one who can find them for me. I need them now, slave." Her voice raised to a shrill little shriek with this last astonishing demand, and the court began to shuffle away in embarrassment, not even waiting for their dismissal. The Amir seemed oblivious of where he was.

"Yes," he said, giggling a little. "Mistress."

"What did you say?" the princess called. Her voice was cool and affectless as an unwearied dove's. "Dosto? Slave?"

"Yes, mistress," the Emperor said, more clearly, and then, suddenly, seemed to become aware again of the court. "That will do," he said briskly, dismissing his public humiliation. "I am not to be called upon."

5

The court scattered in overpowering embarrassment, almost before the double doors had swung shut on them. Khushhal found his way back to the anteroom where the boy Hasan still stood, waiting nervously. He beckoned to his son with the underside of his palm, a small flapping gesture, and together they walked through the mid-afternoon quiet of the palace's public rooms.

"Was that the Emperor?" Hasan said after a time. He seemed nervous; but he usually seemed nervous, shrinking back within his skin from the unpredictable effects he had on people.

"Have you never seen him?" Khushhal said.

"I think I have, years ago, when I was too small to know whom I was meeting and too long ago to remember his face afterwards. Of course I know the noble Akbar the Emperor's son. Or I know who he is, not know him to be greeted by him. But I wasn't sure of his father the Emperor."

Khushhal gave him a sideways glance. "The Amir knows you, it seems. Or he has seen you, at least."

"I don't know when that can have been," Hasan said reflectively, "for it's not to be expected that the Amir's life and mine take similar paths. He is not as I thought he would be."

"It is not for you to think how the Amir will appear, or consider what so great a man as he should be like," Khushhal said. Then he relented, as, with Hasan, he usually did relent, and said, "Of course, no one could expect you not to wonder what Akbar's father would be like. They talk—

at least the Amir talks—of sending Akbar as ambassador to the English in London."

"What for, father?"

"I don't know. I really don't know. Perhaps the Amir has a lot to discuss with the English, and after all, they paid him the compliment of coming to visit him, so it would only be polite to send an ambassador to them with gifts, in return."

Hasan's attention had been drawn by a merchant of cloth, bringing materials into the fortress of the Bala Hissar. By now, they had passed beyond the state rooms and were in the outer shell of the palace, which resembled a market as much as anything, as the tradesmen of the city came to service and supply the court and the palace guard. An oddly silent market; when a baker, now, laden with the bread for the household, collided with a butcher with a bound calf over his shoulder, neither made the smallest protest as they surely would have outside, but walked away briskly, humbled and silenced by the sudden importance of their roles, the gravity of the shady palace. The cloth merchant was a little man, and waddled before three apprentices, meandering helplessly as they half-ran behind him, arms stretched out under the weight of brilliant bolts of rough silk, red and blue and gold. Hasan's attention was taken like a child's with a cloud of hummingbirds. Then he shut his mouth and said, "Where is London?"

"Where the English live, who rule India," Khushhal said, despairing a little. "Though England is far away in one direction and India far in the other direction, beyond the great mountains beyond the empire of the Amir. Do you remember the English, when they came last year, when they lived with the Newab Jubbur Khan for a month, and brought the marvellous clock, the clock of gold and crystal?"

"I remember," Hasan said, dimly. "Those English, they looked nothing like the merchants from India, the ones who come in the spring." Then he brightened, as if sunlight had fallen on his face, and said, "There is another English in the city, though he is dressed strangely, and talks strangely, the women say. Is he perhaps a Russian, that Englishman?"

"Perhaps so," Khushhal said. They were in one of the little courtyard gardens which appeared from time to time in the great rude mass of the Bala Hissar. A pool of clean water at the centre, dripping with a delicious cooling sound into a trough; a plum tree, casting shade in the blunt-bright heat of the afternoon. The cool smell of water on marble, of the shade of a fruit tree; here was luxury, here in the silent quarter of the palace, and Khushhal and Hasan hitched their robes up to their knees and squatted in the cool shade.

"The Amir has very bad teeth," murmured Hasan, as if he were thinking of something else. "I saw as he passed. He started to smile, as he may, and then he seemed not to want to smile, because his teeth are bad, perhaps."

"That is enough, boy," Khushhal said. "Remember you are in the house of the Amir before you insult him so childishly."

"I'm sorry, papa," Hasan said. "I was only making an observation."

"That's all right," Khushhal said. They fell silent for a moment; somewhere, nearby, there was the rush of women's voices, somewhere walled, enclosed and veiled, and they both listened to the lovely liquid sound. "The Amir, you must know, has a task for you. To do with the Englishman—it's good that you know of him, since it concerns him."

"A task for me?" Hasan said. "But how can it be that the Amir should need me to do anything for him? Why has he chosen me?"

Khushhal looked at his slow-lidded son. It was almost worrying, the boy's lack of consciousness of his beauty. In his shy moods, he seemed to be shrinking back from his own face, disowning it, wanting to hide, preferring not to be looked at, not understanding why he was looked at. But it was wilfulness to question the decision of the Amir. Hasan's strangely hot blue eyes—like Khushhal's own, a sign of a direct and pure descent from the Jews, the founders of the Afghan nation—his high smooth brow and small beardless chin, his fine strong hair and teeth, his soft skin. It must have been obvious to Hasan, without too much concentration, what use he could be in the present case.

Khushhal explained slowly what was wanted. Hasan said nothing, merely listened, occasionally nodding. When Khushhal had come to the end of his explanation, Hasan sighed and salaamed to his honourable father. There had not been so much to explain, after all, and it was clear even to Hasan, who was always the last to shut his mouth and understand the point of a story or a joke, that his father did not quite know what Hasan was supposed to do. The Englishman, down there, in his disguise! Wasn't that enough to have found out?

"When shall I go there, papa?" Hasan asked. He concentrated on working out some dirt from under his toenails with the point of his dagger.

Khushhal clapped him on the back, almost making him drive the knife deep into the ball of his toe. "As soon as you may choose," he said. "The Amir will send for you in seven nights."

"Now, then?" Hasan said. He could not see why not, and his father nodded, dismissing him.

6

Hasan flexibly raised himself like a deer from where he squatted, and, salaaming, left his father chewing thoughtfully on a twig in the inner courtyard of the Bala Hissar's inner fortress, waiting on the pleasure of the Amir. He set off towards the Englishman's house. The sentries braced themselves in half-salute as he left the palace by the main gates. He liked that. Hasan knew perfectly well where the Englishman was living. All Kabul knew where he was, knew all about his habits, his interests, the hours he kept and the people he saw. You could, they said in the bazaar, take him anything you found, anything you had. A broken old lamp, a worthless old coin you found in the earth, anything you happened upon, and he would give you money for it with cries of delight like a monkey's howl, and then spend long minutes staring at it before opening his book and scribbling down in it. The boys in the bazaar abandoned themselves in merriment, the soles of their feet to the sky, at this last incredible detail. But he did not seem like a holy man, since he drank a good deal, a shocking amount, and the whole of Kabul, from the storytelling beggars crouched outside the limits of the bazaar to the gossiping nobles in the august silent halls of the Bala Hissar itself, knew precisely what he liked to do after nightfall with whatever boys presented themselves smiling at the gate of his secluded little house. Everyone knew about him. It was true that few had seen him, since he stayed inside like a woman, sending out for his needs; but everyone knew about him. There was an incredible party trick half a dozen boys could now perform, an incredulous account of his gabbling fantastic Persian, complete with the wildest gestures. Hasan was a slow serious boy, not given to laughter, always sitting wide-eyed and solemn while his companions retailed one hilarity after another.

But he had laughed at the gulping mania of the impersonation, and hoped that now, brought up against the original of what was currently the city's favourite joke, he could keep himself from hilarity.

He went directly down the hill from the fortress, ignoring the calls which came his way, and out through the great bazaar. He had lived here all his life, and could burrow through the deep entangled streets as well as any ragged urchin. They called out to him, knowing who he was, wondering at this boy in dazzling imperial white, this boy with the lovely cross face. They knew who he was—his dress proclaimed him—but there was already something in him, despite his blank simplicity, his effortless blank visage, which made the street hang back. They called out to him, but, awed, cast their eyes down before he could respond. They did not want to be the sort of people who called out to Hasan, son of Khushhal, the famous angel of the princely house, and they cast their eyes to the floor, dazzled, in modesty, before he could speak back to them. But he did not respond to their calls, and never had. Even those who called out to him knew this, before they made a sound. He was untouchable, virtuous, noble; the sun shone between the road and the soft pale soles of his feet. He was too good, they said, to walk the earth, and yet he walked the earth, which knew his virtue.

Hasan passed on through the parting crowds. The long twisting call of the muezzin was just beginning, like a great bird singing its inscrutable vowels, and, soon, Kabul would turn with regret from Hasan and, summoned, go to wash, and pray for its own sins. Hasan walked on, into the street of the shoemakers. Here it was that the Englishman had his house. He had taken it from the widow Khadija. The main artery of the quarter, now quickly emptying, was broad and fine, shaded with limes. Every thirty paces or so, a small half-street, blind-ended, like a three-sided courtyard, where the houses were. In the fourth of these was the widow Khadija's house. The houses in this quarter of the city barely had windows or doors onto the street; they were built for the summer's heat, the winter's cold, to withstand a siege. They were solid houses, but not large. Behind the thick walls there was only a small garden and a few square rooms, Hasan knew; his old fencing master had lived in one. But as he stood there, he felt that behind the heavy coarse wall and deep-set tiny door, there could lie anything at all. He stood in front of the Englishman's door. Silly! It was like any other! He felt no nerves. Nervousness was not part of him, but as he stood there, with his innocent cross face, he surely felt something, the barefoot emissary of the Amir with a dagger in his belt, the lovely ambassador between empires. He served an unknowing purpose, a purpose opaque to everyone. He served the implacable veiled purpose of the Emperor's marvellous mind. There was a chatter, from within, like the chatter of birds, of monkeys, of women. But it was not the noise of birds. Hasan raised his soft princely hand to his soft pale face, just once. He pushed at the door. It gave; and, making no noise, he entered the house of the Englishman.

SIX

I

This is the way that Charles Masson came to be in Kabul and how he came to talk the way that he talked, which was the first thing anyone noticed about him.

Five years before, in an army camp in Calcutta.

The parade ground was a desert of musket parts. The company sat, cross-legged, red and sweating, each surrounded by his own little puzzle of greased iron to put back together.

"Now this," Suggs, the Sergeant-Major, was saying through his horrible grin, "is the locking bolt. The locking bolt." He was holding up a small iron object between thumb and forefinger.

The Company, together, grunted a four-syllable noise with their heads to the ground, a masculine grunt which satisfied Suggs. He seemed to think they had replied with what he had said; they could, in fact, have said anything at all.

At the back of the platoon, his gun now in forty pieces scattered, a hopeless archipelago, on a greasy blue cotton tablecloth, sat Charles Masson. He scratched his head. Sweating profusely in his shirt and breeches, contemplating the nightmare iron picnic in front of him, he wondered merely what delicacy to go for next.

"And this," the Sergeant-Major said, grinning sadistically at this further element of bafflement, "is the barrel-loader. The barrel-loader."

There again, that grunting noise, five syllables this time, a downward scale, like a bouncing ball. Masson said nothing, not seeing the need to say an object's name to commit it to memory. In his case, he was as likely to forget the horrid little object after saying its name as before. And he had decided that this was not the sort of information he wanted cluttering up his brain.

A distant door opened and shut. Shimmering a little in the late-morning heat came the figure of Florentia Sale, the commanding officer's wife, her jutting jaw and purposeful stride in no way modified by the pink and white parasol, her virginal dress. As she approached, the men who had seen her started to struggle to their feet. Not Masson.

"Don't get up, I pray you," called Florentia, dragging her panting little dog after her. "Ignore me, ignore me. I should not be here, merely the shortest route, tiffin, you know."

She flashed a steely smile at the men, and strode onwards. Masson silently wished rabies on her dog and—a moment's contemplation after—on her as well. The Sergeant-Major said nothing, and it remained a half-hearted tribute, as the men who had risen got no further than a bent-knee stance before sinking down again to their morning task. Too absorbed in their task; not very interested, either, in Florentia Sale, their commanding officer's commanding wife, a greedy old woman who was more accustomed to tell people not to trouble than she was to receive unsolicited tribute. She passed on, anyway.

"This," Suggs went on, projecting to the far corners of the empty parade ground, "is the musket's thumb-grip. A great help when you come to fire the bleeding thing." He too must be suffering; his great red face twitching and glistening in the heat, his eyes rolling and yellow with the long hours in this steamy blaze, in a uniform suited only to a damp European climate. But he seemed to gain energy from the furious heat, and not to be exhausted by it; his instructions, his striding energy, actually increased as the day went on. "What is it?" he demanded.

"A thumb-grip, Sergeant-Major," they chorused dully, the small diversion of Mrs. Sale's stately passage now dissipated.

Something had led Masson to this point, sitting on a parade ground, sweating into his Company-issue underwear, staring at wing-nuts. A long sickly childhood in a Devon farmhouse, and tales of an uncle who went to sea, bringing back incredible tales of the East. Told and told again. That had been it, surely. There was no desire for money in Masson; he had no wish to go back with his thousands to acquire a country house and respectability. He had no wish to go home.

That was odd, because the urge that had led him here was as hungry and unfilled in Calcutta as it had been in the grey square unwindowed farmhouse ten miles from Porlock. There, it had been his three young brothers standing between him and what he wanted; here, it was the Company, and his duties, and the wing-nuts. Masson had come to the East in the only way he could. It was not long before the means of his coming were standing between him and what he could see every day. Moments—small unremarked street-moments, unhistoric, unforgettable—where the India he had dreamt of in the long confinement of his childhood and the India all around him combined in a sonorous unison. Moments where no Company intruded, where no instructions were shouted, except the single one, inside him. He was reassured, as he heard that sounding double call, that what he had dreamt of was there after all. Saved, he was, in these moments from a deeper worry, that the fulfilment of the East he had dreamt of was one without his presence, his falsifying gaze. What he wanted was an East which was no longer exotic, but purely familiar, and he feared that, like a practising pianist, it could only achieve that when he was not looking at it. An India he wanted only to the degree that it could not include him; that was his fear, dispelled in those absorbed moments when he passed down a Calcutta street, unnoticed, or at least unremarked, or a curious unfearing boy met his expression with an equal gaze, and held it. Unmoving.

That was what Masson was here for; those sudden clicks of identity when, like a hot blush, he was sure that there was something there, just there for him. It was what he had always dreamt of, in the kitchen of the Porlock farmhouse, hunched over the Vicar's *Arabian Nights*. He was sure now, after a year, that it was only Suggs and Sale that stood in the way of his finding it. Suggs and Sale; they had turned into an emporium, selling only frustration to Masson, representing everything that stood in his way.

Suggs and Sale; he could have started a religion, to declare the pair of them unclean.

2

The long morning came to an end, and the platoon limped off into the guardroom, soggy with their combined concentration. McVitie, the hero of the platoon, was, for once, beyond a quip. He satisfied himself with bending down and rubbing his head with both hands, furiously back and forth, as if his head were unconnected to him, like a man affectionately scrubbing at his dog after a run in the rain. A shower of sweat fountained from McVitie's head, and, stripping himself of his shirt, he sank down limply on the rude benches which ran round the room.

"Well, gentlemen," Masson said lightly. "I don't know how much any of us will remember of this morning's dose of pointless activity."

The platoon ignored this, one of them merely giving a small moan of boredom with Masson's comment. He was unpopular in the platoon, for no very clear reason. His unpopularity was such that his every statement was automatically greeted with a palpable turning of backs. More than that, it had reached the point where Masson himself aimed his occasional remarks squarely at the platoon's disapproval. Not exactly enjoying their dislike, but having earned it, at least he would exult in the power of being able to evoke it most when he chose.

McVitie raised his square head a fraction from the bench, without opening his eyes. "We all learnt what we was learnt, Masson," he said. "It was only you. Don't tar us with your stinking brush."

He fell back, gormlessly, mouth open. Masson contemplated him, the platoon hero.

Elsewhere in the barracks, Florentia Sale was passing out her brisk instructions. She was in the basement of what was termed, inaccurately, the Colonel's house; it was merely a random stretch of the building, a few interconnected rooms with a kitchen and a washing room in the basement, but the Colonel's status required him to have a house, and a house he should have, even where there was none. In the basement kitchen, the heat was bathlike, but Florentia Sale was livid, pale, dry in this dense heat. About her, a foot below her square determined face, the kitchen servants clustered, and listened anxiously to her instructions. "Very important, very important dinner," she was crying, not looking at her listeners. "I want you to imagine—to imagine that you are cooking a dinner for the Governor General himself—for the King of England."

There was a perceptible increase in worry, as the little faces creased. "King?" one of them, the most senior apparently, said, his voice almost failing.

"No, no, no," Florentia said. "I want you to *imagine* that the King is coming. I want you to take as much care over your work as if—"

"King?" the boy said again.

Florentia gave up, her face set like cooling gravy. "Yes, the King is coming," she said bluntly. "Remember—fry the onions well, and slowly. Curry? Curry? Understand?" The heads below her wobbled from side to side, acknowledging and agreeing. "And soup. Soup? Understand? And the fish? How will you cook the fish?" There was another general agreeable wobbling; Florentia took it, apparently, for assent. "How? White sauce? Parsley?" The kitchen attendants looked from side to side, trying to establish seniority; one, in the end, stepped three inches forward and bowed superbly. He stepped back, and smiled ingratiatingly. Florentia sighed, and prepared to begin again.

After the soldiers' tiffin, there was, unusually, three hours at leisure. Masson skipped off as soon as he inconspicuously could. He wanted to go and see Mr. Das.

Mr. Das had a boutique in the bazaar. Masson had been drawn in a year before, by a blue glass vase visible through the open door. Then he had wondered if it could be Roman, with the optimism of the inexperienced. Now, he knew it was Syrian, and not at all old, but Mr. Das had become the nearest thing to a friend Masson had. The shop was a ruin of miniature artefacts, and old Das a fraud, apt to proffer the cheapest bazaar silverware as precious beyond an Englishman's dreams. But he, from time to time, failed to know when a coin from his filthy chests was a thousand years old, and deeply unfamiliar. What he knew and what he did not know was apparent from the prices he set, and, after a year going through his stock, Masson felt that, all in all, he knew more than Das did.

Das didn't trust Masson—that was clear from the way he constantly tried to rook him, as if taking the first step in an inevitable exchange of fraud. It was natural for someone in his position, with a boutique full of frail glass, to be wary of a beef-faced Englishman twice his size in a Company uniform; wary, too, when the Englishman in question, revealed as well intentioned, seemed to turn himself from a curious fool into a scholar within months, and Das looked at his surprising protégé with a habitual reproach, as if Masson had not been entirely honest with him at the first.

Nevertheless, Das had been useful to Masson. That first purchase, the Syrian blue glass vase, had worried Masson while he was paying for it. Until then, his purchases had been small and solid—coins, metalwork, durable little objects of devotion, all easily contained in Masson's pack. Each treasure was accompanied by a set of meticulous notes on the object, based on what the coin-handler could tell him. That was not a trove to attract attention in the barracks, but this vase could not be stuffed away like that. Masson would not display it to the platoon's mockery, and yet he wanted the little vase, wanted it badly, and would have gone on wanting it even if he had known that it was not Roman at all.

Mr. Das was all tact, and saw the problem even before Masson had said anything. After all, what was a common soldier doing with such a fine object, handling it so tenderly? What would he do with such a thing? Masson eagerly fell in with Das's suggestion that he transfer all his little collection to a secure cupboard in Das's boutique, and, as Das foresaw, afterwards made all his purchases from Das. He was a sympathetic fellow, the shopkeeper, only betraying the slightest sorrow in a little wince when he saw the appalling tinsel exoticism of Masson's first purchases, when he had arrived in Calcutta. Das handled the semi-industrial figure of Shiva in rough, tarnished bronze with a display of reverence intended much more to spare Masson's feelings than for the benefit of the god. And since then, he had been of great use—there was talk, even, of introducing Masson to a scholarly friend of his, who might be able to start him off on Sanskrit— and he represented, all in all, the nearest thing to a friend Masson had ever had. His face was sharp-cornered at jaw and chin, like many Bengalis; he had an almost pentagonal, queerly inquisitive appearance.

3

Das was turning a coin over and over as Masson came into his shop. A little man even by Indian standards, half Masson's size, he was respectably dressed according to the lights of his religion. Masson could never quite get used to holding a conversation on serious matters with a man so nearly naked. He liked to be discovered in a scholarly attitude, and Masson sat in respectful silence for a couple of minutes, until Das was ready to speak to him.

"My dear fellow," he said finally. "I wonder what you have to say to this. My mind, I confess, is a trifle stumped."

Masson took the coin and looked at it, wondering as usual at the way Das talked, like Tacitus after a drink or two. The coin was a Queen Anne penny, probably palmed off on Das by a Company private too sharp for his own good. Masson considered telling Das that it was a coin of the reign of the Empress Agrippina before it occurred to him that Das might be testing him in some obscure manner. He told the shopkeeper what it was.

"That," Das said, smartly snapping the coin back into his fist, "was more or less what I had supposed it to be. Thank you, my dear sir. And how may I help you today? A cup of *chai* first, certainly."

He clapped his hands and the toothless dirty old woman who was always in the boutique, fingering the goods—perhaps Das's wife, there was no means of knowing—mumbled off into the recesses of the shop.

"I really want nothing of you, Mr. Das," Masson said. "*Chai* would be splendid."

"Perhaps a perusal of your treasures, Mr. Masson?" Das said as the *chai* arrived. Masson took the stinking sweet orange confection, tea and milk and sugar and water boiled together for half an hour. As always at Das's shop, the water it had been made from was so filthy, the *chai* could have been strong or weak, and Masson had to rid himself of the irrational idea that Das made his tea out of the water his crone familiar washed her grubby old body in. The crone smiled and shook her head from side to side, letting go of the cup, leaving a dirty thumbprint over the clay rim. "Always welcome, always welcome. Or perhaps he would like to see a few minor curiosities I acquired in the course of several perambulations about this great metropolis, hmm? No obligation, my dear sir, merely an oddity or two I feel you would be interested by, and—I confess—one or two more I should be grateful to have the benefit of your undoubted and excellent wisdom regarding their history, provenance, and significance. Queen Anne penny, indeed."

The exchange of business was a necessary preliminary to their conversation, Masson had found. Das preserved some necessary dignity by reminding himself that they had begun in a business relationship, and would not, entirely, get beyond that. It might have been designed, too, to remind Masson that he would not come to know everything about Das, that whatever expertise he acquired about Das's stock, he was always there on sufferance. Das reached across the table, stained with rings, and gestured at a small knife, curved and graceful like a miniature scimitar. Masson picked it up carefully and turned it over. A cockroach ran across the table, making Masson jump; it had been sheltering under the blade, and Masson now discreetly flicked it onto the floor with the tip of the knife. Das hated to see an insect killed, and tutted mildly, either at Masson's squeamishness or to suggest that the thing was of no significance.

The blade was curved, whether for grace or use. Though the handle was encrusted and filthy, the quarter-inch at the blade's edge shone. This knife had been used regularly, and recently. Masson had heard of oriental knives that cut flesh as easily as butter, and placed the tip of his forefinger on the edge of the blade. It rested there, the blade trembling slightly in Masson's hand.

"You are left-handed, I perceive," Das said.

"I use both equally well," Masson said, fixed on the thin contact between finger and blade, insubstantial as a point in geometry.

"That is bad luck, very bad luck," Das said, drawing back from Masson with his shock of red hair and his divided soul. He made a warding-off hiss, like the noise of hot metal in water.

Masson smiled his wide open devouring smile. "On the contrary," he said. "It's a piece of very good luck." And he moved the knife, a small movement, half an inch, putting no pressure on the handle. There was a sudden heat in the finger, and underneath the blade, the colour had fled the dirty finger, a little field of tripe-white as the blood drew back under the blade. Masson made his pain-noise, the same hissing Das had made, the same sound of hot metal in water. The blood returned and welled up, wine-dark, in the little flap of severed flesh the knife had made. White, translucent, an onion's slice. Masson put down the magnificent knife, and sucked his salty finger for a minute. When he took it out, the finger was clean, and white in his dirty hand.

"A good knife," he said, picking it up again.

"Whence does it originate, in your opinion?" Das asked.

Masson turned the knife over again. The handle was so encrusted with rust and dirt that it was hard to see if it were decorated. He ran the nail of his forefinger over the surface, and there was some raised pattern—he followed the line—some arabesque—some writing, surely. By the whiplash feel of it, he supposed it to be Arabic, some belligerent verse of the Koran. Not Indian; he somehow knew this, without knowing how he knew. He guessed at Persian. It felt like damascene work, anyway.

He said this to Das as he was feeling the knife. Das clapped his hands with pleasure. "Indeed, indeed, excellent, quite on the nail, as you would say," he said. "I had an interesting visitor this week, a traveller, who had acquired some curiosities. I cannot account for it, but he was eager to disembarrass himself of some old Persian treasures. That, I think, is the finest of his hoard, alas, and sadly in want of care, but the other objects I acquired from him have their own interest and even, I dare say, some measure of value. Would you, by any chance, care to . . ."

"In a furious hurry, was he, your friend?" Masson said. "And I have no doubt that you found yourself in possession of a large quantity of Persian antiquities without requiring too much of the gentleman?" Das looked outraged at the suggestion that he might be in the habit of consorting with thieves. It took a moment to make him realize that Masson was only casting the first shot in the exchanges over the final price, and for a while he seemed unwilling to show his newly acquired objects at all.

But in the end, he yielded to the undeniable argument of lucre, and Masson was soon looking, with hungry eyes, at an array of metalwork spread out on Das's table. For a moment he was incongruously reminded of this morning's exercise with the dismantled musket, as he pored over the miscellaneous array of mostly Persian, mostly indifferent antique objects. In the end—it took an hour—he settled, besides the knife, for a little silver dish and three unfamiliar coins, interesting in appearance, unaccountably so. As was customary these days, he paid Mr. Das with a combination of his army pay and the restitution of one of Masson's own early purchases, before he had developed a proper eye. This process of secondary haggling occupied another half an hour, as Masson attempted to return to Das some of the worthless trash he had originally passed off on Masson at any price. Das, indignant at being insulted in such a manner that it should be suggested that his shop should ever be soiled with such bazaar trinkets, and denying furiously that he was the first source of the trash, attempted to inveigle out of Masson the beautiful little silver medal he had sold him no more than three weeks before, presumably having realized its worth in the interim. At length an agreement was reached, leaving both Masson and Das sore and suspicious, and they settled down to talk, undisturbed by customers, the army, Suggs, or Sale.

"Mr. Das," Masson began. "Speaking of your visitor last week, if you were to travel and were obliged to live on the proceeds of what you could sell on your travels, what goods would you take?"

"I do not understand your question, Mr. Masson," Das said. He picked his nose meditatively and examined the contents before flicking it at the floor. "I have no need or desire to travel, as you well know, I am sure."

"Indeed, indeed," Masson said. He persevered. "In a hypothetical situation, however, if you were obliged to travel, and the only means of support you had was the sale of what goods you could carry, what would you take with you to sell?"

"Ah," Das said, now having got the point. "Like my friend, earlier this week, in flight from his own shadow and selling his worldly goods at a highly disadvantageous rate, I can assure you."

"Disadvantageous to him, Mr. Das."

"Indeed, indeed," Das said. He had a disconcerting habit of taking up Masson's expressions and repeating them, a minute or two later. You could see the quick boy he must have been. "Well, I am sure you are aware that this is a simple matter of working out the relationship between value and bulk."

The conversation ran its course; they agreed on silver, as being most easily disguised and most universally valued. "But why," said Das, "why, my friend, this sudden interest?"

It was time for Masson to go. He consigned the Persian dish to the cupboard where he stored his things, saying a silent goodbye to it, and thanked Das for the *chai*. He left the knife with Das. The heat and damp were insufferable, and, returning to the barracks, Masson lengthened his journey by remaining in the shade. Anyone watching him might have thought there was some superstition which directed his route, like a child leaping the cracks in the pavement. Certainly he drew the attention of the Calcutta streets; the red-toothed men squatting on their haunches chewing paan and spitting consumptively followed him with their incurious eyes. They wondered at this peeled-raw man, ugly and gawky, shrinking into the darker side of the street, hugging the wall like a conspirator, looking down, hiding something.

4

Masson was hiding something, as it happened. It was his plan for escape. It had seemed audacious, impossible, but now Das, with his idle conversation, had found something for him. Until now, Masson had seen no way to be in the East, where he wanted to be, other than by the way he had chosen. The surety that he could only find the East he had dreamt of by remaining where he was, serving the Company at the Company's request, all at once left him.

Masson was entering the camp lost in thought, and hardly saw the Colonel's wife rapidly approaching; he was halfway through the little door let into the gate when he became aware of her, and had to withdraw his step to stand, respectfully, outside while she bustled up. No weather seemed to slow or trouble the grim, sweatless figure of Florentia Sale, and she came from the knife-edged sunlight of the yard into the dark of the lodge, and, bending through the keyhole door, out again into the street where Masson stood waiting respectfully. She moved jointly, at quite a lick, like an aged racehorse. She normally passed without acknowledgement, but as he stood there, her bonily unwielded figure seemed to unfold telescopically, and she became aware of him.

"Soldier," she said, her eyes fixed on a point firmly beyond Masson's shoulder. "Find my husband, if you please, and give this to him." She produced a sealed letter from her swinging reticule, and tapped Masson on the chest with it. He took it from her, nervously. "Most important. Don't lose it. Don't forget it. I know how you chaps can be with anything remotely important."

And then she was off like a horse from the slips. She set off not as if she were going to the bazaar in an idle moment, or to bully some collector's little wife over tea, but as if she were carrying a small bomb with a short fuse. Masson looked after her in her steaming wake with something approaching admiration. She had not looked once at him in the course of their encounter. Masson looked around him at the street, the lodge. Empty, apart from natives. He looked at the letter. He felt just like dropping it in the gutter, into the Calcutta detritus. It was a pact with himself, and with Calcutta; with India; with the Asia he had dreamt of, which, if he stretched out his hand and closed his eyes, thrummed under his fingers as securely as it had when he was lonely, and alone, and fourteen, in Devon. He not only knew now that he was going to escape into India. Such a little escape, like stepping over a low brick wall without looking down or looking back. He also knew how he was going to do it, and if dreaming of escape is no more than the normal human condition, knowing how you are to escape is tantamount to escaping. After all, men do escape, from time to time; it is not merely a dream. Masson accepted an instruction, gravely; he looked at the direction on the white sealed paper—*The Colonel Sale*, it said, and *Urgently Required*, in Florentia Sale's urgently spiked hand—and then, hardly thinking about it, he cast it into the drains and entered the camp, whistling. That was how things were to be, from now on. It hardly mattered how long his escape would take—six months, a year. Now, he knew how to escape, and to that end bent all his silent powers.

5

It took, in the end, a year. The ten days in solitary did not dent his resolve, or make him feel that there was danger in his undertaking. Of course Florentia Sale, unobservant and disdainful as she was, had recalled that the private soldier she had entrusted with the urgent duty was red-haired. Failing to convey a despatch—and Florentia Sale, for this purpose, counted as carrying much the same importance as her colonel consort—was a punishable offence. Masson didn't care. Solitude was what he was accustomed to, and what he frankly preferred to the grim miasma of the barracks, the foglike aroma of the bodies of the platoon. Bodies; the heroic McVitie and twenty-five others, sweating through the Calcutta nights. It also taught him something useful—and Masson was determined that, from now, what he heard and saw and was told should above all be useful to him in his future life on the other side of that low wall. It taught him that he was conspicuous and would, wherever he went, be seen and remembered. It was not just a question of red hair, which could be dyed or covered. Masson was intelligent enough to see that. It was his whole person, which could not be changed. Most people in the world were inconspicuous, readily formed a crowd. Masson did not. He stood out in a crowd like a pianoforte before an orchestra. His secrets, prompt as his red hair, made him obvious and memorable. That could not be changed. It was worth knowing, that was all.

It took a year of acquisition and learning and planning. Not even Das was told what he was about to do. He had a new interest, introduced with a carefully casual air, in silver. Particularly old Persian silver. If Das remembered their earlier conversation, he did not give any sign of it. Masson bought what fragments he could, until he had decided in which direction he wanted to go, beyond the British pale, beyond the North-West Frontier, where no one would pursue him. There, it was quite probable that Persian silver was no rarity, that he would find it worth less than in Calcutta. He switched to bazaar-ware, less pleasing, more saleable. He even bought, though he had to force himself, the grim imitations of European silver with which the Calcutta silversmiths hoped to supply the daily needs of the British. Once or twice, Masson even found an opportunity while on kitchen duty to take Company silver; it was hideous, but beyond Jalalabad, these lumpy saltcellars, these squarely elaborate knives and forks might well entrance a remote nabob. Once, a great silver plate was missed, and the barracks turned upside down; nothing was proved, and by then the massily encrusted trophy was safely entrusted to Mr. Das, who, if he wondered about the sudden accumulation in the dank little cupboard, said nothing and did nothing. In any case, little as Masson trusted the shopkeeper, even to him it must be apparent that these trophies were too conspicuous to sell behind Masson's back. Nor did he seem to wonder when Masson started to take Persian seriously, and within a year had absorbed and learnt enough of the oriental *lingua franca*—all scholarly pretensions to Sanskrit forgotten—to converse very fluently with any of Das's occasional casual visitors, passing through in a two-year journey from Peking to Isfahan.

Too fluently—strangely fluently. A change came over Masson when he spoke Persian and his Persian personality, as he slipped into the most beautiful language on earth, its long floating ambiguous rose-petalled paragraphs like the long twisting full paragraphs of a sad nightingale's song, was not the Masson who emerged, haltingly and secretively, from the terms of the language he had spoken all his life. Masson wanted desperately to engage those wary old men in conversation, who so clearly saw Calcutta as Masson did, saw it as a stage on the long latitudinous journey and not, as the English did, as the great white Imperial jewel at the other end of the long road from London. It was not just that, nor the fascination of talking to a man whose manner and form of life Masson would so shortly pursue. It was the fascination of speaking Persian. There was the wonder of the beautiful language, so full of improvisation and fluid song, so little trammelled by the false bridges and carapace of grammatical structure, laid out in tables. But beyond that, Masson, speaking, improvising, in Persian, felt as if a new personality had been vouchsafed to him, and he observed this flirtatious anecdotal multifarious new Masson from outside, observing the transformation with an inner astonishment until the visiting bright-eyed merchants began to draw away, nervously.

In these last months, his raucous comrades, like the whole establishment, lost all their terror. From the august Florentia Sale down to the ravenous black rats, big as terriers, everything seemed to fade like cloth in the sun. They were wraiths, all at once, whose future, unknown to them, had no substance, like nervous disinherited relations about a deathbed. He had set no term on his time here, and would have gone on, quite happily, his eyes fixed on that astonishing shining destiny.

6

It was a Tuesday. It had been raining all day; not in bursts, but a steady hot rain, without any lessening or thickening, like a hot falling river. The streets steamed upwards and stank. The platoon had been on guardroom duty all day, and was at work in a desultory skiving manner, polishing and shining, with blacking and cloths. McVitie was striding around the guardroom like a deposed king, unquestioned, while the platoon worked. He rolled round the guardroom, his thumbs in his belt-loops, treating the platoon to a long and haphazard account of his adventures with women. He was thirteen—no, twelve—and she was twenty-four, a maid, and blooming, and he made her squeal. And then with her sister Molly, she took the great length of it, complaining like a stuck pig, fit to wake the dead, but she took it, again and again and again. And then when he was fifteen, the vicar's daughter took him by the hand and led him behind, behind a tombstone, that was right, and she made him take it out to show her, though she were no more an fifteen herself, and she knew how to suck it clean, to give um delight and save her maidenhead, so she said, but he bent her over and took her from behind, where there weren't no maiden-head neither, and then from afore, and then—McVitie guffawed at his own wit—there weren't no maidenhead there no more to trouble the vicar's daughter.

The platoon sniggered sycophantically. Masson managed a smile, of sorts, at McVitie's dingy memoirs, stale and weary as the unfaulting rain.

McVitie suddenly stopped in his flow; his gaze, narrowed and intensely felt, but stupid beneath his white eyelashes as a pig's, had settled on Masson.

"Why am I telling you all?" he said, as if a brilliant thought had come to him. "Someone else's turn." He picked up a tin of blacking and threw it hard, at Masson. It hit him, hard, on his arm. "Tell us of all your judies, then."

The platoon roared; the one thing that made Masson entirely conspic-uous was that he was the one man in the platoon who never came on the trips to the brothels in Company Street. Few of the platoon went every Sunday afternoon—perhaps only McVitie—and some went only for form's sake, like little Morgan, who turned out on high days and holidays, and saved half his pay for his widowed mother in Carmarthen. But they all went sometimes; it was only Masson who never went. He was aware, and scared, that to the rest, his never going must look dangerously like a principle, or something worse.

"I prefer to keep private matters private," Masson said, unable to stop himself, and even to him it sounded priggish and unconvincing. The pla-toon guffawed again; there was a hard, forced edge to their laughter, as if brought out for McVitie's approval. Whatever it sounded like to McVitie, to Masson, half-smiling, it was the noise of hounds baying.

"Prefer to keep *private* matters *private*," McVitie said, mimicking in mincing tones. Then he said it again, to make the men laugh harder. "*Private* matters *private*." His face seemed to close up with malice and tri-umph. "I bet you do. Till the hands come calling of a Saturday night. I bet there ain't nothing left private of you then. I bet you lay it all out on a tray for um then, begging for it, ain't you? Bent over the stile, begging for it, ain't you? Bet you miss all them great big farmhands, eh, boy? Tell you what, boy—"

The laughter, now rising to a howling pitch, died suddenly as the guardroom door was flung open and Suggs, the Sergeant-Major, stood there bristling. McVitie, who, horrifyingly, had actually been undoing his belt, sat down abruptly and reached for a boot to polish. Suggs stood and glared at them for a minute, then stalked off glintingly. The door stood open.

Masson was trembling. He could not see how McVitie and the platoon had come to see what they had seen; no notion of his had betrayed what he dreamt of, only an omission. No: he knew how. There was a fear in him; and the fear was bound up with the revelation of McVitie, fresh and wet with sweat, his huge eyes pouring out hate at Masson, his shirt undone three buttons revealing the firm white freckled flesh within, the graceful, perfect whiteness of the bare feet. He hated himself for this, and knew McVitie, somehow, had seen the way Masson had once looked at him. That was the source, surely, of the terrible intimacy of hatred which fell between them, and Masson could only resolve what was quite impossible, never to look directly at McVitie ever again.

Ten minutes after lights out, Masson took himself off to the latrines to write up his notes. That was his practice. It was the only time of day when privacy could be guaranteed for a quarter of an hour. Outside, in the hot Calcutta night, a dog howled; somewhere very close, just outside the gates, and a human voice or two was raised as if in answer. Sweat seemed to drip from the blue air. The lights were put out by Suggs on his rounds, and Masson felt quietly in his kit bag for the precious little volume; a bound book of blank pages, with the stub of a pencil tied into its spine with a piece of string. Masson now felt in a different pocket on the kit bag's inside, and found the little silver medal he had bought from Das a day or two before. Noiselessly, in his summer combinations and barefoot, he swung out of bed and padded off to the latrines. Most of the platoon was already asleep.

Alone, Masson lit the stump of candle he had pocketed with a flint and a taper, and settled down. He allowed himself no more than fifteen minutes; more would mean too great a risk of discovery. Masson did not care about punishment, but he feared for his vital notes, which, if discovered, would surely be destroyed. He opened his notebook at the first clean page, and examined the silver medal. Mughal; no doubt. He began to write a note, starting with where and when it had been bought. He wrote in a tiny hand, resembling the busy progress of carnivorous ants across the page. It saved paper, and, should the volume be found, at least the notes would not be read. There was nothing in the notes. But Masson preferred secrecy.

The candle flickered, as if in a small breath of wind, as if the door to the latrine had fallen open. Masson stopped writing, looked up. There was no sound. He started to write again. Mughal; late Mughal, the seventeenth century. *Awreng-zeb, reign of,* he was writing.

"Busy, Charlie, then?" McVitie said. He had quietly opened the door, and was standing there leaning against the wall, observing Masson while he wrote. He was in grubby brief summer combinations, his legs and torso naked. Behind him, in the shadow, an acolyte stood guard. Masson knew who it was; Hastings, the shifty cheat with no idea in his head and foully stinking breath. Talking to him always made Masson wonder whether some small oriental rodent had died in his throat, and stuck there. Masson looked at McVitie, his terror too huge to try to hide.

"I thought you came out here of a night to give yourself a thrill," McVitie said. His voice was gentle, even cooing. "What's that you're writing, then, Charlie, your diary?"

He leant forward, and took it, gently, irresistibly. He flicked to a random page.

"17th March," he read. "Got up, did guard duty, polished my boots, ate my stinking rice, retired early . . . 18th March, watched McVitie take a bath; I'd spread my buttocks for his gurt engine, I swear I would."

"Give that to me," Masson said, furious. There was nothing there but dry notes on coins, and he felt himself invaded by McVitie's fantasies. At the door, Hastings, the halfwit lickspittle with the perpetually stinking breath, turned nervously. McVitie continued in the same relaxed, reassuring tones.

"I hadn't quite finished, Charles, my dear fellow," he said. "Wait. There's another interesting entry here, isn't there. Where were we? Oh yes: 20th March. Got up, frigged myself stupid thinking on my darling McVitie and his pillar of love. After tiffin, went and stole the regimental silver."

"That's rubbish," Masson said, but all at once, with the flush of blood to his head, he was betrayed. McVitie looked at him, a half-smile of delight about his mouth.

"Joe," he said to the sycophant at the door, not raising his voice one notch, "I think you might owe me ten shillings. Your faith in human nature was entirely misplaced, it seems."

"That's rubbish, and you know it," Masson said, but he felt a terrible sense of plunging, and he could feel himself beginning to bluster, as his hands took on a frightened life of their own.

"Don't you worry, Charlie," McVitie said scornfully. "I wouldn't split on you, no more'n I'd read—" he handed back the little volume, "—a lady's diary."

Masson took it, trying not to snatch. Perhaps that was all. But McVitie seemed in no hurry to go; he stood there, in his customary lounging position, one hand proprietorially fingering his heavy crotch.

"What do you want?" Masson said, attempting firmness.

McVitie affected astonishment. "Want, Charles? Why, I don't want nothing. Can't a fellow stand where he finds it comfortable, like? I'm not in your way, am I, Charles, my boy? Not preventing you from doing anything you came in here for, am I? You want to get on with your diary, I ain't stopping you, am I? You want to take a shit? Don't mind me, my son. Because I'm just planning to stand here—" and with that, with a single gesture of his thumb, he pulled down the drawstring waist of his combinations, tucking them deftly behind his hairy ginger testicles, "—and do what I came in here to do. And I hope—I sincerely hope—you're not thinking of stopping me, are you, Charles? Not thinking—" McVitie paused, looked down at his stubby, fat, suddenly ludicrous erection with an expression almost sorrowful in its intensity, "—not thinking of refusing a chap, are you, Masson?"

McVitie started frigging his cock there, six inches from Masson's face; a slow brutal rub with his heavy fist; Masson could smell the sex and sweat of it, there, in his face.

"Let me go," Masson said, standing up decisively.

"No one's stopping you," McVitie said, smiling quietly, baring his teeth. "Nothing's stopping you. Except what you want." Masson stepped forward, and McVitie tripped him, and, as he stumbled, was quickly behind him, ramming his arm up behind his back in a half-nelson. McVitie pushed Masson to the floor, grunting in his ear. Against his face, Masson felt the stone floor of the latrine gritty and wet and warm. On his back, kneeling, McVitie took a handful of Masson's hair, tugged his head back and slammed it against the flagstone. A hand—McVitie's—was tugging at his combinations. There, in front of his eye, was a pair of boots—the waiting, surveying Hastings. In his back—low in his back—there was a finger, a hard prodding finger, pushing bluntly, blindly, and there in his ear was a voice, McVitie's, a muted whispering cry, saying, right there in Masson's ear, "Answer to your dreams, boy, answer to a maiden's prayer." He kicked once, trying to cry out, and behind him something—the candle—fell and everything was darkness. In his mouth, McVitie's fist, which he bit. But it was only cloth and metal, and he could not hurt McVitie, he could never hurt the invincible McVitie, he knew that now.

7

All at once, it was over; they were gone. Masson lay there in the dark, and it seemed to him that hot liquids were dripping from him—salt, and blood, and sweat, and hot liquid shit. It took an age to stand up, and when he did, unaccountably, it was his joints and bones and right shoulder which most hurt. He found some water in the dark. In the bowl it was warm and thick as sputum. He could feel between his fingers how dirty it was. He washed himself, there, in the dark, trembling as he did so, washing as best he could. When, an hour, a good hour later, he stumblingly felt his way back to his bunk, he could hear the room was silent; not silent with sleep, but all holding their breath, pretending unconsciousness. And then he knew they all knew.

The night was hot, and wet. The rains would not be long returning; the air was soaked with the hanging moisture, waiting to fall like a restrained cataract. One more bucketful of water, gathering in the gathering clouds, and the whole would fall on the brown city. The platoon turned, and sweated silently, and waited for sleep or morning. There was silence in the room. No one snored, all that long hot night.

It was Masson whom the platoon would not look at the next day; Masson whose bruised and broken gaze no one would meet. McVitie had gone too far, but McVitie always went too far, and the cowed esteem, the enforced popularity with which the platoon observed its hero was as it had always been. Only there was a bandage round his hand, where Masson had bitten him; he had bitten him, which was something. But it was Masson no one would look at, Masson whose ready excuses for his night-torn face were not listened to, or needed.

That afternoon, he had only an hour, but he knew that would be enough. He walked out swiftly, having spoken no word to anyone all day, or met their gaze. Outside the gates, the cobbler who was always there was hammering with his poor tools at a poor pair of shoes; squatting against the wall, frowning in concentration. It was a posture, Masson thought, which only natives could take up; he himself could squat for a minute or two on the balls of his feet, but it was a physical impossibility to squat with his feet flat on the floor, and it was never comfortable. But natives could squat like that for hours. If there was some sort of anatomical peculiarity which enabled this, he did not know. It was some kind of favour, like the one which meant that natives did not sweat, even in the most hellish of Calcutta's wet heats. The man seemed quite happy in his naked concentration, bashing the shoe into bits; and next to him was a street tailor, stitching at a shirt and taking care with his left hand not to let his work fall into the dirt. And next to him was a woman, cooking some gloop in a little vessel for any passer-by with an anna or two. In this city there were cooks, wastrels, builders, tailors: there were those who told your future or your health with an inspection of the soles of your feet. Street-corner physicians, handing out phials of watercress liniment—an infallible cure for poor digestion—next to one prescribing the same bottle for impotency, memory, the swelling sickness. The restorers of virginities, the makers of marriages, the ordainers of caste, water diviners, sweetmeat pedlars, both gilded and plain; milkmaids, mendicants, thieves; scribes, storytellers, world-renouncers, whores, those who pursued no trade, and those who pursued a trade as yet unnamed. All at once it struck him how terribly few the British were, how thinly scattered over the surface of India, like an exiguous dusting of fine sugar over a cake. These were good lives he seemed to see, here on the street. Useful lives. It was time to go.

He took himself off to the bazaar and bought two substantial panniers. What else he needed, he knew where to find it. And then to Mr. Das's.

"My dear fellow," Das said, rising in alarm at Masson's blossoming bruises and one missing front tooth.

"I walked into a door," Masson said briefly. "It was a door called McVitie."

"My dear fellow," Das said again, giggling a little in shy concern. "I hope, at the very least, that the door named McVitie came off rather worse than the man named Masson."

Masson had no time for this. "No," he said. "No, on the whole I came off a great deal worse than he did. Look here, Das, I need something today. I need what's in my cupboard."

"Need what, precisely?" Das said, smoothing his hands down his *kurta*. "*Chai,* my dear fellow?"

"I doubt I have time," Masson said. But the crone had been despatched with a double clap of Das's hands. "Look, I need it all, today."

"Not leaving Calcutta, my dear sir?" Das said. A veil—almost an expression of cunning—came over his face.

"No, indeed no," Masson said. It was best not to start on farewells. "No; merely a fellow collector. I wish to show him my purchases. Merely that."

"A fellow collector," Das said musingly. He fixed Masson in his gaze. "One who finds himself unable to come here, for instance, who wants to see everything you possess."

"Yes," Masson said. He shrank from his real reason not to tell Das that he was leaving. It was not that he was afraid of being betrayed; he simply did not want to say goodbye. He recognized how cowardly this was, and was satisfied to know that Das certainly knew he was leaving.

Das suddenly seemed to switch off his amiability. "Very well," he said. "You know best." He stood and led the way into the gloomy recesses of the shop. In the back was Masson's cupboard, and Das unlocked it gracelessly. It took half an hour to wrap each trinket, coin, plate in the long stretches of cloth Masson had brought to lessen the noise, and then pack it all into the pannier.

There was one thing missing at the end. "The knife," Masson said flatly. "There was a Persian knife."

Das was crestfallen. "Ah—a knife? Are you entirely sure? I don't recall. Everything is there, my dear fellow—are you sure it isn't there already?"

"No," Masson said. "It isn't there. It looks," he went on, reaching over Das's shoulder to retrieve the knife itself from a high shelf, "it looks uncommonly like that."

Das stared at him, blank, pentagonal, his expression quite veiled. Masson took the knife and, as if to demonstrate his disdain for Das and everything Das could supply, he bent down and pushed the pretty knife brutally down the side of his boot. It was not a dirk, made for such a purpose, but something richly damascened, curved, polished. A knife for display as much as use, a precious thing, and Masson pushed it brutally down the side of his boot. Das seemed almost on the point of protesting, but shut his mouth.

8

Calcutta at this time was not an old city. The monuments were few, and put up by the English. There was a sense that those who lived here were not born here, and would not die here, if they could help it; there was a sense that everyone in this city was a temporary inhabitant, camping out with what would suffice. From the Colonel's lady to the most abject beggar in the streets, everyone in Calcutta had ended up here, and stuck. It was a thick knot on the silken rope which connected the Bosphorus to China, and that was all. There was no history here, and it aimed to be an English city, with its churches and lawns, its solid official palaces and square garrisons. But all around, the great sea of Indian life washed at the bulwarks, patiently.

Masson walked back swiftly, an undirected rage preventing him from seeing how much the people stared at him. It was an anger which, at the top, he directed at Das, the thief. But he knew that Das alone was not the cause of it. It was like when you were young, and your brother hogged the blanket in the cold night. That was the same feeling of anger, and you felt angry with your brother. But it only took a moment to see that your brother's problem was the same as yours. What was the real thing that made you angry? It was the fact that you had no bed of your own. To be alone, you had to walk for an hour to your secret place, to sit at the hollowed-out roots of a gorse bush with a briar pipe and stare out to sea. That was the cause for anger. But to be angry, you had to turn on your brother, whose wish to be alone ought to be no less than yours. He was grown-up now, and still he had not had his wish, and still he was turning, in his mind, on people whose small wrongs deserved no blame.

Tonight would do. It would have to do, or wait ten days for the next good chance. It would do because he was on guard duty. All day he had been hiding the unpleasant thought from himself that the roster had thrown up Hastings as company at the gate tonight. Waking, nothing had seemed worse than the idea that McVitie's frightened crony was to spend the night-time watch with him; six hours with the feeble stinking dog. He had wondered whether Hastings would seek to change his duty, but then saw that he would not dare; half of McVitie's bluff was that no one would challenge his right to act as he wished. If Hastings tried to avoid him, that might seem like an admission that they had done wrong.

All day that had seemed like a grim prospect. Now, returning head down through the temporary Calcutta streets with the ornamental dagger chafing brutally at his ankle, the duty seemed like a piece of luck. All at once, the escape seemed harmlessly to fall into place. Masson knew, now, how he would go. Exactly how.

"Going to piss," Hastings muttered. It was some way past midnight. The garrison was silent; outside, the city had quietened down to its muttering minimum. Inexplicable small noises, a general murmur, and occasionally, from the distant noise and hum, a clearer sound emerged; a lowing cow, a dog singing across the rooftops and being answered, nearer at hand, a cooking pot being upset in the dark street outside and cries of lamentation following. In the garrison everything was silent. The body had gone to bed, and everything was dark, except the swinging lantern at the guardhouse.

Hastings and Masson had said nothing to each other from the moment they had reported for duty. Hastings would not even meet Masson's level gaze. It was another hot night, and the air was freighted with water; the rain would burst again soon. When Hastings passed within the little circle of the lantern's light, his frightened face was masked with sweat, and flushed red. Masson would not lower his face. He wanted to see, one last time, what fear and wrong in the face were like.

"Don't be long," Masson said coolly.

Hastings looked at him, amazed; the Masson of yesterday would have said nothing, let him go as he chose. He passed out of the circle of light where the black-blooded flecks of insect life danced in the hot air, and was swallowed up by the garrison's dark. Masson, too, moved back away from the light, into the furthest corner of the guardhouse, into the heaviest shadows. Now the gate looked abandoned. He got out his pipe, and put it in his mouth without lighting it. The company slept, unguarded; Florentia Sale in her ramrod bed, by her ramrod Colonel. McVitie slept, and dreamt his iniquities, his hard white body wet with sweat, never realizing what Masson was dreaming for him, what he was going to leave for him, out here in the guardhouse. Masson bit heavily on the stem of his pipe, and thought on, dreaming up the dreaming garrison. Suggs, now, slept fitfully, his narrow mind turning through its narrow knowledge, from one musket part to another, knowing nothing else, not caring what lives he had set free with his narrow knowledge. They all slept, except Masson and the hateful Hastings; and his turn would come, and then they would none of them exist, none of them breathe. Only in the occasional memory of the long-gone escaped hero of the platoon; they would only exist when Masson chose to think of them. And he would not.

There was a noise beyond the swinging lamp; a heavy crack somewhere above, and another, and then another. It was the return of the rain. The rain which now would fall unceasing for months. And then there was another noise, there in the dark which was the yard of the building; a hissing shuffle, Hastings coming back. Masson drew back into the deepest shade of the lodge. He was quite invisible. Hastings's worried face loomed into the light, and looked around, his eyes big and frightened.

"Masson?" he said, tentatively. "Where are you, Masson?"

Masson said nothing. Hastings looked about him, wildly, and reached up to unhook the lantern. Masson reached for his flint, and struck it in the darkness. Hastings stopped dead, and stared at the single flame, licking at Masson's face.

"Christ, you scared me," Hastings said. "What are you doing back down there, then?"

Masson said nothing, sucking at the flame through his pipe.

"I thought you'd gone, I thought you'd done a bunk," Hastings said, giggling nervously. "I thought you'd run for it."

Masson took a deep inhalation. He let himself go giddy for a moment, and the weighty scent rising from the new wet earth and the noise of the rain, like the roar in the forest, pushed him from all sides. He opened his eyes, and there was Hastings, the coward, the fresh wet face filled with fear in the lamplight, black with flies.

"Where are you from, Hastings?" Masson said, finally, calmly.

Hastings stared. "I'm from Lincolnshire. My people are shopkeepers. Why—"

"Why are you here, Hastings?"

"I ran away. Give a fellow a chance, now, Masson, and—"

"You got what you wanted, then, Hastings?"

"I don't know what you mean," Hastings said. He turned away, made a pathetic half-stride to attention, and stared out into the yard and the dark. The rain was falling like applause.

"I got what I wanted, last night," Masson said gently. He stooped, while Hastings was facing in the other direction; stooped with his left hand and loosened his left boot to reach for what was there. "But you knew that. Or you wouldn't have done what you did. You wouldn't have stood and watched what you watched, and done nothing to stop it. And your friend—what is his name, now?—McVitie—yes, I've always wanted him to do what he did. And he always wanted, didn't he, to do what he did. So he was happy and, you know, I wouldn't have minded telling him, if he had stayed to ask, that I was happy too. I wish he'd stayed to ask. It would have been polite. But I worry about you, Hastings. I worry about you. What did you want? Did you get what you wanted? Did you enjoy watching what you watched? Did you want to be me, or did you want to be him, and were you happy when you watched? Were you?"

Masson spoke quietly, calmly, and all the time walking up slowly behind Hastings. Hastings was trembling, as if with rage, and he would not turn, but stared into the court. Masson advanced, a careful game of grandmother's footsteps, and he gripped what he had in his hand.

"He didn't mean it," Hastings said, finally. "He didn't mean it. He gets like that. He doesn't know what he's doing. He doesn't. He'll say sorry, and it'll be all right again. He doesn't know what he's doing."

"But you, Hastings," Masson said. "Do you know what you were doing? Do you?" And then he let his voice change, let all the fury he had in him flow into it, and with a great black hiss, he leapt on Hastings's head, tearing his hair back, baring the stretched gargling throat, and from behind he brought his ceremonial knife with his left hand, and drew it quickly across the throat. For a moment it seemed to him that he had done nothing, and in a fury of panic he brought the knife down again, and hacked twice, three times more, as the black blood spurted, and Hastings made the noise of a drowning man, a strangled cry no one could have heard, and his watery eyes popped out of his head. Masson would not hold him while he died; he dropped him in the dust, there, in the dark corner of the lodge, and leant to wipe the knife on the now useless uniform, ignoring the rattle of the tongue's root in the throat, the bloating bubbles where no break had been. He half-opened the gate, and walked swiftly next door, to the stables. There, in one of the stalls, he had hidden his panniers, and now quickly loaded them onto the Colonel's horse. That was a foolish risk; he did not care, knowing he would not be caught. The horse was woken easily, and saddled. Everything was silent now;

only the rain, thundering, and Masson wrapped himself in a cloak and mounted. The horse submitted to be ridden. It walked gracefully out of the stable; it stepped gracefully, unseeingly, over what lay rigid inside the gate of the garrison. Masson pushed, and rode out onto the deserted swamp of the street.

He did not quite know how to navigate his way out of the city. There were no landmarks, no hills. The English buildings were familiar, but they seemed like islands in the middle of a constantly shifting mire of native dwellings, thrown up overnight and torn down as easily by rain. He turned his back on the English steeple, and went into the half-defined streets of the poor native quarter. Here, he felt as if his panic and fear were leading him astray, and the horse picked its uncertain way through the ruts and pits, watched warily, incuriously by the squatting early inhabitants. The rain had stopped, and the sun was up now in the clear air, the immediate heat sending birds up from the sodden earth into the cooler sky. The horse trod on through the mass of bodies and bivouacs, its head lowered as if already exhausted; Masson felt like a general passing through the disastrous aftermath of a battle.

He came, in time, to the river; the informal settlement ran all the way to the bank, and already at this early hour, there were washerwomen, pounding shirts between rocks. It was not a sacred river. The flow was slow and slippery and brown with the overnight rain, a polished surface with its own turbulence, and over it the heavy white birds flew, ungainly as chairs, draped with cloths. Masson paused for a moment. The dawn was rich and pink and noisy now. He should be going, he knew that. But there was no fear or panic in him, no terror of discovery. He knew he was safe now, and he watched the river for a moment. It was empty of boats, but as he watched, a strange thing approached; a table, upturned, floating down. And in the table stood a man with a long pole. A small man, perhaps a boy—with the sun in his eyes, Masson could not tell. How his vessel stayed afloat, Masson could not see; the table drifted along, pushed by the current. The man in his makeshift boat stirred confidently, ineffectively at the river like a cook at his gigantic soup, and the river drove him onwards. Masson stopped and watched him go his cheerful way, and as the strange craft passed, the man shielded his eyes, looked directly in Masson's direction and gave a huge benevolent wave before turning back to his rudder. He was going the way of the river. Masson watched until he was out of sight, and then pulled at the horse's reins. He turned his back on the city; all that fucking filth. The horse lifted its head from the grass it had been peaceably cropping, and, with a nudge of the knees, set off.

9

". . . and I travelled seven times seven months, over the plains and the lakes and the mountains of the world, and then I left the Empire of the English where the servants of Engelstan pursued me night and day, whose eyes can pierce a cloak and a new-grown beard and see the soul within, whose horses run like the wind to hunt the virtuous and the bandit alike, and in seven times seven months I came over the mountains to the Empire of the Afghans, and the rest you know."

The four bazaar-boys sitting at Masson's feet squealed in outrage. They did not know, they did not, and the story was not there, not finished yet. Masson sighed; the little courtyard where they sat was ankle deep in cherry stones after the long afternoon. The boys had sat and listened, entranced, to the whole story, their eyes bright with the evil witch Sale and the demon McVitie, the demon in human form (how they hissed at his entrances). No, they did not know the rest, they wanted to know everything, the tale of the seven times seven months, and how Masson came to the holy city of Kabul, and, above all, how he met each of them, since, like children, more than anything they loved to hear the tale of their own selves, their own story.

There was a noise outside, the noise of the door of the widow's house being pushed open gently. Masson stood to look inside, to see who it was. It was too dark to see; only a white shape, a brilliant white shape, moving in the house like a spectre. Masson called a greeting, and the shape tensed, was still for a moment and then emerged. It was a boy. He stood at the entrance to the courtyard and looked at Masson. For some reason, the four boys squatting cheerfully on the floor fell quite silent, and scrambled quickly to their feet, their heads lowered. For all the world it was as if they were schoolboys discovered in riot by their master. The boy himself looked bewildered at this tribute he had not asked for. He hardly glanced at the others, only at Masson. It was Masson he looked at. Masson saw only one thing: he had very brilliant deep blue eyes.

"My name is Hasan," the boy said, simply, regally. Masson's mouth moved, but it would make no sound. He looked at Hasan and realized that he was in the presence of an angel. And then, of course, he understood fully what he had never known before; why he had been sent to Kabul.

SEVEN

I

"She has gone, has she not?" Castleford inquired.

"Who?" another member of the Club said.

"Gone where?" a third supplied.

Castleford shrugged. "Miss Garraway," he said eventually, after taking a deep draft of claret. "It must be a year or more since I set eyes on her. Did she marry?"

"No doubt," a voice supplied, not greatly interested in the question. "Stokes can satisfy your curiosity, when he comes, I dare say."

"Where is Stokes?"

"Lying low, I dare say," Castleford said. "I heard Franklin is out for his blood."

"Franklin?"

Castleford sighed. "Where are our beefsteaks? There was an essay on a life of Milton, I believe, so very misguided, in Stokes's journal, and Franklin wrote a reply, and Stokes was heard impugning the gentleman in the wildest terms. And now Franklin has declared that his honour is in question."

"Why was Stokes so very interested?"

"Ah . . ."

The Club was the place, if any existed, where literary men would gather, and comment on comments which had been made on other comments; those comments in turn made on comments on some ancient and unread work of literature. It had been in existence for some ten years at the time of which we speak. At its foundation, it had had a name less unspecifying, and had, at its first meeting, been termed the Hatters' Society, for reasons beyond even its oldest members' recall. A name so whimsical, however much it suited the humour of the initial meeting of the society, could not be expected to last many days beyond it, and for the entire existence of the society, less an initial two weeks, it had been universally referred to by all connected with it merely as *The Club*. Its members fancied that from their embarrassment sprang a peculiar authority. Boodles was only Boodles, and it was more than the dinners at the Beefsteak, which were forever tethered to the ground by its label, but only the former Society of Hatters was *The Club*. In goodwill, we cordially overlook the curious fact that in London and its environs at this time, there were seventy-three gatherings to which miscellaneously employed gentlemen and near-gentlemen resorted, from rural Streatham to bucolic Hampstead, every one of which formerly had a name of some attempted whimsy, but which now was referred to by its members, in fancied distinction, as *The Club*.

The Club, however—that is to say, the one with which we are presently concerned—confined its membership to the literary world, and it is as well to confess, in the case that the reader may otherwise entertain inaccurately elevated notions of the distinction of its circle, that Stokes was its most remarkable member. At first, the splendid outlay of taking rooms for the Club had been considered, but it was not long before it became apparent that the back room at Mrs. Meagles's would do quite as well, and an informal arrangement was reached. At present, the other members of the Club were waiting for Stokes's arrival.

"The old Colonel lives on, does he not?"

"The old Colonel?"

"Who?"

"Colonel Garraway. Living on poetry and opium," Castleford agreed. "Stokes was very merry on the subject."

"Where is Stokes?"

"Yes, we want Stokes—" and, in a moment, the whole table was banging with knives and forks, plates and spoons, and chanting for Stokes. Mrs. Meagles appeared at the door and looked, fondly, at her gentlemen; and in a minute, the rumpus died down, and they were left looking rather foolishly at each other.

2

Stokes, in fact, was still at home. His rooms, or "diggings," as he tended jovially to refer to them, had a habit of surprising his occasional visitors. To begin with, unlike the ubiquitous Stokes himself, they were extremely difficult to find. Stokes often resorted to a joke when describing their location. "Not at the Temple," he would say musingly, one eye on his audience, "but there again, you know, not quite not at the Temple, either." Whether anyone succeeded in running Stokes to ground on the basis of this habitual and bewildering witticism was highly doubtful, and, on the whole, if one absolutely had to see the distinguished editor of the *Dundee Examiner,* one had to dress up in one's stiffest clothes and brave a rout at the Duchess of Dorset's, at Lady Woodcourt's, at the best houses in town.

Nevertheless, like any badger, Stokes had his hole, his diggings, whence he periodically emerged grumpily clutching his latest growlings against popular opinion. "Ah," his cronies would call, "here is Jove, with a new thunderbolt in his fist." And Stokes would waddle, sourly, into the room. In any case, his rooms were—it was confidently asserted—off the Strand. Not exactly in the Temple, but there again . . . You took an unnoticed turning off, into a malodorous and undistinguished tributary to the great flow of the Strand, and then another, into an enclosed warren of footpaths, packed tight underfoot, where no light came. The last approaches to Stokes's diggings were so narrow that, he had occasion to remark, he could never have contemplated acquiring a fat mistress. Even the most direct and upright of men found themselves, in these last stages, turning sideways and sidling towards the editor's rooms as if fearing to be wedged quite stiff between the dank dripping walls of brick. Finally, you turned into an almost unnoticeable doorway, and into a court, dark and gloomy with soot, overlooked by sorrowful, black, unwashed windows, a court whose bottom tilted alarmingly to one corner, attempting to drain away whatever happened to fall, unrequested, on Flat Hand Yard. It

struck the infrequent but imaginative visitor as akin to the deck of a sinking ship; an impression only fortified on further acquaintance since,
viewed in social terms, a sinking ship was precisely what Flat Hand Yard
was. On each side of the court there were doors, each leading to an indis-
tinguishably drab staircase, and on the third floor of the very gloomiest
and dullest of these staircases, the illustrious editor of the *Dundee Examiner* buried himself away and contemplated the world, assured that he
would not be disturbed or dislodged. Visiting Stokes was an undertaking
of an archaeological ambition. As soon as the casual visitor turned off the
Strand, he inevitably felt like a small boy irreverently digging a dignified
nocturnal beast out of his hole, and crying *garn!* The animal might,
despite all sorrowful external dignity, at any moment turn savage, and
dole out some awful unanswerable punishment; since, whatever subterranean associations were awakened by the experience of visiting Stokes,
in his own mind, he inhabited a dwelling so lofty as to be among the
clouds.

Nor were Stokes's rooms themselves any more appropriate to his
station in society. Undeniably the rooms of a deep-thinking man, they
exhibited too consistent a squalor to awaken any external admiration.
The bare-boarded floor of the passage was invariably stained with the
detritus of the streets, with food, and even, Stokes himself claimed,
the blood of his victims. The paper the walls were hung with was brown-
black and mildewed, and hung off in great limp sheets where Stokes
had failed to reattach it with drawing pins. At these lacunae was revealed
a damp plaster the unhealthy mottled colour of a corpse's flesh. The
windows were thick with grease and dust, letting no light in and requiring
the constant burning of lamps, whose smoking wicks, presumably, added
to the thick veil of filth which smeared the panes of glass. Over everything, a thick pall of dust lay; from time to time, under its own weight, it
fell from the curtains in massive sausages with a soft thud, like snow from
a roof. The piles of books lay, disordered, everywhere, and everywhere,
too, the scribbled-on pages of Stokes's great work, unorganized, unconsidered, almost abandoned in disgust under a further random pile of
grease-smeared glasses, the remains of chops, one week old, adhering
nauseatingly to the plate, as festering wildlife roamed bravely through the
undergrowth of Stokes's swamplike rooms.

Among the filth and detritus, there were, admittedly, some fine things.
Most of them you had to fish from the bookshelves and open up to

discover—Stokes's library, despite the pristine unattended chaos in which it subsisted, was a first-rate illumination of what Stokes himself would readily describe as his own first-rate mind. The china was not bought, but family, and was too fine to treat in Stokes's casual, gentlemanly manner. On the one wall where no bookshelves were, hung a brown and yellow portrait of a man; too dark initially to distinguish in the gloom of the room, but which close inspection showed to be an encrusted and glitteringly observant portrait of Rembrandt. "*Perhaps* a Rembrandt," Stokes would idly say. "Probably—well, not quite a Rembrandt, but not quite not a Rembrandt, either . . ." Most people dismissed Stokes easily, but were wrong to do so. There were objects in his room, as in his conversation, which revealed what he, writing in the *Dundee Examiner,* customarily termed "a true nobility of mind." And then—there they were, unarguably—there were his clothes; and how such a shining fantastic sleek ensemble emerged, at five sharp each day, to confront London and astonish even those old enough to remember Lord Petersham in his prime, was almost impossible once you had seen the stinking midden in which Stokes lived.

He was lying on the ottoman, swathed as profoundly as a pasha; his nightclothes, a brilliant red, were still beneath there, the collar drawn up against his neck like a scarf. His glittering pointed slippers, curling at the toes like those of some evil genius of the pantomime, were as villainous as a moustache. On his head, a weird fantastic helmet, a terrible oriental crest conjured out of a Chinee cambric square and a soiled yellow nightcap, wound up and round by Stokes's grotesque unoccupied fancy into the semblance of a turban. He had rolled himself up like a Gloucester bun in an enormous red and green padded robe, which trailed on the floor and lay behind his head like a pillow; what gigantic figure of a man such a garment could have been made for, one could not say, but it dwarfed a Stokes, who lay, a little sulking child, within its Brobdingnagian folds. With one hand, he negligently riffled the pages of a new book; with the other, he plucked idly at the purple Cashmire shawl flung over the gold velvet ottoman, as if considering whether or not to incorporate that too into his fabulous matutinal ensemble.

From the staircase came the sound of heavy boots, pounding up. Stokes closed his eyes again, accepting the undesirably inevitable, and settled back. It was no surprise to him that his novel, so long promised, could never get any further; for months now, he had had in mind a fine scene in which the witty and charming Lady Belinda, the independent-minded chatelaine of Marplot Manor, engaged in a chapter-long argument with Arian Callipie-Goss, the humorously wide-bottomed hero who would carry the bitch off at last; how Lady Belinda would wittily defend the popular modern French novel as the highest form of literary endeavour against a satirically drawn setting of a romantically decaying garden, Stokes could feel without even raising himself to the now tormenting sight of the quill in the inkpot. He had the splendid chapter's first line: "Arian Callipie-Goss was what our ancestors would have termed a gentleman; one troubled with no more profound concerns than the constant vagaries of fashionable metropolitan opinion." He had the last line: "Lady Belinda's laugh was more than ever like a bubbling teapot as she vanished with swift entirety behind the gloom of the nearest elm tree." He had the whole chapter complete in his head—complete in every respect—and it was the fault of the world and its demands if, rather than that, he had to spend his time in the writing of admittedly very fine and penetrating essays for the *Examiner* on the folly of Reform, the folly of the acquisition of new oriental possessions, the folly of turning away from the classical virtues in poetry. He opened his eyes to see a blue and white china teapot being set down by his vile manservant, six inches from his head. He looked at it. It made no sound, bubbling or otherwise.

"I see you've succumbed to the mysteries of the Orient," the visitor said, after half a minute in which Stokes made no sign of recognition, acknowledgement, or even movement.

Stokes turned his head on the cushion where it lay. "Oh, it's you, Stapleton," he said eventually. "What the devil do you mean? How do you do? And what in heaven's name do you want of me that you are obliged to come here?"

"I was talking of your corsair's attire," the visitor said, picking one item out of the list of Stokes's unremarkably uncivil queries. "I came to chivy you out into the streets and meet the fellows at the Club. Do, there's a good chap."

Stokes's visitor was a relatively young man, so odd in appearance that he appeared perpetually restless, as if he had grown accustomed to contemplating a nascent astonishment in adults and frank alarm in children. Somewhat over six feet in height, he was too prodigious, it seemed, for any tailor to fit with clothes; his hands and feet shot out from his clothes as if they were trying to escape from their owner. Once out of his gloves, his long white tremulous fingers vibrated and twitched like the mandibles of an insect. His eyes, a vague bloodshot watery blue, wandered cease-lessly about the room and his nostrils and mouth rippled up and down from side to side, as if he were keeping some small and active animal warm in there. Only one side of his face was properly shaved. The other had been left in its native state, and was adorned with what the vulgar call "bum-fluff"; whether it had been left in such a state of nature through impatience, drunkenness, or, as Stokes once ingeniously suggested, because the light in Stapleton's bedroom fell only on one side of his face, and he felt unequal to the requirement of trusting his own, vaguely trem-bling right hand in darkness, seemed propositions equally probable. It was his cockscomb of hair, however, which made the London streets stare, and the rudest of the street-arabs throw stones and jeer; a brilliant white-blond shock, standing straight up on the left side, as if Stapleton had just that moment woken up from a long and refreshing sleep in a pool of sugar and water. His claim on the notice of the public was that he had written something between five and ten novels; he lived at Chelsea. It was said that he had contracted an imprudent marriage with a placid Cam-bridge barmaid, but none of his friends had ever seen such a creature. There were those who affected to believe that such a woman could not exist. Stokes said bluntly that, if she existed, she could only be Stapleton's nurse.

"I fail to see," Stokes said, "what you mean by my 'corsair's attire.' I was always rather an enemy to the fashionable Orient. I was never, indeed, east of the City in my life."

"Very good, Stokes, very good. The mysterious promise of Essex, eh? The great rubies of Hornchurch? The harems of the nabobs of Kent? The opium dens of, of, of . . ."

"The opium dens of Shadwell? There are, of course, opium dens in Shadwell, Stapleton. Yes, very good, excellent, quite, quite," Stokes inter-rupted, since, once Stapleton's fancy had been caught in an idle way, he could continue weaving, quite happily, for hours. "What, I said, do you want of me?"

"A social call, dear boy, merely that, merely that," Stapleton said. "I am quite hurt, quite hurt. I say, I heard of you bearding the lion in his den. Splendid, splendid. Or not in *his* den, to be honest, the den of the old dam—the old lioness huntrix—the old—er—at the Duchess's, I mean. On Tuesday."

"At which Duchess's? Look here, Stapleton, what do you want?"

And now Stapleton really looked hurt. He reached out for the teapot Mullarkey, the manservant, had brought in. It was hot and full, but there were no teacups to hand. He set it down again. "I only called in to see if you felt like a spot of dinner with the fellows at the Club. Now, Stokes old man, do get out of your Arabian Nights' garb and come with me, and pretend for one moment that you belong to the more civilized portion of the human race, and not to some un-Christian tribe of Hottentots, of Moguls, of, of, of Editors, there's a good fellow."

This was the proper line to take with Stokes. His immediate response was to pull the Cashmire shawl entirely over his head and groan power-fully. Stapleton recoiled physically in his chair; his long and pale-jointed fingers flailed with violently ineffectual purpose as if at some invisible game of cat's-cradle. It seemed to him that Stokes's huge groan was one of gathering strength, and might be followed by an outburst of violence. But Stokes, in practice, reserved his outbursts and attacks for the livid pages of the *Dundee Examiner,* and in a moment he threw back the shawl. He glared balefully at Stapleton, sighed heavily, and rolled his eyes.

"I expect you think this is fair treatment of one who first gave you the opportunity of placing your work before the public," Stokes said eventually.

"Now, now, Stokesy, fair dos, old man," Stapleton said. Then he thought better of it, perhaps recalling that ten years after that auspicious event, he had seen eight novels appear under his name while Stokes, so brilliant in promise, had yet to appear in the bookseller's lists in any other guise than an anonymous commendation of another's work. "Opportu-nity—too poor a word, old man! Gave me an opportunity? Gave me expectations, my dear fellow! Why—you discovered me!"

"Quite so," Stokes said, rising from his slumping ottoman like the uncreated Adam in a particularly preening mood. "And now I propose to go and dress, after which I shall be quite at your service. Old man."

Into the innermost recesses of his diggings, its most intimate cham-bers and antechambers, swept Stokes, leaving the dusty air hovering with mild indignation; wrapped in his red and gold and green negligé, his ruby and emerald déshabillé with cap and turban and all, he carelessly took with him the shawl over the ottoman which his left hand still clutched, and in his wake, a whole pile of books and knives and plates teetered for a second before crashing explosively. A great fountain of untouched dust rose up from the catastrophe, unremarked by Stokes, and Stapleton was left twitching, as all the dust in the room rose, and shivered, and furiously danced in the lamplight. "Occupy yourself," Stokes called back, departing from the scene of his grisly levee. "Ten minutes, my dear fellow, ten minutes. Mullarkey!" And the manservant, solemn and slow as an acolyte, emerged from the scullery to attend the mysterious rites of his master's wardrobe.

3

Stokes was as good as his word in the matter of the ten minutes, although how the shining fresh dandy with his brilliant white linen and sparkling pink face could have emerged in so short a stretch of time from the shambling man-midden by any process less radical than peeling, Stapleton could not claim to conjecture. As they left Stokes's rooms, the ageing pageboy standing at attention by the door to contemplate, with sinister complacency, the fruits of his labours, Stapleton had the sensation of being hauled up forcibly from the dank and slimy depths of a stagnant pond. They passed from Flat Hand Yard through the complex series of alleys, gennels, runnels, dry and semi-dry sewers which led back to the Strand, and Stapleton could only feel, contrasting his own rusty frock coat and dun-coloured, stained, and abjectly frayed breeches with Stokes's immaculate polish, that their exit from so insalubrious a quarter must provoke, in the multitudes of the Strand, a curiosity bordering on a sensation.

"I hear you have a new novel out, Stapleton," Stokes said when they had attained the Strand with, it seemed to Stapleton, remarkably little fuss. A small group of beggar boys, grinning vilely, now assailed the odd brace. "No, no, away, off with you, you know better than to trouble me. Well, Stapleton?"

"I do, indeed. Next month, I believe."

"Excellent, excellent. What a busy person you must be, in your cottage in Chelsea. And the title of the forthcoming work?"

"Zoe. It's a romance of old Byzantium, you know, Stokes. Jolly interesting—the subject, I mean, not the novel, I couldn't honestly speak for the merits of—"

Stokes paused for a second, knocked his cane hard against the wall of the Bag o'Nails inn to dislodge some detritus, and took his hat off for a moment. "Unseasonably hot, ain't it?" he said. "I put my hat upon my head/And went into the Strand/And there I met another man/Whose hat was in his hand."

"Jolly good, Stokes, impromptu like that."

"Merely quoting, old man," Stokes said, evidently gratified by his own honesty. "Remind me—what was the subject of your last novel?"

"*Uggdryth*? Oh, that, Stokes, oh, a romance of life among the Vikings. I meant to get them to invade Britain, but, you know, in the end, they were so interesting that—"

"And before that?"

"You must remember that one, surely? I think you had the goodness to notice it in the *Dun Eggs*. Medieval China."

"I remember, now you jog my poor fading memory. Very pretty—willow trees and pug dogs and the girl threw herself into a brook. And before that?"

Stapleton thought hard; his fecundity impressed and baffled him, whenever he was brought to contemplate it. "Abyssinia," he said finally.

"A romance?" Stokes said.

"Among the early Christians there," Stapleton agreed.

"Did you find it necessary to travel to that benighted realm?" Stokes asked gravely.

"Oh, no," Stapleton said. "All out of books, you know, Stokes. Well, I'll square with you on that one like a chap; it was all out of three pages of Gibbon, and the rest—" Stapleton began to flutter with his hands as he suddenly wondered what end Stokes had in mind in examining him so seriously on his literary works, "—I say, Stokes, you're not quizzing me, are you?"

"Not for the world," Stokes assured him seriously. "And the rest—where did you acquire so broad a knowledge which, surely, must have proved necessary to the writing of such an informative volume?"

"Oh, I made it all up," Stapleton said. "Invented. The whole caboodle, anthropophagy, sacred tigers, ritual dances with cowcumbers, all of it. Did very well, so my bookseller assures me. All out of my noddle."

"Excellent, excellent," Stokes said. "You didn't even feel the need to consult Bruce? Well, you know best. Here we are."

So it was that Stokes and Stapleton entered the Club with startlingly different countenances; to anyone in the room, since they were all mutu-

ally acquainted, what had passed between them would have been immediately apparent. Stokes's bland and sleek severity was one he only
attained immediately after the melancholy necessity of conveying some
very bad news, like a pagan priest returning, clean-handed, from a human
sacrifice. Stapleton, judging from the twitching, flailing, blood-drained
expression of horror, was the recipient of Stokes's worst. It did not take
the Club long to come to the correct conclusion that Stokes had some
moments before found a way to assure Stapleton that his newest produc-
tion was to be handed what the Club informally termed "a stinker"; that
Stokes, for reasons of his own, had decided that, in the opinion of the
Dundee Examiner, Stapleton would not "go," under any conditions. The
sympathy of the Club, befitting literary men, flowed directly, if discreetly,
to Stokes the assassin.

4

The manners of the Club were that dinners were ordered, and eaten,
without reference to one's fellows; so a gathering of the Club would last
for some hours, and at any moment only one or two of the members
would be eating, the others sitting back, discussing, and smoking. The
other convention of the Club was that its doings and discussions were not
referred to subsequently, that conversation should be free and uncon-
fined. Stokes was famous for remarking, witheringly, to a very junior
member of the Club who had thought to refer to some former conversation over dinner in society that "Gentlemen, when they meet each other
in a *mauvais lieu,* do not customarily boast of the fact, or so I had
believed." In no other area of discussion was this freedom so generously
exercised as when the conversation turned to the subject of prospective
members of the Club.

"I have an inclination," one of the younger members was venturing,
"to propose Mr. Carrington for our little society."

"The fellow who went to Canada?" Stapleton said. "Yes, indeed—a
very amusing fellow."

"I read his book," Stokes started, but so quietly that no one paid him
any attention.

"A great diner-out, at any rate," Carlyle said. "I meet him everywhere,
and everywhere he dances attendance on me, and flatters and flirts with

me so prodigiously I blush like a virgin of sixteen. Yes, I like him excessively—there is nothing more appealing than deference in the young towards their betters, I find."

There was a general sniggering at this favourite joke, since Carlyle was the oldest young man yet seen in London.

"I read his book," Stokes said again, and again was over-ridden.

"What was it he claimed to have lived on for a year?" Castleford inquired. "Was it the meat of seals, or whale meat, or—well, I recall I was most impressed, and thought how much he must enjoy his London beefsteak now, excellent, thank you, Mrs. Meagles. Yes, why should we not enjoy the company of so superb a popinjay? It would be amusing for a season."

"I *read*," Stokes said very markedly, "his book, but I am not, I fear, qualified to talk about it—a great fog of oblivion has mercifully arisen between me and it, and when I made the gentleman's acquaintance and he asked me for my honest opinion, I fear I had nothing to contribute. Not that it matters greatly; in reality he was asking me for my admiration for his daring feats, and not for my opinion on his ability to describe them. Well, whether my admiration was to be had or not—and I must say, it was not—hardly seemed to matter to the gentleman, since he proceeded to enlighten me in the richest possible detail about the various culinary approaches to blubber until I pushed away my own dinner, quite untouched."

"An entertaining fellow, though," Castleford said nervously.

"That I do not concede," Stokes said. "But on its own, that recommendation—gentlemen, I thought we had always been firm in our resolution that literary distinction, and literary distinction alone, would admit a man to our number. Carlyle, you are very young, but when you attain my degree of venerability, you will come to appreciate that an explorer of some distant and desperately dull region of the earth arrives in London with the tale of adventures at the most predictable intervals—I should say every two years. And they drive London mad with enthusiasm for three months, and then they and their book disappear from our minds, and nothing more is ever heard of them. I am most unwilling to sentence myself to the prospect of dining with so very temporary a phenomenon for the rest of my life, and still be listening to the bestial doings of the Esquimaux in thirty years' time. Come now, who was that fellow—you know, surely, who I mean—"

"You must be more precise, sir."

"The fellow who came from Bokhara. And Kabul. Went there, rather. Was that not a mere two years ago? Now, what was his name—"

"Yes, I recall—"

"Ah—"

"His name was Burnes," Stokes said. "You see, gentlemen, the point I make—how wild we all were for his exotic tales, and how quickly it is all forgot. No, no, no explorers, no heroes for me, or, at the very least, not at this dinner table. Do you think so meanly of your own merits that a man who buys a camel and goes a thousand miles to a place of no conceivable interest should be of our number?"

"Burnes," Stapleton said. "I recall. I read his book. Very fine—the camels—the dyeing of the beard in disguise—the savage Ee-mir throwing his wives into pits, all that, Stokes—really fine stuff. I read it in a day and a half, found m'self very much better informed at the end of it, very much amused. Yes, what did happen to the fellow?"

"Was there not some talk of his wooing one of the Garraway girls?" Carlyle offered. "We were talking of them before you arrived, Stokes. Perhaps they married: they are both of them quite vanished, after all."

"I believe not," Stokes said. "Yes, that was the talk, but I think it came to nothing, if it were anything but tattle in the first place."

"Good luck to the fellow," someone said, quarrying a sole with his fork. "A fine catch, that girl, for a daring fellow."

"Five thousand a year, and that great place in Gloucestershire."

"The wilds, the wilds, the barren moors and steppes of Gloucestershire," Stokes put in. "I know of that great place. Highly picturesque, I grant you—a highly picturesque state of semi-dilapidation—but far more in the line of a necessary liability on whoever takes the girl than a dowry. But gentlemen. Gentlemen," he went on, pressing his forefingers to his temple in an exaggerated gesture of pain. "What is this? I had not thought that this was a club where the names of ladies were bandied about by members so lightly."

"We weren't bandying her name about," Chapman supplied. "We were doing no more than bandying her fortune about. But we're quite prepared to start on her, if you would prefer."

"Do so," Stokes said; his timing was good as ever, and brought a great roar of laughter from the table. "That, in truth, is the only reason I allowed myself to be roused so rudely, to be chivied out, in the vulgar expression, by our friend Stapleton, and brought down to this disreputable den of thieves; I felt the need to listen to a lady's name being dragged through the mud."

"Five thousand a year," the youngest member of the Club put in, dreamily chomping on his dinner like a printing press on paper. "For that, I'd marry Queen Adelaide."

"Five thousand, and a castle. A highly picturesque castle—"

"Moat and drawbridge, seven hundred years old—"

"Seven hundred years' worth of repairs and rebuilding. Myself, I think the fellow had a narrow escape. Enough to swallow up a trifle like five thousand a year," said Chapman. "As well marry the National Debt. Unless you prefer to live in, as Stokes so wittily says, a highly picturesque state of semi-dilapidation—"

"Quoting, dear boy, merely quoting—"

"I am sorry to hear it, sir; I had thought the theft of wit beneath you, unless you meant it as a compliment to our learning. But each day to wake and find that you have shared the ambrosia of your sposal bed— have, in the hours of darkness, actually pleasured yourself upon not your youthful bride, but half a dozen furry owls."

"Sell the damned place, and live in Hanover Square with two trim chestnuts and her old nurse for the rest of your days, then."

"The nurse would not have been the problem, I fancy," Chapman said in tones of horror. He paused, until he had silence, and then said it again. "It is hardly a matter of a nurse. There is—let us admit the dimensions of the case—a father, as well."

"Yes, indeed," Stapleton said, and the table all started to guffaw. "There is, I believe, a sister, too."

"Of whom nothing is known," Chapman said. "I talked with her once for an hour, and even rose to the intimacy of holding her fan and pocketbook at the end of it. And still nothing has been reported back by explorers to that icy region of the globe."

"The old Colonel seemed barely to know where he was when I saw the old fellow last," the youngest member, whose name was Carlyle, put in. "I dare say he was a great hero in his youth."

"A great hero of Waterloo," Stokes said. "Or so they say. The old Colonel no longer possesses the capacity to talk sense on the subject of this morning's breakfast, let alone so very remote a historical event. Certainly, Waterloo was in another country and a very long time ago."

"What do you mean, Stokes?"

"I mean," Stokes said, taking a substantial draft of claret in lieu of breakfast, "what really matters, for those who are interested in such stuff, is the girl and her prospects, and not her father's—*habits,* shall we term them. Let us be frank, and say that his life cannot be worth ten years' purchase. Not five, in fact. Now, for myself, I should not have taken the girl, with father or without, with five thousand, or ten, or fifteen, even if she had moated castles enough to fill Gloucestershire. I presume the fellow fled whence he came, to our Indian possessions, the second he realized the facts of the case, and I am not entirely sure I should not have done the same thing myself. But for those who like that sort of thing, I should say Miss Garraway offers an excellent property, with substantial holdings and views of three counties. Eh, Chapman?"

"Quite right, Stokes," Chapman said, loyally.

"But for heaven's sake, let us have no more talk of explorers," Stokes wound up. "And, now, gentlemen, a competition. I believe the old Colonel, in his youth, wrote and even published a volume of verses. Let us turn our minds to that, and, gentlemen, you have your challenge. A sonnet, in full Garrawavian style, date circa 1816. Subject? To the Moon? To Cynthia? Which has the more authentic—ah—period charm? Well, you may decide. Gentlemen, let battle commence. And Mrs. Meagles— the claret needs refreshment, and subsequently, so do I."

5

The sonnet was done, and the dinners concluded severally, and the prize awarded. The business of the afternoon, such as it was, was concluded, and now all those sad captains departed; leaving singly and in pairs, according to some notion of precedence. Stokes, last to arrive, was first to take his leave, and the Club took its cue, and melted away into the great paragraphs of the London streets. First, the lions, to their busy quills and their crowded desks, and afterwards, the evening acclaim of some drawing room; then the rising men, preparing in their heads a sentence of denunciation to top or tail this afternoon's essay, thinking it through even as they said their farewells; then the comfortable, the idle, the family men returning to the family board. They all went, singly, and in pairs, to their several purposes, and finally over the empty table, all that was left of the Club was its two eldest members, comfortably settling into their chairs.

"They did not stand upon the order of their going," one said.

"*Macbeth,*" the other said triumphantly. "Indeed, not, although the parallel is inexact: I fear we would not make very promising assassins, the pair of us. Increasingly, you know, as I grow older, I think *Macbeth* truly the best of Shakespeare. How marvellous that scene—"

"Rot, sir," the first said. "For myself, the more I think on it, the more I doubt that very much of it is from Shakespeare's hand at all. Come, now, can you prefer so absurd a farrago to *Hamlet?*"

"I can, sir, and I do," his companion said, but since this was an old and a comfortable argument between the two of them, he changed the subject. "I saw old Robinson died."

"No age at all," the first said.

"Sixty-one. Still, his best work long done."

"Indeed, indeed. I recall him as a boy, no more—did he not make a fourth in our party in Scotland? Heavens above—that must be thirty years or more ago."

"A dull fellow."

"Nonsense. Do you not recall the rumpus we created in Edinburgh, drinking until dawn, and me challenging that odd Scotch fellow to a duel? He played his part, did he not? We have lived, you and I, we have lived."

"Did you hear the clock chime, just now?"

"Six, I believe."

Mrs. Meagles entered; this was the moment she evidently took pleasure in, when the Club had dispersed, and there was no one left but her two easy old friends. With them she did not stand on ceremony, but took her seat, and from her capacious skirts produced her work, stitching, picking, her head bent over.

"We have lived too long," one said, quite suddenly. "There is no place for us, here, now."

"Come, sir," his companion said. "It will not do to be gloomy. And we are not dead, and old Robinson is, and soon to be forgotten."

"We are forgotten, too," the first said. "My books make no more noise than if I dropped my manuscripts in the river, now, and no one cares. I thought I would change the world once, and the world has changed, but without me. Who cares for wit now, or poetry, or Pope? No, I have wasted my life, and it is too late now to pretend otherwise. Had I a son, I should advise him to take up the profession of a bargeman, or a burglar—anything but poetry."

"I shall not stay, if you prefer to entertain the blue devils to me," his companion said. "This is too bad, too severe a judgement upon yourself, and not one anyone but yourself would make. Forgotten?"

"Yes, forgotten," the first said. "All gone now, all into oblivion. Ten years I spent, you know, sir, Englishing Juvenal, and I felt at the end as if I had written it with my blood: I dreamt, ten years long, of doing something which would stand by Pope's Horace, and at the end of ten years, the world did not notice, and now it never will. What does it want? A story of love, in which the squire's daughter marries the squire's neighbour; three volumes of virgins and dungeons, skeletons and phantoms; poetry no gentleman could keep in an unlocked cabinet, odes to obscenity, sonnets at which one blushes at the matter, and blushes again at the scansion; novelty after novelty, and what is old is cast aside without a thought that the ancients are still with us because there is nothing more to add. We have lived too long, you and I, and have lived to see everything we held dear fall into oblivion."

"You must not listen to our young men," the other said. "We were young, too, once, and in love with novelty. They will learn, you know, and discover what you have done, you and I, and Juvenal, at least, will not be forgotten. The battle is not lost, not lost at all, but we will not live to see its end: what we did, we did, always, in trust."

"The battle was not lost, and there was no battle—we offered a fight, and they turned away, not seeing us, and left us, proclaiming to the empty air. I am sick at heart, sick at heart."

"Tell me how Robinson died, at the last."

"I heard something of it," the first said, slowly. "You know his health had been weak for some time, and he had exhausted himself. He improved, quite markedly, and took it upon himself to travel to Bath, for the waters, and his physician thought it an admirable idea. There was no prospect of anything but improvement, and he seemed quite past the worst, and he set off. The first day, his spirits were high—his wife, you know, told me something of this—but in the course of the second, he seemed out of sorts. No doubt those abominable roads. They stopped for the night at an inn, and Robinson took to his bed. In the night he was uncomfortable—it was a wretched little inn—and in the morning, there was no thought of moving him for the moment. Still, it seemed no very serious matter, a day's delay. His wife hardly thought it necessary to send for a physician, indeed. The end came in the most unfortunate way: the landlady's daughter, who was deputed to sit by Robinson, left her post for an hour without notice, and while she was gone, Robinson struggled out of bed, for some purpose, and fell, quite heavily, striking his head. It was an hour before he was found, and unconscious, and then it transpired that no physician could be had within two hours' ride of the place, and that did for him. A sad end. I saw no notice of his death."

"No," the other said thoughtfully. "Of course, he had not published for many years. I thought his last book rather fine, his book on Derbyshire. He was always an admirer of the picturesque. His widow?"

"There is no money, I think," the first said. They relapsed into gloom; the evening, outside, was deepening. Mrs. Meagles, who had been half-listening, laid down her work, and picked up a sheet of paper, left there, and read it with some attention.

"A bagatelle, my dear lady," one of her gentlemen said, kindly.

"I think—" Mrs. Meagles said, looking up, and her eyes were shining, "—I think it most beautiful. May I keep it?"

6

Mr. Castleford's Winning Entry in the

Garraway Sonnet Challenge Cup (Prize, 5 shillings)

Moon not at me, bright lady of the night
Lest 'neath thy silver spell I lose my mind
Blest lunacy! No more long Day's coarse light
Shall fade my dreams: thou, Goddess, art more kind.

[caetera desunt]

EIGHT

There are some women on board here. They suffer as we do from the violent motion of the seas. They complain, less quietly than we do, about the inevitable worsening of the food as the ship heads southwards. Their wardrobes have long since lost their initial crispness, and will soon abandon any pretence to elegance. Their desperation is plain to see.

One of them asked me about India. "Tell me about India," she said, one evening, as the table and floor bucked like a horse, unbroken; her eyes flinched in her head as she tried to keep the conversation, at least, steady. "What would you like to know?" I asked. She pulled, in distress, at her fingers; she had thought that her possession of the fact of India would be enough to start me off, and hardly knew how to tread further. "Are there wild beasts?" she said in the end. "Snakes and tigers and mongooses?" Poor girl, she knew nothing but a child's picturebook for India, where there were snakes and tigers and mongooses. Or mongeese. And that—the correct plural for mongoose, an animal none of them has ever seen—is a conversation which someone on board ship starts up at least once a day. I know which it should correctly be, mongooses or mongeese, but keep my counsel; they should have their entertainment, after all. Her name is Miss Brown, the girl who had heard of the tigers of India; she is very plain, I assure you.

Eight days out of Portsmouth, the wind suddenly stilled, and the jolly breeze which had blown us along seemed to have some more urgent task to pursue in some other quarter of the world. For the first week, we had blown along like a tin boat on wheels, scudding under the unresisting clouds. I sat on deck for long hours, watching the land recede, and then the little wind-flecked sea, and then more sea, and more, until we were flying along and there was nothing to show we were moving at all, nothing except sea and sky and the tight sting of the wind on the face. The slap of wind on canvas and the bright rebounding light of sea and sky, like the beating of sheets of tin. I will not say what I felt, as the boat took me further and further from you. I know you felt the same, as if England were a great ship, pulling you northwards away from me into icy-hearted regions where the breath of the warm-blooded freezes in the air like speech.

There was a deal of jubilation around me. I saw it as if from an enormous height. For everyone on board the *Jane,* our swift progress was cause for joy. We were out of Portsmouth like a hungry hound, released from its traps. To the prow runs a small boy, wild with joy, and at the prow he swings his cap and cries *huzzah!* to the blue empty world. His family looks on, indulgently. Where is he going? Why, to the tropics, to India, to cross the equator, a feat he will not stop boasting of if he lives to be eighty. A feat he himself has achieved, he knows, standing with his legs braced, riding the deck, being taken where the winds want the ship to go. He swings his cap in the wind, and cries *huzzah!,* and all at once I am thinking of my Bella. At first, you are troubled by the salt, drying and cracking on your unwashed skin; it is not long before the taut tang on your cheeks starts to seem ordinary.

Eight days out of Portsmouth, the air stilled, suddenly, and we were becalmed. A painted ship, upon a painted ocean, as the poet says. The wind grew irresolute, mild, quiet, and then fell altogether still. The noise of the tiny waves at the flanks of the ship was of a thousand cats, lapping at a vast lake of milk. After a few hours, a succession of ladies ascended to the deck, pale and grateful. They were the less hearty names on the list, who had been laid low by the Channel's mild briskness. For a week, chicken broth had been carried down to them, and reports of their health had been carried back up to us. Now, as the ship slowed and we all felt for the first time how very hot it truly was, they ascended, one by one from their incarceration as if they would be pleased for the ship never again to make any motion, up and down, side to side, forwards or backwards, but to stay here in this millpond for ever. The famous Miss Brown was one of these; she, at least, had the tact not to express any overt joy at her own improvement, knowing that the improvement in the state of the individual had been achieved at the cost of the common weal.

You see, Bella, I am grown quite the philosopher, am I not? If this were a correspondence, I should ask you to pass on my reflection to your sister, that she could offer her reflections in turn on this important principle in life. But this cannot be a correspondence; it will be longer than I care to think before I can even hand these pages to anyone who can take them to you, and many, many weeks longer before I can hope to receive a packet directed by your dear hand. It cannot be a correspondence; we must guess at what each other may be writing, or feeling, seeing, or thinking at any moment, and write our pages in the dark. No, not quite that. Did I say that we must guess at what the other is thinking? No. I think I know that, and I hope you know, too, what I am always thinking of.

Shall I describe for you my quarters? I think you never were at sea in your life, were you? Well, they are very superior, and very neatly, cleverly arranged. The first time I was at sea, I thought directly of Gulliver in his padded case; a cabin is a beautiful jewelled toy, fashioned by giants. Everything in it that can fall, or be thrown, must be fastened down, so everything has its place, and everything is secured by a series of ingenious little clasps and grips. Once, in rough seas, I forgot this, and was struck on the head by a boot I had carelessly let fall to the floor. It is not necessary to be reminded twice. The bed is set into a little niche, curtained during the day, and one feels very snug when "tucked in" as children say, at night; even if one has been put to bed, not by a mother's dear care, but by the brutal attentions of the tattooed Welshman called Elliott who has been assigned to you.

I have my little shelf of books, secured by the same neatness of touch. In these long voyages, these long dull voyages, with no entertainment but the vagaries of the sea and our fellow passengers, books are highly prized, and a curious reversal of values takes place; it is the least readable, the least digestible of tomes that we most strongly desire, as promising to eat up the greater portion of our hours. The easier delights of a fashionable novel are universally shunned; they eat up room which, on board a ship, must always be precious, and offer no substantial exchange, few hours charmed away. Ecclesiastical histories, the baffling philosophical inquiries of the Germans, the darkest mystics, and, above all, learned disquisitions on the culture, language, and customs of primitive peoples: these are the sorts of works that we fight over so eagerly. I have brought Gibbon, and find myself constantly waylaid by the most improbable people, asking with considerable anxiety when I hope to have finished with my current volume. No one on board has brought my book to read; none, which punctures my vanity, is quite sure they know who I am, though one clergyman thought he had known my father as a young man. Impossible; my father never was a young man.

The Captain of the vessel is a smart young man called Taylor; I deduce that he is nearer the beginning of his career than its end, not merely from his fresh-faced aspect, but from his behaviour. He is attentive, civil, constantly interested in the smallest details of shipboard life, and his restless inspections above and below decks are, I perceive, the object of some merriment among the crew. Is it, perhaps, his first command? He is up early, and down late. Often, I am woken by the swabbing of the decks; in the warm rocking dark of my enclosed bed, an attractive trickling noise summons me from my deep or restless sleep. I pull back from my dreams, which are full of visions of floating and rocking in oceans of air, and for a long half-sleepy moment, wonder what that noise is; and then I realize where I am. It is the slosh of water overhead, the sibilance of the deckhands' brooms, the attendant run of water down the flanks of the ship. And if I lie there for a minute before the intrusion of my man Elliott, I always hear the nervous click of the Captain's boots, pacing the deck, ensuring that what is done is done correctly. Yes, on the whole, I think his first command.

2

There is, I fear, no story here; no narrative to tempt you onwards. Life on board a ship is only of interest to the reader when things go wrong, and I am very much afraid I have no mutiny, and may have no typhoon to interest you. The crew are civil, well disposed, and healthy; they will not slit our throats, or make Captain Taylor walk the plank. Bad weather is the most you, as a romantic reader, may hope for from my journal, and I cannot bring myself to wish for, invent, or summon up a storm, even for *your* amusement. Even when the winds started up again—and it was as astonishing, as *imprévue* an event as their disappearance—we still felt becalmed, marooned, suspended in time. Our lives, in this nowhere place, are abandoned for a time. The smallest events will do to mark the passing of the days; was it two or three days ago we saw the school of dolphins? Was it on a Monday the seaman was flogged? And time moves at a strange pace. After three days, I felt that I had been at sea for ever, so thoroughly did I know my shipmates; and yet, weeks later, I think sometimes that no time whatever has passed since then, that I am cruelly abandoned, three days out of England, three days' journey from my Bella, in perpetuity, bobbing on an unmoving ocean, and each day that dawns is the day that has already ended, beginning, once again.

We are entirely at home, now, and the way we speak has altered. Only the clergyman still talks of "ten o'clock" in the morning; for the rest of us, the only divisions of the days are the number of bells. Fo'castle, galley, port, and starboard, they trip off our tongues readily, if not quite naturally just yet. I remember the first time I was on board ship, that I would not say "for'ard" or "bosun" in company until I had practised saying it, alone, in my cabin. I brought it out, and it evidently seemed quite natural to my listeners. But I felt for some days like a fraud. They are words which one reads in novels, and, unless one has been to sea, has no idea of their exact meaning. Actually to speak these words with the affectation of confidence is to feel that you have been turned, against your will, into a character in a novel. Mrs. Robinson has stopped saying "the sort of hut arrangement, over there, at the front end of the boat," but you can see in her eyes she does not believe in a Mrs. Robinson who knows port from starboard.

The Captain, as I said, is not quite at ease here, not quite certain that it is he who should be in his place. He rattles around, and in the way he inspects and pokes and barks, and then looks at the mildest and least of his passengers like a nervous hound, as if for some sort of approval, it is easy to see that he does not yet trust himself, even when he is in the right. He rattles around like a hazelnut in its shell; almost a tight fit, but not entirely so. At night, he slides into his place at the head of his table and looks about him nervously, as if the man with a proper title to the position will at any second walk through the door. The ladies try to keep the conversation going; he, poor fellow, cannot direct it. Every night, he shows himself as much at the mercy of the table as a rudderless vessel in a busy sea. He cannot quell our clergyman, whose only subjects for conversation are the casual injustices of bishops; he cannot draw out the terrified English virgin; he knows not how to amuse or instruct, to introduce a new subject, and only appears at ease when someone politely inquires about the progress of the board, or small domestic concerns. He hardly knows, I fear, who any of his passengers are, and we were obliged in the end to introduce ourselves and give an account of our lives to this point. It is a relief, all things told, when we can decently retire and I am left alone with my Romans.

3

I was interrupted, there, as I wrote, by a timorous knocking on the door of my cabin. It was Miss Brown, the plain—I assure you, she is most plain—English virgin. By strange coincidence, since she knocked as I was writing the word *Romans,* she was returning the first volume of Gibbon's history, which I had lent her only the day before. I rose, and asked her to sit, but she remained just inside the door, clutching at the book. To say something, I expressed admiration for her application, though it seemed to me that her rapid progress through the Roman emperors could only be ascribed to inattention rising from boredom. Any book may be read in a day if its reader is thinking continually on ribbons, bonnets, and unattached clergymen. She shook her head—Oh no, it was not a question of that; she was not a great reader; she was disturbed to have to say such a thing; but a most shocking disaster had occurred, which she would not for the world have—She quickly fled, leaving the volume on the shelf, without explaining the nature of the most shocking disaster, but I had not approached it less than five feet when my nose twitched, and all became apparent. In short, Bella, she had been overtaken by a fit of nausea, and had vomited into the precious volume. It must have made a poor receptacle for her most inward sensations. Poor Miss Brown; she can hardly now ask for the loan of subsequent volumes, and if any other passengers ask me for the soiled first volume, I shall feel free to refer them directly to her. I wonder what drew on the fit; I like to think that it was not the motion of the sea, but the eminent historian's description of the imperial vices. The stomach that turned at the mild turbulence of the English Channel could not, surely, remain calm when provoked by the recitation of the vices of the Emperor Elagabalus. But I will not prise apart the pages, to discover at what point the Empire earned so sincere a criticism; *dal ventro,* as Ariosto says. She has taken the solution many English spinsters have ventured, and is travelling to India in the hope of meeting some latterday Clive, some nabob Midas who will touch her, and with his golden touch turn that chilly marble into flesh. I confuse my mythologies; perhaps you have to see the poor girl to understand how apt the confusion can be.

You see, I ramble on, having nothing to say, and yet feeling that I want to say it to you. To say that nothing. It was white, your skin, so white, and when I touched it, I remember how it flushed under the hand, like a red gentle bruise, fading. I could write my name on your back with my finger, and the letters rose up before fading again, so quickly. I wonder where you are, and what you are seeing, and whom you are speaking to, and how the world seems to you, now. And what you remember of me; that, most of all.

Three days have passed, now, since last I wrote. We have been beset by periodic squalls; not brutish, but tiresome. It is not long now—a matter of days—until we put in to take on fresh water and supplies, and the food has grown monotonous, to add to our troubles.

The food—I draw back, almost, from mentioning it. Not for your sake—I hardly worry about whether I shall weary you or not—but for mine. The food has narrowed to what the salt barrels can yield, and the occasional, necessary lime which we take in water for the sake of our health. And I dream of food which cannot be had. Most of all, over and over, I dream of watercress. A strange fad, a strange thing to crave, out here. I cannot remember ever having a great taste for watercress when it was there, but I fall asleep in my rocking shaded bed, and all at once, with no interval of dreaming, I am waking again, and my mouth is closing over a sandwich, soft English bread, cool butter, a mattress of crunching cress, refreshing as water. My teeth close on the pillow, and I rise and make do with what the ship, three weeks out of harbour, can provide.

We are all fretful, dull, disinclined for company, and confine ourselves to our own quarters as much as we can, where we lie—I mean, of course, where I lie, knowing nothing of my fellow passengers' leisure hours— and contemplate the creaks of the ship's timbers, its rich brackish smells.

Over dinner, we are inattentive, bring out stale anecdotes, make the same inquiries of the Captain we have made a hundred times, have to ask our self-absorbed neighbour three times for the mustard. The Captain asked me, last night, what expectations I had of India, and I was obliged to remind him that it was familiar terrain to me. He begged my pardon briefly, and then asked me, once more, for what precise purpose I was travelling; and that question I could not answer. I was coy and scandalized to be asked such a question as one of the husband-hunting ladies would be; we are travelling, I must remind you, in what we old India hands so vulgarly used to call "the fishing fleet." I blushed, and stuttered, and coyly brought out some implausible explanation, and the Captain seemed satisfied.

4

There are great difficulties in our history—there are always great difficulties, are there not? But you are not dull and plain, like Miss Brown, and I am not wicked or rich, so there is an end to the matter. Our difficulties are the ordinary ones; the facts of the world, and five seas between us. Those are small matters. I hope you see it in the same soothing light.

I am constantly soothed by the contemplation of the sea. I had quite forgotten a strange fact; that one begins a long voyage like this worrying how the long days and weeks are to be passed. But in a week or two, all distractions seem to lose their charm, and even their necessity. Between each paragraph of this journal, hours, days, pass. Gibbon is laid aside. What enchants and holds the mind is the sea. It is uncharted, holds no distinction between one state and another. One wakes in the morning, and goes out on the shining fresh deck, and the sea and sky are quite different to the sea and sky as one last saw them. But the change has come overnight. When I sit on the deck and watch our progress, it seems to me that no alteration comes; only the tiny changes of light and shadow, of the height of the wave and the dark depth of the ocean. I sit and look for hours, Gibbon limply in my hand, and it seems to me that I am looking at the pelt of a single vast beast, turning and turning.

Our clergyman has expressed interest, to this point in our journey, only in what he already knows. I dread coming across him in this little boat, and sometimes walk with my eyes downcast, affecting to be deep in thought. At dinner, there is no such escape, and he is quite capable of beginning a conversation with some reflection on Beeston of York's unworthy preferment, or a comic tale of one cleric or another. He must be admired for his ability to turn the conversation to ecclesiastical matters on the point of a penny. To give you an instance—one from several weeks ago, now—Captain Taylor asked me some detail concerning the uniform of the Sikh cavalry, over the eternal porksteak. I confessed I did not know, and could not recall—it was a trivial matter, which he had raised for something to say. Before I could promise to search through my poor library for any help, however, the worthy reverend struck up like a band in the Park. "You remind me, sir," he called, "of the late poet Churchill, whose parishioners were said to approach him and ask questions regarding the scope of one of the *latter* commandments—before ladies, I need not specify which one—for the mere purpose of being diverted by his confusion and ignorance. There are many most amusing tales of the late gentleman in his pastoral role; indeed . . ." It is best to give way under these nightly onslaughts; intervening would only prolong them, since he is determined to have his way and edify us with the adulteries of dead clergymen.

Lately, however, he seems to be widening his field of interest. One night, at dinner, he remarked suddenly that we must be approaching the equator. "Indeed, sir," the Captain replied, as well he might, since we had discussed the matter every day for a fortnight. The Reverend Lannon's remark was proof positive that he had taken no notice of the conversation at table. "Are there," he went on, "any interesting natural phenomena which may be observed at the equator? I am most interested in natural philosophy, you know, sir, and would be sorry to miss any particularly valuable opportunity of observation." He looked around him at the table, as if he had made some particularly intelligent remark, rather than simply assert his own intelligence. "My son informs me," the kindly Mrs. Robinson answered, "that there is a curious observation to be made of the manner in which water falls to the drains. In the Northern hemisphere, when the plug is removed from a basin of water, the water falls away in a definite anticlockwise direction. South of the equator, I understand, the water swirls in the opposite direction. Do I mean clockwise, or anticlockwise—Sophy, my dear, which do I mean?" "But at the equator, madam?" Mr. Lannon put in. "Does it follow its own whim?" "No, sir,"

Mrs. Robinson continued, patiently. "It falls directly downwards, without any circular tendency." "No swirling," the august ecclesiastical figure amplified. "That should prove most interesting. But, sir, I worry—do we not move so rapidly that we shall pass the equator in a moment, and we shall have no opportunity to observe this interesting phenomenon? If there were some thought given to the possibility of, of stopping, of—" he dared a new phrase, "—of dropping the anchor at the exact point of the equator. Is the sea particularly deep there, sir?" There was a terrible snorting from the head of the table, and Captain Taylor seemed to be suffering from a mouthful of wine which he had swallowed too hastily; if he were not so very serious a man, I might suspect him of laughing at his passengers.

"The Captain has promised," Miss Brown said, to cover the Captain's confusion, "that our crossing of the line will be marked by some ceremony. A naval tradition, you know, sir." "Ah—really?" Lannon said. "What form does the ritual take?" "That," Miss Brown supplied, "is a matter swathed in mystery. We are not to know, until the line is crossed." "Nothing too . . . *pagan*, I trust," the clergyman roguishly said. No, it is nothing too pagan, as far as I recall, just some tomfoolery with a bucket and mops and a sailors' pantomime, but the clergyman's mock-objection had the unmistakable effect of making the table turn from him with its usual mild distaste.

5

It ought to be clear where we are by now; there ought to be landmarks. One line of latitude is passed, and then another, and then another. We, at least, are excited by these announcements. The small boys on board have all their own charts, on which they have traced our path, and make perfect nuisances of themselves demanding admittance to the secret wisdoms of wind, moon, and stars. We pass the tropic; we will pass the equator, in time, with attendant celebrations; and then another tropic. These facts create considerable excitement on board, but they are lines which man has drawn on the globe, and therefore not exciting to me. When the captain assures us that today, we pass the tropic, I look at him, and he is only a man, telling me of lines he has decided to draw on the unbounded ocean. It is no slur on Captain Taylor, our ineffectual commander, that I am not interested by these abstract facts of geography and navigation. I am uninterested by these facts, because they are the inventions of men. I look at the sea, and am only interested by the wordless great world.

To me, you too are a world. I never understood before now how little distance I had previously travelled. A woman's body is an uncharted universe, of which I had heard. Travellers had brought me back reports, and I nodded credulously. But reports will not do. The empires of the flesh, the rich yielding regions of the breast, the vistas opening up when my lips were laid on yours. A journey between worlds, undertaken in a moment; and to return from these marvels is, I now understand, no less a journey, which I am only now undertaking. I long for the refreshments of you; my watercress girl.

Some days have passed, with no change in our condition that I can perceive. The weather is fine, and we send along merrily. I sit up on deck, an unread and unreadable book in my hands—I fear I shall never advance in Gibbon beyond the sack of Rome, and will not long remain master of what I have read, so rapidly does my mind seem to empty itself of anything resembling rational thought. The vessel sends along merrily, the only still point in this landless salt world of waves and clouds, wind and sky. I get along famously with all the passengers, I must admit—I know not why, perhaps some deceptive appearance of sympathetic listening is to blame. So, as I sit on the deck restfully, I seem to become a sort of safe-box, into which any passing hobbledehoy may load all his grievances and secrets. Mr. Lannon had to confess he did not find the amiably smiling Mrs. Robinson easy company, proposing that perpetual mildness may prove sharper than a serpent's tooth. I thought what nonsense he talks—uncharitable nonsense, too—and sent him, amiably smiling, on his way. Mrs. Robinson was next in line, to offer the reflection that the relation of companion and confidante could not always be easy, if the confidante herself were allowed no opportunity to unburden herself into a kind, a *listening* pair of ears. And I must know—"you must indeed know, sir," Mrs. Robinson said, insistently clasping at my sleeve—that certain young persons could be abominably selfish in their habit of constantly dwelling on their own problems, while never allowing that her interlocutress might have problems far, far, sir, more pressing and distressing which she might care to tell, were it not—At this moment, Mrs. Robinson, the poor sad lady, dissolved into tears and damply hastened off. I reflected only that *interlocutress* is a hard word to pronounce with conviction, sincerity, and an aspect of burning self-righteousness, but Mrs. Robinson carried it off with celerity and grace. She is nicely educated and neat rather than elegant in appearance; I suspect that in the distant past, she may have been a governess. Next was Miss Brown, who fears that the Captain does not like her, and, having no better occupation, desired reassurance. I shall not tire you with her conversation on this most important subject.

6

An event has taken place; an interesting and significant event. Captain Taylor was late for dinner yesterday, and that is most unlike the underoccupied and conscientious fellow. We hung around, picking at old and stale topics of conversation like overfed hens. At length, we received word that we were to go in without our host. It was a dull half-hour at first. Captain Taylor is not much of a host, but it is curious how his nervous incapacity at the table animates us all, as if we all compete to find some subject which will engage his interest and divert us all. Without him, we were somewhat morose.

His entrance, too, was unexpected. In ordinary circumstances he sidles in, apologetically, sliding into his chair with eyes lowered, like a virgin at her first ball. Tonight, he was flushed, grand, and displaying as much firm front as a Cherokee brave, and he appeared flanked by the awful appendage of two solemn midshipmen. He dismissed them with a brisk wave of his hand—I think he will do very well at sea, to be truthful—and sat down, making his brief and silent grace before starting to eat, hungrily and briskly. Conversation sputtered on, like the little flames on the surface of an old ashpit. Mrs. Robinson was the first to address him, and her contribution, as ever, was tactful. "The calls on a captain's time must be most pressing and various, sir," she remarked, as if passing a general observation. The Captain did not immediately respond, but seemed sunk in gloom and roasted potatoes. Silence fell, and he was, all at once, raised from his inattentive state. "Ha—hum—you were addressing me, madam?" he cried, his mouth quite full. Mrs. Robinson repeated her comment patiently. "Indeed, indeed," the Captain replied seriously. "And not all of them are happy ones." "I hope you are not troubled by dangerous concerns or—or—mutiny—or—" the clergyman put in foolishly. "Merciful heavens!" Miss Brown cried in a single ear-piercing squall, and Captain Taylor irritably shook his head. "No, sir. Merely a question of naval discipline. That is all." "In what shape or form, sir?" Miss Brown asked tremulously. "Naval discipline," the captain said firmly. "That is all."

He waited until the ladies had withdrawn before telling us what we gentlemen, at least, had all guessed—that a case of—ah—

(Bella, now a local difficulty presents itself. I shall spare you some things—indeed, I freely admit, I have already spared you much—and I do not care to think of you reading what gentlemen talk about, not always: so I proceed in my own manner, satisfying my own odd humour, and you may choose to understand my meaning, and I may choose to think of your unsullied thoughts. Forgive me: I think of your white skin, your wide eyes, your clean small ears, and it is from my own thoughts that I am raising this protection—so—)

—a case of—ah—*theft* below decks had come to light. "I consider it most important in these cases," the Captain said sagely, "to act immediately, and severely. Once such *dishonesty* takes hold in a ship, it spreads like any contagion, until no man can consider his purse immune from the thief, nor his hand free from the temptation—no man, I say." He fixed me with his eye in a most unusual way, and I felt struck with awe, for no reason whatever. It seems to me unlikely that *any* man is subject to this temptation, and I could not quite summon up the vision in Captain Taylor's eye, of a hold full of fifty seamen *thieving from* each other with no dissenter or refusant. But I dare say he is right. There is no telling what a man may be driven to at sea; and he, it is plain, is no stranger to deprivation.

The two hands were whipped yesterday in full view of the men, whose attendance was required. I suppose it serves as a general admonition. The ladies were absent, of course, so I feel it my duty to set down for your benefit a spectacle you shall never see. It was a most interesting example of discipline. They were sentenced to thirty lashes each, though there had been some intimation that one had been coerced into *theft* by the other, more strong-willed fellow, and could have been considered less at fault. By particular order of the Captain, they were tied together, face against face. They swivelled as they hung from the spar like a huge grotesque doll with two backs. Their shirts were rent from them, and two brawny hands stepped up with the whips dangling from their hamlike fists. I noted, not for the first time, how hardened by work all sailors are; those to be beaten, and those who were to be beaten, had not an ounce of spare flesh on them. Weeks of shinning up and down the mast had left them all very much the same; they were hard and seamed and dark as cricket balls. They were whipped each in their turn, so that they howled in the passive face of the other. Their welts began to bleed horribly after only five or six strokes, and when the watching hands observed this, a murmur began to rise among them. To my surprise, it was a sympathetic noise, expressing no distaste except at the punishment. For a moment I wondered whether they considered the guilty pair had been unjustly arraigned before realizing that, in fact, *they* did not consider the crime particularly severe. This is a strange world, here, and quite unlike the great world. When you place your feet, one in front of the other, the floor beneath you feels firm as earth, mostly; it is only on consideration that you realize that beneath that is the sea, which is never still, never. And boys are whipped for—well, Bella, for a disgraceful act—and their crew-mates think they have done nothing much wrong. I looked away from their torn backs, at the Captain's intense expression. But there was no certainty there, either; his eyes glittered feverishly, and he rubbed himself from time to time, as if cold. The whipping was exciting him. I looked away, altogether, towards the sea which is always there, and always the same, always changing.

7

In four days we put in at St. Helena. It is a matter of considerable anticipation among us. I suspect at least one of our number of harbouring antique sentiments on the subject of Bonaparte. He is a stalwart old Bristol cloth-merchant voyaging out to India for no reason but curiosity. The self-styled French Emperor's final place of confinement, I have noticed, exercises a passionate hold over a certain sort of Englishman of the later middle years. However ignoble Bonaparte's end, the prospect of arriving at his final resting place awakes in our Bristol merchant, and many like him, a curiously passionate feeling. He strides the decks, and inspects the horizon as if there were new lands bubbling up from the oceans for him to conquer. I fear, however, that the predominant feeling in his breast at the name of Bonaparte is not a brave unspeaking idealism, but a sentimental remembrance of those days of his youth when he could still feel abstract passion with any warmth. Certainly, he grows very heated on the subject of individual liberty, and whenever a recalcitrant deckhand must be flogged, he mutters darkly about "rights" and "universal brother-hood," those cant words of forty years back. The deckhands, however, regard him with an undisguised amusement; he respects them to the point that he is unwilling to walk across a newly swabbed deck, in case he soils it anew. The spectacle of this defender of the rights of the ordinary seaman picking his way delicately across the deck never fails to amass a small crowd of idle hands, barely suppressing their disdain. For him, they are Men and Brothers, though he does not address them in any way; for them, he is a fool who has abdicated the place assigned to him by divine providence. Already he trembles at the name of St. Helena, and, like a lover, shows great wit and ingenuity in his ability to introduce the name of the beloved, *Napoleon,* into any conversation. When we put in, he will be easy prey, I can see, for any rude native of that remote place who is quick enough to sell him some old scrap of stuff and pass it off as the tin-sel Emperor's last pair of drawers. His name is Tredinnick. "My home is at Bristol," he observes. "But I am a Cornishman." He addresses this fre-quent remark to me in particular. I perceive he sees some bond between our remote portions of the kingdom; a bond, however, which is not apparent in the slightest degree to anyone but him.

Some days have passed. St. Helena is now at, or somewhat beyond, the horizon. We were blown severely off course by a storm. At least, it seemed to me a storm, but the old hands refused to admit it. The Cap-tain, indeed, showed me the barometer, which for days has been low, and I had to agree, clutching to the table as the ship lurched and plummeted, that the barometer was admitting to *grand pluie* but not *tempête.* It is storm enough for me, however; and I know that any account of a voyage must contain at least one storm to entertain the reader, and I am happy to be able to oblige you. That is not a great deal of consolation, as I yawn and puke over a chamber pot, but it is something. Once or twice, I have had to leave my cabin and go up on deck, far preferring to be tossed about where I may cling to the mast, in the open air, to being flung about like a pea in a drum and have my head broken. The sea is black; quite black; it hurls itself upwards in great spurts, as the ship's flank lolls into it, a rain-storm falling upwards. There is a great terror as the ship labours up the great wall of the wave and then pauses for a moment, a long long moment, nauseously, before plummeting down to a deep hole between peaks. I am writing this in a moment of peace and calm, but it is difficult to forget the feeling of your own toes, scrabbling involuntarily within your boot for some simian hold on the deck, not moving one step forward or letting go of your grip with the left hand until the right is firmly around the next piece of rigging.

The storm is abated now, and seemed strangely distant as soon as we passed into calmer waters. All through it, the hands seemed cheerful rather than filled with fear, as I was, and the more audacious of them even made a point of climbing the rigging in what seemed to me impossible seas; it will take a long time before I forget the image of a boy of fourteen, clinging to the topmost stretch of the mast as the ship lolls crazily to one side and he, still grinning, is poised over a great marine abyss. The storm—very well, then, the great rain—continued for three days, driving us hither and thither about the island of St. Helena, before abating. The ship sailed serenely towards the remote post, as if nothing had disturbed its calm progress from one end of the earth to the other. It was only the human cargo, and the more respectable part of that, which seemed to have gone through a terrible ordeal. I feel I am a brave sailor, but was shaken almost into pieces by the three days of howling gales. As for the others—Miss Brown, Mrs. Robinson, the Reverend Lannon, and Tredinnick, the *soi-disant* Cornishman—I need not describe the harum-scarum wreckage of their appearance when, finally, the seas calmed and they palely ascended from their terrible confinements.

The skies cleared, as if by prior arrangement, and, hovering, floating between a blue sky and a calm blue sea, there was the single mountain of St. Helena. Sometimes you sense a geography which you cannot see, and thus it is with this strange, remote peak. It rises from an underwater plain, a mile deep, precipitous as a tower. No other island—no other land—rises within hundreds of miles. The islanders cling to the steep sides, the utmost peak of the huge tower which rises from the cold depths, and peer out at the world like prisoners. The ship anchors at the mouth of the harbour, under Munden's Battery, and, by long custom, an official party is despatched in a boat. No further progress is made until application has been made to the Governor, and leave to proceed be given in the form of a signal from the battery of heavy guns. There is an awe-inspiring aspect to this distant place, near four and a half thousand miles from England; in itself it is a sublime and picturesque island, but the awe which every visitor feels on approaching it derives, I think, chiefly from its isolation.

8

We are here for some days before proceeding on our long voyage. It is a remote place, but a civilized one. The Governor invited me, and the Captain, and Tredinnick, but not, to his open disgust, the Reverend Lannon, to spend an afternoon on his estate. It is not quite an English house in appearance. There are profound cracks in the walls and everywhere a torn shabbiness, as if the walls had been gnawed by gigantic pigs. But the Governor and his unruly brood of children live here cheerfully enough; his wife questioned me with great *brio*, as she would no doubt describe it, about the currently fashionable books, the current fashions in bonnets which prevail in London. These were not questions I could answer with any conviction, and I wished that I could have you by my side. Not, I add, for the first time. The boys run wild, and are fascinated only by the minute differences between the ships which put in here; and, happily, the Captain was able to still them, like Circe, with tales of shipwreck and storm and details of yardage. It was the only occasion on which I have seen him entirely at ease in company, and he was conversing with eight-year-old boys. They are a good-humoured crew, as I suppose they must be, living out here and clinging to this natural beacon, and parried all Mr. Tredinnick's questions about Bonaparte's last days with brevity and wit. I expect they are quite accustomed to the questions visitors ask of them about the late Emperor, so-called.

After dinner, we took a refreshing turn in the gardens of the Governor's house. The grounds are laid out with great taste, an English garden which surprises you with its variety of oriental plants: the magnolia, minosa, myrtles thirty feet high, bamboo, gum tree, and cabbage tree grow alongside the more expected laurel, yew, cypress, fir, and oak. It is a most pleasant place, and soon I found myself asking the Governor's wife about Bonaparte. "Did he come here?" I asked, and when I heard myself expressing such a banal curiosity, I almost winced. She, however, took it very well. She is a bland, good-natured, stout mother of six; blamelessly respectable, they say she nevertheless will not pass up any opportunity to dance. I rather like her, though she would not quite "do" in London. "Indeed he did," she assured me, smiling. "We were quite friends. We were not his gaolers, after all, and I suppose he understood that this place would be his final resting place. And it was for us to make his last years comfortable. We had no vengeance to pursue with him. Have you seen his tomb, sir?"

I stopped to examine a blossoming aloe hanging over the serpentine path; it was, surely, not the correct season to see such a thing, and the Governor's wife laughed mildly at me, and explained that here, there are no seasons, but a constant flowering and shedding and leaving in the mild unchanging climate. "Do you suppose he was happy, at the last?" I asked. "In this desolate spot?" "Desolate, sir?" the Governor's wife said. "Isolate, certainly. Yes, I believe he was happy. He was surely a great man, and if he lost the world, then he could console himself with the knowledge that few, since Alexander, have had a world to lose. *He, dolphinlike, bestrode the ocean, and lands like plates* . . . Forgive me, sir. I once knew Shakespeare, but . . . We were quite friends, the Emperor and I, as I liked to call him— you have no idea how agreeable and amusing it is to call a man Emperor. And now you will think the worse of me. We were friends. But we talked of small matters, of the concerns of a small country town, set down somehow in the middle of a great ocean. Marriages and betrothals among our little flock, and the shortages of foodstuffs, even of ladies' fashions on the island, and how they would look next to the fashions this year of London, or of Paris; these were the concerns of our conversations. We did not fight the Battle of Waterloo over and over, as old soldiers are said to be fond of doing. The Governor, my *caro sposo*, you know, sometimes tried to tempt him to do so, with silver pepperpots and the saltshakers, but he would smile, and talk of something else entirely. He was greatly interested in the tittle-tattle of our little parish, you know, and of news of the great world, not at all. When ships came, he was invariably afflicted with the blue devils, and retreated to his residence, scowling. He was right so to do; some of those who came, you know, sir, would chivy him out like a curious bear, to see him growl. And once the ship had left, he would come out again, climb Rupert's Hill in his funny, breathless, stumpy way, and as he came down from the peak, it was as if the sun had risen in his face once more. There is one curious fact I always like to share with our visitors; he was very fond of gold, and most understanding of a lady's hunger for display after nightfall. I never met his like. Forgive me, sir; that is a foolish thing to say, for of course, the world never saw his like. Naturally, it did not. All that I can add to the world's estimation is the poor opinion of a poor lady, set as far apart from the world as a lady can be, and tell you that I grew to be fond of him, truly. As a man, you understand, as a man. And, sir, when does your ship sail for India?"

We set sail on a fine evening, replete with water and fresh stores. I had gorged myself on watercress for days, and was happy. The sea, for the moment, was like a glass. You will laugh at me for dealing in worn-out poetry, Bella, but I can do nothing with the truth; the sea truly was like a glass, and I could not see what propulsion drove us onward. Behind us was the little island, and the lights of the town were beginning to twinkle in the evening air. This, then, was what it came down to; the man who strode Europe, and dreamt of striding the world, was reduced to this little scrap of land, this emerald atom, floating in the velvet sea, and was satisfied at last. The island receded from view, fell back by degrees into the saltly tropical marine night, and by degrees I felt myself withdrawing from any interest in the company on board ship. I went below, as darkness fell, and I stopped caring about Tredinnick and Lannon, Elliott and Captain Taylor; even about Miss Brown. Losing everything. Losing—well, what have I lost? There, too, is something I shall spare you, but now I have made a strange decision, and there may no longer be any reason to spare you anything. But still I pass over some things: in these pages, for my own sake, I shall set down only what pleases me in myself, and that, most of all, is my memory of you. For me, now, there is no world, but only you, set down in these pages. There is no *Jane,* there is no society, and, like Bonaparte on his little island, I can count the world well lost, knowing what I have gained.

I shall not see them again. I am going back to Kabul. I did not tell you. I am telling you now. I am going back to Kabul.

But shall I tell you something else, Bella? Something truly strange? My strange decision? I know now that you will never read this journal, that no one shall. I had planned to despatch it to you on my arrival in India, but I have a better plan. Tomorrow, I shall go to the prow of the boat, and look at the white beating sea, and feel the wind on my face, and hear the cries of the hands and the gulls, tangled up in the rigging. I shall take this little book, and throw it as far as I can, casting it to the waves, commending it to the care of the deep. And the salt water shall wipe away the ink, and dissolve the stitching, and the fish will nuzzle the little book into pieces. And the waves shall wash away my sins, and no one will know of them, and nothing will be heard of them but in the great cavernous halls of the ocean, the echoing infinite chambers of eternity.

Write to me, Bella. I think of you every moment of the day.

BURNES

To tell, he longs to see his son, were strong
But let him say so then, and let him go;
But let him swear so, and he shall not stay
We'll thwack him hence with distaffs.

—The Winter's Tale

NINE

I

Imagine, now, a plain. The most dun and dreary, greasy and grey plain in the world. It is relieved by no virtue of freshness, no green, no water. No palace here, no shade, no pantomime Orient (though we are in India), no cool oasis, no sight or promise of rest. There is no field of rice to be seen, no lush verdure clouding the earth, nothing upon which the eye, gritting up with dust, may pause and be soothed. Raise the observing eye up, now, as if on some high crystal stair, some glass silent Babel, hundreds and hundreds of feet into the lowering grey empyrean, and now imagine again, as far as the mind's eye can see, nothing, but nothing, but the slow curving earth. A flat grey brown eventless plain under a flat grey eventless sky. At the furthest grey horizon, that may be an immense range of broodingly dark mountains, rearing up like thunder as the eye focuses on them. Or the eye may be forming some movement out of mossily green thunderclouds, reaching down like sickening black mountains to the earth. No rain falls here, and the long thunder bears no fruit. Nothing lives, except a single hopeless beggar, squatting in the dry filth. He can only be waiting for death; this landscape gives no alms. A perpetually darkening light, a vast dusty plain a thousand miles from any sea, here in the unloved empty heart of Imperial India. Somewhere in this huge vacuum, the Governor General is advancing on his progress.

There he goes; there, miles away, near the baking horizon. He, of course, cannot be seen; his entourage cannot be seen. What can be seen is dust, and he emerges from a cloud. From here, however, from our falcon's view, it looks more like a movement of insects or an extraordinary meteorological phenomenon than the movement of men, or gods. All that can be seen is a vast brown cloud, rising from the earth and taking its single direction; an arrowed cloud, taking its single direction. Some great event is occurring down there on the plain, and wrapping itself in a cloud of earth while it takes its patient, tremendous form, like the manifestation of the wrathful Jehovah before Ezekiel.

From here, the huge slow storm of the earth, risen in wind, announces the progress and hides it, ostentatious and secretive at once. Swoop down, now, to this dun linear cloud, and there, at the head of it, as if emerging from the smog, is the Governor General himself. He rides at the head of his procession like a jewel set at the head of a mace. He is set in his palanquin and lolls, nodding, from side to side. Occasionally his head jerks firmly upright. Etiquette and the requirements of the vast entourage have combined, and mean that he must rise before five each day, and in this late-afternoon thickening gloom, he is feeling the weight of his early rising. Before and beside his gilded elephant strut barefoot bearers, flailing their moghul pennants (but to whom, no one asks). Stern-faced, they raise and lower their feet with swift deliberation, as if in imitation of the Governor General's elephant. Behind Lord Auckland's elephant are the elephants of his domestic party, his sisters and his courtiers. Emily and Fanny are doing their best to remain poker-stiff, firmly staring in their upright palanquins. But two hours on an elephant is as much as either of them can stand, and—after four times as long as that—they pine, they simply ache for the opportunity to complain, even more than the chance to rest. Emily, in particular, does not seem to be looking at anything, and there is nothing there to be seen. She seems, rather, to be fixing the scene—the landscape—all India—with her newly acquired gimlet glare. The gimlet glare is meant to assure the bearers that she is not tired, but stoic under these cushioned conditions; it does not quite succeed, and she looks like someone concentrating very hard on her physical sufferings.

And then the courtiers—the cousins and aunts, each in a tonjaun, the young men from John-Company, as the natives say, the illustrious connection of Lord Palmerston (so very great a disappointment, this young man, such a very distant connection in any case and dim and argumentifying as your everyday country curate)—and—and—and. There are so many men and women in the court of the Governor General, so many courtiers and attendants, each at the centre of his own little court. Every man has one hundred and twenty bearers, and many of those bearers have bearers of their own, fanning—as Emily is apt to say—the third footman's body servant's lapdog for two rupees a month and a red silk *kurta*. The Governor General never goes for a walk on his own; it is as unimaginable as God turning out without his seraphim. George, as his sister is always recalling, is a surprisingly mild boy, once you get to him. But if he is unchanged from her vision of him as an adored fifteen-year-old elder brother, his circumstances are now quite altered. His nazir, and his elephant jemaudar, and his mahout, and his syces, and his elephant coolies, and the bearers and wallahs and advisers and aides all have the faces of thunder, of archangels barring the path. He can never be alone. His life is one of ceaseless, palatial, sublime discomfort.

Behind the gubernatorial party, that vast train of bearers and underbearers and bearers' bearers' bearers rises up and is swallowed in mud and choking dust. The Governor General's discomfort is considerable, but at least he does not ride in the dust kicked up by a preceding half-mile of procession. He rises before six and departs, and the last of the followers only moves from its overnight camp two hours later. It is like the unfolding of a gargantuan squeezebox; a process which is just now reversing itself. Lord Auckland gives a peremptory signal. It is not his decision, in fact, since he has been in urgent communication with the nazir's messenger boy. The boy, running alongside the Governor's elephant, has been trying to inform him that the nazir, that tremendous personage, now wants to make camp for the night. George seems to agree, and his elephant is hauled to a halt like a ship being tugged to shore. The other elephants shuffle to a standstill, and following the lead of the Governor's great steed, fall slowly to their knees. Behind them, the long alarming series of cannonadings and collisions, yells and crushing of animal against man come to a stop. The Governor's party descend, very gracefully, from their mounts on the unfolding portable stairs used for the purpose; against the singing yowl of the camp's native languages, their English chatter is suddenly spiky with consonants as the song of crickets.

2

Elphinstone and Macnaghten are already arguing, as ever. The pair of them have formed a bickering twosome for days now, Macnaghten and Elphinstone, Elphinstone and Macnaghten, each throwing his long-hoarded experiences and adventures at the other. The others in the Governor's party have taken to avoiding, not at all politely, the two dull old men. Now, they seem to be taking up where they left off after breakfast, trawling over their long-ago travels and bringing up their favourite stories, in guise of intense scholarly debate. Macnaghten is a fine handsome ancient—so, in fact, is Elphinstone. Elphinstone is a prinked, polished dandy, whose old age shall be made to shine with *huile antique* and one of Truefitt's best nutty-brown wigs. Macnaghten is more rumpled, more the brilliantly impossible young man grown wrinkled and grey and rancid. They do not look alike, and yet they are obviously gruesome varieties of the same pompous type; to watch them argue is to think of a dead magpie in a ditch, and its live glossy brother, hopping around with offensive perkiness.

Neither Elphinstone nor Macnaghten can make up his mind to come to a conclusion on any subject, and their arguments, interrupted by the day's travels, continue placidly from one week to another. Both find themselves possessed of the sort of ageing handsomeness against which a guiltily shifting expression acquires a high gleam. The Governor's party habitually moves away from them, once they start talking; on this progress, however, each independently fancies that he has found a more deserving and interested listener than his habitual interlocutor. This more deserving young man is a recent addition to the party. At this moment, he is doing his best, nodding and smiling and making small polite interjections in the exchange, turning from Macnaghten to Elphinstone, and back to Macnaghten. He is disagreeing with neither of them. It might be politeness; it might, on the other hand, be a variety of arrogance, the certainty of a man who knows his company is not worth arguing with or persuading. He knows he is in the right. Elphinstone, as it happens, is appealing to the young man while haranguing Macnaghten. Macnaghten is presently at something of a disadvantage, since he is dismounting from his elephant, and trying to disagree all the while. Emily and Fanny, the

Governor's sisters, are helplessly shaking with laughter at his attempts to descend, tip the boy, correct Elphinstone's ancient and decrepit memory, and smile condescendingly at the young man all at once.

"Where are we?" Fanny says, rubbing her rump discreetly with the point of her parasol, like a placid cow scratching herself against a gate.

"Goofrein, madam," the nazir says, rushing up with his own little entourage. "One moment—" hits a boy, "—yes, madam, indeed, Goofrein." And then he dashes off again, to supervise the erection of the tents.

Emily looks around her at the sandy waste. "I shall never, never understand," Emily says to the group in general, smiling brightly, "why such a place has a name at all. There is nothing here—nothing at all."

"Not nothing, sister," Fanny says, stretching. "Look—there."

"No, not nothing," Emily says, squinting and observing a small assemblage of buildings. "A tank and a little mosque, as usual, and a holy man, naked and painted. The same, every day. I wonder why we travel, to see the same mosque and the same tank in the company of ten thousand of our devoted followers."

"Fifteen thousand, at the last count," Fanny says. "Five thousand for me, and five for you, and five for George."

Lord Auckland hears his name, and turns momentarily from his deep conversation with one of the company wallahs; sees, as Fanny smiles, that it is nothing of significance, turns back to the day's dull business. Emily is dry with thirst and itchingly hot. She sees that Fanny's dress is stained in the upper arm, and curses the fashion for tight sleeves—so very undesirable a mode if travelling in India, and probably one long abandoned in London in any case. She is reminded, too, that her wardrobe has now been deprived of another gown; she foolishly wore a new silk gown to call on the little ranees the day before, and it was quite ruined by their hospitable custom—carried out with distinct relish—of pouring attar over the departing guest. And now not even Myra will wear it. The next time, she will wear muslin to visit the little ranees, and hang the incivility. Both Emily and Fanny are plump-cheeked, snub-nosed, bright-eyed; they look like a pair of intelligent, curious porpoises.

Elphinstone and Macnaghten are working up to a terrific display of learning and memory. "Great enthusiasts, great enthusiasts in the black arts of divination," Elphinstone is saying. He is recalling his days in Kabul, thirty or more years back, for the benefit of the new young man. "I recall that they attempt to divine the future by examining the blade bone of a sheep, by examining the marks in the blade bone of a sheep. Most popular, very much like our own practice of examining coffee grounds, or so I imagine. Did you, sir, ever hear of the continuation of such pagan practices?"

"Coffee grounds, sir?" Burnes says—for of course it is he whose novel presence has excited the conversational display of these venerables. He is only half-listening.

"No, sir, the examination of the blade bones of sheep," Elphinstone says. "I wonder if you ever saw such a thing, in your travels in the country of Kabul. My recollection, now, is of the customs which pertained over a quarter of a century ago."

"I do not recall," Burnes says briefly.

Macnaghten triumphantly runs his hands through his haystack hair, delighted at this. "Of course, Elphinstone, it was a very long time ago you were in Kabul. Are you sure it was there that you saw such a thing? Or was it at Astley's circus in London? Very easy to confuse these things, sir, very easy indeed, as one gets on in years, as we are. A colourful court; a cleverly put-together spectacle. Very much the same thing to that interesting thing, the ageing memory."

Elphinstone rises above this in his polished patrician carriage. "I wonder, sir, if you recall, then, what method the Kabul court uses to foretell the future. All civilized and, indeed, uncivilized societies have great interest in divination, as you know, sir, and whether for use or amusement, you must have seen some way in which they seek to peer into the future. If not the sheep bone, then I wonder what, what, what . . ."

Burnes is unengaged. "I recall that they are very fond of fruit, and leave the stones where they lie, after they have been spat out. Perhaps they divine the future from the pattern the stones form on the ground after an orgy of fruit-eating. In truth, sir, I could not tell you. I am certain you know much better than I."

Macnaghten is triumphant, and leads his old sparring partner off to watch what strikes them, it seems, as the unendingly interesting spectacle of the mahouts putting up the Governor's tent. Burnes watches them go.

3

"Mr. Burnes," calls a lady's voice. He turns, and it is the Governor's sister Emily. She and her sister, Fanny, have set up a temporary shelter, a sort of preliminary tent consisting of three parasols, stuck firmly in the ground and leaning against each other to provide a degree of shade; they recline gracefully, though pinkly, on a waterproof ground-covering while the proper tents are constructed. By them sits Emily's lapdog, panting; a pretty little white dog, curled and fluffy, hot as a muff. She scratches the back of his neck, sympathetically. By them, two body-servants lift and lower the heavy feather fans, six feet in length, which do something to provide a mild cool breeze. Burnes walks over, and bows. The sky is heavy and thick and dark, but the sun's heat somehow penetrates; it is as hot as if under a blanket, and Burnes surreptitiously attempts to get into the wafting of the fan.

"At your service, ma'am," Burnes says. "I admire your fortitude, but nothing seems to trouble you, no discomfort."

"You are kind to say so," Fanny says smartly, "but Emily does nothing but complain; you must have been lucky not to hear any of it."

"The worst of it," Emily says, "is not the heat or the dust or the tedium of travel. It is being denied any kind of consolation. You must know, Mr. Burnes, that every rajah we visit takes it as his duty to load us with emeralds, and we return the favour with interest."

"Naturally," Fanny chips in. "That poor man yesterday—we are, after all, proposing to take away his kingdom."

"To give him protection, and leave him in authority," Emily corrects. "And so very little a kingdom after all—I am quite sure, he would be just as happy with a largish sort of garden to rule over." The dog wriggles, helplessly; her hands are firmly around its middle. "It really is not the same thing at all as invading by force, you know, my dear Fanny. That is the worst torment, for me; to be handed these beautiful jewels, and leave the tent, and immediately have to hand them to John-Company. I am truly desperate to hang on to some of the things we have been given— and, after all, they are giving them to us, and not to some dull old man in a counting house on Cheapside. I am quite certain they would be horrified to discover that our discomforts are not modified by the pretty things they so carefully choose for us."

"They could hardly be worn, Emily," Fanny says. "That gigantic peacock head-dress—it would cause quite the wrong sort of sensation if you wore it in London. How people would stare."

"I should like that, a little," Emily says wistfully. "And it is, after all, only a variety of tiara. But I only saw the thing for a few moments, and it was whisked out of my hands. One of these days, I shall be driven to drop an earring in my reticule, or hide an entire parure under a thick shawl, and be satisfied that I have gained something, at least, from my years of servitude in this place. Tell me, Mr. Burnes, do you have any idea what is in store for us? I have hardly had a chance to talk to George—to Lord Auckland—for days."

Burnes is distracted; one of the natives from the Company, busying around the Governor with a serious air, waving sheaves of paper for attention, is familiar to him. He gives up; there are many brilliant young men, studious and attentive, who have crossed his path, and he is not sure when they have met and when they merely resemble other brilliant young natives. "Forgive me, Miss Eden. I believe—now, do not take this as gospel—I believe we are to camp here tonight, and the Governor General will receive, either here or at tomorrow night's camp, the representatives of Runjeet Singh. You will have more jewels to relinquish, I fear. But they may not come tonight; they may not come tomorrow. The Governor General counsels patience."

"And Shah Shujah, too, I believe," Fanny suddenly says. "Shah Shujah is coming, too."

"Shah Shujah?" Burnes says. He must have misheard. "Forgive me, Miss Eden—you said that Shah Shujah is coming here?"

"So I believe," Fanny says, shrugging. "I think that was the gentleman's name. I find these names so difficult, and so easy to confuse, but I am all but certain that I have it right now. He is a pensioner of ours, is he not—a nice old Pretender to some distant throne or other? Colonel Wade, at Ludhiana, you know, was telling me about him, some weeks ago—a harmless old man, now, I believe. What a lumber room of discarded emperors we have at Ludhiana, to be sure. Can there be fewer than four of them there? And when they meet in the street, how do they decide who shall bow first, or bow deeper? A great puzzle. As for Shah Shujah, I fear I cannot satisfy what curiosity you may have. What he does here, no one knows. Except George, of course. I expect he knows."

Burnes is cautiously astonished. Shah Shujah to come here . . . That wicked old man, the wicked old King of Afghanistan, has not been thought of for twenty years. Burnes had known, in Kabul, never to mention his name; that, in fact, is the only reason he knows that the wicked old man is still alive. Twenty years ago, Shah Shujah-ul-mulk lost one of those ordinarily ferocious wars, and fled for his life, abandoning his court and half his followers to the vengeance of the victors. And since then, as far as anyone knows, he has been living a life of determined viciousness in a secluded palace somewhere, living the extravagant life of a ruler with nothing but monkeys and wives and—as the Eden sisters so pertly remark—nothing but a ten-acre garden over which to rule. No one has thought of him for years; probably not even the victor of the vicious little war, who now rules in Kabul, and whose name is Dost Mohammed. Burnes never met or heard of him; he was a nothing, surrounded by emeralds. And now he is to come here, and meet not only with Lord Auckland, but quite possibly also with Runjeet Singh, the great prince of the Sikhs. Something strange is happening, all in all, in the Governor's camp.

He bows to Fanny, who has no idea what she has just said, and walks towards the Governor's group. He is tired of the endless civility which these progresses require; civility to the native princes, civility to the servants, civility to the ladies, endless fan-holding. There is something going on here; there is something worrying. Shah Shujah to be unrooted from his lush jewelled pretend court, and come to accept homage. Burnes needs to be there, to talk to the Governor. Things are going wrong, and the Governor, whose mind is too easily made up, is making his mind up in a disastrous direction. Burnes can feel it. And, besides, he is curious about the native follower he glimpsed, and half-recognized.

4

Behind, the tents are being erected with cries and wails and panicking flurries of movements, as the thirty or forty men whose task it is to raise and lower the domicile form themselves into random groups. Fat Ali starts a song—no, a chant, and quickly the others join in. They all come from different places, some country boys, some street beggars, and they barely have a language in common; their faces, too, are an anthology of the variousness of the human expression. This one crafty, this one slow, this one humorous or kind or sour, from all over the world, from one side of India to another, and their skin is every shade you can think of, from the palest lemon of fat sweating Ali, who is always starting on a joke and never quite finishing it aright, to black clever Romesh with his clever white eyes and his thoughts of the green slopes of home. They are all so different from each other, they represent to each other an anthology of the possibilities of India, of the possibilities of the world. They are interested in each other's unfamiliarities, and listen to the tales of their lives with patient wide-eyed interest. How quiet and dull and indistinguishable the Europeans seem to them, in their hot clothes and their identical short tempers, their pale square faces with no expression. Ali's song is one they all know, the sort with a silly line which he sings, and which is then repeated by them all. There is a joke in it about Bustan, who chases after girls; they all chaff him that the plump white memsahibs in their insect-crushing black boots are what he really dreams of. He takes it in good part, having no alternative, and they sing the rude song, knowing that the English will not understand.

> The cup passes around, the blessed cup
> > around the blessed cup
> *And what joy, it brims with wine, with wine, the sacred*
> > with wine, the sacred
> *But what is this? I cannot drink, no I cannot*
> > no I cannot
> *For there by me is Bustan, who will drink first*
> > who will drink first
> *And he is no man, for when he lies with women*
> > he lies with women
> *He lowers his lips to their hairier mouth*
> > to their hairier mouth—

As they sing, their voices crack with their bold merriment, and the ropes of the tent tremble with hilarity.

> *—And the man who drinks his fill at that font*
> > at that font

I will not share a cup with him, not any cup
not any cup.

And with delight, they start up again, mocking poor Bustan, the youngest and silliest of the group, who gets drunk quickest, who stares after women, who knows nothing of the world and asks the most questions. Bustan blushes—he blushes most of all when it comes to the word *cup*, which has an inexpressible double meaning. But he does not hide his own pleasure; it is nice to be noticed and joshed in this way, and treated as a pet by the gang, and everyone knows there is no truth in it, for no one, and not innocent Bustan, would care to do what the song jokes about.

Macnaghten and Elphinstone have exhausted their topic of argument for the moment, and have no audience but themselves. They are fanning themselves angrily and inadequately with their handkerchiefs, and staring anywhere but at each other—the horizon, a camel, the sky. It hardly matters what has caused this momentary fracture between them; it is something which occurs five times a day, or ten if the group is not travelling. They can argue about anything; whether gunpowder was invented by the Persians or the Chinese, whether there are truly six or seven colours in the rainbow, whether water or tea or curry is more cooling in the frightful climate, whether, indeed, the climate is frightful or, indeed, after some period of residence in India (as Elphinstone said, mopping his purple brow as the punkah-wallah did his best) proves beneficial to the constitution by stretching it. Whatever it is, they have now concluded one argument without persuading each other in the slightest, and are looking around for a new subject.

"Pray, sir," Elphinstone says in the end. "Do you understand the song the bearers sing? It sounded, almost, like a sea shanty, in pattern only, I mean. You take my meaning, of course."

"It is a love song," Macnaghten says stiffly. "The principal singer misses his beloved."

"How curious," Elphinstone says. "I was certain that I heard the word *cup* repeated, which made me think it was a drinking song of some sort."

"The principal singer misses his beloved," Macnaghten says, drawing himself up, "and turns to drinking, in solace. A rare but interesting form, the love song which is also a drinking song. I am surprised, sir, that in your many travels, you never heard an example. Perhaps you did, without understanding the full purport of the song. That is always a possibility, when Europeans travel widely without the opportunity to study any one thing at leisure, as you will agree."

Elphinstone takes a deep breath; the bearers, almost finished with the tent, embark on their vulgar song for a fifth time through.

"I must go and talk to the Governor General," Elphinstone says finally, brutally. And off he goes.

5

The weather over the far hills is thickening and darkening. In a moment, the thunder rolls distantly, a remote roar and patter, like the applause at the theatre. In front of the Governor's tent, the boys run together, and in seconds have put up a trestle table, silently. There is a pause, and then, from behind them, the kitchen boys with their dishes. In this livid yellow-edged light, the silver gleams as if under water. The exhaustions of the day require some kind of replenishment, and the table being laid for the Governor's party to stand and pick at is a heavy one; it is some time before a proper dinner may be prepared, and the cold game, claret, dry cakes, cheese, cold roast quail, curried fish, and rice is intended to support and sustain the delicate hungry constitution of the party before they dine, no more than that. The boys load up the table swiftly, and stand back in their orders. One of the under-chefs comes from the kitchen tent to inspect the restorative mezzo-meal; he stands there with a critical eye, because his job is to find something wrong. He limits himself to ordering the rearrangement of three or four of the dishes, and then claps his hands. The kitchen boys retreat. As if in response, the weather provides a larger, more distant, rumbling applause. The storm is approaching.

The Governor General is still deep in conversation, hardly noticing that the table is ready for him. Around him, the party is rising in various degrees of eagerness; those who have no appetite for food make it very plain by their demeanour, and it is odd to know something so very intimate about each member of the party. Nobody steps forward to start on the food; of course, there is no formal precedence here, no taking of the ladies to the table. It is quite the pic-nic. But still, it would be a brave man who reached for the cold roast duck before the Governor or his sisters had exercised their first rights, and the party circles the table at a distance of twenty yards, not seeming to observe it, passing remarks about the weather and the discomfort of the camp and the journey. By the tent, Burnes sees, again, the native in European dress he had remarked earlier. He is separated from the Governor's little group, and is clearly not a kitchen servant or a domestic; it is not clear why he is standing there, with his undirected gaze and his preoccupied way. Burnes stands and looks at him, puzzled and preparing to go and shout at him to find something to do. Then, all at once, it strikes him; he is standing there, civilly, waiting to be recognized by Burnes. It is Mohan Lal. Paler and plumper than he was when they travelled to Kabul together, and now very elegantly dressed, in the most unshowy of Calcutta fashions, but unmistakably the same fellow. Just as he realizes this, Mohan Lal raises his head, and looks directly at Burnes; he sees, evidently, Burnes's recognition, and gives back a half-smile and a short bob of the head. That is enough for him, it seems. He turns sharply, and disappears between the narrow channel between the two largest tents, melting away with his hands clasped, disappearing once more into the expanse and confusion of the assembling greater camp.

"Did you see that fellow?" Burnes says to Fanny, bending down. "That native fellow in the black coat?"

"Which one, sir?" Fanny says. She and Emily had been watching, with some amusement, the gathering of the locusts around their patient, persuadable brother. They hardly ever get near him, these days; but then, neither does anyone else.

"I thought—I was quite convinced for one second—that an old travelling companion of mine, from the old days, was standing just there. I had no idea he was with us. I wonder if you knew anything of him."

"Forgive me, sir," Fanny says. "I did not observe him."

"His name is Mohan Lal," Burnes says, letting it drop.

"So difficult," Emily says. "These native names. Away, Pug, off with you."

Emily's lapdog receives a gentle kick in his side from his mistress's satin slipper, and off he goes. He has had a long day of wriggling and squirming in her sleeve, and it is good to be put down on earth and run around. Everything here is new and interesting smelling and fresh; and there is rain coming, which will be good. He remembers and knows that much. Up to the table where he can smell food; Lord, how hungry he is, and surely something soon will drop from the sky for him. He tugs at an ankle, but his teeth close on—they bite down on cloth—but there, underneath, is metal, a spur. He lets go and runs off, whining a little at the pain in his mouth, and the officers turn and look at him and laugh. No matter. He runs on. Soon he is among strangers, where the legs are bare. Here, he will not bite; he knows that the ones with bare legs are not so good to him, will throw him no cake or meat, and if he bites them in play, they will kick him, and hard. He remembers, dimly, this lesson, and runs on, pausing to piss and mark the places he is running over. In a moment, he comes to a quieter little corner, somewhere where nothing much is happening, a little silken corner, at the edge of a tent. Somewhere he can curl up and not be disturbed, he hopes. Somewhere in his head there is the memory of a silk dress and the soft white hand of his mistress. He lies down anyway. He feels odd, not quite right; there is a pain somewhere in him, a sharp and bad pain. Somewhere deep inside him; not a paw-pain or a nose-pain that can be eased by a rub and a scratch. He lies down, whining quietly, and sniffing, having nothing else to do.

Elsewhere, the Governor General is deep in conversation with the men from the Company, and the pale and thin connection of Lord Palmerston. They all look distinctly nervous and preoccupied, but they always do. They may be discussing dinner, or some trivial affair. Or they may be contemplating the tremendous event approaching. Some tremendous event is approaching, surely it is; some splendid durbar. To summon Shah Shujah, that empty and forgotten potentate, down from the Imperial lumber rooms of Ludhiana to meet with the Governor General and the great King of the Punjab, Runjeet Singh; what is approaching is some new Field of the Cloth of Gold, and Burnes does not know, and has not been told, what such an event signifies. What such an event (which, in any case, he knows nothing of) *could* signify. All he knows is what he was instructed by one of Palmerston's minions, that, on his return to India, he is to travel once more to Kabul. For what purpose, he does not yet know. He received his instructions from a clever young man with mobile hands and a tight smile in one of Palmerston's gilded anterooms, and nothing else but an injunction to secrecy. He has no idea what he is needed for in Kabul, but it has something to do with this tremendous event.

The Governor General and his immediate circle are in sombre, undemonstrative black. Around them, a sea of glittering body-servants and mahouts surge and swell. They pay no attention to their servants.

Burnes, abandoned, is acutely self-conscious, with nothing to do, and abruptly feels embarrassed. The Eden sisters are watching him, from beneath their parasols planted in the earth, with some interest.

6

"What news of the Queen?" Fanny says suddenly. "How pretty she must be, and what a very romantic notion, a little Queen of just nineteen. It is difficult to conceive of anything which would more quickly destroy a girl's notion of modesty and good sense than being hailed as the ruler of so great an empire. She must have her head turned, very quickly."

"I wonder about that," Burnes says, turning and smiling. "They say that if she is ever to dance, a gentleman of the household is sent to intimate to a sacrificial victim that his invitation would be graciously received by Her Majesty, and he is led forward, quaking with terror, like a lamb to the altar."

Emily rearranges herself on the cushion, squishing her bottom around, and laughs, heartily. "Exactly how matters ought to be arranged for the whole of humanity. In my youth, how I would have loved to have sent my papa forward with his tremendous august majesty, to tell the finest young man in the room that his invitation to dance would not be taken amiss. How very rational a way of arranging matters that would be, rather than what actually happened, which is that I stood simpering for hours in the corner with the other great girls, pretending to admire the flowers all through the cotillion, and burning all the while with shame."

"Nonsense, Emily," Fanny says, accepting a glass of sherry and a hard biscuit from a tray carried by one of the bearers. Still, nobody is touching the cold food laid out with such lavishness; the whole party is circling and waiting for Auckland's attention, or his hunger, to be attracted. "You never lacked for partners. And as you would arrange it, it would be the gentlemen who stood around admiring the flowers and waiting for your gracious invitation, which would be no very great improvement."

"I have never met a gentleman who could simper with conviction, it is true," Burnes says.

"You have been lucky not to spend time with our friend Elphinstone, then," Emily murmurs. "But I worry for the poor dear Queen. If asking a gentleman to dance at a ball presents so very awkward a situation, how is she ever to marry? What gentleman would dare to ask so very personal a question? Is she to despatch Palmerston to indicate that a proposal of an intimate nature would meet the Queen's favour, or is she planning to make the first move herself? One can see how Queen Elizabeth remained unmarried all her life—no one would have dared say a word, and the poor woman never thought of proposing herself. Do you know, I wonder where on earth my poor Pug can have got himself to?"

Burnes laughs, and changes the subject. "You must, I suppose, have met the great mass of Englishmen in India, Miss Eden."

"It certainly feels like it."

"I wonder if you know anything of a gentleman whom I used to know. I should very much like to have some news of Gerard," Burnes says. "He was my travelling companion to Kabul, you know, and since I have arrived in India, I have had no word of him. I should very much like to know what became of him."

"Ah," Emily says. "Gerard. Yes, indeed, Gerard the doctor, poor man."

"Poor man, indeed," Burnes says, smiling.

"The last time I saw him," Emily says, "I played quite a trick on him. Truly, now, I am ashamed. A merchant in the bazaar, one of our merchants, you know, a box-wallah, had the idea of a raffle for goods. A splendid idea, but quite out of fashion in London, I expect. You must forgive our poor notions, in this remote and dim country. Well, in truth, it proved as unfashionable an enterprise in Calcutta as it ever could have done in London. Not one ticket was sold. I forget, precisely, what the goods were—Fanny, my dear, do you remember?—no—I recall—a handsome set, a handsome dinner set, quite out of the ordinary run of things in this country. After that, I forget. Perhaps a pier glass, but I am certain that they were very handsome things, so I know not why the public took against the notion so. In any case, it came to the attention of Dr. Gerard, who was a very careful man, as well as being, as you must know, highly contrary, that only one ticket had been sold for these splendid goods, and, although he had no desire for any of the goods, he saw that a modest outlay would acquire these fine things to a certainty.

"Now, at that time he was a regular attender at Governor's house, since one of the ladies there was in an interesting condition, and he confided the state of things to her, who confided them in turn to my sister

Fanny and to me. We have, you know, some devilry in us, and without telling anyone else, we bought four tickets to the raffle—20l. in all—and sat back to wait for the result. Dr. Gerard was certain that his was the only ticket that had been sold, so imagine his horror when the day of the raffle came, and our tickets carried off the first three lots, and he was left with nothing, having spent 15l. He was good enough to forgive us, even when it became clear that we did not desire the prizes in the slightest, and had given them all to our maids."

"Not the dinner set," Fanny says.

"No, not the dinner set, that is true," Emily says. "We kept that, although I cannot remember that we have ever used it."

"Poor Dr. Gerard," Burnes says. "And he so very argumentative. Do you know, madam, where he is at present? Still in India, I hope?"

Emily looks up in astonishment. "Dr. Gerard? Why, sir—he is dead. Did you not know? I thought that was your purpose in asking. Dead six months back, of the cholera. That was my reason in expressing my guilt at our poor treatment of the man—that was the last occasion on which we had any sight of him. It was a quick case, in the end. But many come to such ends, here, and with so old a man, with no connections, there could be few to mourn him, or talk of him afterwards. He went with you to Kabul, you say, sir? I did not know that."

"He was not an old man," Burnes says, shocked out of politeness.

Emily looks surprised at Burnes's bluntness. "No—perhaps not so very old a man. Tell me—do you know what the Governor General can find so very pressing a matter to discuss that he cannot send to inquire after the health and comfort of his two poor patient sisters?"

Burnes bows, and walks away, ostensibly to discover what the Governor General is talking about, but in reality to stop talking to the Eden sisters. The tents are up, now, and he walks between them to the edge of the camp. The dust the procession raised is still hanging heavily in the air, and only slowly subsiding. He looks at the greasy blanketing sky. All at once, it seems to him not like a black Indian sky, but almost an English one. If it were not so very hot, the sky might seem nothing more than an oppressive sky over Gloucestershire, with its dense drifting black patches, and, beyond, thinning paler grey. An English sky, transported halfway across the world. It is only the earth which is different. All at once, he misses Bella; misses her very much indeed. What skies she is under, he does not know, and never will.

TEN

At this point, the scholarly reader will be wondering what, exactly, was going on, and what, precisely, lay behind the forthcoming meeting of pretenders to the throne of Kabul. The relevant correspondence may be found in the library of the India Office, I expect. Not, however, wishing to overestimate the reader's curiosity or energy, it is fair to describe the flurry of correspondence which had been taking place in the previous year or so. What the point of all the correspondence was between people who, on the whole, lived within the same square mile of London and who saw each other every day is a question we do not pretend to be able to answer. But it took place, and may be consulted by the reader of investigative temperament. So, back to London.

It will be recalled that Lord Auckland's brother-in-law was Barling, the President of the Board of Control. Whether he was inspired by the lessons the Duchesse de Neaud drew from Burnes's book, or not, he took it upon himself to write to Carling, that influential cousin-german of the Prime Minister, and point out that the region now known as Central Asia was taking up some £3.5 million of British exports, and it was worth considering a more forward policy towards Afghanistan. Unknown to him,

Darling was simultaneously writing to Farling, to express his view that the region was of such potential importance to the nation—indeed, he understood that already it bought up to £3.5 million of British goods annually—that it would be best to resist the siren voices and adopt a position of masterly inactivity. Garling, who had actually read Mr. Burnes's book, was strongly of the view that the Amir's strongly expressed hostility towards the King of the Punjab, a useful ally of the English, made him a dangerous and unsuitable ruler of a substantial kingdom, and that the only wise policy would be to replace him, if necessary by a show of force; a view which Harling read, agreed with (which was the reason Garling had decided to write to the President of the Board of Trade in the first place), and repeated in Cabinet. This was not the view of Marling, who, in a strongly worded letter to Carling, argued that the division and hostility between the rulers of Kabul and the Punjab was a useful stalemate, and that peace in the region could best be maintained by sitting back and watching them snipe at each other ineffectively. Farling then set pen to paper, to express his own view—but no purpose would be served by summarizing any such debate, and it may be consulted in the archives. Suffice to say that the reasons to intervene, and not to intervene, were conveyed with the greatest possible appearance of sincerity and conviction to Palmerston and Melbourne, who listened courteously before putting their heads together, having been convinced of nothing more than that they had been presented with a decision which ought to be made.

A decision was made by Cabinet with all due solemnity, and a letter of considerable seriousness was despatched to Calcutta. Five months later, the letter was received by Calcutta, and its contents read with great interest by the Governor General, and its recommendations for the conduct of the meeting between the Governor General, Shah Shujah, and Runjeet Singh duly noted, but it is only fair to point out that the meeting on which London's views were so strenuously expressed had occurred some two months previously, so there is not a great deal of point in saying what the letter actually contained, or in pursuing the necessarily leisurely correspondence further.

ELEVEN

I

He was not much of a soldier, and now he knew he never would be. Once, perhaps, he had imagined that India would be the making of him. In England, he had considered the famous careers of all those who had left disgrace behind at home, and gone to India. In a Surrey regiment those heroes had not seemed remarkable, but India had been the making of them; rogues became adventurers, and a disappointing or deplorable man had seemed quite different under a sultry sun. There were dozens of stories like that, all luring boys from a sense of their own failure. Ten years in the East would do it. He had envisaged himself, returning, rich and hard and unsmiling, a man with the saturnine expression of one with diamonds in his inner pockets, whose laconic conversation would reveal nothing of the secret of how it was that such a man had been made in India. The certainty in him, for the months before his departure, was that in the service of the Company, he would acquire riches and character. He set off from Yorkshire, and, as he set out westward on the York mail-coach, sitting on the roof and clutching his hat in the January wind, he was all too conscious that he was still a boy. But he knew fervently that he would return quite changed, or die first. How riches and character would be obtained, he did not know precisely. In England it was always said that money went to money. There, to become rich, you had to be rich first; and to acquire strength of character one, no doubt, had to have some strength of character in the first place. That was England, however. In India, he would leave the boy he had been behind. He had suffered under the knowledge that he had been, until now, someone who had always followed his elder sisters' suggestions, who would not go to the woods at night. They were so black, and something might be there, or nothing apart from him. He would not go to the woods at night. He cried at hunting and would not be blooded, he flinched to shoot a magpie, he felt himself humiliated and ridiculed when his mother asked him to hold up his hands, that she might better wind her yarn. India would be the solution to all that.

Today, he was not quite so sure. He had been in the Company's regiments for three years, and had no more acquired strength of character than riches. He could perceive it in others, and those who shone on the parade ground were as immediately obvious to him as the riches of a potentate whose robes bubbled with diamonds. And he could see, too, those who, like him, would never be rich or brave. There was no country in the world which could transform someone like him.

The day had been worse than usual. At inspection, the barrel of his musket had been dirty. "Digging for potatoes, again, soldier?" the inspecting officer had bawled, his face inches away. "Digging for potatoes and too hungry to find a spade? Clean it." He had cleaned it, squatting on the ground, and an hour later presented himself, alone, for inspection. The officer was bored and irritable at being called away from his snipe and claret, and took a cursory glance before ordering him to clean it again. He was sure that it was clean, but a careful look in the failing light showed that the officer was right, he had not done the job thoroughly, even now. He was sunk in misery, and the others left him alone, away from the fire. If he could clean his musket, and always have it clean from now on, he felt, then everything else would follow. In the middle of his shame, a feeling of promise emerged. If he could prove himself, in one small thing after another, then he would start to get better, and in a year, in two years, he too would be a brave good soldier. Bravery came not from the single heroic deed, but from a sense of your own duty in the smallest things. He would clean his boots, and clean his musket, and obey orders smartly and correctly, and in five years' time he would return, rich and fascinating as any Mogul. This, now, he would get right, and his life would be told and retold like the life of a saint.

It was proving difficult, however. Night had fallen, and as he peered into the barrel of the gun, he could no longer see the old dirt which must be lodged there. The others were around the unnecessary but habitual fire, swapping old stories and abusing their officers. He was sure they were laughing, too, at him, the disaster of the platoon, and would not draw near. They were yawning, and would soon be turning in after another long dusty day. In any of the others, this kind of punishment would call out some kind of sympathy. If the officer required him to clean the weapon again and again, however, he was sure that his fellows would see it impatiently. He was someone who would always hold the others back.

He got up quietly, unobserved, and slipped off. Behind the tents, there was a group of native bearers squatting equably around a little fire of their own, but he could not and would not join them. There were no lamps nearby, just the big hot Indian night, howling, silently. Then he had a good idea, and sat down in pitch darkness, unobserved. He fumbled for his flint. Here, quietly, he would make a light and see for himself what, by now, he was sure of, that his musket was unquestionably clean. In the silent dark of this corner of the camp, he lit a splint and peered down the barrel, sure that this time, at least, he would display himself as a fellow with the makings of a good, conscientious member of the platoon.

2

The most stupendous day in the history of the world opened in rather a leisurely fashion, like the adagio prelude to a furious overture. By the end of the day, the fate of the world would be decided; it began, like any other, with everyone waking and groaning and pulling the fragments of their consciousness together from wherever they had fallen in the course of the night. The rains had broken while the Governor's camp slept, but it brought no relief. Rather, it was as if a bucket of soup had been dropped over the entire plain, and what had been unbearably hot began to steam. They woke at six, as usual, to a landscape already steaming; the night-clothes and sheets stuck together. And towards them, in august fury, rode the two supplicant princes with their glittering storming entourages, like beasts of the field enveloped by a cloud of insects; rode through the night towards the Governor's camp from their diverse corners of the world, with all the splendour of princes who know that, this day, they will draw a line on the map, and divide the continent between them.

Macnaghten woke with a jolt, and Elphinstone, three hundred yards away, woke at the same moment. They sat up in their different tents, with an identical jolt, at the same moment, like two puppets tied together with a long string. By them stood a different sardonic attendant, looking at his master drily, awaiting his master's instructions. The two of them woke, simultaneously, as if plucked upwards by a single string, and spoke before either of them was quite awake. "No, not at all," Macnaghten said. "Quite, quite mistaken," Elphinstone said. They woke, and were already cross.

Another hot sleepy day to fight your way through, Emily thought, and it was her first thought on waking. She was not shaken awake; there was no need. She woke, as ever, quite suddenly, with a feeling that she had cried out. By her bed there was already a little crowd, the girl with the tea and the girl to wash the Governor's sister and Myra with her attendants, to dress her. Emily never woke with the illusion that she was anywhere but where she was; that cruel consolation had long before been taken from her. She would not have that back; there was nothing worse than those days when she was first in India, and had woken and for a moment believed herself in a Worcestershire bed, and that sensation of delicious heat nothing more than the promise of a delicious hot Worcestershire summer day. That cruel trick the mind played had gone now, and she was glad of it. Now she woke, and immediately knew what she had to face: a day of being dressed, and strapped, and sponged like a horse; a day of pepper flying in the soupy air, of mud and dirt, of gazing at muddy, dirty, tired complexions and never a fresh clean English face in the fresh clean English air; a day of being civil to princes, of accepting the tribute of a mound of jewels without seeming to notice, a mound of jewels one would happily have swapped for one crisp white English apple from a crisp cool English orchard; a day of feeling sticky at every point in the body when flesh touched flesh, of unpeeling one's sticky limbs from each other where they touched; a day of having oil poured over your hair and face and dress in pretended compliment, and having to look grateful and pleased; a day of talking to the ladies of one prince's court after another, and never an idea of who each of them was, and never an idea of what one was supposed to be talking to them about, since George would never let on what the true business of the day was until it was quite concluded; a day of facing a harem of ladies, all giggling quietly between their hands, and trying not to be put out of composure (and how would they like it if one started giggling at them?). A day of having to force down the most disgusting food, of sugary pastes covered in gritty silver paint and brown bitter meats boiled in a pot, a dish which would throw up more jointed legs than seemed altogether plausible in an animal, and having to be polite about it, and never be able to say, firmly, the thing she longed to say, "To eat such things is not the custom of my people." Never knowing whom she should be talking to; the ladies of the court always came in a single body, clutching and mobbing each other in a little bright knot, for all the world like a great unopened tulip, and the important wife could be any of them, from the snub-nosed eight-year-old to the wrinkled old crone she had once taken, initially, for a grandmother or an old nanny. The long peppery day stretched in front of her. It was very unlike her, but now, she closed her eyes and sank back into her damp spongy bed. "Where is my dog?" she said at last. "It rained in the night," one of the girls said, having no response. "Much cooler."

But the Governor General—the man on whom half the world, it seemed, was now bending its thoughts—the Governor General woke, and . . . for a moment, as George slowly surfaced from his sticky sleep, he thought he was at sea. The gentle rocking motion to which he woke each morning had never struck him like that before, and he opened his eyes in a state of confusion. He came to his senses consecutively, with a series of corrections. The rocking stopped, and by him, patiently, was the boy with the morning *chai* and the little old man whose task it was to lay hands on the bed and silently rock George into wakefulness. Not at sea, but in a camp; George stared up at the canvas, and collected himself. The next thing was to recall who he was; the Governor General. The next was to summon up his own name, George, and what he was doing there. The purpose of the day swam into his consciousness like an eel, and with it the thought which always came to him last, as he woke in the mornings. The last thought, as ever, was a single word, and the word was this: *Peshawar.*

"Thank you," he said to the lowly attendants, and as he did so, clutching his *chai* to his nightgown, translucent with sweat, the higher attendants, the bath-wallahs, entered with the accoutrements of ablution. And as the flaps of the inner tent opened and closed behind the tin tub, a glimpse of the high authorities of the Governor General's suite could be glimpsed. They ought to be grave and silent and tall as angel execution-ers, George felt, but they never were. The connection of Palmerston (so very distant a connection) was glimpsed squeezing the shoulder of an adjutant, and the rest of them were joshing and laughing like undergrad-uates at some long-established joke. They awaited the Governor's instruc-tions, and he would make them wait; George pondered the odd fact that they would only ever do what they had agreed to do anyway. He did not have the power, he had reluctantly concluded, to give instructions or to summon unwilling princes, and, indeed, had not particularly wanted these princes to come; he had followed the advice of his underlings, or as other people might have put it, their instructions. But if he did not have that power, he had, at least, the power to make his giggling entourage wait. He had, at least, the power to decide to bathe, and rise, and eat, if not entirely the power to decide when he should do these things, and he watched the tin bath being filled from steaming kettles, thickening up the dense soupy air one degree further, with a sense of smug half-sleepy half-satisfaction.

3

Laughter erupted, outside the door of the tent, from the Governor's suite—no, from further away, from the soldiers who were forever loung-ing outside.

"What is that?" Auckland asked petulantly. "What are they laughing about?"

"A silly fellow shot himself last night," the mahout confirmed.

Auckland raised an eyebrow.

"Shot himself in a ridiculous way," the mahout went on, rattling the story off in case the honoured Governor General's bath should be con-cluded, and he dismissed with his marvellous narrative not fully told. "He was trying to see down the barrel of his gun with a candle, and it went off."

"No matter for . . . merriment, sir," Auckland said, who had problems with his Ms and Fs.

"No, indeed, Your Lordship," the mahout said, retreating into one of his lowest bows, his arms opening wide and round like the arms of a mechanical toy. But the effort not to laugh at such a story was too great to be quelled even by the full gravity of the Governor General, and he soon burst out again, as the boy with the *chai* cast alarmed looks at his boldness. "He was a foolish fellow, sir, a fellow no ornament to the Company, who promised nothing much. And last month the fellows stole his boots as a jape and he came before you on parade in his stockinged feet, he had the audacity, and was whipped for it—"

"I recall," Lord Auckland said, as the mahout hugged himself with laughter at the memory of the silly fellow, in his breeches and his stockinged feet, being lightly, so lightly beaten, as if in jest, and still howling.

"Well, he was no soldier and promised nothing," the mahout said. "Every day, a different different fault, an inventive fellow in his failings, one might say. Never the same fault twice. Gracious heavens, Lordship! And yesterday he had not cleaned his gun, and was told to clean it, and instead he lay in his tent and slept until it was quite dark. And he could not see to clean it, so he lit a candle, and he held the candle to the barrel of the gun, and he peered, careful careful, into the barrel so he could see all the way down to the powder, and then, and then . . ."

The mahout could not go on, the story was so funny.

". . . and when the Colonel came in, he saw—he saw—who it was—he saw—" The mahout paused and, dropping an octave, corrected himself statelily, "—*whom* it was—and—" *presto*, "—and remembered the fellow. And the Colonel looked up at the wall of the tent where the brains were painted, and the Colonel said, without even thinking or seeming to think, that this was one mess the useless fellow had made that he would have to be excused, excused from cleaning up . . ."

"Gentlemen!" the Governor General called over the boy's head. The attendant was already doubling up with laughter, and converted it neatly into a deep serious bow, retreating around the advancing suite. "Well, good . . . morning, gentlemen. I hope you, at least, have something rational to tell me today. I am . . . most undisguisedly tired of listening to the most abject nonsense. If there is a . . . man who suffers . . . more than I, or who wastes every hour of the day enduring the silliest conversations, at the conversational . . . mercy of the lowest of his body-servants, I pity him, gentlemen, I pity him."

"We are quite sah-pwised," the most senior of the junior adjutants put in jovially, pink-cheeked and chuckling with excitement. "Sah-pwised—

like the Goddess Venus at the forge of, of some old Gweek fellow, Lord Auckland—"

"Caught out, disturbed in our slumbers, quite unawares," another cried.

"And if it had been one's enemy, one had all been slaughtered, all slaughtered in one's beds," the terrific swell added, going a little too far, and feeling constrained to add a falling and rather apologetic "no doubt, no doubt, Lord Auckland," and blushing. The Governor General decided to be indulgent, however.

"Not that we have any enemies, eh, what . . . Frampton?" he said. *Frampton* was a particular trial to the Governor's tongue. The whole suite collapsed in sycophantic hilarity. "Caught out, eh? Caught short with our breeches down." This was almost too much for the entourage, who might have been at a country raree show, so concertedly did they contrive to split their sides. Really, the Governor General thought with forgiving delight, of all the Governor Generals they have known, how much the most must they admire me, to want to please me so much. "So I presume we have a . . . visitor. Rather early in the day to call, I should have said."

"A visitor, indeed," the entourage chorused.

"The Lion of the Punjab—"

"Arrived in the night, an hour before dawn, cool as you like—"

"Sitting there, demanding to be fed and watered, stuffing away, pleased as Punch—"

"Bacon and eggs—"

"Bacon and eggs—"

"Never seen the like—"

"Not at home, Governor, not at home, one could always say that, one supposes—"

"Is this—"

"The fellows are saying he said, is this, is this—"

"Is this your English beef?"

"Is this your English beef!"

"Vewy happy, most happy indeed, to wait on Your Lordship's pleasure."

"Very happy indeed. Head to foot in cloth-of-gold, and nothing to say for himself but more of your English beef, sir, more beef, sir!"

"More beef!"

"More of your English beef!"

The hilarity swallowed any kind of explanation, and the entourage clung on to each other, helpless with mirth.

"I advise Your Lordship, however," the connection (rather a distant connection) of Palmerston said, entirely straight-faced, "not to delay paying your compliments to Mr. Runjeet Singh. It might be entirely wise to pay one's civility in person, and soon. After all, I fear that a delay of an hour might very well lead to tragic consequences. At the current rate, it is very strongly to be thought that a further pig will have to lay down its life, and the pig-keepers advise me that the sties are in a most mutinous state already. Whatever their gruntling feelings on the prospect of dying to please the English private soldier, there is a distinct sense of disgruntled, disgruntled muttering when they consider on whose plate they may now end up. The sense of duty so carefully inculcated in Your Lordship's pigs is flagging, sir, distinctly flagging. I will be frank, Governor General. To ask for a further hoggish volunteer to sacrifice himself in the cause of the Lion of the Punjab's fierce although somewhat idle curiosity about what to him must be the exotic and fascinating processes of an English breakfast may very well lead to distressing and unfortunate scenes among the porcine members of Your Lordship's suite. I apologize, I truly apologize, for speaking so frankly."

"Kedgeree—"

"Kidneys—"

"He is a marvel, a true marvel."

"Very well, gentlemen," the Governor General said. "Let it be so. You have . . . my word that what thirty minutes shall achieve in the inner gubernatorial recesses shall suffice, and I shall be with you very shortly. I had heard . . . much of Runjeet Singh, the Lion of the Punjab, but— kedgeree?"

"Kidneys—"

"Bacon—"

"Bacon and eggs, if it please Your Lordship."

"And," Lord Auckland continued, serenely delighted. "We shall do . . . more for him. We shall make him . . . feel that he has had the supreme honour of keeping us waiting for his august presence, rather than, let us say, appeared at an absurd hour of the night and caused us to be dislodged from our . . . most comfortable beds. Not only that, I propose to make the ultimate sacrifice myself, and, in the . . . matter of breakfast, throw myself on the King's . . . mercy. As for you—you will shift for yourselves.

There . . . may be something next door. Liberty Hall, gentlemen, Liberty Hall. Half an hour, if you please."

The Governor General in his damp nightgown bowed, and the entourage, chuckling delightedly, retreated. The flaps of the tent closed, and he allowed the attendants to pull his nightgown over his head. And the Governor General stood naked before his bath.

4

He was as good as his word, and half an hour saw him striding out of the tent. The entourage was in high good humour—it had taken quite ten minutes for their overt hilarity to subside over the cold breakfast—and they formed themselves into the rough precedence of the suite casually behind the Governor General's fresh morning face. It was an inexplicable, casual order, made up of a series of tiny historical unspoken negotiations between rank and birth, so that the connection of Palmerston's (rather a distant connection) had burrowed and pushed and been pushed until he had arrived at his customary place in the caravan, rather in advance of what, elsewhere, might have seemed his superiors, and at the point where no one in front of him would give way. They formed themselves into an informal knot, punctual and pragmatic rather than orderly, and Frampton, the waggish swell, the junior magnifico whom everyone rather liked, brought up the rear, chatting happily like a spaniel with its tail up. There was nothing formal or ostentatious about the Governor's progress through the camp, and yet the little groups of soldiers and attendants shot out of his way sharply, saluting.

In one of the tents, two soldiers sat in their combinations, absorbed in their work of polishing the buttons on their dress uniforms. They spoke from time to time.

"Nice day off for us," McVitie said.

"Makes a nice change," the other one agreed.

"All that fucking marching," McVitie pointed out. "All that fucking standing around in the fucking dust."

"And for what?"

"You said it."

They continued with their polishing, contentedly.

"That cunt," McVitie said.

"What cunt?"

"That cunt. What's his name. Shot himself."

"Cunt."

"I'd have shot him, saved him the trouble."

"Didn't mean, to, though, did he? Didn't fancy a bit of the old felo de se?"

"Might have meant to. Might have wanted it to look accidental."

"Didn't have the fucking iron for it, though, did he?"

"Not a fucking drop."

Next to the two of them, a naked body raised itself from its bed, and regarded McVitie and his crony balefully.

"Some fuckers are trying to get some fucking kip around here."

"Fuck off," McVitie said, amicably, and the soldier lay back again. "Who's this fucking wog, then?"

"What fucking wog?"

"This wog who's come to see stammering George."

"Some wog."

"He's called Sugar and Milk," the supine private called out. "That's his fucking name."

"Who the fuck asked you, you cunt?" McVitie said. Then he turned back and said, "What's he want, then?"

"Fuck knows. I know what's in it for us, though."

"Skive and a kip, I should say."

"There's two wogs, aren't there?"

"Fucking thousands."

"Skive and a kip."

"Skive and a kip," McVitie said, and all the long luxury of courts, of great beds, of great idle eternities was in his voice.

"I should fucking say so."

The Lion of the Punjab had finished and departed by the time George and his men reached the tent which had been set aside for the visitors' pleasure. The curtains were drawn aside and they swept in, but there was nothing there but a long table, strewn with dirty dishes, and, across the canvas floor, the detritus of coffee grounds and fish bones and broken crockery. The servants paused at the appearance of the Governor and his men, and, as one, flung themselves panting to the dirty floor.

"Damn them," Auckland said. "Where are they?"

"A wetweat," Frampton offered, cheerily, but it was at least fifteen minutes too late for joking, and he shut up briskly.

"Where are they?" Auckland said again, tetchily.

The most nearly senior of the men in the tent made a hopeless silent gesture at the tent walls, and lowered himself again.

"I see," Auckland said, and with a quick steely look sent a boy on his way. The others shifted uncomfortably at this slight, and said nothing. "And the other one?"

"The other one, sir?"

"Our pensioner. Shah Shujah."

"No word, sir."

"Send to . . . find, gentlemen. Yes?"

The messenger was quickly back. "The King of the Punjab has returned to his settlement, sir."

"Send for Runjeet Singh, then, send for him," Lord Auckland said. "No, better—let us pay him the compliment of visiting him in his lair. That will flatter him. Let us make obeisance . . . My sisters?"

"They are following, sir."

"Very well." And Auckland was off, leaving the great of the Empire to sort themselves out and follow in some sort of order.

A new camp had been established in the night, somewhere outside the Governor's little canvas citadel. Some tactic, some meaning lay behind the placing of the King's camp, some fifty yards from the outer boundaries of the camp. Not too far, but not exactly adjoining, either. The Sikh tents were pointedly magnificent, swathed in brilliant crimson silk and flagged at every corner with pennants the colour of a dreamt sun. Their shape was not as the British tents, and not practical in the slightest; they were gay and grand as an oriental court in a Persian painting, and shone even in the muddy light like Brighton Pavilion. There were seven tents, altogether, grouped like mushrooms that had sprung up in the night, and around, a solid glossy field of Stubbs-splendid horses.

A messenger approached—not one of the King's, but one of the Governor's own men, deep in a bow, inspecting the ground. Auckland paused and waited.

"Great Governor, sir," he said. "Whose presence waters the barren lands of our poor country, under whose wisdom every savage pagan finds cool shelter, in the light of whose eyes—"

"Yes, yes," Auckland said. "What do you want?"

"—in the light of whose eyes—" the messenger continued, unable to stop himself for a moment in his automatic path. Then he recollected himself and said, "Shah Shujah is here."

"Here?"

"He is approaching with his suite, from the north. He has sent word."

"I see," the Governor General said. "When he arrives, tell him that I am with the King and that he . . . may join us at his leisure."

The entourage looked appalled.

"Sir," Burnes piped up—he was at the back of the group, only having attached himself to them in the course of their progress through the camp. "Are you proposing that Shah Shujah and Runjeet Singh meet?"

"Indeed I am," Auckland said. "That, in fact, was the precise purpose I asked them to attend us here."

"Sir, we had no idea you were proposing to bring them together," the nazir said, seriously worried.

"I see no problem," Auckland said. "They are my guests, are they not? They will behave themselves like gentlemen."

"Is Your Lordship quite determined on what I must call a reckless course of action?" Burnes said.

Auckland wavered in his course.

"I must remind Your Lordship of the fact of the Mountain of Light," Burnes went on, pressing his advantage.

"Remind me, sir," Auckland said. "You are speaking in riddles, and we do not have a great deal of time."

"The great diamond, sir," Burnes said. "The Koh-i-Noor, the Mountain of Light."

"More diamonds, Burnes? Have we not enough diamonds yet? Are they proposing to give my poor sister a diamond she will never wear?"

"I think it most unlikely, sir," Burnes persevered. "It is the greatest diamond in the world, and worn constantly by Runjeet Singh. If he were to be wearing it today, and it seems most probable, it would be out of the question that we could risk the consequences of guiding Shah Shujah into his presence. Sir, you may do as you choose, but there is no prospect of any serious conversation taking place while the late King of Afghanistan is obliged to look at his rival, with the Mountain of Light on his arm."

"Oh, come, come," Auckland said. "They are quite grown up, are they not? Is the King of Afghanistan so very weak a man that he envies another man his diamonds, no . . . matter how fine? Does not Shah Shujah live in Ludhiana, and am I to suppose he never chooses to meet his generous host? They are not ladies' . . . maids, you know, Burnes."

"I assure you, sir, the Koh-i-Noor is too great a fact to be passed over, and we must not allow Runjeet to flaunt it in the face of Shah Shujah. Do you not recall, sir—it was once the property of the Afghan court. That was the price of Runjeet Singh's friendship to the King when he was fleeing for his life, twenty years ago. I have no doubt whatsoever that Shah Shujah is of the opinion that Runjeet Singh stole the object from him, that he extracted it by leaving the poor man no choice. Sir, Runjeet Singh wears it for a single reason—he has no fondness for jewels. He wears it to remind himself and us that his neighbours have no power over him. It is as good as wearing Peshawar on his sleeve. We cannot ask him to remove it, but we may not risk asking Shah Shujah into the presence."

Burnes had talked too much. The Governor General stood there, twenty yards from the Sikh tent, white and clenched and furious. Nobody said anything.

"Most gracious Lord," the messenger, surprisingly, started, but it was far too late. Auckland exploded.

"Does everything in this country come down to jewellery?" he cried, speaking fluently in his rage. "Am I, the King's, the Queen's representative in this place, being told that I may not run an affair of this import as I choose because one damned fellow objects to another damned fellow's taste in personal adornments? Are we to be sent running from one damned scented fool to another the whole day long because of some idiotic brooch? A diamond, sir, a blessed diamond—I have been in this country not five years, and I hope never to see another diamond as long as I live. Are you seriously telling me, sir, that a King, a former King, but a King, will not talk sensibly because he has one diamond fewer? Are they not damned keen to offload every single piece of highly expensive carbon they happen to have acquired on my poor sister? Has anyone, pray, thought to ask Shah Shujah whether he truly feels like this, or if he is prepared to act as the King he once was? Sir, you astonish me. To propose, to m-m-me, the Governor General—"

5

It was then that the largest of the tents opened up, and from its depths, like an insect from a flower, came a tiny little old man. He was first, but behind him came a swarm of men. He was radiant in gold, and behind him the violently clashing purples and yellows and reds and blues of his turbanned court crowded and jostled, aching the eye. The Governor fell silent, and, at a little sign from the nazir, the others dropped back a pace. Runjeet Singh came forward; shrivelled, bent, dark, but white-haired, his kindly face was twisted and broken around his sightless eye. There was something awesome about him, tiny as he was; his face, asymmetrical, torn off to one side by some ancient violence, was pointed, alert, keen. He wore no weapon, but in his face there was everything he had ever seen, and in the single dark knowing eye of the warrior there seemed buried every man he had ever seen killed.

He came directly up to Auckland, smiling benignly, and made a single, odd gesture of the hand, smoothing across the neck and throat. Burnes's eyes moved, with difficulty, from his fantastic face, and saw that it was there, set in an amulet on the little old arm, a stone dull and irregular, translucent like a white jellied fruit but shining, a piece of matt glass—no, of crystal—no (the mind shifted with some difficulty)—truly, a diamond. Truly—the mind was still shifting, slowly, incredulously—a diamond. You could see Lord Auckland changing his mind. Behind him, the entire entourage stared at the diamond, and, as one man, boggled, and their collective opinion moved in line with Auckland's, and no one said anything at all. Shah Shujah should not be permitted to enter the presence of this astonishing thing and its astonishing thief. Nobody should. It was beyond what humanity could be expected to bear.

"Do you like my diamond?" Runjeet Singh asked perkily. Auckland was transfixed. "Nice, isn't it? I always wear it, you know. I could see you were interested in it. And my English, you see, do you not think it fine? I have been told so—fine—no, *magnificent* was the word. Well, there's quite a story behind that, the diamond, I mean. I must tell you later, do remind me, won't you?"

"Gracious King," the Governor General started. He ran through his long prepared speech of idle compliments. The King listened, smiling, nodding from time to time, as if one piece of flattery were more particularly apposite than another. The Governor General finished, and the King produced his own speech in the same, incontrovertible style. It all took twenty minutes.

"Now, let's see," the King said cosily. "Where shall we go? I must say, we all most enjoyed our breakfast, terribly kind of you, but now I feel bound to return the honour. I do hope you will come to my quarters, most comfortable, you know."

It had been decided that the King would be invited to the Governor's quarters, but Auckland weakly agreed, and the whole assembly moved behind the white-haired little old man, snuffling from time to time like a tiny white mouse, into the silken palace.

"I expect your ladies will be joining the remainder of my court shortly," Runjeet Singh said kindly. "I know they will be delighted. Your two sisters, I understand? And no wife? None at all? My dear fellow—well, do sit down. All of you? Well, well, as you wish. I do hope," the King said, settling down, "that you are not suffering too much from the heat. I myself dislike it a great deal, and, you know, in the Punjab we have a far more agreeable climate, quite moderate, you know. Now, let us see."

"Great King," Auckland began, pulling himself together. As long as you spent in the East, it was difficult not to be reminded from time to time of the Arabian Nights, and here, sitting in a silken tent, surrounded by fierce shining men with scimitars, talking to a wise king with the face of a wounded animal and the fantastic tongue of an afrit, the feeling that one was in the middle of some superb story was stronger than ever before. Burnes watched the Governor General work his way round slowly to the subject of Kabul and Dost Mohammed. There was, in truth, little to say, and Runjeet Singh nodded encouragingly from time to time, like a kind master reassuring a slow pupil construing one of Virgil's trickier passages. All that needed to be done was to suggest to the King that he enjoyed the full support of the British, and turn his thoughts towards the matter of Kabul. He could be useful; and there was nothing more desirable than that he be given the impression that the English found him not just useful, but indispensable.

"We know very little of the Dost," Auckland concluded. "He . . . may be a good ruler. But our concern is that there is a king of the Afghans whom we can trust. That king . . . may be Dost Mohammed, or it . . . may not be. We simply do not know."

"As soon trust a monkey with a banana," Runjeet Singh put in levelly.

"That is our fear," Auckland said. "Great Lion, we are exceedingly grateful for your advice. May I be . . . frank? Our concern, here, is for your security. We . . . fear that you may have a neighbour with designs on your provinces. An assault on a friend so great as you is, to us, as an attack on a most beloved brother, and we would always seek to avoid such an eventuality."

The response was astonishing. Runjeet Singh screwed up his little face and raised his little fists. "Peshawar belongs to me!" he cried. "It was always Ours, always!"

"We are entirely in agreement," Auckland said smoothly. "At the . . . forefront of our minds is the need to secure what is rightfully our neighbour's. I mean you, I mean Peshawar. We have, of course, a secondary concern, which you will regard as . . . more selfish, but which we strongly wish to share with you. You see, Your . . . Majesty, we are being entirely honest and open with you on this subject, as we hope to be in all our dealings. We look at our . . . maps, and we see our great and powerful neighbour in the Punjab, who is our friend, and another great and powerful King in Persia, with whom we enjoy excellent relations—sir, let me . . . finish, please—and between the two, there is a tract of land of which we know nothing. If there were someone ruling over Kabul whom we could trust—whom we knew something of, who we could be assured could bring to a barren and lawless land the prosperity, justice, and peace which your greatness has given to his own kingdom, how very different our lives would be!"

Auckland was clearly rather pleased with himself, but, Burnes noted, he had broken the great rule of never mentioning any other oriental ruler in the presence of another with anything but denigration. Runjeet Singh was scowling. "The Shah of Persia," he hissed.

Auckland tried to recover. "Sir, I did not mean to compare the Shah of Persia with you, or to suggest for a . . ."

Auckland was stuck on his consonant, and sat and gasped for his M.

"The Shah of Persia," Runjeet Singh said again, scornfully.

". . . for a . . . m . . . m . . . moment that the relations we have established with him can possibly rank with the regard we have for your unexampled wisdom, under the shade of which we hope to, um, drink camel's milk and feed each other with dates in, um, an eternity which may cause us to think that we are already in paradise with the houris . . ."

Auckland was hopelessly out of his depth here, and Burnes could only hope that his wild compliment would be taken by Runjeet Singh as the sort of thing that Englishmen routinely said to each other.

". . . but the point remains, that we are strongly of the view that it would benefit both of us if there were a king in Kabul who did not look with envy on Your . . . Majesty's undoubted possessions, and who preferred our . . . friendship to the . . . friendship of others. We believe that there are those who approach a ruler such as Dost . . . Mohammed with their sharp teeth hidden in a smile, and are concerned that one whose experience and wisdom is so much narrower than a king such as yourself, sir, may see only the smile. That is our concern, and we greatly . . . fear for the consequences if you find yourself with a neighbour who is hostile to you, and to us."

"Of course," Runjeet Singh said, "you cannot be unaware that the Russians are already received with great expressions of friendship by the Shah of Persia, of whose friendship you seem so assured."

Auckland swallowed a blunt riposte. "Your . . . Majesty's perceptiveness and information are a constant source of admiration and astonishment to Her . . . Majesty, Queen Victoria, and we are most humbly grateful for your wise comments."

"Very well," Runjeet Singh said. "So, I am here to discuss the barbarians whose howls and execrations from beyond Our walls pollute the air of Our territories."

"Yes, sir," Auckland said.

"The man who calls himself King of the Afghans—you wish to remove him?"

"We wish to be assured that the ruler at your gates is a man deserving of our enduring trust, and of yours," Auckland said, avoiding the question.

"I see," Runjeet Singh said. Then he thought hard for a moment, and said something. For a moment, the court of the Governor strained forward, not having understood or quite heard what the King had said: but at this moment, he had dropped into his native language. A prince, prepared, stepped forward and translated, an innocent expression on his face. The King of the Punjab sat back with a calm expression, observing his courtier drop the royal bombshell. "And, His Majesty has just said, Your Excellency is proposing," the prince said, "that the present ruler of Kabul be disposed of, and his lands be given to His Majesty the King of the Punjab."

The whole of the Governor's entourage almost fell over with astonishment. How Runjeet Singh could have thought that he had been summoned to be offered an entire country was beyond credulity. What on earth the Governor General had said to put this appalling notion into the King's head could not be recalled. Auckland flushed, and now there was almost nothing to say. It was not at all clear that Dost Mohammed should be removed, but if another ruler were to be installed, then no one would want to create an empire for a ruler who, despite all protestations of friendship, might turn into an enemy at any moment. For a moment, Auckland could be seen wondering what effect the name of Shah Shujah would have at this point; then his eyes flickered down to the diamond, and he was silent. His mouth opened and closed, but he was utterly silent.

"Well, all that can be decided," Runjeet Singh said kindly, returning to English. "This is all most interesting."

"Thank you for the great honour of your presence," Auckland said, choking. "I hope to have the honour of entertaining Your . . . Majesty's party this afternoon, to dinner."

"With pleasure," Runjeet Singh said. "Very great pleasure."

The party, dismissed, withdrew backwards, bowing, the little white mouse grinning and waving from his pile of gold and silk. Outside, the Governor turned smartly, and strode off, almost purple in the face. No one dared say anything, but trotted sharply behind him. As they entered the main body of the camp, they almost collided with the Governor's sisters and their attendants, clean and fresh and rustling in their pale pink silks. Auckland stopped sharply.

"F . . . F . . . Fanny, Emily, go and pay your damned compliments to the King's damned women. Now, if you please, not next week."

The appearance of a flock of birds, all scattering in one movement, Burnes thought, was produced only by the alarmed frantic movements of the women's hands, as they all fluttered at once. Fanny and Emily, snubnosed in their bony pink dresses, gazed at their once-placid brother speechlessly.

"And I hope they are all thrown onto his fah—fah—fah—fah—fah—*funeral* pyre," George shouted. "And damned soon. Meredith—my quarters, now, if you please."

The Governor General and the nazir and a frightened-looking Company fellow strode off, leaving the others standing in silence.

"Gwacious heavens," Frampton opined. "What a fool that old King must be."

"What is it? What, pray, has taken place?" Macnaghten said, bustling up and fastening his stock. Everyone ignored him.

"He can hardly have been serious," Burnes said. "Even Runjeet Singh can hardly be expected to believe that he was called here to be offered an entire country, which in any case isn't in our possession."

"Gwacious heavens," Frampton said again. "What a bwute."

6

Elsewhere, in the women's quarters, Fanny and Emily were sitting, and making stilted conversation, and politely ignoring the pile of jewels which had been unceremoniously dumped at their feet in tribute. Their dresses were unutterably ruined with oil, which was starting to itch horribly.

"I do hope," Fanny said, "that your journey was not too tiring."

The women of the Sikh court broke into tremendous giggling, their hands flying up to their faces, their little eyes peeping out at the two cross pink ladies.

"It is so interesting to travel through a country so beautiful as India," Emily persevered. "I have long heard reports of the loveliness of your nation, and have long nurtured the ambition to make the journey there, but, as my brother said only this morning, the Punjab has been gracious in sending some of its loveliest sights to us. I mean you," she finished crossly.

Really, was there nothing these idiots would not giggle helplessly at? Anyone would have thought that she had made a joke, and she could not stop herself glaring at them. But all at once, like deer who have heard a distant shot, they stopped, and looked, alarmed, to their right. Through the walls of the tent there came a tremendous noise, a tremendous, baffling, roar. It came from the tent of the King and his court, and it took Emily a moment to realize what it was. It was the noise of thirty men, laughing and laughing and laughing.

TWELVE

I

The long day was over. Burnes was acutely conscious, from the ache which ran from his ankles all the way up his thighs, an ache which seemed more of a premonition than the result of a previous day's busy diplomatic pursuits, that another long day was about to begin. In a few hours, in a very few hours. By him sat Mohan Lal. Burnes had succeeded in running him to earth by nightfall, having suffered the whole long day under the conviction that he must corner him and talk before another night had passed. Mohan Lal had seemed to present himself, waiting in the shadows as Burnes walked by, and it was the Englishman who had the feeling of being unearthed. They had walked for a while through the camp, but Burnes had become selfishly aware that the astonished gazes being cast at them by those still sitting about the fires were making it difficult to talk frankly. Making it difficult for him, that is; the Indian discoursed calmly, evenly, and might have been anywhere. It was Burnes who found himself stuttering, unsure of his ground, lowering his voice whenever they drew near a group of European soldiers. To do the camp justice, it was not often that it had the opportunity to see an officer and a native talking, however stiffly, with some appearance of equality, even, from time to time, laughing together, and after half an hour of this un-familiar promenade-spectacular, Burnes took Mohan Lal's arm and guided him firmly towards one of the tents of the sepoys. The two or three soldiers within got up and left silently, at a glance from Burnes, and the two of them settled down quite like old friends. They had not talked in such a way on their journeys; now, they conversed like two men who have shared considerable discomfort. Once, Burnes recalled with shame, Mohan Lal had been a supercilious ass: now—set against the Edens and the Macnaghtens—he appeared pleasant, calm, and intelligent. It was a pleasure, all in all, to absent himself from the Governor's entourage in this fashion. Discomfort, at the time, often raises barriers of privacy and awkwardness between men; afterwards, when time has passed, the mem-ory of those same discomforts and dangers draws men together in an amusing shared tale to tell, even, it seems, the recall of a happy time of privation. Happy, of course, because it is now safely past. Burnes had, in London, told his tale so many times that the terrors and miseries of the long trek could not be awakened by one more retelling, however inti-mately acquainted his listener was with his story's details. Looking now at Mohan Lal, happy and pleased to see his old companion, it occurred to him that the Indian, to whom he had given hardly a moment's thought since his return from Kabul, must in his own way and in his own circle have been buffed and polished by the coarsely agreeable attentions of celebrity. They were as two men who have shared discomfort and suf-fered together—physically suffered, at every physical passage, surface and extremity—and now, to their mild surprise, had been brought together again by chance, and had found themselves made intimate by what they had largely chosen to forget.

There was only one awkwardness between them, once they were seated and alone, and it was the subject of Gerard. In other circumstances the man might have become a pleasant shared joke; but now he was dead, and they did not mention him.

Burnes had just finished telling the story of the ingenious fraud which the junior of the Misses Eden's jemaudars had perpetrated on a pink-faced griffin, fresh off the boat. It was a long tale, involving a herd of goats and an outraged mullah in the Bombay hills, and rather an old one, since the jemaudar in question had been dismissed at least six months before. But Burnes judged it would be new to Mohan Lal, and pleasantly lost himself in the elaborate retelling—as he reached the raucous climax of the story, before his mind's eye passed a herd of goats, heading purposefully towards the helpless Englishman, their black heads nodding like harebells in the wind. Whether the story was new to Mohan Lal or not, he was civil enough not to say anything, but assumed an expression of shining amusement.

"Very good, Burnes-ji," Mohan Lal said affectionately. "The poor fellow! Well, we must not dwell on the discomfiture of others, and I dare say he will rise to be general before you and I are old."

"I think it most unlikely," Burnes said. "They say he apologizes to his body-servants as they dress him. That hardly promises anything very much."

"No," Mohan Lal conceded. Then he brightened and said, "Two emperors in one day, Burnes-ji! There is something to boast of!"

"Yes," Burnes said. "I was awfully hungry, of course—I could almost have had a third."

Mohan Lal gazed back for a moment, before seeing that it was a joke Burnes was making and breaking into a broad smile.

"But I have to tell you," Burnes went on, not quite convinced that the Indian had really understood the joke, "that it will be much more impressive once retold. All those emperors, I mean. Actually to be in the presence of these men—well, you are somewhat ashamed to be caught out by such an easy, obvious trick. You feel like turning to the court nazir who has shown you into the Presence, and saying, well, sir, is that the best you can do for me in this line? You feel tricked, deluded, but, after all, these little men, scratching themselves, picking their teeth, bored, human, sleepy—they are emperors, after all, or so it would seem. I wonder. Yes, on the whole it is very much more impressive an experience when you come to retell it, and can conveniently leave out the unheroic facts, the member of the retinue who caught the hiccoughs, the King of Kabul losing his place in the opening speeches and having to start all over again."

"So tell it to me," Mohan Lal said, surprisingly. Burnes looked at him. Mohan Lal shrugged. He reached into his tunic and extracted a box of the small beedees which he had always smoked. Burnes had quite forgotten this habit of Mohan Lal's, or thought that he had; but as the first whiff of the heavy tarry smoke reached him, he was taken with a small but penetrating pleasure. He was pleased, after a fashion, by the reassurance that his body, as it were, had held the memory, patiently, for him. "Why not? I, too, would like to hear of Shah Shujah and Runjeet Singh, to know how they strike the onlooker, and I am not likely to have the chance to see them closely."

"You have never seen them? Why not?" Burnes said. "You saw Dost Mohammed, did you not?"

"That was there," Mohan Lal said. "Here, in India—are there not so many hundreds of people with a better claim than mine to talk sense to these kings? Oh, very well, Burnes, I confess—my eyes have indeed fallen on Runjeet Singh. Once, once. I have travelled since we last met, and have seen that great king. But Shah Shujah-ul-mulk—never. He is a mythological figure, a king from lost ages, not forgotten, but an emperor veiled in rumour and lies. Of him, I have heard nothing that I know certainly to be true. I know he is still alive, and I know what everyone knows, of the base conduct of his reign. But to see the beast now—that, I had never conceived of, and am as glad to talk to one who has talked with him as I would be to talk with a man who had milked a manticore. So talk, Burnes, tell; and make it impressive in the retelling."

2

Where to begin? Shah Shujah had not made his presence known, and only the reports of the Governor's own attendants announced his arrival. By the time Burnes had grown too impatient to wait any longer, and went on his horse to the far side of the camp to see Shujah-ul-mulk's arrival for himself, the party had withdrawn into their tents. Shah Shujah's encampment was as glittering and expensive as that of the King of the Punjab's, on the other side of the camp. It presented an expanse of brilliant white canvas no dust had ever soiled, but unlike his rival's, it was quite silent and deserted. At some distance, the horses grazed peacefully with their silent attendants; here, the tents were firmly sealed and silent as tombs. Burnes stood at the edge of the greater camp. Behind him was the usual uproar of the camp being erected or dismantled, the barks of animals in pain or hunger, the cries of hawkers, the howls of dogs and sepoys, the kitchen clank and hiss, the snatches of song both alien and familiar, and an English soldier, somewhere nearby, whistling an old English song. The tumult struck him now as brave, a bravery exerted in the face of a vast hostile emptiness. Before him was that white woven city, and it might have dropped from the dark sky onto the plain in silence. He found himself fingering the buttons on his tunic. It was not exactly fear that he felt, nor concern; he felt almost reassured by the inexplicable certainty that something would flow out of this innocent encampment, that, starting from its innocent candour, things would start to change and go wrong.

The Governor General was still immured in his tent, which was as silent as Shah Shujah's. Burnes, at a loss, took himself off to the officers' tiffin. There, the talk was that the Governor could not possibly see his newest visitor until sunset.

"First, you see," Frampton insisted, "there is the dinner with that fwightful ass the King of the Punjab, and I doubt—I sewiously doubt—that Auckland will have got things quite at order—d'ye see—quite stwaight in his own head before then . . ."

Frampton was generally an amusing fellow, but, like the rest of the party, he was quite thrown by Runjeet Singh's casual assumption that he was to be offered the Afghan throne. Like the rest of them, too, he took refuge in enumerating the Governor's commitments for the day and setting out what there could be no debate over, the Governor's unalterable timetable. They all drew back swiftly from the appalling events of the morning.

"And he's been enclosed for quite an hour now, an hour and a half," Frampton went on, taking a swift doglike bite of flat bread as the gesticulation of his left hand opportunely passed his mouth. "An hour and a half—and what can he find to—well, there you have it. Thwee the old fool dines in camp . . ." Frampton had a means all his own of pronouncing the word *three,* much more resembling the cough of a horse than any recognizable word, ". . . thwee hours at least, and then I suppose the other damned old fool can hardly be delayed until tomo'ow—hi, you, sir, more cuwwy, yes, you, cuwwy, now . . ."

A terrified bearer ran out backwards, bowing and muttering all the while.

". . . and I don't suppose we'll see him again. Damn those potentates. Anyone would think that we were heah at their—"

Frampton broke off, and those who were not already standing did so. The Governor General entered the tent in his usual apologetic way. He looked refreshed and calm, though he could not have been able to sleep . . .

Burnes looked at Mohan Lal, nodding as if he were being told what he already knew.

"I see," Mohan Lal said. "He had come to the conclusion that the offer of Kabul to Runjeet Singh need not be mentioned again."

Burnes was startled. "Perhaps so," he said. "Frankly, I don't know that to be the case."

"But it must be so," Mohan Lal said, "since he could not offer it and could not withdraw his apparent offer. It is not his to offer, and he cannot contemplate breaking off good relations by what must appear the act of a blunt withdrawal of generosity to so very highly valued an ally. So the third possibility remains, that of saying nothing, which always, I find, acts as a reassurance in the short term in such cases."

"You may be right," Burnes said. "He certainly said nothing to me. But it seems rather a dangerous decision to me, to send Runjeet Singh away in the belief that we have made him a promise which cannot possibly be kept. Not withdrawing the offer of the Afghan lands must seem very much like repeating the offer."

Mohan Lal lit another beedee; his shoulders were shaking with mirth. "Burnes-ji," he said eventually through the black clouds of tobacco smoke. "Burnes, Burnes. Come now. Do you suppose Runjeet Singh so big a fool as not to know that? I have no doubt that he was trifling with you in the most deplorable manner. He was amusing himself with your Queen's emissary, to see what mettle this Akh-Lam is made of. He looks harmless, I know, like one of your English white mice with one eye put out. But it is not for nothing that he wears the Mountain of Light on his arm. Depend on it—he was trifling with you, as a beautiful girl flirts with a bachelor duke, and fancies, for the moment, that the power all lies in her hands. And in some ways, he is powerful, and he knows the world. He knows how it works, and what lies are told in it, and he knows what lies to tell, when he chooses. And he knows—he knows this above all—he knows how to lie, which is a gift not given to everyone. He has a thousand ways of lying, a thousand and one. He could tell you a different lie every night, like Scheherazade, and in a thousand nights and one night, like Scheherazade, he would have his will, and you, who have listened to them all, would be helpless before his lying will. He knows Kabul is not yours to give, and he knows that, were it to become so, you could not give it away lightly, to a man like him. He knows that you would prefer a real white mouse as a monarch in Kabul, and knows that he does not present a very convincing portrait of a weak leader, willing to do your will over the Afghans. He looks like a white mouse, I know; he is called the Lion by his flatterers; but there is no beast on earth like him, and no man, either. No, he knows you did not mean to offer him Kabul, and was not accepting the offer you did not make. In some ways, Burnes, you have not spent long enough in the East. So what does he want? Well, my dear fellow, he wants you, above all, to know that you cannot trust him, and cannot rely on him. He does not want to be relied upon, nor, at any point in the future, to be called upon. It is easier, all things considered. So I presume the matter was not raised over dinner."

"No, indeed not . . ."

3

Three o'clock came, and the Governor's party, assembled in the Governor's tent, was startled by the absolute promptness of the Punjabi party. Nothing, indeed, was said, and Runjeet Singh, tiny and resplendent, refrained from demanding any more major tracts of Asia.

"So tah-some, this perennial dining *en garçon*," Frampton muttered to Burnes as they sorted themselves out and sat down, but in truth no occidental drawing room could have produced so opulently feminine a spectacle as the massed nobles of the Punjab with their hooded eyes and limp manners, their obscenely long eyelashes, from whose faces and breasts carelessly-arranged pearls fell like battle honours. The Governor's more upright entourage watched the Sikhs eagerly, to see if they would repeat their breakfast debauchery, but so far from attacking the food, they picked at the roasted quails coyly with their little yellow hands, extracted half-chewed morsels from their mouths and examined them sceptically, picked at their pointed little teeth with their pointed long nails. It was a great disappointment to the English, who hid it under a brave display of gourmandism. And nothing was said, and the two courts parted in two hours with all the final expressions of mutual esteem the occasion demanded . . .

"And Shah Shujah?" Mohan Lal gently inquired.

"Yes, then to Shah Shujah, beastly old man," Burnes said. "You have really never seen him?"

"Never," Mohan Lal repeated.

Burnes hardly knew what to say. "An odd old fellow," he said.

"But beastly."

"Beastly. In the ordinary sense, not in the white-mouse-or-lion sense. Beastly."

"I see, I see entirely. Go on."

"Well, I can't say very much. It was a bare hour he granted us. He granted us—yes, that is the word, the right way round. He granted us the honour, and meant us to feel that. No, I am wrong. Sometimes an emperor is truly imperial. Perhaps those without an empire most of all. Yes, he is an emperor to his fingernails. You felt that if you lived a hundred years, and saw every man with any claim to be considered as royalty, every king from one end of the earth to the other, never again would you lay eyes on so completely regal a king. It seems absurd, I know—he is no king, after all, and he has nothing to rule over. He struck me as a man with no power but what his manner can express and imply, and if he is less congenial than *other* monarchs you and I have known—"

"You have, of course, known rather more than I can hope to, Burnes-ji," Mohan Lal chipped in, smiling drily.

"True—perhaps one or two more," Burnes said, reminding himself that the Indian was not susceptible to being teased. "In any case, I claim no exhaustive theory of the behaviour of monarchs, so very small and remote a class of men are they. A man with a kingdom and a succession ensured may descend to affability; a king with nothing but a pension afforded him by a European power he knows nothing of except that it is despicable, cannot refrain from reminding you of the king he still is in his mind. He kept us waiting—he would not deign to look at us, even as he spoke to us—he offered us no refreshment, nor invited us to sit, and dismissed us as if he had a hundred envoys to see that afternoon. The Governor General was in a rare passion."

"Burnes-ji, you are telling everything too fast, too fast. So he kept you waiting . . ."

"A full twenty minutes outside. The bearers all came to stare, and I doubt they will ever talk civilly to us again, now that they have seen we are men whom a native prince can treat in such a way. And then we were admitted to a tent, an empty tent, an antechamber to the Presence, where we were kept another half-hour. And only then—"

Burnes stopped. The wind was getting up, and the sides of the tent they were sitting in slapped furiously around the guy ropes. He did not know how to convey what he had seen, that Shah Shujah was a bad man, filled with cruelty and rage. Fine as other princes of the East had always seemed to him, he had never before seen one who, if offered, however silently, the return of his lost country, treated the messengers with such disdain and dislike. Perhaps it was the look in his eyes, a strange desperate weak look; perhaps it was the unmistakable way the ex-King's court edged away from him. They were paid to stand by him, his attendants, and they could not stop themselves looking at him nervously. And that told you something about Shah Shujah. They knew him, and would not trust him. He was a man undeserving of support, and those who knew him would not, in the end, support him.

4

Burnes said this, or some of it, and Mohan Lal nodded and sucked on his pungent beedee.

"He wants too much," Mohan Lal said. "Well, he wants everything, and that is too much."

"That is what I thought, more or less," Burnes said. "They said almost nothing to each other—I mean, no business was pursued. There is nothing to say, of course. He has come here, and he knows what we are thinking of, without our having to say anything. And he knows what his being summoned here means. What he does not know is what he is to say, so he sits like an ass and pretends to summon the Governor General and dismiss him, and gaze serenely over the tops of our heads in between. Lord, what are we doing?"

Mohan Lal smiled. "The Lion of the Punjab, and then the Ass of Ludhiana. Quite, quite. You think he has destroyed his chances of becoming a British hero?"

"Auckland was certainly very unamused by the performance," Burnes said. Then he caught something in the way Mohan Lal hung fire. "You don't agree."

Mohan Lal stood up and went to the flap of the tent. There was no one outside to listen. Most of the camp, it seemed, had retired. "No," he said, turning. "No, I think he has probably not destroyed his chances, and I think he has assessed the situation well enough to know fairly precisely how badly he can afford to behave. Which is very badly indeed, although you and the Governor General have not quite realized this, yet. He is absurd, of course, as everyone knows. But he has had twenty years to brood over his neglect, over what happened to him, and to plan how he will behave when events turn his way. He is acting as he wants to, as he thinks best, because he feels that at some time soon, you will decide that you have need of him, and will do his bidding, because it coincides with your needs. You saw his manner; come, Burnes, think what plans have been growing in him during his years in exile in Ludhiana. And now he thinks—no, not that nothing will prevent him regaining what was once his, but that he could soon be beyond the opinion of the British, of the Afghans, of everyone. I am certain of what he believes, as certain as if I believed it myself. God made him King; men deposed him from his anointed place. Now men will make him King again. It is as things must be. Burnes, Burnes, you are tired."

Burnes had yawned, hugely, involuntarily. "I am so sorry," he said. "I feel—not tired, in truth. I feel old, so terribly old."

"You are tired, I expect," Mohan Lal said. "A tiring thing, bowing before one emperor—but to bend the knee to two in one day! Even a fellow as fine and strong as you must find it so. A tiring thing, to bow and kneel and kiss the hand of the anointed one, and to listen to the meaningless compliments for hour upon hour."

Burnes, all at once, was overwhelmed by Mohan Lal's thoughtful kindness; it was true, he was quite drained of vitality, but no one in the camp ever exerted himself to inquire after another's exhaustion. It was too universal a condition, and one which, surely, Mohan Lal must be intimately acquainted with. Burnes felt almost moved by the man's solicitous care. Well, that was what came of having your country ruled by an alien and remote power, and seeing the best of your countrymen turned into servants about you; you learnt to see another man's situation finely, clearly, and whole, and remembered to inquire about it. And then Burnes was struck with shame; because he knew nothing about the man, knew nothing about his circumstances, his family, his history, his life, and it had never occurred to him that he might politely inquire.

"I think you are right," Burnes said. "Yes, it must be the paying of compliments. That, and standing so straight for so long, of course. I start to pity the poor body-servants who surround us from the moment we rise to the moment we retire—I feel I know how they must ache, after having danced attendance on emperors the whole livelong day. But they, our servants I mean, they never seem to complain. Not that they would complain to us, that would hardly be expected, but they hardly seem to complain among themselves either. One hardly feels that they are dissatisfied, and yet their lives seem so hard. Yes, perhaps it is the paying of compliments which drains the vital fluid so."

"I think your servants are probably most heartily grateful for their lot," Mohan Lal said. "I should not compare yourself, talking to kings about matters of the utmost importance, with an unclean fellow who is delighted to be taken from his poor hovel and given food and bedding, and in exchange, all he is expected to do is clean the boots of Your Honour, whom he must regard as the kindest of masters. I truly think you have by far the more physically onerous task. The vanity of emperors is a bottomless well, which no man can ever hope to fill with the grossest and most fulsome compliments."

"Do you think, now, to speak frankly," Burnes said, "that these old kings believe what they are told? Or do they merely permit us to convey our appreciation as they accept treasures they can have no possible need for, because that is what the courtly form dictates? Auckland enters a tent, and says to the old King of Afghanistan that he has long desired to be admitted to the Presence, which is a lie, since I don't think he gave Shujah-ul-mulk a moment's thought until six weeks ago. He tells him he is powerful, which he is not, unless you count the whims Shah Shujah chooses to exercise over his little court, which largely amounts, I suppose, to deciding the colours of the Imperial flowerbeds at Ludhiana. He goes on to say that he is wise, when he is clearly an old fool who could not be trusted to pass judgement over a man who had stolen sixpence. And finally Auckland has to tell the old man, with a completely straight face, that he can now see for himself what all reports have suggested, that the King of Kabul is as beautiful as the day, when in fact he closely resembles a moulting crow held together with rubies. I present you with the encomium in the briefest synopsis; Auckland found it necessary to continue in this preposterous vein for half an hour. Now, my point is this: we only find it possible to convey these extravagant sentiments because we know it means nothing, and go through the customary gestures of obeisance because we would not otherwise be permitted to talk to the old fool of subjects we felt worthy of our attention. But does he know this? Why else would he condescend to listen to such cheap trash? Can he possibly believe it to be sincerely intended? Would he, in fact, like it all to be perfectly true?"

"May I ask you," Mohan Lal said, "what he said in response to the Governor General's gracious address?"

"Well," Burnes said, "I was hardly listening, so badly were my feet aching. But it seemed to be another waterfall of nonsense, beautifully expressed, how powerful and wise and gracious the English were and old George handsome as the sun. The most ingenious flights of fancy, you know, but a meaningless stream of drivel, all things told."

"Come now," Mohan Lal said. "You believe all that, do you not? What is your objection to what the old man said? Are not the British extremely powerful, to rule this vast country? Are they not wise—surely, sir, you believe in the wisdom of the British rule, when placed beside the insane and unjust governments which would quickly arise again, were the British ever so foolish as to withdraw their administration? Is it so very extraordinary to regard the Governor General as a remarkably fine-looking man—somewhat dressy, I grant you, but handsome, decidedly handsome. Come, sir. What, precisely, do you object to in what Shah Shujah said? Do you not believe it all to be entirely true?"

Burnes was stuck. "Yes," he said thoughtfully. "Yes, I suppose I do consider it to be well founded. Perhaps it is simply my Scotch distaste for any form of fulsome compliment. But surely you must see that he would have said it all even if none of it were remotely the case."

"And you would still have believed it," Mohan Lal said. "You would. There is no power in the world, even the cruellest and most arbitrary, which does not believe itself to be merciful, compassionate, and wise, or would not listen with keen appreciation when it is described in such a way. Indeed, those are the qualities which we choose to emphasize when they are least apposite. We are men of the world, are we not? We both know that to seduce an intelligent woman, we comment on her beauty; to lay siege to a beautiful woman, it is best to compliment her on her intelligence. And so it is with rulers. To curry favour with the cruellest, we praise the quality of their mercy; the weakest and most vacillating like to hear of the strength and swiftness of their judgement. Those whose position is as fragile as a feather blown hither and thither by the wind, will always prefer those supplicants who arrive and tell them that their position is impregnably secure. Come now, Burnes-ji; you believe what you are told, because it is what you like to hear, and the princes of the East know this. They tell you what you most need to be told. And none of it may be the case, and all of it will be believed. Avidly believed. Drunk up, like water in the desert."

Burnes sat in the warm flickering darkness. Mohan Lal's eyes glittered at him, as if excited with his certain knowledge, and he felt something had been taken from him.

"Well," he said lamely, "I shall certainly never listen to a compliment from you again."

"Yes, you will," Mohan Lal said, almost scornfully. "And you will believe it. Tell me—when I said to you, a moment ago, that even a fellow as fine and healthy as you would be tired after such a day, did you not believe what I said—believe it without a moment of doubt? Yes, of course you did."

"And you didn't mean it?"

"Ha. Of course I meant it," Mohan Lal said, brushing this aside quickly and unconvincingly. For a moment, the man seemed to look at Burnes as if at an inanimate object, as one might look at a sign in the street; not at what he was, but what he meant.

"What are we doing here?" Burnes said, almost to himself.

"That, Burnes, I cannot tell you. I do not know why anyone leaves his house, to travel ten thousand miles, when all the poetry that has ever been written, all the poetry since the beginning of the world all tells us the single lesson that we would be happiest in our own homes, since that is where happiness is born, and where it lives. What poetry cannot answer is the question that follows from that, whether we men actually want to be happy, or whether we would prefer to be restless. In your case—in the English, excuse me, the British case—I would say that when you have gone home, when you are all old and thinking about what this adventure, this whole centuries-long adventure meant, what it meant to you . . . well, things do not always mean something, but perhaps your adventure, perhaps it meant something. You will sit at home and look into your fires and draw your Cashmire shawls about you, and think that you came here for one reason. Of course, now, you tell yourself all sorts of fairy sto-ries—you are here to sell us your wonderful English goods, you want to set us free, you want us to grow up, you want to educate us and make us worship three gods instead of forty thousand—"

"Only one God."

"I stand corrected, Burnes-ji, and I am sure your one God is much more sensible than ours, who are quaint, who have the heads of elephants and monkeys and have blue skin. They are all very good reasons to tell yourself at the time, but they are not, at the bottom, the real reason you came here. You came here not to make yourselves rich, not to make us better and Christian and clean and dressed in Bradford cotton. You believe all this, I know. But when you are old and tired and sleeping in a thousand years' time, you will start to realize that you came here and took possession of what was not yours for one reason. To surrender it, to give it up. That is the only reason. Do you not know your Shakespeare, Burnes? Have you never seen *The Tempest* in your London theatres? Do you not think it strange that, so very long ago, before your English kings owned anything at all, your English poet was dreaming of giving it all up, of surrendering what was not yet yours? Of what never would truly be yours? You are not adventurers; you are all Prosperos, waiting for the day you can give it up, drown your book, and return nobly. We endure your presence, because we see that when you look at us, you know that we will take it all back one day. And you want us to. That desire is so strong in you, it makes you build an empire; because if you never had an empire, you would not have one so nobly to surrender. That, Burnes, is what you are doing here. You asked me, and you did not think that I had an answer. But I have an answer, and that is what you are doing here. And now you are tired, and I shall leave you."

"Come to Kabul," Burnes said. He was so tired, he spoke almost without willing it, as a man asleep still moves his limbs.

"Kabul?" Mohan Lal said. "Once more?"

"Yes," Burnes said. "Once more. It may prove—well, I do not know what it may prove, but those are my instructions, and I want you by me. Come again to Kabul."

"Very well," Mohan Lal said. He seemed to have expected exactly this instruction. "We will talk tomorrow." He got up, gracefully salaamed, as if to a superior, and then he was gone, leaving Burnes to the dark, and the fire, and thoughts of the great wrong empires.

In the night which took hold between the fires, and the tents, there was a strange frantic movement. A small flurry of white jumped, and snarled, and lay still; then the movement was repeated, and repeated, and repeated. For a few minutes, the boy Bustan stood alone in the darkness, fifteen feet away, and tried to see what it was. It was some kind of animal, he could see that. It grew still. Bustan took a brand from the fire, and approached cautiously. There, slavering, looking up in pain, was a small white dog, its coat stained everywhere with thin yellow shit. It cowered away from the light. By it lay a fat long rat, dead and chewed by the dog. Bustan had no way of knowing it, but it was Emily Eden's lapdog. Its name had been Pug. All Bustan saw was a small shitty dog, foaming and dangerous, which would bite. He retreated smartly. In its poisoned confusion, the dog saw a man, a hard painful flame, approaching and retreating. It seemed, the man, to pick something up, beyond the light the dog would not look at, and then, so painfully, to return, to stand there, unmoving, for a second.

Bustan shot once, and the dog fell immediately. The shot was heard all over the silent sleeping camp. The soldiers on guard, close by, heard it, looked at each other, and when no more shots followed, they continued their long night of watch. Bustan went back to his tent with his gun, never thinking that he had done anything but what had to be done. Night had fallen, and everywhere, now, under the blanketed hot moon, men slept heavily, and they did not dream.

THIRTEEN

"I want Peshawar," Dost Mohammed said, all on a sudden, sitting up. "I want Peshawar. We shall have it," he said, correcting himself into the imperial plural. "We shall have what is Ours."

He looked around him, shining with approval for his own resolution. Peshawar was the Emperor's, there in the middle of the night. It was a part of the empire. And the British would help him recover the lands. That was his brilliant pre-dawn thought. They would take it back from the stinking faithless Sikhs, and give it back to him.

In the imperial bedroom, things were stirred a little by the imperial resolution. At the foot of the bed, the guards were rising from their nests of robes, flailing at their *jezails,* to fight off what must, surely, be an assassin. The Amir sank back in his bed. He had spoken aloud, thinking that Akbar his son was in the room with him. He had spoken, and Akbar, in that waking second, had been by him with his alert black eyes, listening closely to what his Amir had to say. But Akbar was not there: he was out in the high hills, riding through the night, unsleeping and brave.

Around him, there was no one: no one but his servants. The Emperor's secretary slept on, oblivious of his Emperor's call, in the long low cot. The guards went to wake him, a sullen resentful move. Outside, it was the hour before dawn. A nightingale sang on, pursuing its thousand tales in the starless clouded garden. The Emperor sank back, his marvellous mind, too, singing on and on and on, like an empty glass under a salt-wet finger. Peshawar shall be Ours again, he thought. It shall be Ours.

And the Dost slept, and while he dreamt, about the borders of
    his kingdom
His enemies clustered and took parley with each other and they
    dreamt too
Dreamt of taking a new jewel for their new crowns and when
    they woke they boasted of their dreams
They said they would seize the city of Kabul for their crowns, and
    in the black cities they had built
In the black cities of Ind of Persia of Engelstan of Muscovy
    and worse
In the streets of the City of Kali the goddess of the godless in the
    streets of London and Qom and the city of Peter
And other cities beyond the mountain, beyond the mountains
    where no swallow flies
They talked of Kabul and thought by taking it they would come
    to rival it
That they would steal a nation and rival that nation's greatness.
And the great Amir slept on, and knew of these plots and knew in
    his sleep
That their plans would come to nothing, their plans against the
    holy city, the God-anointed King
He knew this while he slept. And Akbar rode in the night
Rode through the King his father's dreams. And Akbar rode into
    the high mountains
And looked out from the peaks at his enemies' empty plans, and
    turned to his people.
And Akbar spoke, and this is what he

FOURTEEN

I

It had taken almost until mid-morning for the early mists to clear. The country, seen from this high point, was dimpled and rippled like a morning bedspread; the downs undulated with little pockets and valleys, each of which had kept hold of a white pond of thin white mist. An hour or two ago, the two riders had seemed to swim through thin bright cloud; now the September sun had cleared the air into a sharp hardness, as if of some mineral purity. The mist remained only in the pockets of the downs' lower points. Even now, however, the mist, which thinned and shifted as they looked at it, had no solid contours, and while it so patchily lasted, it was all but impossible for the observer, perched high on a mound, to gauge over what expanse of land his view extended. Each hill was fringed, as they are in lower countries, by a line of trees; but no building or landmark allowed the eye to judge how far there was still to go. The trees, the patches of furze and gorse, and those otherworldly pockets of mist barely specified any distance or any shape. It could have been an ell of green and white cloth, on which the distant copses seemed the roughest darning, a cloth laid over an uneven surface, which at any moment might be pulled off again. The observer, resting now after his long ride, felt that it could be any distance at all which stretched before him. Whether it was a ten-mile stretch, or a short mile, or even a toy green landscape in front of the gaze could not be told; those might be pockets of cotton wool, down there, deceiving the eye. He felt that his gaze was being deceived, when it would be more true to say that it was not being given a great deal of help. Nothing in this whole helped to fix the distance, but the observers: two men dismounted from their horses, which now stood wearily chomping at the tight short grass. Half an hour ago, the whole country was obscured by mist; in half an hour, the whole country would be laid out clearly before him; but Stokes, standing when he would much rather be lying in a state of indecorous frailty on the damp ground, thought that his weak and trembling legs would be most unlikely to be able to endure much more time on a horse than that. He had been riding for hours, and he took a sideways glance at his companion's burning vitality, undiminished since their dawn start, with envy and dislike.

"The horses shouldn't rest too much, or they will chill," Castleford said briskly. "Fine prospect, don't you think?"

"Very fine," Stokes said. "It will surely do the horses no harm to rest a moment or two longer. I was not thinking, I admit, of their welfare when I proposed a pause in our furious flight. You ride like a highwayman, Castleford."

"Thank you, sir," Castleford said politely, not saying what he thought of Stokes's riding. "You could see all the way to Leintwardine steeple if the weather were clearer. It promises to be set for fine, however."

Stokes bent down stiffly in his borrowed tight boots and breeches. "You know I am no countryman," he said, picking at a little purple flower. "What is this called, now?"

"Ah," Castleford said, inspecting what looked to Stokes like a trefoil purple buttercup. "That, I think, is what the common people call Robin's-root."

"And this?" Stokes pointed at a clump of a vivid, yellow-spiked shrub.

"My nurse used to call it maids'-bane," Castleford said. "Still does, I dare say—she lives on yet, brewing up roots in a damp old cottage in Maddendale. Maids'-bane—yes, I think so—if not that, then something very much like it. But I dare say you would prefer something in botanical dog Latin, in which case neither I nor my old nurse can help you. A pretty thing, though, don't you think?"

Stokes relapsed into silence, having no views on the subject; it was the sort of conversation for which he maintained a private word. He called it *baggling,* to himself, and he carried on these small inquiries about small dull things for the sake of conversation over dinner, out riding, whenever trapped with people he did not know well. All that *baggling;* it was better than talking, and Stokes was satisfied that in carrying it on, he was doing his duty, and when Stokes asked a dull fellow about the most desirable itinerary to follow around the northern Lakes, the name of a vulgar little flower, or encouraged a stupidly talkative duchess to recount the plot of some currently fashionable novel, he was satisfied that they were delighted with his company, and had no doubt that he had hidden his contempt for them beyond their powers of perception. He was quite satisfied with his baggling at this point, but there was none further to be had out of this untenanted landscape, unless he was to start asking Castleford what the common people around these parts called the grass, the earth, the sky.

"I suppose so," Stokes said, in response to a raised eyebrow from Castleford, and with a tinge of envy watched the fellow swing himself easily onto his horse. It was one of those clear, bright, country mornings which anyone, even Stokes, could see could be made to sound idyllic, a perfect morning for riding over the bare bright hills. For Stokes, in his borrowed breeches, on his borrowed horse, painfully aware of his pinching tight boots, the idyll and the pleasure were there to be observed, and he could see that the landscape and the air were beautiful, in much the same way that he could see the joy and excitement in Castleford's shining riding face. The pleasure was there, and Stokes could see it, a round golden thing, just out of his reach.

"Castleford, my dear fellow," he said, squinting against the sun. "Let us confess that you are a more dashing horseman than I. Do not flatter me; let us see things as they truly are. If I keep up with you, then I ride in most abject terror of my life; if you ride at my pitiful pace, there can be no enjoyment in it for you, and your horse grows impatient. Let us ride at our own pace, and meet at Leintwardine steeple—Leintwardine, you said?—in an hour or so."

Castleford was clearly torn. "Very good of you, old man," he said finally from his height. "Awfully dull for you, though, to be deprived of company?"

"Not at all, not at all," Stokes said. "I am such a dull fellow in the saddle, I should get on better alone. And I perceive you long for a hard ride, and I am depriving you of your pleasure. Let me ride at my own pace, and we shall meet in an hour—an hour?"

"Very good of you," Castleford said. "If you ride in the same direction, you will see Leintwardine steeple before long. Well, don't let the grey rest too long, or she will stiffen up."

And Castleford was off, his coat-tails flapping, like a man with a coach to rob. Stokes watched him go, and presently mounted the mare and set off at a mild aching trot as his host receded into a furious buzzing atom, diving up and down over the little hills.

Stokes was not a great countryman, and it was only his inability to think of any reason to refuse the invitation which had led him to come down with Castleford to his sister's house. He had been there for four days, and thought he would shortly go mad with the dullness of these country days. There was no prospect of being left alone in the library, nor of having a moment alone with his papers to continue work on his book. At every dank corner of Mrs. Doughty's house lurked a lady, eager to waylay him with the same question, endlessly repeated. "I believe you write, Mr. Stokes?" *Not at the moment, thanks to your solicitous attentions,* Stokes felt like answering. But he had contrived to produce a series of polite responses for four days now, and patiently to meet the expansively-expressed regret of his fellow guests that they had not heard of him, or read any of his books ("But, madam, I have written none," he had said); to hear the interesting information that his new friend, indeed, could not describe herself as a great reader with the appearance of equanimity. It was the realization, which always struck him at this point in his occasional forays into the country, that there was no escape from this crowd of inquisitors, that led him to accept Castleford's invitation to ride. At the moment, in the middle of a cold morning, aching all over, the idea of sitting in a library and allowing himself to be insulted by the most ignorant and foolish of the denizens of the house seemed almost agreeable. The worst of the torments, of course, was the certainty of ignorance: the unpleasant sensation, as he looked now at the landscape, that he would not know whether he was looking at hops or barley or wheat, that he did not know the names of flowers, could not discourse knowledgeably on the merits of horses or distinguish breeds of sheep at a glance. It was not that he particularly wished to possess these apparently universal skills; but it was disagreeable to be reminded constantly of what in normal circumstances he would not think of, that in this world, he was considered almost abnormally lacking in the most commonplace knowledge. Behind all these thoughts, of course, there was the idea of returning to London, but, much as Stokes longed to return, he had made a pact with himself that he would stick it out, and what honour he possessed forbade him from reneging on that.

The country had seemed quite bare of habitation, but as he rode over the next hill, something unexpected came into view, a mile or two to the west. It was what seemed to be a park, wooded, set low down in a dip; a curious place to build a house, and Stokes reflected that it must suffer greatly from the damp. It seemed quite out of place in this landscape; there was nothing to be seen in any other direction until you got to Leint-wardine, and someone, once, had decided to wall a stretch of land about, to grow a picturesque wood and set a house at the centre of it. Stokes paused for a moment, looking at it. What it was, he had no idea; a still, undisturbed palace lay at the centre, he was sure, but nothing could be seen. He hesitated, thinking of Castleford riding at full tilt towards Leint-wardine, but then, decisively, he wheeled the horse about, and turned towards the odd little park. To view a curious old house would be just the thing; to see something out of the ordinary, to have a tale to tell over the interminable dinner. Castleford would wait an hour or two, and he rode, not quite knowing what he should find there.

2

Depending on how you counted, Queen's Acre had between forty and seventy rooms. Some of the upper sixties, it is true, could not be entered, so full were they of the detritus of previous generations, and, whatever their size, were best regarded as lumber rooms. Fifty usable rooms, then. Bella lived in four. The rest of the rooms were shrouded in darkness, and nine-tenths of the house kept locked up against the unimaginable day of a ball, a great house party, against the day when someone should come to call. It never happened, and Bella lived peacefully in her four rooms, going from her chamber to her drawing room to a little library. When the weather was fine, she walked in the park, but went no further than that. Whether there was anyone to call on, she hardly remembered; she had never been a great rider, and now, "with her years and size doubled," it seemed an unlikely sort of idea. Bella and the seven steady old horses in the stables stayed inside, munching contentedly, not troubling each other's placid lives. At first, two years before, she had lived here as her father had lived here, with the whole huge house kept open, the fourteen unused bedchambers aired and ready. But soon, she stopped moving far from her suite of rooms, lost interest in what might lie at the far ends of the house, and gave orders over the course of a few months for the house to be shut up, part by part; the Prince's rooms, first (one distant Garraway had been proud of his friendship with a Prince of Wales, no one could ever agree which one). The chapel next, to the housekeeper's mild disapproval. The white and gold music room (her grandfather's wedding present to his new wife) was shut up, and the loose-strung harp muted in unseen dust. The library next, once Bella had had removed what she would ever need, the damp old nursery suites, the long gallery with its long-faced ancestors, and then the bedrooms, one by one, starting with the most distant, damp, and unusable, and finally her father's, and Harry's old chambers. All shut up, forgotten, dreaming. The ballroom was closed last; for a long time, Bella liked to go down there and sit in the vast Adam acres. It held no memories for her, no romance; they had never held a ball there, and the grand dark room seemed to hold possibilities. The rest of the house was nothing if not historical; this, for a time, had felt more like a future. But in the end, she saw that she had no use for this either, and had it locked. The four rooms were all she needed, and she hung their Chinese-papered walls with paintings of green unpeopled landscapes.

It was not a convenient house, nor a famous one, nor—in the eyes of most judges—a beautiful one. It was merely extremely old and untidy. It had been built, incomprehensibly, so low down in a hollow of the landscape that it would have been damp even without the inexplicable addition of a moat. A cold caught at Queen's Acre proverbially lasted a week longer than one caught in the healthier air of Leintwardine. The only advantage it drew from its position was that it could not be seen until the rider was almost upon it, and the house slept undisturbed. Most of the house was of Queen Elizabeth's time, with all the lightless boxy proportions and eccentric adornments that implies; there were parts of it somewhat older than that, and still less usable. Bella's bold grandfather had attempted improvements, and the improved taste of his day had done its best to bring light and grace into the house, with a great deal of gilded plasterwork and airy windows which, however, still had to open on no very remarkable vista. It was elegant, but not noticeably successful; the awkward and untutored shapes of the rooms could not be altered, and the original grotesque dark picturesqueness had, Bella imagined, been sacrificed without gaining a great deal in return. Whether through motives of disappointment with his improvements, or for more bluntly pecuniary reasons, Bella's grandfather had stopped short of his original grand plan, and the gardens remained in their preposterous symmetry, geometrical and ugly, admired by no one and loved only by Bella. Her father, the despair of the agent, had done nothing; the only sign that he had lived here were his additions to the library, and a box of grandiose plans to transform the house into a Gloucestershire version of the Regent's Pavilion at Brighton, never fulfilled or seriously contemplated.

No one came here. Every other house entertained a steady stream of supplicants; the itinerant and unhoused who roamed the country left Queen's Acre alone. Anywhere else, men were always turning up at the kitchen door with their look of desperation and unnecessary trades. But no one appeared at Queen's Acre, offering to mend the clocks, or sharpen the household knives. It was too far out of the way, and buried out of sight, and the only mendicants who found their way here were the most lost and despairing of their breed. The country neighbours knew of it, of course, but no one much had visited since the old Colonel's father's day. It was too inconvenient to reach, too uncomfortable, and its inhabitants led so very quiet a life that the gentry hereabouts assumed, correctly, that they had no taste for company. It slept on, without annoyance or disturbance, much as it had done for three centuries.

Bella's days were simple, and undisturbed, and the very few people who lived here existed in a small way. The household matters were few, now that the house was sealed up, and her needs were served by a staff of five. There were no decisions to be made, it seemed; or perhaps the housekeeper and the agent now did as the gardeners did, and made decisions as they thought best, and did not trouble her. It was all for the best, now. She, absorbed in her new life, assumed that her servants disapproved of her mildly, that they would rob her in small ways, but would organize the life of her little warren in a manner which left her in peace, and that would be best, all things considered. Her life had shrunk to what she deserved, and she was happy; she must, surely, be happy, since she never considered the matter, and if they did not even trouble to consult her over her dinner, she ate whatever the cook sent up placidly, like a child. She had lived like this for two years now, and there was no reason why she should ever live in any other way. There was no one to see her here, and she lay on the sofa and read novels quite early in the morning, with a diminishing sense of wrongdoing.

A visitor at Queen's Acre was a rare occurrence, and the housekeeper watched the approach of a solitary rider towards the house with considerable curiosity. From the upper window, Mrs. Bruton could see that he sat awkwardly in the saddle, and bounced up and down like a townsman. Poor beast, she thought, thinking of the horse, and, gathering up her mending, went down to see what the man could want here. By the time she reached the little stone bridge over the moat, the man was dismounting and looking about disconsolately for a groom to take charge. He was in his middle years, pink and balding, and entirely unfamiliar to her; it was difficult to suppress a smile of amusement at his elaborate urban bow in her general direction.

"A handsome house, madam," the fellow said. "If you would be so good—I have a great interest in these old houses—it would give me great pleasure to see over it. My name is Stokes, madam."

Mrs. Bruton nodded, agreeably. She supposed that some letter had preceded the fellow; it was so difficult to know, and as far as she knew, it might be lying unattended to by the agent, on madam's escritoire, or even dropped, unheeded, in the jar in the kitchen where the cook tended to put anything which the outside world supplied. Such a request had not been heard at Queen's Acre for some years, and though the housekeepers of more celebrated houses might have had a practised routine for gentlemen touring the county, she was not quite certain what to show this visitor with his sour London face and—all too apparently—in someone else's breeches. Still, she was fond of the old house, odd and ugly though it might seem, and much as she enjoyed complaining about all the twisting staircases and the terrible winter damp. It would do no harm to have a diversion from darning for an hour or so. She fished her immense bunch of keys from her wicker basket, and, goutily limping, led Stokes through the arch into the courtyard.

The housekeeper seemed dirty and unfriendly to Stokes, in whose imagination all housekeepers of country houses were clean, practical, and cheerful. If her appearance was disappointingly unrosy, and her apron not, as Stokes's beliefs required, clean and crisp and white, she also proved disgracefully unwilling to enlarge garrulously on the family. In

Stokes's opinion, a housekeeper ought to be extraordinarily loyal, and to need no encouragement to chatter about the virtues and kindnesses of the young masters and mistresses of the house. In the novelist's part of his mind, he was already wondering what place there might be at poor languishing Marplot Manor for a far more satisfactory example of the breed, and as they entered the house through a narrow stone door, he was already constructing the beginnings of a little story wherein Lady Belinda's old retainer might demonstrate a series of splendidly subordinate virtues. Life, he thought savagely, has far too few heroines, all in all, and was already cursing what promised to be another wasted hour, far from civilization.

"Is the family at home, madam?" he asked as they proceeded up a narrow back staircase.

"The family?" she said, over her shoulder.

"Yes, madam."

"No family, sir," she said. "Only my lady."

Stokes left it. They came to a door, and the housekeeper fumbled with keys for some time before finding the right one. Stokes followed her into a long low room. The furniture was all covered with dustsheets, and the saloon—as she announced it to be—presented the appearance of a room filled with gigantic blancmanges. She said nothing else, and Stokes stood and nodded encouragingly for a while.

"Very fine," he said in the end. It was too dark to see much, but, apparently satisfied, the housekeeper turned and led him out. Stokes resigned himself to more unassuageable country boredom.

"Do you care for pitchers, sir?" she said.

"Pitchers?" he said. Surely she was not going to show him the pantry?

"Pitchers," she repeated. "Pitchers of the fam'ly. This is the long gallery."

"Highly picturesque," Stokes supplied. In his view, all collections of family portraits were much the same, and none was very interesting to anyone not intimately related to the subject. The first in the dauntingly long line was a dirty unlearned portrait of Queen Elizabeth, apparently standing on the surface of a pond.

"The old Queen," the housekeeper said. Then she moved on to the next, a pasty gentleman in a ruff and hose, and said, "This is the old squire, from the old times."

"I see," Stokes said. "The house seems to me to have something of the flavour of—forgive me, madam, I forget the name of the house—the very celebrated castle, the Sussex house of the Harringtons. It is a great mystery, is it not, how some of these splendid old houses become the target of *virtuosi* and the object of aesthetic celebrity and others—others, such as this, truly no less beautiful—somehow remain to be found. A great mystery, madam."

"I don't know about that," she said, scrutinizing him. He resolved to make no more effort with his London charm. This could decently be cut short; he had enough for his evening story now, surely.

"A splendid old house," he said, briefly.

"This is his son," she went on. "This pitcher. They say he drowned in the moat, searching after the old King's treasure."

"Does his ghost still walk the house?" Stokes inquired, hopelessly.

"Not that I heard," she said. "This is old Thomas Garraway."

"Garraway?" Stokes said, surprised before an ambitious but not very lovely portrait of a fat archer with two greyhounds. "Garraway, did you say, madam?"

"Yes, sir," she said. "He was the old Colonel Garraway's great-great—let me see now—well, great-something-grandfather."

Stokes was silent, but thoughtful. He remembered now; an appallingly picturesque house in Gloucestershire, moated, inconvenient, too large for use. He recalled, too, the surprising disappearance of Bella Garraway from society, retired to the country with her poor health. He almost wasted another comment on the woman, then did not.

3

Bella set down her novel with a yawn. She rose, stretching her back, and went to the window. The house was so normally silent that her attention was drawn by small noises; she could distinguish the creaks and groans of an old house from the activities of the housemaids without effort, and she knew without having to consider when a voice and a tread in the wooden corridors was an unfamiliar one. She wondered, idly, who it could be; a man's voice, perhaps an irregular carpenter, talking to—surely—Mrs. Bruton. Yes, that was certainly Mrs. Bruton, with her keys rattling and her low Gloucestershire voice. She concentrated, and as the voices grew nearer, she realized with some surprise that the man's voice was that of a gentleman. She went back to her sofa, closed her novel, and placed it neatly on the table.

There was a low exchange of comments outside the door, Mrs. Bruton's unmistakable knock, and then she came in, half-shutting the door behind her.

"There's a gentleman, madam," Mrs. Bruton said, setting down her basket and keys. "He says he is acquainted with you, though I'm sure he only came to see over the house. I said you were indisposed."

She held out a piece of pasteboard, with Stokes's name on it. Bella took it; it meant nothing to her.

"I am quite well, Mrs. Bruton," she said. There was no reason to turn people away; she was no hermit, here. "Show the gentleman in."

Mrs. Bruton obviously disapproved, but did what she was asked. Stokes, entering, was no more familiar to Bella than his name, and she rose with a general but rather vague smile.

"An unforeseen pleasure, to find you here, Miss Garraway," Stokes said, accepting her invitation to a sofa. His voice fell on her strangely, but it took her a moment to recognize how long it had been since she had heard anyone who did not have an accent. "Forgive my unannounced intrusion."

"A pleasure to see an old friend," Bella said idly. She supposed she had met him, in some long-ago London drawing room; it all seemed so far away and unimportant now. "Most kind of you to pay a visit. Thank you, Mrs. Bruton. If you could be so good—yes, thank you, that will be all. I will ring."

He was looking her up and down, in a manner which seemed barely decent, as the housekeeper unwillingly retreated from the novel spectacle of a visitor at Queen's Acre. Of course, Bella thought, she had changed a great deal, and since he could only have known her in her London days, he would not necessarily be prepared for her matronly transformation, and his eyes seemed to be searching for the girl of five years ago in what she knew was a fat red country face. He appeared disconcerted, at a loss as he inspected her, as if searching for the right word to describe her so altered appearance. Coarsened, she silently supplied, you find me greatly coarsened, sir.

"An unexpected discovery, I have to say, madam," Stokes—was that the man's name?—went on. "I had heard of the great beauty of your house, and thought your housekeeper might be good enough to admit me. I had no idea that it was your house, or I should not have ventured to pay a visit in so very irregular a way."

"You are interested in old houses, sir?" Bella asked, trying to find her way in the conversation; he was so very much at her advantage.

"Most passionately, madam," he said. A silence fell.

"And I hope Mrs. Bruton was able to satisfy your curiosity?"

He looked at her oddly; perhaps that sounded less than civil. It was so hard to know.

"Indeed," he said. "I am in the country for a few days, a guest of your nautical neighbour. Admiral Doughty," he enlarged, seeing Bella's blank expression.

"Yes, I recall," Bella said. "I fear that the country hereabouts can offer few diversions to one accustomed to a London life."

"There is a lack of sound and fury among these harmonious hills, true," Stokes said, "but I never spend two days in such surroundings without reflecting how very much more rational a mode of existence you live than we poor cits in—"

Stokes broke off. There was an odd sound, somewhere nearby; a thin wailing cry. For a moment, he thought absurdly of his question to the housekeeper about the ghosts of the house. The cry was muted, as if by the closing of a door. It was only the strange sound which made him see how silent and empty the house truly was. Bella looked at him, composedly, as if she had heard nothing.

"—we poor cits," he persevered, "in our sooty little rooms."

She wished he would go now. Looking at Stokes in his absurd unfitting garb, Bella could not think that there was any truth in what he said—and she could not imagine that anyone, on the briefest examination, could describe her life, at least, as rational—and she replied with an equal and opposite untruth. "I greatly miss London, I confess, sir, but circumstances have forced my retirement, and I must make the best of it."

"I am sure your friends all greatly miss you, madam, and I will be pleased to carry the report that I have seen you and found you well. That will surely be a great consolation to the grief and concern which was so generally felt—I mean on hearing the news of your decline in spirits."

"That is most good of you, sir," Bella said. She felt unequal to talking about her health with this fellow. But conversation, in fact, was not something which withered with lack of practice, it seemed, she thought complacently, and she allowed her odd visitor to range over the dullest subjects for a few minutes like the hostess she once might have been. Only at the end of the conventional ten minutes did something go wrong, and it was not her fault, but Stokes's.

"I hope your father is well, Miss Garraway?" he asked brightly.

"I am afraid my father died, near on two years ago, sir," Bella said, untroubled.

"Miss Garraway—I am most heartily sorry—I had not heard. I would not for the world . . ." Stokes was thrown into confusion, and it was his abrupt change of demeanour which finally recalled him to her. Yes, she remembered him now; a literary man, an argufying sort of individual, always talking at the corners of London ballrooms, never deigning to dance, never seeming to notice the unserious diversions of his society.

"Really, sir, it is of no consequence," Bella said. She did not quite know why, but she felt like providing him with an excuse for his blunder, however false. "My father was in very poor health for some time, and so entirely had he withdrawn from the world that his end was little remarked by anyone but his family. It was not to be expected that you would know of it."

"I am most sorry, nevertheless, to have been the occasion of any pain to you," Stokes said, and, as if wretchedly certain that he could not retrieve his slip, stood up to go.

Bella levered herself up, and rang for Mrs. Bruton to show him out. There could hardly be anything but a thick silence now between the two near-strangers, but Bella surprised herself by breaking it, and hearing herself inviting Stokes to call again before he left the country. Perhaps it was his confusion at the last, but she felt a little sorry for him, and did not mind at all that he immediately accepted, with an unexpected and genuine pleasure. When she was alone again, she did not return to her novel, but went over and sat at the escritoire. A letter from her sister had lain unanswered for a week now, stuffed into the half-open top drawer, since Bella had had no news to convey, no sentiments to express; but if, now, she had an event to interest Elizabeth, she found, after sitting for a while in absent thought, that she did not quite want to mention it, and the letter she sealed after an hour contained nothing but the usual mild reflections about the weather and the servants. There was so much, in truth, that Bella did not think about; there was so much that did not enter her thoughts, so much that lay unconsidered in a life that was now past, that might have been that of a distant acquaintance. What she had once done was simply not present to her mind; her London life, her girl's life, was as remote and unimagined as China. Her happiness was of an oblivious, uncontemplative nature, and as the indifferent days went by, she was entirely absorbed, like water falling onto a verdant land.

When Bella sat at the little desk, which faced the wall, she could see the window in the mirror. The light here was subdued, blocked by the steep-rising slopes which surrounded the house, and the look of the outside world, in the mirror, was of some dim swimming underwater landscape. She sat, hypnotized, and did not see the door behind her opening. The maid came in with her luncheon, and set it down.

"Has he been good?" Bella asked, without turning round.

"We've been very good, haven't we?" the maid said, in that especial emphatic way, and realizing from the way she spoke that she had brought her son in with the tray, Bella turned, a ready smile on her face. Bella's child hung back at first, until he saw his mother, and then his smile matched hers, and he ran forward to kiss her, stomping in his infant way as he went. She spread her arms out for him.

"You've been a good boy, haven't you, Henry? You've been a good boy for Mary?"

"Good boy," Henry said, delighted.

"You've been quiet all morning," Bella said. "I was listening, and you didn't make a sound."

"Very good boy," Henry said, in a full, satisfied tone, as if he were supplying a deficiency.

"What have we been doing?"

The boy seemed too full of joy to speak at first, and then the nursemaid helped him out. "We cut paper shapes—and then—"

He started on a long complicated explanation, his new words falling over each other like his hilarious run, and, though Bella could not understand everything, she nodded seriously, her big eyes fixed on his, her face holding his excitement.

"If you are good," Bella said, "you can come and have tea with Mamma, and then, before bedtime, we can go and look at your flowerbed with Mary. Would you like that?"

"He's turning into a proper little countryman, madam," the nursemaid said. "He was talking about his flowerbed all morning."

"I do hope he isn't a nuisance to the gardeners," Bella said.

"Oh, no, madam," she said. "Good as gold, he is."

"Today?" Henry said.

"If you are good," Bella said. "Would you like to hear a story?"

Henry nodded.

"A sad story? Or a merry one?"

"Sad," Henry said.

"Yes," Bella said, wondering a little. "Yes, a sad tale's best." The nurse left, noiselessly, and Bella began. "Once upon a time—beyond the horizon—beyond the ninth horizon, and the ninth horizon beyond that—there lived a beautiful princess in a great glass palace. She lived alone, since her mother and father were dead, and she was very lonely. Now, in the garden of her palace there was a magical tree, surrounded by walls of glass. Its trunk was gold, and its leaves were silver, and when it bore fruit, the fruit was emeralds and diamonds and rubies. Nobody knew how long the tree had been there, and people said it was older than the palace itself, and older than the memory of men. The glass garden was the princess's favourite place, and she went there, often, to be alone. And one day, she was sitting underneath the tree, and found herself saying, 'Tree, leaves, roots, and fruit, tell me who can cure my wound.' For she was so very lonely and unhappy that she felt her unhappiness like a wound.

"But when she spoke to the tree, something strange happened. There was a rustling from the leaves, although there was no wind, and the branches seemed to creak, and then the princess heard a voice. She looked around her, but there was no one near her, and then she understood that it was the tree, speaking to her. And the tree said, 'Princess, I can cure your loneliness. But first you must kiss me three times: once on my roots, once on my trunk, and once on my leaves. And if you do that, I shall fall and die, but in my place you shall have a child, whose hair will be black as coal, whose skin white as frost, whose eyes blue as the sky.'

"At first the princess would not do this, because she loved the tree, and did not wish it to die. But the tree said again what it had said, and slowly the princess thought that her loneliness mattered more to her. 'If you do this,' the tree said, 'you must chop up my trunk, and make of me a cradle for your child, and then I will have served my purpose.' So she kissed the tree three times, as it had asked, once on the roots, once on the trunk, and once on the leaves, and all at once, the tree fell on the grass, so gently it hardly made a noise. And as it did so, the princess heard a call from the highest tower of her palace, and she ran inside. Up and up the stairs of the highest tower she went, until she came to the upmost room: and there, lying in swaddling clothes, was a baby, whose hair was black as coal, whose skin was white as frost, whose eyes were blue as the sky, and the princess was so filled with joy she cried . . ."

Henry was a good boy, and responded as seriously to the idea of stories as of treats. Bella's story wound on, as the cradle grew into a bed for the child, then a marriage bed, and then a coffin, and that was the sad story, winding and unwinding behind the boy's blue eyes, blue as the sky. It was when he frowned in concentration that he took on the look of Burnes. In some ways he was different every day. His life changed from hour to hour as he learnt something new. To have a child was to place a being under a glass, and watch the swarming invisible events of a small new life, the instantaneous quick changes, and each day left behind for ever. She, now, had no new days; each fresh newness was in him, and she was pleased. She never thought of Burnes. She had a child.

He listened silently to the very end of the story, which was his own story, and in a moment she kissed him, patted him on the head, and let him return to the nursery. It was so hard to say goodbye, and whenever she sat here, in her room, whatever activity seemed to occupy her, in her mind was always the idea that she might set it down, go to the nursery, and kiss her boy, for no reason whatever, as if she had been separated from him for months. Sometimes she did that very thing. She never regretted it.

4

The housekeeper turned back without a comment, dropping Stokes's proffered shillings gracelessly in her basket, and left him at the entrance to the house. Stokes stood there for a moment, with his horse. He tried, in his routine way, to begin the retelling in his head, to start to practise the anecdote he would tell at dinner. "I had an odd—no, an interesting— adventure today," he began, but then it obstinately halted. He had had an odd, no, an interesting adventure today, that was true, but what was it? He tried again; poor Bella Garraway, so changed, so dull, and once she had been . . . Well, what had she been? What, in truth, had he seen, now? What was there that could be told to Castleford and his dull sister and their dull guests? Something—some story, true—had been vouchsafed to him, and he knew that there was no betrayal like the telling of it to people he despised. People—he surprised himself—people unlike Bella. He had had an odd, no, an interesting adventure. There it was, undeniable, but behind him, and for once it would not become anecdote. No, he would not return.

The house was odd and ugly and indescribable, but it had opened its great gates to him, once, and closed them now behind him. Where the romance had been in the previous hour, he could not quite say, but there was a distinct whiff of the fairy tale about it. No stranger had walked through those gates for months—no stranger had been admitted by those gates, rather. He could feel it as if he had hacked his way through a hedge of roses. The house had opened, once, mysteriously, to him, and in there was something he had been shown, a riddle he had to solve. He felt that. He had left Bella no more than five minutes before, but now it seemed as if he were looking back at the end of a very long life, at a single pure memory; he felt as if now he could say that it had only been a quarter of an hour, but he had never forgotten it. The transformed girl, the fat girl lying in her panelled warren, buried deep within the dark house. What was she waiting for? What kept her here? The air, in those rooms, was thick with thought, but between him and Bella's thoughts there was an absolute barrier. For a moment, he had been made to forget his breeches, his discomfort, his country boredom, and had felt like a hero. He had overcome the first tests his quest had presented, and had fallen at the last. Already Stokes wanted to return, but as he rode away, he felt inexplicably that that was something which the house would not permit. The house had appeared, before him, and offered its strange spectacle; if he returned, trying to enter for a second time, it seemed altogether plausible that the park, the palace, the moat, might have disappeared. He rode off, preparing to make his excuses to the waiting Castleford.

FIFTEEN

I

On 23 September, 183——, by the side of the road not many versts from the small Crimean town of ——, a gentleman of respectable demeanour but clad in a decidedly rusty black coat and breeches, no longer of middle age, was pacing up and down, and periodically gazing down the empty road to the distant horizon.

"'E won't come no sooner for you being impatient for 'im, sah," his companion observed. This was a sallow and gaunt manservant, well dressed but rather exhausted looking, with sunken cheeks and heavy bags beneath his eyes.

The landowner made no reply, except to extract from his waistcoat pocket a gold watch, as round as a turnip. Like his clothes, it was made somewhat in the fashion of twenty-five years before. He examined it closely, and then replaced it.

"Patience is a godly virtue, sah," the manservant supplied. The gentleman gave a great sigh, and, fanning himself with the back of his hand, went to sit down heavily by the side of his elegant manservant, who confined himself to the habit of turning his garnet ring round his little finger.

We will leave the gentleman sitting there, while we acquaint the reader with his history, occupation, and character.

His name is Nikolai Mikhailovich Layevsky. The estate he occupies, of the middle size of a few hundred serfs, is some twenty versts from where he sits, by the side of what the locals loosely call "the Moscow road." Fifty years ago, his father, who was ultimately of the old nobility, moved to the Crimea, then newly taken into the empire, in search of new land. For more generations than he could count, the family of Mikhail Petrovich Layevsky, the father of the present Layevsky, had farmed the earth in the ancient lands of Muscovy, and no Layevsky had ever thought that any-thing, for his sons and grandsons, would ever be any different.

The family's estates had been enough for centuries, but some time in the late eighteenth century, Mikhail Petrovich became troubled by the depletion of his land. Although the estate was large, each time a daughter of the family married, her dowry included a certain number of serfs and a portion of the estate. Mikhail Petrovich grew convinced—he would not assess it, but he was sure—that his estate was no bigger than half what it had been in his great-grandfather's time. Since this diminishment had come about through no fault or extravagance of his own, but only through his behaving as the head of a family ought to, this was a constant worry to his sense of honour.

From time to time, Mikhail Petrovich had heard reports about the land to be had in the Crimea; tales of its abundance and beauty, and also reports that vast and fecund tracts of lands could be had for absurdly small sums of money. Mikhail Petrovich was a wise man, who was not easily persuaded by travellers' tales, but after some years of hearing such stories about the Crimea, he started to believe that they must be true. So in 1786, he sold the handsome Muscovy estates of his ancestors, serfs, lands, orchards, and all, and travelled to the Crimea.

Mikhail Petrovich had, indeed, acquired a large and beautiful tract of land for very little, and since then, he and, after his death, his son lived there in great happiness. His son and heir, Nikolai Mikhailovich, was only eight years old when he first came to the Crimea. As they came into the country, Nikolai Mikhailovich was not likely to forget his first memory. He had no education or sensibility, but the natural beauty of the country powerfully impressed itself on his ideas. The scent of the forests and fields, carried on the breeze as they travelled along the rough roads, made him close his eyes and try to commit the feeling to memory; the dense border of bird cherries, meadowsweet, cat grass, guelder roses throwing their scent into the warm breeze. When the party stopped, Nikolai Mikhailovich was allowed to drink from the rivers and, once, even to swim while the family and their servants took a rest beneath the wild fruit trees of the region. He always remembered how clear the rivers seemed, however deep they were, so that a white rock on the bed of a river three yards deep seemed to glisten under the hand as if just below the surface.

The land was as cheap and as plentiful as had been foretold, and Mikhail Petrovich Layevsky easily acquired a substantial and beautiful estate with little trouble. There he settled down with his wife, Agafeya Vasilevna Layevskaya, a modest and benevolent woman, whose keenly felt duties to the poor and the sick never diminished the love she felt for her husband and her three sons, Nikolai Mikhailovich and his two younger brothers, Pavel and Stepan.

When Nikolai reached the age of eighteen, he was sent to St. Petersburg to become a student. The life of the capital did not enchant him; though to us, it may seem that society there is quiet and even somewhat dull, Nikolai Mikhailovich found himself longing for the simple life of the Crimea, and repined for the smell of grass, the song of birds, and the clean taste of the water on his father's estate.

Nor did the life of the mind hold much appeal to him, and, when his father died, five years after his departure, he returned home with a sadness in his heart which only masked the relief he felt at taking up a life which was truly his own. He married the daughter of a country neighbour as soon as mourning was at an end, and settled down to a quiet existence, interested only in his voluminous correspondence on agricultural innovations and hearing trivial gossip about his serfs.

His two brothers took quite different courses in life; Pavel Mikhailovich took up a commission in a Guards regiment, and was killed in the course of 1812. Stepan Mikhailovich was sent to the Corps of Pages at the age of twelve, and, growing up to be a generally agreeable young man, found no difficulty in obtaining a place at court.

"How can Stepan bear such a melancholy fate?" Nikolai Mikhailovich would lament to his family whenever his brother's name was mentioned, while the samovar bubbled, and the perfumed pine logs crackled and spat in the fireplace. "Ribbons and silk stockings, bowing and precedence!" Stepan Mikhailovich, who became a great dandy, as devoted to his corset as to his mistress, and was rumoured in St. Petersburg not to know a single word of Russian, would certainly have lamented as long and sincerely over the tedious life led by his brother in the depths of the country.

Thus was Nikolai Mikhailovich's life for nearly twenty years.

In 1815, the barley crops failed.

In 1819, a very dirty and wild-eyed monk appeared from nowhere and lived in a shed for several weeks, until it became apparent that he was preaching sedition to the serfs.

In 1826, a cow gave birth to a two-headed calf.

In 1829, influenza took hold of the estate, seizing several victims, including Mme Layevskaya, whom Nikolai Mikhailovich genuinely loved.

A cuckoo may be found in the most remote and secure of nests. When Nikolai Mikhailovich told his eldest son, Pavel Nikolaievich, that his mother had died in the night, the boy stared over the breakfast table at his father, shedding fat tears into his spadelike beard, and said, "Then I suppose I must go into the army." It stopped Nikolai short; he did not see the necessity at all.

Pavel Nikolaievich had been named after that heroic uncle, dead in the mud, defending Russia from Napoleon. As soon as he could walk, it appeared that, whether by name or by nature, he was to be a soldier. His favourite occupation while still in skirts was to hoist a branch over his shoulder, in imitation of a gun, and to attempt to drill the chickens, as if on parade ground duty. He never walked when he could march, and rode so early that his swaddling served double duty as his saddle, as the saying goes. Long afternoons were spent in the meadows re-enacting the Battle of Borodino, and amending the conclusion, with the aid of dozens of children from the village. Nikolai Mikhailovich complained regularly about these battles of his son, since they took labour away from the fields, but saw no means of combating Pavel Nikolaievich's enthusiasm for all things military.

Upon the death of his mother, Pavel Nikolaievich prevailed in his wish to be a soldier. His application to go into an imperial regiment as a cadet succeeded, since it was supported by his uncle, Stepan Mikhailovich, the court dandy, and Pavel travelled to St. Petersburg to pursue his ambition.

That had been five years before, and now we see Nikolai Mikhailovich, a little older, a little greyer and shabbier, his nose grown big and warty as a pickled gherkin. With his manservant Arkady, he is sitting at the side of the road in September, a third of the way into the century, awaiting Pavel Nikolaievich, returning from his regiment for three weeks' leave.

2

Heavens, how dull it was! A black-legged hen wandered out from the fields into the road, and started pecking at some piece of dry root, tugging at it without success. Nikolai took his handkerchief out, and mopped his brow; it was hotter than it should be, even at the end of this long summer, and he hoped Pavel Nikolaievich would not be many more hours.

Arkady rose, stretching himself, and peered down the road. "I see something, sah," he said at length. "I definitely see something approaching."

Nikolai got up quickly, and looked in the same direction. He leapt up so sharply that he startled the doves in the trees, which stopped their cooing and rattled off in a flock, into the sky. Yes, that was certainly the coach coming! And with that, all the irritation at being kept waiting dissolved at the anticipation of seeing his fine young son for the first time in five years.

To stand and wait like this is the strangest of feelings; not far from boredom, and yet not boredom, since your feelings are a turmoil of excitement and worry. Nikolai Mikhailovich stood, his feet tingling, and stared at the road he had known with all his senses for fifty years as if he had never seen it before. But Arkady was right, there was a coach approaching, throwing up a cloud of dust like a cockfight, approaching at half the speed of thought. It seemed forever, but suddenly the coach was within sight, within earshot, and then, all at once, the sharp reek of the sweating horses. Pavel Nikolaievich, a splendid and shining sight in his brilliant imperial uniform, his cloak tossed negligently over his shoulder, leapt down from the tarantass in one easy movement and embraced his father warmly.

To look at them, the father so dusty and shabby, the son so shining-fresh and handsome, you would have thought that it was the elder who had travelled for two days. But the eager anticipation which precedes a reunion of this sort produces different effects on different people, and, though they had both longed to see each other in very much the same way, Nikolai felt exhausted by his eagerness, just as Pavel's had rejuvenated him. They held each other at arm's length, and looked at each other; and then you could see, in the way they both raised their eyebrows, that they were father and son.

"Very pleased to have you back, sah," Arkady said.

"Let me introduce you to my friend Vitkevich," Pavel said quickly. Nikolai let him go from his embrace, and looked at the long dark figure just now getting out of the tarantass. "He has been so good as to travel with me, and is kind enough to stay with us for a week or two, while he is surveying the land hereabouts. I have written to you about him. My friend, Vitkevich, you know, of whom my uncle speaks so well."

Vitkevich was a tall young man of saturnine appearance, wearing a stovepipe hat and splendidly flaring whiskers. In a long black travelling cloak, he seemed encumbered by his possessions, and Pavel had gone on talking to allow him time to dismount and assemble himself. He fussily tugged and pulled at his cloak, rearranging it, while all the time giving blunt, unconfident gestures towards the coachman now handing down the dusty wooden trunk, fastened with frayed brown leather straps.

"Mr.—" Nikolai Mikhailovich said. Then he recollected himself. It was true that he was not accustomed to company, and especially not to company with foreign names, but he knew, all the same, how to behave. "Mr. Vitkevich, I am delighted to make your acquaintance. Did you have a pleasant journey?"

"Wretched, wretched," Vitkevich said, gesturing to the coachman. "This fellow . . ."

"Arkady, Arkady," Nikolai Mikhailovich said, and his manservant leapt forward to deal with the coachman. Here, in the road, the dust hung, subsided, and the horses, foaming-black and sweating, waited edgily for their water. Nikolai felt terribly tired, and, looking at his son, he realized the cause of the anxiety which had kept him from sleep these last few nights. In the air, a cloud of dust and seed hung in the heavy bright sunlight, as if a thousand old carpets had been taken up and beaten by a thousand beaters. The afternoon resumed its cautious course, disturbed by the wild arrival of the tarantass down the road; the air, quivering a little in the heat, was stirred by the large lolloping of a dark rabbit, venturing back across the road.

"Look, Vitkevich," Pavel suddenly said.

"You are here to . . . my son said . . ."

"To survey the land," Vitkevich said. Pavel beamed, as if proud of his friend.

"You mean to buy land here, then?" Nikolai said. "I may assure you, there is no land in the empire—"

"No, no, sir," Vitkevich said, somewhat petulantly. "No, I have no plans to buy land. I merely have the intention of surveying it."

"Vitkevich is deep, papa, deep in the knowledge of agricultural reforms," Pavel Nikolaievich added quickly.

"And the question of the serfs," Vitkevich said. "That is my central subject of interest, to pursue which, your son has so kindly invited me to stay with you for some time."

"The question of the serfs," Nikolai said. "Well, sir, you will find us as up-to-date in our farming as any estate in the empire, and our serfs, I dare say, as happy in the lives God has given them to lead as you or I. But you will see for yourself. Now, sir, we must not delay."

Arkady bowed with his low, embarrassed bow, not precisely directed at anyone, but beyond the little group.

The house of the Layevsky estate, Boguslavo, was not at all old; it had been built thirty years before by Nikolai's father. But it had a restfully traditional air, like the houses of a previous age, and everyone who dwells in such a house finds it calming in every season. A long sinuous road, firmly laid and with well-kept ditches, led from the gates of the estate to the yellow-painted house. On either side of the road, fields of long grass were shimmering gold in the afternoon heat. Peasants greeted the tarantass with a single raised arm and a doff of their caps; they were all clean and healthy looking, well fed and smocked. Their faces had that ruddy flush which only good plain living and a benevolent master may supply. In the air, a sunlit cloud of dust raised by mowing and threshing hung, and the whole scene was bathed in a soft, blurred radiance. To Layevsky, who had not seen his ancestral home for some years, the scene was like a glimpse of heaven. He had spent the previous years confined to St. Petersburg, and although he had grown accustomed to look upon the thin, pale, refined sickliness in which the majority of that city's inhabitants pass their days, he had not forgotten the healthful life of the country and its refreshing beauty. By the road, now, a female serf, plump and pretty, her gold-blonde hair wound up about her head, smiled and waved with all her loose-shouldered arm at the gentry, swaddled up like invalids in their tarantass. In the field behind her, an older man, peacefully binding up the harvest with slow, deliberate movements, broke into song. It was "Rush-light," and others, across the field, took up the tune. A partridge, there, was put up by a scythe, and through the golden-hot afternoon, molten like honey, it flew for safety, its wings going clattering through the air. Pavel shut his eyes for a second, as if hoping to save the afternoon in his mind for ever. It was so beautiful, the day he remembered from his childhood, and so different, and it was only he who had changed.

"Look, Vitkevich," he said as the tarantass drove on, not quite knowing what he was urging on his friend's attention.

Vitkevich had been sniffing helplessly for some time. It was clear that the atmosphere of Boguslavo affected Layevsky and his friend in quite different ways. "To you," he said through streaming eyes, "this may represent a vista of uncommon beauty. To me, it only represents a hundred opportunities for improvement."

Nikolai Mikhailovich shot his son's friend a startled glance from the box where he sat.

"I could not imagine a single way in which this place could be improved," Pavel said. He was overflowing with happiness, and nothing could intrude on his joy. "In any case, you do see the beauty of it—you see what I see, or you guess at it."

Vitkevich grunted, as if this were merely quibbling.

3

Presently, the vehicle drew up in front of the house, and, without waiting for it to stop, Pavel leapt out. From the shady entrance, Masha stepped forward, her clean round ruddy face filled with excitement. Pavel embraced her warmly, and then stepped back to look at her.

"How well you look, dear Masha!" he said. "How often have I thought of you in Petersburg!"

"Pavel Nikolaievich!" she said, gazing at the splendid officer she had known all his life. It seemed as if the transformation from the youngster with dirty knees, demanding sweetmeats from the kitchen stores, to the fine young officer with his superb whiskers, was too much for her to understand, as if it had happened in a moment. "Pavel Nikolaievich!" she said again, too burdened with happiness to express herself, and then, all at once, burst into tears of joy.

Pavel embraced her again, laughing, and then turned round. "How badly you treat my dear Masha, papa!" he cried. "See what few pleasures you permit her, that a single kiss from her little nuisance can make her cry so!"

Nikolai Mikhailovich stood back, delighted. Nothing could please him more than that Pavel would resume his old friendship with the cook, whatever changes had occurred in Masha's life and position in the last years.

"Little nuisance," Masha sniffed. "Yes, my own little nuisance. I promise never to call so fine an officer such a thing, ever again."

"If you promise to call me nothing else," Pavel said, kissing her tears away, "I promise that I will never be unhappy again. Dear Masha! Vitkevich, Vitkevich, what are you doing? Come and kiss my dear old Masha, of whom you have heard so much!"

Vitkevich was peevishly sniffing, and extracting himself cautiously from the vehicle.

"How terrible the roads are, here," he said. "My poor body is black and blue with bruises. Truly, I have never known the like, and you know I am not one to complain at physical discomfort."

Pavel laughed and laughed, as if he had never heard anything so funny. "Never mind that now, you ass," he said. "Get down and come and let Masha kiss you. Don't mind him, Masha, that's just his way. You will grow to love him as much as I do, I promise. Come here, you old bear."

"Ass, bear—my dear fellow, I can hardly be both. I am most heartily pleased to meet you, madam," he said, bowing deeply and offering a languid hand in her direction as Pavel released her. Masha seemed to doubt that she would grow to love so very queer a fish, but she took his hand, and bobbed at the top of his brilliantly shining coiffure. Nikolai came up, and gave a single, quick, proprietorial kiss on the top of her forehead before leading the way into the house.

Over dinner that night, Nikolai thought, he would put the proposal he had determined on to his son Pavel, to go shooting the next day.

Masha had laboured hard over the dinner. For some days, Nikolai had been aware, from her steady troubled expression as much as from the rows of game, fruit, and fish hanging in the cold-larder, that her mind was made up in one respect at least. She, and the household, would welcome Pavel home with a dinner of which anyone in the empire could be proud.

Nikolai had made no specific instruction regarding the food. However, he was pleased that Masha had made the decision herself to kill the fatted calf, as it were, on his returning son's behalf. The dinner might not be able to rival the elegant culinary dissemblances and contrivances of the St. Petersburg soirées Pavel was used to. Nikolai felt, however, with a strength of emotion not usual for him, that his estate and Masha's best efforts could, at any rate, provide a dinner which would not be surpassed in the quality of culinary virtue and honesty.

Pavel, accustomed and, perhaps, fatigued by dishes which attempted to disguise the origins and substance of their constituent parts, might prefer this honest cooking to a cuisine which aimed mainly to deceive the palate. He might even find true novelty and delight in a dinner where the food was not perpetually entombed, *en gelée, en croute, à la mode,* but abundantly itself.

So powerfully had Nikolai Mikhailovich felt the charm of the unadorned productions of his own stretch of earth that, for some days past, he had found himself involuntarily turning into the cold-larder where the game and hams hung. Here, too, the soft cheese swayed in its muslin bag, dripping peacefully into a bowl. Looking at the limp partridge and heavy, glossy hare, noting from the single twisted-off claw that two of the pheasants had been shot three days ago by Vanya, and the last of them on Friday last, Nikolai felt his pleasure to be complete.

As he stood in the cold-larder, walled against the heat and farm-noise of the day, feeling the sweet warm smell of animal, earth, blood, fruit, he was convinced that the ends of simplicity were served best by the larder, and not by the dinner table. It was then, in the quiet tense days before Pavel's arrival, that he decided to take Pavel shooting. After Masha's splendid, prodigal dinner, Pavel Nikolaievich would welcome the proposal. It would be a treat for his son (in his mind, muddled a little by the good raw smell of the dinner to come, he thought for a moment of his soldier son as still a small boy, playing war, only, in the fields). But it would also be an education; a re-education; a reminder.

His son and the curious guest retreated to their rooms, and slept. As Masha tiptoed upstairs, she heard the comforting sound of Pavel snoring in his room. No one had slept in that room since Pavel left, and she smiled, still tearfully, at the comforting feeling that the house was full again. With no one there but Nikolai Mikhailovich, it was not the same. She still counted herself among the servants, as no one, and although everyone knew that her place in the house was not as it had been when the mistress was alive, she was not someone who would ever have wanted to be treated as the mistress of the house. In former times, she would have said that she knew her place, but the truth was that now, she did not.

She stood at the top of the stairs, listening to the comforting sound of Pavel's snoring. How tired he must have been! In a moment a pair of arms embraced her from behind. She had not heard the master tiptoeing up the stairs.

"Nikolai Mikhailovich!" she whispered.

"Still crying, my little bird?" Nikolai said. "Is it so sad that Pavel Nikolaievich has returned to his father's home?"

"No, I am not crying for that," she said seriously. "I don't know why I am crying—"

"You are crying because you are a very good girl," Nikolai said, kissing her tears away. "And because—"

"Please," Masha began. "Do not tell him—do not tell him about—he would not like it. His mamma . . ."

"He loves you as much as he ever did, and you have always been a second mother to him," Nikolai said. "Do not fret."

"But you will not—"

"No," Nikolai said, holding her to him. "I will not tell him, if that is what you wish. Now, there is so much to be made ready, is there not?"

"Yes, Nikolai Mikhailovich," Masha said, and, wiping her face on her apron, went downstairs to the kitchen to prepare the great feast. Nikolai watched her go, and then went into his study to polish his guns, which were kept there.

4

The family reassembled shortly before dinner in the salon. When Nikolai came in, wearing a new stock and a clean white shirt, in his son's honour, he found Vitkevich bending awkwardly over the card table and inspecting the titles of the books. He was still sniffing furiously. Layevsky stood there in the doorway for a moment, then saw that there was no reason for him to feel shy in his own house, and walked in, coughing slightly. Vitkevich straightened and threw him a quick hostile glance before bowing with ceremonious coldness.

"I hope you are quite comfortable, sir," Nikolai said.

"Quite so, quite so," Vitkevich said. "I slept but little, but I had an adequate rest. I find it difficult to sleep in the afternoons, sir, however tired I feel. Thank you for your kind solicitude."

"We so rarely have guests, sir, you must forgive any rustic neglect," Layevsky said. "I do hope you will be patient and treat us as you would any simple peasant. Tell me, how is Petersburg changed in the last twenty years?"

"I hardly know, sir, so recent has my acquaintance with the city been," Vitkevich said. "I believe it to be much as it was, however; still filled with duchesses and subalterns, and the constant pursuit of merriment. So tiring for one of my fragile disposition."

"I am sorry to hear you suffer from poor health," Layevsky said. "It is nothing too serious, I hope."

"Wretched," Vitkevich said. "There is nothing more fragile than— well, you do not wish, I am sure, to hear of my poor troubles."

Nikolai bowed, having no response to this. "No, do tell me," and "Yes, it would be rather dull," were equally impossible. Vitkevich turned and walked to the end of the dark wood room, and stood there with his back to his host, gazing out of the window. Pavel came into the room, looking refreshed and pink from the bath.

"Mr. Vitkevich was telling me he suffers from poor health," Nikolai said. "I presume, sir, you are confined to Petersburg in your army duties."

"No, papa, not one bit of it," Pavel said. "Vitkevich, you must learn to complain less. Some day, someone will believe what you say. Poor health? Papa, the man is a lion; he goes for days living off the land, and drinking water from puddles which the beasts of the field would turn their noses up at. Complaining, I admit, complaining without cease, but he is strong as an ox. Vitkevich, admit the fact; your poor health is a fiction. It is your favourite occupation, to guard it and complain of its tenderness, but living as you do, travelling through uncharted wastes, fighting and brawling, there is no question that you have anything but the most robust constitution. I heartily wish I was as strong as you."

"Nonsense, nonsense," Vitkevich protested, and turned back to the view. It seemed as if this were a familiar exchange between the two of them. He picked up a book from the set on the walnut card table. "Do you care for Balzac, sir?" he said to Nikolai. Nikolai made a slight bow, not immediately understanding what Vitkevich was referring to. "I *adore* Balzac," he went on, putting the book down again.

"I heartily wish I had the strength," Pavel went on, ignoring all this, "to lay siege to all those belles. That, Vitkevich, is a more impressive witness of your physical hardiness than any number of campaigns."

"Some day, Layevsky, you will go too far," Vitkevich said. "And I believe your cook has come to summon us to dine."

Masha was standing in the doorway, nervously smiling. She had removed her apron, and her skirt and blouse were clean; her face had been scrubbed and her hair pinned up. And perhaps she thought, standing there, that the family would not mind too much if . . . Nikolai gave a deep nod to her, and smiled in an embarrassed way, not looking quite at her, and led the way towards the dining room. He walked past her, not taking her arm or bringing her with them, as if it were quite normal that the cook of the house should come to the salon to summon the family to table. She followed them, a few steps behind, then, at the door of the dining room, seemed to lose her nerve, and went back to the kitchen. She did not know why she had believed for a moment that Nikolai Mikhailovich would ask her to sit down with his son and their guest.

5

The change in Masha's position in the household had come about quite suddenly, and without her quite understanding it. She had always lived on the Layevsky estate, and all her life had never ventured more than forty versts from Boguslavo. The world began just there, at the end of the road, and was all the same; a strange distant fairy tale, peopled with monsters and wars. In her mind, at the end of the road were tartars, the Tsar Napoleon, and men whose heads grew below their shoulders. What she knew was Boguslavo, and the family within it, and that was good enough for her. Masha's father had been an estate carpenter, and when she was twelve, the mistress felt she was willing, clever, and agreeable enough to be taken into the kitchen. Over the years, the family grew to depend on her sensible abilities, and to love her. She learnt to read and write without any fuss, and for years she quietly ran the house, grateful for everything. She always knew where the best mushrooms could be found, never pilfered, never complained, had half a dozen clever ways with any game bird, and was neat and honest with the household accounts.

The influenza of 1829 roamed through the estate like a savage hungry bear. Beginning with a slight ache and a rough throat, within days it required its victims to take to their beds with a cough which racked their bones and echoed through the still winter night. The first to die was Masha's brother, who, like his father, was a carpenter, and she sincerely grieved for him. At first it only took hold of the peasants, but one night at dinner, Mme Layevskaya began to complain of a slight ache and tiredness, and retired early. Masha, serving the men of the family with a dish of potatoes, did not meet their expression; she did not want them to see any fear in her eyes.

The mistress had always been kind to Masha, and over the next weeks she nursed a steady decline with easy dishes. At first, with simple dishes of plain vegetables; then, after a day when she had watched Mme Layevskaya trying to spear a single slippery mushroom on her little fork, and growing tearful at her weak failure, Masha supplied only beef tea and unsleeping kindness. Whenever Nikolai Mikhailovich came into the sickroom, looking as frightened as if death had already laid his hand on the mistress, Masha was always there, wiping her mistress's delirious brow as if there were no possibility that she would not mend.

A day before she died, Mme Layevskaya seemed to improve a great deal, and even sat up in bed for a time. The household and the family began, prematurely, to rejoice, but Masha said nothing. She had seen the look in the mistress's eyes, and knew what it meant. She only felt sorry for the master, and, besides, by this time, she herself was beginning to feel ill.

She took to her bed a day after the mistress died, and remained there for two weeks. In her, the influenza stood no chance; she was too young and strong, and certain that she, too, must not die, for the sake of the family. And yet, when she returned to the kitchen, pale and thin and tired, she felt guilty above all; guilty that the mistress, who had been so good, had been taken and she spared. For a long time she could not look at Nikolai Mikhailovich's despairing eyes, and concentrated only on running the affairs of the kitchen and the house as well as she could, certain in her conviction that, if she had anything to do with it, the gentry would have no more troubles than they were already afflicted with. The bestial hungry influenza had done its worst, and gone elsewhere; where, Masha could not think.

The spring had always been Masha's favourite time. It began so suddenly, like a bough breaking, a still bird taking flight. One day there was nothing but chill and damp in the air, and the next there was a warm wind, bearing the scents of pine and meadow-grass into the house. On these days, she could never resist leaving the kitchen for an hour, and walking through the clean damp grass, for the sheer pleasure of it. If challenged, she would have had a ready kitchen excuse, but in truth it was her one idle hour of the year.

It was the spring after the mistress died, and she was walking through the woods when all at once Nikolai Mikhailovich appeared, as if he had been hiding behind a birch tree. She blushed, immediately, and dropped a curtsy.

"Masha," he said, as if there were no time to lose. "I am so lonely."

She curtsied again, not knowing what to say to this. She had never heard any of the gentry say anything about their feelings; she had no doubt that they had them, just as she had no doubt about the emotions of animals. She herself had said, many times, "Poor Nikolai Mikhailovich!" after the mistress had died, but somehow their feelings were not like hers; their grief was the gentry's grief, and something more solemn and unspeakable than the practical, intense worry she had had when her brother or father had died. That the master would stand before her and say briefly that he was lonely was something nothing had prepared her for.

"So lonely," he said again, and when she looked, his eyes were filling with tears.

"Poor Nikolai Mikhailovich," she said, astonished at her own daring and almost speechless. She did not understand loneliness, and all at once she found herself wondering whether she herself had ever been lonely. It seemed absurd; there had always been the family, and Boguslavo, and the kitchen to keep her occupied, and the hundreds of serfs she had known all her life. She wondered, all at once, if she had ever been lonely, and then it seemed to her that she had always been lonely, and not understood it because she had known nothing else to compare it with. She was thirty-five, and Nikolai Mikhailovich had said simply that he was lonely, and for the first time she was considering her life, and not his. So strange.

"Dear Masha," Layevsky said, simply, and with a single movement he lowered his tear-filled face to hers, and she found that he was kissing her. Her arms spread wide, and, not knowing how to embrace, her hands fluttered at the air, but she did not move. Nothing came to her mind but a single sentence—*Nikolai Mikhailovich is kissing me*—as if she had to speak what was happening to understand it. There, the scent of birch, the damp good earth underneath her thin boots, the clean fresh air, the taste of tobacco on Nikolai Mikhailovich's soft mouth and beard all fused into one sensation, and, without knowing how or why, her arms curved around him in a long embrace. And since that day, she had, it seemed, become the mistress in the house, and he was so good to her, so very good.

6

"Vitkevich is a great linguist, you must know, sir," Pavel said, once the three of them were settled at the table. He was tearing off a strip of pheasant and stuffing it in his mouth. "He is a true wonder, a marvel—I know not how many languages he speaks now, or how many he will end by mastering. Vitkevich, how many is it now?"

"Twelve," Vitkevich said, not needing to count, as if he regularly boasted of the fact.

"Twelve!" Pavel said. "A genius, you see, papa, and he talks sense in all of them."

"That is a prodigious accomplishment, sir," Nikolai said civilly. "You must be a great traveller."

"No, sir," Vitkevich said. "At one time in my life, I had a great deal of leisure, and devoted it to the study of languages, an endeavour which has proved of some use and considerable satisfaction."

"Tell us your languages, Vitkevich," Pavel said puppyishly. "No—better—translate for us. Papa, you will enjoy this. Translate a sentence through all your languages, one by one."

"Really, Layevsky," Vitkevich said. "This is too bad. Very well, what sentence shall I take?"

"Compliment Masha on her excellent dinner," Pavel said, since Masha had been unable to leave the dining room, and was standing, nervously watching the enjoyment of the gentlemen in the shadows.

"The dinner is excellent, and extremely well cooked," Vitkevich said in French. He paused, and said it again, in Russian.

"Bravo!" Pavel cried.

"The dinner is excellent, and extremely well cooked," he said, again, now in German. He spoke again, nine times, each time in a different language, in English and German, Turkish, Arabic, Persian, and languages no one could identify, each time taking a pause, a sip of water, a sniff. Finally, he returned to French, and said, "How well you cook, madam, and the product of your kitchen and larder is beyond compare. You see, sir—" dropping into a lower, more confidential tone, "when one translates from one language to another, a sentence changes into the habitual modes of expression of that tongue, and alters somewhat, so that by the time one has taken the most ordinary sentence in the world through several tongues, it would hardly know itself, like our Lithuanian tale of the drunk coachman who cracked his master's mirror."

"Bravo," Nikolai said, startled by this austere party trick. "How do you come to be so very learned, sir?"

"My life has been spent between periods of great activity and great enforced idleness," Vitkevich said. "And it was in one of my idle periods that I applied myself to acquire a few languages. Your cook is a woman of great accomplishment, sir," he went on, bowing towards Masha. "It is rare, these days, to enjoy a dinner in the old country style. You know, sir, in my opinion, there is nothing to come near this good simple cooking."

"Thank you, sir," Nikolai said; it was what he had hoped Pavel would say, and he would have preferred his son's compliment to his friend's.

"My digestion, sir," Vitkevich went on. "Well, no one could benefit under a regime which alternated the excesses of city hostesses with the austerities of army life. A stomach which is expected to deal with foie gras one week, and coarse rotten mutton in the open air the next, will rebel, sir, and in the most decided way. I am a martyr to the succession of pastry confection and maggoty meat, and such a meal as this represents a true golden mean. I truly compliment your cook, in her own language."

Masha bobbed, and left rapidly. Pavel gazed in admiration at his friend.

"Your family is Polish, I perceive?" Nikolai said.

"I believe so," Vitkevich said. "I bear a Polish name. But my family has lived on the shores of the Baltic for many generations. Our lands are in the ancient nation of Lithuania."

"Do you care to shoot, sir, tomorrow?"

"Thank you," Vitkevich said. "I fear I would be poor company for you; the rigours of the last weeks, and the long journey, have left me no good for anything. And I am too aware that, once I leave, I have a heavy task in front of me. For the moment, I propose to spend my days on your beautiful estate in rest and recuperation, if you have no objection. *Reculer pour mieux sauter,* you know, sir, *mieux sauter."*

"Well, we need not shoot tomorrow," Pavel said. "The day after that will be quite as good."

"Alas—" Nikolai began. He was about to say that it had to be the next day, since, all in all, he would much prefer to spend a day alone with Pavel. And it was not entirely false; the beaters would probably be needed and expected back in the fields the following day.

But Vitkevich, unknowingly, helped him out by saying, "I should not delay. I suffer so at this time of year from the effects of the harvest that I doubt I should be able to accompany you in any case. And I anticipate that the exertions which lie ahead of me, as well as behind, will be best served by the most quiet life imaginable, while I am here."

"Very well," Nikolai said, relieved. He was damned if he was going to inquire into this fellow's adventures, and left the conversational bait where it lay. "That is most unfortunate, sir, but we shall leave you to recuperate in peace."

7

Pavel had known Vitkevich for three years at this time. He was at the age when he had not met every type of man which the world could supply, and on meeting a man who did not resemble anyone he had met before, he could still feel an excitement which is denied to those who have seen more of the world. His friendship with Vitkevich awakened in him a feeling of pride and pleasure; he thought Vitkevich the most remarkable man he had ever met. When he contemplated the extraordinary fact that Vitkevich had not only chosen him as a friend, but had actually come to stay in his family's house, he experienced an emotion which, the reader will appreciate, is not uncommon in young men before they marry, but which still struck Layevsky as unique and thrilling. But everyone was infatuated by Vitkevich; it was inexplicable, but in the officers' mess, he was as instantly prominent as a dancing heroine before the corps de ballet.

As soon as he joined the regiment, he had heard of Vitkevich. The other junior officers often mentioned him, adding apologetically that he was on leave for a week, as if Layevsky had come specifically to meet this remarkable fellow. No one explained why Vitkevich was so impressive, as if the heroic fact of his existence were too well known to require any recitation of his deeds. Not that he seemed, from the way the officers talked of him, to be a great military hero; rather, when a subaltern made reference to him, it was usually with reference to some exploit which would have been enough to land any other fellow in the soup. The admiring way the mess room mentioned him made it clear that here was a fellow permitted some kind of licence, a chap who could sail close to the wind and escape with honour and dignity, as the mess room shook their heads. They did not trouble to explain quite why this was, and Layevsky, curious as he was, did not feel he could ask for elucidation. Nor did he feel enlightened by their frequent casual references to him; it seemed as if he were a fellow who could speak the simplest words, and imbue them with some kind of fascinating individuality. The first night in mess, the Colonel had remarked, "I *adore* cabbage stew, as our Vitkevich would say," and the entire table had broken up, chuckling and shaking their heads. And they all did it; every member of the officer corps would, from time to time, be prone to say, "If Vitkevich were here, he would say this is *a complete bore,*" or, teasing, say to a junior officer whose batman had carelessly left a cuff-button undone, that he was attempting to out-Vitkevich Vitkevich. What was remarkable about the man, Layevsky could not perceive, and he began to feel mildly irritated by the stream of inexplicable, naïve admiration. He could only see that the most ordinary comments were somehow made brilliant and fresh by their connection to a singular personality, the image of which was too fresh in the minds of his comrades to require any kind of explanation.

The second week after he had joined the regiment, Pavel entered the mess room to find a solitary man there, smoking a cheroot and inspecting a French journal. He bowed to the unfamiliar man, who nodded back casually, and took himself to an armchair. Lighting a cigar, Pavel covertly inspected the famous Vitkevich. There seemed nothing, on the surface, remotely remarkable about the man. Dark, whiskered, slight in build, there was nothing obviously impressive about him. His boots, too, were somewhat in need of a clean, and his uniform far from immaculate. Pavel began to experience the faint disappointment of a traveller who has heard much of the wonders of a remote and exotic city, and arrives there to find the aesthetic rapture he had hoped to experience obscured and clouded by the most banal realities. Watching the furrowed look of concentration, Layevsky felt almost satisfied that he, at least, would not be remotely impressed by a man like any other.

At length, the man set down his journal with a sigh, and inspected Layevsky from top to bottom with a disconcerting thoroughness. Layevsky prepared to introduce himself, but Vitkevich forestalled him with a great groan. "How frightful," he said with a curious quick drawl. "How completely frightful." And Layevsky recognized, in his unexplained comment, the grand original of the many unsuccessful impersonations he had listened to over the previous week, and, quite suddenly, was smitten.

Vitkevich said little, then or afterwards, but every time he said something, however banal, it struck Layevsky as completely imbued with the strength of a personality. Whenever the other fellows made a comment, it was merely a comment, which any of them might have made. They seemed to speak a language like anyone else. Vitkevich, on the other hand, could say the simplest thing, and it seemed always like a statement only Vitkevich could have brought out. The words he came out with— they were undeniably in French, but all in all, Vitkevich spoke Vitkevich. "How charming and amusing it is, to be sent on manoeuvres, all in all," he would mutter, and the table would be struck with admiration. Vitkevich, in every way, was the hero of the mess, the man who set the tone, whose escapades and remarks would be raised and commented on for weeks. For the most part he projected an appearance of mildly complaining laziness, and from his recumbent form would issue a series of startlingly irreverent *bons mots,* but sometimes he seemed to be seized with a demonic energy, and organized the entire mess into a splendid practical joke, like the occasion when he thought of bundling up Nozdryov, dead drunk and limp as a sack of old rags, and locking him in a cell with a chained angry bear. Sometimes he would be seized with a mad, original fancy, and argue that the happiness of the individual would be greatly improved if everyone, by law, were to suffer a week of solitary confinement once a year. He would propose these extraordinary fancies to the mess, quite simply, and then sit back while they argued, with outraged futility, against his eccentric idea. Layevsky was quite certain that he thought each idea up on the spot, and his arguments seemed only to be produced to ward off some terrible inner boredom; but he listened to the man speak, and could not restrain his fascination. He was infatuated.

Vitkevich took no especial notice of Pavel, but he took no especial notice of anyone. He was a negligent, brilliant performer, who no more needed to choose his audience than a great tenor at the opera. Anyone, it was apparent, would be pleased to be able to listen, and Vitkevich was entirely uninterested in the make-up of his mess room claque. Layevsky was surprised and excited, then, when one day, as he met Vitkevich coming from the stables in his stockinged feet, riding boots in hand, the elder man confessed to a feeling of dreadful boredom, and proposed a visit à deux to the brothels of ——— Street that evening.

Pavel accepted with alacrity, sweeping to the back of his mind that he had planned to pay a visit to his dandified Uncle Stepan that evening. For him, an hour's ceremonious call would now have to suffice, and he agreed to a *rendezvous,* as Vitkevich put it, at nine o'clock that evening.

Stepan Mikhailovich occupied a splendid town house three streets behind the imperial palace, and Pavel Nikolaievich made his way there a few minutes before six o'clock. He was welcomed into the chilly marble hall by a sour blue-coated footman, powdered to within an inch of his life and glittering with silver frogs, who took the heaviest of Pavel's winter furs with a lip-smackingly ceremonious air, as one who has been handed a dish of sweetmeats. The footman led him past the daringly prominent marble copy of Canova's statue of Pauline Borghese which Stepan Mikhailovich had acquired in Rome, and up the sweeping stairs. At the top, the footman deposited Pavel in a chilly *directoire* anteroom, and went through to announce the nephew. Pavel was always somewhat in awe of his worldly uncle, and he allowed himself to be summoned through with a sense of mild nervousness.

Stepan Mikhailovich was discovered in a state of *déshabille* and prostrate on a sofa. His carefully undone shirt and loosened stock, however, gave only a momentary impression of carelessness, since when he moved, the surface of his corset could be discerned through the shirt, and the carelessly ruffled appearance of his hair was somewhat at odds with the care with which the dark strips of mouse-fur had been attached to his eyebrows and rouge applied to his cheekbones. He greeted Pavel with courtly casualness, not rising, and waved to a seat.

"You will dine with me, of course?" Stepan inquired, after the state of health of his brother at Boguslavo had been established.

"I fear not," Pavel said. "I have engaged to dine with my friend Vitkevich this evening. Perhaps—"

"How very *distingué*," Stepan said, raising a false eyebrow. "I had no idea we dined with M. Vitkevich these days."

"Are you acquainted with him, sir?"

Stepan shrugged. "He is a great favourite of the Tsar, after all," he said modestly. "A remarkable young man. I had forgotten he and you served in the same regiment."

"I think he is the most remarkable man I ever met in my life," Pavel said with the ingenuousness of the very young.

"He is certainly a man of parts," Stepan said. "Some, naturally, are somewhat surprised to see a gentleman with so very chequered a history gaining so much esteem."

"Sir?"

"I see you have not been acquainted with the gentleman very long," Stepan said. Pavel confessed this to be the case. "A very remarkable gentleman, nevertheless. I cannot think of another man whose crimes have been so completely forgiven."

"You exaggerate, surely, sir."

"Well, I am not accustomed, I confess, to meet treasonous criminals at the imperial court. Yes, treasonous—surely, sir, you knew that in youth he rose up against the Tsar and was exiled for his pains? And to be so utterly forgiven—and, really, he is a most decided, a most intimate favourite of the whole imperial family—I cannot think of its like occurring before. They say he is to be trusted with the most important mission sometime soon. A remarkable man."

There was something not entirely admiring in Uncle Stepan's professions, and Pavel soon excused himself coldly and left the old man to his cosmetics. At nine he made his way to Vitkevich's quarters, and the two of them left the barracks on foot. It was the dead of winter, and the streets were lit only by the bonfires which coachmen had lit at each corner. They made their way swiftly through the dry, crackling, fiery night without exchanging much in the way of remarks, and soon found themselves among the festive lights of ———— Street.

Pavel had been here once before with his fellow subalterns, but to come here with Vitkevich was quite a different experience. Before, it had seemed shameful and Pavel had not felt at all easy as they walked up and down, discussing nervously which of the many brothels they should visit. It seemed a mark of Vitkevich's originality that, without consulting, he merely walked into the first house on the street. Inside the plushly furnished house, a respectable middle-aged woman sat picking at popular tunes with one finger on the pianoforte, while around, young women in showy, bright dresses sat in bored silence. Two elderly men sat in a corner, discussing with each other in lowered voices; they might have been talking about serious affairs, were it not for the frequent, covetous glances they shot at the ladies of the establishment.

Vitkevich banged on the lid of the pianoforte with his fist, and the madam left off her music-making. "Bring us a bottle of your very worst champagne," Vitkevich said. "And make it truly revolting."

The madam made a gesture at the maid and, from her seat, made so very ceremonious a bow, it might have been the envy of Pavel's uncle's powdered footman. They sat down and divested themselves of their furs. Vitkevich made a cursory survey of the room, after which he paid no attention whatsoever to the girls of the establishment, but addressed himself solely to Layevsky.

"How boring all this is," Vitkevich said. "And how very unwise we are, to entrust our health to the Petersburg night and these overheated establishments. I do not wonder that our friends find it better to walk about so nearly naked here."

"I believe you are acquainted with my uncle," Layevsky said. "I paid a visit to him earlier today. He said he knew you somewhat."

"Yes?" Vitkevich said. "Ah—yes. Of course. Yes, a very fine gentleman, a pillar of the court. I so admire his confidence and courage. I so hope that I grow to be exactly like that, when I too am seventy years old. It is not everyone, after all, who would venture out with little strips of mousehide stuck to his face."

Layevsky was startled, as one is when someone else notices a fact which one believes is apparent only to oneself.

"He told me a little of your history," Layevsky persevered.

"My history?" Vitkevich said, clouding over. Then he seemed to brighten, and said, "Where is that terrible champagne? Can it be that they cannot find anything bad enough for us?"

Layevsky let it drop, curious as he was. The evening pursued its course, as they drank several bottles of champagne in a series of brothels, in not one of which did Vitkevich pay the slightest attention to the girls, even when they came and draped themselves around his neck. This proved a terrible torment to Layevsky, who felt he could not express any kind of interest in the girls, or propose that they use the houses for their proper purpose. Nor did Vitkevich tell Layevsky the slightest thing about his life, his history, or his future plans, or say anything which suggested that he might have selected the young man to be his intimate. And yet, the next day, when Layevsky woke with a sore head—they had returned after two in the morning, muzzy and poisoned with all the hilarious bad champagne the brothels of —— Street could supply—that had proved to be the case. The following evening, Pavel had felt the desire to sample the pleasures which had been denied him the previous night, and had, rather shamefacedly, slunk off alone. When he returned, he found a note from Vitkevich, rather peremptory in tone but still thrilling to Pavel's infatuated heart, intimating that he had hoped to be able to dine with him, and suggesting the following night instead. Since then, they had become "the inseparables" in the amused eyes of the mess room, and nothing Vitkevich ever said tended to lessen the intense admiration Pavel felt for him.

8

The morning after Masha's splendid dinner, Nikolai Mikhailovich woke, as was his custom, at six. He put on his high boots and a cloth coat, and went downstairs to take breakfast standing in the kitchen, a piece of rye bread with tea. The hounds were already roused, and baying in the yard expectantly. Pavel Nikolaievich appeared by half-past six, and they set off into the quiet of the early morning.

The spot Nikolai Mikhailovich had thought of for their day's sport was a copse of aspen trees, not far from a stream which ran through the estate. As they set off, their hounds running ahead as if already hungry for sport, Nikolai felt exulted by the quiet solitude of the estate in the early morning. The sun was still low in the sky, and in the clear early-morning light there were few peasants in the fields, just preparing for their day's work. The leaves in the trees rustled in the light breeze, and overhead, a skylark sang, high in the pale sky. Nikolai felt intensely happy, and, without passing any remark with his son, seemed to see the beautiful landscape through the eyes of Pavel. The estate would one day be his, and he was certain that the sight of so much beauty from here to the horizon would fill him with a joy that even he could only guess at.

They sat down at the base of an aspen, on a patch of moss, as smooth and dry as a cushion. Laska, the grey bitch, the oldest of the pack, settled by her master, her ears pricked. Somewhere nearby, from deep in the meadow, there was a strange sound, a whinnying, a high cry as of a child. It was a male hare at play. The rippling sound of the brook, the whispering of the leaves in the light morning wind; the bright morning sun, already starting to be hot; Nikolai loosened his stock and took out a hunk of bread from his game bag, and began to chew it contentedly. All at once, as if set off by a single throw, an alarm, there came a crackling firework-noise from above, and the sky was filled with birds in flight. It was going to be a good day.

The hounds looked up with their master, and all at once started barking eagerly. "Hush, hush," Nikolai said. There was all the time in the world, this long day, for Nikolai and his son to be together.

"Papa," Pavel said. "Vitkevich, my friend, you know—he is really the most remarkable man. I hope you come to like him as much as I."

Nikolai's mind had been fixed on the marvellous shooting to come, and nothing else. His eyes were on the sky, and he listened without quite taking in the meaning of his son's words. When he understood, in a moment, what Pavel had said, he felt abruptly deflated, as if their paths of thought had been running away from each other, and he should have noticed the fact. He looked at his son. He felt that he had misunderstood entirely, but what he had misunderstood, he could not say. He had believed that his son had returned, and returned as he was; but now he knew that he had gone into the world. He should have understood that once a man goes into the world, he never returns as he was, and his son, sitting among the glowing woods of his childhood, thought only of the world he had left, and his childhood was nothing to him. He rose, accepting the fact, and prepared to shoot.

"Tell me of his past," he said, accepting a simple fact in the relationship between every father and every growing son, and asking for what he did not care to know. It was with something like pleasure—not precisely pleasure, but sufficiently like it to offer the beginnings of consolation—that he saw Pavel Nikolaievich turn to him gratefully, and begin to tell a sad, sad story.

Nikolai Mikhailovich felt rather refreshed than anything by the exercise of the day, and after a hot bath and a brief stretch on the sofa in his study, he dressed and went downstairs. The saloon was empty. He went over to the card table, where the books Vitkevich had commented on still lay as he had left them, and Nikolai picked one up. What had he said? He looked at the spine of the book; it was a French novel, one of Nikolai's wife's. Vitkevich had said he adored it, had he not? The house was quiet, and Layevsky suddenly, on a whim, called out for Masha.

"How splendid your bag was today, Nikolai Mikhailovich!" she said, entering without her apron. "Who shot the more?"

"Pavel Nikolaievich had a very good day," Nikolai said, patting the sofa to persuade her to sit for a moment and talk. "As for me—alas, I begin to feel my old age creeping upon me, and my eyesight is not as sharp as it was. Still, I did not disgrace myself, I feel."

"Nikolai Mikhailovich," Masha said, beaming. "I believe you outdid your son."

"I cannot deny it," Nikolai said, grinning broadly. "How clever you are. But he did shoot well, and I must confess, my aim is not what it was. Twenty years ago, I should have brought home twice the number. The woods are teeming with birds; a man blindfolded might have done as well as I today, they are so numerous."

"How modest you are," Masha said, quickly kissing him on the cheek. "And you—"

She broke off in alarm. Vitkevich was standing in the doorway, observing them. She did not know how long he had been standing there.

"Come in, sir, come in," Nikolai said heartily. "I hope you had an agreeable and restful day. I was boasting about our splendid day in the fields to Masha."

Vitkevich, a look of perplexity on his face, advanced into the room and Masha rose to go.

"No, no," Nikolai said. "Stay with us, Masha. You must grow used to our rustic informality, sir. Masha, you know, is considered by all quite one of the family; and, Masha, your tasks may wait for a moment longer."

Masha sank down into her seat again nervously.

"I hope you begin to find yourself rested after your military duties, sir," Nikolai said.

"Thank you, sir," Vitkevich said. A silence fell.

"And your day was not too dull?"

"Not at all," he said, casting a glance at Masha. Again, she gave a little convulsion, as if to go, but restrained herself.

Layevsky persevered; after all, this was his house, and this was his

Masha, and he would behave in what way he chose. "You said last night, I recall, that you have a heavy task in front of you?"

"Indeed," Vitkevich said. "As soon as I leave your beautiful estate, I shall be obliged to undertake some rather special duties, which I expect to be more than usually onerous."

"A great honour, no doubt," Layevsky said.

"No doubt," Vitkevich said. Then he seemed to change his mind about something, and shrugged. "I am undertaking a journey into unknown territory. When I leave, I am to travel to Kabul."

"To—"

"To Kabul," Vitkevich said.

"Forgive us," Layevsky said. "We live so very quiet a life here—you will think us the most ignorant peasants, but is that beyond Siberia?"

"No," Vitkevich said, scowling, and Layevsky cursed his slip; Siberia and Vitkevich were now pointlessly connected in his mind. "No, not in Siberia. It lies to the far south, far beyond the bounds of the empire. The Afghans, you know, sir, the Afghans."

"I am most interested, sir," Layevsky said. "That must be a most arduous and onerous journey. I always believed there was nothing south of the borders but deserts and savagery."

"That is not an entirely inaccurate impression," Vitkevich said.

"And—" Masha said. She cleared her throat and started again. "And what is to be found there?"

Vitkevich looked at her, somewhat surprised at her speaking at all. "I do not know," he said. "That, perhaps, is the reason to travel there."

"I see," Layevsky said. He had no idea what questions to ask on this very strange subject.

"You must realize, sir," Vitkevich went on earnestly, "that the empire cannot remain as it is. Where we sit was not within the boundaries of civilization a hundred years ago, but our grandfathers had the confidence to advance, to our undoubted benefit. And perhaps, now, the time has come . . . Forgive me, I run on, and these subjects cannot interest you."

"The Tsar is sending you to new lands?" Masha said.

"Indeed, madam," Vitkevich said, bowing coldly.

"And what will come of it?" she said, boldly.

"I do not know," he said. "Perhaps nothing. But what we certainly know is that beyond our boundaries, there are Russians living in slavery, the poor subjects of barbarians, and it is our duty—perhaps, madam, a cousin of yours is at this moment living in chains, in the utmost misery, living at the whim of some barbarian Mussulman. It is surely our duty as Russians to venture out. And afterwards . . . well, I am undertaking a journey to Kabul, at the express wish of my Tsar. We shall see what comes of it."

"I think I would not wish for more," Masha said, simply.

"Madam?" Vitkevich said. He looked quite baffled at what had drawn him into a conversation on the Tsar's majestic ambitions with a peasant cook. Masha shrank back.

"I would not wish for more," she said again. Then she was silent again, as if she had said enough.

"For more?" Nikolai said, kindly. "Masha, what do you mean?"

"I don't know," she said.

Vitkevich looked at her, assessing her, and then seemed to understand what she meant. "More land?"

"Yes," she said simply. "I do not know what I would do with more. And it would not be ours."

This thought seemed to strike Vitkevich, and he paused. "I am at the disposal of my emperor," he said. "Madam, I think—I believe—that we are in a state of rivalry in some parts of the world, in rivalry with other powers. I think any patriot will want to extend the virtues of his native soil to impoverished and desperate parts of the world. Of course we may say that we have enough land, and sit here. But . . ."

He seemed strangely at a loss now, and, pausing, took out his snuff-box, sniffed it up, and sneezed four times into his red handkerchief, neatly, like a cat.

"Out there is the world, and it could be ours," he went on. "And one day we may wake, and look out of the windows, and there, advancing over the hills, may be your English redcoats. I do not know what is enough."

"I think we have enough," Masha said again, simply.

"Perhaps we do," Vitkevich said, and suddenly there was a flash of kindness in his face towards the cook, and perhaps he had seen, now, who and what she was. "Perhaps we do, and perhaps that is what I will find out."

"There is Pavel Nikolaievich," his father suddenly said, with evident relief. Pavel had come down from his room and, outside, was restfully pacing up and down the loggia of the house. "Shall we join him, sir?"

Vitkevich bowed, and for the first time that Masha had seen, smiled. The two of them went outside. Masha remained standing in the saloon for a moment, and watched the group through the windows. The sun was almost setting, and when they walked on around the house, she stayed there, looking out of the window. The mistress's garden looked beautiful at this time of day; the clumps of flowers richer in colour than earlier in the day, refreshed by the golden light as if by rain. The flowers, unrestrained, spilled over each other, and here and there in the rich mixture of grasses in the meadow, a burst of brilliant red or yellow, where flowers had seeded themselves and grown, untouched. The loose radiant garden stretched out, and there, beyond, the wilder stretches; the mown fields of wheat, the dark glowing forest, and there, beyond the end of the lands, the rising lavender hills, one after another into the scented blue sky. A bird sang, somewhere deep in the sky, a long curving song like flight itself, and, as if to answer, a distant song, a man's song, drifted from the fields. It was Arkady, in his white shirt, trudging with happy exhaustion from the fields into the garden, and singing as if he never feared anyone would hear him, singing in his bright high voice; "Rushlight." She stood there at the window, and gazed at all the land she could see, all the way to the far horizon. Arcturus was rising, and the Great Bear, and Venus, like a nightly unsought blessing. She had never been beyond those dissolving lavender hills; to go into the world would be as unimaginable as to journey to those stars. She had never wanted to, until this moment. Everything she saw she knew, and had thought that would always be the case. But the explorer had come to Boguslavo, and now as she stood in the beautiful rich silence of the earth she knew, beneath the beginnings of the shining night sky, her mind began to roam, beyond the hills, beyond the Crimea, beyond Russia. Here was enough; but as she stood, and listened to the faint murmur of the men's conversation outside, and looked at the warm blue landscape, she all at once understood why men go into the world; understood that, always, always, men must resolve to stay where they are, and not pursue their wishes into the great world.

SIXTEEN

In the shade of the camel, the adventurer squeezed his eyelids together and tried to see what it was, that thing at the edge of the vast sandy horizon. There was nothing here to see; a vacuum, a great yellow and gold and brown vacuum. But in the desert something glittered, far away. Nothing moved, apart from the shimmering air; nothing lived, apart from Burnes and his animals and his party, sheltering as best they could from the bleak midday light. But somewhere, miles away, an object glittered, like a shard of metal in a pile of sand. Something lived, and towards them, so slowly, it came.

To the European eye, the desert and the white sky were one, a single blaze. But Burnes knew that his bearers saw everything in it. An Afghan, taken from the desert and presented with the sea and the sky, saw nothing; saw a single blank blue, never having contemplated the possibilities of azure. And the desert, to them, was alive with change and distance. They looked at it, and saw what their sweating masters could not, a country rich enough for men to live in.

There were no explorers here, in this awful place, and no animals, and no men bending their heads under the sun. But out there was something.

A helmet, a cuirass, a piece of metal, so distant, had caught the sun, and whatever it was had seen them. Towards them came something; it might be bandits, or anything, but for the moment Burnes sat silently and waited. Towards them came a shard of life, towards them in its shining insect certainty, making its way through this vast waste of sand. Burnes waited there, in this improbable place, to see how such a presence would make itself known. He did not know it, but he was waiting for Vitkevich.

SEVENTEEN

I

This time it could be true.

For two years, since Hasan's departure, the same news had been brought into the house of the widow Khadija. From time to time, one of Masson's boys would enter, and sit with him, and talk for a while inconsequentially, before mentioning quite casually that some English were in Kabul. Once, he had been stirred by this information. A boy would break off from his conversation—perhaps he would be describing, in as much detail as he could summon, his brother's wedding to a girl from the hills, the year before. He would bring his eyes down from their mid-air concentration, gulp, and say, prompted by nothing, that there were English again in Kabul.

The first time Masson heard this news, he had been thrown into a state of excitement, and had hardly known what questions to ask the boy—Mohammed, had it been? Yes, rather a smelly boy, Mohammed. English in Kabul. That thrill that went through him, he hardly knew what to do with it. If he had seen these English in the street, he could not say whether he would run from them or embrace them; to find out who they were, or to take measures to stop them finding him. It had been years now since he had laid eyes upon an Englishman; years since he had spoken English to anyone but himself, pottering about the white-walled little garden of the widow's house. He always said to himself that he did not want to be reminded of what he had been—what he was. He did not want to think of himself as English, any more than he wanted to feel that he was a soldier. Those things had passed, and if he spoke to himself sometimes in an odd spiky language, and could not stop himself from counting out coins in English, that was merely an oddity of behaviour which any inhabitant of Kabul might possess. The widow Khadija gave a polite, neat little sneeze somewhere beneath her veil every time she was about to tell a lie; the beggar at the corner pulled apologetically at one ear, and then the other, whenever he was given a coin; Masson counted and chattered in an angular nonsense language. *Seven eight nine ten eleven*—that was the thing you never got rid of, the counting in your first language. But it was all the same, and meant nothing but that everyone had an idiosyncrasy. No one had the same one, but in this city, that was what they all shared.

He had assured himself successfully, then, that he had become something else. He might have killed himself, there, at the gates of the Calcutta garrison, rather than Hastings; and have found no more regret. If he had ever had roots, they were gone now; left in the heavy clay of obligation and unwillingness, left in the clammy dampness of his ignored past, left in Calcutta. Now he had changed, and all that was over. What he was, he did not know: but he knew he was not what he had been.

And yet the news that the English were in Kabul filled him not just with dread, but with a form of excitement. He did not fear discovery, or punishment; he knew that he was beyond the pale here, beyond what England might approve or disapprove of as definitely as he was beyond the reach of their law. What he feared, perhaps, in his agitation, was a feeling in himself that, if he ever saw an Englishman again, he would not be able to stop himself approaching the other, throwing off his cloak, and saying, "I am Masson." To speak again in English, and be answered; at some level, Masson had to recognize, he longed for that.

It disturbed him, because it disturbed his deepest conviction, that what he most wanted and needed was solitude. In Kabul, he had come to think that the desire which had always driven him was the desire to be alone. He believed, now, that he was happy because he was alone and undisturbed; that here, there was nothing to interrupt his solitude, when he locked his door to the world. There was a solitude in the language which he could not share with anyone in the city, and a solitude in his way of life in this little house. Looking back, he felt assured that solitude was the thing he had always sought, and which he could never find before now. When he ran as a boy to his hiding place, to pull the gorse over him and sit in the warm near-dark, not knowing why, that was his need to be alone, in England. And in Calcutta, when, in precious hours in the crowded city, he had found his way to the English cemetery and wandered among the grandiose tombs, reading and sitting and musing, undisturbed, that, too, had been his deepest want not to be with people. If anyone had seen the private soldier in his uniform, wandering about the graves, they would not have wondered about him, or approached him; he was a person without interest, whose feelings were beneath the interest of any inquiring observer, and that had suited Masson and his solitude. There, in the cemetery on Park Street, he had been left alone with a crowd of the dead, and he read the beautiful sentiment on the graves knowing that whatever luxuriant feeling they might call forth from his bosom, nothing would be returned, and nothing more would be demanded of him than what he felt like offering.

> Rose Aylmer! Whom these mourning eyes
> May weep, but never see
> A night of wakefulness and tears
> I consecrate to thee . . .

How sad that was, and how true! How he was moved by the death of poor Rose Aylmer, a woman he never knew! How wonderfully it confirmed to Masson, those lovely long Calcutta afternoons, that, in solitude, he possessed more than the common run of feelings without demanding anything more of him than he was prepared to give. Yes, as he had recognized since he came to Kabul, he was most himself when he was alone, when he could choose how to expend his feelings, and to be alone had always been what he had most wanted. He had not known that until now, but now he knew it. That certainty was what, on consideration, he felt absolutely assured of, and only two things in the last years had shaken his absolute assurance. The first, of course, had been Hasan, when for a week that desire for solitude had left him with an appalling force. And the second, which he could still less explain, was the bound of his heart on hearing the plausible news that there were English in Kabul. It was not fear alone that he felt. He recognized that it was something he deplored in himself, an urge to speak English to an Englishman. He was better when he was alone; he had always wanted to be alone, had he not? So why this excitement? Why this urge to run into the street and find what he was convinced he never missed?

The news, however, that there was an Englishman in the city was one regularly and confidently conveyed by a succession of bazaar-boys, and it always turned out to be false. There were no English in Kabul, and he had started to think there never would be. This was a safe city for Masson. Beyond a certain distance, all foreigners were English to the Kabulis, and only twice had the reported approach of an Englishman referred even to a European. For the rest of it, the Englishman had turned out to be someone who even the Kabulis had to admit was very unlike Masson in appearance, language, and manners, and Masson settled down again into his peaceful existence, undisturbed, wondering only what power the name of England still had over him, to raise him up from his equable state. He had heard the same news six or seven times since Hasan had so suddenly disappeared. It had always been false. But this time, it might just be true.

2

Masson's hours for company were mid-afternoon to mid-evening. The unwearying curiosity the city had exercised towards him had, over the months, diminished, but not disappeared. After a few frantic months of ceaselessly entertaining one visitor after another, Masson had immured himself, only opening the doors for a few hours each day. He had thought that the curiosity would diminish, but he could not see that it had. The whole city came to see him; to sit and stare and listen to him, from near-babies to toothless old men; everybody had come; everybody still came; except one. And each of them told him the same thing; that the English were in Kabul. They never were; only Masson.

But Masson, now, had seen someone, in the bazaar, and that someone, unmistakably, had seen him. It was two days before. He had his daily round, sitting and talking with the shoemaker, the fruitsellers, the carpet-menders; he listened at the edge of a crouching little group to the epics of the storytellers, gathering little fragments of knowledge. To listen pa-

tiently to the ordinary conversation of the people of the city was knowledge, too; he had heard their stories, knew of their lives, and learnt from
it. What they believed about themselves was always wrong, but always
interesting, and he went from place to place, patiently drinking tea, never
admitting the feeling that he might be wasting his time. And occasionally
the shoemaker, at the back of his fusty little shop, would break off from
his customary long complaint about his wife, and explain in detail exactly
what had been done at his cousin's martial funeral rites, and Masson
would listen, his eyes bright, itching for his notebook. They could tell him
what had been done; he would explain, one day, why. Sometimes they
would say, *Oh, are you interested in old things?* And produce something
from a pile of rags, something strange which they could not explain.
Sometimes it was nothing much—Masson had grown to loathe those
industrial figures of Hindu gods, which were incomprehensible and
therefore curious to the shopkeepers—but sometimes, on the other hand,
it was interesting; an old Persian medal, a Tibetan prayer-conch encrusted with the instructions of opaque, distant devotions. He went on
his morning rounds feeling pleasantly braced, and sometimes his patient
civility was rewarded.

Masson prided himself, now, on being able to distinguish between the
faces of Kabul. All Asia poured through here, and with one look, he could
tell a Pushto-speaking near-savage from a pompous Qizzilbash merchant,
a man with a Turkish grandparent, a blue-eyed hillsman, a face on which
Arab or Chinese or Cashmire ancestry had left its mark. He had often
thought that the small distinctions in faces would reward serious study.
The variety here was so opulent, and all witnessed by the tiny shifts in
eyebrow or nose, that it seemed for a time as if the world was here. Then
one day Masson saw an English face, and knew that was not so.

It was in the great hall of the butchers. By mid-morning, the trade had
fallen to nothing, and it became a sleepy, dusty place. On the flimsy
tables, the butchers and their apprentices reclined, sleeping or smoking,
the rough dark carcasses by their side like old friends. They passed occasional leisurely remarks, but lay for the most part in deep content. The
hard-packed mud floor was covered with baskets of chickens, crowded
together and poking their heads through the net; most, by now, held only
one or two chickens, a sight which never failed to strike Masson as
poignant, as the last survivor waited for its purchaser. The air of the hall
was thick with dust; feathers, fur, dry mud floated in the clear light shin-

ing through the thin slits in the hall's roof. It was Masson's favourite place, and he stood and looked at something a different person could have written a poem about.

There were few customers, now; the time for meat-buying was in the early morning, and only a couple of women navigated their way through the islands of captive chickens. The butchers were used to the sight of the Englishman who liked to come and stand, and sometimes ask them about odd things, but the splendidly robed figure who was picking his way across the hall was unfamiliar to them, and they raised their heads to look at this new figure in mild curiosity. Masson, too, observed the man's progress with interest; he was tall, and dressed in a courtly fashion. For a moment he thought of Hasan in his splendour. The man approached, not showing the usual curiosity, but simply making his awkward way, observing quietly. He was five yards from Masson when he raised his head and, with a shock, Masson saw a head as ginger as his own, and the unmistakable Englishman saw what Masson was. He lowered his face again, and went on, not varying his pace, speaking, or looking back at Masson. Yes, this time it could be true.

It was December, and bitterly cold; the first snows could not be long delayed, and Masson cut short his social visits around the marketplace. He returned to the widow Khadija's house in a state of agitation, and waited eagerly for the arrival of Qasim. Qasim was a good boy, on the whole, and a useful one; Masson overlooked his occasional pilfering, and rewarded the occasional heart-rending tales of the misfortunes of his family with small gifts of money, wishing only that Qasim had the wit to see that they would be as effective if he could make them somewhat shorter. And, after all, his unfounded belief that Masson must be extremely rich had its occasional uses, both domestic and public. Still, he was a good boy, on the whole, and usefully curious about the city. He had been Masson's most regular visitor for some months now, and would probably know about this alarming apparition.

One of the upper rooms had been transformed by Masson into a treasury-cum-study; it was here that he kept his various acquisitions, and here where he wrote. He kept two sets of notes; the first was a bald diary, noting times and places and the briefest comment on any interesting conversation. It was a habit he had usefully fallen into when travelling, and kept up when he was in Kabul. The second set of notes was more elaborate; a careful, formal description of anything he had seen, or anything he had acquired, supplemented where necessary with any information, however obviously false, he had had on the occasion. A goatherd would not hold any correct information about a tomb, and a merchant, even if better informed about his goods, might have reason to mislead his strange customer; still, it was knowledge, and worth recording. False beliefs and the native idea of a plausible lie were of interest. Sometimes Masson made an attempt at a drawing of the object; not often enough. He deplored his lack of skill with the pencil, and his clumsy renderings, even if they were no more than *aides-mémoire*, irritated him. They were inaccurate, and inaccuracy was what Masson disliked most in himself. What his scrupulous notes were building towards was a great work, the most complete and truthful account possible of what no one had ever seen. That he might, in the fullness of time, be misled by his stumbling pencil into misdescription was inconceivable, and Masson unwillingly chose not to attempt a drawing from time to time, believing—he knew falsely—that his memory ought to be good enough.

Today he sat on the floor and could not work. He stared into space, trying to will himself into activity, but nothing much came. There were tasks to be undertaken, descriptions to be done, the events of yesterday and today to be set down. He sat in his pile of blankets in the cold room, a ewer before him and his notebook and pencil in his hand, and thought, unaccountably, of the Englishman he had seen.

3

Qasim came as the daylight was fading, and Masson stirred himself to go down and welcome him. The sight of Qasim's face was always a slight shock, as if there ought to be a different one there, looking up at him. He pushed away the half-formed thought, which was always there, and then it was only Qasim, with his squarish Indian face, looking at him anxiously. They salaamed, smiling, to each other, and then Qasim, with his periodic niceness, reached out and stroked Masson's arm.

"My father asked if you would do him the honour to come to his house," Qasim said, once Masson had called for tea. "He has seen you in the street and begs your condescension."

"I would be honoured," Masson said gravely. "The opportunity to repay the honour your house has done me in affording me the finest flower of the family is one I should seize, and am conscious of the honour done me by your invitation."

Qasim looked at him oddly, and Masson worried, as often, that he had rather failed to grasp where the honour in these transactions was due. Still, it would be interesting to see Qasim's family, and try to understand what, precisely, they thought of him and his unwarranted concern for a mere street-boy, the useless elder son (as he understood it) of the family.

"I think I saw your father," Masson said. "Certainly I was greeted by a gentleman I did not know, three days ago, a gentleman who seemed to show a remarkable degree of esteem for a poor foreign stranger. I suppose that must have been him, then. I did not recognize him."

"I resemble him greatly, it is said," Qasim said distractedly.

"A very handsome gentleman," Masson said.

Qasim brightened. "I could not come yesterday," he said earnestly. "My cousin—"

"Your cousin?"

Qasim nodded.

"Which cousin?" Masson said.

"My cousin the carpenter," Qasim said fluently. "He has great problems. His brother—"

"His brother, your cousin," Masson said.

"Yes," Qasim said, momentarily puzzled. Then he resumed his story. "His brother was robbed and left for dead, and my cousin cannot help him."

"Why not?" Masson said. He was rather enjoying this.

"His family is large and he has no money," Qasim said baldly. "And so . . ."

Masson let him run on in this familiar vein for some time; he found it rather restful. When he had finished, Masson agreed to give him something—the little silver bowl, a remnant of Das's quite without interest would probably do—to sell in the market. They sat for a moment in silence. Absurdly, Masson was waiting for Qasim to mention the presence of Englishmen in Kabul. Finally, he raised it.

"Yes," Qasim said, without much interest. "Yes, there are English here again. I have not seen them. They are with the Amir at the Bala Hissar."

Masson raised an eyebrow. "Important Englishmen, then," he said.

"Yes," Qasim said. "They are the guests of the Amir. What are their names?"

"I don't know," Masson said. "I don't know who they are."

"But they are English," Qasim said.

"Do you know everyone even in this city?"

Qasim made a puffing noise at the absurdity of the idea. "The English," he went on. "My father said they are the English who came before."

Masson dismissed this; when he arrived, he too had been widely assumed to be the Englishman who came before, carrying gorgeous gifts to amaze the court. Probably any European, arriving here, was routinely assumed to be the same as those mysterious visitors, whose purpose and whose nature he had never been able to disentangle from the thickets of rumour and mangled repetition.

"They are friends of the Amir," Qasim said. "They come to pay him homage. I would like to see them. And now, Tschawzzz . . ."

A great grin broke out on Qasim's face; the name of Charles was almost impossible for him to pronounce, and he took great relish in his approximations. Produced like this, it had a single meaning, an invitation to fuck, and Masson never stopped finding it amusing that so ordinary an English name had, in one distant boy's mind, become a synonym for their rowdy congress. Qasim only said *Charles* at these moments, and when he struggled with the name, its knot of consonants at either end, Masson suddenly saw himself as exotically lubricious, and he swiftly, gorgeously divested himself of his robes with all the swagger of a Parisian whore.

The raucous acts occupied the evening, and when Qasim had eaten, he departed, holding the reward of the little silver bowl in triumph. Masson sank back, lighting his pipe, and resumed his thoughts. Qasim never stayed the night, and his departure was normally a moment of pleasure for Masson; a moment to be still, and not to think, in solitude. He could feel the thoughts of the English crowding around his little guilty brain, and he resolved not to indulge them. He blew out the little oil lamp, and lay down, pushing the mattress here and there until he had made himself a nest; he was tired, and soon he slept. He had fended off the thoughts of the English, but it had been a mistake. That would be one set of bad thoughts, and he triumphed over them, forgetting what always lay in his mind. He slept, and, in one wide wave, what came to him was what was worse, what was always there.

4

He who, in his daily life, herds sheep and nothing but sheep, will dream of sheep. Masson, every day, handled coins which spoke of kings; of the precious objects of courts, of jade bowls and lapis lazuli, of the rings of princes, of the seals which the chamberlains of distant and obscure palaces once yielded; he walked and rode into the dry high mountains to stand with careful reverence before the tombs of emperors; he hoarded curved scimitars, the witnesses of conquest; he held holy books, buried in gold, in filigree, in arabesque; he read of diamonds as big as a man's fist, which wars were fought over as if they were empires; he touched and imagined and described and hoarded the properties of the magnificent dead, of the kings of the world, and through this great pile of things walked the ghosts of emperors, looking at the assessing, guilty Masson with their calm cruel eyes. Masson, every day, lived among the wreck of empires and his eyes shone with their treasures: and when he closed them, he dreamt of Hasan.

To be with Hasan was to understand loss. Over and over again, that infinite week, Masson was overwhelmed with it. Over and over again, as the clean bright day faded into the luxuriant cool blue evening, and Hasan buried his face in the breast of the Englishman, Masson felt a terrible want, a terrible longing to be with Hasan. *I long to be with you, so much,* he thought, over and over again; and his love was such that the longing was never fiercer than when he already was. Seven days: seven days of longing for what was already there. A week of desire, so strong that nothing could fulfil it, nothing, not even fulfilment. There was nothing that Hasan did not give, nothing more than Masson could have asked for. It was as if Hasan had entered, and for seven days, poured out the full measure of his existence, selflessly, giving everything, and Masson had a thirst for more, for everything, even when he had and was being given everything that could be given. Loss was in Hasan. And when he went, there was nothing more to be added to Masson's desire: nothing but grief. *I want to be with you, so much, so much: I want to be with you, even when I already am.*

It was two years now since he had seen Hasan. Hasan had spent a single week in the house of the widow Khadija with Masson; seven days and seven nights. In that stretch, they did not move outside, but stayed where they were, telling each other the thousand tales of their lives. The servants were sent away, and the doors were locked, and Masson and Hasan lived lifetimes in a week. He had come through the door, and said, "My name is Hasan," and the other boys, without needing to be told, left as if he had dismissed them. That week; seven days and seven nights, and Masson lived it over and over again, in his poor imperfect memory, in his dreams.

Afterwards, he depicted that moment of Hasan entering the house in the oddest way. It was as if he had found Hasan, and not the other way round. For months—perhaps his whole life—Masson had been burrowing through dark narrow underground tunnels, and now he had edged forward an extra foot and found that the rock above him had fallen upwards to an immense height, and a blaze of light illuminated what had been the close uninterrupted darkness of his existence. And rising to his feet, he had found himself facing a man, standing upright in an immense jewelled cavern, blinking in a brilliant light. A man was there who had waited patiently to be found. The oddest fact was that at no point did Masson conceive of Hasan as having a similar subterranean existence; he walked, surely, in light and air, and it was only his long-held desire for Masson that had led him to descend, his long-held certainty that what he could do, now, for the foreigner was to take him by the hand and lead him, step by step, upwards to the sun and the sky.

Masson could not bear to be separated from Hasan, all those days, and every tiny separation which occurred struck him with pain. When he slept, he longed to wake, to be with Hasan; if Hasan was in the house, but not in the same room, that, too, was unbearable; when they were in the same room, but not touching, the spaces between them were a torture to Masson. Only when they lay together, pressed so tight, pressed so that every surface of their bodies touched, their lips, their flesh, one's eyelashes fluttering against the other's, did Masson begin to feel that they were close enough together. No closeness could fill the longing in Masson's heart, the longing for Hasan; a desire he, surely, had always had, a desire he had not known how to name until he saw the man who could fulfil it.

His memory of the week was not, oddly, of sexual pleasure, although that had been there—pleasure so overwhelming, so unqualified, so pure that he wondered what pleasure had meant to him before. In an hour, Hasan, never seeming to exert effort, moving over him as gracefully as a dancer, as if there were all the time in the world, showing nothing like the usual greed, reduced him to a state of amazed helpless rapture, as if with the small pressures of his hands, limbs, mouth, organs, he had removed all that was solid of Masson, and left what had once been a man abandoned, boneless, trembling beneath him. Masson looked, astonished, into those deep eyes, his flesh turned to marzipan, and the deep eyes looked back with an expression of calm surrender. But in his dreams and in his thoughts that was a willed, a conscious memory, summoned by concentration. The involuntary thought of Hasan that came, always, on waking, was of the man standing naked, or clothed, in a doorway, looking with quiet consideration at Masson, lit by the clear sunlight through an upper window. And then those other hours, those short golden hours, when they lay together, and told the thousand tales of their lives, as if they knew that all that had happened to them before Hasan entered the widow's house would soon mean nothing, and must now be told. Masson talked and talked and talked, and told everything, told of London in his fantastic proliferating Persian, told of the voyage and the sea and the arrival in India, told of Calcutta, and Suggs and Sale and McVitie and Hastings and Das, told of his long journey, of his life in Kabul, told everything, emptying the vessel of his thoughts, telling everything that he had ever seen or heard in a single marvellous rush. And Hasan listened silently, his eyes like saucers, the king of the world listening to the inexhaustible tale of the life of his newest favourite concubine, and when Masson drew breath, Hasan talked too; talked of . . .

His memory failed. Masson did not know, now, what Hasan had told him. And yet his memory was of Hasan telling a thousand and one tales, stroking Masson's hair to keep him from sleep. His memory failed there; the words were like the sentences in dreams, which as they fall on the dreamer's ear are thunderous shining proverbs, and which fade in the helpless light of day. He had once heard everything Hasan had to tell, and now did not know whether he had been told anything at all. He knew nothing of Hasan. That was what, in the two years since Hasan had departed, he had had to realize.

On the eighth day, Masson had woken, and there was no Hasan by his side. He knew, immediately, that he had gone, and gone for good. There was such a sense of loss in Hasan, even when he was there, that when he departed, it was more like a fulfilment of promise than a bereavement. He had had a week with him, and on the eighth day he had gone; but

Masson had always known that would be so. He had not seen him since then, and only after Hasan left had he realized how very large Kabul was, how very many people there were in it, and all of them, except one, were not Hasan. Only once—perhaps only once—there, at the far end of the street, had he seen a man passing whose radiance was unmistakable. Masson had run, and the blessed place where he had walked was empty. For the rest, for two years, he had been tortured with the sight of men who could, just, be Hasan, but who were not. Because there was no one like Hasan, no one in the world, and now he was gone for ever, filling only Masson's dreams. The question Masson never asked himself was what Hasan had wanted from him.

5

Masson woke early, and he had already made a decision; he would go back to the hall of the butchers, at the same time, and wait for the Englishman. It was absurd, he knew, but there was nothing better he could think of to do. He would not go to the Bala Hissar, and to wait in the hall of the butchers was the best thing he could think of. Somehow, he felt that it was not entirely absurd. He had an idea that the Englishman had seen him, and been shocked, and would return to the same place, at the same time, to find out what he could.

He went to the hall of the butchers at the same time, at roughly the middle of the morning, and waited there, pretending to be interested in chickens. And then he was right. Across the hall, in exactly the same way, picked the same tall figure, coming from precisely the same direction, wearing precisely the same stately robes. Masson stood there and waited for the man to approach him. He did not seem to have observed Masson, but, all the same, he came in his direction. When he was five yards away— and still did not seem to have seen Masson—Masson cleared his throat, and spoke to him.

"Sir," he said. The man looked at him, in exactly the same way, as if he had never seen him before, and as if his presence there startled him. Masson started again. "Sir," he said. "I am Masson."

That was not what he meant to say. It just came out. The man looked at him again, and said nothing. For a moment, it occurred to Masson that he might be terribly wrong, that this might be a man who had never heard English spoken. Then he looked again, and saw that he was right.

"You must be English," he said firmly.

"Scotch," Burnes said finally. Masson waited for him to go on, but he said nothing more. Then, idiotically, one of the butchers ran up, clutching a squawking chicken by its heels, and waved it at the two tall foreigners. Burnes simply turned away, as if waiting for a subordinate to deal with an inconvenient interruption, and Masson dismissed the butcher as briskly as he could. Burnes turned back, and looked at Masson levelly.

"These people . . ." Masson said. "It is a pleasure to see a fellow countryman in this place. My name is Masson."

"I have heard that there was an Englishman here," Burnes said.

"I have lived here for three years," Masson said. Then, idiotically, he said, "My name is Masson," again.

"I had wondered what your name could be," Burnes said. "I had heard it, but in somewhat altered form."

"It would give me great pleasure to talk at more length," Masson said. "It is some years since I have met with a fellow countryman."

"I am Scotch," Burnes said again, and bowed. Masson bowed back, oddly aggrieved. "Tell me something. Why does the Amir wear blades of grass in his headgear? Something I have often wondered."

Masson looked at him; it was not an inquiry for knowledge, since in Burnes's assessing look there was no curiosity. He was testing him to see if he knew the right answer, to see what use he could be. "It is a coronation ritual," Masson said. "The Amir at his coronation has three blades of grass placed there, and always wears it. An interesting tradition, though I have not been able to discover how ancient it is; I understand that the practice had fallen into desuetude until Dost Mohammed revived it. It is said to be an ancient rite, but there is no evidence to support the claim. It seems entirely possible that it is a picturesque practice invented ten years ago."

"I see," Burnes said, looking Masson up and down once more. "How interesting. We must discuss more, sir, and at greater length." There was no sign of warmth in this fellow's guarded manner, and, as he walked away, Masson tried to reconcile his two feelings, that now he had been reminded why he had left the British, and that he still wanted to meet with this man. He told himself that, of course, he was curious; he reassured himself that he wanted to find out what this embassy to the Amir was all about; but it was not quite true. In fact, he wanted to sit and talk

English, and he stalked off, pretending to be on some urgent errand, with a feeling of annoyance that was not entirely directed at Burnes.

6

"Hearts," Burnes said, laying the cards down on the floor. "Seven, eight, nine, ten, knave, queen. Ace of hearts, diamonds, clubs, spades. That is fifty-one, is it not? And . . ." He laid the two of hearts on the open pile, and sat back with the four remaining cards.

"At least fifty-one," Mohan Lal said, smiling. "Ninety-eight points, in fact. I am impressed."

He took a card from the other pile, the face-down cards, and compressed his lips together. Over the candle, Burnes looked at his impassive face.

"You force me to play, Burnes," Mohan Lal said. "Ah well. Now, let us see . . ."

Hearts, two, three, four, five; diamonds, five, six, seven; knave of clubs, spades, diamonds, clubs; joker, nine of spades, ten of spades, joker; and Mohan Lal laid his last card down on the pile.

"My hand," he said.

"Naturally," Burnes said. "One day, I hope to win a single hand against you, sir. But I have no expectations of an early victory. You are the devil."

"Thank you, Burnes," Mohan Lal said, gathering up the pile of cards. "I think you are too rash in your play; it is always better to delay, you know, until you can set down your whole hand. When will you learn, Burnes?"

"Well, I could not have done better than that," Burnes said. "Since you would have set down that turn in any case and left me with my entire hand. No, it is you who have the luck of the devil, and not I who lack skill. Another hand?"

"As you choose," Mohan Lal said, dividing the double pack for Burnes to deal. "And how do the accounts now stand?"

"I believe I am in your debt to the tune of a hundred and sixty-three pounds," Burnes said.

"My dear sir," Mohan Lal said. "Another hand?"

The cards were decidedly greasy. They had travelled from Calcutta in Burnes's pack, along with all the other supplies and necessities—cigars, polo sticks, guns, pink hunting coats, gifts for the Amir (rather reduced in opulence from what Burnes had relied on, thanks to a momentary fit of parsimoniousness by the Governor General's nazir)—which had so loaded down their four extra camels. Unlike those other requisites, the cards had proved of use, and since they had arrived with the full pomp of Empire in Kabul, they had gamed nightly. This time, there was no question of being lodged with some minor nobility; they had passed unquestioned through the city gates, and been conducted with great splendour to the Bala Hissar itself, honoured guests of the Amir. Nor had they been required to wait days until being admitted to the Presence; the very next morning, the Amir had sent for them, and on their admittance to the throne room, he had risen—the Pearl of the Age had risen—and walked all of ten paces to embrace Burnes. Now, he was an honoured guest—a cousin, it seemed, from the Amir's warm encomium—and there seemed nothing that could not be achieved with a little deference. The Governor General's idea of ousting this splendid and charming Emperor and installing the dreadful old Shah Shujah to rule over this delightful city and country had been nagging away at Burnes for weeks; now, he felt absolutely assured that nothing so awful would come to pass, and he could lead Dost Mohammed by the hand like a small child to wherever he chose.

They had talked and talked, and after hours of conversation, the Dost had dismissed them to their quarters, where they subsided in exhaustion. And the next day, again, the summons had come, and, again, Burnes had gone and talked, alone, with the great Emperor, his court dismissed. And the next day, and the next, and . . . Was there anything which could not conceivably interest the Amir and his marvellous mind? He had asked endless questions about the new Queen of the English, with all the astonishment of the Islamic king for the idea of a solitary Empress; asked about the diet of the English, for details of their agriculture, for information about the railway now carving up that faraway island kingdom ("on grooves—no, rails—"), about the practices of soothsaying; he talked of the arts of England, of industry, of horses and hounds and hunting, of the domestic arrangements of the English, of the shape of their houses and the manufacture of bricks, of the times of their dining, of the clothes of their women ("Aiee!"), of fishing, of the activities subject to taxation and the means of collection, of the structure of the army, of weapons, of guns, of ships, of communications, of the delivery of letters from the

Queen to her subjects, of paper, of mining, of music, of manners, of poets, of the mending of boots, of the diet of the poor, of India, of the cure of diseases, of Napoleon, of the manufacture of mirrors, of the means of punishment, of transportation and prisons and execution, of the cat of nine tails, of mutiny, of prostitutes, of the building of roads, of the holy sites, of the mullahs of Christ, of Burnes's childhood, of absolutely everything. Everything was inquired into with a fierce gaze and unflagging curiosity, and Burnes had the joyous feeling of wriggling, a small child pinned down and interrogated in the most fascinating way.

Within days they were friends. A dizzying sensation, to realize that one was the friend of an Emperor, and one which Burnes at first dismissed, but had in the end to accept. Dost Mohammed liked him, that was clear, and liked him even when ("And, please, what number of fish might a sea vessel hope to obtain on a single trip?") his knowledge failed. After these long sessions, Burnes was left without resources, could hardly speak more, so energetic had the Emperor's inquisitions been, and could only return limply to his quarters, to rest and mumble. Hence the cards. Anything more demanding was, he found, beyond his capacities.

It was clear he was being a great success, but two things remained to disturb his peace of mind. The gifts from the Governor General had not gone down well, and the Amir had picked through the mean little offerings with a mild expression of distaste, passing the little clock and the ell of cloth to the youngest member of his court without glancing at them. It had taken some days of discreet inquiry before Burnes understood that the memory of Elphinstone's long-ago embassy, bearing gifts of a truly stupendous lavishness, had burned itself into the collective mind of the court and that he, as an envoy from the Indian Empire—from the Company—from the Queen of Engelstan herself—was expected at the very least to live up to that splendour. However surprising this attitude was from a ruler who lived so simply, it was a quite undeniable fact, which was evidently never very far from the mind of the Amir. Still, although Dost Mohammed referred, rather touchily, to the subject from time to time in a manner which left no room for apology or redress, it did not seem to have harmed their prospects in any serious way. Rather a relief; Burnes hardly thought that he was going to be able to acquire any supplementary gifts from the Kabul bazaar.

Considerably more worrying, in the event, was what Burnes had discovered quite by chance; that the Russians were in the city, and presenting themselves daily at the gates of the Bala Hissar where he and the Emperor were so securely ensconced in their mutual admiration. For the moment, they were being dismissed, but, as Mohan Lal calmly said, the whim of the Emperor was a powerful thing, and if, for any reason, the esteem between the Scotchman and the Afghan prince should flag, it was entirely likely that the representative of quite a different empire would be sent for. It was up to Burnes to convince the Amir that the friendship of the English was the thing. Indeed, that was the thing Burnes never permitted himself to forget; that the Amir's professions of friendship concealed a whim of steel. And he had a decided advantage; he knew, and had known for some weeks, that Vitkevich was here, and could guess at his purpose.

7

There, in the desert, he had seen a glittering object approach, and waited. The object approached, divided under the single cold light of the desert sun into a caravan much like their own; divided again, and there was a group of men, in military dress, on horses leading camels. The men dismounted, and approached Burnes and his men. They were Europeans, and Burnes addressed the leader of the group in a series of languages, to no avail. He knew, immediately, that they were Russians, but they refused to speak French with him. The leader, after listening to a series of questions from Burnes with a look of careful inexpressive blankness, made a long speech in what must be Turkoman, fell silent, and examined Burnes questioningly, his head cocked on one side, assessing him; and for all Burnes knew, he could have been talking complete gibberish. They rested together, peaceably, speaking only in their different languages. After an hour or so, the Russians rose, salaamed in the oriental manner, and went on their way. Burnes watched them go. They were going to Kabul, he had no doubt.

That certainty was confirmed when, three days later, they encountered each other again in a dry little village on the road to Kabul. The leader, this time, was on his own, and outside the stables, he bowed elaborately to Burnes and introduced himself in perfect French, explaining rather unconvincingly that it was unwise to be familiar with strangers in the desert. His name was Vitkevich, and he said, perfectly simply, that he was bearing gifts to the Shah of Persia. Burnes did not challenge him; he knew this was not true. The Russians were going to Kabul. The man sniffed constantly throughout their brief conversation, and was formal, correct, cold, apart from one moment. In his hand Burnes held a French novel, with which he was whiling away the evenings. Vitkevich suddenly stopped, his attention seized, and took Burnes's hand. "Balzac," he said. "I *adore* Balzac." And then, as if fearing that he had said too much in admitting his literary tastes, he bowed again and was gone.

Burnes had not seen him again, but had learnt that he was in Kabul now, and knew of the daily, fruitless applications of his messengers at the great gate of the Bala Hissar. That was no surprise; he had immediately sent the intelligence of the Russian party to all corners of the world, to see what could be made of it. A few weeks after his arrival in Kabul, word had arrived from the court of the Shah; the British envoy to Persia had mentioned, in passing, that he understood that the Tsar was sending gifts. The Shah, from the envoy's report, had all but fallen off his throne in amazement, and hotly denied knowledge of any such mission. "Although we cannot doubt," the envoy wrote, "that the Shah is receiving the attentions of the Russian empire in other ways . . ." By the time Burnes finally had this report, it was redundant; Vitkevich and his men had turned up in Kabul. Still, he was concerned. His obsession with Vitkevich's presence, perhaps, was the reason he was so little interested in the otherwise curious information that there was an Englishman living in Kabul, and why he greeted Masson in the market with something not far from irritation.

"There is an Englishman in Kabul," Burnes said, laying the cards aside with a heavy sigh. There was nothing more important than being a good loser, even on this monumental scale.

"I know," Mohan Lal said absently, whether because of his predictably orderly hand, or for some other reason. "I heard about him."

"I met him today," Burnes said. "His name is Masson. He seems remarkably well informed on various interesting matters."

"Masson," Mohan Lal said. "What, did you go to visit him? I wondered who he was, and what he could be doing here."

"No, he approached me in the town," Burnes said. "He seemed to be waiting around in the market, as if he were trying to meet me, to be frank."

"Who is he?"

"I don't know," Burnes admitted. "We hardly talked."

"Burnes-ji, what a poor spy you make," Mohan Lal said. "To discover nothing about a man—hmm. You must try harder."

"I expect so," Burnes said. He could not quite account, now, for his lack of interest in so surprising a presence. "Of course, he might be valuable. The Newab told me that he has lived here for some years, as well as some scurrilous stories about him which hardly bear repeating. He thought that he had come here from India, which seems likely, though he was rather vague about it. I got the impression that the Amir had made it his business to find out all about him and then rather lost interest when he turned out to be nothing very remarkable. Perhaps I should go and talk to him."

"Yes, of course," Mohan Lal said. "He is some sort of scholar, people say."

"The Newab said he was a poet."

"Well, that is how they describe any solitary person with no visible occupation, though why even they should believe an English poet would come to this remote place . . . One thing that they all agree on is that he asks questions incessantly about all manner of things, which to me suggests that he might be worth talking to. You have really acquitted yourself lamentably, Burnes."

"I know," Burnes said contentedly. "Very well, I shall go and pick his brains over."

8

The next day, snow began to fall for the first time that year. It settled heavily, and when Masson left his house in the morning, a weight of snow fell in where it had drifted against the door. He always loved this first fresh snow of the year in this high city, and as he went heavily through the streets, it had seemed to work a transformation on the contours of the city. Everything was rounded, smoothed, and turned into the same substance, and the city was made clean. In the silent muted morning, the Kabul of the day before seemed not just transformed, but made entirely new, and it was a different city Masson wandered through. The noise of the streets was deadened; the smells of shit and spice quite gone, and nothing was here instead except the clean silence of a snowy day in which the loudest noise was the crunching of Masson's own boots through the crust, and the intangible oxygen flavour of snow when you stuck out your tongue into the clear empty air. The heavy clouds were clearing above, driven by a high wind, and the still streets blazed under the brilliant blue.

Masson walked the streets for an hour or so, without stopping to call on any of his habitual cronies and shopkeepers, thinking of nothing very much. It was good to walk in this suddenly unfamiliar city, and everything, from his cold wet feet to the freezing bite of the air when he breathed in, was a pleasant sensation to him. He felt happy for no reason, and even his wet socks seemed absurd and nice to him today. Like a child, he carried out pointless little experiments as he went, and the curious Afghans watched him hop along to leave a line of left-footed prints, or stand for two minutes at the street corner, pursing his lips to blow the thinnest stream of steam into the air with mild, forgiving amusement. Finally, he turned tail and went home, rubbing his hands under his armpits, pink and grinning with the cold.

He was just taking off his socks in his upstairs study when the widow Khadija sidled in. Beneath her veil, there was the groping gesture, like two cats mating in a sack, which was her usual greeting to Masson.

"The foreigner is here," she said in her guttural muffled voice.

"The boy Qasim?" Masson said—since to Khadija, Qasim, whose family were Qizzilbash, and originally from Herat, were not to be considered as the same as her.

"No," she said. "No, the other foreigner, the . . ." she shrugged, another big shifting gesture inside the cloak as her powers of description failed her.

Masson put on a pair of sandals and a dry coat, and went down to the large room at the back. Burnes was standing there, his back to the door, his arms awkwardly gripping each other behind him, his whole attitude one of mild impatience.

"Good morning, sir," Masson said in English. Burnes turned, and bowed deeply. "I am honoured by your calling on me."

"Good morning to you, Mr. Masson," Burnes said. Why it was shocking that Burnes should so bluntly acknowledge that his name had registered, that it was important enough to remember, Masson did not know, and yet it was so. Masson called for tea, and they sat down. There was something rather unreal about the whole encounter, Masson thought. The silence of the snowy city seemed to be concentrated in this room and to lie between them; neither, it seemed, quite knew how to start on exploring what they already knew of each other. Suddenly Masson was aware that Burnes had asked him a question.

"Sir?" he said.

"I was merely wondering how you come to be in this place, sir," Burnes said patiently.

"Curiosity, sir," Masson said. He felt disinclined to share his history with this fellow. "I am a clergyman, and travelled in curiosity, and my curiosity led me from place to place, and finally I find myself very far from home, but profitably so. My interests were originally in the ancient history of the Greeks, and to examine the question of Alexander's campaigns in the region, but since then, my studies have led me to very many—"

"It is unusual for a clergyman to wear Company boots, I believe," Burnes said coolly.

Masson was thrown; and he looked down in bemusement at the bazaar sandals on his feet.

"I noticed when we talked yesterday," Burnes expanded. "In the market. Your boots, sir."

"You are observant, sir," Masson said. "Company boots? You mean, a soldier's boots? I had no idea. How interesting. The fact is—the fact is—I acquired them in a most out-of-the-way place—I acquired them in, in Peshawar on my travels, in the market there. Company boots? How they came to be in such a place I do not know. I saw only boots of European manufacture, sturdy, very useful, and acquired them there. Not being a soldier—"

"Not having been a soldier," Burnes said.

"No, indeed, I was unfamiliar with their exact origin, and did not trouble to inquire. What poor fellow must have surrendered his boots, and in what manner, I do not care to think, but they are a good fit, a good fit. Tell me, sir—I heard there is now a Queen in London."

"Yes, there is," Burnes said briskly.

"I somehow heard," Masson said.

"A great curiosity to a Mussulman, I suppose," Burnes said. "Now, you must see the world pass through this place, situated as you are."

"It is certainly less isolated than might be thought," Masson said, not quite seeing the end of the conversation.

"You must see persons of very many nations, here, I expect," Burnes said.

"Yes, we do," Masson said.

"Hindus? Chinese? Europeans?"

"Sometimes, yes, sir, yes, Europeans."

"Russians?" Burnes said, and there was nothing in his tone to indicate that he had reached the centre of his conversation, but all the same, Masson knew it. Russians? Burnes's eyes focused, seriously, on Masson, and his posture did not alter, but now, Masson knew, with the sensation of being alone with a snake, that now, whatever he said, Burnes would listen to it.

9

The court had no doubt in the matter. The Amir was going to have someone killed, and soon. Who it would be, they did not know; what they would have done, they could not imagine. But, without discussing the matter, every one of them recognized the signs, and waited in a state of continuous terror. None of them left. They did not dare. But the unspoken rage of their Amir was unmistakable, and would end in the way it always ended. They examined each other's sleepless faces and tried to see the face of a victim.

The Amir sat in his throne room and his face was clouded with concentration. None of them would raise the subject, but they knew exactly what it was. Over there, the Sikhs, beating at the gates of the empire, stealing lands, moving forward. Over there, the Shah of Persia at the gates of Herat. The Amir's tranquillity was quite gone. He was a man under siege, and if he could do nothing, then at least he could satisfy his feelings by having a prince of the court executed. And the court waited to see who it would be.

The news from Herat arrived in pieces, unpredictably. Whatever Dost Mohammed's feelings about the ruler of Herat, it was and always had been an Afghan city. Now, it was walled up and besieged by the Persians, moving in. The Emperor received the news, and said nothing. The court did not raise the question, and they all knew what they thought; that the holy city would fall to their murderously perfumed neighbours as Peshawar had done; that from either side, the invaders would move in, would drive forward, and Kabul would fall. Whom it would fall to, they did not know or care. It was all one, and a gilded foreign prince would rule in the Bala Hissar, and they would all be dead.

Dost Mohammed's thoughts went around and around, and in his

sleep and in his waking moments, his marvellous mind paced two great empty halls, echoing with his pain and shame and misery. And the two halls of his thought had names. The first was named Peshawar. The second was named Herat. He thought, and thought, and thought, and nothing could distract him. He took no action; he made no orders. The only glimmer in his dark mind was that something had come to Kabul from outside all this, something that could help him. The British, surely, could save Herat from the Persians, and drive them back from the borders of the Amir's empire; they, surely, would help him to regain what was his, Peshawar. He made a single, infuriated gesture with his hand and the court scattered, grateful that it would not happen today. He sent for Burnes.

Burnes knew, too, of Herat; he knew of the siege through the occasional report from the envoy to the Shah, and from the stories filtering through to Kabul. The envoy could be of no help, apart from one interesting suggestion; he believed, although he could not be sure, that the siege was being pursued with the support and aid of Russian arms. This was not implausible, and, as Mohan Lal said, the information could greatly strengthen their position. If Burnes was painfully aware that under no circumstances could he offer what the Amir so plainly wanted, the offer of British help against his neighbours, he was at least reassured that, if need be, the Russian presence outside the walls of Herat could be demonstrated. Vitkevich, still languishing in the house of the Newab Jubbur Khan, would stand no chance at all of being received at the Bala Hissar; he would be lucky, if it came to that, if he escaped from Kabul with his life.

"I have received a letter from a traveller present here," Dost Mohammed said. They were seated in a small room, one of the Dost's private apartments. It was always hard to understand what kind of purpose each room in the palace served, since all were so simple, and little distinguished what might be a dining room from the stables from a bedchamber. What was needed was brought in and out, and each room was otherwise bare and empty. The only rooms with obvious purpose that Burnes had seen were the throne room and the armouries. Still, he thought that this might be a sort of robing room. The Dost reached forward with a formidable-looking piece of parchment, grandly sealed in blue.

Burnes took it, bowing from the neck, and looked at it. It had the appearance of the most formal communication imaginable, and his eyes flicked through the imposing and lavish Persian encomiums at the beginning to the matter.

"It appears to be a letter from the Tsar of Russia," he said guardedly. This, it seemed, was to be their first conversation about the Russian presence in Kabul.

"Yes," Dost Mohammed said. "That is what it appears to be. I learn from this letter, to my considerable surprise, that you are not, it seems, the only Europeans here. This was presented yesterday, and from it, I discover that there are some gentlemen here from Russia, who say that they come from the Russian Emperor. Now, I wonder what to make of this?"

Burnes looked at Dost Mohammed, but he was giving nothing away. His face was serenely blank. The Russians were lodged in the house of the Newab Jubbur Khan, in the house of the Amir's brother, at the orders of the Amir. Despite their best efforts, they were not received into the Presence, of that Burnes was sure, but the Amir certainly knew all about them. The Amir was testing him, in some unfathomable way.

"I cannot say whether these gentlemen are what they appear to be," the Amir went on. "Can this be what it seems? I would be most grateful for your opinion."

"I think I will need to study it, Pearl of the Age," Burnes said; and at least the Amir was trusting him with the knowledge of this communication.

"Very well," Dost Mohammed said. "What manner of country is Russia?"

Burnes girded himself up for the familiar inquisition, to acquit himself as well he could. It seemed as if Dost Mohammed had, for these last weeks, been saving himself for this subject; his inquiries about the dress of Englishwomen had hidden his concern for what directly mattered to their present concern, the demands the Amir wished to make of Britain. He had not mentioned the Russians before now, or referred to the events taking place at Herat; and it was to this that he turned towards the end of their morning conversation.

"It must be a matter of great concern and grief to Your Majesty," Burnes said, referring to the siege.

"That is so," Dost Mohammed said. "The loss of so great a jewel as Herat would wound the heart of every Afghan, and I, whose grief is greatest of all, feel helpless and friendless as a new widow."

"The actions of the Persian Shah are of great concern to Her Majesty's Government, and we cannot condone any such action taken against the territories of Afghan princes. You are assured that the Shah of Persia has been informed of our displeasure in the strongest terms."

"And yet, what can I, alone, do?" the Amir went on. "A poor, helpless country cannot resist alone the might of the Shah of Persia."

"The situation of Your Majesty fills the heart of every Briton with sympathy," Burnes said. He suddenly felt quite exhausted, and stuck at this point like a soldier in a ditch.

Dost Mohammed rose, and Burnes followed suit, standing still, his hands pressed together in the gesture of supplication while the Amir moved about the room. "Sympathy may not be enough," he said. "No, sympathy will not save my lands."

"Your Majesty is right to think that the love between our nations is deep and inexhaustible," Burnes said. "But whatever my personal feelings on the matter, I am required to remind the Pearl of the Age that my nation cannot enter a course of action which will lead to the destruction of the friendly relations we have established elsewhere. Your Majesty, we are not a warlike people, and we cannot take sides in a dispute like this; it would have the most disastrous consequences, for us and for you. Your Majesty, we thoroughly deplore the actions others have taken against you, but further than that we cannot go."

"Your words are empty, Burnes," the Amir said.

"We cannot, Amir," Burnes said. "I can give the absolute assurance that in no circumstances will we take arms against you, but that is all. What I have said to you is exactly what is being said to your predatory neighbours, who would similarly like our direct aid. We will not fight against you, and I would hope that Your Majesty will consider whether he can be certain that even so small a certainty can be afforded in the case of others, of other emissaries from other—"

"Burnes," the Amir said brusquely. "I assure you that I will not receive other ambassadors while there is a possibility of the friendship of your nation."

Burnes bowed, seeing the threat in Dost Mohammed's words.

"Enough, Burnes, enough," he went on. "That will do."

He swept out into the waiting crowd of courtiers, and Burnes was left alone, bowing, holding the Russian letter. There was nothing more he could have said.

10

By now, Masson heartily disliked the appearance of Burnes in his house. He was under no illusions; Burnes always wanted something of him. There was another layer to his dislike, the unnerving feeling which rose from his boots, that Burnes knew what he was and what he had done. Here, he was safe from Burnes; the man needed him in some way. But Masson had no doubt that, were they a thousand miles to the east, Burnes would have had him shot, and not regretted it for a moment. One day, he thought, whenever Burnes turned up, one day I shall show you what kind of man I am; not a cowardly deserter, not a man who kills and runs away, but Masson. And I shall act, and you will see what kind of man I am, and how you will beg for my friendship . . . In what way this would come about—in what way Masson would show himself—he did not know and could not imagine. And he realized that in his uncertainty lay all his weakness, but still he hated Burnes, and the way Burnes looked at the useful, disgusting deserter in his mountain hiding place.

Qasim had gone. One day he had not come, and Masson accepted it. He often slept in the afternoons, and when he came to, gummy with daylit sleep, Qasim was usually there, hanging about foolishly. That day, he had woken up, and there was no one by him. He had not come, nor the next day, nor the next. In the event, Masson had not been honoured by the table of Qasim's father, and had no idea where the boy lived. He did not come the next day, or ever again. Masson had expected it; it always happened in much the same way, and in any case the boy had been more than mildly tiresome. If he had been less lazy, he might have dismissed him anyway, rather than trusting to the usual loss of interest. It was odd, then, that he felt a little pang at his departure, as if he had cared anything for him. Whatever he thought, there was always the memory of flesh, and that was a memory Masson could have done without. Qasim had gone, disappearing into the absorbent street life of the city, never to re-emerge or—to be honest—to be sought for with much energy. The periodic stirrings of lust would not, in this case, drive Masson out of doors. As the widow Khadija would have observed, another foreigner had arrived, and Burnes was proving a much more taxing visitor to the house. He was bored with him.

"It is a letter from the Tsar," Masson said cautiously. "Here, look, it says—"

"Yes, I know," Burnes said. "I can read it, too. I know what it appears to be. I want to know if you think that is what it is."

"How did you get it?"

"Dost Mohammed gave it to me."

Masson raised an eyebrow.

"I knew they were here," Burnes said. "Of course, the Dost pretended it was all a great surprise to him, but he knows perfectly well they are here, too."

"Is he receiving them?"

"I don't think so," Burnes said. "Actually, I am fairly sure not. In any case, he showed me this today."

"And you think it might not be genuine? You think—what?"

"My dear fellow," Burnes said *de haut en bas*. "I think it is exactly what it seems to be. There is no reason, as far as I can see, to think otherwise. Of course the Tsar would send emissaries to Kabul—that is entirely probable. The only reason I am asking you if this is a genuine letter is that, for some reason, the Dost was good enough to show me this and to say that he thought there was a possibility it was a forgery, and the Russians persons of no account whatever. I admit, it would be most convenient indeed were it so, but I don't think that is the case."

"Well," Masson said. "If that is your view, and the Dost perfectly prepared to hear that it is not from Russia at all, why not simply tell him so? That would simplify matters enormously." For one bizarre moment, he thought of Burnes naked; his thin white body stretched out on the floor before him.

Burnes looked at him in astonishment. It was as if he had seen Masson's grotesque thought. "Lie, you mean?"

"Yes, of course."

"But if it is in fact genuine—"

"If, if, if—it suits your ends, the Amir would believe you, and the Russians be thrown out of town."

The possibility had clearly never occurred to Burnes, and he looked at Masson with what seemed very much like distaste. "I hardly think I can compromise my position by deceiving the Amir," he said. "And when it comes to light . . ."

"Very well," Masson said. He held the letter up to the light, ran his eye over it briefly, and gave it back to Burnes. "In my opinion, this is a forgery. There. You have my opinion."

"I cannot take your opinion, sir," Burnes said coldly. "Sir, I have to say that I know well what manner of man you are, and how you live your life here—I know this very well—and you must not assume that my standards of behaviour are your own."

"That is my opinion, and that is what you asked for. And I strongly advise you against insulting me in such a fashion."

"Sir, look at the seal. That is undoubtedly the Russian imperial seal."

"An obvious trick."

"Even if they could write such a letter, the seal, sir—"

"Very well," Masson snapped, and, seizing Burnes's arm, he dragged him out of the room. "Come with me, and I will show you the value of the damned imperial seal."

Burnes followed him, and they left the house. Masson was steaming with rage, and they stomped silently through the snow. His feet, still in their sandals, almost burnt with the cold. No one was about; no one to see the two furious Englishmen struggling through the snow and the silent streets. Masson would not look at Burnes and his foolish honour; this was nothing to do with him, and he cared nothing whether Burnes or the Russians were received at the Bala Hissar. He did not know what manner of man Burnes was, and he did not know how he lived his life, and he did not care enough to inquire. But he knew he was right, and the stupidity of the man, his endless superiority, filled him with fury.

At length they reached the bazaar, and Masson led Burnes to a dark little stall of provisions. The shopkeeper, who was familiar with Masson, nodded agreeably, but the gentlemen ignored him. Masson walked around him and, from a pile, picked up a bag of sugar. He thrust it in Burnes's face.

"There," he said. On the bottom of the bag was a blue seal; it looked uncommonly like the imperial Russian seal on the piece of parchment. "There, Burnes, your evidence. The imperial Russian seal? Every Russian merchant has one. You have no proof that this letter is genuine, and you have a very good reason to tell the Dost that it is not. And you know that if you do, he will believe you. And you know that if he discovers in years to come that it was perfectly genuine, and calls you to account, you may in all conscience say that there was no reason to suppose it so. There, Burnes, look, and you will see what manner of man I am. Listen to me."

"Very well," Burnes said. "I see I will get no sense out of you, sir. I shall act according to my own lights."

"Do you know what they call you?" Masson said, now beyond all restraint. "Do you know, sir, what all Kabul calls you? They call you *gharib nawaz*. They call you that. Your humble servant. And you must know, Burnes, that they all laugh at you, with your humble servant, your endless *gharib nawaz* and your creeping before the Amir, on your knees. The second you turn your back, they are laughing at you. Be a man, you fool."

Burnes stiffened like a warring cock, his nostrils flaring. With one gesture, he snatched the letter back from Masson's trembling hands and stalked off. The shopkeeper looked at Masson curiously; it was not every day two foreigners came in and shouted at each other, in their strange singing shrieking language, the devil-language of the infidel, and he was interested. Then he had a brilliant afterthought, and dashed to the door as Masson went on his way.

"Save Kabul, sir!" he called after his retreating back. "Save us, sir, save us from our fates!"

The foreigner did not turn, but carried on his way. But the shopkeeper went back and sat down, happy with himself.

II

"How is it that you have seen so little of Kabul?" the Newab Jubbur Khan asked politely.

"Because, my dear fellow," Vitkevich said, "we are effectively prisoners, here, in your house."

Vitkevich had reached the end of his patience. For weeks, now, he and his men had been entirely cut off from the world. No news penetrated the walls of the Newab's house; no knowledge could be gleaned from the ever-present guards, and they sat and waited and told long stories of their past campaigns to pass the time. He felt utterly alone; what he knew of the world outside the walls of the Newab's house was now long out of date. He had his instructions, and he had a sense of what had been happening in Herat, in India, in Kabul. But now he knew nothing of all that. There had been no communication whatever from the Amir in response to his entreaties, and all Vitkevich knew was that the English were here in this city. Everything might be going appallingly wrong, and he—he, surely—would suffer the consequences. Imprisoned, he felt at the mercy of people he now knew nothing of.

They lived in comfort and unspeakable boredom. It would not be so bad if they could simply lapse into silence, lasting days, leaving each other in peace, but that didn't seem a possibility. Instead, they talked, on and on, but always around the same subjects, speculating about when the Amir would see them, and never coming to any conclusion. It was terribly dull. They never had any new information, since none of the Afghans would really talk to them, and the conversation always ran its course and ended with them all saying that they didn't know why they were being kept here and hoped it wouldn't be long.

Sometimes one of them would start reminiscing, set off by a chance remark, and however dull the story of a campaign or a small military adventure, they would all drift over and listen. Vitkevich had heard all the stories more than once, but by some silently agreed decision, nobody would complain if a soldier felt like telling it one more time. Vitkevich disliked telling his own story—he was aware that it was rather more interesting than anyone else's, and might discourage the others—and confined himself to the usual soldier's complaints. The days passed on in this haze of boredom, and even the diversions from boredom seemed to have lost their appeal; dice lay neglected now, novels unfinished or unread. The ennui was too absolute. Confinement in camp always bred a passionate loathing of one's companions, a sort of loathing which focused on the most harmless habits; the way Jirinovsky did not always reach for his handkerchief, but blew his nose on his fingers and would then wipe them casually on the cushion he was sitting on, or Stanchinsky's dozy egotistical inattention, his habit of asking some question about one's history, family, or ideas, and then interrupting after two sentences to pass some remark about himself or to wonder, for the fiftieth time that day, when Dost Mohammed was finally going to see them. Vitkevich was too well acquainted with the irritations of camp life to give way to any of this, and much as he itched to tell his subordinates that he had heard that story a hundred times, or to remind one of them that it was disgusting to talk of one's bowel problems over dinner while scratching one's testicles, he kept quiet. Prison had been very much the same, and although these inner irritations with the presence of other people had a way of building up into huge resentments, it was vital not to give way to them.

Oblovich had the limelight at the moment, and was recounting an adventure that he had had while on manoeuvres. He was an extraordinarily vulgar fellow and had told the story before, but the men were listening in an inattentive way. The Newab Jubbur Khan—now there was the principal source of Vitkevich's irritation, with his charming manner, the perfect host, and all the time refusing to be of the slightest help in any way—had entered the room and stood, nodding at what, presumably, he could not understand at all, as if the rhythms of a story, even in a foreign language, were in themselves interesting and entertaining. Oblovich was glittering feverishly, thrilling himself at least with the much-told story.

". . . but then the wheel of a gun carriage caught in the mud, and the horses turned it over, trying to pull it out. Well, that was a day and no mistake. My batman said to me, that's the third, so we're all right now. And I said, what do you mean? And he said—he was a decent little fellow, a Moscow shoemaker's son, always praying, I often wonder what happened to him—he said that they always said troubles come in threes, and we'd had three that day, and wouldn't have a fourth, God be blessed. So I went to the commanding officer and said bluntly, because I could see that the men wouldn't stand for any more, that we'd better strike camp there, where we stood. That's the sort of chap I am, I never kowtow, and if the Tsar himself were to say something stupid, so if you imagine the Tsar saying to you that the moon was made of green cheese and the grass in the fields was nothing but noodles, most people would say, yes your imperial majesty, no your imperial majesty, but not me, oh no, I'd tell him straight away that he was talking nonsense. So I went to the commanding officer and told him, because I just didn't care, that we'd better stop there, and he stared at me and said that I should return to my place and he saw no reason to change the plans for the day. Well, I went back, and in the end I was right, you see. Because the whole cart was turned over, and we were all standing around scratching our heads and thinking what we were going to do, when all at once over the hill there came thousands and thousands of the enemy.

"Well, I say the enemy, but I don't know exactly who they were, not knowing much about the part of the world where we were. But I can tell you there were thousands of them and they looked like they meant business, all in fur and grinning and spitting and shooting in the air. Now no tribesman is a match for one of the Tsar's soldiers, yes, you've got a point when you say that. But you've got to remember that we were tired and hungry and didn't know where we were and there were thousands of them, all bearing down on us and wanting blood on their swords. So as quick as we could I ordered the men into a square. You'll be asking now why it had fallen to me to be ordering all this, but I'll tell you. It was the commander in chief again. You're not going to believe this, but when they came over the hill, he had no idea. As long as I live, I'll remember the look on his face. You'd have said he'd been turned to stone, just standing there and staring, a fine Petersburg gentleman, but no iron, no iron at all. So it fell to me to organize the men. Let me ask you—what would you have done? I'll tell you what I did in a moment, but I still don't know whether I did the right thing."

"You must have done the right thing," Jirinovsky said sycophantically, "to get out alive. You must have."

"That's right," Oblovich said, delighted. "That's right, son. Well, I'll tell you . . ."

I could tell you a thing or two, Vitkevich thought viciously; I could tell you about bravery. I could tell you what it's like to run away from home when you're fifteen, to fight the Tsar's troops just because you believe in something; to resolve under a hail of bullets that you are going to die rather than be taken, and half an hour later be lying in the enemy's wagon with your body and shame intact; to spend years in exile, to change utterly, to return and burrow your way into the affections and trust of the powers you once fought against; to learn never to trust any-one, and ride with the future of the Tsar's empire on your shoulders; to be brave, and know it, and never to admit to bravery, because that is what anyone would have done in the same place. He told himself his own story, over and over, and listened carefully to it.

When Oblovich stopped talking, the Newab looked round the group to make sure that the story had come to an end, and then bowed directly at Vitkevich, who stood up. The Newab beckoned him outside, and handed him a sealed note—one which had clearly been opened and badly resealed.

"You have a letter from one of your countrymen," the Newab said, not troubling to deny that he knew its contents.

Vitkevich raised an eyebrow, but opened it. It was in execrable French, and from the leader of the English mission. He read it there, while the Newab stood by him, nodding and smiling from time to time. Vitkevich folded it up again.

"The guest of the Amir asks to meet me," Vitkevich said. "His name is Burnes. Do you know him?"

"Certainly," the Newab said. "A great man, and a great friend to the Amir and to every Afghan."

"He proposes to entertain me to dinner," Vitkevich said, seeing the impossibility of this in Jubbur Khan's eyes. Then he had a bright thought. "Sir, see, here, he reminds me that it is the Christian festival of Christmas in two days' time." It was not the Russian Christmas, but the Newab would not know the difference between European calendars. "A very important and holy festival for all Christians. The guest of the Amir, this great man, I do not know how to refuse so very important a man and so very kind and condescending an invitation to so holy a festival."

"Of course you must go," the Newab said. "You must all go, the Amir himself has said so."

Vitkevich would not inquire into this shift of heart. "We will not impose on his hospitality to so very great an extent, and it will suffice that I alone go. I thank you for your consideration and respect for our customs."

"Well," the Newab said, smiling broadly at this flattery, "if your men will consent to remain as my guests at this most important festival, we shall do our best to help them mark it. The day after tomorrow, you said." He wandered off, leaving Vitkevich holding the letter and wondering at what would surely be the men's surprise at being asked to celebrate Christmas on quite the wrong date.

12

The court dreaded the moment when the Amir left his audience with the Englishman. He swept out and his face, every day, suddenly boiled with rage. The court knew the Englishman knew nothing of this. They stood outside the little audience chamber in silence, awaiting their Emperor's pleasure, and his voice was always calm and peaceful, asking reasonable and clever questions—such clever questions, if you listened, you would be more astonished at the Dost's wisdom and knowledge in being able to ask them than you would at the Englishman's answering them. But the court had no doubt that his manner concealed an overpowering fury, and as he came into their midst, every day, his face had already hardened into an expression of demonic conviction.

The doors were flung open and the court leapt back a pace or two. The Pearl of the Age walked out, giving them no sign of greeting, not slowing; they rose from their deep bow and sorted themselves out in precedence in a raggle-taggle way as they scurried after him, like dice being shaken in a gaming bag. Peshawar—Herat—Peshawar—Herat. The Dost led the way in silence, and they did their best to keep up, their eyes lowered.

Outside the women's quarters, the Amir stopped and coughed decisively. A wail came out—the worst of the wives.

"Not now, Dosto," she called. "Not today, in the name of everything holy."

"It is I," the Amir said firmly.

"No, not now," she said petulantly through the screen. "Go away, slave. Tomorrow, tomorrow, tomorrow."

The court stood, stiff with embarrassment. Khushhal cast a glance sideways, and one of the princes caught his look, and immediately dropped his head, unresponding. Khushhal, too, dropped his head, but it was too late. The Amir Dost Mohammed Khan had seen his glance, and turned on him.

"You wish to say something, Prince?" he said, quite quietly.

"No, Amir," Khushhal said.

"You insult me, Prince," the Dost said.

"No, Amir," Khushhal said, in almost speechless terror.

"You insult me," the Dost said, firmly, and the fury was black on his face. The court drooped their heads and felt the full force of their relief. It was done, it was over, and now, this time, the rage of the Dost had fallen elsewhere, and how Khushhal would die, they did not yet care to imagine.

EIGHTEEN

The historian's eye rises up, and inspects the world from a safe distance, and sees things which none of these people saw in total, which all of them had to guess at; they are all prisoners in their place, in the dark, guessing at what might be happening from their little cells, their circumstances. The historian is, on the other hand, their warder, and knows everything. The lines between them are fragile and easily broken; Bella, in her moated grange, cannot know what is happening, in that faraway place. She does not care, but if she did, she still would know nothing of these events. The news takes months to travel, and will never reach her in any case. Auckland in Calcutta knows where Burnes is, and he has his instructions, but they can talk to each other uncertainly and unpredictably, and on the whole leave each other alone. Runjeet Singh hears rumours, and that is all; the court of the Shah is far away, and the solitary envoy there sits, and has to construct his behaviour in accordance with instructions now long out of date. But we, happily, know everything.

Not many people know, for instance, that there is an Irishman within Herat, constructing the city's defences, rousing the populace to defiance. How he got there is a mystery, but there he is, and the city is standing firm. He bears the absurd name of Eldred Pottinger, but, despite that, he is proving himself a great hero, and knows it. Pottinger knows a great deal, all in all, and is certain, too, that if he ever gets out of this monumental scrape, what he knows will set off the most almighty row. He knows, for instance, what his masters only guess at, that the Persian troops at the gates are armed by Russians; and though he does not know what the state of affairs is in Kabul, he guesses that he has discovered something of great value. He is right; the black diplomats in Petersburg, at the court of the Tsar, are horribly aware that they are playing a dangerous double game, and should anyone unfriendly discover that they are simultaneously paying court to the Dost and besieging the city of one of his Afghan neighbours, their plans will fall helplessly to the ground. We know, too, that Auckland has given way to persuasion, and when Burnes arrives from his mission to Kabul, it will be to learn that the general view is that his deplorable friend the Amir Dost Mohammed Khan must go, and, in the interests of the stability of the region, that wise and great king Shah Shujah will be summoned from his palace in Ludhiana, and installed with a full display of imperial power on the throne which is rightfully his, to popular acclamation.

The lines of communication slip and slide, give way, and leave each of them once more in the dark, feeling their way uncertainly, always conscious of the proximity of disaster. Burnes talks to the Dost, and is always conscious of how far he can go, and what he cannot offer his magnificent friend; his hands are helplessly tied, whatever he would like to say. The Amir has the appearance of a man who knows everything, but he does not, and shortly his ignorance of one thing will lead him to what seems like disaster. Only we know everything; they are helpless.

NINETEEN

Yusuf started to explain once more. There were seventeen dishes to prepare, and the explanation was long. By him, the kitchen boys squatted
and chewed, and listened curiously to their chief. He did not feel confident in his explanation of the feast the kitchen was to prepare, and was
not sure that he had entirely understood its reason. The explanation of
the foreigner had been long and complex, and Yusuf had listened and
nodded, thinking that he was taking it all in. Now it was his task to convey
the order to his subordinates, he was not at all sure of the cause of the
feast, or what was required.

A festival, like Eid; that seemed to be it. In the depths of winter, the
Christians celebrated the birth of their God with a feast, and it had fallen
to Yusuf, the principal cook of the Bala Hissar, to prepare this feast to
instructions.

"A holy feast," he said, his eyes shut. "There will be fish and small birds
and mutton."

"Fish?" one of the kitchen boys said, his arms folded.

"I will explain," Yusuf said. "The sauces and the dishes of vegetables
we prepare as for a great feast, for Eid."

"For how many?"

"For two," Yusuf said firmly. The kitchen boys looked at him in puzzlement. Yusuf was a skinny, wrinkled man; everything about him seemed shrunken except his tongue, which was too large for his mouth, and he spat a little as he explained. "For the guest of the Amir, and an honoured ambassador from the Emperor of Russia. For two only."

"How . . ."

Yusuf sighed. He would go into explanations for the sauces and the dishes in a moment. Now he produced his prize object, handed over by Burnes the day before.

"This is an English fish," he said, holding up the solid shining packet. "Brought from England."

"How long does the journey from England take?"

"Many months, but the Englishman explained that the fish will be well. It is—" Yusuf faltered, unable to explain the mysteries of the hermetically sealed salmon. "It is well."

The boys gathered round and examined the tightly bound package in scepticism.

"It does not smell," one of them admitted.

"And a dish of plums, baked together," Yusuf went on. "And—I have it all here . . ."

The explanations went on, and the English Christmas dinner seemed to make more sense as he talked, to become more like a great court feast, to become more like food.

Like beasts into the ark, the dead limbs of animals were carried into the great kitchens of the Bala Hissar, and Yusuf sniffed at them and pronounced them good. Quails, live and peeping, flicking their heads about; five chickens in their netted basket, white and shining in the dim hot light of the fire; half a sheep, flung over the shoulder of a bloody squat butcher. And then the fruits of the tree, the vine, the roots, dried plums and mulberries and grapes, shrivelled and richly fragranced; roots and tubers buried in the warm-scented earth of the fields, piles of mushrooms like little cushions, carried in baskets. And the kitchen gave up its hoard of treasures, bottles of pomegranate seeds, glowing like rubies, bowls of yellow and brown spices, pounded by the least of the boys until the air twitched with heat. The fish was opened, and its meat found to be clean and good, and the deepest of the copper pans was set to boiling, to receive it back into its seething element. The kitchen quickly filled with bowls, each containing a different thing, steeping in unctuous dark liquids, exchanging their rich flavours for the great Christian feast. On the floor, three boys sat, dealing with the birds; the butcher took each bird out, one by one, and with his axe beheaded the chickens, with his clever thick hands wrung the necks of the quails. In the yard, the children of the court watched this favourite entertainment, their mouths open. The butcher brought their little limp bodies back, and the three boys took them, each by each, and calmly began the peaceful work of plucking them, their quiet absorption in the fug of dust broken only by the occasional violent sneeze. The fires roared, and Yusuf went from corner to corner, examining, prodding, shaking his head, until he was satisfied. And then the cooking could begin.

The lamb was spitted, and dripped over the crackling fire; its sauce of almonds and saffron and thread of gold thickened in the care of Yusuf's attentive brother. The pickles were chosen, and sat in their wax-sealed jars, waiting to be opened. Two chickens boiled in a vat of water with roots, with garlic-scented grass; they had long to go, and when the meat had been stripped and the bones pulled out, the rich soup would be boiled and boiled, and produce a few tablespoons of plummy sweet juice. The quails were boned, and placed inside the remaining chickens, their heads poking from the orifice in the high courtly manner, and inside the quails was a forcemeat of lemon and mushroom and the finest dried apricot, the apricots from the summer garden of the Bala Hissar itself; over them, in the end, a sauce of pomegranate, boiled into an oaky brown. The stuff for bread was all there, and the cook already beginning his task, already kneading and mixing and shaping. The slippery dishes of aubergine, the pulpy smooth mash of roots, the melting onion, that could wait; the silver sweetmeats were laid out already on the glittering salver; the cakes and fruit pastries piled high in the third of the larders, the darkest, the coolest one, as well-water ran softly down its walls. And Yusuf returned, satisfied, to the strangest of his labours, to the English pudding he was creating.

The plum pudding was in its early stages, and Yusuf felt exhilarated by this new, this fantastical dish. Five bowls of dried fruit were arrayed before him, each soaking in water and milk, each growing plump. The seven types of nut were in neat little piles, arranged from the bitterest green walnuts to the sweet creamy white nut every cook had a different name for; some chopped to a floury fineness, some to the size of lentils, some halved, some left whole, according to their nature. The eight spices, the cardamom, the seed of the fennel, the cumin, the poppy seeds and the sweet bark of the cinnamon, the pile of cloves with their stony petals and their pebbly little heart where the best flavour hid, the pepper with its strange property, the property of not being tasted, of making every other thing taste more powerfully of itself, and there, in its precious little jar, a precious little stony nutmeg, the single nutmeg in the whole of Kabul, kept for just such a purpose as this. All this would combine, and in the end, there would be a mysterious single smell, the perfume of the cedar tree. The treacle, the honey, the brick of sugar. The eggs rested in their golden straw; the flour and the mutton fat, which in the end would soak up all that sweetness, weighed, prepared, measured. And there, at the end of the pile of raw food, was a single silver coin, as instructed by the Amir's honoured guest, to be placed inside the treacly mixture, placed deep inside and hidden. Everything was there, before Yusuf, and as he took a deep breath and prepared to begin, the boys of the kitchen abandoned their task, and came for an amazed moment to watch the extraordinary task their master was embarking upon.

Their faces glistened in the heat, and for hours, as they laboured, they only shouted at each other. Through the open door, from time to time, came a small child or two in a gold brocaded coat, one of the Amir's small sons, and stood and gazed at the hellish fiery scene. The air was stormy with hot purple flavours, roaring out of the kitchen into the cold mountain air. Yusuf was a favourite with them, always popping a nut or a slice of sugar or a spoon of honey into their mouths (or sometimes, teasingly, a burning-hot pepper root, red as sin, for no better reason than to watch them cry and puff. But that, they found, was fun too). Today he cast them hardly a look as he went briskly from place to place, dipping a finger into a sauce, prodding at the bread, sticking a blackened prong into the heart of a limp roasting bird with the considered accuracy of the compassionate executioner; testing, tasting, eating in fragments the great strange feast, bellowing and roaring and nodding with a benevolent half-smile when, against everything, it seemed to be coming near to the goodness he had so clearly seen. "Out! Out! Out!" he roared at them, and they ran, the children, twenty paces into the yard, where they stopped, and soon, step by step, the boiling fury of the kitchen drew them back to stand and stare, their watering tongues licking their little chins.

And then all at once the feast was done, and everything, as if by magic, came together at the same time; the world, its traders, its ambassadors, had poured its many virtues in homage into this fiery room, and from each corner of the room, the kitchen boys came with their heavy perfect burdens, each after the other placing their perfect dish on the great silver plates. Their histories had prepared them for this moment, too; each boy, each chef, came from a line of palace chefs, and their fathers and their fathers' fathers had poured decades of kitchen expertise into their proud descendants, preparing them for this moment. And the feast, in tremendous procession, began to leave the kitchens of the palace. Yusuf watched it all go, and when the kitchen was left, bereft, ruinous as a battlefield, he sank to his hams and for the first time all day, closed his eyes, closed his ears to the boys' chatter, and abandoned himself to the entirety of exhausted pleasure. The feast was done.

2

Vitkevich was in pain, and held his hurting face as if it were some delicate soft fruit. He had envisaged and planned for his journey, had packed cigars and books, medicines against sickness and ennui, had thought of possible disasters; but he had not thought of this. His whole face hurt, and although he knew that the cloud of pain must be emanating from a single tooth, he could not find which one it could be. Sometimes it seemed a back tooth; sometimes it seemed to him that it came from the other side of his face entirely. He felt like poking a sharp point into his mouth, or even, sometimes, into his ear. He felt that would extinguish the pain.

Oblovich recommended chewing on cloves, and suggested sagely that the pain of a tooth sometimes subsided of its own accord. Vitkevich, cradling the entire right side of his face, nodded, knowing it was not true; this would get worse and worse, and finally his cheeks would explode in a mess of blood and pus and rotting teeth. The sweet woody stench of cloves filled their rooms, until they all grew to hate it—Vitkevich most of all.

They had been taken by surprise by the civil letter from the Englishman, asking Vitkevich, by name, to dinner, and discussed it endlessly. Whether it came merely from the Englishman, or whether it was some sort of despatch from Dost Mohammed, they could not agree on, and had no real means of telling.

Vitkevich suffered his pain, and could think of nothing else. The idea of a feast was so unbearable to him that he would not entertain it—for days, indeed, he had put nothing in his mouth but the occasional clove to suck and thick hot coffee, bitter under the sugar, as if cigars had been extinguished in it. He was not his usual plotting self, and since he would not think of food, he did not think of the feast, or the Englishman. He sat in his misery, a huddled little lump in the corner of the room, clinging on to the fading belief that this pain might go away of its own accord.

"We can always tell the Englishman you're not well," Oblovich said, experimentally. "I mean, one of us could go, just as easily. Better if someone else went, Vitkevich."

Vitkevich shook his head irritably—it was like watching a molten ball of metal topple around a box, so slowly did the pain attendant on his movement fade. The rest of them looked at each other.

"He wouldn't mind putting it off," Oblovich offered. "Just a day or two, I mean."

"Ah farff ingo ha korffaffa," Vitkevich said. Then he reached into his mouth and pulled out the handkerchief he was biting on, knotted and sodden—the pain was so hot, he felt it must be wet with blood, but it was only saliva. He tried again. "I hardly think," he said, his tongue mincing about the least tender parts of his mouth, "that would be wise. If we delay it may never happen. And the excuse for the dinner is Christmas, after all."

"Christmas?" Oblovich said—he was unnecessarily obtuse, really.

"The English Christmas," Vitkevich said. He winced, horribly, and the others winced sympathetically. "Impossible."

"Vitkevich, you cannot go, and you will not delay, and you will not send another man in your place," Stanchinsky said. "Come now, something must be done."

"Leave me in peace," Vitkevich said, and wretchedly inserted the handkerchief back into the horrible orifice. "Good evening, sir," he attempted, in Persian, as the Newab Jubbur Khan entered the room.

The Newab bowed, delightedly, all about. "But that can be cured," he said, when his inquiries about everyone's health had been answered by an account of Vitkevich's present misery. "There is nothing easier. I shall arrange it immediately."

That, in fact, had been Vitkevich's fear—he could, after all, have arranged it himself, were it not that the details of Kabul dental treatment were as vividly present to his mind as any pain could be. He attempted to object as best he could.

"Do not try to speak, my dear sir," the Newab said, cutting through Vitkevich's farffing. No one else attempted to help him out; indeed, they were grinning insanely at the prospect of this coming entertainment. "It only aggravates the pain, constantly to be speaking."

Everything else seemed to be handled in the most infuriatingly leisurely way, but it could only have been five minutes when the Newab returned, smiling benevolently, with a servant of dangerously insane appearance. In the man's hand there was a blackened tool, surely too big to insert into anyone's mouth. He hung back, staring wildly around the room as if searching for a victim.

"There is nothing easier," the Newab said kindly. "I am so sorry you did not bring this to my attention earlier. My dear sir, please, it will be over in a moment—if you could just indicate to my farrier the tooth which is causing you such pain . . ."

"Your farrier?" Vitkevich said, or tried to say, retreating back into his pile of blankets.

The Newab turned to his farrier, and gestured at Vitkevich, still smiling benevolently. The other Russians all shut their eyes, clapping their hands over their faces as one. The farrier advanced, his blacksmith's black implement in hand, and Vitkevich swallowed, hard.

"The wise man learns from pain," the Newab said sententiously, "and then plucks out what pains him."

"Well, tell him to chop my head off," Vitkevich said, but no one understood him through his gag. The farrier thrust a filthy hand into Vitkevich's mouth, pulling out the handkerchief. Vitkevich told himself that he was a brave man—he was—and indicated, silently, the rotting tooth.

Half an hour later, Vitkevich was wondering how his head could possibly have contained so much blood, and now be so empty. Two teeth had been pulled—a good one, by mistake, and then the rotten one. The farrier had gone, jingling the teeth in his dirty fist like dice, and the handkerchief, the blanket, Vitkevich's robes, were sodden with blood. The others were staring at him in awe.

"Gentlemen," Vitkevich said, wretchedly approaching an appearance of insouciance. "I am happy to say that I am quite fit to pay a visit on the

English tomorrow." But he spoke through a pond of blood, and nobody understood what on earth he was trying to say.

3

Burnes had made a great effort, conquered his dislike, and returned, the morning of his Christmas dinner, to see Masson in penitent and apologetic mood. It had to be done; there was no reason, after all, to be rude to the poor man, and, almost as soon as he had stalked off and left him in the marketplace, Burnes had been taken with a feeling of guilt. He must be lonely, and be pleased, underneath his touchy surface, that there were compatriots of his here to keep him company. In any case—as Mohan Lal pointed out—the man was well informed, and deserved to be trusted a little. For all these reasons, Burnes did not wait long before going back to Masson's house to apologize.

He would rather, however, not have had to bring him what must seem like bad news. In the interim, Burnes had been subjected to another gigantic audience with the Amir. He had made what he now suspected was a mistake. He had gone into the hall and, waiting for the Amir to arrive, assessed the hand he held. Burnes had two trump cards. The first was the firm information that the Russians were aiding the Persians in the siege of Herat. They were besieging the capital of the Amir's cousin. The second was something he could say; something he knew to be false; that the Russians in Kabul were, in fact, no emissaries from the Emperor of Russia, but merely adventurers, bearing a false letter, drawn up by themselves and sealed with something from a bag of sugar. He could say both these things, and the Amir would believe them both. What consequences would follow if he lied, he could not imagine; but he could not imagine what consequences would follow if he told what he knew to be the truth.

In the event, he had told the Amir that the Russians were quite genuine, in his opinion; and followed it up quickly with the information about the siege of Herat. Dost Mohammed had greeted these pieces of information impassively. He nodded, and then returned to his favourite subject, the necessity of the British lending him troops to invade the Punjab and regain Peshawar for the empire. Burnes wondered afterwards whether he would have done better to have kept his two pieces of information to himself. That was certainly the view of Masson, when he described the conversation to him. But by now Masson clearly felt that he had done what he could, and merely shrugged, as if to say "of course, of course." Burnes left Masson's little house, casually wishing him a merry Christmas on his way out (Masson had looked surprised, and perhaps he had little idea of the date in this remote and un-Christian place). He did not mention why he left so soon; that Vitkevich was expected at the Bala Hissar.

He returned, as it proved, not a minute too soon. The guards at the gate of the Bala Hissar were clustering like jackals circling a corpse. They were not waiting for him. They wanted to see the Russian admitted; the Russian who, every day for weeks, had been sending letters to the Amir. Burnes's return caused a little flurry of excitement—could they really have such difficulty telling one European from another?—but when that had subsided, the youngest of the soldiers sulkily slung his *jezail* over his shoulders, and led Burnes back to his quarters.

His rooms had been prepared for the feast, and his companions had removed themselves. About the room, the tallow candles were blackening the walls, although it was not yet dark; a splendid carpet had been laid on the floor, and about it, piles of Chinese cushions. There was no one there; it was a banqueting hall, prepared by the afrit of the Arabian Nights, and now only one demon remained: Burnes. He stood in the fiery splendid room, and listened to the noise of his guest approaching through the distant corridors of the great palace. He wondered, standing there, how he would ever recognize him, and the thought filled him with nervousness; he had met him twice only, deep in the desert, and now, he wondered how he would ever know what he looked like. Faces were all the same in their essentials, and, unable to summon up Vitkevich's face, Burnes recalled the story of the family of Darius before Alexander, and feared that he would destroy everything by greeting the wrong man. But then, all at once, there he was, before a small crowd of torch-bearing Afghans, and of course, of course, it was Vitkevich.

Burnes bowed deeply, putting all the warmth he could into it, and Vitkevich bowed back. The soldiers retreated into the anteroom, and stood there, gawping. Burnes decided to ignore them entirely, and they might very well stay there for several hours.

"Do you have any books?" Vitkevich said.

"Books?" Burnes said, surprised at this opening gambit.

"Novels, of any description," Vitkevich said, sitting down without being invited. "My dear sir, I confess, I am appallingly bored."

"A great problem," Burnes said. "Yes, you are quite right."

"Well, we travelled with everything we could need, I thought," Vitkevich said. He had something of a lisp, Burnes noted; not an unattractive trait, but something which contributed to his alert, energetic manner. "Or so I thought, but I was the only one of the party to think of stowing any reading matter, apart from the essentials, and the ten novels I chose, I have long ago read, and much as I love Balzac—I *adore* Balzac, sir—I rather hunger for some other entertainment. Of course, I would happily exchange our small library for yours . . ."

"We play cards," Burnes said, smiling. "I believe we have novels, all much read, by now, but in English, I fear. Save the French novel I already offered you, of course, which I perceive you are too familiar with already. Do you speak English, monsieur?"

Vitkevich shrugged. "I am prepared to try," he said. "I am desperate to try. Perhaps cards would be a better entertainment, but—well, sir, I am not a rich man, and we may have days ahead of us, weeks. In that time I could lose whole estates to my subordinates, if I had estates to lose, of course."

"That is precisely my problem," Burnes said. "I am in debt by a considerable sum now to my guide—I had not thought that whist—what is *whist* in French?—no matter—would be so very dangerous a game, or that it would present the greatest of the perils we would have to deal with on our travels. I think you are wise—perhaps we, too, will turn to the quiet reading of novels in the long evenings. Balzac, I fear, I make no headway with."

"I *adore* Balzac," Vitkevich said again. "I wonder if you have ever read—well, I forget the title, but a marvellous novel. I could read it twice, three times. Indeed, I have, and a fourth reading, it emerges, would be more than even I could stand. But you will enjoy it. An English novel? A pleasant diversion. Let me see. Squire Allworthy, Uncle Toby, *l'homme de qualité* and his ghastly dog Fido, Sir Grandison, Peregrine Gherkin, and there was a novel where a man was *naufragé* and made friends with a negro and another where a man was *naufragé* and his only friends were very small people and very big people and a third book which I did not trouble with and horses. Very rational. No, I fear I have read all English novels, or all that I am likely to read, and I find that every single one of them begins with a shipwreck, for some reason I cannot guess at."

Burnes found himself laughing. "My dear sir, what dull old books you have suffered through. Perhaps we may offer you something more modern—"

"But not if it is mad Belinda in a haunted house—Otranto? Udolpho? Yes, there is another one the poor dear Empress forced me to read."

"No, I am sure we can supply something more entertaining than Sir Charles Grandison with his men, women, and Italians."

"Men, women, and Italians," Vitkevich said. "How I adored that, and now I remember nothing else of the poor boring fellow's adventures. I longed, I must say, to meet that dull fellow in real life and tell him the full story of the dullest periods in my own dull life, to wreak some kind of revenge. If only it were he who travelled to the kingdom of the giants, and if only one of them had had the sense to tread on him very firmly. Well, you will enjoy Balzac and I will suffer through your terrible English novels. You know, I am quite ashamed to confess to such a thing, but it was the Tsarina herself who recommended Balzac to me, and I set upon it with the heaviest heart—the poor woman, she has recommended the most unspeakable books to her whole court, and we all are obliged to read them, since any suggestion from their imperial majesties, you know, has the force of an imperial command. The poor woman—I can hear her now. 'I know,' she would say, 'I am quite assured, quite determined that you, my dear Vit-a-kevich'—poor woman, she is so, so vulgar—'that you, above all people, shall appreciate the many sincere, the many improving beauties of this beautiful and most Christian book, and I know, I am quite assured that you shall weep, you shall cry as I did over so very sad and improving a story.'"

"You are intimate, I perceive, with Their Majesties?" Burnes said.

"Agonizingly so," Vitkevich said. "Well, the imperial literary command goes out, and a book the poor illiterate woman has spent months poring and puzzling over is delivered, and we must read it in two days and then listen to her sad ramblings. Well, unspeakable as this all is, she truly redeemed herself with her enthusiasm for *Illusions Perdues,* and now, sir— do you know, I will not hear a word spoken against Her Imperial Majesty's imperial literary tastes. Poor woman. She reminds me of no one so much as our unspeakable host here, the Newab Jubbur Khan, whom I believe you know. Or so he tells us."

"Indeed," Burnes said. The fellow, all in all, was a gentleman, to Burnes's slight and inexplicable surprise. "Well, I apologize in advance for our national literary effusions, and, indeed for our national Christmas dinner. I have been so bold as to attempt to instruct the Amir's cooks in an English Christmas feast, but I dared not inquire into what they have made of my instructions. It may be a curiosity for your memoirs. I cannot promise more than that." Burnes clapped his hands and ordered a bearer off to the kitchens. "I would be most interested, sir, to hear of your travels; you must have seen quite different lands from us."

"Indeed," Vitkevich said, and, quite evidently, was immediately on his guard. "Indeed, many most interesting places. And we have observed most interesting customs. Do you know, sir, the inhabitants of—now, what was that place we travelled through—my poor memory, quite hopeless—well, some place between here and the Emperor's borders—they have a custom of telling the future from the grounds of coffee, thrown onto the ground? A most curious thing. I had never seen it before."

"We have something similar in London," Burnes said briskly. "What route did you take to arrive at so very distant a place as this?"

"Oh, a very commonplace and uninteresting route, I assure you," Vitkevich persisted. "I wonder if you have ever had cause to have a tooth removed in Kabul? Well, I must tell you . . ."

Vitkevich embarked on his long and dreadful tale of the Newab and his brutish farrier. Despite himself, Burnes was amused, and waited patiently until the end of the story.

". . . but what the fellow was proposing to do with my two teeth, one in perfect health, I could not tell you. Perhaps they are at this very moment on sale as an exotic curiosity in the market here. I like to think so—I would be most curious to see what price two fine Russian teeth (very well, one fine, one rotten) would fetch."

"What very interesting experiences you must have had," Burnes said. "Tell me—"

"Ah . . ." breathed Vitkevich, and Burnes's inquiries were cut short by the arrival of the feast, in high silver state. First, borne in magnificent splendour, was—

"A dish of grass," Vitkevich said, amused. "That, I confess, I have never seen. Not cooked, either. Is that an English custom? To present your guests with grass? A most interesting sort of salad."

"No, I promise you," Burnes said. "I think that must be their own addition. There is some importance, you know, attached to grass here—you know that the Amir wears blades of grass in his turban?"

"I did not know," Vitkevich said. "I have not, I admit, laid eyes on the Amir. Blades of grass? How odd. What can that mean? And they would wilt so. Are they replaced hourly, by minions? Still, it seems odd to begin a feast with a dish only a sheep would appreciate. Ah, things are improving. Fowl—two in one, how interesting—the small bird escaping from the larger one's anal cavity, how charming."

"No, that is its neck."

"I find that even more charming. An English custom? I suppose not. And—ah, that is more attractive, I must say—when did I last eat mutton?—at Bokhara—have we been to Bokhara?—I forget. Well, a very long time ago. Yes, and . . ."

Vitkevich hungrily narrated the entire arrival of the feast. "I have not eaten—" he said at one point, his eyes shining, and Burnes felt that this was the first sincere thing he had said, and might be the only sincere thing he had ever said in his life, "—for *days*. Good heavens, what is that? Some Afghan monstrosity. What a disaster they have made of a fine English dinner, but you and I, we shall enjoy it."

"I have to say," Burnes said, "that looks to me like a very reasonable approximation of an English plum pudding. I am surprised. Please, sir, do assuage your hunger."

4

They ate, at first with cautious delicacy, offering each other this dish or the other, then with increasing speed, taking spoonfuls indiscriminately, mixing the meat with the splendid flaming pudding. Vitkevich kept up a commentary on the food, telling one funny story after another, and swerving gracefully away from any suggestion of where he had been, where he was going, who he was, and what he wanted. For a moment, Burnes had thought that he had come to the Bala Hissar with the beginnings of a conversation, and, like many great wits, would exhaust his store within a few minutes and be reduced to retelling the plots of his favourite novels. But it did not happen; as he gorged, the man grew more and more loquacious, and his conversation as fanciful as if it had been fuelled by wine.

"Have you ever been spoken to by a camel?" Vitkevich would suddenly say. "I had no idea they could be so rational. Now, this was some weeks ago—we were in some need of fresh mounts—"

"Where was this?"

"Ah—I forget the place, precisely—a small town, a trading town, somewhere to the north of here, or possibly to the west—"

"In the vicinity of Herat, perhaps?"

"Herat, Herat . . . no, not there. Well, it was a trading town, and we were trying to acquire fresh camels. They were wretched beasts, and the fellow was asking a tremendous, an *obscene* sum for them. But, as a traveller like you must know, far better than I, sometimes there is simply no alternative, and we were quite at the man's mercy. Well, we loaded up the animals, and attempted to mount. I had reserved the one tolerable-looking beast for myself, but the miserable animal obviously thought itself too fine, and would not kneel. We whipped it and pushed it and beat at its knees, and it would go down for a moment, but whenever I approached it, the animal rose sharply and threw me into the dust without the slightest ceremony. Of course, this was supplying a great deal of merriment to the entire town, and I was growing somewhat impatient. The animal was standing there, looking appallingly contented with its success. I flung down my pack, and went to glare at it. I brought my face up against its own beastly physiognomy, and hissed at it. And it looked at me, and said, quite clearly, *Va t'en*. A dreadful animal."

Vitkevich's imitation of a camel clearing its throat with a *va t'en* was immaculately plausible, and Burnes laughed immoderately. "I am deeply hurt," he said cosily, "by the failure of our national literature to spread beyond our shores, I have to say."

"On the contrary," Vitkevich said, "it is read everywhere."

"I wonder if you know our national poet, Shakespeare?" Burnes said.

"Indeed, of course," Vitkevich said. "Incorrect, of course, but full of beauties."

"And yet," Burnes said, "I feel that his greatest beauties are appreciated only by his countrymen. I wonder if *The Tempest,* for instance, is known at all well in Russia?"

"Sir, I know it intimately," Vitkevich said. "A most beautiful play."

"A curious subject," Burnes pursued. "And an unsatisfactory ending. I wonder, truly, whether Prospero had the right to abandon his island."

"Sir?"

"To have journeyed, even unwillingly, to an uncivilized place—to have educated and taught the natives, and then to abandon them so readily. Or perhaps, sir, you feel that we have no right to impose our ways on a native, alien way of life?"

"I do not recall the play at all well," Vitkevich said carelessly.

"I wonder whether you feel, as I always do, that Prospero's magic was a great benefit, in the end, to Caliban and his island, that he did a better thing in coming there than in leaving it?"

"I do not remember the play at all well," Vitkevich said again. "I am sure you are right in everything you say. Tell me, in your travels, have you found camels or horses the more serviceable beasts? For myself . . ."

Burnes considered himself entirely outdone; and everyone knew that camels were of no use in mountainous country. Although Vitkevich's conversation roamed freely and extravagantly, it was clearly fenced off, and there were some places to which he would not allow himself to be led, even by the most indirect route of a conversation about Shakespeare.

The fellow was a gentleman, Burnes said to himself again, hours later. He was woozy and pleasured with overeating, and as Vitkevich rose to go, they seemed, unmistakably, to be friends; sad, momentary friends, because there would and could be no sequel to this amiable festivity, but unmistakably friends.

"Thank you, sir," Vitkevich said. "I had not expected such a pleasant evening could be afforded me by Kabul. But I see—well, thank you, sir."

"The pleasure is mine," Burnes said in the formal Persian response, and Vitkevich broke into a broad smile. "Tell me—how long do you plan to remain in Kabul?"

The smile dropped like a stone. "That is not quite a question I can answer," Vitkevich said smoothly.

"Well, I wish you every happiness," Burnes said weakly. They stood there for a moment, knowing that they could not decently wish each other success, and then Burnes said a terrible thing. "I expect your return will take you to Herat, where I understand you have friends waiting for you."

Vitkevich did not break his conversational stride. "Our plans are not yet settled," he said. "I wish you a most pleasant Christmas." And then he was gone. Burnes would have done anything to take back his last comment. He was left alone in the room, and the pleasure seemed to disappear like the afrit's palace. He had—he supposed—wanted to let

Vitkevich know what he knew, but now he felt that he had blundered; that he had laid his knowledge open to the Russians, who would now safeguard themselves against it. What would follow, he had no idea; he felt simply assured that he had provided them with something which would enable them to destroy his chances. As the servants came in to remove the remains of the feast, he saw what would happen; he might be here for weeks longer, for months, but his mission, now, might as well be over. And the next day he would send the Russian every single English novel he and his party could muster.

The kitchen boys, unfed in this hall of food, hung back silently, waiting. And as the silver dishes were carried back from the English feast with their fine wrecked freight of meat, fruit, and roots, they flung themselves forward, seizing each one. This was their ancient right, and they fell on them like beasts, like crows, like—better—like fish, crowding to the rich surface of the water. Onto the dishes they fastened their little hungry mouths, and sucked and licked, puckering their mouths, their eyes closed in pleasure at the rich remainders, polishing the imperial silver with their tongues. The feast was over, and, as they fought and pushed over its residue, they gave no thought to it, or to the fine ambassadors, or to the labour they had expended, which had ended in these few scraps. They surrendered themselves to pleasure as if no one was—as if no one ever could be—watching them.

TWENTY

The Russian ambassador was speechless with rage. Never—never in his life—had he stood up in these circumstances. In the vast hall of the minister's golden office, there were five chairs only; and the minister sat on one, behind his vast desk, and four chinless advisers and clerks, behind him, sat on the others. Every other chair had been removed from the room, and the ambassador stood, and fumed. Outside, the London spring continued in its half-hearted way, the birds in the park peeping faintly. The minister turned over one paper after another, in a leisurely, unhurried way, as of one who knows the game is his, and did not speak.

"I wonder if I might have a chair to sit upon," the ambassador said firmly. He was not prepared to be treated like this, whatever the circumstances. The minister looked up, amused, and down again. In a moment or two he reached out, and rang the bell on his desk.

"The Russian ambassador," he drawled, when the attendant came in, "has asked if he may have a chair." He smiled, sardonically, his mouth closed, not revealing his teeth just yet. The attendant left, and the ambassador knew he had been given instructions that, in this eventuality, he was not to return. The ticking of the clock in the room was loud, and the ambassador waited and filled with pointless fury.

"Your gentlemen have been most busy, recently," the minister said finally. He did not look up, and his voice was muffled by the weight of papers before him. Behind him, his officers and envoys engaged the Russian's gaze unabashedly, and grinned wolfishly. "We have been most interested to learn of their activities in—ah—in a most valuable and important region of the world."

"The minister must be prepared to specify the matter under current consideration." The ambassador's English was excellent, once the ear had become accustomed to his rich, gurgling accent. He was clenching and unclenching his fists in the rhythm of his heartbeat, like a washerwoman wringing a handkerchief.

"Indeed, indeed," the minister said. "I apologize for delaying in coming to—ah—the very curious *point* Her Majesty wishes to make to His Excellency. Indeed. Well, it seems that Your Excellency has carelessly omitted to tell us of some events and interests which must directly bear on our oriental possessions. Perhaps you would care to enlighten us, concerning the—ah—the *intentions* of the great power which Your Excellency so ably represents? For instance—let us see—the matter of Herat. I am sure Your Excellency is as pleased as we are to hear that the inhabitants of that unhappy city have been relieved from their besiegement by Persian soldiers. Herat, Your Excellency, a city somewhat to the east of the Shah's accepted territories, and to which, happily, that great Emperor has now relinquished any claim."

"Once the warships of Her Majesty's Navy, in its *wisdom,* had dropped anchor in the Persian Gulf, sir, I hardly feel that the Shah could have failed to see sense, but—"

"Sense," the minister said calmly, raising his calm smiling face, and looked directly into the ambassador's eyes. "Sense, indeed; that is a quality which Her Majesty most sincerely values in her cousins, and her ambassadors. So I wonder if Your Excellency has any comment to make on this most interesting and incontrovertible information regarding the siege of Herat?"

He raised a piece of paper, fluttering it approximately in the ambassador's direction. The ambassador was ten feet from the desk, and would not compromise his dignity by walking forward, like a clerk. "If Her Majesty's minister will be so good as to explain?" he said.

The minister dropped the paper casually on the desk. "We are puzzled, sir, most sincerely puzzled. It seems—no, sir, I know not seems—" His attendants broke into an ecstasy of preening at their minister's learning. "—we have learnt that the Shah was aided in his most futile and detestable attempt at the walls of Herat by outside forces. By Russians, sir, by Russians!" The ambassador looked back levelly as the minister broke into a terrifying shout. He would not budge an inch.

"Sir, your information is erroneous," he said. "This cannot be."

"This, cannot, be," the minister said, purring. "And yet it is the case. Were it not for the fortuitous presence of a most brave English officer within the unhappy city, we have no doubt that the Shah, or rather, sir, the Tsar, would now be in possession of Herat. There is no doubt whatever."

"Sir, these are matters of which I know nothing," the ambassador said bravely. "Her Majesty's minister astonishes me with these unfounded claims."

"Unfounded, sir? Unfounded? Let us move on, before you see how much knowledge of these extraordinary activities we have acquired. Indeed, sir, we found it so impossible to believe that the Tsar could act in such a manner, we dismissed any but the most incontrovertible reports. Let us move on, sir, to another and still more alarming report. What can you tell us of a gentleman named Vitkevich?"

"Sir?"

"Vitkevich, Your Excellency." The minister paused, and looked at the ambassador patiently. He stood in silence, incredulous at this treatment. "We know, sir, that there are Russians at the court of Dost Mohammed, the Amir of Kabul, and that they are presently received with every mark of favour. With every mark of favour, sir. Their commanding officer is named Vitkevich. Now, what can the meaning of this be?"

"I know nothing of any Vitkevich, sir."

"Nothing? Let us see. Until six months ago, we had a most valued envoy to the Amir's court, and the most friendly relations. And six months ago, the Amir made a most unreasonable demand of our envoy, that we should send him troops to invade the territories of one of his neighbours, a most valued ally. Sir, I hope you are listening to this very serious story. And six months ago, our envoy was abruptly dismissed, and the Amir, to our astonishment, began to receive the attentions of this gentleman Vitkevich. This, sir, must not continue. It must not."

"Sir, I know nothing of anyone of that name."

"Very well," the minister went on. "Most serious steps will be taken at any suggestion that military aid is being offered to the Amir. Most serious steps, indeed, are being undertaken at this very moment, of which you and the world will shortly learn. Her Majesty is most displeased at these extraordinary Russian activities, and wishes to learn what steps are to be undertaken to restore the previously excellent state of relations between our two governments. We look forward to your response, sir. That will be all."

The ambassador stood, trembling with rage. Never—never—had he been spoken to in such a manner, and it took him a full minute to realize that the audience was over. He turned on his tail, and stalked to the door. By either side stood a footman, and that was where they remained, making no move to open the great mahogany door. The ambassador stood there, looking from one to another, but they were impassive, and finally he had no alternative; he took the door handle and pulled it furiously. Every single man in the building had known of his humiliation; every one, before it had happened. Never—never—never—but he had lost, and the mild laughter which accompanied his departure told him that everyone in London knew it.

2

Vitkevich did not know it; he stood in the halls of the Bala Hissar, and saw nothing but the moment of his triumph. He had achieved greatness here. The English were long gone, dismissed, destroyed, and here was Vitkevich. He had done everything, and soon the time would come when he would return to Petersburg, and enter the court of the Tsar in splendour and triumph. He closed his eyes, and saw his return, shining clear as a jewel against the black velvet of his mind. The princes of the Amir's court would ride with him to the borders of the Amir's empire, and the kingdoms would open up before him, and the angels would conduct him along the silver road to the deep North. He knew it; but he knew nothing.

3

The two men walked at dawn in the gilded city, among the fantastic golden pinnacles of Runjeet Singh's palaces and temples, picking their way through the narrow paths between the smooth dark pools, drifting with weed. It was cold at this early hour in this northern city, and both wore shawls, wrapped tight about their shoulders. The washerwomen, at work already, ignored the two men; the English and their guides were no longer an interesting sight, after a few weeks living here.

"So it is settled," Mohan Lal said, full of amusement. They were talking of Runjeet Singh's demands, which had been presented to the Governor General the day before.

"It is very much like a dowry," Burnes said. "I suppose that is the customary thing here. I had expected rather more in the way of statements of friendship, but it all seems to be a matter of money and jewels and sheep. Very curious sort of document, but of course we shall go along with it, and ensure that when Shah Shujah is king in Kabul again, his one-eyed neighbour receives everything he asks for."

"So it is settled?"

"It appears so," Burnes said. "If Auckland had ever been inclined to think that Runjeet Singh could evict Dost Mohammed with his own forces, this document would change his mind. One who thinks so much on what he can extract in the way of tribute from his neighbours cannot be the repository of our trust. So we are to join with the Sikh forces—well, let us say things as they are—we are to go into Kabul and install this poor Shah Shujah as our own Amir. Shah Shujah will have his throne, and the Lion of the Punjab will have his annual tribute, and Dost Mohammed will be dead or in hiding, and we, I suppose, will be most happy. It all makes the most perfect sense, to Auckland, if not to anyone else, but you and I will say nothing for the moment."

"And Runjeet Singh's demands?"

"You never saw the like. Well, it is fair to say that he has agreed to send fifty-five loads of rice annually to his beloved neighbour and cousin, once we have succeeded in installing Shah Shujah in Kabul. But in return he demands fifty-five high-bred horses of approved colour and pleasant

paces, scimitars, poniards, twenty-five mules, melons, grapes, pomegranates, apples, quinces, almonds, mulberries, raisins, pistales, all, it is specified, in abundance, two lakhs of rupees annually, jewels, women—no, not
women. But on it goes. Mulberries! Are we to suppose that Runjeet
Singh's preference for Shah Shujah is founded in the belief that he is more
likely to send him mulberries?"

"Few things have ever surprised me," Mohan Lal said. "But I had never
thought to see the great might of the British soldiery embarking on an
invasion for no better reason than to ensure the supply of fruit. Poor Dost
Mohammed."

"There, I cannot agree with you," Burnes said. "He has brought this
upon himself, and has found that his new friends, the Russians, have disappeared from his side like snow in May."

"But if the Russians have withdrawn from Kabul," Mohan Lal said.
"Why are we troubling to invade? What threat does Dost Mohammed,
friendless, present to anyone?"

Burnes could not answer that one.

4

The order went forth, and the Army of the Indus began to draw itself
together. From Bengal came a brigade of artillery and of cavalry, of two
infantry divisions, the 16th Lancers, the 13th Foot, and the 3rd Buffs, came
the Company's European Regiment, two regiments of native light cavalry, and twelve battalions of sepoys. Summoned. And from Bombay, a
brigade of cavalry, a brigade of artillery, a brigade of infantry, the 4th Dragoons, the 2nd Royals, the 17th Foot; the regiments and the battalions and
the brigades received their orders, and drew themselves northwards and
eastwards in their thousands. The orders had been sent, and the Governor General and his suite awaited the arrival of these tens of thousands,
glittering in the clear sun of the northeast.

Macnaghten had never known such success, such utter transformation in his standing. A matter of weeks ago he had been a bore from
whom everyone slid away, however informative what he had to say. Now
he was, it seemed, the most desirable of dining companions, and finally
detached from Elphinstone. Everyone wanted to hear his disquisitions;

Elphinstone, by contrast, gloomily mouthing predictions of catastrophe, could find no one but sepoys willing to attend to him. It was Macnaghten's moment, and he was seizing it with both hands.

Tonight, he had actually been placed next to the Governor General's sister at a most intimate dinner—there were no more than ten of them, in the smaller dining room in the palace which Runjeet Singh had placed at Auckland's disposal. He wanted to hug himself, but for the moment he was doing as he had seen other people doing, nodding and smiling charmingly as Miss Eden told an amusing story of her evening with Runjeet Singh, the night before.

"I knew," Emily Eden was saying, "that the old man was fond of his drink, but it is too much to inflict it on us. He offered me a glass, and, naturally, I took it. No sooner had I placed it on my lips than I felt my lips began to blister. A terrifying concoction. Happily, I was placed on his blind side, and felt no compunction about pouring it directly onto the carpet. Well, sir, in only a moment, he turned to face me, and was most impressed to see how rapidly I had despatched his favourite punch, and ordered another glass for me. That, of course, went the way of the first, the moment he turned his blind side to me, and the third and the fourth. He was truly astonished to see how very well an Englishwoman can hold her drink."

Macnaghten laughed graciously. How delightful it was to sit and listen in this way, to feel oneself admired!

"You know, sir," she went on, "we have placed the highest trust in you in this matter. I hope you are not daunted by the prospect."

"When a cause is just," Macnaghten said sagely, "one's courage may be assured."

"I see," Emily Eden said. "You do not share your friend Elphinstone's doubts as to the wisdom of our action."

"There can be no doubt," Macnaghten said, warming to his theme. "The Amir of Afghanistan has made a most sudden and unprovoked attack on the lands of our ancient ally, has insisted on his most unreasonable pretensions—"

"Yes?"

"—and presents a serious threat to the security of the frontiers of India. It is the most extraordinary mystery how he was ever presumed to be capable of forming any kind of alliance with us. And he is unpopular with his own people. This is not an invasion, you understand, madam; we are restoring the rightful king of the Afghans to his throne. I have no doubt that we will find his popularity among his people quite unabated by time, and he will enter his country to the wildest acclamation."

"And why are we aiding him in this worthy endeavour?" Emily Eden said. The table had fallen silent, to Macnaghten's piquant delight; all ears were on him. There were ten people around the table, and about the walls, twenty manservants, impassively watching their masters like hawks, and, Macnaghten realized for one moment of pure glee, every single one of them believed every word he would say.

"It is to be regretted that those whose cause is just cannot always pursue it," Macnaghten said, assembling his solemn face. "We, happily, are in a position to aid our neighbours, and there is no reason not to do so. It is a small step, and a wise one; it will ensure the security and happiness of a large tract of the world for generations to come."

"And meanwhile," Fanny Eden, safely at the end of the table, murmured to Burnes, "we, and our children, and our children's children, contemplate that most delicious curry growing colder by the moment. I understand congratulations are in order, Sir Alexander."

"You are most kind," Burnes said. "The Governor General had to tell me bluntly, so very tactful were his initial means of letting me know of my elevation. He sent me a letter, which I opened without reading the direction, and it was only when he told me to look at the outside more carefully that I realized what a very tremendous personage I seem to have become."

"Lieutenant Colonel and a knight at thirty-three," Fanny said. "That, at least, is nothing to be ashamed of."

"A consolation, I suspect," Burnes said. "I lost the argument, all in all, and my friend Dost Mohammed seems to have become my enemy."

Fanny Eden looked at him quizzically; perhaps she had forgotten, or never known, the efforts Burnes had made on the Dost's behalf.

"What manner of man is he?" she said finally. "Your friend, Dost Mohammed."

"Very agreeable, I confess," Burnes said. "But unwise."

"At last," Fanny said, as Macnaghten reached the end of his glowing indictment, and the servants, at a gesture from Lord Auckland, moved forward to serve what could only be rather a cold curry. Burnes sat for a moment, with an ineradicable feeling of ennobled defeat.

5

It was an essential part of the charm of the Princess's Thursdays that they were not grand occasions. To an outside observer, they certainly appeared grand; no one could recall one of the Princess Fanny's Thursdays which had not failed to supply at least two of the Grand Duchesses, dividing the salon between them. No one came to the Princess's Thursdays who did not have the highest possible claim to be there, but she and her Thursday *habitués* made a point of speaking of them in the humblest terms. "We shall be very simple, and I fear it will bore you greatly," she would say to a new recruit, offering the golden invitation. "Merely a very few old friends, drawn together by a love of music. I cannot offer you any excitement, but if you wish to make a dull old woman very happy, I should be most pleased to see you at my house one week." Those fortunate enough to be welcomed there were always wise enough to understand what the Princess meant, and everyone knew that the Princess's simple Thursday evenings were occasions at which the highest pinnacle of St. Petersburg society was to be found.

The Princess was in deep conversation with General Scherbatsky one Thursday. At the far end of the salon, a soprano was giving an account of some melancholy Polish songs, but no one listened to the music at the Princess's Thursdays, save the Grand Duchesses and nervous newcomers. The General, too, was a relatively new attender at her evenings, and, taken by his hostess from the duty of listening to the music, was most eager to please. Much as he longed to send his eyes searching about the room, he did not dare divert his attention from his hostess for a moment, and listened to her drawling out the story of the tantrum the Tsar had fallen into the day before as if he were Moses, fearing to miss a word of divine writ. She was a most charming woman; her voice low and musical, her face presenting the irresistible appearance of a great beauty, five years past her prime. No breath of scandal had ever come near her, and she relayed the mild events of the court in a manner that was charmingly flavoured with a touch of indiscretion.

She finished her story with a muted peal of intensely genteel laughter. Her footman had been standing patiently with a silver plate by her side, waiting for her to finish. She turned to him, taking the card from the plate, and he bowed. She examined the name on the card for some minutes, her pretty brow wrinkling in puzzlement.

"I confess," she said finally to the General, "this gentleman is quite unknown to me. A most curious thing, for strangers to present themselves at one's house, but perhaps I am old fashioned in these matters. Can you enlighten me in any way?"

She passed the card to him.

"M. Vitkevich," the General said cautiously. Here was a difficult one: the General knew quite well that Vitkevich had been one of the stalwarts of the Princess's Thursdays. Indeed, before his own wonderful elevation into this happy society, he had greatly resented the status of one of his junior officers. He also knew quite well that Vitkevich would never be received by anyone, ever again. "I am unable to be of any assistance, I fear."

"No matter," the Princess said carelessly. "Ah, Stepan Mikhailovich—one moment, if you please!"

Stepan Mikhailovich Layevsky was passing, and smilingly bowed to his hostess. His corsets audibly creaked as he did so.

"How curious," he said when he had looked at the card. "Yes, I think I know of the gentleman. An adventurer, I believe. Well, he has been travelling in distant lands, and when he returned, it became apparent that he had been making all sorts of representations to oriental potentates which he had no right to make. He has placed us in a most awkward position, all in all. You know, madam, he had the audacity to present himself at court last week, and the Tsar himself—well, I need not say how angry he was. In front of the whole court, he said, 'Vitkevich? I know no such man, except some poor criminal, lately returned from India. Show him out.' An extraordinary man, to present himself here."

"Shall we admit him?" the Princess said. "It may be amusing."

Layevsky bowed. The Princess's whims were not to be contradicted.

"Or it may not," she went on. "No, I think if I start admitting people of whom I know nothing, I shall soon find myself pouring tea for my dressmaker. Tell the gentleman I am not at home," she finished, turning to the footman.

6

What he had not dared to ask for had been granted him. What he had not dared to dream of had been made flesh.

Masson was the last European in Kabul, and now he was preparing to leave. Burnes had gone, his mission failed. The Russians had gone, bearing their tinsel triumph; Masson had gone out to watch their splendid departure, deeply wrapped in cloaks; the pomp of their procession, spurs tinkling, impressed the city, and only Masson saw how empty it was. Soon Dost Mohammed and his court would flee; either that, or they would fight and lose; and the city would be left to the English. Masson had no doubt that the English were on their way, and in force. He had one thing to do, and then he, too, would go. The time had come. In a year, this would be no place for him to be.

Before his departure, he had one thing to do; to destroy Burnes. In these few days, he did not leave the house; he sat in his upper study, and wrote and wrote, hardly sleeping, in an ecstasy of creation. He alone had seen Burnes, and his failure; he alone could tell the story of Burnes at the court of the Amir, and he wrote and wrote, piling lie upon lie, knowing that there was no one to contradict him. With his pen, he would destroy Burnes, and everyone, until the end of time, would know that Burnes had failed, and caused his own failure. He lied and lied, and as he wrote, his eyes opened and stretched with a savage righteous joy. Every monstrous line bubbled helplessly to the point of his pen, and there he was, there was the fool, Burnes, striking attitudes before the Amir, helping the Russians, insulting the Dost's wives, heading towards disaster with every step. Only sometimes did it occur to Masson that he was writing about a real person, and the face of Burnes swam before his eye. He pushed the feeling of regret away, and went on writing. The man who took the seal on a bag of sugar for the Russian imperial seal! Burnes's laughable Persian! Burnes's appalling ignorance! The fool who destroyed his own chances, the fool who knew nothing but how to strike poses of his own honour! Masson wrote and wrote; he described how Burnes ran and hid from Vitkevich, wrapped his head in towels, and called for his smelling bottle. Before his eyes, the scene swam up, clearer than memory. One day, these lies would be as true as history, and one day, one day, everyone would know of the clear-sightedness and wisdom of Masson, the one man who could have helped Burnes, whom Burnes, the fool, ceaselessly insulted. For long hours, Burnes seemed to him like a monster of his own creation, the embodiment of what had hurt him most and insulted him most. Everything he had written had been the dry notation of truth, until now; at this moment, he sat and invented, wildly, and knew that what he wrote would come to be the truth. Every little hurt came to Masson, and he wrote and wrote in a golden fury of righteousness, deep into the night.

He paused for a moment. The candle guttered at a draught. Masson raised his head and listened; a creak downstairs. It was the door to the house, being pushed open. Masson did not fear robbers. He trusted his luck too much, and he waited. A powerful thought came to him, like a hot storm of wind, and he almost trembled at it. He heard no more noise, and waited, silently, trying to tell himself that he had been mistaken; knowing that he had not. Long minutes passed, it seemed, before there, in the room, was his thought. Standing there. What he had not dared to ask for had been granted him. What he had not dared to dream of had been made flesh. Hasan, robed in white, sombre and beautiful, radiant, shining, shining, there. Hasan had returned.

7

The Army of the Indus was assembled, and the fifty thousand men, their thirty thousand camels, waited like a town. Two weeks before, this stretch of the Punjab was barren, bare, and beautiful; now a city, a city on wheels, pulsed and screamed here. It might have been there for centuries; it had acquired, already, its myths and stories and heroes. Everyone had heard of the lieutenant of the 16th Lancers, the magnifico who was followed by a train of no fewer than forty servants; everyone had heard that the 4th Dragoons had assigned three camels to carry the cigars of the regiment's officers, and were delighted to know it. The order had gone out to travel with the barest essentials, but no officer took that remotely seriously. The *on-dit* in the Army of the Indus was that there was no realistic prospect that these damned Indian princes would hold Kabul on their own, and they packed their pleasures in accord with their belief, that once they were there, the Governor General would decide that it was, after all, necessary for them to stay there for months, and perhaps years. Hence the camels for the cigars; hence the immense trains of servants, the beasts laden down with dressing cases and colognes and—if it were all amassed in one place—a lardy mountain of hairdressing unguents. The Governor General would be an utter brute, Frampton opined, if he honestly expected anything else.

"When we are settled there," a lieutenant drawled, "we must send for a pack of foxhounds. Excellent hunting to be had, I understand."

Like a carpet borne by ants, the Army of the Indus inched forward with its vast burden of necessary comforts, followed by a vast and increasing train of jemaudars and mahouts; inched eastwards, a few miles a day, and as it went forward, like a ball of snow, it grew larger and larger, amassing more and more camp followers from each place it rested. The kings of the shifting city observed this process calmly; Macnaghten and Shah Shujah and Burnes, each with his court. Observed, too, the others' courts and rituals with mild, uninterfering curiosity, listening only to gossip.

The army had paused at the bank of the Indus for some days, while the pontoon bridges were constructed. Beyond the borders of the straggling town, the river, roaring like a millstream, stretched away. Macnaghten, who, with the departure of the Governor General, had risen beyond all his expectations, spent his days in his tent; his subordinates brought him papers from time to time, and he examined the communications with his best air of calm authority before nodding. It was terribly easy, to be in charge, and the ceaseless universal deference now afforded him was what had always appeared to him as no more than his due. News was occasionally brought of Shah Shujah, but Macnaghten rarely saw him, ensconced in his splendid palanquin, a mile away, and gave little credit to what he heard. The news that the new King of the Afghans had ordered one of his men to whip an English drummer-boy caused him some discomfort—the boy's crime had been to carry out an errand too slowly (and it was not, in truth, Macnaghten had to concede to his outraged subordinates, the task of English soldiers to run errands for this oriental prince). Other tales of Shah Shujah, his cockfights and dogfights and the summary punishments meted out to members of his entourage, Macnaghten listened to without comment; that was the sort of thing to be expected of these princes, and even those who suffered most directly under their whims accepted them without the fury an Englishman might evince. He agreed, however, that the whims of a potentate must not be allowed to extend to the Queen's forces, and he was persuaded to send a remarkably mild note to Shah Shujah, pointing out that the discipline of English troops was a matter for the Queen's representatives, and asking him to report any further delinquency without taking action himself.

"Dreadful old fool," Burnes said to Frampton when he heard of this. The boy's wounds had been displayed across the camp, to general mutterings of disapproval among the ranks.

"And that fwightful old Shah Shujah," Frampton sputtered through a mouthful of food. "One might have thought he would understand it worth his while to ensure a modicum of loyalty. After all, it is we who are supposed to keep the wetch there. Not that it did the boy any harm—that sort of conspicuous discipline, much to wecommend it."

Burnes could not dissent from this, and the boy had made a perfect nuisance of himself, displaying the results of Shah Shujah's summary discipline to any passing sepoy or jemaudar with indignant delight. Still, one had to keep an eye on this sort of thing; and, as Mohan Lal said, Shah Shujah's reputation for enjoying the sight of these atrocities was remarkable even by oriental standards.

"Doesn't he have his own army to whip?" Frampton said.

Burnes shook his head mournfully; Frampton shook his head mournfully; and, together, they contemplated the sad business of Shah Shujah's army. Macnaghten and Auckland had refused to countenance the idea of a prince of Kabul without any kind of army at all. Even they could see that Shah Shujah, entering Kabul, would have to be able to show some Afghan supporters, rather than a lot of English red-faced mercenaries. The Army of Sugar and of Milk, as the officers' tiffin had christened it, had been put together out of any old passing tinker or merchant or fakir, pressed into some kind of uniform and left to pick up the rudiments of drill at leisure. By now, there were five thousand members of the instant army, wandering around the camp with perplexed expressions; sometimes you came across a pair of them, pretending to stab each other in the stomach with their bayonets in play. Shah Shujah seemed as pleased as Punch with the ragtag army the English had pressed together for him, and from time to time inspected their dismal appearance, carried back and forth on his second-best palanquin. Anyone would have thought the troops, who could not even agree which shoulder to carry their rifles over, were the men who had defeated Napoleon at Waterloo, so austerely approving was their Emperor's gaze. But the important thing was to keep

Shah Shujah happy, and, by means of these endless inspections and turning a blind eye to his extravagant, wilful punishments, that end seemed to be in sight.

"But whipping a drummer-boy . . ." Frampton said.

"How are the bridges?" Burnes said, changing the subject.

"Slowly, slowly, slowly," Frampton said, shaking his head. "Five days behind, five whole days."

From the great looms and pulleys, the temporary workshops on the side of the river, rafts the size of housefronts were emerging, piling up for the huge task of the crossing. Boats had been seized, and lashed together; planks nailed on top into great squares. These littered the plain like dance floors, or the cast-down books of a giant's library. The carpenters sawed and hammered without cease. The army was idle, and sick of pointless drilling to occupy the time; the officers made inroads into their camel-loads of cigars, and wrote letters and journals. The connection (rather a distant connection) of Lord Palmerston so ran out of things to say that he described the crossing, days before it had happened. Ah, well; there was no reason not to write it now, since it would all happen as planned, and after the Indus were traversed, there would be little time to set pen to paper.

"There had been some doubt among us," he wrote, "that the sepoys would pass the Indus, a river appointed by their religion to mark the utmost borders of their empire. But in the end all passed off well, although not with any marked alacrity. The crossing of the great river presented a military spectacle of the most impressive kind. The battering train and heavy shot were towed across on rafts, and then the men crossed the magnificent bridge we had caused to be floated in the river. First, the native regiments dispelled our concerns by crossing with great good humour, cheering as they went, and then our men. The cavalry went on foot, leading their horses by the reins. The bridge swayed considerably, but its broad expanse held. Finally the camels with their attendants; the unaccustomed movement beneath their feet caused them great distress, and several bolted; still, I do not believe that we lost above two hundred, which in such a vast number is not a catastrophe. In truth, it was the most magnificent spectacle I ever beheld, and all accomplished with great ease." He set down his pen; how naturally the anticipation of small losses came to him, and now that he had written it, he felt that it would all come to pass, just as he had supposed.

It was some days before another officer wrote a letter to his wife, back in Calcutta, when the crossing had been achieved. It had been much as his colleague predicted. ". . . the crossing was magnificently organized, but many of the native troops were rather ragged. I fear I was tired, and as we rested on the far bank of the river, watching the column cross, I was suddenly startled by what I took to be a large funeral procession. What put such a thought into my head I know not, as I was thinking of very different subjects. I cannot help recording this, it made such an impression."

He put his pen down, and scratched his head. The letter would go with a bearer the next day, or the day after that. They had crossed the Indus; in a matter of weeks or months, they would be in Kabul, and he would send for Hannah to join him. The climate, after all, was said to be most agreeable.

8

The servants lined up in the empty marble hall, expressly to smirk. Vitkevich formed a poker face, and drew his black furs about him. As the doors were opened to him, never again to reopen, a carriage was drawing up in the courtyard. He lowered his head, as if against the snow which was now forming, but in reality because he did not want his departure to be seen; he could not bear any further snubs, he could not bear, at this moment, a familiar face to look directly into his and force itself to make no acknowledgement. Twenty times a day, wherever he went, that happened; or a lovely face which had once gazed into his eyes with adoration had flushed, and twisted on its neck and looked into the middle distance, until he had passed. He went to the places where that was most likely to happen, and it happened, as he knew it would. He lowered his eyes now, and shrank into his greatcoat, and hurried away from what, undoubtedly, would be some new humiliation. He was a brave man, he assured himself, and now he knew what he was expected to do.

The streets were empty, and the few men in them huddled over their braziers at each corner. Even people who had never heard of him turned their backs. Vitkevich's chambers were not far from the Princess's palace; it had been part of his idea of himself that he would live, and continue to live, in the best part of Petersburg, and now he saw how empty that bravado had been. He had foreseen this, and earlier that evening had dismissed the servants. The doorman let him into the dark, empty, cold flat, and Vitkevich dismissed his suggestion that he light the fires with a final, extravagant tip. The man gazed at the ten-rouble note with astonishment, and retired hastily.

Vitkevich dropped his fur on the floor, and, lighting the lamps as he went with his flint, went into his study. Everything here was neat and orderly. For a moment, he gazed at the blank wall, and he saw what he would rather not have seen: the image of the plaster, painted with a single spurt of the blood his skull held. Onwards. Vitkevich sat down at his desk, breathing into his hands, and took his papers out of the top drawer. Perhaps it would be best to light the laid fire, after all. While it grew and settled, he went through them. There was nothing here, in truth. He drew a sheet of writing paper towards him; as well to say something at the last. Various formulae went through his head; various pieces of grand bravado; it all came so easily, and it was only when he took his quill, dipped it in the ink, and prepared to start that he realized he had no one to write to. The pen, poised above the paper, dripped; a single black blot. A tear for Vitkevich, he thought sardonically. No matter. And then, in a fury, he took a handful of his papers, and threw them into the fire; and then another, and another, watching them burn, to lick and roar at the chimney until it was all done. There was nothing left of Vitkevich, now; and the fire retreated to a peaceful crackle. Everything, now, was done. He sat down for one last time, and faced the sheet of paper with its single black tear. Burn that, too? No. That would do for an epitaph. The key was in the lock of the bottom drawer, and he turned it briskly. There, as he knew it would be, was his old pistol. He wondered, briefly, who would hear the noise of the shot into his head, and who would come running. He had always been brave, and now the time had come to be businesslike.

9

Masson was sated with the days, the weeks of solitary lies; but to Hasan he would not lie. The boy had appeared from nowhere, from the air, and Masson took the unspeaking face of the beautiful annunciation between his two hands and spoke, and spoke. He told him, again and again, that he loved him, knowing that when the next day broke, he would be gone, and said over and over again that now Hasan must be brave on his own. Told him as boldly as he could that he must never forget that this was his country, and it was for him to fight, to keep it his. Told him that the English were coming, and it was for Hasan, the hero, to fight, to kill, to drive the English back to the sea, to drive them back to where they were born. Nothing in Masson's life had ever struck him with the necessity he now felt, of saying this as plainly as he could, and he talked, on and on, to Hasan's listening face. Remember me, he wanted to say, remember to fight, remember who you are, and the angel listened, as if to a confession, as if to something he already knew. They did not have long, and as Masson went on talking, it seemed less and less as if he was wasting what few hours they now had together. He would leave the boy sleeping, in the early morning light, and the boy would wake and find him gone, and there was only one thing he wanted to leave him with. Masson went on talking in his fantastic gabbling Persian, and in the serious silent Asian night, Hasan did not lower his gaze, but went on listening to what he must do.

10

The Bolan Pass fell; and Kandahar fell; and Ghazni fell; and the Amir Dost Mohammed Khan sat in his citadel and heard of the progress of the infidel towards his great city, and knew what must be done. His armies had melted away, disappearing into the hills before the forces of the English, and the Amir thought, and did what he must do.

This, then, was the first of the two virtuous journeys of the Amir Dost Mohammed Khan. He observed his city, and, with a great sorrow in his heart, accepted his task. The princes of the court were summoned from the far corners of the kingdom, and stood before their Emperor with their heads bowed, knowing what he was to say.

"We must leave our beloved city," he said into the silence, and one after another, the princes of the court began to weep, knowing that it must be. Only the Amir Dost Mohammed Khan did not weep, knowing that he was telling his unhappy subjects only the beginning of the story, and not its end.

The noble horses of the Bala Hissar were made ready, and the Amir and his princes, his family and their families, their attendants and the warriors of the kingdom rode out in the night. They left the gates of the mighty palace open for the infidel to find, and did not look back. They rode out of the fortress, and through the jewelled city of Kabul, and out into the mountains, and the weeping entourage followed their unweeping Emperor, riding eastwards, and never looking back. The Amir faced towards the dawn, and his bright eyes were like emeralds in the early light, and were wise. Great was the Amir of the Afghans! And even at this moment, as he rode, as he undertook his virtuous journey, he was calm. His people wept and cried out when they saw in the morning the gates of the Bala Hissar hanging open, and the halls of the Bala Hissar empty like the shell of a nut, but the Amir Dost Mohammed Khan, as he rode out to deliver himself into the hands of the infidel, did not weep, for he knew one thing. He knew that he had chosen to take one virtuous journey; he knew also that there would be a second, and he did not speak of it.

II

The Bolan Pass had fallen; and Kandahar had fallen; and Ghazni had fallen; and the Army of the Indus rested, in something like shock, before the city of Kabul. They had been there, unmoving, for four days. The morning had come to advance into the city. This would be no siege; the low walls of the city lay undefended before them. For days, the curious inhabitants of the city had been paying visits to the camp; some trying to sell food to the hungry soldiers, but most merely to inspect their new masters. Bazaar merchants, street-boys, the veiled women had come; the Newab Jubbur Khan, to Burnes's high amazement, had appeared from nowhere and casually informed him that the court had fled, he knew not where. The city lay before them on a silver plate, a gift. It was Shah Shujah's; it was theirs; and the days were spent not organizing a siege, but arranging a triumphal procession.

Burnes was near the head. Before him rode Shah Shujah and his assembled entourage. Macnaghten and the English went behind, and then a few hundred cavalry officers, their spurs bright in the mountain sun. So, Burnes thought, so this is our achievement; to take what we are being given. The brilliant clean cavalcade left the camp, and when the first of the horsemen passed the low wall, there was a small shock in Burnes. Nothing had happened. It was theirs.

Shah Shujah had not seen his city for many years, but his head was upright and stiff, looking to neither side. Burnes felt that nothing in the city—in his city—interested him but the possession of the Bala Hissar itself, and in the old king's unmoving rigidity, he saw not the dignity of an emperor, but an inhuman lack of curiosity. They went on into the silent city. There was a great weight in the silence; it was not that of an empty city, Burnes felt, and soon he understood why. At the edges of the streets, people were standing; more and more people, not moving, not speaking, just staring. Acclamation had not occurred to them, and the thickening crowds stood and stared at their old king and his new allies in complete, leaden silence. They rode on and on, and when, through the silence, from the crowd, a hoarse hiccupping cry sang out, Burnes almost blushed with the shame of it. Involuntarily, he looked for the source of the single heckle, and found it; an old madman, an old familiar figure from years before. He was behind the mass of the crowd, and half-running along, keeping pace with the riders, and shouting the same thing, over and over. "*Gharib nawaz!*" the old madman was shouting, laughing as he called out. "*Gharib nawaz!*" Burnes had never heard it before; he had only been told by Masson that all Kabul had nicknamed him *your humble servant,* and now, riding behind the deplorable Emperor in this contemptuous metropolis, he blushed with an all-enveloping shame.

Burnes pulled his horse to one side of the procession, to the side of the street, and waited there. The crowd was three thick, and gazing up sullenly. All at once, the madman fell silent, and melted, somehow, into the crowd, and, all at once, the air rang with the people's silence. He had never heard such silence in Kabul, or seen such massed stillness. The whole of Kabul stood on the street; small children, red-veiled women, the merchants of the market, the mullahs. They stood without moving, staring at the empty triumph of Shah Shujah and his glittering foreigners, and made no noise. The procession went on, and soon Burnes, on his horse, was far behind the principals. He wheeled his horse round, facing the crowd, and they parted in front of him. He rode away from the procession, through the empty silent streets. The city had surrendered itself, as it were, to the funeral of some beloved prince, and had closed itself to every other pursuit. No one was there to stare at him; the shops and houses were locked up and silent, and in ten minutes he had ridden to the outer edges of the city. He tugged at the horse's reins, and spurred its sides, and broke into a gallop. It was a bright, empty day, and he emptied his mind of the silent city behind him. The mountains rose before him like a dream, brown and cream and white in the clear high sun, the earth hard as stone beneath the horse's hooves. He was alone, and rode out into the distant bare country like a hunter. It might have been minutes, or hours, before he slowed and slid off the sweating flanks of the horse, the city far behind him. He looked up into the utter clarity of the Afghan sky, and saw something he had never seen before; a single cloud, like nothing he had ever seen before in his life. Across the depthless azure of the Afghan sky, a single, brilliantly white line, shining with the reflected sun, being drawn as if with a piece of chalk. Burnes looked at it, never having seen it before. Far above, tens of thousands of feet above, a jet plane was tearing across the sky. He looked, and to his mind came a single diction- ary thought: disaster. Disaster: evil star. He stood with his neck tipped back, his mouth open, until he ached and the thing was quite gone. What it meant, he did not know.

ANTHROPOLOGICAL
INTERLUDE

I

The room he rented had initially seemed nice, but it hadn't taken long to discover that the little square it looked out on was brutally noisy, all night long. The taxis of Kabul congregated there—how had that escaped his notice?—and their engines, idling, filled the upper rooms with exhaust fumes. It was bad enough during the day. At night, the revving of engines was even noisier, and the drivers seemed to wait until the small hours before testing the noisiest functions of their cars, hooting for no obvious reason. It woke you up, choking in the lingering fumes, and for a moment you had no idea where you were, but you were already angry. Angry with the world, and then you identified the source of your rage. There was no point in going to throw open the shutters to yell at them; he had tried that a couple of times, but the drivers, each squatting possessively on the bonnet of their car, just looked up incuriously, as if at a change in the weather they had not caused and could do nothing much about. He, too, fumed; but less noisily.

In the day, the drivers greeted the Englishman with good humour. He had been there long enough to become part of Kabul, it seemed, and they hailed him merrily, like wrongdoing schoolboys putting on a pretence of ignorant innocence before an angry headmaster. He took it, in a way, as a compliment. Every other Westerner they came across was fair game. Often, making your way across the little square, you came across a driver negotiating with a hapless pair of travellers; they saw someone weighed down with rucksacks, and their eyes narrowed at the prospect of the fortune to be made out of some boy with dollars in his pocket, wanting only to be driven to Peshawar, and perhaps, too, a few cheap drugs. Sometimes, a driver would be nonchalantly naming some gigantic price for the drive, and then would glimpse the English anthropologist leaving his house. The hard, incredulous stare would disappear, and the driver break into a broad cheerful grin at his new Kabuli friend. On the whole, it was agreeable to be accepted like this; he tried to persuade himself to stop troubling about anything else.

2

He had been there a few months when a diversion occurred to him. The laborious work of interviewing, of picking over absurd titbits of Afghan family history for something which could be reduced to diagrams was growing wearisome to him; he started to wonder, in fact, if he was truly all that interested in questions of matrilinearity. The winter came early that year, and, gloomily staring out into the falling snow, an interesting diversion occurred to him; a trip, not to gather information, but just to pace some ancient steps.

Whenever he came to Afghanistan for fieldwork, he always made a point of packing a battered and treasured book. He had had it since he was eleven; an old library book, borrowed and reborrowed from the local public library, and in the end, when he had read it a dozen times, he had reported it lost and paid for the thing. That must have been the first thing he had ever heard about Afghanistan, which now constituted half his life. He first came here in 1961; now, fifteen years of kinship diagrams later, he felt he understood the country less than he had when he was eleven, and reading his stolen library book. No one else he knew had ever read the shabby book in its green binding; it was a shameful pleasure. He always brought it with him to Kabul. Of course, the derring-do tone of this epic of empire had no real merit, but, alone in his room, he had never ceased to be excited by it. He was honest with himself; he brought it with him to egg himself on, to remind himself what had driven him here in the first place. A few pages of Pottinger's heroism, read by candlelight, would reconcile him to a Kabul power cut, and the next day, he would be able to embark on the dull task of sifting solid information from his rambling interlocutors with some measure of zest.

He opened it up, with the usual mild sighing pleasure; he was only looking for a date, but the book fell open at the familiar rabbity portrait of Dost Mohammed, and, without meaning to, he began to read, scratching his Afghan beard. There was nothing more comforting than reading a book you could practically recite, and soon, the room, the metallic stink of exhaust fumes, the raucous outside noises of the Kabul streets receded, and he was eleven again and utterly absorbed for a gorgeous hour. Kabul was always demanding that you spread your own self out, shared it out like titbits at a picnic. You had to be companionable here; reading was a bad, a solitary pleasure conducted in an empty room. The Demands of Sociability; he saw the book some anthropologist would write one day. Not him, though. In the end, oblivious to the task he had set himself, he read beyond what he had wanted to find out, and had to turn back twenty pages. Poor people! There it was: 6 January.

That was about two weeks away. Or a hundred and thirty-two years ago. He checked his diary, and realized that today was Christmas Day. All over the city, the hippies would be celebrating in their own way— probably abandoning themselves to opium, rather than turkey, he thought wryly. He had probably better write to Catherine, a long amusing letter. These days, he was away for too long at a time, and he felt it; whenever he returned, London had always changed in some small, unarguable way. A building demolished, a new shop, a new book or film everyone had read or seen months ago; sometimes even a new phrase of slang (Sloane Ranger!) on everyone's lips. Sometimes it was years before he discovered that some old actress had died and everyone else knew it. Yes, it was a good idea he had had, this retracing of the famous journey. Not very helpful with regard to matrilinearity, rather out of his usual line, but interesting all the same. And there might be an article in it, he supposed. Yes, 6 January. He hoped the weather would not be too bad, then reminded himself that if it were, that, indeed, would be rather the point. His life was grey, and orderly as a filing cabinet. This would be a pleasant change.

Begramee, to his slight surprise, was now a golf course. The greens were covered with snow, but he discovered the reason for the strange smoothness of the terrain when he stumbled into a pit, and found himself sliding through an unnatural melange of snow and sand. This had been the first night's resting place. He stood up, pulling his knapsack back on, and brushed himself down. He had walked only five minutes further when, almost from nowhere, a group of women appeared, running towards him. Kipling's advice came horribly to mind:

> When you're wounded and left on Afghanistan's plains
> An' the women come out to cut up what remains,
> Jest roll to your rifle an' blow out your brains
> An' go to your Gawd like a soldier . . .

But Kipling had had nothing to say about golf courses, and he suppressed the thought. The women ran up, their golden grins shining bright, and, of course, they had no knives. They gestured at him, grinning, and of course they would assume he could not speak to them in their own language.

He greeted them as elaborately as he could, but they did not reply; perhaps a foreigner's Persian did not count in some way. He sighed, and followed them. At the end of the golf course—perhaps on the golf course, it was not implausible—there was a little group of huts, a fire burning in the open, and he followed them into the largest of them.

Inside, there was a circle of men. They paid no attention to his entrance, and he squatted down and joined the group with a general salaam. They seemed to be talking about hunting—no, he concentrated—about the cousin of one of them, gone to America to be rich. Goodness, his Pushto was poor. The story wound its way to a leisurely pause; every time one of them said something which must be meant for Connecticut, he turned and nodded at their guest, amiably. When it seemed to have come to an end, he spoke—he trusted his Persian more— explaining his journey. Only slight embellishment was needed; as always, it was sensible to bring a blood relation into it. In Kabul, he routinely refused the request for the gift of a specific possession—a ring, a cheap watch—with the sad assurance that it was given to him by his father as he lay dying. In the same way, now, he told them with a straight face that he was following the route taken by his grandfather's grandfather, a great English warrior, and hoped to find his bones.

"Engelstan," the oldest man said, nodding. "They came with tanks, with aeroplanes, to fight Dost Mohammed. My father told me, and his father told him."

"Dost Mohammed was a worthy adversary," the anthropologist put in, scrupulously.

"And Macnaghten," he went on. "Macnaghten, the Prince. And when they came to the English, and told them that Macnaghten was dead, dead by his own hand, the English cried out and said, 'How is it possible? How can he be dead, and the sky be as it was before?'"

"Macnaghten," another said, trying the name, remembering the tale.

The anthropologist made a mental note. He would not claim Macnaghten for his grandfather.

4

The food was good at Begramee, though heavy; the fatty stew of lamb and roots incongruously called Lancashire hotpot to mind. He fell asleep almost immediately, and woke sore and aching from the lumpy thin mattress and the hard earth. The day was clear, and the sun on the snow dazzling. He set off after a solid breakfast of thick bread and bitter, burnt tea; the sun was low in the sky still. He had forgotten to wind his watch, and had no real idea of the time. It must have been an hour before he realized he had company. A boy, about fifteen, was following him, twenty or so paces behind; a strange sort of intimacy in the white empty landscape.

For some reason, he did not feel threatened or concerned. He let the boy pace behind him steadily for an hour or so, and then paused, turned back, smiling. The boy did not seem surprised; he continued his steady pace until he had come right up, as if he had been waiting for the anthropologist to notice him before approaching.

"Hello," he said.

"Hello," the boy said. Then, in English, he said, "Hello!" and grinned, hugely.

"Where are you going?" the anthropologist said, as they started to walk once more, side by side.

"I come from Kabul!" the boy said, with huge enjoyment.

"A beautiful city," the man said gravely.

"What is your name?" the boy said.

"My name is Conrad," the anthropologist said.

The boy nodded, and fell back into his companionable stride without offering his own. "Many Americans come to Afghanistan," he said. "I like America!"

"Would you like to travel there?" Conrad said.

The boy laughed uproariously, although there was nothing comic in what Conrad said. He shook his head, over and over.

"I am from England," Conrad said. "Not America. Engelstan."

The boy seemed to agree with this. "Will you be my friend?" he asked after a few minutes.

"Of course," Conrad said. It was important to appear relaxed.

"Can you give me your watch?" the boy said.

Conrad shook his head, and explained that it had been the last gift of his grandfather, on his deathbed; an explanation the boy seemed to accept placidly.

"Once," the boy said, out of nowhere, "the English came here, and fought with us. But now they are our friends!"

"I hope so," Conrad said. "Do you—"

"The English," the boy said. "They fought Dost Mohammed. And Macnaghten. The only man to reach Jalalabad was Macnaghten, and when he reached there he said Sah makeh. Do you speak Urdu? Sah Makeh. Everything over. But now we are all friends. Do you know Jalalabad? Very very beautiful city."

"I am going there," Conrad said. "I have heard much of its beauties."

"Look," the boy suddenly said. "There is my brother!" And he left Conrad's side, and off he went, running heavily through the heavy snow. Conrad could see no one, and he watched the boy running off with a slight sadness. He had been nice. Yes, everyone was friends now, and Afghanistan would be peaceful for evermore.

5

It was on the fourth day that he found the bones. By then he had invented the rules of his journey—the rules of the game, if you liked. To everyone he met, he would quite simply say that the grandfather of his grandfather, a great English warrior, had travelled this way many years before, and he was walking the same way to pay his respects to his ancestor, and perhaps to find his honoured unburied bones. He would say this, and then simply listen to what they had to say in return.

What he never expected was that the bones would be there. That broke all the rules of his game.

The night of the third day, he was listening to the family memories of an old Afghani, sitting in his shelter. Macnaghten had come with tanks; the shepherd in the next village, his grandfather's mother had been English, who had run away to safety and fallen in love with a great warrior, no, another shepherd. Conrad listened, his hands biting with the cold of the January night. The old man finished what he had to say, and paused, his eyes bright.

"The bones are there," he said. "Your ancestor's bones."

"Where?" Conrad said.

"Over the next hill," the man said. "You do your ancestor honour by your journey."

Conrad nodded graciously, supping from the bowl of thick soup; some of the viscous fat adhered to his beard.

"My son will take you there," the old man said. He clapped his hands and a youth in the dark recesses of the hut stood up. He turned his head and rattled out a short, metallic burst of tribal Pushto. The boy sulkily came forward.

"Tomorrow will be early enough," Conrad said, alarmed, but the man seemed set on the idea.

"It is very close," he said. "And today is early enough, to do honour to your ancestor. It is very close, and quite safe."

Conrad gave up, and, wrapping himself up and taking a torch, followed the boy out of the hut. He was oddly annoyed by the assumption that he was worried about safety. The group seemed to approve of this urgency. The boy said nothing, just slouched a pace or two ahead of him, and the anthropologist was in no mood to talk. The night was astonishingly clear; the moon bit at the deep black of the sky, and beneath the feet, the hard snow crunched like gravel. They plodded onwards in the intense hard cold. When Conrad fell, the ground shifting beneath him, the boy came back a little and hoiked him up roughly without making a comment. There was no sound, no light but the brilliant moon; somewhere, beyond the hills, a dog howled faintly. It took ten minutes to reach the top of the steep hill, and then the boy made a rough sweeping gesture. There was nothing to be seen, nothing but a smooth field of untouched snow. Conrad turned to the boy, but he was hunched over a cigarette, trying to get a match to spark. The boy raised his head, and gestured again. Conrad began to walk forward, not knowing what else to do. In a moment he would turn back, assume a solemn expression, and allow himself to be led back to the tent. There might be more to see in the morning, of course. He took another step forward, and then something broke underneath his feet; something friable, empty, like a great bird's egg. He pulled his foot up, and something came with it. He saw what it was, knowing what it would be before he knew what he felt; and it was a skull, its crushed-in roof biting at the sole of his boot, and then, helplessly, he toppled forward with one leg in the air. He fell, ludicrously, hard, and something, again, shattered underneath him; the bones, another set of bones, what remained of another man, and, nauseous, twitching, he flailed about, trying to raise himself without doing one thing, without putting his hands on the field of bones. But from here, he could see one thing: the snow was not smooth and level, as it looked when you stood; it rippled away, unevenly, like a cloth cast over the shattered remains of a broken tea set. It was all bones, heaped up and left where they lay, untouched, contemptuously unburied. He wanted to turn and go back to the boy, unfeelingly pulling on his cigarette, but, as he pulled himself up, he seemed to fall forward, and then, again, under his boots, that sickening breaking sensation, and another, and another, and another. This was what he had come to find, and now he had to go.

6

The next day, he walked and walked and walked, and he got to Jalalabad, and no one paid him any attention as he entered the city. And the day after that he agreed a price with a taxi driver, and drove back to Kabul along the snowy roads—it took four hours—and tried never to think of any of his journey, ever again.

AKBAR

What good is a cow that neither calves nor yields milk?
What use is a son unlettered and stubborn to boot?

—*The Pancatantra*

TWENTY-ONE

I

The sheep in the fields froze for a tiny moment, and then scattered; not running as sheep run, all together, but in different, panicked directions, like a pond when a rock has been heaved into it. They must have seen this roaring monster before—must have seen it every day of their short lives, indeed—but they ran as if this new terror were quite new to them. Their grandfathers had never seen such a thing, and they ran, having no idea what was descending on them.

"Do stop that," Bella said to her sister. Elizabeth had been humming "Hail the Conqu'ring Hero Comes" on and off since they had left Queen's Acre. "It isn't funny."

"It is funny," Elizabeth roundly declared. "Very funny indeed."

Bella looked at her balefully. She had never been in a railway carriage before, and the novelty of it had come from an unexpected direction. The speed of the travel she had heard about, and within a few minutes it had ceased to astonish her. After an hour or so, it seemed merely the appropriate velocity to go at, and Bella allowed herself to be hurtled through the English countryside as if she deserved nothing less. What disconcerted her was a more human aspect of it. She and Elizabeth were enclosed in a small compartment, alone, and there was an unnerving lack of certainty whether they were in public or safely alone, in private. In some ways, as they talked, it felt open to any stranger, like a post-coach; in others, Bella felt as if they were luxuriously alone in a mechanical landau, and she felt a slight awkwardness as they talked, as if at any moment a stranger might enter. Still, she knew what she would say, on her eventual return, when Henry or the nursemaids wanted to know all about it; she would tell them how very fast a train went, because that was what everyone always said.

"I'm sure he will be quite all right," Elizabeth said. Bella looked at her, surprised; she had, indeed, been thinking about Henry, left alone at Queen's Acre for three weeks. How he had cried when she left, although when she had first explained it to him, he had nodded in a serious, adult way, accepting what his mother needed to do; how she had cried, too, once they were safely away from the gates. "By now, he will be in his garden, digging to his heart's content. He will be quite happy, you know. At that age, it is one day after another."

"I know," Bella said. "He would love to come to London."

"He is as well in the country," Elizabeth said, briskly dismissing this impossibility. "And he has never been without his mamma. It does children good. I am so fond of him."

Bella assented to this, silently. The train slowed, quite abruptly, and in a moment stopped. Somewhere ahead, the engine hissed villainously. Bella stood up and stared out of the window at the suddenly unmoving countryside.

"A change of horses, do you think?" Elizabeth said idly.

"It could be highwaymen," Bella said. "Quickly, sister dear, hide your jewels. No, I think they have to stop sometimes; it is more restful to us, and our poor nerves. Do you suppose anyone will remember me, after all this time? And so changed?"

"Not changed one ounce," Elizabeth said in her uncharitable way; she need not have said *ounce* so meaningfully, after all. "Of course they will remember you—you will see. It will be good for you to leave Queen's Acre, to see some new faces and practise your curtsy and forget your country manners."

"No one will marry me now," Bella said, and the thought made her happy. Elizabeth made no comment; the point was so unarguable. "But you are right. Society is good for the soul; it assures one of one's own superiority in every point to the mass of mankind."

Elizabeth rolled her eyes; and she used, surely, to enjoy Bella's jokes. Beneath the window of the carriage, a bright metallic ring sounded, and again. Elizabeth joined her sister at the window; beneath, a workman with a hammer was hitting one of the wheels of the carriage, testing its soundness.

"I know nothing of these things," Bella said. "But I would feel more at ease if they had carried out their examination of the train before we began our journey. What will happen, should we lose a wheel? There are so many wheels—perhaps we will continue as if nothing has happened. Or perhaps we will be thrown into a ditch. Who can say? Not I. Henry would be too overcome with excitement to speak—I shall write to him this night, without fail. He has been pummelling me with unanswerable questions from dawn until dusk, and now I shall be able to answer every one. Or not, more probably."

"Dear little Henry," Elizabeth said. "If only papa—"

Bella raised one eyebrow, quizzically, and there were a number of ways in which the sentence could have gone; if only papa could still be here, to dandle his bastard grandson; if only papa had borne the news better; if only papa had had the strength of character to behave with love, or as a gentleman ought, instead of the shameful half-measure; but he was dead now, dead after years of insensate stupor, and no end would be served by completing the sentence. At the time, she could have softened the terrible blow by telling him that she had married Burnes in secret, as Elizabeth had said she must; but, for no reason that she could see, she had not. She would have been prepared to lie to her father; it was herself she was thinking of. And afterwards she had not seen him again, and no one had told her even that he was dying. How few people had come to his funeral; how sad he would have been to have seen the empty expensive spectacle, the empty carriages lined up outside, sent by all the duchesses whose intimate friendship he prided himself on, and the clergyman, by all reports, ineffectually fumbling about for his virtues. Bella had gone into mourning, quite formally, for a year precisely, her black gowns seen by nobody. A substitute for feeling. He had never chosen to see Henry—that had been his idea of how a gentleman, in these circumstances, should behave—and Bella, now, was hardened to her gratitude at the fact. Henry was so very unlike his grandfather; so unlike, she rejoiced at it.

"Do you suppose they know?" Bella said casually.

Elizabeth knew, somehow, what and whom she meant; the upper ten thousand. "I don't think they do," she said slowly. "No, it was lucky, but somehow I think your disgrace was not discovered. Someone would have been sure to allude to it, I think. The Gilbert girls, no doubt. Both married now—did I say? The younger to a most unattractive clergyman, and glad of it, I dare say."

"My disgrace," Bella said ironically. Really, what an excellent governess Elizabeth would have made. "Dear little disgrace."

"Yes," Elizabeth said, lightening a degree. "Dear little disgrace."

"Elizabeth," Bella said. "You were making a joke?"

"A joke?" Elizabeth said.

"Your disgrace," Bella said. "That, I hope, was meant as a joke?"

Elizabeth frowned. "I love Henry," she said finally. "Of course I do. But Bella, please—let me, at least, call things by their proper name. Is there nothing in the world can make you serious?"

For a moment, it occurred to Bella that Elizabeth had never married, and wondered about it; it was deplorable that her sister's condition was not something she ever considered. But of course Elizabeth could not marry now; whether she had chosen it or not, that was her condition. No man would marry the sister of Bella Garraway; and if he married her, unknowing, then there could be no place in Elizabeth's life for Bella or Henry. Perhaps scandal had touched her; perhaps she had accepted what must be, through love for her sister. Bella had never considered it. Yes, her disgrace, she thought; and the disgrace had touched Elizabeth, and bruised her hard. She settled back into her seat, and presently the train began to move again.

2

The house was as it had been, and this was strange. Bella had expected— well, what had she expected? She had not seen it for five years. A ghost of a house, perhaps, shut up and draped against dust. Or newly uncovered, made to shine for her benefit, its chatelaine, the servants lined up on the steps outside to greet her. But it was as it had been; a single unfamiliar maid—what had happened to Emily?—to open the door, and then the dark hall with its heavy ticking clock, the untouched walnut drawing room, and everything just as she remembered it, and somehow different. After all, the house had only been empty for a week; Elizabeth lived here in her solitary bluestocking dignity. She paused, wondering at her own egotism. It was she who had changed, it seemed.

Elizabeth had been hard at work spreading the interesting information of her sister's return, and, while Bella permitted her cloak and bonnet to be removed by the bobbing maid, she fingered the pile of cards in the silver filigree bowl. A rout—a dinner—another dinner—the notice of a funeral, a man whose name she only dimly remembered. Her name was on all of them, and she went through the pile methodically while the trunks were brought in. They struck her, wildly, as the submissions of tradesmen, begging for her custom. She almost expected to find Burnes's card there; but how should it be?

"We dine at home tonight," Elizabeth said, "and it will be as well to rest tomorrow, too. Very tiring, travelling, and one feels so dirty."

It was still her father's house to Bella. She retired to her room, and sat there, not tired at all. Her things were all about her; things she had not thought about for years, and never missed. Her box of precious things, for instance, there on the dressing table, still locked, mementoes of her life before Henry. She felt no urge to open it up, and in any case had no idea where the key could be; only an effort of memory could recall what she had once placed in it so carefully. There was a knock at the door, and the maid entered with the tea. Bella sat with her eyes closed against the room which held some other past; once, perhaps, a girl had sat here, and wondered what would come to her, and what her life would bring. She had never imagined a life like the one she now had; it had surprised her; and there was nothing in it she would wish otherwise.

There was a small sound as the maid quietly set down the tea tray, trying not to disturb her exhausted mistress; the clink of a spoon on china. It was the same noise as—as something—Bella delved, and it was the noise of the workman, knocking at the wheel of the train, four hours before. It sounded again as the maid quietly arranged the things, and a deeper, stranger memory came to her; the sound she had not understood for years, the sound from her father's study. The teaspoon clinked against the china, and it was as if she were listening again to the regular afternoon tocsin from the next room, as her father drowsily unlocked the opium tantalus and measured out his dose. She had heard the sound every day of her life, but now it brought back one afternoon, as she and Burnes lay there, together, naked, holding each other, as quietly as they could, and listening to the clink of glass on glass, the sound of approaching oblivion.

She opened her eyes; the maid had gone. A false memory. That afternoon, they had been alone in the house. But she could do nothing about it. That was what her mind had decided to recall for her benefit, for her dubious entertainment. Memory, that exhausted repertory actor, going through the exhausted, familiar lines of some tired melodrama. It moved through the now meaningless scenes with a terrible practised proficiency for her benefit alone; and she was in the wings, condemned to watch it over and over, to prompt the leads if they should ever go blank. But they never did; and Bella endured the recurrence, knowing she had no alternative. All memory was distasteful to Bella, even the memory of pleasure. Especially the memory of pleasure. Only Henry was good enough to drive the idle, weary round of memory away; he had taught her, in the end, what love was. Burnes had written three times; long, full, grand letters full of declaration and fine manly feeling. They wearied her, in truth, like a bad novel when there is nothing else to read, but she made an effort and replied in the same vein, hardly considering what she wrote. She knew with complete certainty that he would not return, and, if he did, would not return to her. Henry knew nothing of him, and he knew nothing of Henry.

3

The doors of the vast ducal house were flung open to the world, and every window blazed with light. The faint strain of an orchestra drifted out in the early-evening air; lilting, silken, rich. The street was unmoving, and blocked with black carriages; the street-boys dodged between them, running towards the gates to get a better look. Tonight, the Duke's four hundred guests were punctual to the minute, and had arrived at the precise time requested; the promise of Royalty weighed heavily with them. And the two or three hundred carriages converged simultaneously on the same point. The coachmen put their legs up, and tied the reins to the post, munching a bit of bread and cheese contentedly.

For this most important party, the Duke had shown himself. For some years now, he had withdrawn from society to devote himself to what he had always been most interested in, the acquisition of antiquities. Society, on the whole, did not concern itself with this. Lord John, his amusing second son, had taken over the burden of entertaining with pleasure (the Marquess of Porlock, the heir, was a dull dog, too, it was agreed) and the Duke of Dorset was not missed. Tonight, however, the Duke had issued the invitations, and, for the sake of Royalty, was standing in the salon of his house to greet his very prompt guests. Lord John was here, of course, and, as the ballroom filled, he wandered about, greeting friends more casually than his awesome father whom no one knew. In the background the orchestra played; lilies from the ducal hothouses spilled and swooned from the walls, dripping with candlewax; there had been more than anyone knew what to do with. No one danced yet; there was a twitter of excitement in the dazzling room, heavy with the scent of flowers and women, bright with the light of flames and diamonds. Not since the Regent—no, not since the Regent—the room agreed, and the queue of the upmost five hundred of the upper ten thousand, prompt as footmen, built up as the barker called out their names. They advanced, brilliantly smiling, towards the Duke and Duchess, each of them suppressing a catty thought about the Duchess's ostrich headdress, thick as a shaving brush, secured with brilliants.

"I don't see my old friend the Duchesse de Neaud," Bella remarked to Lord John. She and Elizabeth had been absolutely on the stroke of the hour, on Elizabeth's insistence, and, with pleasure, she found herself rewarded with the attentions of an old suitor. For the moment, before the arrival of the Queen, she noted, the room was rather interested in her, whether they remembered or recognized her at all.

"The Duchesse," Lord John said, and then laughed heartily. "My dear Miss Garraway, what a very secluded life you have been living, not to hear about the poor woman's shame."

"Shame?" Bella said composedly. "Of all my former acquaintance, she is the last I should have associated with any shame."

"A most unfortunate story," Lord John said. "It emerged, all at once, that she had been sadly deluded in the Duc, who was no duke, but a rich tradesman from Soissons. Forty years in the country, and no one thought he was anything but what he said. I suppose after the Revolution, a great many odd fish turned up here, and were welcomed, but none so odd as that. Patriotic fervour made him a favourite at first, and then a clever marriage, and before you and I were born, Miss Garraway, he was universally accepted as what he said he was. It all came out some two years ago. And she, as you say, so very respectable."

"And now?" Bella said.

"Who knows?" Lord John said, giggling. "A sad story, looked at in the proper light, and how foolish the Court appears in that proper light. Of course, there was nothing more foolish about the whole affair than the fact that, once in possession of this information, the pair of them found every single one of their former friends strangely forgetful. One day they were so agreeable, and the next no one could recall their names. And yet they were very much the same persons, and who could but admire the old Duc de Neaud for being so very clever? I forget his true name—I knew it once—no, it has gone."

"Poor woman," Bella said. "And did she know of the deception?"

"No one can guess, and no one seems to know where they are now."

"How odd," Bella said. "What a favourite she was at the Court, without the benefit of her Duke. Could they not, for her sake—"

Lord John gave her a quizzical look. "But how could he be received? Well, I expect they live exactly where they did before, but no one calls, and they come to nothing. I have a whim to invite them again, to see what happens when they enter the room. Not when my father is acting the major-domo, however. Ah—"

The orchestra had struck up the national anthem, and the room, by now crowded, drew back into two bodies, either side of a clear passage. The Duke, who had abruptly left the house, now returned with a tiny girl on his arm; a tiny, cross-looking girl in a brilliant red silk gown, flushed and plain. Her face was round as a bun, and as she passed a remark or two, her regal teeth were ugly, little, and stubby. As she smiled crossly from side to side, it was as if she were not acknowledging an acquaintance, but ordering the deepest of bows. The room bowed at her command, and the noise was like thunder, muffled by silk and feathers. The Duke and the Queen proceeded slowly up the room, followed by the Duchess and the Prime Minister; her importance could be immediately perceived, the only ugly girl among all these ugly old people. It took ten minutes.

The party began again, and the Queen and the Duke began to dance a stately, ceremonial sort of waltz, like a dancing master demonstrating the correct steps with a favoured pupil. To Bella's surprise, Lord John did not move away, but asked for the honour of leading her onto the dance floor.

She assented, with a sense that this was not meant to happen to her. If she had envisaged her return into society, these three weeks Elizabeth had persuaded her to agree to, it had been with a conviction that society, now, had no role for her; and it came down, in the end, to a doubt whether she was now a woman who danced, or a woman who did not. She was no longer a girl, that was clear, nor was she a new wife who could dance without fear of consequence. If she thought of her place now at all, it was with the abandoned girls, the mothers, at the side of the room, observing and curious. To dance with Lord John was so unexpected an opening to her three brazen weeks that she did not quite know how she could carry herself, and she fell into the steps of the dance with a consciousness that, now the Queen had passed through, the room was observing her. Bella Garraway; so sadly changed; and in the arms of Lord John.

"I hope you understand the purpose of this evening," Lord John said.

"The Queen, surely, is purpose enough," Bella said. "I confess, I have never seen her, or only as a cross little princess in the Duchess of Kent's carriage in the Park. Such an alteration from the old King."

"Miss Garraway," Lord John said. "Miss Garraway, you disappoint me. The Queen is stale, a stale amusement, and will grow staler once she marries. No, the Duke has not invited us here to watch us curtsy; it is to mark his marvellous acquisition. You know the Duke, of course?" Bella dissented, and she knew Lord John's father very little. "Well, I think few know him well, but I ought to say that this expense and display is, in his mind, all in the service of a magnificent acquisition he has made. So magnificent, indeed, that I doubt he will mention the fact at all, so I promise to take you to inspect it at some point before supper."

"You are rather mysterious, Lord John," Bella said.

"I mean to be," Lord John said. "Ah—" and he bowed, warmly smiling, in farewell, disappearing like a climbing lark into a white cloud of dancers.

4

Not since the Regent—not since Waterloo—not since . . . The old ladies, sitting around the edges of the room, delved back twenty, thirty years in their memories and all agreed that they could not recall so splendid a London Season. No, not since Waterloo; and the Duke of Dorset's surfacing to pay homage to this marvellous new Queen, after so many decades when her dull or disgraceful old uncles seemed to rule over society, seemed like a magnificent pinnacle of a magnificent Season. The black fans of the dowagers fluttered, and, behind them, the word for the Season was "glorious." No, not since Waterloo.

There was nothing like a faraway military victory to rouse the dowagers of this little London to a fervour of enthusiasm. The news from the East was so thrilling, they named a cotillion after it. The armies of India had roused themselves, and annexed great provinces with surpassing ease. Patriotic fervour made the ballroom glitter, and the most surprising people agreed on the astonishing triumph. Around the room, the name of Kabul was being dropped casually; some pronounced the name with an initial stress, some not; and if they had come to write the name of the city down, few would have agreed whether it began with a K, a C, or even (for even Society may boast a little learning) a Q. No matter; the name was uttered by one shining face after another. In these ballrooms a new reign began; the founding of a new empire, practically; and the eyes of society fell on the ugly little Queen with adoration, as if she had done it all herself.

Stokes's mind was on expenditure, as, these days, it so often was. His dizzying escalation seemed to have crippled him, so great were its attendant properties. The *Dundee Examiner* left far behind, the Hatters' Society long forgotten, his long-foreseen state seemed to require an appropriate method of living, which he was by no means equipped to pursue. The new editor of the thundering paper could not, after all, walk from place to place; he could not with propriety continue to live in Flat Hand Yard with the attendance of a drunk valet called Mullarkey; he could not refrain from the ceaseless burden of entertainment, but it seemed to him that his rapid ascent had conferred honour and obligations without supplying the means to fulfil them, and he felt like a balloonist, gasping at the thin cold air. A carriage; a house in Brook Street; a platoon of servants and an army of new friends he didn't care for in the slightest, all eating their heads off at his expense; and all so that he could pontificate daily in print and be invited to the house of the Duke of Dorset. Soon, he reflected gloomily, he would have to acquire a wife; the alternative, soon, would be the debtors' prison.

He slunk into the great salon unannounced. Despite his absolute promptness in departing from Brook Street, the carriage had proceeded no more than two hundred yards before being blocked by the mob of carriages, all similarly queueing for admittance. For ten minutes, they sat immobile, while Stokes weighed up the absurdity of taking the carriage for a journey of eight hundred yards against what had suddenly become the impropriety of arriving by foot. Finally, he flung propriety to the winds, and walked the last stretch, but he was too late; the Queen's carriage was drawing up ahead of him, and he skulked, kicking his heels. It was some minutes before he could be surreptitiously admitted, lest the Queen's ears be soiled with the knowledge that there were those who arrived after her.

There was a certain gratification in being the last to arrive, in every sense, and Stokes would have had the doors shut behind him for good. Assiduous as he had always been in his attendance, it was only in the last year or so that he had come to appreciate how incomplete his social ascent had been, and he looked back at the hostesses he had once courted with a real sense of shame at having started in so very degraded a condition. Lady Woodcourt would never be admitted here, or the Gilbert girls; it was now almost incredible to him that he had ever thought of such vulgar hours in terms of "society," and Fanny Woodcourt's cards, asking him to think of her at seven on Thursday next, were these days returned with a civil regret. To think of Fanny Woodcourt—the idea! No one thought of her, surely, at seven on Thursdays or at any other time. He had been admitted now to Society, and the only thing that could make him happy was the firm knowledge that the gates behind him would be closed, and no one more admitted. All the same, he ruefully admitted, it might well come to the point where he had to sell the Rembrandt to pay for all of this; and if it proved not to be a Rembrandt at all, he did not know what he was to do.

There was a marvellous emptiness about this party, all in all; there was never any kind of lure found necessary, and no fascinating fashionable guru of the variety that lesser entertainments found so indispensable would ever be promised on the invitations of the Duke of Dorset. Nor, in fact, did Stokes know a great number of people here, but he strolled through the groves with a feeling of some satisfaction. To know nobody here was as sure an indication of the social purity of the gathering as it would be in a costermongers' tavern, and it was with a feeling of positive irritation that he found himself acknowledging the bow of Castleford. The idea that a vulgar companion from the old days might have followed in his wake, and slipped through the doors just as they were closing firmly shut, struck him as inconceivable, and he wanted, more than anything, to ask the blunt question of what on earth he thought he was doing there.

"I thought I should know nobody here," Castleford began companionably. "Tremendous pleasure to see you, a great man like you."

Stokes bowed coldly, before recollecting himself. After all, he could not wander about in solitude for the entire party. "I don't remember seeing you here before," he said.

"Nor I you," Castleford said, apparently equal to this. "Very dull, these things. I wish Royalty would know its place, and stay there; they are the ruin of a perfectly good party, in my view."

"Sir?" Stokes said.

"In the old days," Castleford said comfortably, "the old King would stay in St. James's and those who cared to would make the pilgrimage, and come away feeling very much the better for it. Now—well, look—" he waved his arm in a half-circle, "—they come out, and turn what might be a perfectly pleasant party into a gigantic exercise in tedium. Really, it reminds me of nothing so much as a hen-coop once the fox has got in. Half of them stiff with terror, and the other unable to keep still with frantic excitement. But you are so great a patriot, these days, I hardly expect you to agree."

Stokes bowed. If only someone he knew would come within reach, he could leave this tedious reminder of his former self. "You are less than generous, Castleford," he said mildly. "It is not precisely enthusiasm, I think; certainly, I look inside myself and my emotions are not at all those of a startled hen."

"No doubt," Castleford said. "No enthusiasm whatever, Stokes? You are not swept away in this tide of patriotic fervour?"

"I feel a sense of honour, perhaps," Stokes said. "Your sister is well?"

"Quite well, thank you," Castleford said. "In the country, I believe. I recalled you were always rather an enemy of acquisitions in the Orient, Stokes, but, you know, on reading your recent effusions, I start to feel my memory must be at fault."

"I confess, I had not always thought the Indian expeditions as wise as now appears, but—well, Castleford, you will know far better than I the value of these new acquisitions of Her Majesty. New markets—you see the point of that? Come, Castleford, a fellow can change his mind."

"Of course," Castleford said. "But I was always a proponent of Empire, you recall. Great heavens, is that not—"

It was, indeed, Bella Garraway, and Stokes, briefly taking his leave of Castleford, went to greet her.

5

The world is waiting to be born. A new Queen in London, her little teeth gleaming at her suitors in her ballrooms. In Boston, far on the other side of the world, the stevedores are saying something they never heard before one year ago; they unload a ship, and chalk O.K. on the side of it. Ten miles from them, no one would understand it, but they like this, a jocularity they never think will spread into every language in the world, given time. The dancers, at this moment, are still dancing to something their grandfathers would recognize, and tonight's ball will finish with a novelty which is no novelty, a decorous old round dance, this season's sensational "Kabul Cotillion," but in other parts of Europe, the orchestras are assembling to make sounds never dreamt of before, and men, with their ink and their manuscript paper, are dreaming, they are plotting ways to bring the old eighteenth-century dream of harmony, civility, and proportion to an end for ever. Emily Eden sits with her pencils, and sets down in laborious chalks and tints what she can see, tidying up and making picturesque the sights of the world; soon, a Frenchman will do something which will make her effort seem pointless, and before long, when the Europeans want to record the fabled East, they will take a box of M. Daguerre's, point it, and that will be good. England is being carved up, with lines of steel and thundering, steaming engines, pouring smoke into the blue English air, and the deer of the English parks look up, and run as fast as they can from the roar.

Akbar wants his father's lands returned, and that is the extent of his desire, and he never thinks that his act will change the world, as surely as photography. After Akbar, no one will look at the world again in the same way. Our lands are ours, they will start to say, and the tale of Akbar in his splendour will be told from shore to shore, wherever men embark from ships and start to rule. From now, the poor bewildered people will hear of Akbar, and they will know that they are not helpless, that they can rise up, and take back what was always theirs. And Akbar will fulfil the desire of the English, to lose their Empire, will drive them back with their engines and their photography, their post offices and their belief in the equality of men; he will make his people poor again for no reason. They do not know that the English would give them civilization, and they do not care; they want only to be Afghans. The world is changing. For now, we are in a London ballroom, full of a dream of glory, but the world is already altered, and takes no account of the wishes and dreams and pride of men. It starts to change, now.

6

Even the orchestra talked of Kabul.

As the third viola was accustomed to point out while they rosined their bows in the back bedroom of some town house, turned into an impromptu band room for the evening, *orchestra* was a flexible term. Some of these here dances stretched to no more than four or five players, the squire having the front to whine about the idea, the very idea (as the third viola said, his voice rising in mockery) of them taking a break, and no supper neither. And what the point of that was the Lord only knew.

But tonight the old Duke had done himself proud, with an orchestra which would do in any theatre in town, bassoons, drums, and even a trumpet, and four fiddles to a part, as the orchestra all agreed, taking their break in the Duke's library. "You see," the third viola, the oldest hand in the business, explained seriously, "there are them as think one fiddle looks too stingy, and stretch to two, never thinking that, it stands to reason, two fiddles on their own, they can't play in tune with each other, now, can they? But four—now that's an orchestra. This is what I call a party. It brings the old Prince to mind, it really does."

The trumpet player blew a rude noise through his mouthpiece, as if testing it, and the others all sniggered. "My old pa saw the Regent," the contrabass said. "He said he was like a great sausage, all corseted in and lumpy. Laugh? He said he couldn't help himself. And the old sod never paid up, that's what my old pa always says."

"You be quiet and don't talk about what you don't know," the third viola said. "He knew how things should be done, I'll tell you that for noth-ing. And your old pa didn't know one end of a bow from another, so, begging your pardon, even if he was here, I wouldn't give his opinions the house room they don't deserve."

The trumpet, having assembled his instrument, began very solemnly to play the Last Post. The third viola broke off and glared at him. "No, I'll tell you a story," he went on, ignoring this interruption. "It was the day the Regent came and he spoke to me. I'll tell you the story, the proudest day of my life, and then you'll know what sort of man he was. Well . . ."

Orchestras are as full of storytellers as an oriental bazaar, and the musicians listened contentedly to the long-familiar tale of the third viola's triumph. Still, just as in society, men have their season of triumph, when audiences cluster about them, and the moment was not his. The star of the moment waited on one side for his moment. For years, the bassoonist had been a man of no note, and now, strangely, he was not; for as long as anyone could remember, whenever he timidly ventured a story of his past, it had been as good as a signal to the others to start putting their parts in playing order. These days, he was a splendid old fellow, and when he played at the circus, even the conductor sometimes remembered his name. It was odd that a year ago, the fact that he had been a soldier in India for most of his life had counted against him, when you considered how these days everyone hung on his every word. So he listened to the third viola's boring story with an air of content, warbling away in the instrument's highest register as if attempting to see just how disagreeable a noise he could make with the old thing.

The third viola finished, and looked around; the performing habits of musicians are hard to break, and he might have been waiting for applause.

"My old father," the contrabass said with tremendous withering scorn, "said he could never understand how some fat old man could make such a spectacle of himself. Those were his words. A great sausage, that's what he always called him, fat as a pig in a frock, and so pleased with himself, you'd think he was about to burst."

"Ten minutes, gentlemen," the bandmaster said, popping his head round the door.

"It was ten minutes ten minutes ago," the flute said.

"No, it was five minutes ten minutes ago," the trumpet said. "So George, what kind of place is this Kabul, then?"

The bassoonist paused, set down the instrument, and leant on it, like an old wise farmer with a walking stick. "I never saw it," he conceded, relishing the sudden attention. "Never got that far. They say it's a fine place, a fine rich place. And when they say that of a place in the East, they mean it. I've seen places as'd make your eyes water with the gold and the beautiful women—"

"Niggers, though, George," the trumpet pointed out.

"Don't be so ignorant," the bassoonist said. "I could tell you a story or two of the women I've seen. There was one day in the bazaar in Calcutta—you, you ignorant bastards, you won't know what a bazaar is, but you've got your dick-shone-airies, ain't you—and I was minding my own business when this dirty great black with a mace comes down the street and behind him, six little fellows all carrying this litter, and I stands to one side to let it pass, they've got a word for it, I forget, and they all stop by me, and the silk curtain opens, and there's this little face, a princess, a rani, as they'd be calling her, looks out at me, and, blow me down, she says, 'What's your name?' and I tells her, and the curtain falls and it goes on. What that was all about I don't know. But I'll tell you one thing. I'll never forget that face to my dying day, and I'd walk from here to Calcutta if I thought I'd ever lay eyes on anything like that again. Worth conquering the world for, a face like that. Tonjaun, that's what they call them, tonjaun."

"Tonjaun, George?"

"That's what they call the litter she was in."

"Ah," the trumpet said. "But you never went to Kabul."

"No," the bassoonist allowed. "But I know one thing. There's no other nation on earth could have done what we've done, marched in and taken charge, and no other nation could set it to rights like we'll do."

"Makes you proud to be an Englishman," the third viola attempted, to general derision.

"Fine lot of judies out there, I dare say," the trumpet said.

"Gentlemen," the conductor said, coming in again, and the orchestra stood and prepared to return, for their moment.

7

"Soon we'll be ruling the world," a languid young man just behind Bella was saying with the appearance, at least, of irony. "Railways from here to Cathay, no doubt." And as they stood there, the ball drifted past them, offering them tiny fragrant nosegays of thought.

"Georgina Frampton's son, you know, is there, but she is quite sick with worry," another, higher, more fluting voice floated over. "And when you come to think of it, a son lying dead, and no word of it for months or years. A terrible burden for the poor woman."

"Five thousand a year, or so they say—"

"Most sadly changed—"

"I confess, Her Majesty was so good as to confide that—"

"Not since the Regent—"

"Not since Waterloo—"

Bella had more or less finished reassuring Stokes with a general account of the soundness of her health and expressing her obligation for his kind solicitude when Lord John again appeared. She introduced them to each other.

"I am charged to show you my father's new acquisition," Lord John said. "You see, Miss Garraway; I come to fulfil my promise to you. And you, too, sir, if it would interest you. I would not keep you from your supper, of course, but there is too great a crowd at present, and I can promise that even a mob of hungry dowagers cannot entirely devour the feast before we reach it. Would that interest you? My father," Lord John was continuing, as he led Bella and Stokes from the door of the supper room into an empty corridor, "is a great antiquarian, as you must know. His only interest, indeed, as I am sure he would eagerly confess. How much more interested in any number of dead Queens than the one who has been so good as to honour us tonight. I am charged—silently charged, you understand, but I understand his wishes—with taking his most honoured guests to glimpse his latest splendid acquisition."

"I am prepared," Bella said. Lady John, she thought; Lady John.

But the room was not empty; bending over a glass case was the Duke himself, whose departure from the ballroom no one had noticed, and by him the little figure in red. They raised their heads and turned; Bella dropped the deepest of curtsies and Lord John and Stokes, composing their faces, bowed solemnly.

"Most interesting, Duke," the Queen said, smiling in her ugly unconvincing way. "A most valuable addition to your interesting collection."

"Sir, I fear I am disturbing Her Majesty," Lord John said seriously. The Duke stood, unmoving, with a black look on his face.

"Not at all," the girl said. "Please, Duke, continue. Most fascinating."

"If we may," Lord John offered. "Sir, I thought to share your new treasure with two of your guests—Mr. Stokes, you know, cares so much more for the life of the mind than for dancing, and Miss Garraway—"

"Quite," the Duke said. "With Your Majesty's permission? A rare find, a precious thing. The best authorities have examined it at length and conclude it to be a fragment of the poetess Sappho. A very rare thing, but my librarian is convinced of its provenance, and I cannot recall so very important an object being offered to me."

"A national treasure," the Queen said. "Sappho, did you say?"

"Yes, ma'am," the Duke said. "I believe there is a fanciful poem on the subject by the modern poet Pope, but little is known of her or her works, and this is a significant addition."

"Stop hovering," the Queen said over her shoulder to the new entrants. "I detest hovering. Come here, come here."

The three of them advanced, and looked into the case. On a bed of white linen four feet by two lay a tiny scrap of papyrus, brown and ragged. Bella bent over as the Queen pressed her nose, almost, against the glass, and saw that on the little scrap were some marks; she looked some more, and saw that they were two Greek letters—*chth*—and the beginnings of a third.

"*Chth*," the Duke said. "Most interesting. Of course, it is not at all clear what sort of poem this could have formed part of, or, indeed, what word it might have once begun, or ended, or . . . But it must be regarded as an extremely interesting discovery. Fish, perhaps."

"Fish, cousin?" the Queen said, raising her head; they all followed her.

"The Greek word for fish contains this concatenation of letters, Your Majesty. But there are other candidates—darkness, for instance, or rather, more specifically, the darkness of the earth, or the underground, you know, a very interesting and pregnant word, or . . ."

"So disappointing," the Queen said. "Not to know exactly what was in the late poetess's mind, when she took her stylus . . ."

The four of them bowed again at this unexpected display of regal learning.

". . . and set down a poem in the full flood of inspiration. But perhaps I am too romantic, sir—it could be, could it not, that if she were writing of fish—fish, you said—that this is no more than a fragment of the poor woman's instructions to her cook?"

They all laughed, deferentially.

"No, I prefer to think," the Queen went on, evidently gratified at the compulsory success of her sally, "that it was set down in the full flood of her inspiration. *Chth,*" she said thoughtfully. "And fish, too, may be the subject of a most romantic poem, after all. Now I recall—the poetess flung herself into the sea, did she not?"

"That has been the belief of the modern era," the Duke said.

"*Chth. Chth. Chth,*" the Queen repeated as she turned and, Duke in tow, went towards the door, for all the world as if she were clearing her throat. "Most interesting."

She, Bella suddenly thought, will be Queen for ever. She raised herself from her profound curtsy and watched the door close behind the tremendous scarlet woman. Not twenty, and an age, a lifetime of Empire before her, and she knows it. *Chth. Chth. Chth.*

"I shall never forgive myself," Lord John breathed, collapsing into an armchair and giggling mildly. "Had I known—"

"I believe you knew perfectly," Bella said, sitting down more decorously. "And you shall forgive yourself, but I shall not. The Queen—"

"I feel sure that the Court now will be entertained every night with Her Majesty's recitation of a fragment of Sappho," Stokes said. "*Chth.* From memory too, in all probability. I must say, the Duke's fragment is remarkably poetic, when one comes to think of it."

"She read awfully well," Lord John said. "No one else could have done it so convincingly."

"And she seemed so moved by it," Bella said.

"Appallingly moved," Lord John said, his chuckling dying away gracefully. "People say she is interested by nothing but the circus, but we three, now, we will be able to correct this sad misapprehension. She is a woman with a true respect for learning, you see. Miss Garraway—I must tell you this—it is such a pleasure to see you once more in town—we have been deprived too long of your company."

Stokes turned away in mild embarrassment to inspect the Duke's books, and it was too late now either to make his excuses and repair to the supper room, or to join in the conversation; and, after all, Lord John's sudden compliments to Bella were rather what he had been thinking of making himself. He took down a book at random, and began to flick through it. Like the rest of the library, it seemed to be in Latin, and he stood stiffly with his evident tactful fraudulence.

"I am sure you have contrived to console yourself in other manners, sir," Bella said. "It is difficult to believe that you have been lying prostrate, waiting for my return to society; and, after all, I had a very serious reason to disappoint you, regrettable as it may seem to you."

"Yes," Lord John said. "Yes, I heard you had been ill, and I am happy to see you looking so well again. I do hope you will permit me to call while you are in London."

"Lord John," she said, and Stokes could see that this question, so ordinary, had taken her by surprise, and she could not field it immediately. "I would be—I would—I think it may prove difficult, so short is our stay, my sister's and mine, but—I would not be unfriendly for the world, and I am most honoured by, by . . ."

"Miss Garraway," Lord John said. "I quite understand. Let us say no more, but enjoy our evening."

Bella crimsoned, as if Lord John's smiling kindness were too great to bear, and whatever reasons she had to excuse herself from his attentions, it was clear she was not about to reveal them.

"When we meet again—" she began, but Lord John was too quick for her.

"Whether we shall meet again, I know not," he said. "But if we do meet again, why, I shall smile."

"I shall smile, too," Bella said, with a look of relief on her face. "Lord John—"

"Miss Garraway, Mr. Stokes," Lord John said, and seemed to make an effort, and take notice of the editor again. "You must both be hungry. Let us go in to supper, and leave these dusty old relics behind."

Bella followed him; and afterwards, her odd feeling was one of pity; not just pity for Lord John, refused by her for a reason she could never explain, and of course not in any degree pity for herself, but pity, all the same, for Elizabeth. As Lord John took one last look at her, full of regret and tenderness, she felt she knew that what supported a human being was the sense of touch, another pair of arms around one's neck, consoling. And by accepting the single enriching joy of Henry, embracing her every day, she saw now that she had taken that support from her sister, for ever. The touch of Henry was all she needed, and the evident prospect of becoming Lady John was no more substantial than the idea of Burnes's return. But yes; they might meet each other again, they might; and when they did, why, she would smile. That would have to do, as it would always have to do for her poor sister. And Stokes followed her, unregarded, with his gaze, and him she never thought of.

8

The coachman cracked his whip, and the carriage set off into the plum-pudding richness of the warm London night. Bella drew her wrap about her, and thrust her hands into Elizabeth's muff. They sat there for a moment, with their hands jammed together cosily.

"It is just as it was," Bella said. "Just exactly the same. Society, I mean. Did you have a pleasant evening? I saw you dancing without a break."

"I did," Elizabeth said. "I wish I could tell you who took me in to supper—a very agreeable gentleman, and an officer, I slowly gathered. He seemed to know me quite well, full of solicitude for my strength and your health, you will be pleased to hear. His face was not unfamiliar to me, I admit, and for two solid hours I was in a state of terror, in case some kind acquaintance demand an introduction. And Lord John?"

"He is so agreeable," Bella said. "He asked if he might call, and I had to make an excuse."

"Yes," Elizabeth said thoughtfully. "Yes, that is probably all for the best. I hardly know him, but . . . Have you seen the Queen before?"

"No, not since the accession," Bella said. "Whom is she to marry?"

"A German prince, they say," Elizabeth said. "A very handsome German prince, I hope for her sake. And for the sake of the little princes to come."

"No, she doesn't produce a very engaging impression," Bella mused. "I spoke with her, a little, you know."

"You spoke with her?"

"Lord John took us to see an antiquity or two, and she happened to be showing the same interest. I mean that gentleman Stokes and I. A very important personage, now, I understand."

"So I believe," Elizabeth said. "But just as he was. They are all exactly as they were, as you say. Apart from the Duchesse de Neaud, of course."

"Yes, I heard that. I wonder that you did not think of telling me so great a scandal. And who were your partners?"

"Oh, my old dancing partners," Elizabeth said. "The day is fast approaching when, if they ask me to dance, they will be fulfilling one of the cardinal virtues and not expressing an ambition towards one of the mortal sins—the worst of them, too."

"And they could as easily fulfil that ambition, like me, by staying in Gloucestershire and never moving," Bella said. "I refer to sloth, you understand, merely sloth. Still, you have no shortage of willing partners, and that is something."

"Yes," Elizabeth said. "As you say: that is something. Lady Frampton's tomorrow, I believe. She has a son out with the Army of the Indus, you know. Gracious heavens—"

A boy, a street-boy, had taken advantage of the momentary slowing of the carriage, and had leapt onto the running board; against the window, his face pressed violently, gurning and smudging against the glass. Behind him, half a dozen of his familiars ran, barking with laughter. Elizabeth rapped sharply on the glass, then, taking the stick which was always kept in the carriage, on the roof; the coachman noticed, and cracked his whip at the urchin. The boy fell off, and they continued on their way.

TWENTY-TWO

I

This was the worst of the billets so far.

They did not stay more than a few days in any place, riding on without apology or delay. It would not be wise. The English, in Kabul, might or might not know of them, but they would not be pursued or caught, and for that reason, they arrived in a place in the high mountains, commandeered a few houses, and, after a few days, moved on. Where they went next, they never announced; where they had come from, they never told. Sometimes they doubled back on themselves, but for the most part they did not know where they would end up that night. Only Akbar knew, and he kept his council.

The settlements were rarely comfortable, but none had been as raw as this one. High in the mountains, it amounted to a dozen houses built out of mud walls, lodged in a deep horizontal crevice. It was almost invisible until you were upon it, and would do very well for the next week. The villagers were evicted, and were now staying in the smaller settlement over the brow of the hill, with anyone prepared to take them in, returning at dawn to serve the Prince and his retinue of brothers. They were a remote and a helpless people, existing somehow on a few sheep and a scrap of land, vulnerable to any transitory marauders. Their language was strange and ugly, and would be barely comprehensible half a day's ride away. It was difficult to make them understand what they had to do, and they seemed barely capable of realizing who it was demanding the use of their homes. Akbar's retinue had stayed in many places now, and this was the first where no display of awe or obeisance had followed the explanation, where Akbar's name meant nothing. They had no idea where they lived, or who ruled them, and seemed not to care that it had once been their Dost, and was now the red-faced infidel. They gave the court whatever it asked for, but they gave it grudgingly, as they might have followed the instructions of any rich traveller.

It was a wretched hole, and its seclusion was its only recommendation. In the deep cold of winter, Akbar's court shivered. Most houses in the eastern marches of the empire were kept warm with an underfloor heating, a *tawkanah*; the villagers crouched outside and fanned the fires, blowing hot sparks into the hollow underneath of the house. This was a dismal place, and there was nothing to do but place the settlement's two crude braziers under a table hung with blankets, and bury your hands in the depths of the muggy heat.

It was night, and the Prince's brothers were assembled around the table, silently trying to warm themselves. Akbar himself was in the largest of the houses, alone, thinking. The brothers had finished eating, and the villagers had taken the coarse brown dishes away. Four sheep had already been killed for the court's food; this was a poor place, and if they stayed more than another day, then the villagers would have to be sent out to steal another from their neighbours. That, Akbar's brothers generally assumed, was not their concern; the honour bestowed on these ignorant shepherds was payment enough, as everyone would understand.

They were high in the mountains, and as they moved from place to place, never knowing whether they were pursued or tracked, they were hiding the world from them as effectively as they cloaked themselves from the world's hostile intentions. What events were occurring in the rest of the empire, they did not know; whether, when they reclaimed the empire, it would be for Akbar or for the Amir, who by now might have been executed by his enemies, they did not know, and would not speculate. But from day to day they lived, holding out the idea of their return to the great jewelled city with the certainty of faith.

Akbar's retreats into his inner sanctum occurred unpredictably, and the band of princes accepted them as a mark of his eminence. They sat and waited for him. What he contemplated, they did not know; but they accepted the gravity of his contemplation. There was a suspension of the rules of his father's court, here; they were not courtiers but warriors, equal against the invader. But there was an unarguable and undisputed sense of hierarchy, and as Akbar entered, there was a general stiffening as they acknowledged him.

Akbar himself was not, perhaps, an inspiring figure; slight and small, he passed unnoticed in a city crowd. And that was his power. When he closed his hand on a dagger, his fingers were thin and delicate as some exotic white vegetable; impossible, too, to believe that a hand so clean could inflict damage, and there had been dozens who looked up, amazed, from the savage gash in their stomachs to the fine-boned Baroukzye face as if, somehow, they had been betrayed. Akbar was graceful and fastidious as a girl, cleaning himself devoutly, like a cat; constant small acts of grooming were characteristic of his habitual demeanour as he shook off the dirt and mud of the world. Even out here, he washed. The villagers were each day handed a full set of robes, and wondering, their women made their way down the hill to the three murky ponds, to pummel the great Prince's apparel into a white never seen before in this high filthy settlement. In the coarse mud house he had commandeered, a pail of water stood, constantly refreshed, and the cousins who stood outside the door, watching and waiting, listened to his occasional splashing and puffing with a satisfied sense that this man was not like them. No one imitated him; no one could; not even Musa, his current favourite, who was summoned nightly to share the great Prince's bed. And catlike, too, was his stillness in thought, his ability to appear in a room unseen and to slink from it. He was small and slight and feline; as he grew, his father's court had inspected him, wondering at where in the outer shell of his being his ferocity showed itself. They peered cautiously into his mild pensive eyes, and soon they all remembered an old proverb. *The cat walks alone, and his cousin is the tiger/and when the cat grows, walk from him; for he will turn and eat you.* They remembered it, and it seemed ancient to them; but Akbar might have inspired it, and planted it newly in their minds with the appearance of memory. There had, they knew, never been a man like Akbar before; never.

"I was sleeping," Akbar said, entering quietly.

"It is good to sleep," Khadi offered. Khadi, like most of them, was some form of brother or cousin, and, like most of them, he found it wise to offer quick approval of all Akbar's actions. "Did my brother dream?"

Akbar came and sat at the table, pulling impatiently at the horsehair blanket until his hands and feet were thrust into the heat under the table. "I dreamt," he said. "I dreamt of my father."

"A good dream," Zemaun hazarded. "A propitious one."

Akbar turned his head and regarded him with pity. "I dreamt I killed my father. He came to me in my dream with his arms open, and I killed him, and in my dream, I was not sad, but calm."

The princes drew back. Khadi was bravest, and quickest. "The honoured Amir is alive," he said. "Your dream is a good one, Prince; it says that none will kill the Emperor but his son, and when death comes to the Amir, his son will be there to live on. Dreams are wise, and they often say things which are contrary to their seeming appearance. To dream of the killing of a father speaks of the honour you bear him, and tells us that he lives on, beyond the hills."

"Fool," Akbar said, reasonably. "It may mean that I wish to kill my father. A dream of bad luck. I slept badly. The food here is unfit for dogs, and my dreams were poisoned by it."

They sat for a while, toasting their limbs nervously. Hours could pass in this way, as they waited on Akbar's pleasure.

2

Nadir came in the night, and, they later gathered, had waited patiently until dawn, and Akbar's rising. When the court rose and wandered out into the bright mountain air, there was Akbar, and a stranger, crouching. Akbar was listening intently to the man, and they retreated. It was Nadir, and they went back inside, wondering what this could mean. No one had tracked them down until now, and how the Prince's cousin, the son of the Newab Jubbur Khan, had found his way here could not be guessed. They put it down to the profound contemplation of Akbar, one of those plans he had not shared with them.

Akbar listened intently to what Nadir had to say. The sun was barely up, and the long shadows on the mountains were blue-edged and sharp. Below on the hills, a boy shepherd was singing; an aimless, multiplying song which filled the valley; a song for himself and his sheep, a song which would last out the day with its improvisations and changes. The land was quiet and unmoving, and it seemed as if he sang with the landscape, as it echoed each soft falling strain. Akbar sat and listened; listened intently to Nadir, talking, but, behind that, to the noise of his father's morning lands as the sun rose slowly, showed its broad expanse.

Presently Musa came out of Akbar's hut, yawning, his robes wrapped about him approximately. He had woken and found Akbar gone, and, not knowing what else to do, had gone in search of him. He did not know what would happen when Akbar tired of him; he had been around for long enough to know that some of his cousin's favourites stayed, and some, inexplicably, disappeared. Some of the Prince's entourage had had their day basking in the sun of his favour, Musa had slowly learnt from the direction and unexpressed meaning of their gaze; Zemaun, for instance. And others disappeared. The chalk-clean morning was beautiful, and still, and empty. This beautiful land; and his Prince would fight for it. But when the day came when Akbar tired of him, Musa, too, would stay, or he would go; and until that day came, he did not know which it would be. And until then, all he could do, whenever he woke and found his Prince gone, was to rise swiftly and follow him. Akbar gave a swift, angry gesture, not turning, but for a moment Musa did not understand as he gazed at the two men and, behind them, the opening morning. The Prince repeated the gesture again, with a short fierce hiss. Perhaps it would not be long, before the day came. Musa went back inside, with his fear that Akbar was beginning to find him tiresome. It was best to leave the Prince to his task, listening to the news from Kabul.

"They live outside the gates," Nadir said. "The English, I mean. They have set up there."

"And the Bala Hissar?"

"Shah Shujah lives there, the pretender. They say he insisted on it, and insisted that he would live there without any English. The English agreed—no one knows why. Perhaps they think that the people will come to see him as their king, and not the king the English chose. It is so changed. He loves riches, the usurper, and the great halls of the palace are hung with gold and jewels, with frippery. He is protected day and night. The people hate him—they know they pay for all this, and groan under the weight. They hate the English, too, and talk always of Dost Mohammed as their Amir, with love and sorrow. Sir, you know, when Shah Shujah rode first into Kabul, the people all came to see, and they stood in silence. Not one man cheered. He fears for his life, and will not ask the English for their protection. They live outside the gates like beggars."

"Do they fear me?" Akbar said, quite calmly.

"They will learn to fear you," Nadir said with simple tact. "They do not know where you are. Cousin, there is no need for you to flee from place to place; they are not searching for you."

"I am not fleeing," Akbar said scornfully. "Flee the English and their foolish six-months' king? Nadir, if I chose to stay and fight, I would stay and fight. We must travel for one reason; to let the people know that I am here, and one day, soon, they will fight for me. You will see; the mountains will rise and fight for me. That is all."

"Sir," Nadir said. He had no idea, it was evident, how true this was. "The people long for your return."

Akbar nodded, accepting this without argument. "And the Amir?"

Nadir took a deep breath. "I saved the best news until the last. It took me days to find you. Everywhere I went, I showed this jewel—look," and he opened his fist, and within it was a blood-red stone, an imperial ruby, "and the people, when they saw it, they opened up and told me in which direction I must go to find you. It took me days to reach you, and what drove me onwards was the thought that I would be the one to tell you this. The Amir is alive and safe. He journeyed long and far and finally, in his wisdom, he found the English court. They say Shah Shujah begged for him to be killed, but the English would not kill him, they were merciful. He lives in India, and is afforded every comfort of a greatly honoured guest. They are merciful, the English, and they will pay for their mercy. He is wise, the Amir."

"They will pay for their mercy," Akbar said. "Yes, that is true. And they did not blind him?"

"Sir, it is not their custom, to blind a defeated enemy, but to give him honour. Your father is safe."

Akbar accepted this. Behind them, the court had crept quietly from their houses, and had listened to what Nadir had to say. It seemed to them, observing their Prince, deep in thought, that he had accepted a duty from his father; that, knowing he was alive and waiting, Akbar now understood that it was for him to reclaim the kingdom. When that would be, no one knew; but now they knew it would happen, at a time when Akbar wished it; and the lovely earth stretched before them to the horizon, to the dawn, to the mountains breaking like waves of stone.

3

Nadir stayed that night, at the expressed desire of Akbar, and in his honour, Musa, the favourite, was led forward to tell a story. The noblemen sat and listened quietly to an old story, an old story they all knew, and from time to time they nodded. There was comfort in it, a comfort they could not have explained.

"Once there was a rich man in the mountains with three sons. Each of the sons had a plot of land; Aslam, and Nadir, and Khalid. Khalid was the youngest of the sons, and one day a terrible disaster came upon him. The rivers rose, and swelled, and the banks of the river broke and destroyed the lands of Khalid. The lands of his brothers, the will of God did not touch, but from that day Khalid was a poor man with two rich brothers.

"Now each of these men had a child. Khalid had no luck in life but the gift of a fine handsome son, and his name was Jubbur. Nadir had a son too, whose name was Ayub, and Aslam had a daughter. Jamila was as beautiful as the sun in the sky and fair as the moon when it walks through the still night in the mountains. Jubbur and his father were poor men, and they worked the land of their rich brother, their rich uncle, Aslam. And one day Jubbur looked up from his toil, and saw his cousin Jamila as she walked to the river, and saw that she was beautiful, and he fell in love.

"It was strange, but Jamila, too, saw her cousin, and she, too, fell in love, although he was a poor man and could not hope to win her. And she came to speak with him, and their love was as strong as iron. Their love was forged in the heat of the day, and by nightfall, nothing in the world could break it. Jubbur went to his father, poor Khalid, and he told him of his love for Jamila. But Khalid was sorry in his heart, for he knew that this could never be. He tried to persuade his son that it would be best to forget Jamila, but Jubbur said he could not, and in the end Khalid had no more words, and could only shed tears for the sake of poor Jubbur, his son.

"Now Jamila's father Aslam was a proud, rich man, and when Jubbur came to him and told him that he loved his daughter and he wished to marry her, Aslam fell into a rage. He dismissed Jubbur in a fury, telling him that what he wished for could never come to pass, and that Jamila was promised to another; she was promised to her cousin, the son of the other rich brother, whose name was Ayub. Jubbur went out, full of grief, and that day, he went to Jamila and told her that he would win her, if it took years, and this is what he would do for her sake. He would mount his horse, and ride to India, and there he would work and work until he too was rich. It might take years, but then he would return and claim Jamila for his bride.

"Jubbur was as good as his word, and that day, without saying a word to anyone, he mounted his horse and he rode without stopping to India, far, far beyond the hills. He worked and he lived there for many years, and in the end he did what he had promised; he built up riches beyond those even of his uncles. Many years passed, but he never forgot his promise to Jamila. He lived there in solitude, with his riches, and he thought of her every day of his life. And one day he knew that the time had come, and he mounted his horse and returned to the mountains where he was born.

"He rode for days and weeks. His heart rose in his breast as he saw his old home and the lands of his father, and his father's father, and as he rode towards the side of the mountain where his family had always lived, he met with an old man, the servant of his uncle Aslam. Now the servant did not recognize Jubbur, so rich and magnificent was he, and bowed down before him. Jubbur did not enlighten him, but asked him in a kindly way whose fine lands were these. The servant replied to him, that they belonged to two brothers, to Aslam and Nadir. Jubbur pretended to think, and he asked the old man if his master Aslam did not have a daughter of famous beauty, whose name was Jamila.

"Jubbur feared that in saying this, he had revealed himself, but the old man did not seem surprised that the beauty of Jamila had spread into far countries, and this is what he told the poor unfortunate Jubbur. 'Yes,' he said. 'My mistress is named Jamila, and, you are right, she is as beautiful as any woman now living. She is married to her cousin, Ayub. How happy they are! And blessed with three fine handsome sons. No one could be more fortunate than they, in truth.'

"Jubbur heard this, and said nothing, but it was as if the old man had pierced his heart with a dagger. 'And Aslam and Nadir,' he said. 'Am I wrong, or do they not have a brother, Khalid?' 'Yes,' the old man said. 'Yes, that is true. Poor Khalid! He lost his fortune, and then the worst happened to him. His beloved son, Jubbur, left him, without a word, and in loneliness the old man died of grief. And no one knows what happened to his son, or why he left so cruelly. The world is strange, and it is not given to us to understand everything that happens in it.'

"Jubbur said nothing, but he watched the old man go, and knew that everything he said was true. He looked for one last time on the lands of his ancestors, and he knew that there was nothing more for him here. So he turned his horse, and, weeping as he rode, he returned to India, riding by day and by night. No one knows what happened to him, but it is certain that he died alone, still thinking of what he had lost, and how little he had gained."

The story was over. It was done, and told, and its meaning hung in the air like smoke. The princes sat in silence, and presently, one by one, they looked at Akbar, and his cheeks were wet with unmeaning tears. And the next day they would move on.

TWENTY-THREE

I

Was he a griffin, or was he not a griffin? He certainly looked like someone who had only just stepped off the boat from England, and to talk to him, you would come to the quick conclusion that he was the most naïve of neophytes. From his own confession, he had spent no more than a week in Calcutta before setting off for Kabul, and, just as they did with every fresh-faced wide-eyed new arrival, here in the East for the first time, the old hands listened to the jokes, the observations, and the complaints which they all made patiently, forcing a smile or a show of interest. Yes, it was strange that one ate so very fiery a dish as curry in a hot climate, they all agreed, as if the matter had never been discussed before. Yes, it was indeed curious how, when one stepped off a boat after months at sea, the Indian earth beneath one's feet appeared to swell and pitch; they nodded vigorously, letting the boy believe for the moment that he had made an original or an interesting observation. There was never any need for a conversational dismissal; when the next boat arrived, it would bring a new crop of naïve young men, all of whom would make exactly the same comments, and the previous arrival would listen and be struck with terrible embarrassment at his own unoriginality, too late for apology.

This one certainly looked and sounded like a griffin—he was such a griffin, he seemed not to know the word. Everyone was talking about the evening at Macnaghten's when his only comments were, "What is a *shikar*? What is a *jezail*? Was that tiffin? What is the difference between a jemaudar and a mahout?" and finally broke into one of Frampton's best stories, entirely innocently, with, "What is a griffin?" How Frampton had blushed; no one had used the word, out of consideration, and it could only be presumed that he had overheard one of them drop it, and perhaps even with reference to him. On that basis, there was no pinker griffin yet observed. But then there was his name, which somehow seemed to qualify him as an old hand in the East. Was he a griffin, or was he not a griffin? The single fact which seemed to raise him above the usual status was his name, and the camp silently agreed that they could not quite think of Burnes's brother in the usual condescending way. What he was, they could not quite determine, but they treated him with a wary respect.

Certainly, no new arrival had ever been given the honour of a tour of the cantonments by Macnaghten himself.

"Hm—you must not think that—that this is our normal mode," he was saying to Charlie Burnes, pottering through an inexplicable pile of rusty buckets. "We hope to be in more respectable shape—altogether more reliable shape—who left this here?"

But the soldier walking briskly past lowered his hand from its quick salute and sauntered on, not apparently realizing that Macnaghten had been addressing him.

"All assembled and ordered in so very great a hurry, you know, and the many inconveniences we now labour under, it was only to be expected, became apparent after it was altogether too late to alter the arrangements. Here are the kitchens, you see, and who thought to put them in so very distant a quarter of the cantonments did not consider the consequences for our appetite—so very unhealthy to eat food gone cold, but what is to be done I cannot say."

"Could not the kitchens be moved?" Charlie Burnes offered brightly.

"It sounds so easy, but whether to move the kitchens, or our domestic quarters, and what is to be moved to make way for that, and in turn something must be moved for the sake of the second chicken . . . the second displacement, I mean, sir," Macnaghten said, kicking off a persistent domestic laying fowl, "displacement, displacement. A most delicate problem, and the men must suffer (while everyone seems to be in possession of their own most obvious solution) with food which reaches them at blood temperature at best, cold food, a most dissatisfactory, unsatisfactory state of . . . These are the armouries, and, ah, here is Sergeant, Sergeant . . ."

"McVitie, sir," the Sergeant said, saluting sharply.

"McVitie, of course," Macnaghten said with relief. "A fellow Scotsman, you see."

"No sir," McVitie said.

"And these . . . chickens . . ." Macnaghten offered feebly. "They are your charge?"

"No sir," McVitie said as the birds flocked about his feet, pecking pointlessly at the dirt on his boots.

"That will be all, Sergeant," Macnaghten said. "You see, we will be in much better order in six months' time, once we have finished . . . I hope you are finding the East of interest?"

"Very much so, sir," Charlie said. "Although I hope to have the opportunity to travel more before I must return."

"Quite so, quite so, a young man like you, a great chance. And this is the sepoys' mess, and this their midden . . . A very fascinating place, Kabul, you know," Macnaghten said, turning away from the embarrassing sight of a native woman squatting over the midden. "And what is very unusual in the East, one with a healthy climate, a great relief after Bombay. When you have been here as long as I have you will very much appreciate this climate. How did you find Bombay? You were there a week, I believe?"

"Calcutta. Very interesting, sir. Rather different from my expectations—so very different that now I cannot recall precisely what those expectations were . . ." He laughed lightly. "But the society so very agreeable . . ." Charlie Burnes trailed off, lost in momentary thought; perhaps, like every griffin yet born, he had met a captain's daughter on his second day in the country and by the Thursday had been swearing everlasting loyalty to her before being whisked off to this remote and incommunicable place.

"And these are, are, more chickens," Macnaghten said. "You are at Lady Sale's tonight? I believe so?"

"Is she rather a tall woman?" Charlie said.

"Not preternaturally so, but, tall . . . yes, I think we may agree on that description, all in all."

"A fine view of the city, sir," Charlie said.

"Of the?"

"Of the city," Charlie said.

"Of the city," Macnaghten said, wonderingly. Then he looked over the canvas roof of the officers' mess, glistening and sodden with rain. "Quite so, a very fine view of the city. How long do you hope to spend with us, sir?"

2

The cantonments had been established for months now—nearly a year, in fact—but they had taken on the decayed, frayed air of an ancient settlement without ever starting to seem remotely permanent. The city had acquired a new suburb of tents and huts, and outside the gates of the city, the cantonments squatted. It seemed surly, temporary, and so strangely irrelevant. The British settlement produced no real change to the city. Only in the streets of the bazaar did it appear that the nature of the city had changed, as a red-faced Englishman lurched from corner to corner, half a head taller than anyone seen here before.

In the cantonments, there was a simmering air of resentment at the discomfort and squalor they lived in. Burnes and Macnaghten and the grandest generals had commandeered houses in the city itself; not the Bala Hissar, in which Shah Shujah and his seedy entourage roamed like tatty old tigers. That had been the insistence of the pretender, and no one had known how to refuse. The present situation, in which the army managed as best it could in the hastily thrown-up huts and field latrines, seemed satisfactory to no one, but it seemed set to continue indefinitely. Once a day, Macnaghten and Burnes rode up to the Bala Hissar, and were graciously admitted to the Presence, and two hours later rode back, fuming. Shah Shujah was a fool: and the Bala Hissar was the price of his foolishness. What they could do was live with the situation as best they could, since there seemed no prospect of anything improving; and what "as best they could" meant was, in their shabby temporary settlements, to put up the appearance, at least, of living like kings.

Goodness, how they were all knighted! How the gracious honours flowed in their directions, and with what a casually lipsmacking air Sir

William asked Sir Robert to pass the salt to Sir Alexander! Heavens, how they shrugged when complimented on their elevation, and, heavens, how they gloated over it and insisted on their handle in the most ordinary communication! The tale of how Sale, the day after the letter had come, had quite naturally said, "I must ask Lady Sale about that," went round the camp like a barking whippet. "I must ask Lady bleeding Sale!" they all said, laughing. Sale affected to believe, and told anyone who showed any interest, that the men all called him "Fighting Bob," but he was mistaken; on the whole, they called him "that cunt."

And how the entertainments had multiplied, until they overlapped and overlaid each other, and the most distinguished persons in the cantonments found themselves dashing from one hostess to another, so as not to offend or show favouritism; and how infuriating that it was driven by nothing more than Lady Sale's unquenchable desire to write, over and over again on scraps of paper, the interesting information that "Lady Sale would be most delighted if Sir Alexander Burnes would do her the great kindness . . ." Like besotted lovers, they could none of them stop writing the name of their beloved on paper; and the object of their love was their own astonishing transformation.

That night, indeed, was for Lady Sale. She was the most indefatigable of the suddenly created hostesses, and was happy to spend long afternoons bellowing in Hindustani at the hopeless cooks this place could supply with the final aim of a dinner for the great of this place. If she wanted to believe herself and her salon at the unchallenged pinnacle of Kabul society, so be it. She approached entertaining in a decidedly martial spirit; "Lead the charge, Bob," she always hooted as her guests went in, and, "Ladies, I sound the retreat," at the end of her dinners, and they all somehow managed a faint smile at this tiresome military fantasy. The means by which she outmanoeuvred the utterly depleted arsenals of her rivals would have aroused the admiration of Clausewitz; mounting engagements to which the few other hostesses of the place could not rise, emerging each night from her impregnable battlements with an air of glowing exhilaration, anticipating nothing better than the next encounter. Whether anyone wanted to challenge this asserted supremacy was a moot point, but it had to be admitted that none could. Lady Sale, tall and stiff as a grenadier, with a glint in her eye as she bore down to extract a promise from some wavering guest, would not brook a refusal. She was formidable, and exactly the sort of officer who, in the heat of battle, most risks being shot in the back by her disgruntled subordinates. But she never turned her back, and she strode the muddy ways of the cantonments like one who, unable to doubt that everyone heartily loathed her, was nevertheless assured of her absolute security.

Elphinstone had been secured for this evening's entertainment, and Macnaghten, and Burnes, and Frampton, and Burnes's brother, and, of course (what went without saying), Sale. Fighting Bob quailed before his wife's terrible elevation, and it was impossible to imagine what on earth they found to say to each other when the guests had departed and they were alone. Perhaps, Frampton was in the habit of speculating, they merely continued shouting at the baffled servants; that mode suited them so well, after all.

The guests were absolutely prompt, and stood in what served as the drawing room of the Sales' house in near silence. Each of them held an aperitif of some garnet-pink liquid, but no one was drinking from his coarse thick green goblet. Lady Sale had been quick to turn this necessity into a tradition, as if for generations the Sales had offered their guests nothing but pomegranate juice before dinner, but no one with any sense ever drank it. The lazy kitchen boys had failed to pick out the pith, which floated like scum on the surface, and left the juice with an unpleasant tang, bitter as earwax.

"We are waiting for Frampton, I believe," Lady Sale announced. "Where can he be? He is not one to disappoint. Tell me, Mr. Burnes, have you had a chance to hunt yet? A shikar is something no new arrival in India should long neglect—it is Sale's passion. I do not know if anyone is planning one."

"A shikar?" Elphinstone said. "For myself, I am too advanced in years for such amusements, but I recall, in younger days . . . I wonder if I have ever told you of the day in '26 which turned into a shikar of the most thrilling variety? The Colonel's plan, that day—the old Colonel, you understand, the old Colonel—his plan was for a few hours' pig-sticking, and I am sure that none of us, least of all myself, considered it at all probable to conclude as it did, with my bagging a ten-foot tiger, a 'man-eater' as we vulgarly call them. The most extraordinary thing, all things considered. Well, you see—"

"Frampton," Lady Sale interrupted, greeting her last guest with an air of decisive relief. Frampton stood apologetically in the doorway; in his hands was a bough of some fruit tree. He looked, despite his whiskers and his high-waisted scarlet uniform, like nothing so much as a pagan god.

"I have heard of pig-sticking," Charlie Burnes began apologetically, but nobody, even Elphinstone, paid him any attention.

"What is that you have there?" Lady Sale said peremptorily.

"Most sowwy to be so delayed," Frampton said, bowing quickly around the group. "Extwaordinawy thing. I found this laid upon my cot like a love-offewing. I thought myself quite past the time to attract such attentions, and in any case, there are no unattached ladies in the camp at all likely to make so womantic a gesture. An extwaordinawy thing. I count myself baffled."

"What is it?"

"Mulberries," Burnes said, taking it from Frampton and weighing the dark fruit still attached to the bough in his left hand. "You are not alone, Frampton. I found exactly the same thing, left in my private quarters, when I returned from my audience with Shah Shujah today. I was at quite a loss to think who could have left it, and the servants denied any knowledge of it."

"A mulberry branch?" Lady Sale said. "How amusing. How curious. Had you brought your offering, too, Sir Alexander, it might have furnished an agreeable supplement to my cook's dessert. But I am sure you both would prefer to keep your romantic offerings. How mysterious and fine a thing to discover. Or perhaps—" she gave a little trill of laughter, "—perhaps it is no more than a gesture of welcome from the people of Kabul, and they seem very shy in temperament to me, it is not impossible that they prefer to offer it in secret than openly. I recall when Sale and I were in Allahabad, the people, you know, they truly loved us, and one day we returned from exercise, and—"

"I do not think that it is a romantic gesture," Macnaghten said. "Or a hospitable one. I found one, too, in my private quarters yesterday, and thought no more of it. I cannot think what it means, but I fear it has some quite specific meaning not apparent to us."

"Of course," Elphinstone said, "it is said that west of Peshawar, the mulberry branch is a sposal symbol. Many travellers, you know, sir, have observed it, but for myself—"

"Nor that," Macnaghten said heavily. There was an awkward silence, as they nervously passed the mulberry branch from hand to hand, inspecting it as if some explicit message might be written among the leaves. They shifted about, not having anything else to add, but not feeling that the subject was at an end.

"Let us go through," Lady Sale said decisively. "Bob, lead the charge." The steward was at the door, and they sorted themselves out—the excess of men forming a kind of tail at the end of the procession—and quietly went into the dining room.

Lady Sale's dinner was subdued at the start—not that that was unusual, and the Sales clapped their hands for a succession of dishes with their usual chilly enthusiasm. Cold curried soup, roasted river fish, and a fricassee of what game birds the country could supply, and their guests offered each other each dish with punctilious courtesy. The subject of the mulberry branches did not recur, and they cast about for a better subject; the inadequacies of servants, the discomforts of the camps, a private soldier caught stealing from his fellows. The food was good, but somehow it was not Lady Sale's; she had been provided with it, as she had, newly, been provided with her title, and she seemed a guest at her own table, her display of grandeur not quite convincing. It was as if she itched to turn her plates upside down to judge the style of the establishment, and her guests always felt, obscurely, that though the food here was good, if she had been left in charge they would have found themselves eating the cooking of a child, and dined off baked pastry shapes. It was with relief that the table heard one of Charlie Burnes's inquiries, and fell on it gratefully, as on fish pie after a monotonous procession of curries.

"I am sure I have been told this before, but what is a shikar?"

"A shikar!" Frampton said. "Yes, that is an excellent ideah. Let us mount a shikar for our young fwiend, to show what pleasures Kabul can supply. It must be utterly dweawy, to be cooped up here with nothing to break the monotony, and I am sure, it is weeks since we thought of such a diversion. A hunt, a shoot, Mr. Burnes, nothing more. It is so affected, to be sure, how one slips into these pieces of jargon, and I fear that the newcomer must think we use these words for no other weason than to confuse and baffle."

"Shikar—an interesting word," Macnaghten began, but nobody paid him any attention.

"Of course," Lady Sale said, "there is no wooded country hereabouts, and the absence of coverts must inevitably change the quality of any hunting, but let no one say that there are no country pursuits in Kabul, or that we were dull dogs. The game is bountiful, and well rewards a morning in the hills. Some laughed, indeed, at our bringing a pack of fox-hounds, but to my mind, that was a part of our luggage which has proved of the greatest efficacy in maintaining the enthusiasm of the men for their present situation. Not that the men hunt, of course, but the diversion offered by a morning's sport does tend to restore the spirits and return the weary officer to us with a new sense of purpose. So often, I have noticed, what initially seems a luxury when the camels are being loaded turns out to be of vital importance and great value. I recall, when we were in Allahabad—Sale, is it Allahabad I mean?"

"I believe so," Sale said, turning from the other lady at the table with mild, assenting regret.

When Lady Sale had finished her story, and the table had added similar instances of apparently idle pleasures, Charlie Burnes said diffidently, "Is there any hawking to be had here? I should so much like to see a sport so associated with the East."

"I fear we are too far to the West here," Burnes said. "They seem to enjoy it in the East, east of here, I mean—I remember a pleasant morning I spent near Peshawar, as the guest of a great nabob—and again in Persia, true, but not here. My friend Mohan Lal and I went on numerous hunts when we were first in Kabul, and they knew what was meant by hawking, but they had not the skill or the curiosity."

"I hardly blame them," Frampton said. "Of all the deadly dull sports, hawking is the worst; to thwow a small bird into the sky and then unleash a bigger bird to kill it never stwuck me as an amusing diversion, so lacking in any exercise is it."

"I greatly enjoyed it," Burnes said. "I confess, it is lacking in exercise, and there is never any serious question about the outcome of the sport, but there is something courtly and pleasurable about it when practised in a strange land."

"Have you ever been on a true Afghan hunt, Sir Alexander?" Lady Sale inquired.

"In the past, on two or three occasions," Burnes said. "Our old host, the Newab Jubbur Khan, was very keen that we should see it—an odd and laborious business, and sometimes not very sporting. The usual way is to dig a sort of man-sett near a spring, and wait there at night to shoot the deer that come there to drink."

"Not my idea of a hunt," Sale said.

"No, not very sporting, but their principal interest is in shooting for food, and our concerns for sporting behaviour do not strike them as being sensible or even capable of being explained. There are more dashing forms of field-sports, of course."

"I should so much like a shikar," Charlie Burnes said. "May we have one?"

The table all laughed at Charlie's simplicity. "Of course, sir, of course," Macnaghten said. "Perhaps the day after tomorrow? I think the hounds would benefit from the exercise, and I am sure it would be of no difficulty to persuade some of the men to act as beaters. A true Afghan hunt. Elphinstone, you know, in his book about Kabul, describes the hunt, and, I must say, for once he did not make any obvious errors—if you wish to know what one consists of, I am sure Elphinstone has a copy close to hand, or—" this evidently occurring to Macnaghten as an eccentric alternative, "—you could always ask one of us about it. An excellent idea. The day after tomorrow, gentlemen?"

The guests here excused themselves a good deal earlier than in London, or India, Florentia noted when they had all gone. She strode about the rooms with the appearance of strict purpose, although the servants apparently needed no instruction or supervision as they cleared the dining room. Sale was in an armchair with a thoughtful cigar; he gazed into space, taking a consoling puff from time to time.

"I can see young Burnes will prove a great addition to our society, in time," Florentia said, picking up a gewgaw from the makeshift card table and putting it down again. Sale grunted; he had been thinking of Bath, autumn of 1822. You always regretted the ones who got away, and wasn't that the truth. What a fine filly she had been! "It is so sad that we can afford him no prospect of a suitable wife, so far from any civilized society."

"I expect he can wait," Sale said.

"Wait he can," Florentia said. "I expect I was thinking more of ourselves; how agreeable it would be to have more feminine adornments to our little parties. If only one could import the officers' wives!"

Sale looked at her in mild surprise. His wife, he supposed, had always rather enjoyed the lack of any serious competition on that front. "They come in bundles, and you will soon have more than you know what to do with," he said. "Now that we are settled, it seems as if more and more of the officers are sending for their families, and soon, my dear, society here will be as interesting as that of Calcutta. I know, like all ladies, you constantly feel the lack of gossip, but—"

"Not that," Florentia said. "I merely feel a lack of civilization can be discerned in a settlement which is predominantly male, and I dread to think what misbehaviour can spring when so little moderating feminine influence may be felt. I tremble for the consequences, Sale, I truly tremble."

"My dear," Sale said. "Not all ladies have the heart and spirit you do, and this can only be a temporary situation. Why, only yesterday, five more ladies arrived to join their husbands."

"Those," Florentia said, taking a finger and drawing an angry streak in the dust on a glass bowl, "were not ladies, by the most generous estimate. Boy!"

"A curious business, those mulberry branches," Sale said.

"Were you left one, too, Sale?" Florentia asked.

"No," Sale admitted. "No, I seem to have been overlooked."

Florentia seemed as dissatisfied as if she had been snubbed. "I dare say it signifies nothing so very important," she said finally.

3

Burnes sat at his desk, and looked levelly at the private soldier standing at ease before him. This was his least favourite part of the week, and why the task had fallen to him, he did not know. Military discipline had up until now been quite outside his interest or expertise; but, as Macnaghten had finally managed to explain, many of the lapses the men were likely to fall into could best be dealt with by Burnes. They were in an unfamiliar place. Those who would normally be charged with enforcing discipline were, it must be admitted, no more familiar with the customs and beliefs of the natives than the men. "Local sensitivities, you see," Macnaghten had said, coming with relief to his final point. "Local sensitivities, Sir Alexander. That is the matter at hand. Of course, I myself would be pleased, ah . . ." "You are so very busy a man, sir, I quite see the point," Burnes had said, unwillingly. So it came about that although—"Of course, of course," Macnaghten had said, waving the point away—ordinary breaches of discipline would be dealt with in the normal way, by the commanding officer, from time to time cases would arise where "local sensitivities" would require an explanation and a reprimand from Burnes. Quite why—Burnes thought, looking at the resentful private soldier before him—nobody else could explain why it was undesirable to take an Afghan nobleman's wife as a mistress, he could not say; but the task had, in this instance, fallen to him. It was the morning after the Sales' dinner, and he, surely, had better things to be doing.

"You must see," Burnes said patiently, "that our presence here must excite feelings of hostility and resentment. Do you see that?"

"Yes sir," the private said, staring directly before him at the wall.

"You do see that," Burnes said. "Whatever we may think of the matter it cannot be pleasant to find yourself, overnight, governed by a foreign power. Do you understand?"

"Yes sir," the private said.

"Where do you come from, soldier?"

"Bristol, sir."

Burnes paused, to permit the picture of the man's home town to rise up in his mind. "Imagine, for one moment, that an army of Afghans appeared at the gates of Bristol."

"With your permission, sir, Bristol, no gates, sir."

"Be that as it may," Burnes said. "Imagine for a moment that an army of Afghans arrived in force to take over your city."

"With permission, sir—fight them off—a lot of heathens sir—no match for a hundred men of Bristol sir—"

"That," Burnes said, "is not quite to the point." The man subsided into mild muttering, in which the words "lot of wogs sir" could be discerned. "It is important that I make you understand quite why your conduct, if it continues, will create a quite unnecessary problem. To that end, I am trying to make you imagine the situation from a point of view which is not your own. Is that clear?"

"Yes sir," the private said.

"Now," Burnes said. "There is no doubt in our minds, you understand, that we are here for the best of reasons, and we hope, in time, to make the inhabitants of this city understand quite why we are here, and, in time, to appreciate our presence. How do you suppose that we may best achieve this end?"

The private looked dumbstruck.

"I would like to know," Burnes continued patiently, "by what method you consider that we can convey our goodwill and honourable intentions to the disgruntled natives of this place."

"Don't know sir," the private said.

"Think, man," Burnes said. The man was astonishingly stupid, all in all; how he came to penetrate a Kabul zenana was decidedly baffling. "Very well; I shall tell you. We shall achieve this end by behaving extremely well. That is all. Careful, consistent, honourable behaviour; that is all we can do to assure them that we have not come to rape their women and steal their goods. Do you understand?"

"Yes sir," the private said.

"Now," Burnes said slowly. "Now, I wish you to imagine, once again, that you are at home, in your city, in Bristol. Are you married, private?"

"No sir," the private said. "Not married sir. No cause to be sir."

"Do you have, for instance, a girl?"

"No sir," the private said. "Been in India five years sir. A man like me sir."

"Let us leave that to one side," Burnes said steadily. This was not going at all well. "I would like you to imagine that you are back in England, in Bristol, with a loving wife and several children. Your life is steady, and peaceful. One day you discover that your wife has been entertaining an Afghan warrior each day. I would like you to tell me what your feelings on the subject would be."

"I'd kill her, sir," the private said.

"And then?"

"I'd kill her, sir," the private said.

"Soldier, if you please, I would like to suggest that your feelings towards your wife's lover, too, would be less than amicable," Burnes said. "You would be filled, would you not, with a feeling of great resentment and dislike directed not merely towards him, but towards the entire occupying forces. Whatever benefits your new masters brought you, or were planning to bring to you, your feelings would be those of anger and hostility. Now, I would like you to think of the consequences of your actions, and think what the lady's husband is likely to be thinking, not just of you, but of us all."

"There's a difference, though, sir," the private said.

"I am not very interested in excuses, soldier," Burnes said. "How did you come to meet the lady?"

"She came to me," the soldier said. "I never thought of such a thing, but she came to me in the market and she took my hand and she took me to her house. I never wanted—sir, she is wronged, and I did no wrong."

"May I remind you that you took another man's wife as your mistress, and he is greatly aggrieved by the fact? Greatly aggrieved. I would be most interested to hear why, in these circumstances, you consider you did no wrong."

The soldier seemed almost tearful, and Burnes waited, his chin resting on his two hands.

"If I was in Bristol—and if I had me a wife—and if the Afghans were there and ruling over me—and if one of them came and took her as his mistress—sir, I know it wouldn't be for cause of my neglect, and not because, I mean, in those circumstances, sir, she couldn't say justly that a beauty like that lay abandoned and unhappy because I, the husband, you understand, her husband, spent his nights away from her bed, and not—" The soldier gulped, and for a moment Burnes could almost believe that there was some compassion and not just idle lust in him, "—not because he left her lying there while he went and took his pleasure elsewhere, with, with boys, sir, with boys. I'm telling you the truth, sir, he doesn't deserve her. With boys, sir."

"Soldier," Burnes said. He steadied his voice. "You understand that we are in a very strange place, and one whose ways must seem to us different from our own in many ways. That is no concern of yours, and no excuse for your fornication, unhappy as the lady's existence must inevitably seem. Whether you are the first man to have taken a woman to his bed out of motives of selfless generosity, I leave you to ponder. What I am concerned about is the gentleman's outrage, not what must seem to us his disgusting behaviour, and the consequences of that outrage. You will mend your conduct immediately, and it is only fair to warn you that your punishment will be severe and exemplary. That will be all."

"Sir," the soldier said, downcast; he wheeled, saluting, and left the room with an anonymous soldier's briskness. Why these tasks fell to Burnes, he could not say; it was not the first such case with which he had had to deal, and he knew perfectly well it would not be the last.

4

Burnes and his brother lived within the city, in a requisitioned merchant's house; the merchant and his family had, he gathered, removed themselves at the approach of the British. The house had been rapidly colonized and stripped bare in the interim, and Burnes had found a dozen families camping in different rooms, who accepted their eviction with surly equanimity. It was only after some time that he learnt, from the servants, that the owner of the house had only left a week before; the squatters had established themselves so thoroughly, and many of the rooms were blackened and greasy; like most Afghans, they had not thought twice about lighting fires in a windowless room.

The house was handsome and substantial, built, like Jubbur Khan's, around a courtyard, in the middle of which a single mulberry tree grew (Burnes had inspected the tree, but no branch had been torn from it recently; and, in any case, the city was full of mulberry trees). The nomadic poor had taken what the merchant's family had left, and now the house was picked bare, like a bone. Burnes went from room to blackened room, and it seemed blank to him; there was nothing to distinguish a bedchamber from a dining room, and he had to divide up the house randomly. His decisions, it was apparent, seemed very eccentric to the establishment—he had discovered, for instance, that he had scandalized the servants by selecting a room as his bedchamber which had formerly been used for the family's devotions—but the architecture of the house was dictated by principles he did not quite understand, and which he certainly would not share. He did his best to live his English life in a house, a succession of rooms, and was conscious that nothing quite fitted.

Charlie inhabited what had once been the women's quarters, and they still had an occluded, enveloping air; some sense of decency, perhaps, had discouraged the scavengers from taking down the elaborate wooden shutters. It was restful to retreat there, and feel the weather at one dramatic remove, as the dry cold sunlight cast its slow shifting patterns through the wooden veil onto the white floor, or the rain dripped and pattered as if on a drum. Here, the city was simplified to the noises of its weather, and Burnes and his brother came here to be alone, and forget where they were. Charlie was indulging him in this, Burnes knew; but he never suggested that he would rather be out and roaming, gazing at the amazing city with his gullible wide eyes, and for that undemonstrative kindness Burnes was grateful.

"Ahmed asked me if we ate pork today," Charlie said. "He seemed rather interested."

"Yes, they all ask that," Burnes said. "Never wise to admit to it, of course. What did you say?"

"I said I couldn't rightly remember," Charlie said. "True enough. I don't suppose I've had the opportunity since I left England; if I'd thought, I would have marked my last leg of pork with fireworks. Or maybe with a wake and hired mourners. I dream of bacon, Sikunder, every night."

Burnes smiled at the new nickname Charlie had settled on; in Scotland he had been Allie, like every other Scots Alexander, but this, used only when they were alone, gave him an unfamiliar delight. "Cheese," Burnes said. "I can hardly recall the taste of cheese, but I still dream of it."

"Yes, cheese," Charlie said. "Cheese and an apple and a rasher of cold bacon and a book and a bed in the heather. That's the thing."

"Did you not eat pork on board ship?" Burnes said.

"That's so," Charlie said. When they spoke like this, together, their voices curled together like duetting singers, sumptuous with the neglected vowels of their childhood; only in solitude. "I grew so sick of pork, I wonder I miss it now so much. Heavens, we talked about those boring pigs, grunting and shitting their days away no more than six feet from my cabin porthole. You would hardly credit there being so much to say about half a dozen pigs as we found, and—you know, Allie, I've known some pigs, and would never have taken any of them as a bosom companion, but of all the pigs in the world, those were the dullest, and, heavens, how we talked about their funny wee ways while we were chewing up one of their brothers. I promise you, we spent the whole voyage debating the question of whether sows' milk could be drunk, and no one could guess why goats, cows, asses, but not sows."

"I would not care for the task of milking an angry sow," Burnes said. "A sow would happily take your hand off with a bite if she were in the mood. Did no one think to try? In any case, the Afghans, I always tell them with a straight face that it is only eaten by the very poorest people in England, and it is said to taste something like beef. That always seems to satisfy them. They are odd, you know, the people here, and you should be wary in talking to them. I thought I understood them, but sometimes I think them stranger than anything."

"They seem strange to me, but you have spent so long in India . . ."

"I know," Burnes said. "It all must seem very similar to you, all strange in much the same way, but—you remember those first days in India, when all brown faces seem very much alike, and in a week, you wonder that you ever thought them at all similar? It all seems strange, I know, and all the customs and habits very much alike in their strangeness, as to those lady novelists who place their haunted castles in Sicily, China, or Scotland indifferently. You will come to see, in time, Charlie. To them, you know, a Hindu from Calcutta is as strange and as exotic as you are, and very much the same sort of animal as a bacon-eating Scotsman. These people are different; you can say anything to an Indian, but here you should think before you speak, because the only thing you can be sure of when an Afghan replies is that he will not tell you what he is thinking."

"They seem like children, almost," Charlie said. "Their sports—you know, Sikunder, I saw the oddest thing yesterday in the street. Two men, very grave and bearded, hopping at each other until one fell over. If only we had known it when we were nine years old—but it seems a curious way for grown men to spend their afternoons, I have to confess. I had the greatest difficulty not abandoning myself to hilarity, but they were surrounded by spectators, all taking it with the greatest seriousness. The most absurd sight, like this—"

Charlie got up, and took his left ankle in his right hand, hopping a little to keep his balance.

"Like this?" Burnes said gravely, and then he, too, got up and took his left ankle in his right hand.

"Exactly that," Charlie said. "A most extraordinary sort of thing for a grown—oof!"

Burnes had launched himself at his brother, and caught him off guard; Charlie stumbled back against the wall, but did not fall, and then they were nine years old again, and in the yard of a Montrose manse. Burnes was helplessly giggling.

"Very well, sir," Charlie said. "I feel constrained to warn you—" hop "—however, that were you relying on any respect from me, that your age, frailty, and—" hop "—worldly distinction entitle you to any—" hop "—consideration, you mistake the mettle of your opponent. Sir—" hop "—you tangle with me at your peril. On guard, sir."

Burnes was giggling too wildly to do anything but hop limply, and as Charlie launched himself at his brother, puffing histrionically like a bull, he was already falling backwards onto, happily, a pile of cushions. Charlie fell with him, bringing the low table with him, and they lay there among the remains of their early breakfast, lost in hilarity. Burnes reached up and, still laughing, stroked his brother's hair; it was so nice to be nine again, and with your brother for an idiotic hour. Their fall raised a cloud of dust from the cushions, and Charlie fell to sneezing; and that was the funniest thing in the world.

"Sir Alexander—achha—Burnes," Charlie managed to get out, giggling and sneezing and wriggling all at the same time. "For services to—achha—to the Lord knows what—achha—"

"For distinguished and dignified service to—"

"Sir Allie," Charlie said. "Anyone would think—achha—you were some kind of important person. Sir Allie. If the Queen could see you now." He grew still, pensive for a moment. "Does the old man know?"

Burnes thought; he wondered who, in England or Scotland, would have heard, and for a moment he was in a quiet London house, looking at a woman, reading the same four lines in a newspaper, over and over. "I don't know," he admitted. "Perhaps they do by now. I wrote at the time. Yes, I suppose they do. I know what they'll say."

"Is that the best you can—achha—"

"Have you nothing of interest to share with us, boy?"

"I suppose you think yourself very fine, now."

Burnes smiled, as they lay there, each grinning into his brother's face. Yes, the old man would be saying something of the sort, running his eyes over his son's letter, grumbling at its length. Perhaps at this very moment, sitting in the dining room at the manse, the windows open for the sake of the Lord's good fresh air and ignoring the shivering footmen. But then Burnes remembered that some quite different time was happening, there, far away, across the world, in Scotland; a different hour to this fine bright morning, and somehow at exactly the same moment. He willingly forgot the world, there, laughing helplessly with his brother. And then, outside, there was the urgent sound of a pack of foxhounds, barking as they ran into the courtyard, and all at once, so sad, as he stood up and feeling the beginnings of an ache in his arm where he fell, he was alone and in Kabul and did not know why.

The shikar, it had been agreed, would meet at Burnes's house and set off from there, though there was no need, surely, for the natives to bring the hounds into the yard. Outside the window, the hounds romped and yowled over each other like a lot of unruly ginger schoolboys; the climate here suited them, and they were quite different from the disconsolate and shabby animals they had been in the Calcutta stableyards. As everyone agreed, they had benefited, too, from the care of their native keepers, who seemed fond of and knowledgeable about animals, and they were now as admirable a pack as any English hunt's; the horses, too, were healthy and well watered, and no longer shrank from a fierce day's riding. Irritation at the kennel-boys' unwillingness to follow simple instructions had passed away, as their own methods of exercise and feed established themselves, and the hounds conspicuously thrived.

A dozen officers and Englishmen were assembling, their horses tied up outside, and the turbanned kennel-boys lounged about the gate to the courtyard, waiting for a tip and a dismissal. Macnaghten and Elphinstone were here, although not in riding clothes; perhaps merely to see the shikar set off. The rains had cleared, and the morning was bright as Burnes and Charlie came out into the courtyard in stockinged feet, their boots in their hands. Frampton sauntered over, saluting them.

"Fine day, gentlemen," he said. "I sincerely hope you have no very determined plans for the day—after you excused yourselves so stwangely early last night, the mess hatched a plan for the day's hunt. Digby, you know, has a spot in mind, a half-hour's hard widing east of here, a secluded valley, pullulating with deer, and we put it to the beawers, and they seemed to have no objection to the place. If that seems suitable, sir, I think we can pwomise you an admiwable intwoduction to the delights of the shikar. But we must not delay."

Burnes and Charlie agreed, and once they had put on their boots with the aid of the body-servants of the establishment, they mounted and ordered themselves into some semblance of precedence, Burnes and Frampton at the front, wading through a turbulent sea of dogs.

"Good morning, sir! And to you, sir!" Burnes called to Elphinstone and Macnaghten, standing in their ordinary uniforms at the gate. "You do not join us?"

"I should take great pleasure," Macnaghten called, "but other pressing demands prevent it. Take care to keep the bearers well ordered, sir. You know what idle fellows they are. And ensure you return with all my men in one, in one piece—the country, you know, it is not, it is not Hertfordshire . . ."

"Really," Burnes said, turning to Charlie, mounted by his side on the roan, "I do believe Sir William the greatest old woman that ever was seen. If he worries so about a day's hunting in the hills, I cannot imagine what use he would be in the heat of battle. Frampton! Call halloo!"

And they poured out of the gates as Frampton spurred his mount,

Burnes and Charlie at the front, the other officers close behind, and the hounds roaring at their heels; two British soldiers at the back with a dozen mounted native bearers on their splendid horses. There was no thought given to trotting through the outer streets of the city, and the people of Kabul ran for cover. It was a splendid day; the rains had swept the sky clear, and over the city, the white block of the Bala Hissar shone against the brown slopes above the city like chalk. They were soon beyond the city gates, and past the British cantonments; the horses pounded the earth like demons, and the saluting soldiers flew past, their faces little white mushrooms by their furious path. They left the road, and were up into the hills, the hounds baying behind them, Frampton calling halloo joyously, the Afghan bearers behind giving hoarse guttural cries from the depths of their throats, and the still air was made wind by their flight. It was no more than half an hour before Frampton called a halt, and they stopped, the horses sweating in the cold mountain air. They were in utterly empty country; Kabul left far behind, and before them the great foothills of the distant eastern mountains, still capped with snow, seeming to float in the deep blue sky.

They paused there silently after their gallop, and no one said anything for a minute or two.

"Fine pwospect, ain't it, sir?" Frampton said. His face was glowing with an enormous grin. "This blasted wasteland of ours."

"In five years," an officer said, "this will be a favourite pic-nic spot for the ladies of the Company."

"No doubt," Frampton said. "But for the pwesent, let us enjoy it while we may. Shall we dismount, gentlemen?"

The tiffin was laid out by the bearers, and, though none of them had breakfasted more than an hour or so earlier, the clear air and the ride had made them hungry again. They fell on the cold food, the roast game, bread, and cold curries with abandon, throwing the bones to the hounds, and even the bearers, some distance off, sucked at fruit and picked at the cold quail with enthusiasm. There was nothing so good as food taken in the clean high air.

"Are there no tribesmen living here?" Charlie said. "It seems quite deserted."

"There may be," Burnes said. "They hide themselves well, timid little fellows; they would run from the sight of us and we would never know.

But it is quite as likely that there is no settlement within ten miles. You will see; this is a land of desert, and its population is deer and birds. If you wish, I shall ask the bearers. Hai!"

A bearer rose, and came over, throwing a bone into the mass of feeding dogs, the expression on his face direct and unservile. Burnes spoke to him in his own language; he frowned and spread his hands, and replied, turning away and going back to his place without waiting for a dismissal.

"The man said there was a settlement of some sort here once," Burnes said to Charlie. "Of infidels, he said, but that may mean anything; probably no more than that they spoke an unfamiliar language. He had no idea what had happened to them; he thought they might have travelled on. Much of the country lives in a nomadic fashion, you know, moving on when someone else challenges for the land, or when no rain comes for a season, or when the snow falls. It is more than likely that there is no one living within some miles, and if there is, they will take some care to avoid a pack of warlike strangers."

"I should like to see a rustic shepherd or two," Charlie said.

"That, I fear, is not very probable; they have good reason not to put themselves in our way. Today, you must be satisfied with some good hunting. Shall we begin, gentlemen? Sergeant, be so good as to pack up the tiffin?"

"Very good, sir," Sergeant Porter said, saluting briskly.

The party had halted at the neck of a valley. At Frampton's orders, the shikar was to be conducted in a strictly Afghan fashion, according to the habits of the Kabul hunting nobility; in part, because the efficiency of the somewhat unsporting method had been tested, and found quite admirable, and in part for the education of their Charlie Burnes, the likeable griffin. They formed themselves into a loose crescent with no particular regard for rank or status, Frampton and Burnes at the centre, Sergeant Porter at the extreme left, the bearers at the right, and, the dogs running before them, descended into the sparsely wooded valley.

They trotted for some ten minutes before they put up a hare, which fell to Digby's gun; then, in quick succession, a brace of partridge from a rowan bush, and a fox which had probably been stalking game and failed to notice the approach from upwind of the hunting party until it was nearly upon it. The hounds set off in chase of the fox, and only Porter saw what darted off in the opposite direction, some hundred yards off; a great male deer.

"Sir!" he shouted, and the party, just riding off after the fox, turned for a moment without halting.

"After him, Sergeant!" Frampton called, without checking his pace in the opposite direction. Porter spurred his horse, and, reaching for his musket, lit off up the incline, a single bearer following him. This would be a fine trophy for him to show the mess; this would be something to boast about.

The body of the party roared off in high spirits, though the fox promised no great sport; they had happened upon it, and all its wiles would not put more distance between them and it than would supply a half-hour's chase. But they had not ridden for more than four minutes when the hounds put up another hare, which led them astray. By the time the hounds discovered the fox's trail again, it had put some distance between itself and them. It was a good hour before they cornered it, in a hollow by a spring, and, in high spirits, they blooded Charlie in the English manner, to the frank curiosity of the bearers.

They rested by the spring for some minutes, laughing and joshing; Charlie refused to wash his face, and, dried with blood, he presented the appearance of a fine warrior to carry back to the cantonments. Frampton ceremoniously presented him with the brush, which he tucked seriously under his saddle, and they all collapsed onto the ground.

"You see," Frampton said. "A fine thing, an Afghan chase. Why we do not exercise ourselves in this way every day, with so little otherwise to occupy us, I cannot understand."

"Frampton," Burnes said. "It seems to me that we are missing someone."

"Yes," Charlie said. "The Sergeant—Porter, is it?—he left us, pursuing a deer."

"I thought he was following us," Frampton said. "No matter. We will wait here, and he will find us shortly, with, no doubt, his twophy."

5

There were no landmarks here; the bare hills rose and fell, unmarked by any kind of incident. There were no signs of habitation, or even a memorable shape of rock by which he could orient himself, and by now, among these smooth hills, rising and falling in their bare brown way, Sergeant

Porter considered himself thoroughly lost. How the deer had managed to evade him, he did not know; there was nothing to hide behind, nowhere to run, and yet it was gone. The bearer trotted wearily behind him, paying no attention to Porter's shouts; there was nothing they could say to each other, and, as if in embarrassment, they hardly looked at each other. Occasionally the bearer rode forward quickly, and gestured, as if he had glimpsed the deer, but though Porter followed his directions, he had not seen anything for some time now. From time to time, a movement at the corner of the eye made Porter wheel, his musket already raised, but it was always a bird, or nothing he could see.

"Useless," Porter muttered, and assented with the bearer's gesture to halt. The deer, he had to accept, was quite gone now, and it would be best to return to the main body of the hunt. He wheeled his horse around. The bearer looked at him questioningly. It struck Porter for the first time that the bearer was not much more than a boy, and would be considered a very good-looking man in London; strange how these delicate looks surfaced in remote places, where the inhabitants would have no idea of the success they would have among the women of a civilized place. "Shikar," Porter said. "Go back. No good. Finish." The bearer shrugged, and dismounted with a single smooth gesture. "Oh, damn you," Porter said. "Why can't you understand what I say?"

It seemed hopeless, and in any case Porter himself was all but exhausted now, so he, too, swung himself out of the saddle and squatted by the side of the bearer. He shrugged and grinned; an easy enough gesture for the native to understand, you might have thought, but he looked back, his face empty of any response. "And no food, neither," Porter said. "A waste of a day, and me in hot water if they have to send out to search for us, chum."

There was no point in talking, but the Sergeant preferred chatting companionably to his dumb associate to sitting in silence in these silent bare hills. That way, surely, was the way to return; since he had split off from the main body of the hunt, his attention had been fixed on the quarry, and not the direction he was riding in, and now he was not at all sure where to return. The land, like his unwilling companion's face, was blank, unspeaking, and silent.

They sat there for a while in silence. There was no noise but the wind; Porter wondered what time it could be. The sun was high in the sky, but it was no warmer; if anything, it was rather colder than first thing in the morning. A movement, somewhere at the corner of his eye, and a crackle as if of branches; over there, at the bottom of the valley, a little copse of trees, and within it something large, like—yes, like a deer. There it was. Porter rose, raising his musket, and strode ten paces towards it. The copse was quite still again, but the deer, now, had no escape. Porter congratulated himself; he would, after all, return to the hunt, the animal slung over his saddle. He lowered his musket, and waited.

Behind him there was a sudden noise; he turned, and the bearer was mounted, and riding away furiously, in the direction they had come from. "Damn you!" Porter shouted; that would certainly startle the deer away. "Come back at once!" But the bearer did not slow down, perhaps not understanding what Porter had shouted, and was soon over the hill. Oddly, he had not startled the deer, and the copse remained silent. That was a piece of luck. Leaving the horse where it was, Porter raised his musket, and, pointing directly at where he was sure the deer was hiding, he advanced with steady, trembling steps, towards his prize.

It was a good bag, in the end. As the afternoon began to fade, the others, two miles away, found themselves with an admirable assortment of game, besides the fox. Frampton even suggested staying where they were, for some further nocturnal sport, hunting hyenas; a thing none of the English had done, but a sport in which they understood the Afghans had established a considerable science. The provisions were exhausted, however, and none of them was equipped for a bivouac overnight; with regret, they determined to return, weary but cheerful.

Porter's bearer had returned alone, and there was no point in waiting longer for the Sergeant. Frampton was irritated, but no more; for him to return alone to the cantonments was not the sort of behaviour anyone could condone, though he quite saw that it might make little sense, in certain situations, to wander about the hills in search of the party. "Damn'd fellow shouldn't have wandered off like that," he said. "We should have done better if we had stuck together. If it turns out he lost his quawwy, I shall be most iwwitated. To inconvenience us and have nothing to show for it, that would be too bad. After all, this is not England—if he should be lost, we hardly have the men to send out for him. This is not familiar countwy, all in all. Damn the fellow. Gentlemen, five minutes?"

"He may be lost, Frampton," Burnes said. "Should we send out for him?"

"Porter? Not he," Frampton said. "A wily old bird like that, never lost in his life. Put him down in the wemotest and most bawwen desert, and he would be quite at home within an hour. Depend on it, he's at this moment in the cantonments, woasting his feet and a pair of cwumpets at a fire, and laughing at us. I am most sewiously annoyed with the fellow. No more shikars for him, gentlemen."

"Should we ask the bearers for their opinion?"

"The beawers? What can they, in heaven's name, tell us, a dull lot of fellows like that? The one who weturned seemed quite unperturbed by the loss of his companion. Depend on it, there is nothing to concern ourselves with. I intend, however, to make the wetched Porter wegwet his conduct for weeks to come. He has quite spoiled my day with wowwy. Shall we weturn to lay our spoils at the feet of our masters?"

"I don't know the bearer who returned," Burnes said.

"No?" Frampton said. "A young man of parts, eager to offer his services to us since he seemed at something of a loose end, and a good wider, I perceive. Handsome fellow, too. I find it encouwaging, that the inhabitants seem more and more weady to join with us in expeditions of this sort. What was his name, Digby?"

"Hasan, I believe, sir," Digby said.

"Well, nothing further to be done," Frampton said. "Let us weturn and chastise the wetched Porter."

6

Burnes did not enjoy or look forward to his daily audiences with Shah Shujah; each time, as he and Macnaghten were ushered into the tawdry halls of the invisible Emperor, he could hardly suppress the thought, "the puppet Emperor"; the tiny figure in his toy-theatre setting, gesticulating and squawking on the tinsel throne. Shah Shujah's method of conducting himself towards the British was far less civil and patient than Dost Mohammed's had been. An observer would have quickly come to a false conclusion; it was Shah Shujah who exhibited all the haughty disdain of a king forced to entertain uninvited visitors; it would have been Dost Mohammed whose grateful civility suggested a debt to the people who had restored him to his throne, and maintained him there.

They were ushered into the audience hall, and kept waiting there unconscionably. It was quite altered from Dost Mohammed's time; that austere space, shining with light and the eyes of the alert Amir, was gone, and in its place was a terrible apocalyptic splendour. It was something Burnes did not try to explain, not quite understanding it himself, and Macnaghten had entered the audience room for the first time without that sense of appalled shock. Macnaghten had not seen it before, and Burnes could not explain what he felt; that here was the worst of Shah Shujah's deeds, the cruel display of riches and power and will. No one would have understood; perhaps only Mohan Lal and Gerard and Vitkevich, who had seen the halls of the Amir, and had known what Dost Mohammed had been. But Mohan Lal was in India, and Gerard was dead, and Vitkevich, he knew not where. To anyone else, to say that all Shah Shujah's wickedness was in this pantomime transformation was to invite ridicule; and everyone knew the stories that drifted down from the Bala Hissar, the stories of the small boys, the courtiers, tortured slowly to death before Shah Shujah's slow-lidded eyes; the Suddozye prince killed before the court by having molten gold poured down his throat. And all of them had heard, and would never forget, the long morning when they had brought the news to the Bala Hissar that Dost Mohammed had surrendered, and was kept in India under the personal care of the Governor General, and listened for two hours to Shah Shujah's demands; listened to the Amir they had, in their wisdom, brought back to his kingdom, shrieking with one death after another, one torture after another, multiplying and repeating, blinding, flaying, boiling, disembowelling, demanding in his furious desire a hundred, a thousand deaths for Dost Mohammed, and they had known then what manner of man the new Amir of the Afghans was, and they had listened in silence. Was that not cruelty enough? But for Burnes, it was not; and the transformation of the room was the biggest sign that here was no man, but an impotent old dragon, waiting for its moment to strike and kill. Burnes entered this room and, for him, all Shah Shujah's wickedness was already here, glittering like an arsenal.

Where had these treasures come from? Were they brought from Shah Shujah's long exile; were they acquired hastily; were they brought up from some underground depository, left in cellars during Dost Mohammed's long wise reign, and only now brought up to the state rooms of the palace? Somehow, Burnes thought this last. In his mind, he saw Dost Mohammed entering his new palace, and with a single disgusted gesture ordering the tawdry display of the deposed king to be buried somewhere unseen. He would like to know of it, perhaps even like to keep it. In his mind, Burnes saw his Amir ordering the cellars to be unlocked, and going in, alone, to contemplate the ruins of kingly vanity.

The room was hung with red and gold; the carpets and hangings swathing the muffled room, dotted about with great jewelled golden bowls, and at the head of the room, a barbaric glittering empty throne—that, surely, could not have been brought from India. Burnes remembered the room before, empty and clean and white, and how the noises of the palace and the world outside filtered in. This was muffled and silent, a sumptuous tomb, waiting for its Emperor to arrive.

They stood and waited in silence. Shah Shujah's custom was to keep them at his pleasure for anything up to an hour. Macnaghten got out his watch, and shook it irritably. There was nothing to be done; tempting as it was to remind Shah Shujah who, here, was in the position of power, the consequences of such action were unpredictable. In India, the old man could be summoned; here, the English could only obey his whim. He was the bare scrap which concealed, in attempted modesty, the reality of the situation, and to cast him aside would not just be to admit the substance of the English presence, but to move their obligations onto an entirely new level. If the old man wanted to believe himself the true ruler of the kingdom, and the price of his belief insolently making Burnes and Macnaghten wait an hour, then that could be endured.

The arrival of the Amir was a slow one, and accompanied with the greatest ceremony. The guards flung open the doors, and the court nazir, preceded by some sort of footmen, entered with a slow marching step. Next, some more footmen, splendidly dressed in long gold coats, whose sole purpose was to scatter handfuls of rose petals in the path of the Amir, and, presumably, to sweep them up afterwards—a ceremonial invention, no doubt, of Shah Shujah's. It was all too easy to imagine the angry exiled king, dwelling in his mind on rituals he would impose, and saying to himself, over the long course of years, "When I am King in Kabul again, I shall never walk on anything but rose petals . . ." And then the court, the hired nobility, walking backwards, bowing constantly. Through all this, Burnes and Macnaghten stood stiffly, not being greeted or acknowledged. The court gathered behind the two English envoys, and, as one, flung themselves to the ground; and then, a long minute after, came the Amir, with his body-servants and his personal guards, taking cross little steps into the room, turning, and up the red-carpeted steps onto the golden throne. At length, the whole revolting procedure was done, and with a single gesture, he commanded the English envoys to begin their twenty minutes of compliments.

At length, business could begin. Questions of court finance were routinely run through, and Shah Shujah's peremptory demands met with the gentlest possible suggestion of the likely consequences of increasing the burden of taxation on the citizens of Kabul; a daily discussion. Shah Shujah's request for the head of Dost Mohammed was as regular a demand, and one which Macnaghten had no answer which could possibly satisfy, it was clear, however often it was repeated; and this was always followed by a lengthy denunciation of the British weakness in failing to find and kill the sons and brothers of his predecessor. A nervous moment; although Burnes knew nothing of the sons of Dost Mohammed, apart from those presently with him in India, he hoped that no one had told Shah Shujah that the Newab Jubbur Khan was a regular and welcome guest of his and his brother's. Finally, in recent weeks, the thoughts of the Amir had turned to his great treasure, the Mountain of Light, and demands had started being made that the British should now demand the return of the Koh-i-Noor from the thief, the swindler, Runjeet Singh. It would not be long, Burnes thought, before Shah Shujah started making demands for the loan of forces to reclaim Peshawar, and the pretence in Calcutta that he was at all to be preferred to Dost Mohammed would have to be dropped. He waited, listening to Macnaghten's steady, well-rehearsed explanations with practised patience.

When the Amir had finally run out of his familiar complaints, Macnaghten, for once, had something to raise with him.

"Your Majesty's aid is most urgently begged by us," Macnaghten began. "It may be a small question, but we feel that Your Majesty may be so good as to wish to help his valued allies and friends in what may prove to be a trivial matter. A valued soldier of ours failed to return from a hunting party yesterday, and his companions were obliged to abandon him by the onset of darkness."

"Speak on," Shah Shujah said, scowling.

"Your Majesty's patience is the wonder of his friends and the terror of his enemies," Macnaghten said. "We are greatly concerned for an English soldier's wellbeing, and wish to find him; if he has been rescued by Your Majesty's subjects, we will, I fear, have some difficulty in discovering him, owing to our unfamiliarity with the region where he was last seen. Were Your Majesty so good as to help us in this matter—"

"You weary Us with matters of no importance," Shah Shujah said. "Where was he taken?"

Burnes stepped forward, bowing, and explained.

"Do not waste my time," Shah Shujah said. "Your servant is dead. He was foolish to go to such a place, and he has learnt his lesson. I can do nothing for you. Pray that his death was swift."

"Your Majesty's gracious sincerity awakes our unceasing admiration," Macnaghten muttered.

Each day, the audience ended in exactly the same way, as Macnaghten said something innocuous or even lavishly flattering to the puppet Amir, and Shah Shujah, out of his repertory, brought a daunting facial expression. He stared at them, as if grossly insulted, and said nothing more. This, it turned out, was the signal to go, and the two of them walked backwards out of the throne room, bowing deeply as they went. The court divided in two behind them, and Shah Shujah watched them all the way to the door with his unforgiving face. And what he would do without them . . .

Somewhere else in the city, in a quiet house behind a simple door, another court sat and listened to a boy. The Prince had returned, and the whole city knew it; knew what the British did not know; knew what the Bala Hissar did not know; knew that their Prince was returned in the night, and waited for the day to dawn. It would not be long. Akbar sat in the innermost room of this merchant's house, and around him were his brothers and cousins. They sat and listened, their attention entirely fixed on Hasan, the son of Khushhal, telling what he had done, proving his loyalty.

TWENTY-FOUR

I

"In six months," Florentia Sale said, "you will return to find us as civilized as Calcutta. You know, Sale, I very much have it in mind to hold a ball this winter."

"A ball, my dear?" Sale said.

They were standing at the edge of the cantonments, saying their goodbyes. Sale was setting off for a six-month spell of duty in Jalalabad, to the east; Florentia, at her own request, was remaining in Kabul. As she very sensibly pointed out, she could be of no use to Sale in his duties in Jalalabad; could be of considerably more use to the ladies of the camp, to arrange diversions and be of help in small ways. Besides, the climate here was so healthy and the life so peaceful, it would be altogether more agreeable for her to spend a winter here, her third. As everybody agreed, there could be nothing more pleasant than the sharp Afghan winter; Florentia particularly anticipated the revival of one of the previous winter's innovations, as Burnes—so admirable, so original—had suggested the possibility of skating. It had been many years since Florentia, long in the East, had thought of skating, but the clever Afghan blacksmiths had fashioned great numbers of skates for the British, and it had proved a delightful diversion on the deep-frozen river; even some of the Kabul nobility had taken to it, and very pretty they had looked, too, with their robes flying behind them and an expression of grim concentration beneath their turbans. And what a pleasure it had been to discover that she had not altogether lost the knack, and in a week could carve a perfect 8 in the ice, to general, gratifying astonishment. Yes, among the many new pleasures they had introduced to Kabul—racing, cricket, concerts—ice-skating was the most gratifying in Florentia's memory, and she looked forward to the first hard frost eagerly. And this winter, perhaps, they could hold a ball or two on Sale's return; it was not impossible.

"You will have so wretched and dull a time on your manoeuvres," Lady Sale said brightly, "I feel it my duty to provide a pleasure for you on your return. Yes, a ball; I really think, now, we have enough ladies here to make it plausible, and no one can say we do not have musicians enough—after waking us with their marches every morning for the last three years, I do not see why we should not make some use of their talents. If only we had a pianoforte, Sale—"

"I doubt, my dear, Jalalabad will supply a pianoforte, or I would be sure to return with one. But you will manage very well—you always do, my dear. Very well, a ball. I quite envy you your quiet six months here; you are right not to want to accompany me into the wilds."

"Abominably selfish of me, I know," Lady Sale said. An Afghan woman, in her heavy blue cloak, came out of the nearest tent, one of the officers' tents, and shuffled past them. They both averted their eyes. "But, you know, I always wish to be where I can be of most use. Ah—here is Brydon. Good morning, Dr. Brydon."

Brydon, on his morning rounds paying compliments and handing out palliatives, gave a deep bow and stopped. "You are departing on your duties, I perceive, General?" he said.

"Indeed," Sale said. "I truly wish—well, whatever my wishes, I am to leave you until the spring. Upon my word, I never had so pleasant a tour of duty as here, one so supplied with every pleasure or with fewer demands on my time. I fear I am in for a rude shock now; I have quite forgotten how arduous a soldier's duties can be."

"You know, Dr. Brydon," Florentia said, "General Sale always says this, but in truth, I am sure, he finds it rather dull here—a strenuous spell of duty quelling insurrection in the hills will be just the thing to invigorate him, so little is there to occupy us here. I never knew a quieter place.

What was it Macnaghten was saying last night—quiet from Dan to Beersheba—yes, indeed. And how is dear Mrs. Sturt? No news as yet?"

"It cannot be many days, Lady Sale; but she is doing very well, and is bearing up with great good cheer. She is convinced that she will have a boy, this time, you know."

"I told her as much, indeed," Lady Sale said with an air of triumph. "One can always tell, Brydon, by the weight of the infant—I always knew, with each of my children. Not many days, you say? Good, good—I shall pay her a visit, this very morning. You know, Brydon, I expect you to act the beau while my husband is absent, and keep us all diverted with new fashions and surprising entertainments. I was in the middle of promising Sale a ball on his return, but so dull are we, that will be far too many months away to provide much of the pleasure of anticipation to us. I expect ingenuity—novelty—ideas from all my irregulars, Dr. Brydon, I warn you."

"You see, Brydon," Sale said, "my wife will brook no insubordination."

"Lady Sale, ha ha, has shown herself so much the mother of invention," Brydon began brilliantly, "so much the queen of our little society, that our poor suggestions can only prove, ah . . ."

"Well, Sale," Florentia said briskly, "off you go—if you dawdle much longer you will find yourself snowed in for the winter. And you will find pleasures enough, I dare say, wherever you find yourself. You return in April, I think?"

"What pleasures can there be where Lady Sale is not?" Brydon said, getting carried away, but they both ignored him; they gave each other a brisk joyless salute, and turned away, Sale to his horse and Florentia, no doubt, to bully servants and lecture the frightened pregnant young wives. Brydon, left standing there, watched them both go, for the moment forgetting where he was and where he had been going.

2

It was two weeks before the information of the attack on Sale and his brigade reached Kabul. It had been in a pass a week's march east of Kabul, as daylight was fading, and no doubt the effectiveness of the ambush had been due to the element of surprise, as the bandits startled a weary and inattentive body of men. Something like this might have been expected, and the one fatality and dozen injuries were not, in themselves, serious; moreover, once the English had retaliated, the encounter had come to a swift end as the Afghans took to their heels and fled. The narrow pass wound and curved, allowing any savage marksman opportunity enough to conceal himself and take careful aim; the sides of the pass were high and steep as cliffs, a deep fissure in a mountain, and as the men marched three abreast, they were ambushed by Afghans, crouching at the brim of the pass high above. Their aim was not good, and the *jezail,* the Afghan musket, was a primitive object, not allowing much accuracy; otherwise, it would have been no harder for the enemy than shooting fish in a barrel. The brigade had no means of protection, and in a few moments, a man lay dead; the English fire, directed wildly upwards, ricocheted against the sides of the pass, and hardly reached the enemy at all. The response itself, however, ineffectual as it was, seemed to impress the tribesmen, and the encounter was swiftly over. Sale himself had a wound in his leg, according to reports, but, the dead man aside, there were few serious injuries and the brigade continued on its path, more warily.

The news of the assault on Sale's brigade was received in different quarters in Kabul. Akbar heard it and nodded grimly; the men had done well, and this encounter was never intended to be more than a warning skirmish. If the battle honours on either side were equal—one of the sharpshooters had concealed himself ill, and the English had contrived to shoot him in the head—the weight of warning must be all on one side, as the English learnt to fear. Whatever they thought them, these exchanges constituted the stately opening moves of a game of chess, which Akbar, hunched over his white pieces, would always win with a cry of *shah mat* as he knocked the black king to the floor. Whatever significance they assigned to it, Akbar intended that in a five-minute skirmish they would understand that from here on, they were engaged in a game of black against white, and disaster upon disaster would visit them.

The news was received by the English more casually than that; a sign of loose idle hostility, Macnaghten confidently said, not entertaining the possibility that war might have broken out. Florentia had continued to hold her dinners, and over her table, the general view was that something of this sort might at any moment occur in any quarter of the world. By the time the news had reached Kabul, the winter had begun, in that abrupt way it did here, with a single, heavy, overnight fall of snow, and

Florentia Sale's dining room was drowsy with three substantial fires. The more learned guests delved into the long communal memory of India, and recalled the disappearance of the thugs; and after all, Florentia reflected out loud, London too had its footpads and mohawks, and Sale was, by all accounts, quite well. A mere flesh wound, requiring only the most superficial attention, and all would be well; Sale had known worse, though for herself she much preferred the wisdom which was now evident, of staying in the safety of the Kabul cantonments.

Burnes excused himself and his brother early, and made his way back through the streets of Kabul to the old merchant's house. It seemed to him that the city was oddly peopled for the late hour; in normal circumstances, the Kabulis retired at darkness, and the streets were deserted by eight o'clock. Tonight, despite the cold, small groups of men clustered periodically; a dark patch, like a copse, glimpsed through the heavy falling snow, and then, as they approached, dark silent Afghan faces resolved themselves out of the lucent gloom, and fell back into obscurity. Some festival perhaps (and the city was always ready to celebrate the birth of some descendant of the Prophet with guns and firecrackers); but the groups were silent and sombre, and watched Burnes and Charlie go past narrowly. They, too, did not speak, and it appeared to Burnes that, in some leisurely, unemphatic way, they were being trailed; two or three men could be glimpsed through the quietly falling snow, walking fifteen paces behind them. Each of them followed them for five minutes or so, before falling back and seemingly handing over to a new band of silent attendants. The jingling noise of Burnes's uniform as he walked briskly in the obscuring snow seemed unaccountably loud, and it was with some relief that they achieved the merchant's house, and ordered the gates tightly shut for the night.

Charlie said a quick goodnight and, shivering, went to the old women's quarters of the house. Burnes, too, went to his quarters, and summoned Ahmed, his usual footman, to light the fires. Ahmed appeared in a matter of minutes, and behind him, an unfamiliar new servant, who stayed at the door; it was a matter of mild irritation to Burnes that the household was constantly augmenting itself without reference to him, and he found himself employing various street-acquaintances of his footmen and cooks for no better reason than his body-servants seemed to think that they, too, deserved followers to demonstrate the grandeur of one who served the English. It did no good to complain about this tendency of his household, and he resolved to leave the matter until the next day.

Ahmed listened for a while, tipping his head from side to side in some kind of agreement while he laid the fire in the grate.

"Yes," he agreed in the end. "There is some discontent in the market. Perhaps Your Honour would care to remain in the house for a day or so."

Burnes looked at the man sharply; he had not considered that this might be a serious matter.

"Do you advise me to remove to the cantonments? We are rather isolated here."

Ahmed seemed to consider the question. "Perhaps Your Honour would care to remain in His Honour's house tomorrow," he at length concluded. "There he will be safe."

"What is the cause of this?" Burnes said. He felt that Ahmed was unwilling to say more. Perhaps he was unwilling merely because he did not know what the reason for this discontent was.

"Nothing, sir," Ahmed said. "A one-day wonder, and soon over. Perhaps Your Honour would prefer to stay in his house tomorrow."

Burnes suppressed his irritation; it might, too, be as Ahmed said, a one-day wonder over some trivial matter, a soldier fighting a merchant in the market, perhaps. Similar things had been known, and nothing ever came of it. He dismissed the thought of removing to the cantonments; and the snow was falling too heavily now to take so alarming a step.

"Come forward," he called to the figure in the doorway. Ahmed cast a vague, worried look behind him as the man stepped forward and bowed. As he stood upright, his eyes cast downwards, Burnes recognized him, without quite remembering where from; a handsome man, delicately featured, a familiar face in the cantonments.

"My brother," Ahmed explained. "He is visiting me, and asked to come and present his respects to my master."

Burnes nodded politely, and dismissed them. Perhaps Ahmed was right; there was some evident unrest about, for whatever cause, and there was no reason to venture from the house the next day. He had been in Kabul long enough to know that the mood of the city changed quickly, and if the cause of this mild hostility proved to be some fool of a sergeant's having seduced someone's wife, or getting drunk and starting a fight, it would all be forgotten in a day or two. Respect was the thing, and Kabul repaid that respect.

It was a cold night, and Burnes woke from his uneasy, dreamless sleep three or four times, shivering deeply. Each time, in the confused small hours, it seemed to him that there was a vague rumble somewhere close at hand, like an army; each time he wrapped himself deeper in blankets and returned quickly to sleep. Once, he woke and in the dark of the room, there might have been another man there, standing somewhere in the shadows, the effect of the light cast by the last of the fire, but, muttering to himself, he brought the blanket over his tired aching head and sank back into the cold darkness.

He woke, and it was morning, and he was alone. Or not alone, because there, his face white, was Charlie, half-dressed with a heavy Afghan robe thrown over his shoulders. Burnes screwed up his face; he felt sticky and stupid with his lack of sleep, and scratched his head, yawning.

"Where's Ahmed?" Burnes said.

"Gone, I think," Charlie said after a few moments. "Ally—"

"Gone?"

"They've all gone, I think," Charlie said. "I can't find anyone. No one woke me this morning."

Burnes yawned again, trying to think. "Oh, for heaven's sake," he said.

"Ally, don't move—something terrible . . ."

Burnes rolled over, away from his brother. He felt exhausted, limp, and unequal to any of this. As he turned, his face brushed against something, and his hair caught in some sort of cold wet twigs.

"Ally, don't look—come away, Ally."

Burnes brought his hands up, and disentangled himself. What—there, somewhere in the night, someone had placed by him—what—a branch of a tree, some kind of—a mulberry branch, winter-bare and spiked. And something else, there, something solid and heavy and stinking; the smell, sharp now, brought up the dream again, some dream of wading through stench; some object wrapped in cloth, the size of a small boulder.

"Come away," Charlie said; his mouth opened and closed, but the quiet terror of his voice seemed to have nothing to do with his white face. Burnes groped his way upright, pulling the blanket around him. The object was wrapped, and could be anything, but Burnes knew as well as his brother what it was. It was a trophy; it was the head, rotting, months old, of Sergeant Porter.

Burnes leapt away, and for a moment the two of them stood there.

Burnes's clothes still lay where he had thrown them, the night before; and then he understood that they had been deserted. Quickly, he pulled on a shirt, tugged on his breeches and boots, and, half-dressed, with a blanket over his shoulders, holding his coat, he followed his brother out of the room. Charlie would not stand there, had fled as soon as he could, and Burnes followed him, shaking, out of the house. It had stopped snowing, and the courtyard was deep in snow over which no foot had trod. The gates were bolted and secure; from somewhere, outside the house, there came a muffled noise of men talking. They hurried across, as if to Charlie's quarters, but Burnes summoned himself, and held his brother's arm for a moment.

"All gone?" he said.

"I think so," Charlie said.

"Have you made certain of it?" Burnes said. Charlie shook his head. Burnes assembled himself, and, taking Charlie with him, he turned and went back. They went back into the house, and, not speaking, went through the rooms. Nothing had been touched, and the house seemed not to have been looted in any way. There was something frightening in this; robbery would at least have supplied a routine explanation. But each room was empty of people; the dining room, the study, the bedchambers; the two of them went through, and there was no one to be seen. In the night, the household had risen, and gone without a word. Even the kitchens were empty, abandoned; food lay about and piles of used dishes. They had fled as one, at some signal. They walked around the house, and then Burnes turned, and walked back the way he had come. There was nobody there, and there might never have been anyone in the house. Only outside the gates; there, they could hear, there was a faceless army of voices.

For hours, it might have been, they sat and shivered in Charlie's quarters, and for the first time, the ghosts of the evicted women seemed to gather about them, accusingly. They sat in silence, listening to what they could hear; the steady murmur outside. No attempt was being made on the house, just an unmoving hostile guard. The fire was out, and they shivered; neither of them made any move to relight it, nor did it occur to them to do such a thing, in the terrifying cold room. It might have been hours of silent listening before, from outside, a voice was raised, and, even in the room, they could hear what it called. "Burnes!" it called. "Sikunder Burnes!" For a moment Burnes shrank, hardly knowing what this meant, and then, like an echo in the snow, he realized that he knew the voice.

"Great God, the sepoys!" he said, leaping up. "They are still there, at least!"

He went briskly to Charlie's desk, where paper and pen lay, and wrote quickly; a note to Macnaghten. The sepoys were still there, would send for help. He finished, and folded it briskly in three, not saying to Charlie what he was doing, and then went out into the courtyard. There was a small door set into the great gates of the house, and, without thinking, Burnes undid it and opened it. There, as he thought, were the sepoys, standing there hardily, and beyond them, twenty or thirty Afghans, squatting in the snow inattentively. Was that all? For a moment he thought of simply walking out, past the Afghans, returning to the cantonments with a carapace of confidence. The nearest sepoy turned, a look of terrible alarm on his face, and Burnes knew what to do; he handed the note to him, and shut the door firmly behind him, bolting it solidly. There was food in the house, and, after all, Ahmed was not wrong, not necessarily wrong; he had fled, but this, perhaps, might be a matter of a day, no more than that. Reinforcements would soon arrive, and the Afghans disperse, and things return to normal, and the shamefaced household would slink back by nightfall.

3

The time, then, had come: the time of Akbar's reckoning, and the princes of the house swept down from the hills, and entered into the city of their father. One by one they came, the many sons of the Dost, under disguise. For many weeks, no day had passed without a party of traders presenting itself at the gates of the city, and entering without challenge. But the English did not look into the faces of these traders, and did not see the mark of the Baroukzye princes in their eyes. Unsuspecting, the English searched the possessions of what they thought to be merchants, and, one after the other, each of the sons of the Amir passed into the city.

At this moment, there was no disloyalty between the brothers, but only a fierce conviction, a burningly held purpose. Each of them arrived, and each carried out the same humble task, at the order of Akbar. Each of the princes went to one of the mulberry trees in the city, and cut off a branch with his sword, knowing that same sword would serve a different purpose, very soon. Then the princes went, humbly, by darkness, and carried out the errand of a servant or a spy. Each of them bowed before Akbar's purpose, and accepted the humblest duty. Each, by darkness, entered into the houses and the inner rooms of the English, and there left the branch of the mulberry. The English saw it, and understood what this meant, and trembled in fear.

Akbar was patient, but he knew, now, the time had come to act. Soon, the princes of the English army would feel the weight of his wrath, would hear the song of Akbar's scimitar, slicing through air. But first, he would send one more message to them, that they would know something of the fury of the princes of the Afghans, the wrath of the Afghan empire.

4

He had lost track of time. It must have been days now. In this dank dark place, there was no sign of day coming and going; nothing to mark the passage of time but the arrival and departure of his dreadful torturers. He was slumped, naked, in the corner of the cellar furthest from the door, shivering from cold and terror and the many shallow cuts all over him. For the moment he was alone; they had left him when his pain had brought him to the point of retching, but now he knew they would return. He thought, over and over again, what he had not stopped thinking for days now, that when they next entered, he would dash at them, desperately, and seize a blade and somehow do away with himself before it could all start again. He thought it, and believed it was possible, not admitting to himself that he had tried before, each time, and each time failed as they pushed him back, contemptuously, and held him down to continue their black acts; drawing the points of their blades across his body as if in the most exquisite calligraphy, one after the other. It was the pain, always the pain; each time, he thought—he knew—that this time he must die of the pain, and each time he did not. Why this was happening to him, he did not know, and for days had been wailing at them that he was not important, that he was nothing but a common soldier, nothing anyone would care about or miss; promising them that if they let him escape, he would bring no punishment down on them; consoling them with his assurance that he knew, he understood that they meant to seize some other fellow in the marketplace, there, a week before; that it was a mistake, that there was no reason for them to go on with this; pleading in English, over and over again, and then, as they returned and returned, turning to the language of his childhood, and calling out in Welsh for mercy to his uncomprehending torturers, these inquisitors who asked no question and did not listen to any answer he could offer. They had been gone for hours. They would return in minutes. He listened; and out of the underground silence, his terrifying fantasy produced the sound of footsteps, outside, coming closer.

5

It is fair to say that nobody appreciated the sacrifice Florentia Sale had made in parting from her husband as much as she did herself; but few silently deplored and regretted it as much as Macnaghten. "Splendid woman," he would say routinely, his voice somewhat trailing off. "Pillar of the, of the . . ." He disliked and feared her, he did not know why, and if he longed for a larger society, it was only because that would enable him to refuse her invitations. At present, that was impossible. She would instantly know whether he was going somewhere else, or merely preferring his own company to hers. And Sale's departure meant that the woman was at something of a loose end, at any hour of the day, and at any hour of the day, expected Macnaghten—expected him! Macnaghten!—to attend to her.

He had been caught, like a rat in a trap. His morning stroll about the cantonments was no longer a safe occupation. It was not precisely an inspection of the state of things, more of an idle curious promenade, to see what the men were up to. An army encampment is always throwing up interesting sights, and one of Macnaghten's pleasures was to walk about, and watch the men digging a ditch, or a hopeful native arriving with a basket of curiosities for sale, or, if nothing better could be provided, a dog worrying a rat. His position licensed this inactivity in him, and for an hour or so each day, he liked to shed his secretary and pretend to embark on an inspection of the cantonments; his interest, however, was less like a general, and more like a street urchin with nothing to do but gawp at the local doings.

That had always been his pleasure, and, surely, a harmless one, but

Florentia Sale had contrived to deprive him of it, and an agreeable hour of solitude. No sooner was he embarked on his promenade than the wretched woman would materialize, and waste his time in conversation of the most hectoring variety. He had contemplated explaining brutally that he was engaged on business, but that was so evidently untrue that he did not dare. The truth was that every other person in the camp recognized his right to idleness, and respected it without him resorting to pretence. There was nothing to be said, and he wished the woman had been taken off by that damned "Fighting Bob," where she might at least have been shot in the passes.

"Poor Mrs. Sturt," Florentia was saying at this moment as they walked the alley behind the officers' mess. "Men, of course, know nothing of true bravery; it is for women to discover that, I may tell you. The dangers and suffering of battle are nothing compared to the usual lot of women. A battle—over in an afternoon. I would a hundred times be dropped in the thick of battle than endure poor Mrs. Sturt's long sufferings. Thirty-six hours, Sir William—think of that—thirty-six hours of constant pain, and no sign of the poor baby. Of course, all will be well in the end, but I must say, I myself am kept awake by her suffering, two nights now. Poor Dr. Brydon, too, exhausted and yet still hopeful."

"Yes," Macnaghten said. "I have often thought, the lot of women is a hard one."

"Sir William," Florentia said. "You never said a truer word. But I must say, the poor woman, in so sadly temporary accommodation, and though, I know, nothing can be done in that regard for the men, or, indeed for her, I really feel that now that we are to be billeted here for some time, it cannot be right that we all live in this extraordinary way."

"As you say, Lady Sale," Macnaghten said, "there is nothing that can be done in that regard."

"Come, now, Sir William," Florentia said. "Nothing? It is so very unsuitable, I must say, for a General Sale to make do in such a manner, at least. And you know, I am the last to complain about discomfort where it is unnecessary, but this is quite unsatisfactory. Now, I am going to break a marital confidence, and tell you something. Do you know, Sale, as he left, said one last thing to me: he said, 'Florentia, my dear, make sure that Macnaghten finds you a proper home for the winter.' Sir William, are there not ample houses within the city for us? I cannot answer for the

General's rage, were he to return and find that his wife had endured one more winter in this impossible, this impossible—"

"Lady Sale, I am most sorry for your discomfort," Macnaghten began wearily—would the woman never leave the subject alone?—but it was at that moment that a sepoy ran up, and, bowing, handed Macnaghten a hastily folded note. "Excuse me one moment, Lady Sale."

The sepoy and Lady Sale stood there while he read the communication. It was from Burnes, and read: *The guard here is insufficient: please supply two dozen men, without delay.*

Macnaghten handed the note over to Lady Sale, shaking his head. "You see my difficulties," he said. "Burnes, there, in the city, demanding men, a constant drain as it is, and now requiring more without a by-your-leave. I have the greatest respect for that young man, but regret the day I ever acceded to his request to take up residence within the city walls. A very able young man, but I fear he has no concept of the demands being made on me from all sides. And, my dear Lady Sale—" now Macnaghten was losing his temper, "—I know quite well that ladies very easily submit to fear and make precisely this absurd request, and, with my respect for you, I should not easily be able to refuse it, whatever difficulties it would present to me. No, we must go on as we are for the moment. Now . . ."

Macnaghten took a pencil from his inside pocket, and scrawled *Quite impossible* on the bottom of the note.

"Return this to Sir Alexander with my regrets," he said to the sepoy, with the sense of being indubitably in the right. "I shall explain further tonight, I think. We dine together, do we not, Lady Sale? And Burnes, surely, will be of the company."

6

The long day wore on, with no news. The sepoys did not call out again, and the only noise from beyond the gate was the slow increase of murmur, the occasional raised voice, the occasional roar of assent. Burnes and Charlie sat in the old zenana, saying nothing, only listening.

At four, from beyond the gates, a tremendous noise broke out, and suddenly it was apparent that the crowd outside was far larger than it had been in the morning. Charlie leapt to his feet.

"They're not—" he said, but then the gates sounded like a great bass drum, and it was clear to both of them that some escalation was beginning. Some kind of ram was being deployed against the gates, and, far from drifting away, the crowd was growing bigger and more driven by fury.

"If I could only speak to them," Burnes said, but he knew it was far too late to think of that; and what had happened to the reinforcements, he did not know. Outside, it went very quiet, and they listened; it was a single voice, raised in imprecation, like the summoning song from the mosque, twisting and winding like a melody. As it reached its cadence there was an explosion; the crowd yelling in obscure joy, and, for the first time, the sound of gunfire, dreadfully close. "There must be—"

He could not stand here, and, although there was nowhere else to go, he left the room. Charlie followed him. They had walked through half a dozen rooms when, somewhere near at hand, inside the house this time, they heard a noise from the kitchens. Burnes stopped and drew his pistol. Making a hushing gesture to Charlie, he tiptoed forward; through the silent dining room, the silent pantry, and there were the kitchens. They halted for a moment on the threshold, ears cocked, looking around; at first there was nothing to be seen, but then, all at once, in the gloom of the far end, a movement—an animal, perhaps—no—

"Who's there?" Burnes called. Nothing moved for a moment, and then a figure came forward. At first he could not see who it was, but as the man moved into the light, unarmed, he recognized him; it was the man from the previous night, whom Ahmed had described as his brother.

"Stop there," Burnes said. The man stopped, and spread wide his hands, in a gesture of friendship. "How long have you been here?"

"Sikunder Burnes," the man said. "I slept in the kitchens, and when I woke, the house was empty. I do not know where everyone is gone. I stayed because my brother told me not to leave until his return."

"When will he return?"

"Sikunder Burnes, I do not know," Hasan said. "I think now he will not return. The men are outside the gates and calling for your blood."

That was something they had not said to each other, and to have it confirmed in speech, so simply, somehow made everything so much worse. Burnes gave silent thanks that Charlie did not understand Persian.

"You must go," Hasan said. "Or they will break in and kill you."

"How can we go?" Burnes said. "The house is surrounded. If we stay they will break in and kill us; if we leave they will certainly kill us. Our best hope is to wait until Macnaghten sends soldiers."

"Macnaghten," Hasan said, thoughtfully. His clean eyes shone white in the murky room. "Sikunder Burnes, there is no hope now that the English can rescue you—there are too many outside for that. I can help you to reach safety—trust me."

His face was familiar, open, and clear; Burnes thought for a second before agreeing.

"Here are some robes," Hasan said. "Take them and put them on—darken your face—and we will go over the back wall. That will be safe."

"We still have to go to the front of the house, through the mob," Burnes said.

"They will be watching the gate; trust me, you will be safe," Hasan said simply.

There was nothing to be done. They stood there in the cold dark kitchen, and Hasan gazed seriously at the two of them. A rat ran across the floor.

"Very well," Burnes said decisively. He explained everything to Charlie. "It will be fine," he said. "I know this man—I think we can trust him."

A blind alley ran around two-thirds of the house, and ended at a high wall underneath the inner orchard. Once Burnes and Charlie were in their dirty borrowed robes, their faces darkened with cold meat juices from the bottom of a kitchen pan, they made their way to the back of the house. The orchard was raised six feet above the level of the street, and below, the alley was quite empty. Quickly, Burnes swung himself over the wall and dropped into the street, followed by the Afghan and finally Charlie. Without saying anything, their blue eyes lowered, they followed the alley around the house towards the furious shrieks of the mob at the front. When they turned, and Burnes saw the faces of the crowd, he almost flinched; but it was too late for that, and he prayed, without turning to look, that Charlie, too, was finding some bravery in himself.

In ten paces, they were among the crowd, and Burnes began to edge through the pressing bodies. It was going to work; he sidled between the men, each with a blade raised or a *jezail* pointed at the heavens, and no one took notice of them. There were hundreds of them, and of the sepoys no sign at all, buried deep within the crowd, pressed against the heavy gate. Three hundred, perhaps; four hundred; perhaps more, and—

A heavy hand fell on his shoulder, and with a single movement, his hasty turban had been ripped off. He turned, as swiftly as if he had been burned, and saw Hasan, holding his turban up, and calling. And then, of course, Burnes remembered him: Hasan. Remembered his face, and knew him; remembered the man who had left with Porter, and returned alone. Hasan: he saw all his wrath and virtue, and heard his voice, now, now, calling with the great high beautiful voice of the angels, summoning the righteous heavens to descend upon them.

"I have him, I have him! Sikunder, Sikunder, here, here!"

And there was a moment of terrible blind stillness, as the crowd, as one, turned to Charlie, and to him.

7

And the dogs of the city devoured his face.

Kabul was still, and from the cantonments the pall of smoke could be seen to hang over the city, marking the end of Burnes. The word had come, and Macnaghten had grown silent; the men were armed, and sent to the pitiful mud walls of the cantonments. There they waited, but everything was quiet. And then more word came, from the Bala Hissar itself. The palace was taken, and of Shah Shujah there was no news. Macnaghten sat, and was silent, and the cantonments waited.

Deep within the cantonments, two women sat and waited. Florentia Sale, at the bedside of Mrs. Sturt. In the younger woman's arms, a baby, hours old, sucked at its mother. There, six hours old, was the only content to be found, and the two women were pale.

"He is feeding well, at any rate," Lady Sale remarked—for something must be said. There was an unnatural silence about the tent; the men were all at the snow-deep ramparts, waiting, and about them nothing. The silence when there is no one there; the silence when no one in a crowd makes a noise; Florentia strained, painfully, listening. She recalled herself; for Mrs. Sturt's sake, an effort had to be made. "A fine boy. I think I can promise you one thing," and her voice rose, ringingly, in assurance, "he will grow up, and grow up to be as brave a soldier as his father."

Lady Sale's head sang with her own bravery, and she jutted her jaw out in defiance.

"Yes, that's so," Mrs. Sturt said casually. Lady Sale looked at her in surprise; she was a foolish woman, but surely she appreciated the danger they were all in? "Yes, he is strong—look, his little hands, how they grasp and tug—yes, I can see him as a soldier when he grows up. Where is my dear Sturt? And Dr. Brydon, too, abandoning us so swiftly—but I am really disappointed in Sturt."

"My dear," Lady Sale said, as kindly as she could, "you know that a soldier has many calls on his time, and even the birth of his son must take second place to such pressing duties."

Mrs. Sturt waved this away and subsided into an enormous sulky yawn she did not trouble to cover. ". . . first son," she finished. "Lord, how fagged I am. D'you suppose it is quite as tiring for them—for him—" she nodded downwards at the baby, "—I mean? He looks as if he has just woken from a good deep sleep."

"I don't know," Lady Sale said impatiently.

"Where can Sturt be?" Mrs. Sturt said. "So unlike him. Everything is so quiet, is it not? I want Sturt by me—I want to talk of names for the little one. Do you think Horatio a nice name?"

"I don't know," Lady Sale said. Really . . . "Perhaps a naval name, rather than a military one."

"That's so," Mrs. Sturt said comfortably. "And I do so feel he will grow up to be a soldier. I wish General Sale were here still."

"Yes," Lady Sale said. "But I start to think he is lucky to be in relative safety, although he would never have credited it when he set off."

"*He* would be kind to me, were he here," Mrs. Sturt said, a note of complaint coming into her voice. "He was so very solicitous about my welfare, he would not leave me lying here quite alone while he went about his duties. Really, I grow cross with Sturt."

Lady Sale gave a silent prayer of thanks for Mrs. Sturt's stupidity; sometimes not being able to understand or think, she considered, could be a blessing.

Sturt was at the walls of the cantonments, with the men; the officers patrolled up and down in the early morning, watching, waiting. The night had risen into the air like smoke, leaving no trace. The city seemed quiet, and the empty hills behind the cantonments were calm as if nothing had happened; as if the riotous fury of the night had never occurred. There was nothing but a pall of smoke over the city to show what had happened. The city had risen, once, its jaw and teeth stretched wide, and bit and swallowed, once, before subsiding again to the deep, leaving nothing behind, and the English contemplated the smooth tranquil expanse with terror.

Macnaghten had withdrawn to his quarters, and had left instructions that he was not to be disturbed, except in the case of the direst emergency. Outside, the nazir himself stood guard implacably; inside, undisturbed, Macnaghten shook, and wept, and from time to time wrote with wild bursts of speed, his hand scrawling loosely across the page. He was not to be disturbed; because what he was writing would, in the end, excuse him, and he knew that he might not have very long. He wrote, not in his usual precise, slanting hand, but in the loops and flurries of a man with no time, and as he wrote, his uncontrollable tears made blots on the page. "I may be considered culpable for not having foreseen," he wrote, and then stopped, trembling; the terror rose up in him like a wave, and it choked in his throat. He tried to start to write again, but could not; his hand rested on the page, and would not move. Go on, he told himself; go on; but it would not. He had to set down what he knew must be the truth, that he had always done his best, and no man could have done better, but he could not go on, setting down the folly of Burnes and the helplessness of his own position; he shook with the effort of keeping his tears silent. There was nobody now but him, and he could not show himself. The great hero, hiding in his tent, waiting and crying.

By the end of the afternoon, he had cried himself out; drained, dry, exhausted, he felt limp as an empty waterskin. He had finished writing his testament, and there was nothing to do now but to take charge, and show himself once more. In the mirror, he caught a glimpse of himself, raw, red, and frightened. That would not do. For the moment, he had no idea what to do but wait, but he called for his body-servants to shave and wash him. They came quickly, and, once they had shaved him, he washed his face alone, slowly. As he put on his uniform, buttoning up, a single idea came to him, and he felt consoled.

The troops were all in position, waiting for something which might never come. They were all wrapped deep in their coats and blankets against the sharp cold, and from time to time stood up and stamped, their breath clouding in the thin mountain air like oxen. The place seemed to have changed. Familiarity had stopped them seeing it, but with the news from the old quarter of the city, it was as if the land had become strange again. It looked like the city they had first seen, unfamiliar and hostile. The country had a bareness about it; outside the city walls, no tree grew all the way to the horizon, and no earth softened the contours. The city was set down in a rocky and bleak valley, climbing the cliffs for no reason, and beyond its bounds, no life, no animals, no orchard subsisted. Who had stopped here, centuries ago, and begun to build? But it was here that Kabul was, and now, that was all the life there was. The country, buried deep in shining snow, closed them in, and the soldiers stamped their feet and watched for what would come next. The skies were clear, but the silence all around them was like the silence between cracks of thunder, weighty and oppressive.

Macnaghten's little court was summoned, and despatched into the city. On their return, Elphinstone, who had remained at the walls with the men, cornered the nazir, and learnt that Macnaghten had sent them to the old quarter, laden with gifts; they had distributed what gilded objects, what gold the camp could now supply. Everything was now quiet, the nazir said, but he was not cheered by what he had seen; and when Elphinstone asked him further about the state of affairs, he learnt that a son of Dost Mohammed's was in the city, and the city believed with a certainty which could not be hopeful superstition, that Akbar's men were camped beyond the ridge, and waiting their moment. How many men? The nazir did not know, and all his bribes had not been able to find out. Many; very many. That was what they had all said, locking away the English gold and shaking their heads. The nazir went, and Elphinstone repeated all this; Macnaghten emerged from his tent, looking shaken and cold, and was told what he already knew, that the city by now could not be bought, and the bribes had been spread to no purpose.

Beyond the ridge, the army of Akbar lay, waiting. After nightfall, a scout was sent out, and returned in an hour to confirm the truth of this; perhaps five thousand men. There was no sign of movement, but the still night seemed full of unbroken thunder, and the guards on the walls stayed as they were, snatching an hour or two of sleep where they could. Five thousand out there; twenty-five or thirty thousand men of fighting ability within the city; no bravery, now, could be enough in the face of a concerted rebellion. Akbar was there, somewhere in the city, and soon would summon his men from where they circled the stony horizon. They waited on his pleasure, their clenched jaws scything and chattering in the deep night cold.

In the morning, a message came from Akbar, and it was an astonishing one; the three bearers of the message, high disdainful princes, each with a long shining dagger hanging from his *kummur-bund,* stood and waited with a taciturn lack of obeisance while Macnaghten read the strip of parchment. The letter, brief and to the point, offered the English a truce. "I had not realized . . ." Macnaghten began, but he stopped in the face of Akbar's terrible messengers. There was no point in saying to these men that he had not realized that Akbar had declared war on the occupiers. Burnes's murder was not a single thing, and now there was no reason to pretend that any of them did not see it for what it was. Macnaghten went to his desk with the nazir, and, while the three princes waited, wrote a courtly letter back to Akbar. In the light of recent events, he felt that it would be useful if Akbar presented himself at the English settlement; he made it quite plain that in no circumstances would such a meeting occur outside the walls of the cantonments, and added that Akbar would find that his security would not be threatened in this meeting. Macnaghten meant it; there were those, such as Frampton, who strongly urged that Akbar, once within the cantonments, should quite simply be shot *pour encourager les autres.* Macnaghten refused this advice. There were dozens of sons of Dost Mohammed, and if they were so foolish as to cut off one head, no one could seriously doubt that many more would spring up in its place, until the English found themselves killing every Afghan. The only hope was to placate Akbar, by any means necessary, and see what he demanded. He explained what he was writing, carefully, to the messengers, and to his slight surprise, they did not immediately demur, as if Akbar had already decided to deliver himself into the hands of the English; whether this was foolishness, or came from a knowledge that they were now quite helpless, Macnaghten could not guess.

They left, and Macnaghten turned to Elphinstone, who had been standing there throughout.

"I need a memorandum from you, sir," Macnaghten said. "There is nothing else for it. You are to write, in your own words, a statement declaring our position here to be beyond hope."

"Macnaghten—" Elphinstone began.

"There is nothing else for it," Macnaghten said again. "If we cannot convince Jalalabad to send reinforcements, and quickly, then we are done for. You are to write a letter, in the strongest possible terms, declaring our position to be quite desperate. That is all, gentlemen."

The truce began, it seemed; and it was only the truce that demonstrated that, now, they were in a state of war. That afternoon, the unfamiliar silence of the city was suddenly broken, as a lone figure wandered its way towards the walls of the cantonments. The men raised then lowered their muskets. This was no soldier; a small boy, bearing two huge baskets of dried fruits. One of the soldiers started to laugh; the pedlars who had gone constantly between the city and the camp had disappeared in the last few days, and this was the first sign that things, perhaps, were returning to normal. And behind the boy came more merchants with their wares, plodding cheerfully through the snow, coming right up to the mud walls of the camp, and waving their wares over the barrels of the soldiers' muskets. All that afternoon, the pedlars came, selling their wares to their enemies, and the soldiers laughed, and bought, and squatted in the mud, chewing bits of dried plum, nuts, tobacco. This was a lot of nonsense. But by the time night fell, they were all gone again, and the same silence had returned to torment them. Now, there was nothing to do but to wait for Akbar, and see what he would do with them. Macnaghten's and Elphinstone's declaration was despatched, and reinforcements begged for; but nobody in the camp thought that they waited for anything but the exercise of Akbar's pleasures.

8

The next day, the enemy descended from behind the hills, all at once, like weather.

The men at the walls raised their weapons, and tensed at the sight; dozens, hundreds, thousands of men, pouring over the brow of the hill. Even at this distance, their blades flashed in the bright sunlight, and the British prepared themselves to shoot. A mass of men, an army, assembled from the far lands, and Akbar's truce seemed worthless. But they did not ride towards the cantonments; they rode directly down the hill, towards the river, and there the mass of men slowed, pooled, stopped, about a mile away. Elphinstone, behind his men, got out his telescope and peered through it. The army had stopped, he saw, at the bridge the British had built the summer before. More than that, he could not see. It was only half an hour later when the army began to move again, and there, somewhere behind, there was a flash and, two seconds later, an echoing roar. The bridge had been mined with explosives, and destroyed.

The army was patient, it seemed, and they gave the cantonments a wide berth, riding about it towards the gates of the city. This, then, was only a display. The men slowly lowered their guns and watched them go; near enough to hear the thunder of the massed Afghan cavalry. They let them go their way, knowing that soon they would be back, and the city swallowed them up.

That afternoon Akbar presented himself, with three attendants—the same three who had delivered his announcement. He was conducted directly to Macnaghten's quarters. Macnaghten stood up to greet him stonily. The Prince was young, he observed, and startlingly clean; his eyes watchful and alert, taking in the whole of the military tent in one sweep. The tent was almost full; with his suite, Macnaghten had filled his quarters with guards, sepoys, and attendants, who closed behind Akbar and the three princes of the court. The business began immediately; today, there were to be no compliments.

"We require Shah Shujah-ul-mulk," Akbar began. "He will surrender to us, and leave the Bala Hissar."

This confirmation that Shah Shujah was still alive, and walled up in his palace, was welcome, but Macnaghten only nodded.

"You are to leave my father's country and return to India," Akbar said. "You will be afforded safe passage. After your return, the Amir Dost Mohammed will be returned safely to us; we require that some of your men shall remain here as our guests until he is safely returned. You will surrender, too, all arms before any of this may happen."

"This is quite impossible," Macnaghten said. "We can agree to none of your demands. Good day, sir."

"You may wish to consider our offer, and the consequences of your refusal," Akbar said. "We are quite willing to wait while you think whether this is not, in fact, the best opportunity you are likely to have."

"There is no point—" Macnaghten said, but Elphinstone was drumming on the desk furiously. Macnaghten looked up, and Elphinstone gave a quick nod. There was nothing to discuss, but it would do no harm to make Akbar wait while all the British were brought to agreement. "Very well. The sepoys will take you to a place where you may refresh yourselves."

When they had gone, Elphinstone leapt in. "Macnaghten, we gain nothing by refusing immediately like this. Remember, Dost Mohammed does not command anybody's loyalty, or only a part of the country.

Agree, and we split Akbar's men, and throw them off their guard. Here, treachery is part of daily life—we should betray them after agreeing to their demands. There is no reason why we should not."

To Macnaghten's surprise, the other officers seemed to agree with this, and in a few minutes assent had been given; agreement would be made, and conditions extracted. Shah Shujah, after all, might prove to hold some popularity, and if Akbar's army could unite against the British, they would surely divide again when asked to support a king so many of them had reason to dislike. Akbar was sent for, again.

"After all," Macnaghten remarked while they were waiting, "they will not have forgotten so soon our generosity, and I do not believe that this is anything but Akbar's request; once the word gets out that he has evicted so generous an occupier as we have proved, there is a strong possibility that his support will melt away. Sir."

Akbar, entering, bowed, coldly.

"We have considered your offer, and consider it fair," Macnaghten said, scanning Akbar's face for any expression of surprise at this sudden change of sentiment. "We are prepared to meet your demands. We will withdraw forthwith. You yourself are to accompany us to the borders of the country, and be responsible for our safety. Four British officers will remain here in Kabul, the names of whom will be supplied to you shortly. The Amir Dost Mohammed Khan will return, and Shah Shujah removed from his present position. We are meeting, you see, all your demands rather than fall into a futile war which could only destroy you and which would damage the friendship between our two countries. In return, I would ask that this agreement remain between yourself and us, and that the other chiefs of the nation know nothing of it. That, you will agree, is a reasonable request in the circumstances. Good day, sir. We will speak again tomorrow."

A flicker of something like interest had passed over Akbar's face as the other chiefs were mentioned, but now he sank back into his calm unspeaking contempt. He nodded, turned, and left.

"We will get through this, you see," Macnaghten said. For the first time in days, he seemed imbued with confidence at his own plans. "He will say nothing, and when his allies learn, their support will vanish. He is not furthering his own interests by plotting in this extraordinary manner."

Macnaghten's suite melted away, taking their leave quietly one by one, and not meeting their chief in the eye. They were returning, as they had to, to the ramparts of the cantonments, and preferred to say nothing of what had passed. In a few minutes, there was nobody left by Macnaghten but Elphinstone; even the nazir had gone. Macnaghten turned sharply to his old sparring partner, but had nothing to say. Elphinstone shrugged, helplessly.

"What is it, sir?" Macnaghten said. "Tell me: what is it you wish to say? You wish to say something to me? Do not fix me with your eye, sir; do not stare so; if you wish to say something, say it. You wish to say something? Sir? Sir? No, sir, do not go—no—sir—this fever—this winter fever—I beg you, sir, go, go now . . ."

9

It was a week later when Macnaghten rode out of the gates of the cantonments in something like triumph, feeling thoroughly justified. In his pocket, he carried a letter from Akbar, and now the terror of the previous week had dissipated into the air. With three of his junior officers, Macnaghten was going to meet Akbar—not in the cantonments, nor in Akbar's lair in the depths of the city, but outside the walls, half a mile from the British settlement. And Akbar, certainly, had learnt what kind of man Macnaghten was, and, without direct pressure, had given way. The nazir had courted the other great princes of the city with gifts and money and promises, and Akbar's support had started to crumble beneath his feet. The letter Macnaghten carried showed that Akbar had learnt of this, and his initial demands had mysteriously diminished to no more than this. Shah Shujah to remain; the British to remain, and leave within a year, at a moment of their choice; the assassins of Burnes to be handed over for execution; and Akbar to receive £300,000 in gold and the military support of the British in future. The settlement was acceptable—more, it was impeccable, and Macnaghten rode out with the certainty that he had achieved more than anyone, more even than Burnes could have conceived possible.

The Afghans had been settled on the field of snow for some hours there, observed from the cantonments. They had set blankets on the snow, and squatted about it; there was no food evident as the English rode up, but it had, incongruously, the air of a pic-nic in the deep snow. Akbar rose, followed by his entourage. There were, Macnaghten noted, three or four of his usual followers there with him, the fine martial sirdars; but there, too, five unfamiliar faces. Akbar's court came and went, and the regular appearance and disappearance of new attendants was, the English thought, a part of his demeanour, to display what sort of men were behind him. Today, Macnaghten did not care; he looked at those faces, and felt he knew what Akbar could no longer be certain of: that some of those men, surely, were no longer Akbar's men, and were his without knowing it.

(And from the low walls, the men of England, of Wales and Scotland, stood, their thin guns raised, and watched the horsemen ride into the snow.)

Macnaghten dismounted; the others followed his lead. Mackenzie, the adjutant, seemed to hesitate for a moment; or perhaps his foot was just caught in the stirrups. Macnaghten advanced resolutely. Akbar stood there, making no gesture of welcome or acknowledgement, and Macnaghten almost felt like making a triple bow to this small imperious Prince.

"Sit," Akbar said. His manner was quite different from those of other princes of the East; the situation did not suggest an exchange of civilities, but in no circumstances, you felt, would he have troubled with trivialities before reaching the necessary point.

"Sirdar," Macnaghten said. "We have received your communication, and are grateful for it. Our principal concern has always been to preserve the good relations between our nations, and feel that on the terms you propose, that good intention may be pursued. It was never the intention of Her Majesty that we should remain here indefinitely, and since we understand that Shah Shujah will be secure in his possession of the kingdom without our continued attendance—"

"Prince," Akbar said wearily. "Let us come to the point. You have received our letter."

"Indeed," Macnaghten said. "For which we are grateful."

"You assent to its terms," Akbar said.

"We assent heartily," Macnaghten said, relieved. Akbar stretched out his hand, his empty small hand; Macnaghten, idiotically, reached forward as if to shake it, but the sirdar shook his hands irritably.

"The letter, sir," Mackenzie said, leaning forward.

"Of course, of course," Macnaghten said, and, fumbling in his pockets, extracted Akbar's letter. He handed it to Akbar, who, after a short glance, handed it to his entourage. For a few silent minutes, they passed it from hand to hand, inspecting it carefully. Macnaghten waited in silence. Finally it returned to Akbar, who handed it back to Macnaghten.

"And you assent to the terms contained in our communication," Akbar said heavily.

"Why not?" Macnaghten said, a little puzzled. Akbar gave a small glance to left and right, almost smiling; it was so difficult to tell, but anyone might have thought there was a touch of contempt in his expression. "Sir, may I beg you of the favour of learning who these gentlemen are? We are familiar with only part of Your Highness's extensive suite."

"It is of no concern," Akbar said. "They are all in the secret, Prince. They all know of our discussions. We are all—" Akbar smiled again, that mild, contemptuous smile, "—in the secret."

The sky and land were silent, all at once, for one moment, and then a great scream; so full of rage and triumph it seemed hardly human, seemed as if it could not possibly come from Akbar's open mouth. "Take them, take them!" he was crying. "*Begeer! Begeer!*" Macnaghten had no chance to move; four Afghans had fallen on him, and were dragging him away, all at once; and before Mackenzie and Trevor could move, the Afghans were on them, and their corky arms bound tight behind them. Macnaghten's face, astonished, looking about like a dog who hears gunshot and cannot understand what it means; Macnaghten, crying out in Persian, "*Az barae Khooda! Az barae Khooda!*" over and over again. Mackenzie heard it, and as he himself was being borne away, and thrown over the back of his horse, he committed it to memory. *Az barae Khooda;* what Macnaghten was screaming as he was pulled away, screaming and screaming like a wounded fox, Mackenzie did not know what it meant, and would not for many months; but in his dungeon, kept like a beast by Akbar, expecting every day his own death, he kept hold of those words, a sentence he did not understand; and in the end, he found out what Macnaghten was crying out as they took him away to kill him. Mackenzie, in the end, was released, and then he found out what Macnaghten's last cry had been. *For God's sake,* he had been crying out, his last words in a language not his own, and no one heard him but Mackenzie, who did not understand. No one saw Macnaghten's end, but that was not the last of Macnaghten; because somehow, as his trussed subordinates were led into the city, into their faces were thrust the last of Macnaghten, on seven dripping poles. The head was thrust against theirs, and Mackenzie was not likely ever to forget the weight of a human head falling against his face, or the heavy fatty film of blue over the eyes, or the look, so alive, so flaming, in the eyes of the man who held the pole and screamed for justice, and revenge, and right.

I O

In the cantonments, the men stood, and looked for command, looked for the reassuring word of order and security. But they did not know whom to look to; and as their minds went through those dead—those lucky dead, they were already learning to think—their minds alighted, incredulously, on Elphinstone. That was all there was, and they lowered their muskets, having no idea what the next day would bring, fearing to contemplate it. Elphinstone, too, stared out at the terrible empty country, echoing with the distant throaty roars of joy, and waited for some word to come from on high. In his mind was a black memory of Macnaghten; the moment when Macnaghten had dismissed them all, and before Elphinstone could go, the commander of the Army of the Indus had collapsed in a hysterical uncontrollable storm of tears and trembling, his fists clenched and flailing helplessly at the air. Even from Macnaghten, Elphinstone, now, would welcome a word, to know what to do, what action to take. But no word came from the head and limbs being passed around the bazaar in those long nights of riot. And in three days, Akbar, so leisurely, sent word, and his instructions were these: that the next day, the Army of the Indus would pick up its belongings, and return whence it came. The next day. The word spread in the cantonments, and from Elphinstone, helpless in his tent, no word came. All that terrifying day, the camp resembled a squirrel colony in the last days before winter, burrowing and discarding and packing and sorting what goods they could, white-faced as they threw what need not be taken into the mud and snow. The men and women and children, the sepoys and the camp followers, all sixteen thousand of them, followed the instructions of the new Prince of the Afghans, and prepared with all the appalled haste they were capable of; prepared to flee wherever Akbar the Great wished to send them. And the next day, at dawn, they departed; and behind them the city howled its raw *shah mat,* and the dogs of the city howled as they devoured the limbs and entrails, the body and face of Macnaghten, the Prince of the English.

TWENTY-FIVE

On 6 January, the Army of the Indus turned away from Kabul and, in the snow, began its march to Jalalabad.

Behind them rode the Afghans, firing on the rear, riding among the column, their long knives raised.

That was the first day, and the snow was crimson with blood.

In the morning of the second day, it was found that many had died in the night of the cold, and many had lost their limbs to frostbite.

In the middle of the second day, Akbar presented himself, and assured Elphinstone that he would escort them to safety.

Three hostages were given to Akbar, and the Army of the Indus halted.

That was the second day, and the snow was crimson with blood.

On the third day, the Army entered the Khoord-Kabul pass. Above them were the tribesmen, shooting down at them, and behind them were the Afghans, their guns raised and their knives falling.

It is said that Akbar rode among the people of his country, and spoke to them in a double tongue; in Persian, he called on them to spare the infidel, and then, in the language of the people, he called on them to kill the English.

That was the third day, and the snow was crimson with blood.

On the fourth day, Akbar rode again to the Army of the Indus, and, in his goodness, he took the women and the children of the infidel, nineteen in number, and removed them to a place of safety. The infidel army watched the women and the children go, and marched on.

That day, the snow fell hard, and the Army of the Indus went forward blindly, falling underneath the blows of wrath, dying in the snow.

Akbar was wise, and he told the princes of the army that under his guidance, all would be well for them; and the people of his nation fell on their enemy without mercy.

The silver of the knives, the black of the night, the white of the snow, the red of the blood.

That was the fourth day, and the snow was crimson with blood.

On the fifth day, the English were seized with a terrible despair, and did not stop, but marched on, through the night. But Akbar had foreseen this, and, there, in the night, they found that the pass was blocked with a great wall the Prince had caused to be built. The Afghans fell upon them from the rear, and there in the dark they died; every man died; every one; under the knives of the Afghans; and in his mercy, Akbar paused at the last, and saw the last man alive over the wall, and let him go.

"Let them know," he said. "Let the English know what Akbar has done. There goes the messenger, and he will bear the tale. Let him ride to safety, with his terrible burden, and the world will know of the deeds of the Afghans, and they will tremble."

The horsemen of Afghanistan gathered about their Prince, and listened humbly. How lucky they were! How great! How blessed are their children and their children's children, whose forefathers were the first to know of the greatness of Akbar, whose deeds will never be forgotten until the world turns to dust.

They rode away, each by himself, his noble heart soaring. That was the end of the fifth day, and the snow from there to Kabul was crimson, crimson, crimson, with the blood of the infidel. The empire was cleansed, and washed clean with blood, and the princes of the empire rode over the fallen warriors, and their wicked bones crushed like dry bread under the glory and might of the Afghans.

TWENTY-SIX

In Gloucestershire it rained.

The seasons here grew together, and the indifferent months passed with the steady slow mixture of weather, and it always came down to rain; slow, dripping, unstopping. The water fell, not torrentially but steadily, and the battlements dripped into the moat, onto the terrace, onto the heavy jutting sills. Water gathered where it could, and dripped into the unattended rooms of that empty house, rotting away the substance of Queen's Acre, bit by bit. The estate was silent, and the house silent too; only a distant crow, cawing its misery into the rain, and the tapping sound of the rain, a single drop, close by, and the greater massed hiss further off. No ghosts walked at Queen's Acre, but the tap, tap, tap of the rain was like the step of a phantom, feeling his way with a stick, and the hiss of the rain was like the far-off noise of crowds of ghosts, feeling their slow undying way through the bowed-down groves of trees, sullen as September. Thousands of them; uncountable thousands, falling from the sky, and making a single sound, and then they were gone for ever, seen by no one. It rained thus at every season of the year, indifferent to the circuit of the great earth about the sun, falling from the cold dark Gloucestershire skies onto the cold dark Gloucestershire earth with no suggestion of summer, spring, autumn, winter. The house knew this, and did not mark the seasons; it was winter now, but that did not seem to matter. It was the day, the first nameless day, which falls after Twelfth Night, but for this house, all days were nameless, and the long season at the heart of winter had passed through the house without anyone acknowledging it. The heart of winter; it had taken hold, here; it never arrived, it never left. Christmas and its twelve attendants, the twelve days following like apostles, were nothing here. There was nothing but the rain, and that needed no acknowledgement.

In her lair sat the mistress of the house, sat Bella. It was the room she spent her days in, and it had, over the years, turned into her life. Two niches had been adapted by the estate carpenter, long ago, and held the five hundred books she liked and read, over and over; a ragged selection of bindings, rather than a wall of imperious unbroached authority, it merely held the books she liked in no especial order. It was nice to reach out, and have one's hand fall upon a book read before, a book certain to please, because it had pleased before. But the shelves of books filched from the long-locked library of the house presented a chaos to the critical eye. The third volume of Dryden jostled with *The Wanderer*, a slender satire about poets drinking from skulls next to a knee-high folio which contained every facial expression known to man with, no doubt, serious explanations in German. Her work was thrown casually over the sofa; a screen cover, begun seven years before, never to be finished, but good to hold and dream. An oak table—barely larger than a loo table—had been placed here, and here Bella ate with Henry; on it, now, the remains of luncheon still sat, unregarded, although the tea things had been brought in ten minutes before. On another table, nearby, stood a half-finished game of Patience, at the point it had reached a week before; she did not think it would come out, now, but left it, with its piles of blunt, bright, regal faces, as it was. Nobody saw Bella but her son, and the servants, and she trusted the love of one, and did not consider the feelings or opinions of the other, so her pink dress was old, and somewhat stained. She stood, now, at the window, and thought nothing. All that she could see was her own; the terrace, beneath, shining phosphorescently in the gloom with wet moss; the moat she crossed once a month; the wilderness which could now no longer be distinguished from the wild neglected lawn, the walks and beds buried under years-long growth as the land took back its own, the smooth hills rising, the sunken dark copse Elizabeth once so loved. She looked at it, and her eye might have been looking at nothing, so familiar was the land this window framed. All her mind was filled with the pat of water, the tick of drops from the gutter onto the sill, popping its mournful tattoo; she saw nothing but the slow slide of a drop down the leaded window; falling, holding, pausing, then joining with another drop and continuing its path downwards. Stop—on—stop—on—following its imperatives, its mysterious path.

Henry was with his tutor, and her hours were long and empty today; they weighed on her. She went back to her chair, and reached for her book for a moment. She read on. *The Doctor is with us. Aunt Nell is in love with him. He ordered his matters, and came to town at Lady L.'s request and mine*—Bella turned back to discover who was writing, and saw the heading at the beginning of the chapter, "Lady G. to Miss Byron"—*and Beauchamp's, that we might sooner come at my brother's Letters.* She stopped. These people; who were they? She forgot. Lady G., Miss Byron, the Doctor, Aunt Nell, Lady L., Beauchamp; they could be anyone. And yet someone had created them, and thousands of readers had cared about their fate, quite as if they had been flesh and blood. She had no idea who they were—in an hour of idle inattentiveness, they had gone from her mind—and for a moment, her thoughts ranged idly, creating them for herself. Lady G., a woman with a toothy face like an ass's and untidy hair; Miss Byron, who talked indiscreetly; the Doctor, who was kind to women if they remembered to weep; Aunt Nell, a beauty of thirty-two; Lady L., a ballroom martinet; poor witty Beauchamp, who had fifteen thousand a year and a stutter which made him sweat and meant that his best jokes were confided to his lucky correspondents. It seemed to her, then, as she lay back in the chair and looked at her land and her rain, that all her life she had been hearing names of men and women, and discovering what properties they might have, what goodnesses they would be capable of, and as her imagination roamed, they came to life and presented themselves to her, and for a season even she herself believed them real.

All at once she got up, and set the book down. She had a strange fancy, now, to take a walk, and see everything that was hers. There was a bell pull set into the wall of Bella's chamber, which she almost never used; the rhythms of her day meant that the servants came quite often enough, to bring meals or remove them, to bring Henry in or to ask for instructions. There was no need to summon anyone; they would be with her quite soon enough, on the whole. But she went to the bell pull, and tugged it; somewhere in the house, a bell would be sounding, and a maid rising without enthusiasm to attend the mistress. It was odd, but now, she felt impatient, and waited to be attended with her fingers drumming on the table.

It was lucky that the bell summoned the housekeeper.

"I have an odd fancy," Bella said casually. "I should like to open up the house, and look at it for an hour or two."

"Madam?" Mrs. Bruton said.

"For no reason," Bella said. "But if you would be so good as to lend me your keys?"

Mrs. Bruton reached into her basket, and extracted the heavy set of keys, handing them to Bella.

"Will that be all, madam?"

Bella dismissed her. She sat there with the keys for a few minutes, as if this was all she truly wanted; and then, all at once, impatiently, she leapt up and left the room. First, her mamma's bedchamber, dusty and cold; here mamma had died, and dying had pressed on Bella her diamond brooch, the brooch Bella always wore. Then the Chinese room Elizabeth always loved best. "When I am grown," she always used to say, "I shall always sleep in the Chinese room, and dream most beautifully, every night." Papa's bedchamber, and—because Bella, now, would omit nothing—his dressing room, bare as a box, and his bathroom. In the washbasin, a spider crouched; Bella benevolently left it, and went on.

The grander rooms were downstairs, and when she had done with the locked rows of bedchambers, Bella went there. There was no one to see her now, and she swept down the stairs, skirt gathered in one hand, nodding to left and right like an empress. And she was eighteen again, and the great ball to mark the end of her childhood was just stirring into life; the faces tipped upwards, watching her descent with adoration. The library, the pilfered library, and here it was that Bella, so often, had stood and wept at her father's fierce reprimands; the music room, that perfect wedding gift, like the translucent inside of a blown egg; the red dining room; the drawing room; the saloon; and then the ballroom. So full of her life, this house; and every memory was false.

Quite false. Mamma had died in London; her father had never reprimanded her, in the library or otherwise; there had been no ball here for two generations; Elizabeth had never expressed any particular love for one room over another; and the memories fell on her like rain. Here was her imagined life, the life in her head, and in the ballroom she paused, and thought that life through from beginning to end.

There was one story she invented which was real: she dreamt it, but she knew it was true. Christmas, now, had come: and it had been at another Christmas she had been banished: and at another Christmas her father had died. After she had gone, he stayed in London. For a while, he had continued as he had done, dressing and going out, with one daughter the fewer. But then his life had started to grow smaller, and he left the house less often. Some days, he would go from his bedchamber to his study, and remain there the whole day, the trays of food returned untouched to the kitchen. No one disturbed him. And his occasional walks became fewer, and fewer, and in a year, he never left the house.

What was he thinking, there, in his dark shrouded study, with his books and his opium? Nothing: oblivion had settled over him, and he waited, patiently, with no one but the ruby witch and his own empty brain. From the study, for months on end, there came no sound but pacing footsteps in the dark and the clink of the bottle being freed from the tantalus. To those black rites none was admitted: in his grief there were no sharers. From time to time, the household met him on the stairs, his eyes blazing in his gaunt white face, and each of them shrank into a deep bow, but for days and weeks, nothing was heard or seen of him, and he backed with a warning expression into his own catafalque.

It was late in the year, two years after Bella's final departure, when the household began to hear new noises from his quarters: deep, rasping, human noises, retching coughs, cries of pain instantly muted, the noise of black matter being torn up from the belly of the old Colonel. Still no one went up; the tray was delivered at the set times, and returned at the set times, and the Colonel was not seen, but only heard. Elizabeth, once, attempted the entry, distressed by the noises of pain, the unremitting evidence of physical anguish, but her offer to call for the physician was refused. The Colonel was weak, and wretched, but his eyes could still blaze contempt, and she backed out, helplessly.

By the time the Colonel could no longer refuse help, it was too late. A maid heard a heavy fall, late one night, from the study, and, neglecting all commands, rushed in. He was lying on the carpet, a thin stream of vomit from his mouth, and his arm at an unnatural angle where he had fallen, hard, against the divan. There was no Colonel now to reject help, and Elizabeth, roused from her bed, sent immediately for the physician.

How the Colonel died, no physician could explain: he was weak, and undernourished, and frail, but none of that need have led so rapidly to his death. But it did: in ten days, the Colonel sank by degrees, his eyes emptying by the day. They could do nothing but supply opium for the pain: and what pain had required the opium of the decades before these last days, no one could say. He said nothing; there were no last words; he did not call for Bella, and Bella did not come. That was how he died, and Bella told herself the story, inventing it as she went, and knowing that she told herself the exact, the incontrovertible truth, incontrovertible as the empty funeral, the lines of empty ducal carriages outside in a display, no more, of grief.

It was there, in the dark empty acres of the Adam ballroom, that she heard it. A strange noise, coming from somewhere far away, outside the house. An unfamiliar noise, unlike anything she knew, cutting through the cold murmur of the rain, the sobbing distant rooks. It was a sound like something breaking, like a huge violin string stretched to its final point and then snapping; a crack and a twang all at once. Somewhere, the noise was loud, somewhere far away, and she sought it again, her ears sharpened; but it did not sound again. It was the sound of something breaking, out there, and as the memory of it faded like an echo, it was like something breaking in her; it might be the sound of grief. She was alone in her silent dark house; she had unlocked everything now, and it was all empty.

Perhaps she stood there for minutes, or hours; the gloom of day was seceding into the gloom of night, and as she stood there, she started to understand that her life here was at last over. Her long, slow, imaginary life. The moment had come to go into the world of substance and flesh. Not to return to it, because now she felt that she had never truly gone into the world. But now the moment had come, for Henry's sake, and for hers. She wanted her son by her, to hold and kiss, but that could wait. What had come to an end there, in the dark January ballroom, she could not say; what newness was beginning, now, she would not guess.

She came out of the ballroom, slowly, and locked the door behind her. The housekeeper was there, waiting, an expression of mild concern on her face, and, wordlessly, Bella handed her back the keys. Together they walked back upstairs. Bella said nothing until they were almost at the door of her chamber, and then she turned to her, smiling a little.

"I think, next week, we must go to London, Henry and I," she said. And then something odd; the housekeeper bobbed, as if she had been expecting Bella to say this very thing, and perhaps she had; perhaps she, too, had heard the crack of the breaking string. "I trust you will make the necessary arrangements? The beginning of the week, I think."

She went alone into the chamber, and shut the door behind her. Lord, Lord, how tired she was, all at once. The windows were wet with rain, and she went to look out. She had so much to do, now, all of a sudden, but all that could wait. The clock chimed five, singingly; and shortly Henry would be with her. She hoped he had enjoyed his day. But then, he always did. She sat down, and prepared to wait for her son.

TWENTY-SEVEN

The fort at Jalalabad was the colour of rock, and rose from the earth like a desert outcrop. Massive, square, and blunt, it seemed hardly to have been built by men. Its asymmetrical blocks and buttresses presented, rather, the appearance of something formed in the course of aeons by the slow processes of geology, and discovered by explorers, who then inhabited it. It was lost in this terrible waste, like a system of caves. The fort was all but invisible until the traveller was almost upon it, melting into the yellow-brown rock; it emerged, from nothing, a sudden gigantic mountain, its walls like smooth cliffs. No army, the centuries had learnt, could break these brutal facades, and each assault broke over it like the Wind of a Hundred and Twenty Days; ferocious, howling, and in the end devoid of substance.

For the moment, the British were here, and for the moment, they hid and crouched inside like rabbits. The sentries were posted, and watched at the gates for day after day, but nothing came. Night after night fell, and the officer of the watch came to General Sale and told what he had seen; nothing. From the west came no further word, and the English were immobile within their walls. On Sale's table were three letters. The first reassured him that no help was required or needed; he had read it, and ordered preparations to be made for a sortie in force. The second, a week later, had demanded support, and contained Elphinstone's declaration of the utter hopelessness of the position in Kabul. They were still readying themselves, however, when the third letter had arrived with its unspeakable news. Sale read it, and learnt that the Army of the Indus was in full retreat. He ordered his men to stand down, seeing in his mind's eye the loss of not one, but two armies. And then they waited in the desert silence. But no word came, and nothing appeared on the horizon.

It was the afternoon, and the watch had just changed, when something was seen. Something, out there, in the bleak deserts which surrounded the fort. The officer of the watch was summoned, and raised his telescope. Out there was a small wavering shape, moving with incomprehensible languor. From here, the figure hardly seemed to be progressing forward; it drifted and swayed like a galleon at anchor, seen from shore. The officer of the watch sent for Sale, who appeared within a minute, his coat unbuttoned. The shape resolved itself; it was, incredibly, a rider. For some minutes, they thought it a riderless horse, but then they saw more clearly what the burden on the back of the animal was. That burden, lolling about—left—right—back—forward—until it seemed impossible it should not fall—that, that was—it was a man, at the last inch of consciousness, and clinging on somehow.

They stood there, watching without belief. It might have been a headless corpse, bound to a limping, exhausted horse. Closer it came. So slowly, but the horse somehow seemed to know where safety lay.

Abruptly, Sale came to himself. "Go and bring him in," he muttered, and turned heel and went. The men stood there for a moment. Behind the solitary black rider making his insensate path towards them, there was nothing and nobody to be seen.

Three officers rode out. From the fort, they seemed unnaturally, indecently lively as they approached the broken figure. They seemed to circle him in nervous inspection. The horse did not stop at their approach, but carried on with its slow awful tread as if it had been blinded. The man on the horse, too, made no kind of effort, lolling and swaying from side to side, drunk with exhaustion. The officers dismounted, and came towards him, cautiously. One took the bridle of the horse, and, with a shudder which could be seen even from the fort, the animal halted, its head falling down almost to between its forelegs. The two other officers reached up to the man, and, between them, tenderly, they loosened him from his seat, and let him fall, so slowly, to the side, into a pair of strong waiting arms. They placed him traverse over the saddle of one of their horses, and then, on foot, leading their mounts, they returned to the fort.

At the open gates, twenty soldiers stood gaping. When the little party was inside, and the man lowered again to the ground, everyone gathered round. None of them said anything as water was brought, and held to the mouth of the man. He was not dead, and drank a little, helplessly, like a child. Most of it ran down the sides of his face, as he coughed and spluttered. Sale pushed his way through, and stood looking at the man lying on the floor; looked at what everyone knew was what remained of the Army of the Indus. "His name is Brydon," he said eventually.

For three days, Brydon was left alone, in bed. His horse did not survive the afternoon. By the end of the week, he was a little stronger, and started to tell his story. The story Brydon had to tell, over and over again, was a single one, and it was all he could tell; it was the story of how an army died. Brydon was the only person who saw that death, and who could tell it at all; but it so often occurred to his listeners, then, in Jalalabad and for the rest of his life, that he could not know everything they wished to know. An army died, there, in five days; but the army was sixteen thousand people; and sixteen thousand stories found their ending there. Sixteen thousand stories; sixteen Scheherazades, telling night after night, would never be done with their telling, and every single story ending in the same way.

Or almost every story; because from the agonizing retellings emerged an appalling, tiny hope. Brydon told his story, and it was simple and brief; and then he told it again, and it was a little longer; and then he told it again, and had remembered something. A junior officer had been deputed to sit by Brydon, and note down what he said. Brydon's face was bruised and battered and wrecked against the clean white sheets, and the junior officer listened to whatever he had to say. Brydon's recovery was not certain yet, and what he remembered must be recorded. In a few retellings, he recalled something; it seemed, out of nothing.

"No," he said suddenly. "Not everyone. Some of them returned with the Sirdar. That's right. The fourth day out of Kabul. Akbar. He said—I think he said—that he would take some of the women back with them, and they would be safer there and Elphinstone agreed. I don't know why. Elphinstone, too."

"Elphinstone?"

"Elphinstone went back, with Akbar, he went too."

"How many?" the officer asked gently.

"Many?"

"How many went back with Akbar?"

Brydon said nothing.

"A hundred? Two hundred?"

"Perhaps twenty," Brydon said.

"Were they killed?" the officer said.

"I did not see them killed," Brydon said placidly. "I saw them being led away, though. That was the last thing I saw."

"Who were they, Akbar's prisoners?" the officer asked. "Whom did Akbar take? Can you remember?"

Brydon shook his head, sinking back in exhaustion. The officer persevered.

"What happened to them?"

"I did not see them killed," Brydon said again, and closed his eyes.

Brydon grew in strength, slowly, and told what he could, over and over, but that was all he could say. The women and children and Elphinstone had been led away, and nothing more had been heard of them, and perhaps nothing more ever would be.

Brydon had been there, but he had not seen every ending to every story, and even what he had seen, he could not always retell. Did he not know, or could he not say, how Frampton died on the first day, raising his arm up to the sky as a horseman rode at full pelt amongst them, slicing his snickering blade down upon Frampton's bare neck, down, again, and a third time as the blood spurted in the air and fell on the packed dirty snow? Or how Macnaghten's nazir, so tremendous a personage, was found on the second morning, his face and hands black with the frost, his lips drawn back in a black animal snarl? Digby was shot in the back, the third day, scrambling up the crumbling sides of the canyon. Brydon never saw how Elphinstone died, in Akbar's prisons, shitting and puking into his blankets, crying and yelping out, and knowing nothing of where he was, died regretted by no one. Perhaps he did not know that McVitie was there, at the last, on the fifth day, was trampled over by the horses, and lay there screaming for half an hour; could not tell how he, too, had ended, taking his own rifle with resolve and shooting himself in the head. Brydon had seen so much, had seen so many men fall, and there were many thousands of stories which he had seen reach their end. But there was only one story he could tell, of how an army, all at once, died; and it stuttered from the tongue of the incurable doctor, again and again and again.

He told that story so often, and each time, General Sale crept into the room as he was talking, and stood, listening, just outside the circle of the candlelight, his eyes wide and empty. Each time of the telling, Sale listened, saying nothing, and when silence fell, he turned away, and left with his face white and sick. No one spoke to him, and he seemed to wish to be left alone. His aide-de-camp followed him from place to place, saying nothing, wishing the old man would confide or break down. It was three weeks after Brydon had reached Jalalabad, and still lying, feeble, in bed, that the aide-de-camp went to his quarters, and sat with the doctor. For half an hour, he questioned him directly, and found out what he knew. Then he left him, exhausted, to sleep again, and, summoning up all his bravery, he went to General Sale and, unbidden, offered him what Brydon had told him. It was what the General, he knew, wanted to know, and terrible as it was, he had to be told. The General sat and looked at the aide-de-camp, summoning up all his resources, and learnt what he feared to know, and feared to ask; that there was every possibility that Florentia had not died in the march, but had been taken hostage by Akbar, and led away by the blood-steeped Prince. That was all that anyone now could know, and where she was now—what she was now—what had fallen upon her could not be told, and perhaps never would be known. The General listened to what his aide-de-camp had been brave enough to ask, what his fear had shrunk from, and, when the officer had talked himself out, his eyes fixed firmly on the wall behind his General, he shook his head, and with a wave of his hand, silently dismissed the man. What thoughts were in the old man's head, no one could know; what look came into the old man's deadened eyes when the doors were shut, and the lights extinguished, and he was alone once again, was not for them to imagine.

There was nothing further the fort could or would do with Brydon, and he was left alone with his amanuensis. He remembered a little more every day, but he lacked for willing listeners. For some weeks, the watch kept an eye on the horizon, waiting for others to appear. Perhaps when the snow melted, the remnants of the army would emerge; perhaps a few had found shelter and safety among the tribesmen of the hills, and in time would make their way cautiously to Jalalabad. But day after day they gazed at the horizon, and slowly they came to accept that no one would come.

Only one came.

One day, after weeks, months of waiting: months which taught the fort, taught every man in it that there is one thing worse than despair, and that thing is hope. It was late in the afternoon, one cold day. One of the unpredictable caravans of native pedlars, a line of slow horses loaded with goods and women, trudged before the fort, and, as it passed, a small child was let down from the horses.

The caravan did not stop. The child stood there in front of the fort, and irresolutely ran after them; but they did not look back. The child stopped, and burst into a storm of wails. The men opened up, wondering, and went for the child. It was a small girl, in Afghan dress, but as they looked at her tear-stained dirty face, it was apparent that she was European. The kind private who knelt by her took his handkerchief, and with a little spit and a few kisses cleaned and calmed her. Her tears died down, and, by degrees, so did the private's. She looked up at them, as if recognizing something, and said a sentence in the pretty rustic Persian she had learnt. "My mother and father are infidels," she said. "But I am a Mussulman." She was fat and well, and proved to be the Andersons' little daughter. Of the Andersons themselves, there was no sign.

Brydon remained in his room for weeks, like the well-guarded treasure of the fort. It was nearly a month before he appeared in public, walking round the battlements with an air of puzzlement. It was as if this now seemed to him a strange way for anyone to spend his life, walled up in a strange land, staring out at emptiness. His presence had become inexplicably embarrassing, and he was avoided by most of the men. His story had been told, and it could not be listened to or endured. The fort had all seen and handled the thing which had saved his life, a French novel which he had placed in his hat and which had been sliced almost in two by an Afghan sword in the course of the army's last day. In time, that would become a relic, like the regiment's salt pot, fashioned from a horse's hoof, souvenir of the regiment's great day at Waterloo. Not yet, however, and no one wished to see it again, or talk of the last days of the army. It could have been them. Only Brydon wanted to go on talking, and Brydon was avoided.

No one cared to disturb the General, and Sale, too, preferred to keep to his quarters. It was nearly two months before any communication came from Akbar. It was brought by an insolent Afghan sirdar. The man appeared, his hand tight on the handle of his sword, and gave the letter to the officer of the watch without dismounting, turned, and rode smartly away. The letter was taken to Sale, and, with a native, he patiently read what Akbar had to say. No reference was made in it to the last days of the Army of the Indus; nothing was said of what Akbar had done, and it seemed sedulously to avoid any tone of regret or exultation. The letter merely informed Sale, with the minimum of formalities, that the hostages were well, and that, in one month, when Dost Mohammed had been returned safely to his kingdom, they would be delivered to Jalalabad. The letter concluded with the information that Elphinstone had died, and here there was, perhaps, a touch of regret and condolence as Akbar added that all that could have been done for him was done in his last illness. Sale could not share any regret; Elphinstone had, by dying, saved himself the worst humiliation of all, to see the disasters of the war laid at his door. And that, no one would have doubted. There would have been no one but Elphinstone left alive to blame; and now, there was no one at all left to blame. It was as well Akbar regretted Elphinstone's death, because no one else would mourn him. The letter said no more; it made no reference to the identity of the prisoners. Sale handed it back to the translator with no comment.

He made no comment, either, when, in the coming days, word was received from the Governor General that what Akbar had requested had been granted. Dost Mohammed was released from his Indian captivity, and was to be permitted to return to his kingdom, to rule if he could. There was nothing else, in truth, to be done. Somehow India had learnt that Shah Shujah, that puppet emperor walking on rose petals, had met his end. They had abandoned him to his enemies in Kabul, and the long feud between the princely families had run its inevitable course, once the English were gone. How Shah Shujah had been killed, no one knew. No one could think, or cared to, how an emperor who had spent so much of his life devising the last torments of his enemies could face his own horrible death. No one could wish that it had been merciful. Jalalabad, and Calcutta, and London, had now supped full of horrors, and if little information had been received concerning the last hours of Shah Shujah-ul-mulk, none was requested. It was enough that he was dead, and certainly so. Enough to know, too, that Dost Mohammed was returning to what had always been his, and that the men and women Akbar had held were returning. Who they were, what they had endured, these things Jalalabad did not know, and were not told. They did not talk of it. They had too much to spare themselves.

The life of the fort was quiet and empty. Watch succeeded watch, and nothing was looked for or seen. It was the most peaceful period anyone could remember, and beyond the blue hills to the west, the gates of the Dost's Empire were closed for ever. Behind those walls, there was silence; or perhaps the empire, made whole again, was roaring with joy. Perhaps it was torn apart by war and murder. But here there was no word, and it was no longer any concern of the English. Dost Mohammed and his court were returned, and there was still no word of the men and women his son had held. Sale sat in his quarters, day after day, and was not disturbed.

It was spring before any word came. A letter was brought to the gates of the fort, from an English officer, Eyre. The hostages were near, very near; no more than a day's march west of here. They were weak, but healthy and in good spirits. Eyre said they had no complaints of their treatment. Their escort had brought them to this place with trust and consideration, and left them there, turning back to Kabul. The hostages were alone now, and wrote begging for the kindness of an escort to be sent from Jalalabad to bring them to safety.

The aide-de-camp brought Eyre's letter to Sale in his darkened room. Sale read it carefully, making no comment.

"Send a party to fetch them," he said tonelessly. "I am glad Eyre is well."

"Sir," the aide-de-camp said. "You have not looked at the last pages of his letter. Look, he has thought to send us a list of those in his party, and look—"

Sale turned over the pages. There was no expression in his face, but his hand was trembling. The aide-de-camp would not say, but he knew what Sale would find in the list, and what he would look for first. He cursed Eyre for writing the names in random order; it would take the old man a few minutes to find the name. Still, he would say nothing. It was for the General to find the name of his wife, buried down there among lists of other wives, children, jemaudars, and discover that she was still alive. There were twenty or twenty-five names there, all familiar; and one of the names was that of Florentia Sale.

Sale opened his mouth, as if trying to speak, but he could say nothing. The aide-de-camp stepped forward smartly, and took the list back from the old General, turning and going before the General could dismiss him. He dreaded seeing the old man cry.

Sale would not move from his room still, and when the watch saw the party approaching, word had been received that he was in the guard-room, and the prisoners should be conducted directly to him. That was Sale's word, but everyone took it for granted that he meant only Floren-tia. The rest could wait. That was all, then, this knot approaching so fast towards the fort; this little knot of humanity, treated with such care and defensiveness, like well-bundled china. The solicitude of the men was evi-dent even from the battlements. They approached, a small band of thirty or so, and, at the orders of the captain of the watch, the great gates of the fortress were flung open, to greet them in like heroes. Behind them, the gates would shut, slowly, slowly, and the story would end. Here they come, then, from the west, bearing no gifts but themselves; and, as they come, the incredulous guards see a face lifted in something like defiance, to claim what heroism they can. Incredulously, the guards look on, as they stand at the yawning gates, and see faces they know; thinner, whiter, harder, but faces they know, as if from some previous life. Mrs. Sturt, looking up as if daring anyone to question her right to be here and alive; she carries an infant in her arms. Here is Eyre, his arm bound up in band-ages, and looking down at the earth, his neck flopping, riding under some invisible burden; and by him, there is Florentia. The men will normally cheer at anything, but now they are silent. The war has wrought great alteration in them all, as it swept through the lands and their lives like the burning Wind, and the strangest change of all is the one wrought on Flo-rentia. Because Florentia looks directly forward into the bright winter sun unblinking, unforgiving, audacious, and she is not changed at all. She is helped from her horse, and led to Sale, waiting for her in the guardroom of the fortress.

The war is not over, but the story is. And in the end, in the stories, in the circuses, it will come down to this; the nurses of the West will hunch by candlelight over their wide-eyed charges and tell them the story, and this is what it will come down to, this last scene. The war is not over; still to come is the revenge of the British, as they ride in force to Kabul, in the righteous angelic fury which, blazing high in them, will turn to flame, and consume the great bazaar of Kabul; and then they will leave, leave the smoking ruins of Kabul, and ride back to their Indian stronghold as if the devil himself was pursuing them, never again to return. That is still to come, but when the nurses tell the story, this is their last scene; a man stiff as a ramrod, waiting in a guardroom, hardly knowing what to expect.

Sale stands there, and the door opens. He can hardly look, although he knows who it is standing there. It is Florentia, his wife. Behind her, the adjutants of the fort crowd together. They could not have restrained themselves if they had tried. He stands there, and his eyes are pained with being kept open, like a wanderer in the driest deserts. He looks at her, and she is just the same. He cannot speak, and cannot move. Fighting Bob; she looks at him, and the expression on her face is just as it was. She has somehow kept the last unspeakable months from marking her. But he looks at her, into her face, and there, there, what is it, stirring the surface of her flesh like a noiseless tiger, moving to pounce, unseen, deep in a grove of bamboo? Some reproach is there, some tight rage, some knowledge which, if she talked and told for day after day, she could never share with Sale. He knows it. By degrees, the officers behind her fall silent. Sale and Florentia are before each other, and for the first time in months, each knows the other not to be dead. Never again will Sale sit and think through the thousand deaths his wife could have died. They are restored to each other, and all, surely, is well. But Sale cannot speak. He walks forward five paces, unable to do anything other, and she looks directly into his face. Before that look, he shrinks. What he can do, he does. He places his hand on her shoulder, and he grips her tightly. "Old girl," he says, his voice drying and choking. "Old—"

More than that, he cannot do. With a few strides, he leaves the room, not looking behind at his Eurydice. She does not follow him. The aide-de-camp walks briskly after the General, wondering, through the parting crowd of officers, expectant at the scene. Sale goes through to the gate of the fort, his head cast down, walking as quickly as he can. There, the tired horses of the party are still standing, still saddled. Sale waves aside the stable-boys, and mounts one. The gate of the fort is opened a few feet again. Sale, followed by his mounted adjutant, spurs his horse and rides out into the desert.

The adjutant has a job to keep up with the old man, who rides like fury. It is a silent hour later before he pauses. The adjutant catches up and stops, but Sale says nothing. The country is bare of habitation, of vegetation, bare rock. There is nothing to be seen but miles of rock, stretching far away to the edges of the sky. That is what they all died for. The fort is left far behind. The two of them sit there on their exhausted horses in the barren cold desert. The sun is starting to set, and finally the adjutant can no longer endure to be silent.

"General," the young man blurts out. Sale's face is turned away from him; he is gazing furiously at the horizon. "General, I congratulate you."

Sale turns finally, and looks directly at the subaltern. His face contorts, twists, wriggles; he is quite unable to say a word. Whether he is trying to suppress something, or to force something out, his face contorts. And then, all at once, he turns his horse away, and digs his spurs in. The subaltern watches the old man gallop away, the dust beneath the hooves rising in great angry spurts, and lets him go; and the sounds of the hooves diminish, fade, fall into silence, as the figure shrinks and falls into the landscape, a man riding, a fly buzzing, a speck of dirt, nothing, nothing, nothing.

This, then, was the second virtuous journey of the Amir Dost Mohammed Khan. The bonfires were lit in Kabul, and another on the horizon, and a third on the horizon's horizon, and so, a chain of fires, stretching eastwards across the curving earth without a break, from the city of the Dost to the Dost in exile. And horsemen rode through the day and through the night to bring the Dost the news of his triumph, passing the message from rider to rider, and happy the man who was admitted to the presence of the Amir, and, kneeling, brought the great news to the ears of his king. The Dost heard the news with joy, and bent to kiss the messenger. He ordered his household to assemble, and before a further day could pass, the Amir made ready for his journey. Made ready for his second journey, the second virtuous journey of the Amir Dost Mohammed Khan; his return to the city that loved him.

With his court he rode westwards, and when the noble horse of the Amir trod on the rich soil of his empire, the Amir and all his princes wept for joy. The Amir halted, and dismounted; and there, in the day, beneath the Afghan sky, he kissed the Afghan earth, knowing that never again would he leave it. His empire was returned to him, and if he did not forsake it, it would repay him with loyalty, and love.

He rode into the ways of Kabul, clad all in white, his white-robed princes about him, and the city roared its joy, its blazing fires, its yelling throats, its guns cracking into the bright summer sky. He rode through the streets, slowly, reaching down from his horse and taking the hand of any man who wished to run forward and touch his great Emperor. There were many such. The Amir Dost Mohammed Khan rode, so slowly, through the press of men, his eyes and his heart full of joy, and at length, he came to the gates of his palace, to the gates of the Bala Hissar. They were flung open, and the Amir paused, and spoke in his ringing voice. "Let these gates never be closed again to my people," he said. "Let them be forever shut against those who wish my people harm." And the empire, all at once, roared its fiery approval.

Later that night, from the portals of the Emperor's palace, the Emperor looked down upon the jewelled orchard city, and was pleased; and by his side stood his son, Akbar, who saved his father's kingdom, and the Emperor was proud. The city, too, was proud, proud of the Dost who had left in grief and returned to them in triumph, and gazed up at the palace of the Dost as at the mansions of heaven. "My son," the Emperor said, and his wise eyes blazed with love and glory, and he said no more.

And so the tale is done, and justice restored, and wisdom and virtue triumphed. Ended, the interlude of the English and their vainglory; over in four winters; ended, that mulberry empire, that season of wrong. And forever afterwards, when the children of the Dost's empire were gathered together, and they told each other tales of the past to while away a long cold night, they would talk of the great deeds of these years. And father would tell son, and when the son grew to manhood, he would tell his son, and the triumph of the Dost would not be forgotten until Afghanistan itself was destroyed. Let the city chant its uncadenced joy; let the nightingales in celestial flocks descant the empire's unending glory. The world shall hear the tale of the retreat of the English before the wisdom and greatness of Dost Mohammed, and the world shall learn what the Afghans are, and tremble at the show of their might. Fear may be learnt: awe may be taught.

The tale is done, and it ends here, with the Emperor in his palace, preparing to rule again, looking down at his great city. With Dost Mohammed, greatest of the Afghans, who barely blinks as guns are fired to mark his splendour, whose reign was of calm and plenty, whose name be blessed in the presence of the children of the Afghans and their children's children and their children's children's children, who, for the rest of his virtuous reign, considers the English from time to time; and his thoughts are strange, as into his mind comes the memory of one face; comes the memory of Burnes, who tried for greatness, whose greatness failed; comes a face, and, when it comes, Dost Mohammed remembers a man with eyes blue as the sky; and his feelings are kind, as he remembers him. Sing, Dost, sing of your worthy enemy, and offer thanks that He who made all things afforded you an adversary worthy of your greatness, and rewarded your humility with empire. An Englishman; and the Dost's mind sings on, in silence, and knows that the Dost, for a time, admired him; remembers him in friendship, and nothing else.

EPILOGUE

The orchestra swelled in its fervent adagio, and General Sale rose to his feet. He raised his hands to his face, clutching his expert expression. For a moment, the hushed multitude could not see what he was seeing, but then a female figure emerged from the darkness at the back of the stage. A low murmur came from the upper seats in the house; she was their favourite, and to see her as Lady Sale exceeded all expectations. The murmur did not drop, but fell seamlessly into a humming, as they all recognized a slow grand tune in the orchestra, and unthinkingly joined in. In the flies, two boys crouched, steadily reaching into the box of torn-up paper, flinging it far over the stage. The paper snow fell prettily over the scene. This was what they paid for, and why they came to Astley's circus.

The two figures stood, ten feet apart, unmoving, waiting for the audience to start weeping. She might have been a statue, there with her hand in the air—and how well she had done, last season, in *The Winter's Tale*! The orchestra grew more impassioned, and the gods sang along, and, now, she was moving forward, towards her husband. One uncertain step;

one more; and then, half-running, she came to him and they fell into a marvellous embrace, face-front to the audience.

"My dearest husband," she projected, her painted face tipped back.

"My dearest wife," he crowed, and the entire house burst, all at once, into furious applause. They waited for it to die down, and then he spoke the last lines of Astley's latest triumph, the reunion of General Sale and his brave wife.

"So Britons shall never come to harm," he declaimed ringingly, "while hearth and home—" he paused, grandly, "—and LOVE is warm."

The curtain began to fall slowly, to tremendous applause. Bella, too, applauded until her hands ached, and Henry, by her side, applauded, his eyes shining at what he did not understand. She applauded and applauded, and she, too, did not quite understand. There were many people in this audience who had seen this scene, over and over; it was quite the sensation of the Season, and sent all London out into the cold city with their certainty made warm. She had never seen it, and only when she was quite sure that she did not and would not care, had she consented to go. It was a treat for Henry, she told herself.

She stopped applauding, and soon everyone did. It was so odd how applause came to an end; at one moment, it seemed as if no one wanted to stop, and the next, everyone had taken their signal, and left off. She wondered who the last person to clap his hands was; there must be a very last person, making a single clap, just after every other person had stopped, but it never seemed like that; it always seemed as if the applause all finished, all at once, by agreement. For a moment, as she took Henry's hand and gathered her things together, she was that person. Going on applauding, alone, clapping her little hands together alone, while everyone else prepared to go; applauding the war, applauding heroism made small and put on stage. She, too, had been in the war, the real one, and perhaps she ought to be the famous Bella Garraway, impersonated on stage to music while thousands watched, their tears streaming down their cheeks.

The audience was of the most mixed variety, and Bella clutched Henry's hand tightly as they made their way out.

"Who was that gentleman?" Henry said when they were in the open afternoon air.

"That was General Sale," Bella said. "He was a great hero."

Henry shook his head, irritably. "Not him," he said. "I meant the gentleman who was greeting you, Mamma."

She looked around; she had not seen any acquaintance. She searched the emotional crowd, and there she recognized Stokes. He caught her eye, and, smiling, came up to them.

"Miss Garraway," he said, removing his hat. "And who is this fine fellow?"

"How do you do, Mr. Stokes," Bella said, smiling. "Say hello to Mr. Stokes, Henry."

"An enjoyable way to pass an afternoon," Stokes said. "I often come to Astley's."

"I would have thought it quite beneath your notice, sir," Bella said.

"One cannot always live in the most elevated intellectual ether," Stokes said. "It entertains, it suffices to pass an hour or two. Poor soldiers! How they must have suffered!"

"A very sad story," Bella said. Then she had a sudden whim, and said, "Tell me, sir, shall I see you at Lady Spencer's rout this evening?"

Stokes scrutinized her. For a moment, she feared that he was thinking of writing about her, so thorough was his gaze. "I had not thought you cared for such diversions, madam."

"We cannot always live in the—ah—the elevated intellectual ether of our own company, you know," she said, and smiled brilliantly at him. How nice to be witty again; she had thought it quite gone from her.

He seemed a little confused, and bent down to Henry. "And you, sir," he said cosily. "Do you hope to be a soldier when you grow up, like General Sale?"

"No," Henry said, and his little face shone with the memory of his quiet acres, of birds flying slowly over the still ponds of his own lands. "No, I'm going to be a farmer."

"A very sensible young man," Stokes said, straightening, and smiled warmly at Bella. "I hope to see you in a few hours, then."

"A very few hours," Bella said. Henry watched him go, and then turned his face up to his mother's.

"Mamma," he said thoughtfully. "I think I only said that because of what he asked me."

"Asked you what?"

"Because he asked me if I was going to be a soldier," Henry persevered. "He's a nasty man, isn't he?"

"No," Bella said. "He's the same as everybody else. It is disagreeable to think people nasty, Henry."

"But if he asked me if I was going to be a farmer," Henry said, "I would have said I wanted to be a soldier. I only wanted to contradict him. Mamma, can you be both? A soldier and a farmer?"

"I don't know," Bella said, and then, not knowing why, she sank to her knees and embraced him. He had seen something simple there, and she had seen everything, every division and distinction and remembered small shifts; he had seen, as it were, the sea, whole and simple and terrible, and she had seen its myriad tints and depths, its shades and movements, all in a moment; seen her story, and his, and theirs, and ours, and understood it all. She had seen history's vasty depths. It was fading now. She was glad of it. She held her son to her body, felt his limbs in their sailor blue, felt them straining as he pulled from her. She had dropped to her knees, and her face was by his, looking at what he saw, looking at the world from where he saw it. His hat had fallen to the ground, but neither she nor he made any move to retrieve it. His eyes were fixed on some distant spot; the child seemed to let his eyes fall on things, and not to look at them. There, there, was what he wanted to run to; he saw one thing, and then another, beyond that, and then another and another. She calmed him by singing, and for a moment it kept him, but her voice dropped, and she sang in his ears, and when she finished, he would pull from her and run into the world. But for the moment, she sang; like the low audience at the circus, she broke into song. She sang him a hymn, familiar, calming balm into his ears:

> And O thou Lamb of God, whom I
> Slew in my dark self-righteous pride:
> Art thou return'd to Albion's Land!
> And is Jerusalem thy Bride?

"Mamma," he said, puzzled, not turning to her, but she continued with her low voice; she poured that calming sound into his ears, and the gods sang along. She kept the tremble of fear she felt from her voice. He should not know what she felt, squatting there in the street: that she, too, had fear in her, and pain, and it was almost to soothe herself that she sang the old hymn into her son's ears:

Come to my arms and never more
Depart; but dwell for ever here:
Create my Spirit to thy Love:
Subdue my Spectre to thy Fear.

She felt him straining, to run from her into the street, and, knowing that one day he would run from her into the world, in sunshine and shade, to conquer, to discover, to find what he did not know and to find what he would never know, she felt her eyes grow hot. One day, he, too, would go into the street, to disappear among the disorder of humanity, to look for what he could never find, and as she watched Stokes go, his head lowered as if in shame, watched him be surrounded, lost in the crowd, she wiped her tears dry on her boy's soft red hair, subduing his spectre to her fear.

"Shall we go now, Mamma?" he said.

"Yes," Bella said, holding him tight. "Lead your Mamma where you want her to go."

He squinted at the street before him as he decided. "That was a good circus," he said. "That was a very good circus. I liked the lions and the tigers best."

"Yes," Bella said. "That was a very good circus. And now where shall we go? Home?"

"No, not yet," he said to his mother. Then he thought hard, and said, "Mamma? When we go, shall we take the omnibus? May we take the omnibus? My omnibus?"

"Yes, my darling," she said. "Yes, today is your day, and, as you choose, home in your omnibus," and as she said the word *your,* and again, *your,* she felt inexplicably close to tears, thinking of what she had lost, thinking of what she now had. In a moment they would go on, where they had to go. But not yet; they would not go home just yet. And as Bella stood up, and brushed her dress, before them, the street was as it always was, and it swallowed them; the noisy and the eager, and the arrogant and the lonely, and the wise, frightened, and good, all at once, making their usual uproar.

Glossary

Afrit	a demon
Anna	an Indian coin of small denomination
Beedee	a small cigar
Boy	sometimes, a palanquin-bearer, from the Telugu *boyi*
Chai	tea
Claque	a group paid by a performer to express vociferous enthusiasm at the opera
Coal-lighter	a small boat
Cutpurse	a pickpocket
Engelstan	England
Footpad	a street robber
Gig	a small coach
Griffin	a new arrival in India
Jemaudar	in general, a leader; specifically, the second rank of officers in a company of sepoys
Jezail	a musket
Juggernauth	an avatar of the god Vishnu, or specifically the triumphant car under which devotees supposedly throw themselves
Kummur-bund	a sash
Kurta	a long shirt
Landau	a large open carriage
Linkboy	an urchin employed to light the way of London gentry across streets

Newab	a lesser rank in oriental nobility
Mahout	the driver of an elephant
Mohawk	a violent delinquent
Nazir	a high native official, the master of the court
Palanquin	a litter, born by four or six men
Qizzilbash	a Persian inhabitant of Kabul
Quluma	an item declarative of Islamic faith
Raree show	a vulgar entertainment
Sepoy	a native soldier in the service of the British forces
Sirdar	a prince
Syce	a groom
Tank	an artificial pond or lake, possibly from the Gujurati *tank'h*
Tantalus	a lockable holder of decanters
Tawkanah	a system of underfloor heating, common in eastern Afghanistan
Tiffin	a meal akin to luncheon
Tonjaun	a variety of sedan
Zenana	the women's quarters

Cast List

(+ means dead before the action begins; * marks a principal character)

* Amir Dost Mohammed Khan, Pearl of the Age
* Akbar, heir to the Dost
* Alexander Burnes, an adventurer
  Dr. Gerard, an adventurer
* Mohan Lal, a guide
  The Newab Jubbur Khan, brother of the Dost
  Futteh, a singer
  The Mir Wa'iz, mullah of Kabul
  Sayad Atah +
  Khushhal, a storyteller
  Futteh Khan +
* Bella Garraway, a heroine
  Colonel Garraway, an opium addict
  Harry Garraway +
  Charles, a valet
  Fanny, Lady Woodcourt, a hostess
  Sir Bramley Woodcourt
  Mrs. Garraway +
* Mme la Duchesse de Neaud, a courtier
  M. le Duc de Neaud
  Miss Gilbert, a spinster
  Miss Jane Gilbert

* Stokes, a journalist

King William IV

Mirabolant, a chef

Mullarkey, a manservant

Stapleton, a novelist

Mrs. Meagles, a landlady

* Castleford, a litterateur

Chapman, a political economist

Mr. Thomas Carlyle

* Miss Elizabeth Garraway, sister of Bella

Emily, a maid

Queen Adelaide

Lady Porchester, a society beauty

Lord Palmerston

Mr. Sandoe, a bookseller

The Newab Mohammed Zemaun Khan

* Charles Masson, a deserter and scholar

Khushhal, a courtier

* Hasan, an angel

Ahmed, a vile old supplicant

The worst of the wives, a Suddozye princess

* Suggs, a Sergeant-Major

* Florentia Sale, an army wife

* McVitie, the hero of the platoon

Joe Hastings, a sidekick

Mr. Das, a shopkeeper

* General Sale

Miss Brown, a husband-hunter

Elliott, a maritime valet

Captain Taylor, a novice

Mrs. Robinson, a companion

The Reverend Lannon, a cleric

Mr. Tredinnick, an old republican

The Governor of St. Helena

The Governor's wife

The Emperor Napoleon Bonaparte +

* Lord Auckland, the Governor General of India

* Emily Eden, sister of the Governor General

Fanny Eden

An illustrious connection (rather disappointing) of Lord Palmerston

* Elphinstone, a bore

* Macnaghten, another bore

Myra, a ladies' maid

* Shah Shujah-ul-mulk, deposed King of Afghanistan

* Runjeet Singh, the Lion of the Punjab

Ali, a mahout

Romesh

Bustan

* Frampton, the most senior of the junior adjutants

Mrs. Doughty, Castleford's sister

Admiral Doughty

Mrs. Bruton

* Henry Garraway

Mikhail Petrovich Layevsky +

Nikolai Mikhailovich Layevsky, a Crimean landowner

Agafeya Vasilevna Layevskaya, his wife +

* Pavel Nikolaievich Layevsky, his son

Pavel Mikhailovich Layevsky, his brother

Stepan Mikhailovich Layevsky, his brother

Arkady, a manservant

* Masha, a cook

* Vitkevich, an explorer

Mohammed, a rather smelly boy

Qasim, a boy

Khadija, Masson's landlady, a widow

Jirinovsky, a Russian officer

Stanchinsky, another Russian officer

Oblovich, another Russian officer, a teller of dull tales

Eldred Pottinger, the hero of Herat

The Shah of Persia

Yusuf, a chef

The Russian ambassador to the Court of St. James

Princess Fanny, a hostess

General Scherbatsky

The Duke of Dorset

Lord John

Queen Victoria

Musa, Akbar's favourite

Khadi, an Afghan prince

Zemaun, an Afghan prince

Nadir, son of the Newab Jubbur Khan

Charles Burnes

Dr. William Brydon

Sergeant Porter

Digby

Ahmed, a footman

Mrs. Sturt

Mackenzie, an adjutant

Trevor, an adjutant

Aide-de-camp to General Sale

Miss Anderson

Errors and Obligations

Anachronisms and plain falsifications have on the whole been indulged in when it pleased me. The full story of the First Afghan War is too intricate and too peopled for a novel, and it was always my intention to write a fiction. My characters are often rather unlike, and sometimes, as in the case of Masson, very unlike their originals. (In reality a Londoner, an accomplished artist, he certainly never committed murder or sodomy in his life, and he, and his descendants, deserve my apologies.) Some of this high-handedness may be justified by the utter vagueness of the sources on the most basic matters—the best authorities, for instance, do not even agree whether Vitkevich's first name was Yan, Ivan, or Paul—but by no means all of it, and on the whole I have preferred my inventions to the known facts. Although some of the most apparently extravagant episodes in the novel are simple historical truth, much of the narrative is quite wrong, if viewed as an account of history, and a reader interested in the course of the First Afghan War will want to turn elsewhere to discover the real events. The reader should probably know that Dost Mohammed really did have a wife who called him "Dosto" and "Slave"; a Company officer really did have a vision of the Army of the Indus as a gigantic funeral procession before its departure. Sometimes, the war threw up something I would never have dared to invent, and this is one of only two or three moments when I have directly quoted a participant in the war (the officer was Hamlet Wade). But much of the preceding story is complete invention: this is a pack of lies, though the outlines of my imaginary war occasionally coincide with those of a real one, in which people died.

The issue of what language my characters would have been talking in is not one with which I wanted to trouble the reader; Persian was the general *lingua franca,* which would have been spoken at Dost Mohammed's court. Pushto was a more rustic language, not widely understood by the

English. The Russians would, of course, have used French to talk to each other as well as to the English.

There are a couple of very specific debts which ought to be acknowledged here. The journey undertaken in the Anthropological Interlude was carried out by Mr. Louis Dupree, the author of one of the best studies of post-war Afghanistan, but my fictional character has nothing otherwise in common with him. I would also like to express my particular obligation, at the end of the novel, to Patrick Macrory's *Signal Catastrophe,* which describes a performed version in a London circus of the Sales' reunion.

I incurred many personal debts writing this novel—too many people to name, and some of them, who are deeply involved with the continuing tragic history of this great country, would prefer not to be named. I would particularly like to thank some fellow novelists, whose unselfish friendship, love, and support have been unfailing. Alan Hollinghurst, Candia McWilliam, Rachel Cusk, Barbara Trapido, and Lynne Truss were unstinting, and when I wrote, what would give them pleasure was always in my mind. The largest debt is to this novel's onlie begetter, Antonia Byatt, who told me bluntly from the beginning that I must write a long novel, and whose interest, certainty, and trust I came to rely on more than I can say. Thanks, too, must go to my editors at *The Spectator, The Independent, The Observer,* and *The Mail on Sunday,* who generously gave me time off to write in a concentrated way. I would particularly like to thank Boris Johnson and Mark Amory of *The Spectator* for their constant loyalty; Mark Amory has, over the years, been the nicest and most patiently sympathetic of editors. Georgia Garrett, my agent, was also the best of readers; Philip Gwyn Jones was an editor whose expectations I wanted to live up to. Practical help was offered by James Davidson, who very kindly wrote a line of Greek verse, my father, Ray Hensher, who tried to remedy my total ignorance about early railways and Company armaments, and Matthew Hamlyn, who was the novel's first civilian reader, whose enthusiasm gave me a great deal of encouragement and whose learned curiosity saved me from many blunders, particularly in the matter of the preserved fish Burnes took to Kabul. The last acknowledgement ought, in all justice, to go to the illustrious dead; but the homages to and thefts from the greatest nineteenth-century writers, from Astolphe de Custine to Surtees, are better left for the reader's indignant discovery.

Bibliography

These were the books in English I found most useful and tempting, which the reader in search of a more accurate account of the First Afghan War and Afghan history in general will want to read. I must acknowledge a particular debt to Jan Morris's superb imperial trilogy, which first interested me in Dost Mohammed.

Alexander Burnes, *Travels into Bokhara* and *Cabool*

Col. William H. Dennie, *Personal Narrative of the Campaigns in Affghanistan, Sinde, Beloochistan, Etc.*

Louis Dupree, *Afghanistan*

Emily Eden, *Up the Country*

Mountstuart Elphinstone, *An Account of the Kingdom of Caubul*

Lieut. Vincent Eyre, *Journal of an Afghanistan Prisoner*

George Frampton, *A Peep into Afghanistan*

Rev. G. R. Gleig, *Sale's Brigade in Afghanistan*

Benedict Grima, *The Performance of Emotion among Paxtun Women*

Peter Hopkirk, *The Great Game*

John Kaye, *History of the War in Afghanistan* (the standard nineteenth-century history of the war, and still indispensable, largely because Kaye seems to have burnt a large number of inconvenient documents.* I used the third edition, with Kaye's final supplements and footnotes)

Mohan Lal, *Life of the Amir Dost Mohammed Khan*

Peter Levi, *The Light Garden of the Angel King*

Colin Mackenzie, *Storms and Sunshine of a Soldier's Life*

*He said a fire had broken out in his study.

BIBLIOGRAPHY

Patrick Macrory, *Signal Catastrophe*

Charles Masson, *Narrative of Various Journeys in Balochistan, Afghanistan and the Panjab*

Christine Noelle, *State and Tribe in Nineteenth Century Afghanistan*

J. A. Norris, *The First Afghan War*

T. L. Pennell, *Among the Wild Tribes of the Afghan Frontier*

George Pottinger and Patrick Macrory, *The Ten-Rupee Jezail*

Florentia Sale, *Journal of the Disasters in Afghanistan* (the edition I used, edited by Patrick Macrory, also prints Dr. Brydon's journal of his famous journey)

The Sirdar Ikbal Ali Shah, *Afghanistan of the Afghans*

Gordon Whitteridge, *Charles Masson*

M. E. Yapp, *Strategies of British India*

Henry Yule and A. C. Burnell, *Hobson-Jobson*

A NOTE ABOUT THE AUTHOR

Philip Hensher is a novelist and critic, and the author of four other works of fiction, including *Kitchen Venom,* winner of the Somerset Maugham Award. He is a columnist for *The Independent,* and chief book reviewer for *The Spectator.* He lives in South London.

A NOTE ON THE TYPE

This book was set in Monotype Dante, a typeface designed by Giovanni Mardersteig (1892–1977). Conceived as a private type for the Officina Bodoni in Verona, Italy, Dante was originally cut only for hand composition by Charles Malin, the famous Parisian punch cutter, between 1946 and 1952. Its first use was in an edition of Boccaccio's *Trattatello in laude di Dante* that appeared in 1954. The Monotype Corporation's version of Dante followed in 1957. Although modeled on the Aldine type used for Pietro Cardinal Bembo's treatise *De Aetna* in 1495, Dante is a thoroughly modern interpretation of the venerable face.

Composed by Stratford Publishing Services, Inc.,
Brattleboro, Vermont
Printed and bound by Berryville Graphics,
Berryville, Virginia
Designed by Virginia Tan